P9-DTO-352

MONA SIMPSON'S
ANYWHERE BUT HERE

"No one would guess that *Anywhere But Here* . . . is a first novel. Mona Simpson writes with confidence, with a swagger. She is already a master." —Anne Tyler, *USA Today*

"A brilliant novel . . . *Anywhere But Here* is a book about two women, but Simpson makes them seem like the world."
—Laurie Stone, *Village Voice*

"There have been many novels about mothers and daughters . . . but Simpson has found a very special, achingly real, yet often funny way of portraying such a relationship that speaks directly to our times. . . . We are in the presence of a major new literary talent."
—Barbara Bannon, *Cleveland Plain Dealer*

"A raw, amazing, heart-breaking portrayal of a sort that hasn't turned up in anything else I've read." —Alice Munro

"It has all the bite and poignance of a life unfolding . . . a moving, extraordinary achievement." —Gail Caldwell, *Boston Globe*

"Mona Simpson has a remarkable gift for transforming the homely cadences of plain American speech into something like poetry. A stunning debut." —John Ashbery

"Simpson's prose is at once effortlessly casual in tone and also an instrument of genuine subtlety. . . . Her novel takes your breath away."
—Elizabeth Ward, *Los Angeles Herald Examiner*

ANYWHERE
BUT HERE

by

MONA SIMPSON

■ □ ■

VINTAGE CONTEMPORARIES

VINTAGE BOOKS • A DIVISION OF RANDOM HOUSE • NEW YORK

■ □ ■ □ ■ □ ■ ■ ■ □ ■ □

For Joanne,
our mother,
and
my brother Steve

First Vintage Contemporaries Edition, January 1988

Copyright © 1986 by Mona Simpson

All rights reserved under International and Pan-American Copyright Conventions. Published in the United States by Random House, Inc., New York, and simultaneously in Canada by Random House of Canada Limited, Toronto. Originally published, in hardcover, by Alfred A. Knopf, Inc., in 1986.

Some stories in this work were originally published in the following publications: *North American Review* and *The Paris Review.* "What My Mother Knew" was originally published in *Mademoiselle.* "Approximations" and "Lonnie Tishman" were originally published in *Ploughshares.*

Library of Congress Cataloging-in-Publication Data
Simpson, Mona.
Anywhere but here.
(Vintage contemporaries)
I. Title.
PS3569.I5117A8 1988   813'.54   87–40088
ISBN 0-394-75559-6 (pbk.)

The author wishes to thank the Corporation of Yaddo, the MacDowell Colony, VCCA, the Transatlantic Henfield Foundation, The Beard's Fund, the Kellogg Foundation, and *The Paris Review* for their support during the writing of this book. Also, the author would like to thank Allan Gurganus, Elizabeth Hardwick, Robert Asahina, Robert Cohen, Lionel Shriver, and George Plimpton for multiple and generous readings.

Author photo copyright © 1986 by Thomas Victor

Text design by Marie-Hélène Fredericks

Manufactured in the United States of America
10   9   8   7   6   5   4   3   2   1

CONTENTS

There are three wants which can never be satisfied; that of the rich wanting more, that of the sick, wanting something different, and that of the traveler, who says, "anywhere but here."

—*Ralph Waldo Emerson*

ANN

■ □ ■

■ □ ■ □ ■ □ ■ □ ■ □ ■ □ ■

1

ANYWHERE

■ □ ■

We fought. When my mother and I crossed state lines in the stolen car, I'd sit against the window and wouldn't talk. I wouldn't even look at her. The fights came when I thought she broke a promise. She said there'd be an Indian reservation. She said that we'd see buffalo in Texas. My mother said a lot of things. We were driving from Bay City, Wisconsin, to California, so I could be a child star while I was still a child.

"Talk to me," my mother would say. "If you're upset, tell me."

But I wouldn't. I knew how to make her suffer. I was mad. I was mad about a lot of things. Places she said would be there, weren't. We were running away from family. We'd left home.

Then my mother would pull to the side of the road and reach over and open my door.

"Get out, then," she'd say, pushing me.

I got out. It was always a shock the first minute because nothing outside was bad. The fields were bright. It never happened on a bad day. The western sky went on forever, there were a few clouds. A warm breeze came up and tangled around my legs. The road was dull as a nickel. I stood there at first amazed that there was nothing horrible in the landscape.

But then the wheels of the familiar white Continental turned, a spit of gravel hit my shoes and my mother's car drove away. When it was nothing but a dot in the distance, I started to cry.

I lost time then; I don't know if it was minutes or if it was more. There was nothing to think because there was nothing to do. First, I saw small things. The blades of grass. Their rough side, their smooth, waxy side. Brown grasshoppers. A dazzle of California poppies.

I'd look at everything around me. In yellow fields, the tops of weeds bent under visible waves of wind. There was a high steady note of insects screaking. A rich odor of hay mixed with the heady smell of gasoline. Two or three times, a car rumbled by, shaking the ground. Dry weeds by the side of the road seemed almost transparent in the even sun.

I tried hard but I couldn't learn anything. The scenery all went strange, like a picture on a high billboard. The fields, the clouds, the sky; none of it helped because it had nothing to do with me.

My mother must have watched in her rearview mirror. My arms crossed over my chest, I would have looked smaller and more solid in the distance. That was what she couldn't stand, my stubbornness. She'd had a stubborn husband. She wasn't going to have a stubborn child. But when she couldn't see me anymore, she gave up and turned around and she'd gasp with relief when I was in front of her again, standing open-handed by the side of the road, nothing more than a child, her child.

And by the time I saw her car coming back, I'd be covered with a net of tears, my nose running. I stood there with my hands hanging at my sides, not even trying to wipe my face.

My mother would slow down and open my door and I'd run in, looking back once in a quick good-bye to the fields, which turned ordinary and pretty again. And when I slid into the car, I was different. I put my feet up on the dashboard and tapped the round tips of my sneakers together. I wore boys' sneakers she thought I was too old for. But now my mother was nice because she knew I would talk to her.

"Are you hungry?" was the first thing she'd say.

"A little."

"I am," she'd say. "I feel like an ice cream cone. Keep your eyes open for a Howard Johnson's."

We always read the magazines, so we knew where we wanted to go. My mother had read about Scottsdale and Albuquerque and

Bel Air. But for miles, there was absolutely nothing. It seemed we didn't have anything and even air that came in the windows when we were driving fast felt hot.

We had taken Ted's Mobil credit card and we used it whenever we could. We scouted for Mobil stations and filled up the tank when we found one, also charging Cokes on the bill. We dug to our elbows in the ice chests, bringing the cold pop bottles up like a catch. There was one chain of motels that accepted Mobil cards. Most nights we stayed in those, sometimes driving three or four hours longer to find one, or stopping early if one was there. They were called Travel Lodges and their signs each outlined a bear in a nightcap, sleepwalking. They were dull motels, lonely, and they were pretty cheap, which bothered my mother because she would have liked to charge high bills to Ted. I think she enjoyed signing *Mrs. Ted Diamond*. We passed Best Westerns with hotel swimming pools and restaurants with country singers and we both wished and wished Ted had a different card.

Travel Lodges were the kind of motels that were set a little off the highway in a field. They tended to be one or at the most two stories, with cement squares outside your room door for old empty metal chairs. At one end there would be a lit coffee shop and a couple of semis parked on the gravel. The office would be near the coffee shop. It would have shag carpeting and office furniture, always a TV attached by metal bars to the ceiling.

Those motels depressed us. After we settled in the room, my mother looked around, checking for cleanliness. She took the bedspreads down, lifted curtains, opened drawers and the medicine cabinet, and looked into the shower. Sometimes she took the paper off a water glass and held the glass up to see that it was washed.

I always wanted to go outside. My mother would be deliberating whether it was safer to leave our suitcase in the room or in the locked car; when she was thinking, she stood in the middle of the floor with her hands on her hips and her lips pursed. Finally, she decided to bring it in. Then she would take a shower to cool off. She didn't make me take one if I didn't want to, because we were nowhere and she didn't care what I looked like in the coffee shop. After her shower, she put on the same clothes she'd been driving in all day.

I went out to our porch and sat in the one metal chair. Its back was a rounded piece, perhaps once designed to look like a shell. I could hear her shower water behind me, running; in front, the constant serious sound of the highway. A warm wind slapped my skin lightly, teasing, the sound of the trucks on the highway came loud, then softer, occasionally a motorcycle shrank to the size of a bug, red taillights ticking on the blue sky.

I acted like a kid, always expecting to find something. At home, before supper, I'd stood outside when the sky looked huge and even the near neighbors seemed odd and distant in their oc-cupations. I'd watched the cars moving on the road, as if by just watching you could understand, get something out of the world.

At the motel, I would walk around to the back. I'd stand look-ing at the field, like any field. The back of the building was or-dinary, brick, with glass meter gauges. There was a gas tank lodged on a cement platform, pooled with rusty water. The field went on to where you could see trailers and a neon sign for Dairy Queen in the distance.

The near and the far, could have been anywhere, could have been our gas tank, our fields and sky at home. Our yard had the same kinds of weeds. Home could have been anywhere too.

"Ann. A-yun," my mother would be yelling, then. It all ended, gladly, when she called me from the door. She was finished with her shower and wanted to go for supper at the coffee shop. Our day was almost done. And we enjoyed the dinners in those coffee shops. We ordered the most expensive thing on the menu and side dishes and beverages and desserts. We were anxious, trying to plan to get all the best of what they had. We rolled up our sleeves, asked for extra sour cream and butter. We took pleasure in the scrawled figures added up on the green-lined bill.

Mornings, we always started out later than we'd planned. The manager ran the credit card through the machine and filled the form out slowly. My mother drummed her nails on the counter top, waiting. Then she sighed, holding the credit card form in both hands, examining it a second before signing. "Okay," she said every time she handed the paper back, as if she were giving away one more thing she'd once had.

We'd drive off in the morning and I'd look again, at the plain building, the regular field. I'd forget the land. It was like so much other land we'd seen.

My mother had clipped out pictures of houses in Scottsdale, Arizona. We loved the colors: pink, turquoise, browns, rich yellow. The insides of the houses had red tiled floors, clay bowls of huge strawberries on plain, rough wooden tables.

We went out of our way to go to Scottsdale. When we got there, my mother drove to the Luau, a good hotel, one they'd listed in *Town and Country*. I sat in a chair on one side of the lobby while she went up to the desk. She came back and whispered me the price.

"What do you think? It's a lot but maybe it's worth it once to just relax."

"I think we should find somewhere cheaper."

"There might not be a Travel Lodge in town," she said. "Well, think, Pooh-bear-cub. It's up to you. What would you like to do?"

"Let's find out if there's a Travel Lodge."

She sighed. "Okay. I don't know how we're going to find out. There's probably not. In fact, I'm pretty sure. So what do you think? What should we do?"

I worried about money. And I knew it was a bigger system than I understood. I tried to pick the cheaper thing, like a superstition.

"There's a telephone. Maybe they have a phone book." We were standing in the dark Polynesian lobby. A phone hung in the corner.

She did the looking and it was there, Travel Lodge, with a boxed ad showing the bear sleepwalking, in the yellow pages, listed as being on Route 9. "Nine where?" my mother said, biting her fingernail, clicking the other hand on the metal shelf. "Now, how the heck am I going to find that? It says right out of town, yeah, I'll bet. I didn't see anything, coming in."

"We don't have to go there." I felt like I'd done my duty, checking. I looked around the lobby. It seemed nice. I was beginning to hope she picked here.

"Well, come on." She pulled her purse strap over her shoulder. "Let's go. We'll go there. We should." She had that much worry, apparently.

But driving to the Travel Lodge, not even halfway there, in town, at an intersection near a gas station, we had an accident. My mother rear-ended a car on a red light.

I was sitting on a curb of the intersection, pulling at grass behind me banking the closed filling station. Nearby, the cars were pulled over to one side and a police car with a flashing red light was parked, making traffic go around them. The policeman stood writing things down as he talked to my mother.

She was moving her hands all around her hair and face. Then she folded her arms across her chest, but one hand couldn't stand it, it reached up to tug at her collar.

"I was going to just stay at that hotel, I *knew.* I was tired. I know myself. Now, God, tell me, really, how long do you think it will take to be fixed?" She bit a nail.

The policeman looked into the dark gas station. "Problem is, it's a weekend," he said.

My mother looked at me and shook her head. The policeman walked over to the other driver. She was a woman in shorts and a sleeveless shirt. She seemed calm.

"See, I'm not going to listen to you anymore," my mother said. "Because I know best. You try and save a few pennies and you end up spending thousands." She exhaled, shoving out a hip.

It was ten o'clock and finally getting cooler. We were hungry, we still hadn't eaten dinner. The other woman, having taken the numbers she needed, left, waving good-bye to us and to the policeman.

"Calm down, Adele," she said to my mother.

My mother pulled a piece of her hair. "Calm down, well, that's easy for you to say. Jeez, calm down, she says, when she's going to sue, she'll get her kids' college educations out of this, I know how it's done."

The woman laughed and slammed her car door shut. She rolled down her window. "Barry's Hanover might have a mechanic in on Saturday," she called to the policeman.

"Mom, I'm hungry." My rump was cold and it seemed we might be there all night.

"Well, we have to stay," she said. "If we'd just checked in, then we'd be there now, probably eating, no, we'd be finished. We'd probably be having dessert. But now we have to wait."

"For how long?"

"I don't know."

The policeman came over to us, still holding his notebook. "We've done all we can do until tomorrow," he said. "Now I'll take you wherever you want to go and you can just leave the car here and call in the morning and have her towed."

"They're probably not even going to have room left at the hotel now," she said to me.

The policeman had freckles on his arms and his hands, like my mother. He put the notebook in his back pocket. "Now, you are both welcome to stay with my wife and I for the night, if you're worried. There's plenty of extra room."

"Oh, no, thank you, though, we couldn't."

"Because it wouldn't be any trouble. And my wife makes a mean apple pie." He looked at me.

"Thank you, but no, really." My mother inspired offers like that, often. I didn't know until I was older how unusual that is. "But would you mind dropping us off at the Luau?"

"Yes, ma'am," he said. "Nice place."

We both sat in the backseat while he drove. The windows were covered with chicken wire. "I just hope they still have room," my mother said, stretching her fingers out on the seat and looking down at their nails.

The thing about my mother and me is that when we get along, we're just the same. Exactly. And at the Luau Hotel, we were happy. Waiting for our car to be fixed, we didn't talk about money. It was so big, we didn't think about it. We lay on our stomachs on the king-sized bed, our calves tangling up behind us, reading

novels. I read *Gone With the Wind*. Near the end, I locked myself
in the bathroom, stopping up my face with a towel. After a while
she knocked on the door.

"Honey, let me in, I want to tell you something!" I made myself
keep absolutely still. "Don't worry, Honey, she gets him back
later. She gets him again in the end."

We loved the swimming pool. Those days we were waiting for
our car to be fixed, we lay out from ten until two, because my
mother had read that those were the best tanning hours. That was
what we liked doing, improving ourselves: lying sprawled out on
the reclining chairs, rubbed with coconut suntan oil, turning the
pages of new-bought magazines. Then we'd go in the pool, me
cannonballing off the diving board for the shock of it, my mother
starting in one corner of the shallow end, both her arms out to the
sides, skimming the surface as she stepped in gradually, smiling
wide, saying, "Eeeeeeeee."

My mother wore a white suit, I swam in gym shorts. While I
was lying on a chair, once, she picked up my foot and looked
down my leg. "Apricot," she said.

At home, one farmer put in a swimming pool, fenced all around
with aluminum. That summer, Ben and I sat in the fields outside,
watching through the diamond spaces of the fence. Sometimes the
son would try and chase us away and throw rocks at us, little sissy
pieces of gravel.

"Public property!" we screamed back at him. We were sitting
in Guns Field. We kids all knew just who owned what land.

Every afternoon, late, after the prime tanning hours, we went out.
Dressing took a long time. My mother called room service for a
pitcher of fresh lemonade, told them not too much sugar, but some
sugar, like yesterday, a pinch, just enough so it was sweet. Sweet,
but a little tart, too. Come to think of it, yesterday tasted a little
too tart, but the day before was perfect. This was all on the telephone. My mother was the kind of customer a waitress would like
to kill.

We'd each take showers and wash our hair, squeezing lemons
on it before the cream rinse. We touched up our fingernails and

toenails with polish. That was only the beginning. Then came the body cream and face cream, our curlers and hair sprays and makeup.

All along, I had a feeling we couldn't afford this and that it would be unimaginably bad when we had to pay. I don't know what I envisioned: nothing, no luck, losing everything, so it was the absolute worst, no money for food, being stopped on a plain cement floor in the sun, unable to move, winding down, stopping like a clock stopped.

But then it went away again. In our sleeveless summer dresses and white patent leather thongs, we walked to the district of small, expensive shops. There was an exotic pet store we visited every day. We'd been first drawn in by a sign on the window for two defumed skunks.

"But you can never really get the smell completely out," the blond man inside had told us. He showed us a baby raccoon and we watched it lick its paws, with movements like a cat but more delicate, intricate features.

More than anything, I wanted that raccoon. And my mother wasn't saying no. We didn't have to make any decisions until we left the Luau. And we didn't know yet when that would be.

In a china store, my mother held up a plain white plate. "Look at this. See how fine it is?" If she hadn't said that, I wouldn't have noticed anything, but now I saw that it was thin and there was a pearliness, like a film of water, over the surface.

"Granny had a whole *set* like this." She turned the plate upside down and read the fine printing. "Yup, this is it. Spode."

I remembered Granny almost bald, carrying oats and water across the yard to feed Hal's pony. But still, I didn't know.

"Mmhmm. You don't know, but Granny was very elegant. Gramma isn't, she could be, but she isn't. We're like Granny. See, we belong here, Pooh-bear-cub. We come from this."

I didn't know.

A week after the accident, we had good news. The bill for our car was far less than we'd thought and my mother paid ninety dollars, off the record, to fix the other woman's fender. They both agreed not to contact insurance companies.

This was all great except it meant we were leaving. The car would be ready in a day. My mother sat on the edge of the bed, filing her nails, when she put down the telephone receiver, gently. "There's still a few things I'd like to see here," she said.

We went out to the pool and tried not to think. It seemed easy, lying on towels over warm cement. I'd gotten tan, very dark, the week we'd been there. My mother had freckles and pink burns on her cheeks and shoulders, and her hair was streaked lighter from the sun. That day, my mother got up and went inside before I did. She had to be careful in the sun.

I was in the pool, holding on to the side, kicking my legs in the water behind me. I was worried about my knees. Lately, I'd noticed they were fat, not knobby and horselike, the way my mother's were. So I was doing kicks to improve them. Around the pool, other women slouched in deck chairs. I thought about my knees again. At least tan fat looked better than white fat, I was thinking.

Then my mother called me. "We're going to see a house," she said, shoving a towel into my hand. "Hurry up and jump in the shower."

We waited, clean and dressed, outside the Luau. My mother told me that a real estate agent named Gail was picking us up. There was something in her tone, she didn't want to explain. So I went along with it as if it was nothing out of the ordinary. And there in Scottsdale, it really wasn't. It had been so long since anything was regular.

Suddenly, Gail was there and she honked. I climbed into the backseat and my mother sat next to her in front. They talked quickly, getting to know each other. My mother said we were just moving, from Bay City, Wisconsin, and that she was looking forward to the warm air.

"I couldn't stand another winter." She rolled down her window and glanced outside. "I love Scottsdale, the dryness."

Gail Letterfine was very tan with light gray hair, bright clothes and turquoise Indian jewelry. "You're going to love this house, it's absolutely cream of the crop. I haven't had anything like this to show for over a year."

She drove us to the top of a hill. The land was brown, dirt. There were no lawns. I just sat in the backseat, not saying anything. I wished I had *Gone With the Wind*. I knew I shouldn't say anything, in case I contradicted my mother. I could tell she was lying, but I wasn't sure. And I didn't know why. She liked me to talk, around strangers, like a kid. But I was mad, sort of. So I just stared out the window.

Gail Letterfine parked the Mustang on the pebbled lot near a fountain. Pennies overlapped and glittered on the bottom. Just from where we were, I could tell this was something we'd never seen before. We didn't have houses like this in Bay City. A maid opened the door, a woman I knew was a maid from her black short dress and white apron. We'd never seen a maid before, in person, at least I hadn't, I didn't know anymore about my mother. When we got along, it seemed we knew everything about each other. But now, I felt like my mother glossed over things. She knew how nervous I could be.

The maid went to get someone else. Gail Letterfine opened a door and it was a closet. "Coat closet," she said, loudly, as if it were her own house.

The living room was huge, with red clay tile floors and high ceilings. There were long windows on two walls and you could see outside, down the hill. There was no furniture except a black grand piano and chairs against the walls.

The woman of the house came to meet us. Considering where she lived, she looked like an ordinary person. She had plain brown permanented hair and a nice face. She was wearing a gray dress and stockings.

Gail Letterfine introduced her and the woman took us through her house. Out windows, we saw the backyard, brown and dry, with an oval turquoise swimming pool. Clay pots of strawberry plants stood with thick, heavy berries hanging down over their rims. Every time we entered a room, the woman stood in the doorway while Gail Letterfine pointed out features. In the kitchen, Gail opened every cupboard, where we saw canned soup

and Jell-O mixes just like in my grandmother's house. Gail went
on about the sink, the refrigerator and the stove. Then she started
in on the plumbing. From the way my mother shifted, you could
tell she was less than interested.

"What about your appointments?" My mother cupped her hand
around a painted Mexican candleholder on the kitchen table.
"Are they for sale, too? Because they all go so well, they're what
make the house."

I wondered where she'd learned that word. The woman shook
her head. "No, I'm sorry." My mother liked the woman who lived
here, her quietness. There was something tough in Gail Letterfine. With her espadrille, she was now pointing to the molding
around the kitchen floor. My mother would rather have talked to
the woman in the gray dress. Perhaps that's why we'd come here,
because my mother missed her friends.

The bedrooms and bathrooms were regular-sized.

"Our daughter's room," the woman said, in the last doorway on
the hall. "She's gone off to college."

My mother nudged me, "This would be yours." We wandered
into the adjoining bathroom, which had a vanity and a makeup
mirror. Starfish and shells cluttered the tile rim of the sunken tub.
My mother frowned at me, "Not bad."

They walked back down the hallway to the dining room. The
woman in the gray dress had, quietly, offered them tea, and my
mother answered quick and loud, "I'd love some."

I stayed in the room. Outside, water slapped the edges of the
swimming pool. A light breeze was making waves. I sat on the
hard single bed with stuffed animals bunched up by the pillow.
Two pompons fluttered on the bulletin board.

I leaned back and imagined the girl away at college. I thought
if I lived here, with this bed and this bulletin board, the regular
desk and dresser, I would have this kind of life. Nothing to hide.
The girl left her room and went to college and people could walk
through and see it.

I actually breathed slower and believed my mother had
changed her mind about California, that we were really going to
live here, in this house.

It was nice lying on that bed, listening to the soft shuffle of water through the window screen. I felt like sleeping. Then a few minutes later, I woke up hungry. I got up and went down the hall. I was thinking of the woman in the gray dress. For some reason, I thought she would give me cookies and a glass of milk.

They were sitting around the dining room on beige chairs. My mother's knees rested together and her calves slanted down, parallel, mirroring the woman's across the room. My mother was sipping her tea, holding it a long time to her lips, appreciating it.

"Could we put in a bathhouse? I'd love a little cabana out there."

Gail Letterfine lifted her silver glasses, which were attached and hooked behind her ears on a thin silver chain, and wrote down my mother's questions in a hand-sized notebook.

"You'd need a permit." She tapped the arm of her chair with a pen. "That's not hard."

"But I would like to know."

"Who can I call? Let me see. Oh, I got it. Mangold."

My mother floated up to where I was at the sliding glass doors. She rummaged her hand through my hair.

"But you like it," Gail Letterfine said, slamming the notebook closed.

"Well, my husband's coming in next week, and of course, he'll have to see it, too."

"Of course," said the woman in the gray dress, nodding as if she understood perfectly.

"But I'm sure he'll like it." My mother nodded, too. "I think this is the one." She lifted her eyes to the high corners of the room. "Mmhmm, I'm sure of it. What do you think, Ann?"

I was reeling, as if I'd just woken up to trouble, when she said her husband. The sentence went through me like a toy train, three times around the track and no time, coming in, could I picture it right. Ted sure wasn't coming. Not after we'd used his credit card like we had.

"I'm hungry, Mom," I said. I was disappointed by the woman in the gray dress, too. I felt like I'd been promised food and then not given it.

My mother ran her hand through my hair again. "Well, we better be off and get this little one something to eat." She smiled. She liked it when I said bratty, kid things in front of other people. We both did. It made us feel normal. She liked people to think she spoiled me.

On the way back to town, Gail Letterfine drove us to see Frank Lloyd Wright's work site in the desert, Taliesin West. I didn't see what the big deal was. They were excavating. There were huge piles of dirt, like you saw at home where they were developing for the new highway, and dust around everywhere. It was so hot, the piece of thong between my toes stung the skin.

"I love the atmosphere," my mother said, tilting her face up to the sun before naturally drifting indoors, to the air-conditioned gift shop. That was one thing about my mother, why she was fun; she valued comfort. We never had to stay in museums too long. If we didn't like something, we left and went somewhere else, like a restaurant. She wasn't too strict about discipline.

Metal bells of all sizes hung from the gift shop ceiling. "People come from all over the world to buy these bells," Gail Letterfine said. "You're lucky to get them at that price. They're going to be collector's items."

My mother bought one, taking a long time to pick the size. "Won't it look nice in the house?" She winked at me.

I scowled.

Gail took us out to a late lunch. We ate a lot, we each had desserts, extras. We acted the way we did at motel diners, not minding the prices, but this was an elegant restaurant, and expensive. They weren't going to take our Mobil credit card. My mother argued primly when Gail tried to pay the bill and I kicked her, hard, under the table. That night, my mother made me watch while she rolled down her stockings and put her fingers on the bruises. She said she'd known all along Gail would insist. And Gail had, tearing the bottom strip off the bill. "It's a write-off, you know," she'd said. "No prob."

She'd left us in front of the Luau.

"So tomorrow morning, I'll bring a contract to breakfast. Just a

work sheet. So we can start talking terms. Toot-a-loo," Gail
called, waving her plump hand as she drove away.

We watched her car go. All of a sudden it seemed sad, leaving
Scottsdale. Suddenly, I really did like Gail.

"Well," my mother shrugged. "We really don't need dinner,
that was plenty. Should we just walk around a little?"

We ambled down the streets slowly, because we were full from
eating too much and because it was late afternoon and there was
a light, warm breeze and because we were leaving tomorrow. My
mother led me through an archway, to some shops on an inside
courtyard. She found a perfume maker, a blind man, who blended
custom fragrances. He showed us essences of oils, leaves, grasses
and flowers.

"All natural," he told us.

He kept the essences in small glass bottles lined up on glass
shelves. I dawdled while he worked with my mother. He mixed
drops of oils on a glass plate, then rubbed them on the inside of
my mother's arm with the tip of an eyedropper.

Finally, they got what they wanted. I had to laugh. The mixture
was lily of the valley, wild penny rose, lilac and ordinary lawn
grass.

"It's like my childhood," my mother said, holding out her arm.
"What I grew up around. Smell."

They decided to call it Joie d'Adele and my mother ordered a
hundred and fifty dollars' worth, eight little bottles, the smallest
batch he made. She asked if he could mix them overnight, because we had to leave Scottsdale the next morning. He was an
odd-looking man. His face hung large and white, creamy. He
wore brown clothes and he moved slowly, with his head turned
down. But he liked my mother, you could tell. Some people did.
You could see it. Strangers almost always love my mother. And
even if you hate her, can't stand her, even if she's ruining your
life, there's something about her, some romance, some power.
She's absolutely herself. No matter how hard you try, you'll never
get to her. And when she dies, the world will be flat, too simple,
reasonable, too fair.

As soon as we got out of the store, we started fighting about the money.

"We can't afford *that*," I whined, turning on one foot to face her. "A hundred and *fifty* dollars! For perfume! Plus the car and the hotel!"

"Well, you should talk, how much do you think your raccoon is!"

We'd made our way, walking and yelling, to the pet store, where the baby raccoon hunched in the window, his paw stalled in a bowl of water.

"He's a hundred and he eats! He'd eat up fifteen dollars a week in food, at least! The perfume would last, it would last me five years probably. I take care of things and they last. You see what I wear. I haven't bought one new thing in years. But they were all good to start with."

That was a total lie. She bought things all the time. I stood knocking on the glass, trying to make the raccoon look at me. I'd been thinking of starting my new school with the raccoon, riding a bike with him wrapped around my shoulders.

"So, I guess we can't afford him either, then," I said.

"Just remember, I'm the one who has to catch a man in this family. I'm the one who has to find you a father."

"You can buy perfume in California."

"No, not like this. There are only three in the world like him. One is in Italy and the other is in France. He's the only one in the United States."

"According to him."

"Stop kicking stones like that, you're ruining your sandals. And when they go, we can't afford another pair."

We both understood that neither of us would get what she wanted, the raccoon or Joie d'Adele. It was fair that way, both deprived.

That night we packed. My mother wrapped the Taliesin bell with care, bundling it several layers thick in hotel towels. When she paid our bill it was higher than we expected. "Three hundred." She frowned, raising her eyebrows. "It's a good thing we didn't get that raccoon, you know?"

Gail Letterfine was due to pick us up at nine o'clock for breakfast. We were gone, far away in Nevada, before the sun came up.

A lot of times, I've thought about it and I feel bad that I didn't let my mother buy her perfume. For one thing, I feel bad for the guy, early in the morning, trusting, having his eight bottles of Joie d'Adele carefully wrapped. Now I'd like to smell it: lily of the valley, penny rose, lilac and grass. It's been years since we've been home. He must have been very hurt that we duped him. He might have assumed the worst and he would have been wrong about that; my mother really had liked him. It was only me.

Years later, when we were living in California, we read his obituary in *Vogue*. It said he'd been the only living custom perfume maker in the States, so he had been telling us the truth. Apparently, he hadn't trained anyone under him. If they'd listed the name of an apprentice, I'd have sent away and surprised her.

"Awww, we should have bought some from him, remember when I wanted to get some of his perfume?" my mother said, when she showed me the little article. "It would probably be worth something now."

"By now, it'd be all gone."

The weather changes quickly on my mother's face. She shrugged, nose wrinkling. "You're right."

But I do feel bad about it, still. That bell is precious to her. She's moved it everywhere; that bell has hung, prominently, in the now-long series of her apartments.

"People come from all over the world for the Taliesin bells. We're lucky to have one. They're collector's items." I've heard my mother say that fifty times. She believed every word Gail Letterfine told us, as if we were the only people in the world who lied.

It did something for my mother, every time she let me off on the highway and then came back and I was there. She was proving something to herself. When she drove back, she'd be nodding, grateful-looking, as if we had another chance, as if something had been washed out of her.

Years ago, when I was small, she chased me to the kitchen table and swiveled between her long arms on each side of it.

"Now where are you going to go?" she'd said.

This was when we were all living in my grandmother's house back at home.

I ducked under the table and saw everyone's legs. Jimmy's blue uniform slacks, Ben's bare knees with scrapes and white scars, my grandmother's stiff, bagging, opaque, seamed orange stockings in black tie-up shoes, my mother's tall freckled legs in nylons. The muscles in her calves moved like nervous small animals. I knew I couldn't get away. So I lunged out and grabbed my uncle's blue legs, holding on hard, sobbing in yelps, not letting go. I thought Jimmy was the strongest one there. Carol stood with her back to us, wiping the counter with a sponge.

Jimmy ran his hand over my head and down my spine. He hugged me hard, but then he pried my fingers off and pulled me away from him. His face was blank and large. "I have to let your mother have you."

My mother was screaming, "Jimmy, you give her to me. She's my child. Mine."

Jimmy pushed me forward with his knuckles on my back, and then she had me. When she shook me against the refrigerator, Ben ran out the door. None of them looked while we fought. They turned their backs. Jimmy left then, too, the screen door slamming. Carol followed, shaking her head, and they were gone—a family.

I fought back, I kicked and bit and pulled hair. I fought as if I were fighting to live. She always said I turned animal, wild. And there was something in that. I could feel something, the way my lips went curled on my teeth, the backs of my knees.

Later, I'd be in bed, swollen and touchy, not moving, and the house would seem absolutely still. The sheet felt light, incredibly light on my skin. My grandmother made up her own bed for me, with new sheets dried out on the line. They helped me after, but then I didn't care anymore.

When I was better again, up and running around, my mother still hadn't forgiven me. She drew it out. Those days she ignored me, came in the house like a stranger, as if she had no relation. She left me to my grandmother's care. She'd roll up her pants from the ankles and push up her shirt sleeves to show her cuts and bruises.

"Look what she did to me," she told the mailman on the porch. "She's wild. A little vicious animal."

Maybe it was the same as later, for her it was all one circle, coming back to the same place, when we made up. In the middle of the night, she woke me and wanted to talk. She looked hard into my eyes, sincere and promising, touched me where I didn't want her to touch, told me again and again that she'd never leave me, when I wasn't worried that she would.

"Okay," I always said.

The last time my mother let me out by the side of the road was in Nevada. I don't know why she stopped after that, maybe just because we were almost to California. It was different to let me out on the highway than it would be someplace we lived. I was old enough to get in trouble.

That last time in Nevada was different, too. Because she left me out on the road just a mile or two up past an Arco station. I could see the building in the distance. She let me off and drove out of sight, but this time I didn't cry. I started walking, in the ditch, back towards the filling station. I wanted to make a phone call.

There are more important things than love, I was thinking. Because I didn't want to talk to Benny then, he was just a year older, there was nothing he could do.

I got to the gas station. I didn't have any money, but my mind was made up. I went over to a teenage boy who was leaning against a pump, sucking an empty Coke bottle, and asked if I could borrow a dime. He dug into his jeans pocket and pulled one out.

"Don't have to pay me back. You can keep it." When I was walking to the corner of the lot, to the telephone, he said, "Hey. Hey, girl. Where're you from?"

The dime activated the telephone and I told the operator collect

call from Ann. Then I stood there waiting for the phone to ring.
The static of the line was enough: I could see the old black phone,
where it sat on the kitchen counter, breathing silently before it
rang. I knew the light there this time of day, the way the vinyl
chairs felt, warm and slick from the sun, on your thighs. I thought
of the cut cake under the clear glass cover, frosting melting down
onto the plate, like candle wax. The empty hallways were clean,
roses in the carpet down the middle, strips of wood floor showing
at the edges. Clean white lace covered all the dark wood surfaces
in the house. Out windows, the yard moved, never still, shim-
mering, the fields rustled a little, the old barn that used to be a
butter factory just on the edge of view.

The phone rang once. I heard it going through the empty
house. Maybe my grandmother was out in the yard or at the Red
Owl. She could be watering at the cemetery. I was sure, then, no
one would be home. And Ted would be working, Jimmy might be
on the road.

"Hullo?" My grandmother's voice sounded so exactly like her
that I almost hung up. For the first time, the telephone seemed
miraculous to me. I looked around at the poles and wires on the
dry hills. We were anywhere. I didn't know where.

"Collect call from Ann?" the operator said. "Will you accept
the charges?"

"Why sure. Ann, tell me, where are you?"

"I'm fine. I'm in Nevada."

Then the operator clicked off the phone. It was like other
people on the old party line, hanging up.

"Well, tell me what you've been doing." She was perplexed. I
could hear, she was trying to find out if I was in trouble.

"I don't know. Nothing much. Driving."

There was a billboard across the highway, the paper peeling
off, flapping. It was a family, in a red car, advertising the state of
Nevada.

"Well, are you having fun?"

"Yeah, I guess."

"Tell me, is there anything you need, Ann?"

That made me wince, so I couldn't say a word. I held the phone

a foot away from me. I wanted to go home, but I couldn't ask for
a thing. It was too hard to explain.

The house there seemed small then, still and away from everything. I tried to get my normal voice.

"No, I just called to say hello."

"Well, good. That's fine. We sure do miss you around here."
She was tapping something. She kept her nails long, filed in ovals
and unpolished. She tapped them against her front teeth. "Is your
ma nearby?"

"She's in the bathroom," I said.

"Well, I love you. We all do." Then she was quiet from the
embarrassment of having said that.

"Bye."

"Shouldn't I hold on a second and talk to your ma?"

"Nah, she takes a long time in there. With her makeup, you
know."

"I suppose she hasn't changed then."

"No."

I hung up the phone and the house back at home closed again,
silent and private. I couldn't see inside anymore. It was small and
neat, far away. I sank back against the outside wall of the phone
booth, letting the wind come to my face. There were low blue
hills in the distance.

"Hey, girl, wanna take a ride?"

I crossed my arms and began to say no, but just then my mother's car started coming back over the horizon and so I turned and
waited. She slowed down up the road where she'd left me.

Maybe that was why this was the last time it happened: because
I wasn't there. The car crawled, slowly, towards the station. She
was looking for me. I stood kicking the pavement, in no hurry for
her to get there. The fields were plain and dry. Air above the tar
pavement shimmered in ankle-deep waves. In a bucket by the
pumps, water sparkled, dark and bright.

When my mother saw me, she stopped the car and got out.

"Ann, you nearly scared me to—"

The boy whistled. I smiled and stared down at the blacktop.
He was looking at my legs.

"Ann. Get in the car," my mother said.

In my seat, I still saw him. I closed my fist around the dime.

"Who were you calling, tell me."

She was looking at me, waiting. I had to answer.

"No one."

She sighed and started the car.

"Just hold your horses until we get there, okay? Your grand-mother's old, leave her be. She hasn't got that long anymore."

I dragged my cupped hand out the window and the moving air felt solid, like a breast.

She was better. I could tell. She drove evenly and her shoulders dropped. Her foot pumped gradually, modulating the speed.

"Are you hungry?" she said. "'Cause I am. I could go for a little something."

All those times on the highway, it was doing something. I lost time there in the ditches, waiting. Minutes out of my life. It was as if I had millions of clocks ticking inside me and each time one stopped. I left one clock, dead and busted, on the gravel by the side of the road, each time.

I didn't say anything. The highway was clean and straight. I rested back in my seat.

"Huh, what do you say, Pooh?" She was trying to make up.

I held out, I was quiet. She clutched the steering wheel and the blood drained from her knuckles. I squeezed my fist. I could feel my palm sweating as if it would rust the metal of the dime. I wouldn't look at her.

But thinking was too hard. She was my mother and she was driving and we were almost to California.

I was quiet as long as I could be, but she would still have me for a long time. It was easier to talk.

"There's a sign," I said, finally. "A Travel Inn Hobo Joe's."

"Hungry?" she said, glad and loud.

I thought of the french fries, the chocolate malteds, as much as I wanted from the menu. "Starving," I said.

2

BEL AIR HOTEL

■ □ ■

I wonder what we looked like then, that day we drove over into California. My mother could probably still tell you what we were wearing. I remember she looked at me and then at herself in the rearview mirror as we neared the border. She wriggled in her seat.

That morning, she'd shouted, "Look at those fields. Should we stop, Annie? I think they're tomatoes. Yep. They are. Look at those beefsteaks!" She'd skidded to a stop that would have been dangerous if the highway hadn't been so empty. We'd climbed out and picked tomatoes, eating them right there in the field.

We stole vegetables all across America, anything we could eat without cooking. My mother spotted the trucks.

"Oh, Ann. Look. Sweet peas," she'd say. The trucks of peas were open-backed, the vines clumped in bundles. We followed those trucks anywhere, turning off into towns we'd never heard of and then waiting till the first stoplight, when my mother sent me out with a five-dollar bill to the driver. The windows of the cabs were high and I had to jump to knock. The drivers never touched our money. They shrugged and smiled and said, You go on ahead, take what you want, then. And we loaded up the whole backseat of the car, from the floor to the roof, with the sweet, heavy-scented vines.

Sometimes on the highway, loads of peas would drop off the truckbeds and bounce on the concrete like tumbleweed. We pulled onto the gravel shoulder and ran out and chased them, laughing on the hot empty road, the flat country still on all sides of us.

That last morning in Nevada we'd bought nine melons, big melons, each too heavy for one hand. We'd tasted samples from toothpicks on ragged, wet paper plates. We'd never imagined how many kinds of melons there could be. And they were all sweet.

But when we crossed the Nevada border some men made us stop. We couldn't take our melons into California. It was still not noon and already hot. We pulled onto the shoulder of the road. When the man told us we couldn't bring our melons in, my mother stood out of the car and cried. She talked to him, saying the same things again and again, while he shook his head no. He seemed to have all the time in the world. A green fly landed on his forehead and it took him a good forty seconds to lift up his hand and shoo it. I backed the car onto the grass and started hauling out melons. My mother screamed. I was twelve years old. I wasn't supposed to know how to drive.

We didn't have a knife or anything. We split the melons open, smashing them on the legs of the sign that said WELCOME TO CALIFORNIA, and we stood on the concrete platform eating them, the juice spilling down our arms.

Our shirts were still sticky and sweet smelling, but the bad, sour side of sweet, when we drove into Los Angeles. My mother had called ahead for reservations at one of the hotels she'd read about, but she wouldn't go there right away.

"Huh-uh. Look at us. And look at this car. We can't go like this. We're going to clean up a little first."

"They're used to it, they're a hotel, aren't they?"

"Honey, the Bel Air isn't just a hotel." She had the tone she always had when she was too tired to fight. "You'll see."

"Why can't we wash up there?"

"*Because.* That's why. You just don't. Listen to me once in a while." Then it seemed she'd brought me all the way to California just to make me mind.

She parked in front of a restaurant near the campus of UCLA.

"This looks like a good little place. And we can have a bite to eat. Hamburger Hamlet, it's called. Cute."

She took our gingham dresses from the trunk. They were still in their dry-cleaning cellophane. Two men leaned against the building. They had tie-dyed sheets spread out on the sidewalk with buckles and leather belts for sale. We stood there staring down, entranced. They were slow and graceful, smoking.

"What are you looking at? Come on," my mother said. The ladies' room was upstairs in the restaurant. "Those kids are on drugs," she whispered. "They're hooked on marijuana." My mother had read about drugs. She always read the magazines. Now she listens to talk radio. But even then she knew what drugs were.

In the rest room my mother plugged her steam rollers into the wall socket and unpacked her cosmetics and soaps, lining them up on the counter. She used the row of sinks as if this was her own huge dressing room. She turned on a hand dryer and touched up her nails, holding them under the warm air.

She washed, shaved her underarms and ripped open a fresh package of nylons. She clipped the hot rollers into her hair. She stood in pantyhose and a bra, starting on her makeup. She didn't dally, watching other people. Strangers touched their hands under thin streams of water in the sink farthest from us and my mother didn't notice. She was driven. The will to be clean.

"Ann," she called then, looking for me in the mirror. I was standing by the door. "Comemeer."

"My name is Heather," I said. While we were driving she told me I could pick a new name for myself in California. It would be my television name.

"Heather, then. You know who I mean." She sniffed me. "You smell," she said, and handed me a towel. "Let's have some scrubbing action. Get undressed and hurry it up."

I washed standing on one leg, the other foot on my knee, swishing the towel around lightly. Other women disciplined their eyes to look away from us, cut a hole in the air and avoided falling into it again.

They saw me as a Theresa Griling. It's a long story, this girl I knew at home. I was beginning to understand how someone could become a long story.

My mother didn't notice the other women, but she saw that I was embarrassed. All of a sudden she saw that. And it must have seemed like a defeat. She'd driven all that way and now we were here and I was ashamed of her.

She sighed one of her sighs. "Comemeer," she said. She brushed blush on my cheeks. "Listen. Nobody cares, do you hear? They don't give a hoot. They can think we wanted to wash up before we eat. They can see we've been traveling. They don't want you to stay dirty."

I must have looked pale standing there, because she pushed some lipstick over my lips. They were chapped and I wouldn't stand still, so she smeared a little and licked her finger to clean the edge of my mouth. I ran over to the sink and spit. I tasted her saliva, it was different from mine.

I felt something then, as I stood watching my spit twirl down the drain. I wanted to get away from her. There was nowhere I could go. I was twelve. She'd have me six more years.

My mother examined us in the mirror and sighed. She held my chin up and looked at us both. She'd been right. We did look much better. She gathered our things back into the suitcase and snapped the buckle shut. "See, all done," she said. "Doesn't it feel good to be clean?"

We found eight car washes in Westwood that afternoon but they were all the drive-through kind. My mother wasn't going to trust them with our Lincoln. She would now, but we were new then.

"You wouldn't do it by *hand*?" She was standing on the black-top talking to a boy who looked as if she were asking for the world. "I mean, I'll pay you. *Ex*-tra. I just don't want those hard detergents on it. They'll hurt the finish." She ran her hand on the car top. It was still smooth and new. This was a long time ago.

"You can wash it yourself, lady," the boy said, walking off. He walked with his head tilted slightly back, as if he owned the sky.

My mother sat down again in the car. "You know, I guess we

could," she said. "I guess we could do it ourselves." She started
to unpack the backseat.

"Heather, go." She gave me a five-dollar bill. "Give him this
and say we want rags for the windows and stuff to clean the seats.
Oh, and ask if they have a little vacuum cleaner, too. Go on."

She already had our one suitcase out and the trunk open. My
mounted child's ice skates were on the pavement next to a tire.

The boy stood hosing off the wheels of a Jeep. "Hurry up," my
mother yelled, but I kept sluffing. I didn't care about the car
being clean. If it was mine, I'd have just left it dirty. She would
say I never learned to take care of a thing.

I stood with the five-dollar bill stuck in my hand, looking down
at the cement ramps by the gas pumps.

"Could we please buy rags and cleaning stuff and also possibly
rent a vacuum cleaner?"

The kid laughed. "What kind of cleaning stuff?"

I shrugged. "For the outside and for the seats."

"Gonna do it yourself, huh?"

"She wants to."

He put the hose down, not turning it off, so a stream of water
dribbled down the blacktop. He stuffed a bucket with rags and
plastic bottles. "You have to pull up here for the vacuum. You
just pull on up when you ready."

"Thank you."

"I don't know how much to charge you for this stuff. Five dollars probably be too much. You not going to use that much fluid."

"She might. You better take it."

He laughed. "She might, huh? She always like that?"

My top lip pulled down over my teeth. "Oh, no, she's usually
not that bad. We just moved here. Just today."

"Oh, I see. Well, makes sense. Anxious to get the car cleaned,
huh?"

"Yeah."

But we kept looking at each other, his chin tucked down
against his neck and his eyes dropping open, until my mother
called.

"Heather, hurry it up. It's already four o'clock."

"That your name, Heather?" He picked up his hose again.
"Yeah," I said. "Thanks."

Torches flared on both sides of the road that led to the Bel Air
Hotel. The path wound in and out of woods. My mother drove real
slow. She parked underneath the awning. I moved to get out but
she stopped me and told me to wait. She rested her hands on the
steering wheel the way she used to for years on top of my shoulders. The valet came and opened the doors, her door first and
then mine. She wasn't shy to relinquish the car now. There was
nothing embarrassing in it. It was clean. The leather smelled of
Windex.

At the desk a man shuffled through his book. "We've put you
in the tower, which is a lovely room, but there's only one bed. A
double. I'm afraid it's all we have left."

My mother let a frown pass over her face, for appearances.
We'd slept in doubles all the way across America. She didn't like
to sleep alone. I did. She was frowning for me to see, too.

"That will be all right." She shrugged.

Following the valet to our room, we let ourselves relax. I
bumped against the wall and she let me bump because I was
clean. The stucco seemed to absorb amber evening light.

We walked through an outdoor courtyard. There was a small
café; white tablecloths, white chairs, the distant slap and shuffle
of late swimmers. People at the tables were drinking, lingering in
daytime clothes.

We climbed stone steps to the tower. My mother tipped the
valet and then closed the door behind us. I crossed my arms over
my chest. She looked at me and asked, "What's the matter with
you now? Don't tell me even this doesn't satisfy you."

She stood looking around the room. And it was a beautiful
hotel.

But I was thinking about us on our hands and knees, our butts
sticking out the car door, scrubbing the melon juice stains off the
leather. The afternoon canceled out now. My mother was not that
way. She could hold contrasts in her mind at once. She must have
found me horribly plain.

"It's nice," I said.

A green and white polished cotton canopy shaded the four-poster bed. My mother kicked her shoes off and collapsed. I sat on the window seat, my leg swinging over the side. My jacket hung on the back of a chair where I'd left it. She hooked it with her bare foot and brought it to her face. Then she tried it on, adjusting the collar, turning it up.

I looked at her—she was standing on the bed, barefoot, her toenails polished a light shade of pink, glancing in the mirror. "Take my jacket off," I said, cranking the window open. It wasn't warm but my arm was pumping as if I needed air.

"It fits me. You don't know what a cute little shape I have, for a mother. Pretty darn good for my age."

"Can we afford this place?" I wasn't looking at her anymore. My face was out the window, gulping the night. I watched the waiters move, beautifully, around the glows of candles on the little tables. One man cupped his hand over a woman's to light a cigarette. My mother's fingers spidered on my back.

"I'll worry about that, okay? I'm the adult and you're the child. And don't you forget that."

"Don't I wish I could."

"Well, you can. So start right now." She laughed, half a laugh, almost a laugh.

"I'm hungry."

"Should we call room service?"

"No, I want to go out."

I hardly ever said things like that. I was afraid I would be blamed for wanting too much, but that night it seemed I had to go outside. I didn't like being just with my mother all the time. You were alone but she was there. My mother must have felt that too, but I think it was one of the things she liked about having a daughter. You never were all alone.

"I don't know, I'd just as soon have something here, now that we're parked and all. To tell the truth, I'm sick of this driving. You don't know, you haven't been doing it, but it tires you. You can't believe how my shoulders feel. They ache, Heather-honey, they really ache. Twenty-one, twenty-two, let's see, we left the fifth, do you realize, we've been on the road sixteen days. No, the fifth to the, today's—"

"We can go here. You don't have to drive. There's a restaurant down there."

Her head turned. She looked a little startled; she always did when she was interrupted from one of her long songs. "Oh, okay. Fine. That's fine. It's just this driving, seventeen days, day in, day out, eight hours a day behind that wheel and boy, you feel it, you feel it right—"

I stood up and walked to the door, my jacket hooked on one finger. "Let's go."

"Well, would you just wait a second, please, and let me wash my face? And I want to put on a little bit of makeup."

I sat on the steps and listened to her vigorous washing. She slapped her face, her feet thumping on the bathroom floor.

"It's going to be a few minutes," she said.

And it was. The sky went from deep blue to purple to black in the time it took my mother to get ready. I sat on the steps watching other people come to the café, sit down and drink, clinking their glasses together. I saw a man reach across a table and rummage underneath a woman's hair, as if there were something to find.

My mother was humming, standing with her back to me.

When she stepped outside, I sniffed loudly to let her know I didn't like perfume. I was wearing my regular afternoon clothes, and she'd put on a long dress, with a slit up the back. She was the adult, I was the child. She wore pearls and heels, her hair was teased two inches out from her face.

I rolled up the sleeves of my shirt. I have the kind of arms you roll sleeves up on. My mother is softer, plush.

"Well," she said, making noises around her, the pearls, the cotton swishing, "are we ready?" She was talking in an octave higher than her normal voice, a voice to be overheard.

"What do you think?" I shoved my hands in my pockets and started down the stairs. She clattered behind me.

"Wait, wait, would you? Go a little slower, please. You don't know what it's like up here. I mean on these heels." She put her hands on my shoulders. "My balance isn't what it should be. It's

fine, in the morning, I'm fine. But by this time of day, you're just
going to have to slow down. Please."

"Why do you wear them, then?"

"Honey, you know. They look nice." She caught up to me and
grabbed my arm, falling a little. "At my age, they expect you to
have a little height. And who knows, maybe I'll meet someone
tonight, you never know. And I'd hate to meet the right man when
I had on the wrong shoe."

But my mother seemed to gain balance when we waited at the
café entrance. I was glad to be with her then. I was glad to have
her in those shoes. I stood close by her, when I was shy.

"Two for dinner?"

"Please," she said, her chin high, following him. She knew
how to do these things.

We got a small table at the edge of the courtyard with its own
glowing candle, like the rest. We didn't look at each other at first,
we looked at the people around us. I didn't see any free men for
her.

My mother opened the menu. "Wow," she whispered, "a wee
bit pricey."

"Room service would be just the same."

"Not necessarily. But that's okay. We're here now, so fine. Well,
I know what I'm having. I'm having a glass of wine and a cup of
soup." Even that was going to be expensive.

"I'm hungry," I said. I was mad. I wasn't going to have any
soup or salad. If we could afford to stay here then we could afford
to eat, and I was going to eat.

The waiter came and my mother ordered her glass of wine and
cup of soup. "Is that all, ma'am?"

"I think so. We had a late lunch."

I ordered a steak and began answering the waiter's long string
of questions. Baked potato. Oil and vinegar. Beans instead of
rice.

My mother kicked my shin, hard, under the table.

"Didn't you want a hamburger? I don't know if you saw, but
they have them."

"No, I'd rather have a steak."

"Oh, okay, fine. Whatever you want. It's just that you said you wanted a hamburger. You said it this afternoon."

Then the waiter left us alone. My mother leaned over the table and whispered. "Didn't you see me winking at you, you dummy? Didn't you feel me kick? I can't afford this. What do you think you're doing? Jesus. You saw what I ordered, didn't you? Don't you think I'm hungry? Am I supposed to starve myself so you can have a steak?"

"Why didn't you order yourself a steak?"

"Boy," she said, "I can't believe how dumb you are sometimes. We can't *afford* this."

"So why are we here? Why aren't we somewhere we can afford? I asked you upstairs and you said I shouldn't worry, that you were the adult and I was the child."

"Well, children order hamburgers when they go out to expensive restaurants. That's all they're allowed to order."

"Then, why didn't you change it? Go ahead. Tell the waiter I can't have my steak."

"I don't believe you. You shouldn't have ordered it! You felt my foot under the table, you just wanted your steak. Well, fine, you can have it now and you'd better enjoy it, because believe me, it's the last steak you'll get for a while."

She sank back into her chair, her arms lapsing on the armrests. Our waiter arrived with her wine.

"Everything all right?"

A smile came reflexively to her face. "Lovely, just lovely."

She'd had it with me. She pretended that she simply wasn't hungry. As if not wanting things was elegant, but wanting them and not being able to get them was not.

She leaned over the table again.

"If you were so hungry, why didn't you order more at lunch? You love hamburgers. You usually always order a hamburger."

"I do not *love* hamburgers."

"Yes you do." She sighed. "Why can't it ever just be nice? Why can't we ever just have a nice, relaxing time?"

"In other words why can't I just want a hamburger, why can't I

want what you want me to want. Why don't I always just happen
to want the cheapest thing on the menu."

"That's what I do, why can't you?" she said. "Don't you think
I'm hungry after all that driving?"

"You can have some of mine."

"No." She shook her head. "I don't want any. It's yours. You
ordered it, now you eat it." She looked around the café. "There's
nothing for me here. I wanted to just stay in and have something
quick from room service. Not get all dressed up. I just wanted to
relax for once."

Our food came and I stopped looking at her. I started cutting
my steak. It was thick and glistening with fat. I put all four rounds
of butter in the baked potato. Steam rose up in spirals. Then I
shook on salt, spooned in sour cream. It looked delicious. She
took a sip of her soup.

"So how is it?"

I said fine, still looking at my plate.

"How's the salad? You haven't touched the salad."

"Uh-huh," I said, still eating.

"Try the vegetables, you need those vitamins." She put down
her spoon. "Would you like a taste of my soup? It's delicious,
really, these little bits of carrot. They're grated very finely. I wonder what they use. It tickles your throat when it goes down, like
lots of little sparks."

She was even smiling.

"No thank you," I said.

She did the talking while I ate. "You know, you're really right.
This is a lovely place. Lovely. The pool over there, can you hear
it? That little glup, glup, glup? And this air. I love these warm,
dry nights. I wonder how cold it gets in winter. I know we won't
need really heavy coats, coats like we had at home, but do you
think we'll even need any? Light coats? Sort of raincoat-ish? I'd
love to have a trench."

Then I set my silverware down. I guess I was finally full. Now
I looked around, too, and up at the starless sky. "The air is nice,"
I said.

"Are you finished with that?"

"What? Oh, the steak?"

"I thought if you were I'd try a bite."

I shoved the whole plate over to her side. I passed her the salad and the dish of vegetables.

"Oh, no, I just want a little bite."

"Try the vegetables. They're very good." I knew if she finished my dinner, that would be the last I'd hear about the bill.

She sighed and settled in her chair. "Oh, it is. Very, very good." She leaned over and whispered to me. "You know, for what you get, these prices really aren't so bad. This is enough for the two of us, really. You know?"

Later the waiter came for our plates. All that was left was parsley. "I'll take that," my mother said and grabbed the sprig from his tray. He must have thought we were starving. But my mother really always had liked parsley.

"Will that be all? Or can I get you some dessert and coffee?"

My mother winked. "No coffee, please. But I think we'd like to see a menu for dessert. And would you like a glass of milk, Young Lady?"

I looked up at the waiter. "I'd like coffee, please. With cream and sugar."

He left, to bring the dessert tray. My mother looked at me suspiciously and smiled. "Ann, now tell me, when did you learn to drink coffee? Were you just bluffing or did you learn? Look me in the eye and tell me true."

We shared the cup when it came. She took a sip, then I took a sip.

"With you," I said. "I learned from you."

I could see her looking at me, wondering. But she let it go and she let the bill go, too. Now, I'm glad she did. You grow up and you leave them. She only had me six more years.

3

THE HOUSE ON CARRIAGE COURT

■ □ ■

We were leaving the house on Carriage Court and Ted the ice skating pro. We'd met Ted when we took skating lessons, first to firm my mother's thighs, then just for fun. All day the air conditioners in the arena hummed like the inside of a refrigerator. On the door of my locker hung a picture of Peggy Fleming; on my mother's, Sonja Henie. Framed photographs of Ted during his days with Holiday on Ice hung in the main office, next to the list of hourly prices. In them, he didn't look like himself. He was young. He had short, bristly hair and a glamorous smile. His limbs stretched out, starlike, pointing to the four corners of the photographs. The lighting seemed yellow and false. In one of the pictures, it was snowing.

In spring, three years before we left, my mother had gone to Las Vegas and married Ted. She came back without any pictures of the wedding and we moved into the house on Carriage Court. She said she hadn't wanted a big wedding, since it was her second marriage. She'd worn a short dress she already had.

When my mother and Ted came home from Las Vegas they took me for a ride in Ted's car. He turned into a development on the west side of the Fox River and they told me they'd bought a new house. Before, we'd lived all our lives with my grandmother.

"Guess which," my mother had said, looking back at me from the front seat. Ted drove a white Cadillac, with a maroon interior and roof.

I knew, I could tell from their faces. They'd bought the rectangular house with no windows. "I hope it's not that one," I pointed.

"Because that one looks like a shoebox." They didn't say anything, Ted just kept driving. Finally, my mother sighed.

It turned out a young architect had built it. He loved the house. He was only leaving because the house was too small for another child.

After we moved into the house on Carriage Court, my mother and I stopped taking lessons. Ted could fill up the ice with other students and that way he made more money. I quit skating altogether. Eventually, my mother stopped, too. Then Ted went to the rink himself every day, like any other man going to a job.

My mother and I seemed different in the new house. I was always in trouble. Neither of us could remember a time anymore when I wasn't always in trouble. There were rules. We were not supposed to open the refrigerator with our hands, which would smear the bright, chrome, new handle, but by a sideways nudge from an elbow. "Here," my mother demonstrated, showing me how to pull my sleeve over my fist like a mitten if I really had to touch the handle with my hand. Now that she was married, my mother decorated the inside of the refrigerator. All our jars were lined up according to size.

Sinks and faucets were supposed to be polished with a towel after every time you used them. Then the towel had to be folded in thirds and hung up again on the rack. Ted went along with all this, I suppose because he loved her.

And now that we lived on our own, we had the same thing for dinner every night: thick, wobbly steaks, which my mother served with baked potatoes. She also gave us each a plate-sized salad. Ted thought salad dressing was gauche, so we sprinkled the lettuce with salt and red wine vinegar. We didn't have any furniture in the house, except for two beds. We sat on a bed and balanced the plates on our laps.

My mother read health books. She read books by Gaylord Hauser about how he kept movie stars on sets in California looking fresh at four in the afternoon by serving them health food protein snacks. She served us protein snacks. Once a week, she broiled a châteaubriand, which Ted sliced for her. She arranged the pink rectangular pieces on a plate and kept them in the refrigerator under a sheet of Saran Wrap. We ate them cold, with salt. She made us steak tartare for breakfast. She bought ground tenderloin and mixed it with pepper and capers and two egg yolks. We ate breakfast at the counter, standing up. We spread the meat on buttered whole wheat toast.

There were nights I remembered before they were married, when Ted and my mother had eaten late in the gray television light of my grandmother's living room. They sat in chairs with standing TV trays. I saw them when I came down for a glass of water. Then, the rare, thick steaks, moving on their plates when they touched them with knives, running with the shiny, red-gold juice, seemed to make my whole face swell with longing.

Now, in the new house on Carriage Court, I wanted anything else. All meat tasted the same to me. It tasted the way my skin tasted, like a sucked piece of my own arm. I asked my mother for tuna casserole. But she only laughed.

She told me other people ate tuna because it was cheap. Plus it wasn't healthy. Anyway, she and Ted liked meat.

"Very few men are as clean as Ted," my mother told her friend Lolly. There was nowhere to sit in the new rectangular house on Carriage Court, so they stood, holding their coffee cups. Lolly was another woman from Bay City who'd gone away to college and then come back home to her mother. The way my mother sighed and drummed her fingers on the bare wall, it made you think she was a little sorry Ted was so clean. She might have wished he weren't always malleable. She sighed again. Still, she wasn't sure. There was a row of unpacked brown boxes, and I perched crosslegged on one of them. "I'm neat," my mother said, "I just always have been. I can't *stand* messes."

That was a total lie. But Lolly nodded, sipping her coffee. I was thinking of the inside of my mother's purse, of all my mother's purses. In the house on Lime Kiln Road, she'd kept them in a closet, lined up on a shelf. In each one was a nest of old things, brushes, hair, bobby pins, makeup spilled and then hardened, so that the old orange powder and ink stained the lining, broken pencils, scraps of paper, little address books, all worn and woven together into something whole. But no one saw inside them except me.

"Honey, if I've told you once, I've told you a hundred times, don't sit on those boxes, for God's sakes! You don't know what's inside where! I swear, if I open them and find broken dishes, you're going to go out and work to buy new ones."

I jumped off and went to the kitchen. I had no doubt that I'd always be in trouble from now on. There were so many things to remember. Even when I tried I made mistakes. A minute later, I was in trouble in the kitchen for eating grapes from their stems, instead of breaking off my own little cluster.

My mother reached down, out of nowhere in the morning, and laid her cool hand like an envelope on my forehead.

"Where does it hurt?" We didn't have a thermometer in the house on Carriage Court; she would have to decide. She worked and she always ran late in the morning, so she would have to settle this fast.

"All over," I said. "My throat."

She was looking out the window, running through the day ahead, far away, in the out-of-town school. She didn't want to make a mistake. Well, it could never hurt to rest, she seemed to be thinking. She sighed. "Okay, stay here and sleep. Just stay home. Tomorrow, I'll write you a note."

Now that we lived in the new house, I stayed home alone when I was sick. The moisture from my mother's hand felt good on my forehead and the distant slamming of the front door sounded like relief in my side. I spread out in my bed and moved, falling slowly into another red warm sleep. It was familiar to be sick, I was returning to a place already known. Turning in bed, under the cool sheets, all the sick days seemed the same, crystallized like cabins along one lake, spanning all my childhood years. Outside the smallest hung my red and blue plaid jumper, my first-grade Catholic school uniform, and in a corner my grandmother stood shaking a thermometer, reading it by the window light, where a beating hummingbird fed at the red glass dropper just on the other side of the screen. In another cabin, I was nine and pretending to be sick: the distant bell rang, faintly, and a test was being given in the gray-green public school. In the fourth-grade trailer, children handed papers back from the front of every row. The harder glittering objects of my healthy passions expired in my exhaustion. I loved the familiar here. The nicked wood of my old dresser, the kitchen table from Lime Kiln Road. I wanted my own mother's hand.

When I woke up, snow fell softly at the window and the black and white television was on. Lucy and Ethel were trying to steal John Wayne's footprints from the cement outside of Grauman's Chinese Theatre in old Hollywood.

I stayed in bed and watched the reruns and time fell off in half-hour segments. Then I got up to get something to eat. The kitchen was dry and bright with sun. It was late morning. Everyone was out to work. I made a big breakfast to make me feel better. I scrambled eggs and mixed up frozen orange juice. I finished and went back to my room. I wasn't sure anymore if I was sick or not.

And then I heard the noon bell from school. Out my window, there was an aluminum fence and a vacant lot two yards down. I saw my friends from school come back on the path for lunch, their parka hoods down, their black rubber boots unbuckled and flapping.

I ducked. I didn't want them to see me. I wasn't sick enough not to care.

I decided in the glittering noon light that I would get dressed and go to school. I'd tell my teacher I was sick in the morning but I felt better now. I would bring a note from my mother tomorrow. Afternoon was easier anyway. Geography and science and an hour of reading before I would come home, at three o'clock with the others.

I went to my dresser and got tights. Standing up too fast made my head spin and I had to sit down on the bed for a while before it was still again. Then I went to my closet and pulled on a dress over my head. I felt dizzy and hot inside, but I went to the bathroom and brushed my hair. I could hardly feel it. It was like brushing someone else's hair. I steadied my hand on the cool tiles.

I went to the front closet and got on boots and my coat and mittens—I wanted to be all ready to go. I stacked my schoolbooks up on the kitchen counter, my pencil case on top. I stood in the closet and rummaged through my mother's and Ted's coat pockets for money. I took a dollar from Ted's jacket, the paper folded and soft as a Kleenex, and put it in my mitten. Then I sat down in our only chair, waiting for it to be time.

I was floppy in the chair. I felt whatever strength I had seeping out into the upholstery. The walk would be the hard thing, then I would be at my desk at school. Finally, it was time to go. Early, but time. I got up and went to the kitchen to get my books. I was counting things off. I took the balled gray string with my key from my pocket and locked the door behind me. I walked down our driveway to the street. The snow had soaked into the ground already. The plowed, wet pavement seemed very bright.

With each step I felt less sure of myself. I felt myself walking like my grandmother walked, as she stood up out of her car when there was ice on the drive, dizzy.

I turned around and went back home. I closed the door behind me and locked it, pulled off my boots and hung up my coat. I took my clothes off and got into bed again. I fell into a light, warm sleep. Now I didn't care.

I woke up later, hearing the shouts of my friends on the path, coming home from school. They looked fine, themselves, through for the day. You weren't finished with a sick day at three o'clock. You didn't get through being sick until the next morning. I'd still be wearing my same pajamas tonight when my mother and Ted came in from outside. I felt the back of my neck under my hair. I turned on the TV again for the after-school cartoons.

It was dark then and I was glad, because all the other kids would be inside, doing homework and getting ready for supper. There was something about the stillness of our house, though. It was empty and dry and I wished my mother would come home.

The front door slammed. I knew it was my mother, not Ted, from the way she moved around in the kitchen, the double echo of her high heels. I heard the pan I'd left on the stove clatter against the porcelain of the sink. The refrigerator door opened and closed. Then her footsteps were coming and she stood in my doorway, clicking on the overhead light. I was still watching television, another "I Love Lucy," an older one, back in New York.

"So what did you do all day?" She looked over the room, her hands on her hips. "Besides making a mess. I thought you might at least vacuum or do a little *something* around here. I can't do everything, you know. I can't work and shop and clean and then come home and clean up again after you. You could've eaten a can of tuna, like I do for lunch, but no, you had to dirty a pan and there's crumbs all over the counter." She clicked the TV off and I felt the loss of the small apartment, the tiny furniture, like a quick pain.

"I'm sick, Mom."

"You're not that sick. I'm sick too, I have a sore throat and I still went to work. Now, come on, get up and you're going to clean that kitchen."

Maybe I should have vacuumed. I could have. Maybe I wasn't that sick. There were obvious things I didn't seem to see. I never in a million years would have thought of vacuuming.

I started doing the dishes. It was easy. I felt warm inside and dizzy. I kept scrubbing and scrubbing at the pan, looking out the window into the dark. The water felt good on my hands.

My mother came up behind me and touched my hair. "I'm sorry for yelling like I did. I guess I'm tired, too, you know? We both just need a rest."

We weren't popular on Carriage Court. My mother and Ted didn't talk to other people. You saw the others out grilling in their front yards and settling sprinklers on the grass after dark, but my mother and Ted stayed inside. Our first summer, a posse of three fathers from the end of the block came to tell Ted how to mow the lawn. I stood behind the screen door, listening. They were all nice, looking at their hands while they talked, their shoes shuffling on the porch. Ted was nice, too, inviting them in for a drink.

When the men moved towards the door I ran to my room and cried. From the open windows I heard the shouts of a kickball game starting up. I wouldn't go outside then, everyone would know. They must have known already. They probably thought of me as the girl with the overgrown lawn.

A little while later my mother came in and sat next to me on my bed. "Aw, honey, I know just how you feel."

I pushed her and she faltered and fell off, onto the floor. It took a moment to get up. "Oh." She was genuinely shocked. I studied my hand. I was surprised, too. I didn't think I'd pushed her that hard. She looked at me again, brushing off her white sharkskin slacks. "Oh, you little monster."

Her arm came near my face and I hit her.

After that, she left. I heard the two of them moving in the kitchen, but no one came to my room. The house seemed unusually quiet, I could hear the refrigerator humming. Finally, I got tired of being in bed and walked to the garage. I took out the lawn mower. We had the thin, manual kind you pushed, because my mother thought they were more elegant. We had a black one. My mother hated the noise that motors made, mowing.

It was really hard. I'd cut an uneven row of four feet, when Ted tried to take it from me.

"I'll do it, Ann."

My mother stuck her head out the screen door, holding the handle, as if, now that I'd hit her, she was afraid. "Annie, he made arrangements with the Kokowski boy to do it tomorrow morning. It's all set. We even paid him already."

But I couldn't think of anything else except getting the lawn done then. Ted had to pry my fingers one by one off the black handle. I was surprised when he held them, palms up, in his hand. The fingers and knuckles were red and scraped; I was bleeding. He looked down into my face, not letting go.

"Take it away from her, Ted." My mother, still inside, poked her head out, yelling. "She'll kill herself with it. Look at her, she's going crazy."

Ted's voice was gentle, almost a whisper. "I know you want it done now. I understand that. But I'll do it. Let me do it." I thought there was something wrong with his smile, though, his teeth looked like a zipper.

I stepped back, crossing my arms. I was looking down at my

tennis shoes. The right one was ripped over the toes and there were grass stains, too.

Ted was stronger than I was. Each of his lunges mowed a five-foot row evenly.

"Oh, Ted, don't now," my mother called. "Why? We already paid him."

"It's all right, Adele. It won't take me long."

She let the screen door drop shut. "I just don't see why she always has to get her way. Every time she throws a tantrum, we give in."

I ran to the end of the block to the kickball game. When the Kokowski boy stole second base, he saw Ted on our lawn.

"Hey, your stepdad's mowing your yard. I was supposed to do it tomorrow."

"You better give him his money back," I said.

"So, how come he's doing it now? He sure waited long enough before."

"Want to fight over it?"

He said no, forget it, even though he was bigger than I was. I'm glad he did because the way I was right then I know I could have hurt him.

I lay on my stomach on the kitchen floor, drawing. My mother moved at the counter, washing food. It was four o'clock on a Sunday and the world, from our windows, stayed still.

For a long time, I colored my picture. All my drawing took a long time. I didn't like there to be any white left on the page. My third-grade nun had tacked my pictures up on the bulletin board in the hall. She had dunked my head over a drawing on a table to see the first-place blue ribbon in the crafts fair. She told me I was the best artist in primary school because I was patient. Then another boy moved to the district, a boy they didn't like because he couldn't sit still and because he wore clothes that were too small for him. Tim drew all the time, on everything. He could pencil psychedelic drum sets on the edge of his lined paper in three minutes and they pulsed against your eyes. Nobody else thought he was any good, but I didn't mind moving so much when we went to Carriage Court, because of Tim. I knew he was better.

I still drew at home, on the floor, and my mother never looked at the pictures. No one saw them except me.

That day she was standing at the window by the sink and I stopped. I put all my crayons away in the box and turned over the picture to the floor. Her shoulders were jumping.

I went over and touched her. She didn't seem to notice. "Mom," I whispered, ever so quiet, not wanting to disturb anything.

Then she looked down at me. "Was it better just the two of us?" She bit her lip, then shoved knuckles into her wobbling mouth. I looked up at her, still holding the end of her sweater. She'd stumped me, guessed what I always meant. If it was still just the two of us, we were going to move to California. So I could be a child star on television.

But I thought of Ted, then, the familiar sound of his car coming up our driveway, everything the way it was.

"Tell me, Bipper, were you happier without this man?"

"He's nice," I said.

"Do you really think so?"

I nodded, eagerly. We took the afternoon to make a surprise; we were both dressed up when he came home at seven for supper, the kitchen floor was waxed and glistening like ice. We must have seemed expectant, heads tilted, beaming, when he came to the door.

He looked from one of us to the other, bemused. "What's up?"

"Dinner in a sec," my mother said. She opened the broiler, poked the meat.

Then Ted did what he always did, he carried the black and white TV in from my room to the kitchen and flicked on the news. I crowded near my mother to fix the plates.

"Do you think he sees?" I said. Everything in the kitchen was clean and polished. We'd opened a new box of Arm & Hammer baking soda in the refrigerator.

"Absolutely." She nodded. "Comemeer." She walked over to a clean place on the counter. When I'd put away my picture, in a cupboard, she must have found it. Now she was looking down hard at it. I had been drawing grass, the individual stalks. There was still a field of white. It was only half finished.

"I thought it would be of me," she said.

I was in trouble all the time now.

On weekends, my mother and Ted slept late. I always snuck outside before they woke up. "A-yun," my mother called me one Saturday, yelling from the porch like other mothers. I wouldn't have gone in, but there was a whole kickball team of kids looking at me who went running when their mothers called.

"Be right back." I dropped the ball, knowing, as I said it, what the chances of that were.

My mother, seeing me, pulled her head back into the house like a turtle and slammed the door. Ted's car was gone from the driveway, that was bad. I walked slowly, staying out as long as I could. She stood just inside the door, in the entry hall. Even though it was a cool, bright day, our house seemed stale, as if the air was old. My mother was wearing nothing but Ted's old gray sweat shirt that she slept in.

"You really think you're the cat's meow, don't you," she said, looking at me and shaking her head. "You think you can just play, while I work and work and work. Sure, that's what mothers are for, isn't it, to slave away so you can have a nice house and clothes and food in the refrigerator when your friends come over. Sounds pretty good. Well, I'm sorry to tell you, but you're not going to get away with that anymore. You're going to have to start pulling your own weight."

Through the kitchen windows, the sky was clear and young, the palest blue.

"It's my fault too, I spoiled you. I should have let you cry when your father wanted to go dancing. I should've gone with him."

I started walking and her nails bit into my arm.

"Oh, no you don't. You're not going anywhere. You're going to stay right here and clean, for a change. You can see what I do all day Saturday and Sunday and that's my vacation. I work all week while you're playing."

"I go to school," I said.

She bent down over the vacuum cleaner. Hoses and brushes sprawled over the kitchen floor.

It was the same vacuum cleaner we'd always had, the Electrolux my father had given me rides on when I was a child. He'd pulled me on it all over my grandmother's house, bumping from the carpets onto the floors. We got it for free because it was my father's sample, when he worked as a vacuum cleaner salesman. "You go over EACH square FIVE times. THEN you move on to the next one." The kitchen was the only room in the new house that didn't have wood floors. The floor was black and white linoleum, checkered. It went on and on. There must have been hundreds of squares. I was counting up one side, to multiply with the other. "See, now watch carefully." My mother put all her weight into banging the long brush against the molding. Her legs moved with bitter, zealous energy.

"Mom, it's one o'clock. Why don't you put on some pants."

"Because *I've* been working all day, that's why, Little Miss."

"You've been sleeping is what you've been doing. And you go to anybody else's house and their mother's wearing pants. I don't care what you do, I just think it's ugly, that's all."

"Well, then, I'll tell you, Honey. Don't look. Because I'll wear whatever I want in my own house that I pay for—"

"Gramma paid for it."

"Ooo, you little—" She lifted the vacuum cleaner nozzle over her head ready to swing, but I jumped back and then she sucked in her breath. "Oh, no. No. You're not going to provoke a fight so you can run outside and get out of your chores. Oh, no you don't. You're a smart kid, but your mother's smarter. Now here. You take it. Let me watch you."

She turned the vacuum cleaner on again. I picked up the handle and brushed it softly against the floor, my ears dull to the noise. Next door, someone was mowing their lawn.

"Come on, let's get some muscle in there. Boy, you can't do anything right, can you?" She grabbed it out of my hand and started banging the metal brush up against the wall again, her whole body slugging. "See, that's the way. Now, do it."

A few seconds later, she called from the back of the house,

shouting over the noise of the machine. "Five times. And remember, I'm checking. So it better be clean. Or else you're just going to do it over again."

I looked down at the floor. I thought of the years in front of me when I would still need a mother. The hundreds of black and white squares. And I vacuumed hard, slamming the baseboards.

After six squares I looked behind me at the kitchen floor. Rows and rows and rows times five. I heard water running for my mother's bath. The rushing water sounded musical, tempting. I looked back once and decided, I'm not going to do this. I left the vacuum cleaner going so she'd still hear the noise and I ran outside.

It wasn't the same as before. I didn't play kickball, because my mother could call me there. I ran the other way, past the vacant lots down to where they were building the new highway. In the woods, I remembered I could slow down. My blood was still jumping in the backs of my knees. Below, yellow bulldozers crawled in the sand. Sometimes men hiked up and gave us dollars to keep our eyes on the surveyor's stakes, not to let anyone pull them out. The woods were going for the new highway, but we helped the men for a dollar.

I lay down and put my hands up beneath my head. Clouds moved slowly. I lay there, chewing on a piece of grass. I closed my eyes and tried to forget about myself. When it got dark I'd have to go home. I'd be in trouble again.

A rainy day after school, four, four thirty. Something in my throat. I was alone in the house. They wouldn't be home until six or seven. The house was empty. The kitchen was dry and clean, no food in the refrigerator. It was a night we would go out to eat. Outside, it seemed damp. I sat in my bedroom, in the back of the house, facing backs of things. Fences, other people's yards. There was nothing in my room but one bed and the old TV.

I took my clothes off and I sat on my bed, looking at myself. I hadn't made my bed that morning, so it was a mess of sheets and the wool blanket. The old TV on the floor, a portable black and white, was playing softly, on to a comedy from the fifties. I had the volume turned down low so all I heard was the rise of the same laugh. I'd look at the screen then, when I heard it, and watch the actors, a man and woman staring at each other. It was the same gray and white light, the television, as the sky outside, the rain on the window. I felt my arms and legs, from my shoulders to my elbows, my knees, down to my arches. I was thin, slight.

It seemed damp in the house and I was alone.

I went to my mother's bathroom and I took an oily compact mirror from her makeup bag. Back in my room, the warm blanket felt good on my skin then. I held the greasy mirror, looking at myself.

I felt colder then. I hid the mirror under the blanket and rubbed my legs from the hip bones down to my ankles, the outsides. I clasped my fingers around my ankles. I was alone. Alone. No one was watching me. I didn't feel like I would go anywhere anymore, like California. I knew I'd stay here in the back of the house, facing the backs of things.

My mother looked out the window while she warmed up the car. Anything not to see me. When she got mad enough at me, she took me to my grandmother's house.

Even in my dreams, when I was chased and running, I saw yellow lights in a kitchen, the blue back of my grandmother's dress as she bent over to reach a low cupboard. My grandmother was almost always home.

My mother slowed the car when we turned onto the old road. The sky was darker, the road was uneven, there were no streetlights, only stars. We heard wind in the tall trees. When we walked inside, my grandmother was sitting at the kitchen table, her silver glasses low on her nose, picking the meat out of hickory nuts, collecting the soft parts inside a glass jar.

The plates she used for every day were white with a faded gold line around their rims. The china was scratched from knives and some of the plates were chipped, but I'd known them all my life. She brought out a blueberry pie from the cupboard, still in the square pan, covered with tinfoil, the blueberries black and glistening, caught in a net of glaze like a dark and liquid lace.

My mother sighed, exhausted, holding her coffee cup and looking around the room. It was a place where she recognized everything, the position of the house on the land, the stars out the kitchen windows and the clean, ironed hairpin lace doilies. She did not like the house, she would never have chosen it, but it was the only place I saw her thin shoulders fall, where she hooked her jacket on a peg instead of buttoning it up around a hanger. Her legs swung under the table and her smile came easily to me, no matter what I'd done, no matter how bad I'd been. She was tired and home.

We heard the distant running noise of the highway and the nearer etching of the crickets by the side of the house, and in the kitchen, the refrigerator and fluorescent lights hummed.

"I was watching Welk," my grandmother said.

"Oh, should we go in there, Mom?"

"Ugh, no, it's all reruns. I've seen it before."

My mother stood up when she thought she should go, slowly, as if she didn't want to. The beds here were made with tight sheets dried on a line outside and then ironed. You could hear the wind through the walls. But she had to go. She was grown up and married. We waited for a moment by the screen door, looking at the car. My mother had to go out and get in it. She turned on all her lights. The car glowed like a lit cage. We watched until we couldn't see her anymore.

In the downstairs bedroom, there were hundreds of pajamas and nightgowns in the dresser drawers, most of which had never been worn. People gave them to my grandmother for Christmas and her birthday and Mother's Day. When her husband was alive, she'd received them on anniversaries, too.

"I don't know what it is about me that makes them think of pajamas." She lifted up a pink gown from a box. "Look at this. I don't wear such fancy stuff. I wish she'd come and take it back."

My mother had tried to outdo the others, with silks and quilted satin, crocheted inserts, ostrich plumes and matching robes.

"It must be something about me," she frowned.

I picked cotton men's pajamas, my grandfather's, like the ones my grandmother wore. The huge legs dragged on the floor and the elastic hung loose around my waist.

We had cornflakes before bed. We didn't talk. The train whistled, gone as soon as it was there, shaking the ground, moving north. The upstairs smelled of fresh-cut pine. It had been like that for years. I looked out the window on the landing. The oak leaves were close and big like hands; between them you could see stars.

I heard the toilet flush, then footsteps to the back door, where my grandmother called in her dog, shutting the screen again, when he was shaking against her ankle. She snapped the porch light off. The dog's tail beat against the wall as she talked him into settling down. She bent down in the corner, patting him. He always had huge particles of brown lint in the corners of his eyes. I suspected she let him sleep upstairs with her when she was alone.

"Yas, yas, you, sure, you're a good dog, yas sure, yas you are. Sure, that's a good dog, down, go down, yas. At's a good Handy, yas."

She paused for breath every few seconds on the stairs and I heard her hand clasp the banister.

"Are you asleep?"

"No."

"Are you too warm or too cold?"

"No."

"I can get you a blanket."

"No thank you. I'm fine, Gramma."

She lowered herself slowly, the boards creaking under her, to her knees. She poked her elbows in on the bed and said a prayer. From across the room, it was just words. Then she rattled her pan under the bed and crawled in.

"Well, it does feel good to be in B-E-D."

"Yes."

"Well, good night then."

"Night."

When my grandmother said I love you, which she did only rarely, she waited a long time in the dark. Time enough passed so that I stopped waiting for it, and I would be almost asleep and then she said I love you in an unwavering, normal voice. I thought she said it that night. But I didn't really know if I heard it or not, I could have been asleep, dreaming, so I never answered. My grandmother was so shy.

The next morning, when I woke up, I heard her moving around the kitchen, getting pans out of the oven drawers. Wind was blowing upstairs near my bed, branches were beating against the walls. The crackling sound of the radio came up through the floor. It was dark out the windows. I woke up hours earlier than I ever did at home. My grandmother cut a piece of buttered toast into four squares and arranged them around a yellow scrambled egg. My grandmother's eggs came out the way they were supposed to, not like my mother's. At home, we each made our own breakfast. We spread steak tartare on toast or stood at the open refrigerator and ate cold châteaubriand. My mother cooked the steaks at night and Ted sliced them, so we'd always have protein in the house. The kitchen in my grandmother's house was old-fashioned, with pale yellow cupboards and mint green trim. At home we had all the modern features. But I was more comfortable here at my grandmother's. Still, I didn't know if I would have wanted it to be my house.

The radio was on and there was a storm. We thought of driving up to Lake Superior for the washups. My grandmother and I collected rocks. We'd found minerals and geodes in caves and cracked them open ourselves. When my grandmother took her European tour she brought a chisel and came home with rocks from all the famous places. She wrapped them in colored tissue paper and taped labels to the bottoms on the airplane. Rock from the Acropolis, Rock from Pillar of the Coliseum, Rome. Sometimes we drove to small Indian towns around Bay City for their museums. We'd met rock hounds, old women with pointed sneakers and no socks, their skin gathering at their ankles in tiny folds like nylons, on Lake Michigan, bending over the gray sand, looking for petoskeys.

"Well, should we call your ma?"

"She's not up yet." I was looking at the big round clock over the refrigerator. In the new house, we had to go wandering around to alarm clocks to see if one had the right time. I'd dig Ted's watch out of his pocket in the closet. There was a tiny black traveling alarm by my mother's bed. She slept with one arm draped over it.

"We could call her from up there, I suppose. 'Course then what can she say?"

"Can we take Handy?" I asked. My grandmother got Handy the way she'd gotten all her dogs; Handy was our dog first. I'd wanted a dog because I had a crush on our morning paper boy. I used to take the garbage out when I saw him coming up Carriage Court. But I thought it would look more natural to be walking a dog. After a while, though, my mother decided I wasn't taking good enough care of Handy and besides, he made a mess. She decided that the dog needed more room to run, so we gave him to my grandmother. My grandmother fussed, saying, Oh, I don't want another dog, what do I want a dog for? Handy was the name we'd given him. My grandmother took our dogs and kept whatever names they had.

"Why sure. Does a wanna ride, Handy? Sure, sure a does." Handy began thumping his tail against my grandmother's ankle.

I put on one of the heavy men's wool jackets still left from when my grandfather wore them out to the mink. We took gloves and scarves and loose, baggy clothes. Neither of us would have dressed like this if we were staying in Bay City. My grandmother wore big cotton housedresses or overalls and flannel shirts the days she stayed home, but she owned nice, tasteful suits, knits, with matching purses and jewelry for the days when she had to drive into town, even for ten minutes, to buy something from the department store or to pick up a roast from the butcher.

The dog whimpered and beat his tail against the vinyl of the backseat, and I sat in front with the map spread out on my legs. In a town we didn't know the name of, we stopped in a Swedish tea shop. "Well, should we call your ma from here? They must be up by now."

I found a cuckoo clock by the cash register. Birds and nests on eaves were carved into the blond wood. It said half past eleven.

"Not for sure," I said, although it was about now that they usually got up on Saturdays. My mother would open the back door and sneak out to the garage with a bag of garbage, wearing only a T-shirt. After she pranced in, she'd stand for a minute at the back door, looking out to the dazzling sunlight on the yard. In summer, the sprinklers would already be going on the lawn next door, making thin rainbows over the grass. But it was raining and they were probably sleeping late. At our house, when we got up on a weekend and there was rain, my mother sighed and we all went back to sleep for a few hours.

We decided not to call my mother until we were farther north, in Michigan. It seemed safer in another state. Walking to the cash register, we passed two men in outdoor clothes with a radio going on their table. "Storm's still up," one said to the other.

My grandmother was a shy person, but she made an effort. "You're not going to the lake, are you?"

"Yes, ma'am. Up to Superior. Gonna get the washups."

"Why, us too. You must be the real rock hounds."

We followed their truck. We drove and drove, through towns with Indian names, down main streets one block long. We passed a road sign advertising the butter factory that used to rent our old barn; it showed a picture of a Michigan summer: blueberry patches, a bear, high clouds over a lake and dark green pines—the paper peeling off the sign, flapping in the wind. We were halfway to Canada.

We each sat on one of the twin beds, taking turns talking to my mother.

She shrieked so loud my grandmother held the receiver out a foot away. At that distance, my mother's voice sounded hilarious, like a tiny recorded puppet's voice.

"Lake Superior. My God, Ted, they're at Lake Superior, those two. Well, when are you coming home?"

My grandmother kept the phone away from her.

"Put her on," my mother said, "put on my little wee-bear-cub. I miss my Little Bit."

The corners of my grandmother's mouth lowered. I took the phone. My grandmother and I were both laughing then, and I tried to stifle the sound.

"Pooh-bear, are you there? Are you all right?"

"Yes, Mother, I'm fine."

"Do you have enough to eat, Bear-cub? And what are you wearing? Do you have warm clothes?"

"Yes, Mother."

"Well, you be careful out there on the beach. Don't you dare go at night when it's dark. And be careful of the other rock hounds and watch out for those undertows, because, believe me, Twussy, they can be atrocious, they just pull you right out, I'm telling you—"

"We'll be fine, Mom, we're not swimming, we're just walking on the beach. And we're going down to dinner now, so I have to go."

"Okay, well, have a good time and take care, you two. And hurry home because I miss my little Twussy Thing, Pooh-bear-cub. I'm lonesome just thinking of you way up there."

"Is it still raining where you are?" my grandmother asked.

"Storming. I'm in bed already." My mother giggled.

Downstairs to the dining room, my grandmother and I could hardly walk.

"Well, how do you feel, you little, you little Pooh-bear-cub, you," my grandmother said. "Oh ye gods."

"My little Twussy Bear, I'm soo lonesome, sigh." We kept bumping into each other, and then against the walls.

"We shouldn't talk like this," my grandmother said, trying to pull her face straight. "But oh, the things she says. Twussy bear. Now what is a twussy bear?"

Ten at night and the storm was still going. We sat in the dining room in a corner, next to a window. Finally, we were quiet. That was what always happened when we talked about my mother. First, we couldn't stop laughing, we were hysterical with talk. Then it burned out and we each sat quiet, alone.

"Gramma, was she always like this?"

My grandmother turned and looked out the window. Her profile was sharp and even, like faces of men on backs of coins. Outside, waves opened and lit the shore. Rain splattered on the glass.

"Oh, there was always something not quite right about her. Something a little off. She wasn't quite all there."

"Even when she was a little girl?"

"I've thought that to myself a thousand times, and I just don't know anymore." A waitress brought a basket of bread to our table. We knew it was warm. Neither of us touched it. "I think even when she was real small, there was always something missing."

I looked around the room. There were rock hounds at most of the other tables. Canvas bags and flashlights lay next to their feet.

We ordered big meals: fried steaks with pats of butter melting on top and peach pie, warm, under cream, on a soft, dissolving crust. "Nutmeg," my grandmother said, tasting it. "Good." Afterwards, we both drank coffee. The times I'd tasted my mother and Ted's black instant espresso, I spit it out. But we drank cup after cup with cream and sugar and it was delicious, sustaining us, as we waited for the storm to clear. The waitress kept circling the room with the silver pot.

In every person's face, there is one place that seems to express them most accurately. With my grandmother, you always looked at her mouth. Her teeth seemed to balance at the very tips of each other, just touching, her lips held and nervous while she listened to a question.

"Oh, no, we're just amateurs, shucks no," she said, frowning, to a table of women at our left. In groups, she was the shyest one at first, always, but eventually they looked to her to start them laughing. The ladies at the table promised to wake us up if the storm broke.

"That's room nineteen?" one of the women shouted, as we stood up to leave.

"Us, why no," my grandmother teased, "but Elma, you go and

knock on nineteen in the middle of the night and just see what the gentleman says. And tell us what you find there." The women were still laughing as we walked away.

We went to feed Handy two pieces of steak we'd wrapped in a paper napkin and to let him outside by the car to make. But he whimpered in the rain, so my grandmother spread newspapers from the trunk over the backseat floor. When we left, we felt sorry for him staring out the car window. With his paws up, he looked tiny and pitiful, wet; his head, with the hair packed down, seemed no bigger than my fist, the size that's supposed to match a human heart. We took him under my poncho and carried him to our bathroom, where he beat his tail against the door. "Ugh, you are a wet thing, you," my grandmother said, lifting him onto her jacket.

The wind was still blowing when we finally went to bed. At the very northern edge of land, where it was dark and late and storming, sleep seemed the easiest state to exist in. I went to sleep there fully trusting the world not to harm me. I don't know if I ever felt that safe, before or again. My hands lay softly on the bed that night, my ear to the pillow as if that was where the comforting sound of rain came from. We were far away. I liked going to sleep knowing it was cold and no one was outside and we were so far away from anywhere else where the sky might be clear and other people might be living other lives.

When we woke up the next morning the storm had broken and the air was sweet. There was only a light rain. We dressed quickly and took our equipment from the car. I carried Handy in my poncho. It was still dark, but the sky was lightening a little over the lake. In the distance, we saw spots of other flashlights. Waves shellacked the sand and brought new rocks and driftwood. The lacy foam receded and we tracked down, looking for agates, banded with gray and blue, the colors of the air here. They were everywhere in the sand, caught in the masses of seaweed. We walked slowly, our eyes careful on the ground. Every few minutes one of us would stop, bend down and pick up a stone. We found agates and arrowheads and just granite smoothed by water. We each came over to see when we found one, held it in our hands under the flashlight. My grandmother walked to wash hers in the water first. I licked mine to see and then put it in my cheek, sucking, until I found a new one.

It was as if the stones renewed us. We could have walked and walked, bending down forever on that beach. There were miles to study. Handy ran along near us, going ahead, then looking back, his barks soft and lost in the louder noise of waves. I hadn't seen an ocean yet, but this lake seemed enough. We couldn't see the other side, but we knew over the pencil gray line of the horizon was Canada. Canada—just the sound of the name. It seemed it could end all our problems.

A man at a filling station kept looking at my grandmother. It bothered me. He leaned on the front of the car and he took a long time to wash the windshield. My grandmother blushed a little when he stared. She picked up the Kleenex box on the car seat between us and set it down again.

"Gramma, why is he looking at you funny?"

She shrugged. "Well, shucks if I know."

Then I remembered something. There was a picture of my grandmother when she was young, wearing a white lace dress, her braids ending in two pencil points at her waist. She was holding a black dog with a huge ribbon around its neck. My mother and my aunt Carol said she was beautiful. They said they felt in awe of her. I'd never seen it. To me, she just looked like a grandmother.

"That guy likes you, Gramma."

"That old fellow. Shucks no, he's too old for me."

But when the man filled the tank, he kept looking in through the window, the nozzle in his hand. My grandmother gripped the steering wheel and she looked down at the spokes, her mouth working, smiling in spite of trying to frown.

"It's Chummy with that Public Service hat." My grandmother walked to the window and pulled back the curtain every time we heard a car. Public Service was the name of the gas and electric company in Bay City. The men wore yellow hardhats. She meant it wasn't my mother.

Then she pointed with her fingernail where I should erase. My homework spread over the kitchen table. She stood behind me, checking the arithmetic of my problems, her glasses low on her nose.

The back of my hand was in my mouth, something I'd done all my life. It drove my mother crazy. When I was young, I bit my nails and she pretended to give me a manicure, rubbing my baby fingers with quinine. It worked, but the gesture simply adjusted itself. Now I moved my lips over the back of my hand. This made my mother more upset. "I should have let her stick with the nails, who cares if she ruined them and had ridges all her life like Juney Miller, it'd be better than this," she told Lolly once. "Ann, take that mouth off of your hand. You're going to get thick awful lips like a Negro. If you do that where other people can see you, they're going to think something's really wrong with you. And I don't think you even know when you're doing it anymore."

"Yes, I do."

"No, you don't. You think you do, but I've seen you doing it when you thought you weren't."

My grandmother watched and didn't say anything. I did another page of problems and she looked over it, checking my additions and multiplications in the old math.

"We have fun," she said. "I know you like it by me."

Then we heard my mother's car in the driveway. My grandmother touched my hair, just then. That was the kind of thing she almost never did.

"I know you haven't got it the easiest with your ma. I know how she can be. I know it."

I looked down at my sheet of problems. I said, "Sometimes," and then my voice stopped.

"I know, I know it, but shhh now."

The screen door banged and my mother rushed in, with Handy beating around her ankles.

"Well, hello, hello." My grandmother collected my school papers together. We sat around the kitchen table. My mother rested her chin on her hands. She fiddled with her bracelet. She seemed tired again.

"So, tell me, what did you two do?"

We told her little bits. We drove up to Lake Superior, we had supper and went to bed. When we woke up, the storm was over. My grandmother took out our rocks from the canvas bag and spread them on the counter. She wrote labels and taped them on rocks while we talked. She'd finish them before I had to go. When we walked out to the porch, a rusty streak of red held in the sky. It was one of those dusks that was cool but not cold, the sky so brilliant it made the houses and barns, everything built, look small.

We stood on the porch, in no hurry to leave, while my grandmother took the leash down to walk Handy. As soon as she lifted it off the peg, Handy jumped up on her, yelping.

"Ya, you be quiet, you," she said with a false sternness.

The highway was barely visible but we heard the constant running noise of travel. My mother was wearing a straight cotton dress with a cardigan and I had on dungarees. It seemed to me then, as we stood there, for a long time on the verge of leaving, that we shouldn't have really had to go. Something had gone wrong.

My mother and I should have both been girls who stayed out on the porch a little longer than the rest, girls who strained to hear the long-distance trucks on the highway and who listened to them, not the nearer crickets. We would have been girls who had names in their heads: Ann Arbor, Chicago, Cheyenne, San Francisco, Portland, Honolulu, Los Angeles; girls who looked at the sky and wanted to go away. We would have been the kind of girls who thought we, more than other people, saw the sadness of things, the poignance of lush darkness around stars, but who finally sighed and, calling the dog with a mixture of reluctance and relief, shut the door and went in home.

My grandmother looked at me as my mother slid into the car. "Go on, get in now," she said.

But she wanted me and I wanted her and she couldn't have me because I was my mother's. She was too old to take care of me. She would die before I was grown.

As we backed out of the driveway she bent down to Handy. My mother turned on our lights.

My mother was born on an old kitchen table, now in the basement, cluttered with tools. Her high school dresses hung packed together over her red ukelele in the upstairs closet, the closet with one high window that showed sky and clouds and telephone wires. Her father's mink sheds stood rusting in the field out back. My mother blamed the house on Lime Kiln Road for things gone wrong in her life. She had hated being so far in the country, she remembered walking miles in the snow to Saint Phillip's Academy, the sound of her boots the only sound for an hour in the hollow, blue air. She had felt embarrassed, bringing boyfriends from college to a dead-end road, when the car had to pass by Griling's house, junk and old auto parts in the front yard, and children whose matted hair made their eyes look huge and hereditarily dumb.

"Well, who could I meet? Out here? Gram talks about Ellie's June this, Ellie's June that, well, I remember when June was in high school, Ellie bought the smallest little house in DePeer and June grew up with all the doctor's kids and lawyer's kids. They could have moved, too, but no, Gram and Dad stayed there. And look at June now. Look who she married. And she didn't even go to college."

"She married an undertaker. And now she's got twelve kids."

"Listen, it's the undertakers who make all the money these days. More than the doctors even. They don't have to pay the malpractice insurance."

"So would you want twelve kids?"

"I think I would." She said that quietly, shy. "I always wanted a big family. I think I would have liked to be a homebody."

That shut me up.

□

"So did you really have fun, tell me true, I won't tell her. Did you really have fun or was it just all right?" She bumped over a curb. "Whoops."

Then the car was coasting, and she let me turn the radio on. "It was all right," I said.

She was intent, looking at me. There was something about when she looked at me, it made me blush, I couldn't help it. It always seemed like I was lying, no matter what I said. The blood poured to my cheeks. "What did you have to eat? Did you have a steak up there or just those Polish pasties?"

"We had pasties."

She made a face. "Well, I broiled a château," she said, moving the wheel with one hand, easy. "We'll see that you have a good steak tonight."

A week later, my mother ran to my room. She'd told my grandmother what I'd said and they'd fought on the telephone, my grandmother cried. "Ann, tell me true now, did you lie to me, because she said you had New York steaks, the best they had on the menu up there, and she paid twenty dollars for it." She looked at me, shaking her head. "Don't do that, Ann, don't play us against each other. She's my mother, too," she said.

The winter I was six years old, my mother was gone. She went to California, without me. My grandmother and I talked to her on the telephone in the kitchen, asking her when she'd come home. She told us she was recovering. I pictured her in a white hospital like a kitchen, with violets in a water cup. "Not yet," I told the nuns at school when they asked if she was home. They asked at the end of the day when we stood in line, waiting for the bell to ring. They touched the top of my head and their palms felt cool and dry. Every day my grandmother's Oldsmobile would be banked right in front of the school, waiting. She leaned over and opened the door and inside it was warm, the motor running.

One day, a friend from my school came over and we ran through the fields chasing monarchs with butterfly nets and my mother called and said she was coming home. "Just when you had your friend and played nice," my grandmother said, putting down the phone. The jars of butterflies sat all over the counter tops and on the kitchen table, holes punched in their tin lids. Their wings seemed to beat as we breathed.

The day was there then and I was scared. I didn't want her to come. I waited outside, I was wearing all white—white shorts, white T-shirt, white anklets and white sneakers—and when I saw the car coming down the road, I hid behind the garage in a lilac bush. I didn't want her to see me.

But then—then the car door slammed and before she had to come look for me, I ran out and she was there and I was at her legs and she was young and beautiful and so much fun and my mother again.

"My baby's all white, oh, you smell, you smell like perfume."

The white VW gleamed in the sun and she carried me, hers again, my legs sticking out from her back. I felt sorry for my grandmother that day, moving around the kitchen in a blue print dress, there was flour all through the yellow light, she was baking, rolling out dough. She cut around our fingers, making cookies the size of our hands, all day she looked down at her work on the table, because I was not hers to watch anymore.

For a long time, I didn't like Ted. He seemed to get in our way. Before Ted, my mother and I were waiting, preparing. We were going to go to California.

My mother taught me how to diet and smile right so all my teeth showed and to practice, looking in the mirror. I knew how to eat right so if a Hollywood agent came to Bay City, he would pick me. I thought of it every meal. Every meal I didn't chew with my mouth open because I didn't want the Hollywood agent to pick another girl.

But then, my mother went to Las Vegas and married Ted, and in the new house she didn't talk about California anymore.

She gave me her old Sears jacket and she bought herself a new one. It was a zip-up jacket, too big for me, mustard-colored, plain. I walked around in it after school, in the fields, the underdeveloped parts of the new neighborhood. I thought I would just stay there in a plain jacket and no one would ever see me. My mother had told me I was a girl with potential, but now it seemed nobody would ever know.

One night we were driving—my mother and Ted in the front seat, me in the back, to the Lorelei for prime rib. I sat by the dark window and didn't say anything. We passed intersections, the colored lights slick on the road.

"Ann," Ted said to me from the front seat, looking in his rearview mirror, "your mother tells me you'd like to be on television."

I sank further down into the jacket, I could feel my neck flush with blood. She'd told what I wanted. I was ashamed. I was embarrassed to want something like that.

"I know a man who works at WBAY. I can ask him to get you on a local commercial, would you like that?"

My mother leaned her arm on the seat divider. "Just think, you'd be on TV."

Something opened like a clam in my chest. I felt so happy.

"Yes," I said.

"All right, I'll talk to him."

My mother raised her eyebrows and clicked her tongue. "Here's hoping."

We kept driving in the dark but it was different. I watched the red disks throb on stakes by the side of the road. I looked for the skeletal antennas of the radio stations out in the fields, in the country, broadcasting through the night. We felt safe together in Ted's car, we could feel ourselves moving.

I got Mary Griling to come to Carriage Court. It was easy because I was older. I drew her a map and she rode after school on her brother's bike that she had to stand up on so her feet reached the pedals. At our house on Carriage Court, we had a new Instamatic camera. We still didn't have any furniture, but my mother and Ted bought equipment. We had the camera and a radio that picked up international channels. We set the large radio, with the antenna extended, in the middle of the living room floor.

I got kids to come to our house and I took pictures of them.

Younger kids, eight- and nine-year-old boys. Mary was the first girl. I didn't know why I did it. It was just one of the things I did.

Mary was different from the other Grilings. Her collars were straight and her dark hair fell evenly onto her shoulders. My grandmother said she was lucky she was pretty, that could help her, God knew nothing else would. I'd watched her coward little kicks during football games, and in school I'd seen her stand by the window, watering plants on the ledge. Careful, she always seemed to be concentrating. I didn't live on Lime Kiln Road anymore and I didn't go to the same school anymore either. But once when I was there playing tag, I held Mary's wrist and pulled her by a tree. Clouds moved above us, it was going to rain before supper.

She came after school before it was dark, that still time of day. I took her through our empty house to the big bathroom, the one my mother and Ted used, and locked the door. I told her she had to do what I said. I told her to take off her shirt and stand by the wall.

I said the same thing to the boys. I was always amazed when they did it. People are so easy to boss.

Mary looked down and unbuttoned carefully, her chin tucked against her collarbone like a bird cleaning itself. I took a picture. Her bare chest was incidental; what I liked were her shoulders curling down, her distracted eyes as she stood with her hands hanging useless at her sides.

They all looked up at me while I did it. They seemed frightened, their faces sunk back, except their eyes. I asked them to lie on the long, fake-marble counter by the sink. They always looked so serious.

Mary rubbed her tennis shoes off, one by one, toes pushing down the soft heel of the other shoe. Kids are so shy. She was lying there, looking up at me, her eyes large and muscular, wet like a fish's eyes. That was what made me want to touch them, that tremble. Some flinch. They were afraid of me. The boys tried to look brave, setting their teeth, breathing in. It's amazing the power people give you. Mary Griling just lay there, her face flattened, I could do anything to her and she looked up at me, weakly and kind, a nerve pulsing in her cheek. The muscles gathered in her stomach. My fingers turned heavy and sensitive, as if all my blood poured down to their tips. I lifted the elastic band of her skirt and looked down at her face. She was peering at me, more and more humbly, the veils of her eyelids closing, knowing she was giving herself up. I could have reached down and killed her, she was just lying there, trusting me.

"The others did this, too?" Her rib bones rose, the highest part of her body. She pulled her stomach in, shy.

"Yes." I'd said there was a club, all the girls on Lime Kiln Road. I didn't tell her there were boys.

I had Mary, good little Mary, serious Mary Griling who worked hard to be neat, to do well in school, in my house alone. She was lying there under my hands. I touched the pancake of her breast and something fluttered beneath my flattened palm. Then I pushed her skirt and her underpants down to her ankles. She flinched while I took the pictures. I was watching her face turn funny.

"Is that enough pictures?"

"Okay." I put the camera under the counter, where my mother stored the Ajax and extra soap. But she still stayed there and I looked at her. The tiny muscles of her upper thighs clinched when I touched her. She looked at me as if my finger was on the wet muscle of her heart. Then I licked my finger. It tasted like flour. I put my hand in her mouth and ran two fingers over the bumps of her gums. I felt like I owned her, then. With the boys it took longer. I stood over them until they shuddered and cried, biting their lips until they bled, arching up and down on the counter, in my hands.

She sat up, sideways, with her legs hanging down and then she jumped. I looked back at her, her buttocks pressed towards each other as if she could feel me watching. She dressed against the wall, in the corner.

"Does your father see you undressed?"

She was clasping the top button of her blouse. "No," she said, guarded but obedient, duty-bound to answer.

"Want me to help you?" Her shirt hung down, lopsided.

"I can do it by myself."

I was thinking of Griling's messy house, the junk in the front yard, piles in the closets. She finished dressing. Her collar folded down, even. I smoothed it carefully, against her neck. She looked up, not knowing if she should be afraid of me.

"You can't tell anybody about today," I said. "I won't show the pictures."

"All right," she said, not sure.

Then she left, walking in one line through the kitchen to the front door. As I watched her go, she seemed to collect mystery again, to draw it back into her small body. Her head was dark as she rode down our street on her brother's wobbly bike. The boys always looked over their shoulders at me, asking, dipping their eyes. I knew they'd be back, I didn't wonder. I hadn't had a girl before because I worried they would tell their mothers. But Mary Griling had no mother.

"I'm really bleeding," my mother said, turning to me in the car. "It's just all over. And thick." My mother said absolutely anything to me. It was as if she were alone.

"I don't want to hear about it," I said, "and could you please keep your eyes on the road." We were driving from my grandmother's house, just the way we did a hundred times after she married Ted and we moved away. The stars were small and dim through the windshield. I sat against my car door, worrying.

I had homework for the next day. We turned off our old road and onto the highway, we drove by barns and silos, we passed a high blinking radio antenna in a deserted field. Then I remembered that my science book, which I needed, was in my locker at school. That made me exhausted. I couldn't possibly finish.

"I have a Super in and a Kotex and it's still going right through. I can feel it. Yech." She made a gagging face. "You'll never believe what that man did. I still can't believe it. Open the glove compartment, Honey."

When I didn't, she reached over and opened it herself. "There. Look at those bills. Those are all our bills, Annie, un-PAID. You need clothes, I need clothes, I don't have anything, I go to work in that old junk, in rags, five, ten, fifteen years out of date. I should really go to work looking a little nice, too. But this man, with my money, with our money, goes out and buys himself a new car. Yeah, uh-huh, you can imagine, Annie? He thinks he needs a new used Cadillac. The old one wasn't good enough."

"Could you please be quiet?"

"I'll say what I want in my car," she said. "Don't get fresh with me now, Ann, because I can't take it from you, too. And you should know a little about these things."

She jerked the steering wheel and the car bumped over a curb, turning.

"Where are we going?"

"We're driving past the Lorelei."

The Lorelei was the restaurant near the ice skating rink where the three of us used to go on Sundays for prime rib. They were supposed to have the best prime rib in Bay City, thick and tender. Now Ted ate there without us, after night skating. We drove slowly into the gravel parking lot. Across the road was the pale green dome of the arena, BAY CITY painted in large black letters.

"There's his car," I pointed. Ted's maroon and white Cadillac was in its usual spot.

My mother pulled behind it and turned the motor off. She walked out and peered in at his dashboard. "There he is. That man. Oooh, when I think of it. The dirty devil."

"How do you know he bought a new car?"

"How do I know, they called me, that's how I know. Van Boxtel Cadillac called and said, Well, you must know about the gold Cadillac, it's all set, ready to go. I laughed and said, No, I didn't know a thing about any car. But then I drove out and saw it there on the lot. A gold Cadillac, barely used. A '65."

I still didn't say anything. My mother started up the engine again and tried harder.

"Do you know what this means, Honey? This means no money for us. No clothes, no toys, no nothing. This is it. He's spent all your money, what should have been for your lessons and your clothes."

"So, why don't you go in and talk to him if you're so upset."

That seemed to subdue her. "No, that wouldn't be a good idea." She shook her head, turning the ignition. "He's in there drinking with his friends, he wouldn't say anything in front of them. I know this man. This man is a creature of habit. I'm just going to go home and go to bed. And you, too. Don't say a word about any of this, do you hear me? Not a word, young lady. See, I'm not going to tell him they called, so he won't know I know. We'll just wait and see how he tells me, we'll just see how he tries. Now do you understand? Not one word. Because that could spoil everything. *Eve*rything.

"Let's set the alarm for five and get up then. Come on, Pooh, we'll be fresher in the morning. Our minds will think faster."

We were never done with our work, it seemed, all those years with Ted.

We fell asleep, alone in the house. But I didn't sleep good sleep anymore, the way I had when I was younger, at my grandmother's. Now, I had cowering sleep. I snuck under the covers, exhausted, stealing time and comfort I didn't deserve.

It was the fourth or fifth time that winter I'd lost my key. My mother was furious when she drove her car up the driveway and saw me, sitting on the porch. She slammed her door and marched out.

"Your lights," I said.

"Damn." She almost fell, she turned around so fast. "You're ten years old, Ann, you ought to be able to keep one key."

She opened the door and let us in. I stood in the front hall, stamping my feet. My mother set the thermostat up. My hands had swelled and turned red.

"Somebody's going to break in one of these days with your lost keys and then you know where we'll be. In the poorhouse."

"There is no poorhouse in Bay City."

She sighed. "I'm going to have to string it around your neck. And how would you like that, for all your kids to see?"

"Go ahead." I started for my bedroom, then turned around. "What happened with the Cadillac?"

She sighed again. "I don't know. I just don't know yet."

□

When I first saw the '65 Cadillac, snow was blowing in tiny balls across the gold roof. The Cadillac sat like a huge painted egg on our driveway. There was one streetlamp in front of our yard and as I walked up the road, I could see the glass and chrome glitter. I went up close. It had molded fins and I walked the length of the car, running my hands on the sides, brushing down snow. I pulled off my mitten. Through the windows, the inside looked safe and closed and tended like a home. I lifted up the chrome door handle and it gave with a soft click. Ted never locked things. His office in the arena, his cars; in summer he left our back door wide open. Inside, it smelled rich. I didn't sit down because my clothes were wet and my boots were muddy with slush. The car had thick tan carpets and no plastic mats. I reached over and opened the glove compartment. It was there, what I was looking for and afraid to see: Ted's glasses, folded together in the beaded case that said LAS VEGAS IS FOR LOVERS. The car was his, definitely. I closed the glove compartment and then I shut the door, lifting the handle so it would fall quietly.

I was afraid to go in the house. I would have stayed in the car, but I didn't want my wetness to ruin the leather. I did what I did all summer. I went around the garage to the side of the house and listened against the wall. In summer, if I heard fighting, I wouldn't go inside.

I had my own key, another copy, stuffed with the string down my pocket, and I let myself in. No one called when the door slammed and I stamped my boots in the front hall. The kitchen was dark and the counters were dry and perfectly clean. I opened the refrigerator. There were only jars of things and one head of lettuce in a plastic bag. I guessed we were going out for dinner.

"I'm home," I said and then I heard something in my bedroom at the back of the house. It was dark in there, it took my eyes a second to adjust.

"I AM your little lotus blossom." My mother was banked on my bedspread, talking baby talk, with a light mohair blanket thrown over her. "Won't you get your lit-tle lotus blossom a glass of wa-wa?"

She still hadn't seen me.

"Get up, Mom, it's suppertime." I switched on the overhead light. Ted was sitting on my bed next to her as if something was wrong. All of a sudden, I thought she was sick. Perhaps this was what happened when people were dying. She still didn't notice me. She smiled up at Ted, her face swaying. "Wa-wa for the little lotus flowa."

Ted turned to me. "Your mother is drunk," he said, smiling his zipper smile. "She's had too much to drink."

"I am not drunk!" she screamed as Ted stood up to go to the kitchen, to get her a glass of water.

"You're disgusting," I said, looking straight down at her. Then I took dry clothes into the bathroom and locked the door.

Later, Ted knocked and asked if I wanted McDonald's. I said no, I was going to take a bath.

I packed a blanket and pillow in a brown paper grocery bag and put on my boots and coat over pajamas. I stuffed my robe in the bag, too. It was nine o'clock and our whole house was dark and asleep. I slipped out the front door and walked towards the Cadillac. There was a new lawn of snow on the ground. I knew my mother's car in the garage would be safer, but it was old and the seats were vinyl and one of the windows wouldn't go all the way up. Besides, the doors would be locked.

I wanted the Cadillac. I sat on the front seat and let my legs dangle outside while I pulled off my boots. I laid my robe and then the blanket and pillow on the backseat and I wrapped the boots in the thick brown paper bag. Then I crawled low so no one could see me and pushed the locks down into the doors.

I felt safe there with the snow falling in one bank on the slanted back windshield. The leather warmed under me. The streetlamp lit the snow. I closed my eyes and thought about driving all night on a dark road, the car moving smoothly, my mother and father sitting in front, my mother's arm falling down over the seat on my stomach, patting my hands under the blanket, telling me to Don't worry, go to sleep, it's still a long ways away. They would wake me up when we came to California, before, so I could see us crossing over, riding in.

Then I jerked the way I sometimes do and it feels like my heart should stop but doesn't. The streetlight was glaring and now it was hot in the car. It was still night. I took off my pajamas and sat, naked, in the driver's seat, with my hands on the wheel, making it swivel. I slid down to reach, but I was afraid to touch the pedals with my feet. I thought I might make the car go. I could feel the leather sticking to the moisture of my skin. I wondered if my body would leave a stain. I moved my thighs and my arms as if I were making an angel in the snow. That way my print wouldn't be recognized. I would seem to be someone larger.

Then I heard a noise. There's a difference with the things you imagine, that make you jerk in your sleep, and the things you know are real. I crowded down in the footspace and put my pajamas on again. I took my boots out of the paper bag and pulled them on my bare legs. They were heavy rubber boots, much wider than my legs. When I sat up, I saw it was the snowplow, dragging chains, coming down our street, mowing the banks like hedges on either side, blocking all the driveways.

I ran back in the house and to my room. The alarm clock was still ticking, too early to ring. My mom and Ted's door was closed and I could hear them inside, breathing. No one knew I had been gone. I couldn't fall asleep again, so I dressed for school. I sat on the kitchen floor against the refrigerator and worked on my homework. I noticed the kitchen windows coming light and I was still working. It seemed like I had endless hours. I worked out all my math problems and copied them over on a new sheet of paper, the numbers neat like houses on blue lines. I read my reading, called "The Sound of Summer Running," about a boy who didn't have money for new sneakers. Finally, I was finished. I stacked my books up in a neat pyramid and sharpened all the pencils in my case.

For the first time I could remember, I was ready to go to school. All of a sudden, I was starving. I pulled up my knee socks and went to the sink. Ted had remembered to defrost. There was a two-pound package of ground sirloin in the sink, the blood running in jagged lines down the white porcelain.

While I was spreading the meat, my mother walked in, wearing black tights with a hole in one toe and a tartan plaid skirt, looking at her side, tying the matching sash. Ted walked out behind her, all dressed, saying Good morning, Ann, and nodding as he buttoned up his coat. He didn't eat breakfast with us anymore. He drove to the Lorelei and ordered eggs.

We stood at the window over the sink, watched him stamp to the garage and come out with the shovel.

"Look at the size of those icicles," she whispered. "It's like a wonderland. I'd like to chop off a few and keep them in the freezer." We both watched Ted shovel the driveway. He waved when he trudged up and leaned the shovel against the garage. We could see him through the windshield, unfolding his sunglasses and putting them on. He backed the Cadillac out slowly and as panels of snow fell off, it looked like something huge, coming up from underwater.

"It really is a beaut."

I was eating my steak tartare standing up. "So I guess you're not mad about the car anymore." It was still early, but I wanted to be at school before the bell rang for once.

"Oh, Ann, I was all wrong about that. We were wrong about him, we really were. You know what he was going to do—he was going to drive it home and say, Here, Adele, Happy Anniversary."

I sat against the wall, to pull on my boots.

"Really, Ann, we should be ashamed of ourselves. He really only meant the best. We spoiled his surprise."

I heard my mother in the living room click the radio on. Then she came galloping into the hall, saying, "Snow day, put your books away, school's out, snow day! Go out for me once and just hit those icicles with the shovel. We can take them out in summer, on a tray, with fruit around, wouldn't *that* be a centerpiece?"

"You're so *tan*, Ron," my mother was saying. Ron Hanson was Ted's friend from Holiday on Ice. His hair was bleached blond, with tinges of green, he laughed from his waist, placing one arm over his stomach as he bent down, and he had effeminate hands with long, spoon-shaped fingers. My mother talked about him endlessly with Lolly. But Ted was a reserved man with few friends. The three years we lived in the house on Carriage Court, we saw Ron every winter Holiday on Ice came through Bay City. This time, they were in from California and so Ron was staying in our back ironing room.

Now he was in the kitchen, leaning against the counter, with my mother and Ted, drinking. I could hear their ice cubes shifting in their glasses.

"It's those pills, I'm telling you, Adele, you should get them, you really should. You and I have the same skin, that same, pay-yull skin."

I was in the bathroom, standing on the rim of the tub with my arms up gripping the shower curtain rod for balance, so I could look at my body in the mirror. It didn't look to me like me. There were smudges of fat where I didn't feel fat. Water in the tub was gulping out after my bath. I kept looking, trying to look a different way.

"What's the name of those pills?" my mother said. I stopped and stepped down onto the rug. Didn't she know pills that changed your skin, things like that, were dangerous?

"I just call them pigment pills, that's what they really are. But it's a prescription. I'll write it down for you. I found a man who'll give them to me, but they're not inexpensive. They're rather dear, in fact." He laughed. I imagined his hand on his red shirt, his thin fingers spreading.

My mother knocked on the bathroom door. I picked up a brush and ran it through my tangles to be doing something.

"Open up." She rattled the doorknob. "It's locked. Honey, I've told you, don't lock this door. It's dangerous. If something happened to you in the tub, we couldn't get in."

"What's going to happen to me in the tub?"

She was standing, looking at me in the mirror. She smiled and patted my naked butt. She cupped her hand and ran it down my thigh.

"Don't."

She looked down at me. "Why don't you run out there and say good night a second. Go on."

I looked at her as if she were totally crazy. "No."

"Go on. Why not? Don't you think they've ever seen a naked little girl before?"

"I'm ten years old, if you haven't noticed."

"Well, you're still a little girl to us. At our age."

"In case you don't know, it's not very nice to walk around naked. People don't do that, Mom."

"Oh, come on, a little girl with a cute little bod like yours, it's just cute, that's all." It made me wince, hearing her say Lolly's word. She ran one finger under my arm to my elbow and smiled, secretively. Then she stiffened up again. "Go ahead. Come on, Ann, do it for me."

"Why."

She sighed, impatient at having to explain herself. "Because I'd just like them to see what a cute little shape you have. Come on, won't you please, Ann? Just run out. Just for a second."

"Forget it," I said. I had my pajamas there, folded on the toilet seat top. I put them on, buttoning up all the buttons.

My mother sighed. "Boy, I can see you're almost into the terrible teens. Can't ask you to do anything anymore."

I put on my robe and tied the belt, tight. "I will, however, go in and say good night."

My mother followed me into the kitchen, still looking down at me with pride. Her gaze was like a leash as we walked. Ron and Ted leaned on the counter. We still didn't have any furniture in the house.

Ron was holding up a hinged metal fish whose sides shimmered like dark mother-of-pearl. He said he found it in Baja. I asked Ron if, when he went back to California, he would buy us one of the fish if we gave him money now. I'd noticed that most people would give me the thing when I said that. They'd just give it to me. Adults relinquished shiny, pretty things to children. They were embarrassed to be caught liking them too much. I could see Ron looking into the segmented fish, deciding. He wanted to keep the fish—he wanted it that much. It hurt him, the thought of giving it up. I decided then that this made him different from other people. He loved his toy the way a child would.

"I'll get you one if I ever go there again," he said.

"Ron, are you married," I blurted.

"Now, Anny, what do you think?" he said. His eyelashes dipped down, teasing. "Of course I'm not married. I'm waiting for you to grow up."

I ran to my bedroom, screaming.

That night my mother came to my bed and just sat down. It woke me, I could feel her looking at me. I bent my knees under the cover and sat up. She pulled the blanket down off my shoulder, down one side. She pulled one knee out and looked up and down my leg. "You are a long-limbed beauty," she whispered. "You're my jewel. I have to take you somewhere they can see it."

A clear night, my mother and I piling into the car to drive to dinner.

"What about the TV commercial?" I said.

It took her a minute to look at me. She was distracted. Then she sighed. Ted was back in the house, getting something. She leaned from the front seat, her face working, eyebrows, mouth.

"So be nice to him. Play up to him a little. I bet if you're real cute and quiet, he'll do it for you. Don't kid yourself."

"Why can't I ask?"

"I wouldn't. Just be real cute and make him *want* to help you. You've got to learn to make men want to do you favors."

When he came into the car, I asked. "Ted, what ever happened with, you were going to ask a man you know if I could be on a commercial for TV."

He looked over at my mother sharply. She stared straight ahead, hands on her lap.

"Oh, Honey, I did ask him and he said that none of them were made locally, they get them from Chicago and then they dub in the Bay City names. They don't make them here."

"So I can't do it."

"No, I'm afraid not."

"He could, he could get you on if they made them here, but they don't make them here," my mother said, scolding.

"Oh."

A year before we moved to California, I asked my mother for a bikini. Theresa Griling couldn't get one because her older sister who planned their money said her suit from last year was still good. My mother took me shopping downtown, but Shreve's didn't have real bikinis. All the two-piece suits came up too high and most of them had white pleated skirts. When we'd tried on bathing suits, we both stared at me in the store mirrors. In a bathing suit I looked older. "Oh," she said once and put her hand on my waist. I shirked away then. I couldn't have said why, but it felt weird, that touch. It moved as if her hand were burrowing in. After that, I said I didn't want to try on any more.

Then one day I rolled my bike into the kitchen and Lolly was standing there holding a bikini.

"Malibu-wear," my mother said, putting her hands in the bottom, spreading it open between her fingers. "This is the real bikini, all right. Try it on. I put it on me and it was a little small, so it should be just right for you."

I changed in the bathroom with the door closed and walked out, suddenly cold.

"Very shall-we-say-svelte." Lolly and my mother looked at each other, talking over my head.

"What do you think?"

"Love it," said Lolly.

"Comemeer." My mother kneeled down on the black and white linoleum floor and pulled the bottom up as if she were shaking me into it. She pinched the shoulder straps and looked at Lolly. "Just a nip or two on each side.

"Okay, my little Bipper," she said, tapping my butt as punctuation. I was dismissed. "Very cute. Adorable, in fact. Why not, you know. If you've got a cute little body, why not show it?"

Lolly slapped her own butt hard and the cotton made a soggy sound. "This bod needs some work. A good two weeks of diet and exercise before I'm ready for show and tell."

□

I rode my bike to the public swimming pool with Theresa and Benny. They both still lived on Lime Kiln Road. Every morning that summer, Ted drove me across town before he went to work, turned in the bumpy dead-end road and left me off. I always walked slowly up the yard to my grandmother's house. I liked the minutes alone there. The trees, bushes with shiny leaves—I remembered everything.

I thought I had been happy when we'd lived in the white house, out in the country. But I was dumber then, there were things I didn't know, even about downtown Bay City, where my mother took me to a boutique called The Id. I didn't know if I could be as happy here now, as happy as I had been once. I kicked the gravel stones up the driveway.

Benny lived over the long yard in the next house. Like everything on Lime Kiln Road, I had known him all my life. His mother and father were always Carol and Jimmy. Benny was pale, with thick white-blond hair and scrapes and scars on his skin.

I remembered sitting with Benny on my grandmother's eaves trough, saying our first words. My mother had taught me to say yellow, but Benny said lello. Lello was Benny's color and Benny had to be right. Our parents thought of us as exact opposites and marveled that we played together so well. For years we were together, me trailing behind, always a year younger. I behaved better at school; I was quiet, meticulous, but Benny knew things, the things kids were supposed to know. He was a genius at running and accidents. He could run fast and hard as if his lungs were pure and inexhaustible.

In schoolrooms, he knocked things over. He was accident prone. Once, jumping off the garage roof trying to fly with two paper kites tied onto his arms, he cut himself over the eye. Mothers on Lime Kiln Road loved Benny. You could see him with a white bandage on his forehead, sitting on a front porch, reading or tossing a ball to some rapt younger kid. For a long time he tried to teach Netty Griling how to read.

He knew the names of things. Bugs, trees, things on the radio, parts of machines. He seemed born knowing how to drive. Later, he danced easily, he could throw a perfect stone, a football, he understood rock 'n' roll.

These things mattered, they counted, we both knew. I admired him, he would always be older.

Theresa and I rode behind Benny. Every mile or so he would lazily turn back and circle around to us. It was a clear warm day with soft nimbus clouds drifting in the sky. I had the new bikini rolled up in my towel. At the pool, we paid a quarter for a wire basket and changed in wooden cubicles where the half-size doors were old and chipped and the concrete floor was gritty. You pinned the safety pin, with the number on it, somewhere unnoticeable, like the side of your suit. In the cubicle, all of a sudden I was surprised how small the bikini was. I stayed there awhile tracing a name cut into the pink faded door.

Theresa gasped. "You got a new suit, a bikini." She poked her elbow into my side. "Why didn't you tell me?"

I shrugged, all of a sudden not wanting to be noticed.

We lay in the sun for a while and it was the way it always was. We had to rub the white cream from a silver foil tube on Benny's shoulders and Benny's nose: Benny burned. I went dark. With the new bikini, you could see my tan line. I snapped the elastic of the bottom. My grandmother, my aunt Carol, my mother—all of them looked at me in summer as if I were amazing. They all freckled in our family, freckled and burned. I was dark from my father.

Benny ran to the line at the diving board, and Theresa and I moved back to the metal fence and put our hands behind us. Then we jumped in, cannonballs, our arms hugging our knees.

Something amazing happened then, to the spot I jumped in, the spot of blue in the pool. I was underwater, coming up, and there was a swarm of boys around me, touching, pushing, patting my breasts with their flat hands. Legs and arms were on all sides of me. I felt as if I couldn't get out; they were touching me up and down. I splashed, pushing my shoulders up for air, for breath, and the world changed and stood still, when I came above the water, splashing, trying to move towards the cement side. Something had my leg and was pinching the muscle of my calf. I saw the stillness of the sky, the pale green high water tank with BAY CITY written on its belly in black letters. I was alone.

I pulled on the metal steps trying to climb and their hands were on my legs. One was pulling my bikini bottom.

I screamed up, "Help me, these guys!" to the lifeguard on a white chair.

I didn't have time to think, I just pulled with my arms. Above me, the lifeguard moved one dark leg over the other. The bottoms of his feet were yellow. He picked up a white whistle off his chest and finally blew it. By then I was out, stepping, making my first footprint on the concrete lip.

"Okay, guys, knock it off," he said.

In the green water, the star-shaped cluster split and disappeared. Their skin looked white and strange, fishlike under the surface. I stood on the concrete, my arms across my chest, looking up at the lifeguard. I was back to myself. This was Ashwaubenon Pool in Prebble Park; I'd been here before, all summer, days and days. I kept standing there, waiting for the lifeguard to talk to me. He was motioning at the deep end, where a boy's arms were beating the air, as he tried to get to the side.

I looked at the shadows in the green water. For a second, for a split second, I had opened my eyes and with the pressure of resistance underwater, for a second, the thought had come, *they like me*, and it was warm and the water was soft and enclosing and I was someone else, being directed, floating.

Theresa hauled one leg up out of the pool; she padded, dripping, and stood next to me. The lifeguard finally looked down and shrugged. "You know, you're asking for it in that suit. If you don't want it, don't ask for it." He grinned. His legs were swinging beneath his chair. It was the first time I'd thought of the bikini; that was what had been different.

We lay down on our towels again, by the fence, and closed our eyes. You could feel yourself drying, just under the wind. I listened to the pumps below the concrete, the steady machines.

Benny stood dripping on us. "What happened?"

I kept my eyes closed and pretended to be asleep. Theresa sat up on her towel and told him.

"I know you're awake." Benny kicked me with a wet foot. His feet were so white. He was frowning. "Those guys are creeps."

"Saint Agnes creeps," Theresa said. None of us ever went to Saint Agnes. It was the rich Catholic school.

Theresa and I turned on our stomachs and opened a magazine and Benny went to buy us all Dreamsicles. Theresa took her sister's magazines; they were swollen and frilled from having been wet and dried so many times. Underwater, those guys were faceless, swirling around like sharks. They still poked up, sometimes, laughing. But I was safe, things were the same, while I stayed on the concrete. It would only change in the water. When Benny came back, the Dreamsicles were already melting inside their paper wrappers.

"Here." He threw his balled-up T-shirt into my lap.

Theresa carried my pin and hers and waited at the counter to get our baskets. She came in the stall with me when I changed. The ordinary dry shorts and top felt good. Then we were standing outside, against the metal bars by our bikes, waiting for Benny. Theresa touched the inside of my elbow. "You better not wear that suit again here."

"He owns the *very* largest real estate company in Bay City." My mother smiled to herself. "And it's growing. Boy, are they growing."

She moved the wooden spoon in the pitcher of lemonade as if her arm were some electric appliance.

"So, why are we going over there? Are we buying a new house?"

"Shhh," my mother said, her eyes casting down the hallway to detect Ted, who hadn't left for the day yet. Ted taught skating classes now on Saturdays and Sundays. He was hardly ever at home. I looked down to the empty rooms. I wouldn't have minded a new house, that was for sure. Two years and we still didn't have furniture. For a while, they'd said they were going to put in a pool, but that fell through, too. Most of what my mom and Ted planned didn't work. It turned out they couldn't get the bulldozers in to dig the pool without going through another yard. And when they asked the neighbors, they said no.

"No, silly, shush." She looked around the small yard, then, at the two trees, the fence. "He's just a friend of mine, that's all."

It took her a long time to get ready. She touched up her finger- and toenails with light pink polish. We drove to the old section downtown. My mother explained that the company had bought a house for its office and remodeled. We walked up the stone path-way and Dan Sklar opened the door, even before we knocked. Wind chimes hung over our heads on the porch.

The office was empty, he was the only one there and he didn't offer to show us around. My mother leaned against a desk and smiled at him. "Well, so, how are you?" she said. Her bright voice made me angry, she had a way of smiling and looking at the other person and paying absolutely no attention to me.

Dan Sklar slumped over as he stood. He looked like a tired person. His small nose was sunburned and peeling.

"The Japanese gardens in front look fan-tastic," my mother said, leaning back and crossing her arms. "They're gorgeous, very elegant. Just like they are over there."

Over where? I wondered for a minute, and then I knew what she meant. I looked at her. There she went again. She'd never been to Japan. She looked down at the rug, into the shag.

"Have you been there?" he asked.

"Mmmhmm."

I knew better than to say, When? or anything, and anyway, what did I care. She'd lie to me, too, in a minute. She was like that.

We were standing by a sliding glass door. Outside, young maples moved slightly, trembling in the stillness. My mother picked up a paperweight and held it in her hand. "A-yun," she said, still looking at the paperweight, turning it, making it snow. "You didn't get a chance to really see the rock garden. Dan's rebuilt a re-yall authentic Japanese rock garden outside." Vowels and consonants rolled and spiked in her mouth, and her eyebrows lifted as if she were talking to a very young child. "Why don't you go out and explore."

I just looked at her. Then at him. It was getting so I always turned to the other person to help protect me against what she said.

But he nodded at me, weakly. "There's a waterfall in back," he offered.

"I don't want to go outside," I said. I pretended to be dumb.

"Oh, well, okay," she said, looking down at the carpet. She lifted her eyes then, up in a straight line to Dan's face. She tossed her head and took a breath.

"Why?" she said.

He couldn't have missed the sharpness in her voice. But his eyes meandered out the glass doors, to the garden. It was high summer, just turning.

"Huh?"

"Why."

"Why don't I want to go outside?"

"Yes. Why don't you want to go outside?"

I shrugged. "I guess I don't feel like it. Is it like a federal case, I have to have a reason?"

"It's just a nice day and I thought you might like a little sun, that's all." She exhaled through her teeth. "But, no, not you, anything to be contrary, to be the center of attention."

Dan Sklar's head turned. His breath came out of his mouth so slowly, it was like something ticking.

"Adele," he said, "leave her."

But then the same thing happened that always happened, when someone tried to stick up for me.

"No, I'm not going to leave her because she's going to have to learn."

Dan Sklar swiveled his chair so he was completely facing out the window. We could see his back and his hands. He'd picked up string from his desk and he was lacing it, cat's cradle, through his fingers. Behind him maple leaves fluttered and moss on the ground seemed wet. Then my mother made a face at me. The face was like a mask: sour and menacing, recognizable, at the same time. The lines around her mouth carved deeper. Her cheeks pushed out, round and young. She looked like she was innocent and just now saw me for what I was: a devil.

I walked across the carpet, quiet—because of my sneakers. I opened the sliding doors and moved outside past Dan Sklar. He didn't matter anymore. He wasn't going to help.

The sun was weak but a definite yellow on the sidewalk. This part of town was still, today, and empty. As soon as I was outside, I was glad. I didn't know why I hadn't left earlier, I should have. It was like stepping into another room, with clean, aquatic light and thinner air. Across the street was a small bank and its empty parking lot. Down the road, pigeons sat on the painted game circles of the playground at Saint John's School, where I used to go. The spires of the steeple intersected with telephone wires.

Then I heard my name. Dan Sklar slumped in the open door, his arm above him on the wall. "Ann, there's a pond with goldfish down on your left, and in back, there's a waterfall."

"And all over the sides, he's planted flowers. Oh, and Ann, you'll never believe, there are lily pads on the pond. Remember, when you were a teensy-weensy girl, we used to go see the farms and the lily pads?"

I just stared.

She was talking to him. "We were living at Mom's and she was always the first one up at five or six, you know. So we just jumped in the car and went to see the farmers milking their cows. And she used to love lily pads, where the wee little frogs sat."

I stayed where I was sitting, on a stone. I drew my knees up and hugged them. "Okay," I said.

They shut the sliding glass door and pulled the beige curtains closed. My mother poked her head out once more.

"Ann, be careful where you step. Don't squash any flowers. Look where you're going."

The wind chime moved above the door as if someone was running their fingers through it. This old neighborhood was near Saint Phillip's Academy, the Catholic high school where my mother had gone. She had taken me to Dean's, the place she'd gone after school for hamburgers and malts—that was around here, too. I felt in my pockets, even though I knew already, I didn't have any money. I could walk off, but then I'd only be in more trouble later and there wasn't anywhere much I could go. There was a car lot a few blocks away. From where I was, I could see the string of flags rippling.

I tried to be very still and forget about myself. I pictured a refrigerator sitting in Griling's dump, the sun on its dry white sides.

Then a boy I knew from my old school rode by on a bicycle. Paul, whose father was a beekeeper. I didn't want him to see me. For two years, he had sat behind me in the row of small desks at my old school, where I went before Ted and the house on Carriage Court. It was possible he would go by and not know me. It was years now since we were in school together. I stayed, crouched there on the rock, like the Land O' Lakes Indian. A fly settled on my arm, but I didn't move.

He looked at me and kept walking his bike. Then, a few squares of sidewalk later, he looked back and stood there. "Ann," he said. "You're Ann August, aren't you?"

I stepped forward, my hands conscious and awkward at my sides. We sat down on the steps together by the goldfish pond. There was a patch of smooth black pebbles. I took a handful and pitched them in one by one.

"You're at Oak Grove now," he said.

"Yeah. Public school."

"I see your cousin around. Ben. I used to come over to your house in first grade, I remember once we caught butterflies."

"Yeah, I remember that." I was embarrassed all of a sudden. I didn't want him to ask what I was doing here.

He was hitting two rocks together. "You were living with your grandmother then, out there. You told me once you liked your cousin better than me."

"I'm sorry."

He shrugged. "Doesn't matter. We were just little kids."

"Do you still live on a bee farm?"

"Yup. Got a thousand more bees now than we did then." He

opened his hand and counted on his fingers. "Clover, alfalfa, wildflower, orange blossom, grass"—his fist was closed—"and mixed. I get out honey myself now. I have my mask and my gloves and my own colony."

"My grandfather had mink," I said, stupidly.

"Yup, I remember the sheds."

We both just sat there with our elbows on our knees and our chins in our hands.

"I guess I better go now," he said, standing. "Do you ski?" he asked suddenly, looking at me while he kicked the kickstand up on his bike.

"No."

"Oh," he said. "I ski now."

I nodded. Nothing seemed surprising. I fingered the concrete sidewalk, still cool despite the thin yellow from the sun. I liked him but I was glad he was going, because I didn't want him to be there when my mother and Dan Sklar came out.

It was a long time. I walked around to the back, telling myself that when I'd stepped on every stone, when I'd seen and said the name of every flower, they would be finished and we could go home. But then I was finished and nothing happened. Birds sat on the telephone wires not moving, even when I threw stones.

One of the stones landed with a loud ringing on the roof of a car parked across the street. I felt that sound in my heart. I waited then, terrified and stiff, to be caught. But time stayed still, the rectangle of sun, like a room around the parked car, changed, slowly sliding into shade.

Then the old heavy trees on the street began rustling and it started to rain. I skipped to the door then, holding my elbows in the other palm, like eggs. Sure, she would come out now.

But she didn't. I watched the birds fly off telephone wires into the dark trees. The wind chimes on the porch clattered wildly. The pond of goldfish ruffled up and stayed itself at the same time, like the skin on a pan of milk, scalding.

I walked to our car, getting soaked. The rain felt like dull needles. The doors were locked. I stood for a moment looking into the dry, kept inside of our car. My book was there. Then a line of lightning cracked the sky and I ran back to the porch. I put my ear to the wall and I didn't hear anything moving. It seemed impossible now that my mother was inside; still, our car was there. I couldn't seem to hold the two things in my mind at once.

A few minutes later, there was a strange light, slanting as if it came from the ground behind the house. I still sat, damp, in the porch shade. But everything in the yard, stones, the black telephone wires, our car, the tiny, waxy, mossy flowers, seemed to shine hardly, as if their colors were only painted and there was metal inside them.

The sun was in the sky again and the dark clouds, now marbled and veined with light, moved fast. Once, my grandmother had been driving with her husband in the old Ford. They drove into a storm. I always thought of them at one place on the black highway, a firm yellow stripe down the middle, my grandfather with his glasses at the wheel, my grandmother, in a blue dress, looking down at her hands in her lap, and the car, half in rain, the back half dry in sunlight. She'd told me that once and I thought of it a lot. It was just one of those things I used.

I sat in a square of sun, pitching stones in the pond again, trying to rouse a goldfish. They never came to the surface, but sometimes one turned underwater, a quick apostrophe of flame, like sun on a coin for a second, then extinguished again by the green. I looked up and followed the telephone wires, down the road to the string of flags marking the car lot. Something about the stillness of the air made it already late afternoon. My clothes were almost dry now, except for the elastic of my underwear and the rims of my sneakers.

Finally, then, while I was still looking at clouds between telephone poles, printing my thoughts in black square letters on the sky, the door closed behind me and my mother came out alone.

She smiled hugely and stopped a moment, rolling her head and smelling the air. "Mmmph," she said. Then she looked down and found me. She wasn't angry anymore. She stuck her arm out in the air, her hand open, and clicked her tongue—the way she had when I was little. It was a signal for me to come running and take her hand.

But I only stood up slowly.

"Do you have any coins?" I said.

"Coins?" she repeated, not changing her face—the stupid smile was still there. "Why? Do you feel like running over to Dean's?"

I thought of that a second, the silver glistening behind the soda fountain, and the day seemed to close up, small again. We'd get into our car and go, normal. I could taste the beginning of sweetness at the back of my throat.

"But before that, for here. To throw into the goldfish pond."

She stepped lightly over to where I was. She was wearing white patent leather thongs and her pink toenails looked like the washed insides of shells.

She looked in her wallet, but there were no coins. Then she lifted her whole purse to one side and shook it so everything fell to the corner. She rummaged and extracted a dime and a quarter. She gave me the quarter.

"Go on, it'll work even better," she said. "The more money, the faster you get your wish."

My mother looked around the yard. "Isn't this fantastic," she said. Her smile stayed, too big, as if she couldn't stop it.

"It's all right." I shrugged.

"Well, I think it's really great. The authentic Japanese. Really, really great." Then I knew what it was—that smile and the way she was talking—it was as if she was proud.

She closed her eyes and threw in the dime. It landed half on a lily pad, and wavered on its edge a moment before sliding under. She was crouched down so her sharkskin slacks hiked up and I saw the shaved nubs of blond hair on her ankles. Even her ankles had freckles. She was mumbling to herself, moving her lips the way she did when she said prayers. There was a flat, gold leaf on the pavement. She picked it up, examined it against the sky, then set it on the thinly pleated water. We both knelt down watching it move.

□

A long time ago, once, my mother drove me far, I don't know where it was, to a brick hospital, just the two of us. It was on a long lawn, like the dairy, a low, brick building that went on as far as you could see. We parked in the parking lot in back. My mother told me she had to have a test for TB. I was young enough to misunderstand.

"For TV? For TV?" I kept saying. "You have to have a test for TV?"

"No," she said. She was distracted.

I had to wait, sitting in the lobby on a chair, while she went somewhere else. A long time later, she came out in a wheelchair, a nun in a white habit pushing it behind her. "Come on, Ann," she said, without turning her head to me. The nun didn't say anything; they both looked forward. I hurried up to go and ran a little to keep next to them. The nun left us for a moment in a long hallway. There were glass showcases on both walls. I held on to a small piece of my mother's sleeve.

"See, I'll have to come and live here," she said. She looked at the handiwork in the cases and sighed. "I guess I'll learn how to knit and crochet and make things like that. That won't be so bad. I suppose I'll like it after a while."

She looked down at her hands and smiled.

"What about me?" I said it quietly, almost a whisper, and just then a huge roaring started in my head.

"You'll get used to it. I won't be able to take care of you anymore, I'll be too weak. But I'll knit something for you, maybe a sweater. You can come and visit. Mmhmm. I think I'll knit you a sweater."

The nun came back and said, "We'll have the results on Thursday." Thursday, Thursday stuck in my mind, a purple word.

The nun wheeled my mother to a cement ramp outside the building. My mother stood up and took her purse from next to her on the wheelchair. It was a white patent leather purse with gold clasps. We started walking to our car. My mother looked back, once, at the nun in her white habit, the veil moving a little in the breeze as she turned. The roaring was still in my head, in back of one ear, and I didn't say anything. It was spring that day, there were irises and daffodils planted along the edges of the hospital lawns. There was a watery breeze like on Easter. My mother drove home and never mentioned any of it again.

I was sitting on my bed, watching television. My mother came into the room. "Oh, there you are, I called you, didn't you hear me." She rubbed away a tear with a cuff. "You scared me. You know yesterday I was watching you from his sliding glass doors, and you were just standing there on that long grass by the sidewalk, you weren't even in the nice garden, sort of shuffling your sneakers on the ground, in that jacket, with your hands in your pockets and your head down. I saw you looking like that, unhappy, sluffing around like a little old man, and I thought, nothing is worth it, you're my jewel. Honest, Honey, you are. You're my absolute precious, long-limbed jewel. I have to get you somewhere they can see you." Her face folded and she started crying. "In that plain old jacket, with your head down, kicking, I thought to myself, here's this beautiful, long-limbed girl with potential stuck in a nothing town. You look like a boy in those jeans and that scruffy jacket, some boy at a gas station in some nowhere place."

One day, I came home from school and the house was furnished. It had everything. I walked from room to room, switching on lamps and sitting on sofas. I ran my hands over the polished tabletops. The house had still been empty that morning.

When my mother came home she explained that it was only rented and temporary. She didn't like the blue and green color scheme, but it was the best they had. She and Ted wanted to invite the family over for Thanksgiving.

For three days we shopped. Ted went to work every morning, as usual, but my mother and I drove to the country to buy pumpkins. We placed orders at butchers' and bakeries. My mother said she'd give me a note for school saying I was sick.

□

My mother's sister Carol lifted her eyebrows, her hands modest in her lap, counting the different kinds of forks and knives fanning out on both sides of her plate, while her husband Jimmy started a story. All of Jimmy's stories were about sex or machines. The same thing with his jokes.

"This widow was lonely," he was saying, "so she goes to her husband's grave and digs up his you-know-what and nails it in her bedroom so it sticks up through the floor. She makes a little trapdoor for it, so, during the day, she can put it down. You know, for company."

"Oh, Jimmy, not with the kids here." Then she looked at me and laughed. "You know, you just can't stop him." Carol was eleven years older than my mother. She looked like a country woman, with her tight curls and undistinguished color of brown hair.

My grandmother shook her head as if she'd just tasted something bitter. "I don't like to hear such stuff." Her voice thumped like the weight of her footsteps when she walked around her house at night.

My mother carried in a pewter soup tureen. She bent over the candles, serving. The soup was from fancy cans we'd bought in the gourmet department of Shreve's, cans imported from France. "It's madrilene," she announced. Jimmy was rolling back his sleeves, still telling his story, but in a softer voice. Jimmy had respect for a few things. One of them was food.

He winked. "And so another guy, a neighbor, he catches on. He looks through her window one night and sees. So he goes in the next day with a saw and a shovel and two-by-fours and he builds himself a little room under the floor where her husband's thing is. He throws that out."

"He doesn't bury it properly?" My cousin Hal carefully unfolded his napkin on his lap, over his knees. Hal was thin and straight, all right angles. You could tell Hal hated his father.

"Okay, say he buries it."

"So," my mother said, sitting down. She smiled and slowly lifted a spoonful of soup to her lips.

"The house looks very nice, oh, so much better," Carol said.

"Every night, he crawls into his spot and he's ready. And so they do it. And this goes on a few months. And then one night, she comes with a knife"—and Jimmy lifted one of his own knives, the butter knife, for emphasis—"and she goes, okay, Harry, come on, we're moving. I bought us a new house."

"Dad," Hal said.

"They're at it again." Carol's head twitched back and forth, resigned.

"No more now," my grandmother said. "You had to have your one, so now you've had it."

Jimmy Measey was still laughing, sputtering, repeating the gesture with his knife. "Come on, you're going to a new house, fella."

He looked over at Benny, who was pretending to smile like he understood. Benny got this smile whenever his dad looked at him, a thin smile you felt you could wipe off with a rag. When Benny was little, his father used to tease him around other people. Once we were sitting at a restaurant, out for steak dinners. Jimmy kept telling Benny how good chopped sirloin was, how that was what he should really want, how nothing in the world was as delicious as chopped sirloin. Jimmy thought that was wildly funny, tricking Benny out of his steak, making fun of him for not knowing the names. Benny had that same wan smile then, when the whole family was laughing, as a waiter set down his hamburger. Benny was afraid of his father.

"What's this, tomato broth?" Jimmy said.

"It's madrilene," Ted said quietly, looking down.

"Yeah. S'good." Jimmy speared a lemon slice with his fork. "Now what am I sposed to do with this?"

Carol nudged him. "Just leave it, Jimmy. Leave it on your plate."

Hal smiled deliberately at my mother.

The next two courses came on small, hand-painted plates. Everyone finished the endive salad and the salmon mousse before my mother. She smiled and talked, eating slowly, looking at each bite before she put the fork in her mouth. She was really enjoying herself. It made me happy. Then Ted cleared the small plates and followed my mother into the kitchen.

"Don't you want us to hold on to our forks, Del?" Carol was asking.

My mother shouted back. "No, there's plenty clean. Just look to the left of your plate."

I brought out the pâté, each plate garnished with a limp-stemmed violet from the refrigerator. We'd paid fifty cents each for them at Debago's nursery.

Jimmy looked at his watch. "It's been almost two hours and all she's done is make me hungry."

When I set down their plates, Carol and my grandmother giggled and shook their heads. Jimmy lifted his violet. In his big hand it looked like a specimen, something dead.

"Addie, what's this flower for? Am I supposed to eat it?" he yelled into the kitchen.

"Shhh," I said.

My grandmother frowned. "It's like those fancy little butters you two used to get from the factory, such little portions," she whispered.

Then my mother glided in and they all hushed. She was beaming. Ted stood behind her, pulling out her chair. She still thought her dinner was a success. I looked at her cheeks, high and proud, and I bent over and started eating my pâté. It tasted delicious. I felt like telling her people laughed. They were hungry. But it was so good and she was happy. Why couldn't they just wait?

"So, tell me, how is your work, Adele? How do you like the new school?"

My mother sighed. Whenever my grandmother asked her questions, she sighed and she slumped back into her chair. "Well, Mom, I don't like that drive out there every day in my old car with the window that doesn't roll up. Ann knows. But these administrators are bright, just out of college, most of them. It's a good team." She looked down at her hands on the tablecloth. "I have plenty to do this weekend still. Those darn reports. Ann, maybe tomorrow we'll drive downtown to the library and both just work."

Jimmy Measey was talking to Ted about moving the water softener store to Three Corners, because they were tearing up the
road for the new highway.

Ted never talked about his own work at all, as if he were embarrassed. I didn't blame him. It didn't exactly seem like a job.
My mother once told me Ted was an orphan.

My mother rustled in her chair and stood up. "Ted, could you
please come in and carve? And Ann, would you mind taking our
plates?" We both stood up beside her, the family. I felt behind us
they were laughing at the way we did things. It seemed unbear-
able for my mother not to know. She was trying so hard.

In the kitchen, I tugged her arm. "Mom, I think they're really
hungry. It's getting late."

"Well, I hope they're hungry." She'd stepped out of her shoes
and she was leaning with both hands on Ted's shoulder, watching
as he cut. "Oh, it's perfect. Just pink enough. Per-fecto. Honey,
you take the bread basket out. Go."

"It's prettinear ten o'clock. Ugh, I don't like to eat so late." My
grandmother smiled at me then, as if it were all right to complain
about my mother. I was supposed to know she didn't mean me
too. But I felt so sorry for my mother. I wanted them all to leave,
before she knew anything.

"Ta-da," my mother said, setting down the platter of sliced
steak and new potatoes. Her face stalled, waiting for compli-
ments.

"Well, that looks very good," my grandmother said.

"Adele, you don't mean to tell me that after all this time, we're
not even going to get a turkey," Jimmy said, laughing but not
really.

My mother looked around the table at each of us as if the lights
were just turned on. She looked down to Ted, as if for help.

"Jimmy, this is châteaubriand, ordered five days ahead from
the butcher down at Krim's, at eight ninety-nine a pound, it's the
best meat you can buy in the whole world, I hope that's good
enough for you."

"Come, let's shush and eat," my grandmother said.

"Well, Adele, it is Thanksgiving. It's ten o'clock, we have been sitting here since five waiting. If you'd told us, sheesh, we could have had it at our house. Carol would have baked a turkey."

My mother's chair screeched across the floor. She left, running into the other room, her dress a black swatch in the hall. "You can't do anything right with them," I heard her sobbing, as Ted followed. He was smiling his awkward, zipper smile when he stood up.

Benny and I both sat, very straight, with our hands on our laps.

"Oh, Jimmy, if you would only once just be quiet. You know how she is."

"Carol, I don't care what's wrong with your sister, I want a turkey on my Thanksgiving, all right? And if we can't eat now, you can get your purse and we'll go." Jimmy stood up, stuffing a slice of meat from the platter into his mouth with a hand, his napkin still tucked in his collar. Blood dripped on my mother's tablecloth.

Hal got up, making a noise with his chair, and walked down the hall towards my mother.

"Should I fix you each a plate?" My grandmother looked back and forth between Benny and me. The food was resting in the center of the table. Parsley and lemon slices garnished the potatoes. It was a beautiful platter, neat like a field.

Benny told her no.

"We're old enough to wait," I said.

Jimmy shook his head, looking at me. "Your mother."

It seemed we waited a long time, still there, and then I heard Ted's voice, shaped and kind, like a curve around my mother. "Before it gets cold," he was saying. They came back, Ted and Hal on either side of my mother. Standing, her face lit with the candlelight where she'd been crying, my mother seemed beautiful and strange and I felt sorry I hadn't run back to her with Ted. She wasn't looking at me now.

"Shall we eat before it's cold?" she said. "Hal, why don't you start the vegetables and I'll serve."

We ate quietly, careful.

"It's wonderful, Adele. This whole meal has been wonderful," Hal said.

"Yes, it's very, very good."

"Thank you," my mother said, primly.

Jimmy leaned back in his chair. "Well, Adele, for the very best meat available in the world at eight ninety-nine a pound, I'll tell you something. It's not bad."

My mother's face hung in the air a second while we waited. Then it grew to a slow smile. She couldn't help but laugh. She looked over at Carol. "I don't see how you put up with him."

"Well, you know, Adele, sometimes I don't either. Sometimes I just don't know either."

They never went to bed that night. I heard them. They moved from room to room on the new furniture, the way people turn over and change positions while they dream. I think they were amazed. They had been married three years but they had never had any furniture.

The next morning my mother came in and sat on the edge of my bed. She looked at the room behind her.

"I think he's running around," she said. She was nodding her head in assent with herself.

"Who is?"

"Shhh. I'm sure of it."

"You're nuts." I turned around to go back to sleep.

Her hand pried my shoulder up. "I don't care if he is, I hope he is. If we caught him with another woman, boy, that would really be it. That would really help."

"What?"

"In court. Then we'd get everything and we could move." She shook her head. "It's no more than I deserve, Gramma paid for the house, it should be mine. She's *my* mother."

"What are you talking about?"

She looked down at her foot. A slipper dangled off the bottom, she was bouncing it on her toes. "Today, at noon, Horst is going to call and ask him out with some girls. We'll just see what he says. I'll bet he goes."

"Who's Horse?"

"You know, Horst, downtown. The tailor. He's the one who took up your raincoat."

The morning was slow and pretend. We all stayed around the house, doing nothing in the kitchen. My mother offered to cook Ted an egg. He refused, but he stood next to her and let her pour him more coffee. She made me cinnamon toast. That was the kind of thing she never did. She hated white sugar. We all ate the leftover château straight from the refrigerator. One of us would open the door and leave it hang while we stood chewing.

Then, at noon, the phone rang.

"It's for you, Ted." My mother handed him the receiver and walked to the stove. My mother rubbed the same spot on the counter, over and over, with her dish towel. I sat where I was, blowing the sugar on my plate, then writing my name with a finger.

"No," Ted said, into the phone. "I'm not interested in that."

Then he was off. He took his coffee cup from where it was on the counter and went back to the screen door hinge he'd been trying to fix. I walked into the living room. All the candles had melted down, the wax flat on the plates like fried eggs.

"So, what was that all about?" my mother asked.

"It was Horst."

"What did he want?"

"Nothing. He wanted to go out somewhere."

"Oh, well, are you going?"

Ted put the screwdriver down. "Adele, you heard what I told him."

"Oh, well, I was just wondering. I mean I was right here, are you sure your answer wouldn't have been different if I wasn't around just then?"

I went back to look in their bedroom. The bed was tight and untouched. They never had gone to sleep.

A nun's flashlight carved out a cave in the darkness and we followed. The old orphanage had closed. Now, they'd built an annex on the west side of the Fox River, small wooden cabins where older girls, girls who'd been in trouble, lived by themselves, four of them with one nun. My mother and Lolly and I walked through the woods to a benefit dinner in one of the cabins.

My mother nudged me. At the small round table there were candles, that was most of what we could see. The windows were dark and it was dark outside.

All around us girls hovered in white high-necked blouses, their long hair pulled back in plain liver-colored rubber bands, lipstick a little over their lips and dabs of nail polish on their nylons. They seemed tall and awkward, they didn't know what to do with their hands. They'd made our meal and they hovered, waiting to take our plates away and wash them. But I knew sometime, once, they were bad. When one leaned down to pour coffee, my mother touched her sleeve and asked a question. She looked up, distracted, and then explained. As a project, they'd made the centerpieces. Ours was an old 45 record melted down, that's how they got the edges to frill. They put the candle in the hole.

My mother nudged me and whispered. "You could do that."

After school, downstairs, I lay in the cool basement. There was a bed with an old bedspread and a television. I lay on my stomach and watched the reruns in the cool dark. I heard my mother coming down the stairs. She had a load of laundry in her arms. The pipes banged, as she set the machine going. Then she came towards me.

"What are you doing down here? Why do you always come down here when you could watch the big TV upstairs? Are you ashamed of something?" She was talking a certain way. I kept looking at the TV, not moving, though a commercial came on.

"And why do you bounce up and down like that with your hips, people don't do that, it's vulgar."

I still didn't answer. I was barely breathing.

"Did someone fuck you?" She said the word long, with air in it. I wasn't allowed to say it. "They did, didn't they? I can tell. Tell me, Ann, who did, tell me, who fucked you. Because they really ruined you."

I saw her then like an animal, her teeth huge in her face, her body stiff and small. Her feet clicked on the cement basement floor and she moved back and forth with her hands on her hips, her head bent forward, stalking. She wouldn't come any closer. It was as if I had a smell. I made myself stay the same.

"No," I said.

"Come on, tell." Her eyebrows lifted and fell once and she kept her smile. She was excited. "Tell me who did it to you, who fucked you."

I still didn't look at her. "Oooooh," she came towards me with her arm. "Stop twitching like that."

I got up and walked past her to the stairs. She grabbed my arm and I shoved her away. "Leave me alone," I said. She made marks on my skin. "What's wrong with you."

"Nothing's wrong with *me*," she yelled at my back. "I go upstairs in my own house. I'm clean. I don't twitch. I have nothing to be ashamed of."

I locked myself in the bathroom. In a few minutes, she knocked and scraped on the door.

"Ann, come out here a second.

"Ann, I have something to tell you. There's something we have to talk about.

"Open this door. Otherwise, otherwise, I'm going to open it, I'll get the key."

Circles. My head was against the cool tiles of the bathtub. The door had a gold metal doorknob. There was no keyhole, there couldn't be a key. She said she was going to get a key. But there was no keyhole, there couldn't be a key. But she said there was a key.

I pressed myself into the corner, like something molded there. I tried not to hear, not to think. And then, after, there was always a lightness, a feeling of air inside, like you are an impostor, eating only the appearance of things, living in holograms of light. There in the corner, almost gone, I had one feeling above my stomach, like a flutter. No one but me could ever know about this time, not if I wanted love.

Later, Ted came home and everything was normal again. My mother acted nice to me, she made sautéed mushrooms for over our steaks. She seemed to have forgotten. I watched her, but it seemed rinsed away, all gone. We were friends again, I was her daughter, she liked me. And I was relieved, happy in some recovered way. She picked up my hand and squeezed it. And all evening, there was that lightness. I wasn't hungry, I wasn't interested, I wasn't tired.

I didn't want anything. I'd lost my attraction for gravity and I couldn't get it back by myself. I knew it would always be there again in the morning, after sleep. But for that night, I didn't care. I didn't want a thing.

We drove past the shopping center, the used car lot and my public school, out on the highway, to where it wasn't developed yet. And then when we were at the place we'd gone for the benefit dinner, the place for girls, my mother let me out on the ditch by the side of the road and turned around and drove away. I stood waiting for her to come back. I was sure she would come, but I was trembling anyway. I couldn't control my teeth, my hands. I didn't have anything with me, money, anything. I took off my mitten. Inside was one soft worn dollar bill, pale from washing.

I was just wearing my jacket and jeans. I sat on a post. I didn't see my mother's car coming back. I watched the other cars in the distance, each one was a sink of hope, I squinted my eyes so I thought it was ours and let myself feel the sweetness of belief wash over me, but then it would come close and be green or red or yellow or blue, and all the time, inside, I really knew.

I thought of going somewhere. I looked behind me at the woods. The snow was melting on the ground. The tree trunks seemed to all rise, black, from the same level plane. It was hard to look at them. It was late afternoon, their black bark looked lush, holding gold on their thin sides. They glinted like fish in the air and soon it would be dark.

Then down the road, on my side, coming towards me, two girls were walking on the gravel, their hands in their jacket pockets. Their heads were down. I couldn't see any more from where I was. Their feet kicked up clouds of dust. I thought they were coming for me. They were girls who lived here in the woods, in those cabins, and my mother had told them I was bad and they were coming. At the exact same time and with a feeling like a finger pressing down, leaving an impression on my heart, I knew that they were coming for me and I knew that I was imagining it, that they weren't, they didn't know me.

I bolted. I saw a flash of metallic blue, but then I was on the other side of the highway, up the embankment, in the woods, before the blue car passed. I stopped for a moment, still. All my life I'd imagined one death—slow motion, a clear day, pale blue sky, white clouds and a dull gray highway, a yellow stripe, the long bounce off a rounded blue fender, then the soft fall, dead, then nothing. All in sunlight. I'd never told anyone and I wondered if every person carried their own death with them, like something private and quiet, inside a small box.

I started to walk in the woods, still looking down for a white car on the highway. I knew where I would come out, on the other side. I didn't think past that. At the road, I could hitch. The sky was white and blue now. The trees had lost their gold.

When I came out I was on another highway. Trucks and cars passed by. I'd never hitchhiked before. As bad as my mother thought I was, I hadn't really done much. I was still too scared.

A truck zoomed by and the wind almost knocked me over. I stepped up and stuck out my thumb. I looked ahead of me. Three women, mothers, drove past without picking me up, and I looked down at myself and thought how I must look. My jeans were splattered with mud. Then a truck came and stopped. Feet above me, the cabin door sprang open. The man said he was going as far as the bridge. The seats were leather and cracked, I could feel the tape on the backs of my thighs. The whole cabin smelled of oil. It was a long, easy ride. We passed Dan Sklar's office and I saw a white car like my mother's outside on the street, and Saint Phillip's empty playground. The sky was colored with feathery pink clouds when I got out.

"Say, where're you going?" he said, when I stepped down.

For the first time I thought he might be dangerous. He wore a pale brown uniform with darker brown piping and a clover with his name, BUD, over his left breast pocket.

I jumped down the three steps and pushed the door shut. My

ankle twisted and I landed in a puddle. I started running and
didn't look behind me. Suddenly, lights flooded the place between
me and a brick wall. It was the truck moving and I turned around,
stuck.

His head was in the rolled-down window.

"Girl, where are you going? I don't like to let you off like this.
It's getting dark."

I looked at my shoes. They'd gone from white to brown with
streaks of mud and coal, in just one day.

"I'm going to my grandmother's house."

"She live around here?" His head moved back and forth.

We were downtown, by the quarry. There were old stores here,
small stores with gray worn wooden doors and bars across the
screens, the only color labels from the orange companies. Ruby
Beauty, Sacramento, Indian River.

Two huge piles across the water, the bright soft yellow of sulfur
and the smaller mounds of coal; he was staring.

"Yeah," I said.

He waited a minute as if he were deciding whether to believe
me. His face stayed in the window. He had short white hair and
wide bones. I thought I saw him wince. He was thinking he was
acting selfish, he shouldn't leave me, but he wanted to get where
he was going.

The small red lights of the truck flashed on and he turned.

I'd lived in Bay City all my life, but I'd never seen this corner.
I fingered the dollar in my mitten. I went into the grocery store
and the door tinkled above me. It was dark inside except for the
wide, white iceboxes along the one wall.

I stood by the cash register, choosing. I bought a package of
Milk Duds, a piece of beef jerky and a bottle of chocolate milk
with a straw. I opened up my folded dollar and I gave it to the
man. He waited while I stood there, before he slid off the wooden
stool, butt by butt, to stand.

Then I climbed the cement steps to the bridge. This was somewhere my mother could be driving and see me. She'd brake the
car, get out—the world would stop in light. There was no one else
on the sidewalk. My footsteps were soft in the dark, I could hear

them. Cars flowed in one stream, their small red lights like sequins. For a second, they looked to me like dark separate muscles
of one long thing, then they were cars again. I took my mitten off
so I could feel the steel metal sting of the banister. There was a
three-foot wire mesh fence and I could see through to water.
Smoke came from the tailpipes, it was cold enough to hold in the
sky. The noise was steady. I looked down. There was splintering
ice on the rushing, dirty brown water. It looked like root beer
when you took the lid off in the summer.

On the other side factories lined the river as far as you could
see. The sky was still a luminous blue. Small windows in the
factories showed yellow. And on the ground, trucks, dumpsters,
plows and cranes stood still, parked on the coal lots, their orange
shapes scattered, left cranked up in open positions, empty-
handed. Dirt fell in a fountain from one of the cranes like a huge
timer.

Then I looked down again. The sidewalk I was walking on now,
halfway across the water, was steel mesh, too, I could see down
through it, and then it was as if something uncorked in me, the
air rushing inside my ears. I looked at my dirty sock and my dirty
shoe from the puddle and the sound of water below was like the
reflection and echo of something, and I stopped. I closed my
eyes.

Cracks on sidewalks, red lines of ants, uneven places, grass
growing up around concrete, the worst thing is you are alone. You
always know. When you can't even sink, you can't stop, you can't
let yourself. The dream of stopping, the desire, is like a pill.
There is no one to hold your dead weight, so you always come
back to yourself and you have to move again, your right foot and
your left, the same.

I bit my lip until I tasted blood and gripped one hand over the
other. One step and one step and one step. The underneath roar
and the creak of steel were loud like sound in one closed room
running in lines over itself. I bit the Milk Duds like pellets. I felt
my tooth; there was a chip. That made me incredibly sad. I kept
the piece in my hand. It seemed singularly important that I have
it and not lose it to the water. Finally, I was light, a feather on the

other side, ground again. I walked by the dark coal plant, I kept
walking. I could smell the coal, it smelled like winter. An old
neighborhood, these were bad streets, every block the flashing
lights of a tavern. A brilliant Schlitz sign, water falling, white and
blue, tripping over itself, behind it, I saw that the sky had gone
dark. Then I was on the highway, on the shoulder, in fields, unused earth.

The earth creaked, I stepped on a branch, above me the sky
shifted like a wooden door. It started to rain and the drips were
themselves and echoes all around me. Along the road, there were
stakes with shiny reflector disks to keep the cars from running
off. I walked in the marshy ditch, passed the bowling alley, taverns, long fields between lights. There was an old red brick hotel
where they put chairs out in the summer, in front of each door.
Once the son was my grandmother's paper boy.

In the gravel car lot of the Starlight, a pickup backed out and
a guy rolled his window down and whistled and I started running
through the field. By the tracks, there were woods, birch and
pine. It was very dark now. I knew where I was. But there were
noises all around me. I kept biting the hard Milk Duds. I promised I wouldn't look back; I felt touches on my shoulder blades;
there was air, different from other air. Some air was curved and
shaped like an arm, with viscous weight when it touched you. It
touched behind your knees, your neck, the soft part of your cheek
that bruises. I was walking over a mulch of disintegrating leaves.
There were warm spots and long cooler corridors, as in a house,
but I was walking fast, tripping. The points in the sky were stars.

I came to a clearing. A weaker light showed through. The trees
were high and feathered; they sighed and dripped, scraped and
wheezed, shifted their weight. Finally, I stepped out. There was
a long field, water coming out of a cement pipe that we crawled
through in summer. Past that was the railroad track.

My cheek brushed against a cattail and I saw my foot sink into
a puddle. When I pulled it up out of the swamp, I heard water.
The weeds moved under the dark surface like swollen hair. I
pulled the cattail hard with my hand and the silver seeds blew off

onto the tall grass like scattered wishes. I sat on a rock and took off my shoe, pulled down my sock. Sitting still the noises were louder. There was one sound, loud and continuous. Air has a voice like water, but I didn't know if it was the wind or a faraway train or trucks on the highway. I didn't know if there'd ever been such a thing as silence. The wind rippled on my arms. It was always there, the sound, like inside a shell, but you had to move and then stop to hear it.

I walked with one shoe. I got over the pipe with my knees. The mud of the other side felt silky, good, on my bare foot. Then I was at the tracks. The moon was a long way down, centered between the two ties. I balanced on the rails. The smooth metal was good on my foot. It would take me to the end of Lime Kiln Road.

I kept going and going with my eyes closed, my own sounds, a scuff and a meech, two steps, endless, echoing in my ears, indistinguishable now from the outside, the way the lines of the sky and land finally merge at night and then go on and on, ringing forever.

There was a train. I was in the ditch, holding on, shaking, deaf and blind. After, a long time after, I was cold and wet. My heart was still beating, loud, like underwater.

Then I was at my grandmother's door. The house was dark and quiet, cool, wrapped in wind. I heard branches ticking against the high windows like fingernails. I decided to sleep in the Oldsmobile. I didn't want to wake her up. There was something perfect about her sleep.

The dark in the garage was a different, grayer dark, there was no light inside the blackness. There was a deep scent of rainwater and earth from the geranium planters, filled with soil and roots. Each summer, she took them to the cemetery, planted. I found the handle of the Oldsmobile door and lifted it. I went around to the other side, but the doors were locked. I could see the shapes of the lawn mower, the old hand plow, Benny's dirt bike, all the tools hanging on the wall. Then there was real noise, outside, metal, and the wind taking the garbage can lid down the drive. Something was in the garbage. I pressed myself against the old wood wall and waited. There was a long screeing sound. Raccoons. I stepped outside. Their handlike paws moved intricately below them, as they looked up at me. Their fingers worked without them, over the garbage as if it were jewelry, precious, expensive things.

I stood on the hard grass of the yard and started calling.

"Gramma. Gramma. Gramma."

I kept going and going. Now was too late to stop. I heard my voice coming from all over, the wood of the roof, the high tenting trees, a wind from the railroad tracks, crickets in the fields, all the sounds started anywhere but in me.

A light at the top of the staircase flicked on. My grandmother stood at the small window and opened it.

"Who's there?"

"It's me."

"Who are you?"

But the light pulled off and she was coming down the stairs. Then the kitchen was chalky yellow, the same room I'd seen by itself in dreams, and the dog barked inside the door.

My grandmother opened the screen an inch. "Is it?"

"Gramma."

"Oh, good gracious, come in."

Then it was over like any dream, I was cleaned, I was warm, I was safe. I was wearing loose silk pajamas my great-great-aunt Ellie gave to Carol for Carol's honeymoon at Niagara Falls in 1946, the elastic big on my waist. I pulled the covers up in the small cold bed while my grandmother sat downstairs in the kitchen corner, calling Ted on the telephone, telling him she had me here.

"Your mom's not home," she said, kneeling in front of her bed, shoving the pan underneath with the regular sureness of a cook. "Lan-knows where she is. Ted says she's out somewhere looking for you."

We each sighed and went to sleep. Later, we heard noise. Doorbells rang from two places through the house. Someone was at the front door. It was not the kind of house where you went to the front door. Even the hoboes in summer knew to use the back.

I stood up to the window and the sky was lit with a huge moving stripe of light.

"Shhh, just stay down where you are. I'm going to go to the hall window to see. If anyone comes, you just run in the attic."

She walked slowly and pulled on the light by the window.

"That's your mom down there. Ye gods, who knows what all she's got with her. You just sleep. I'm going to tell her she can just come back in the morning."

I walked to the high window. My mother was standing where I had been on the lawn, her hands on her hips, staring up at the house. She looked small. She was wearing her suede jacket and her sunglasses were still on the top of her head. Dan Sklar stood behind her, his shoulders curling down. The light was coming from the top of a squad car. Two policemen crowded on the porch. Then I heard my mother shouting through the walls.

"Just let me have her, you don't know what I've been through tonight! She scared me near to death. I almost had a heart attack, I can still barely breathe."

"You can have her in the morning then. She's here fine, now. Just leave her sleep."

"Mom, she's mine, she's not yours. Give her to me." My mother was beating her jacket pocket with a fist.

My grandmother closed the door, I heard the bolt locking. The policemen shifted their feet, their fingers in their belt loops. Then they all left and it was quiet again.

The inside of the tin bread box, the polished silver metal, was bright with sun, brighter in the creases. The outside was pink and smooth, painted. I stood for a long time, looking into the metal, the sparks of light in the tin, playing.

The screen door rang and my mother stood there to pick me up. My mother acted nice to me then. It was just us in the car, she and me, and it was early. She drove fast on the highway, the sun was bright, but still cool.

We sat on the same side of the booth in the restaurant on top of Shreve's. Our knees touched under the fabric of our skirts. I was wearing funny clothes, a skirt of Aunt Carol's, my mother's college sweater from the upstairs closet.

The waiter stood for a long time, pouring champagne into our orange juice, and we leaned forward, watching the glasses.

"So. I think it's time we really think about going." My mother smiled at me. Our seat was by the window, over the Fox River. The bridge was splitting in half, the huge metal sides lifting in the air, for a boat to go through underneath. From where we were it was all silent choreography, light blues and darker blues, steel.

"What?"

"We've been talking about it a long time, I think we should really go."

"Could Ted get a job out there?"

My mother put her cup down in her saucer too hard. A pool of dark water filled the plate to its rim. "He's not coming with us." She shook her head. "You and I are really elegant. We can pass. He couldn't fit in there. Not in a million years."

The champagne and orange juice bubbled in quaint, tall glasses. Two tiny paper umbrellas rested on the ice cubes. When we raised the glasses and toasted, the backs of our fingers touched.

My mother called the Los Angeles School System. She stood with a yellow note pad next to her, talking on the phone in the kitchen. I was home, too. My mother had called us both in sick. While she held the receiver, saying, "Mmhmm, mmhmm, yes, mmhmm," her hand thumped against her side.

Then, when she hung up, she started hopping around the kitchen, clapping.

"Yippee! We're going to make it, Ann-honey. You just see. We are. I know it."

"What did they say?"

"Well," she started, kneeling down next to me and gathering her breath, picking up my hand. "It looks like I'm going to get a job. He said to me, *Well,* for someone with your credentials and experience, there should be a spot, for sure, somewhere in the system. I just have to send all my things in. You know, my papers.

God, I'm going to have to work on that. But, let me tell you, Ann, he was impressed. You don't know, but your mom's pretty special. Really, Ann, you don't know, but not many women my age have an MA."

She looked down at her hands. She was shy about it. I felt, I don't know, kind of proud.

She stood up. "Say, remember that boy from TV who was here once for the Cerebral Palsy telethon? Let's just give his agent a call and see about getting you on a series. Let's see, it was Ellen Arcade in Riverside, I think." My mother had a long, perfect memory.

She sucked in her breath when she got off the phone. I was absolutely still; I knew the less excited I looked, the faster she would tell me.

"Well. She *said* there's not a thing she can do while we're here. *But,* she said, the minute we get to LA, to call and she'll make us an appointment."

We skated around, skidding over the black and white floor in our socks, our hands clasped together in the center as we spun.

"So what do you think, Ann? Isn't it something? Everything just seems to be falling right!"

When we stopped spinning, I was so dizzy I collapsed against the kitchen counter and hit my head. I remembered the rented furniture, the kitchen which seemed so still and permanent and permanently ours, branded by afternoon light. We would be leaving. The house on Carriage Court wouldn't be our house anymore. That made me sad and tired with the burden of decisions. We wanted too many things.

Then, there was a contest. The spring before we left, the Red Owl Grocery Stores gave you one stamp every time you bought your groceries. They had new bags printed, saying YOU MAY HAVE ALREADY WON. You had to get an A, B, C, D and an E stamp, with consecutive numbers on them. The winner would get ten thousand dollars. My mother and I didn't really become interested until we had a consecutive A and B. Then, we got a C.

We stood outside the Red Owl Grocery Store pasting the stamp in and looking at our card. I licked it and smeared it on, and my mother pressed it down with her thumb. Our grocery bags sat around us on the parking lot.

"Oh, I think we're going to win, Ann, I can just feel it." My mother sighed before she opened her wallet, carefully, to slip the card in. "On second thought, why don't you keep it."

I slid it in my back pocket and felt the tiny raised shape of it under the denim.

Ted sat watching TV when we ran in. We showed him our card, climbing over him, on the couch. He smiled. "They're not going to let you win. The thing's rigged. They just want to get you in the store to spend your money."

"Yeah, mmhmm," my mother said, shaking her head and winking at me behind his back.

Three or four times a night, my mother would think of some small item we needed and we would get in the car and drive to another Red Owl. Ted would shake his head and smile when we decided to have hot fudge sundaes at midnight and when we drove to the other side of town to buy the ice cream and, at another Red Owl, the fudge. When we came back, he'd lift his book down from his face and look at us, bemused. He wasn't absolutely convinced we wouldn't win.

So the night we came racing from the car with thirty dollars' worth of groceries we didn't need and the fourth consecutive number, the D, he smiled and examined the book. In his subdued way, Ted was becoming excited for us.

Before I fell asleep, my mother tickled my back. I lay facing the wall.

"What would you like when we get the ten thousand, I suppose I should say if," she said.

"Go to California," I said, "and boots."

"Do you really want to go to California?"

"Yes."

"Well, maybe when we get the money, we'll just move." I thought I knew what my mother was thinking from the light way her fingers drummed and swirled on my back, her wrist dragging behind. She was thinking of the beach, the wide road dipping down to the ocean, all the things we'd seen on television. But she worried. She pinched my shoulders to keep me awake. "Would you like that, honey?"

"Yes."

"Sure?"

"Yes."

"Okay, good. I would, too, I think. I think I would too."

We bought marshmallows, detergent, whole wheat bread, Rock Cornish hens for the freezer, shish kebab skewers, new sponges, herbal teas, raisins for me to take to school, but we still didn't get the fifth consecutive number on our stamps. We didn't even see an E. We began to talk and compare with people around us in the checkout lines.

Ted became smug with renewed conviction. "That's it," he said, laughing, his arms bursting up extravagantly like a jack-in-the-box, suppressed too long. "They let you come just so close and then you go buy up the store, hoping you'll get the last number."

That was the night we came home with seven bags. My mother nodded, agreeing with Ted. She sighed when we'd hauled the bags in. We still had all those groceries to put away.

"He's right, you know," she whispered to me later, sitting on my bed. "Sure, they're going to try and rig it. If they let you win, they're going to have to pay up. This way the people keep coming in and buying. Of course, they'd rather have you lose. And I think he's right—I don't think there's an E in Bay City. Uh-uh. But I have an idea. Probably a lot of people here have everything but the E. So I thought tomorrow I could call in sick for both of us and we can drive up to Door County and go to a few Red Owls there."

"Okay," I said, grateful, looking up into her eyes. My mother was so smart. I felt excited, lying in my bed.

We didn't tell Ted. We wanted to come home that night with the completed card and surprise him. Mr. Know-it-all. We waited until he left in the morning and then I ducked down under the dashboard until we drove out of the neighborhood. All the kids were walking to school, I didn't want them to see me. I wouldn't be there all day, it made me feel creepy.

But it was all right as soon as we were on the highway. Fifty miles north and we started stopping at every little town and asking where the Red Owl was. Penfield, Egg Harbor, Fish Creek, Kiwaunee, Sturgeon Bay; we bought small items at each one; gum, razors, toothpicks, matchsticks, new soap. We walked into each store several times, taking each thing separately to a different cash register.

"What if they see?"

"Just say you forgot. You went out to the car and thought, Damn, and just remembered. So you ran in again."

In a little town named Malta, we got an E. It wasn't the right E, it wasn't consecutive, but it was our first E. We went to Malta's three Red Owls, in each aisle, hoping we'd get the right E, E 56614. We picked the items carefully, superstitiously, as if the difference between a package of ovenproof tin foil and a box of animal crackers would make the difference in our lives.

My mother sighed, opening the clasp of her purse. "We're running out of money," she whispered. We made our final choices, taking a long time. Holding the things in my hand, I believed they each had magic, a destiny, souls of their own. My mother chose a tin of anise candies. I picked a set of sixty-four crayons. "When are you going to use those?" My mother sighed, but she let me buy them.

We met outside, from our separate cash registers. After six more purchases in Malta, we had one more E, but not the right E, *the* E. My mother broke down. We walked through the store once more, this time both of us in the same register line.

"Look," my mother said to the checkout girl. There was a kind of laugh she used when she asked for something outrageous, a helpless, this-is-crazy-but kind of noise. "You won't believe this, but we just need one E. We need E 56614. Then, if we get that, all we'd need is the C. If you have it in there, could you just please give it to us? We've got the three already, and we only need two more. She's not going to let me go home without it."

My mother pressed down on my foot, hard, with her shoe. She looked at me for the lie. We already had the C.

The girl said she was sorry but the stamps came in an order, a mixed-up order, but she had to give us the top one in her pile.

"Oh, couldn't you please just look through your stack a second and see?"

"No," the girl said.

"Please, I'll give you ten dollars." My mother held the money in her hand and the girl stood shaking her head no. She looked sadly and clearly ahead of her into the keys of the cash register. "No, I'm sorry, ma'am, but I can't."

In back of us a woman was bumping her metal shopping basket forward. "That line's moving twice as fast and this is the eleven or under," she said. "Meanwhile I pay the baby-sitter at home."

My mother took her money back. "Come on, Ann, let's go."

"That's three eighty-nine for the groceries, ma'am."

"Forget the groceries," my mother said. She was mad. She was always mad when she couldn't convince someone to make an exception for us. We climbed into the car and she slammed her door. "That dummy. 'No, I ca-yunt,'" she mimicked.

We drove home and both took naps until dinnertime. After, when we were watching television, Ted looked at us each and said, "Well, aren't we going to have our nightly run? What'll it be? Dessert? Charcoal for next summer's barbecues?"

Ted was hopeless. "Very funny," my mother said, keeping her eyes on the set.

My mother fell in love with a car. It was a used car, but barely used, a beauty. It was only a year and a half old. My mother said the owner had only driven it once a week to go to church. A dealer was selling it, but it was still parked on the owner's curving driveway.

After we gave up on the contest, we drove out to buy ice cream cones at Dean's every night. We rode by the car, after. My mother smiled and shivered slightly whenever she spoke of the car. It had a white exterior, a white roof and two navy blue lines, thin as pencil marks, running down its sides. I always felt like tracing them with my fingers. It was a Lincoln Continental Mark III.

"I think it's the most elegant car in the world right now," my mother said. We'd parked a few houses down and we climbed out to look closer. It was a private driveway, so we kept very quiet, walking. There were dark bushes on either side. The neighborhood was still and lush, perfumed with fallen roses. The dark seemed to gather, secret in the hedges. There was a haze of dusk in their pointed intricate branches. The car had a light tan, creamy interior and an elaborate dashboard with polished wood panels. We pressed against the windows to see more. My mother softly tried the door and grimaced at me, quickly, when it opened in her hand. We slipped in. I was on the driver's side. We each sat in our seats for a minute, I rested my hands on the wheel.

"It even smells good," my mother whispered, "feel the leather." We ran our hands over it, lightly. Then we got out and gently closed the doors again. We each turned back to look at the house we were walking away from. It was large and old and closed.

"Apparently, she's in her sixties," my mother said. "A very dignified woman, I've heard, *very*. He's a dentist. Now, Gramma could be more like that, she could dress up a little and join clubs. But she'd rather just stay out there in her old clothes and make her own little supper and rake her leaves." She sighed. "She's really a loner, you know, Ann? And she'll always be that way, until the day she dies."

We drove past the car every night that spring. The first week in June the weather turned. It was cool when we walked with our ice cream cones from Dean's to the car. My mother switched on our heat.

"Listen, there's something we have to decide." Her tone seemed more solemn than usual, there was something older and sweet in it. It was what she would someday become. "We can afford either the Lincoln or California, with the money we have saved and what I'll get from the Teacher's Retirement Fund. But we can't have both." We stared out the windshield in front of us, licking our ice cream cones, placid as cows. She'd said that softly, as if she were apologizing. "Now, if we get the car," she went on, "we'd still have the house and remember, Honey, we're at the top, here. There, you'd always be one of the poorer kids. I won't be able to compete with the families who have fathers. So, you have to think what you want, Honey. It's up to you."

Sometimes it seemed years, it had been known between us, decided, we were going to California. But we'd never really said it. It was our secret, a nighttime whispered promise. Now we were sitting in the car in the waning summer daylight, early evening.

My mother shifted her ice cream cone to her left hand and started the ignition again, driving with her right. We rode slowly through Bay City. The air was moist now as I dragged my hand out the window. I was wearing clothes I'd had for a long time.

Spells can be broken by the person who started them. Some things, once spoken in the daylight, can never be the same. I didn't want to leave, but I didn't want to give up California, either. I never wanted to move from my seat. I wanted my mother to keep driving and driving. She was talking, humbly now, mentioning rent, school systems, putting the house on the market. "Dan Sklar would handle it for me," she said.

But if we stayed, we wouldn't have California anymore. We couldn't whisper at night about moving there when we were sad. We'd never believe it again.

My mother had given me choices all my life and I'd never learned to choose. I always tried to figure out first if there was a way I could have both things. My mother's face was obvious. I'd learned a long time ago to pick the thing she hadn't picked, the one she didn't want. That way she would get me both, because she couldn't bear to give up what she wanted for me.

My mother loved that car. She had to have it, I knew she wouldn't be able to relax until we bought the Lincoln. She pulled up slowly and parked in front of the house with the Lincoln in the driveway. She looked over at me, down into my face. "What do you think, Ann? Which do you want?"

"California," I said.

"Rather than the Lincoln?"

"I think so."

"Well, be sure now. Think a minute."

"I'm sure."

Her hands dropped from the steering wheel to her lap. She stuffed the napkin from her cone in the car ashtray. "Okay." We both looked out the windshield at the darkening bushes. "You really think you can make it on TV?"

"Yes." My hands clutched the car seat under me. I was bluffing, I didn't know anything. I was twelve. I had no idea if there was anything I could do.

"Okay," she said, apparently satisfied. She looked relieved. She backed the car slowly and turned around. "All righty. Well, then, I guess we're going."

We both went solemn. We drove and didn't say anything. I kept thinking of her asking face, peering down at me, and how now she was settled, looking straight out into the dark. It already seemed too late to change our minds. When we pulled into our driveway, a light was on in the neighbor's garage and the door was up. One of the older boys lifted the hood of a car open, he was bending into it, searching the machine parts with a flashlight. I knew what would happen to him, to the people who stayed.

We came out of the Red Owl carrying grocery bags and the cars had their lights on already. It was drizzling slightly and the brown paper bags were damp by the time we got to the car. I had on Benny's junior varsity jacket; it was big and warm, the sleeves too long for me.

My mother sighed once and looked around. That was all. We stood a moment with the groceries on the car top before she opened the doors. You look at a place differently when you're leaving. I jammed my hands into the deep felt pockets of Benny's jacket.

"You know we can still change our minds." My mother started the car and sat back in her seat. We both put our hands near the heating vent.

We drove out into the traffic. It was still early, five o'clock, and not yet dark. The wet pavement made the car wheels hiss and the drivers ahead of us went slow and cautious.

"I know."

My mother turned onto the highway and pulled on our lights. "Okay, okay," she said to herself, when a passing car honked and blinked. She wasn't going the direction of home, but I didn't care, I didn't have anything to do. We'd both started the year in Bay City knowing we wouldn't finish. I liked wearing Benny's jacket. I felt the inside, serrated seam. We were going over the bridge, the steel underneath roared every ten feet, it was like hearing the hollow height and water. Then we were on the other side of town and my mother drove out to the cemetery.

People were coming home from work, there was traffic. We turned off the road, through a black, wrought-iron arch and then under the trees. My mother's car bumped on a groove, meant to make cars go slow. It always seemed quiet in the cemetery, and that evening there were no other cars. Green vertical pumps stood every few feet on the lawn, to fill cans with water, and most of the boxes were planted. The grass was shiny, bright green under the drizzle.

My mother slowed and parked as close as we could get to her father's stone. It was alone, the only one on a small slope between two oak trees. The other land was all bought for our family.

It was a pink granite stone, smooth on the edges, polished. Years ago, in summer, when we'd come to water the geraniums, Benny and I had slid down the sides. Now, my mother and I stayed in the car with the rain coming down over the windows. My mother left the heat on but turned the motor off. She kept her hands on the steering wheel.

"Should we go out?" I said, after a little while.

She shook her head slowly, no, over the steering wheel, her chin puckering into a frown.

I shifted in my seat, inside Benny's jacket, and looked out the windshield; there was fog on the ground, blurring the distant lights down the hill and behind us on the road. The trees above us were dark and heavy; they seemed very old.

Finally, my mother pulled the lights on again and we drove out, the long way, down the winding path. It was the only time I'd been to the cemetery with my mother. I wondered if she came by herself.

We worked on the house. We painted my bedroom floor white and hung curtains to match my flowered bedspread. Ted fixed the fireplace. Now, my mother bought fresh flowers and candy to put out in bowls in the living room. The house was nicer than it had ever been, so people would buy it. But it wouldn't last. We had to mop

up my white floor each time before people came to see the house,
the new bedspread in my mother and Ted's room wrinkled like a
sheet if anyone sat on it. The days we'd stayed around the house,
though, cleaning and painting and fixing things, were when Ted
and my mother and I got along best, most like a family.

After summer school, once, I was in my room, in play clothes,
leaning over to tie the laces on my sneakers. Ted knocked on the
door. He was home early, he wasn't usually home at that time.

He sat on my bed next to me. For a while, he didn't say anything. It made me think that in all this time, he and I hadn't been
alone much. Just the two of us, we didn't know what to say.

He held his hands in his lap and looked at them. "Your mother
is leaving me," he said. "I suppose you already know that."

The tiles of the floor, painted white, spun when you looked at
them too hard. It was cool in this room. My room touched the
farthest back in the yard.

"Ann, do you know what a homosexual is?" He looked at me
hard, waiting, like the teachers wait, a whole side of their heads
still, after they ask a question in school. "Well, a homosexual is
a man who likes men better than women. Your mother is saying
that I'm a homosexual and when you're older and she tells you
that, I want you to know it wasn't true."

"Okay."

"That wasn't the reason."

I couldn't look at him. "What is the reason?" I mumbled.

"What?"

"If that's not the reason, so what is the reason then?"

I sat next to him looking down at the floor.

"I don't know, Ann. You'll have to ask your mother. Someday
you'll just have to ask your mother. Maybe she'll tell you."

We kept sitting there, on my bed, staring at the wall. Then he
picked up my hand.

"I'm sorry to see you go, Ann. Because in the years we've lived
together, I've grown to love you. I've come to think of you as my
own daughter."

I smiled to myself and tried to keep it from showing. My chest felt warm, as if he'd given me something important to keep. I didn't want to move, I was sitting in a small square of sunlight.

"I'm going to miss you," he said.

I looked down at the floor between my sneakers. Ted was an orphan. My mother had told me he didn't know who his real parents were, but every Christmas he sent a nutted fruitcake, carefully wrapped, to his foster parents in upstate New York. He sent it early so it would be sure to get there on time.

The sky in the windows, that had been plain and blue when I'd started to put my shoes on, was bright and almost dark now. I didn't want to go outside anymore. Then we both heard my mother's car bolt up the drive, the slam of her door. Ted dropped my hand back in my lap.

Lolly and my mother sat in the basement, laughing. They'd made a pitcher of Bloody Marys and it stood on top of the washing machine. They were sorting my mother's old suitcases of things into boxes. All we could take with us was what would fit in the car. Stuff my mother owned but didn't know where to put lay on a carpet in the basement. I sat on the top step where they couldn't see me.

"He's left and gone back and left and gone back. And he knows if he did, she could ruin him."

"You mean she'd get half of everything."

"Half, more than half, the house, *ev*-erything that he's worked so hard for and built up himself from scratch. I don't blame him for wanting to hold on to it."

At night, I walked back down to the basement where they'd been. I pulled a string to turn on the light. It was just one bulb. I rummaged through the cardboard boxes. In the pile marked *Take* were my baby skates and an old suitcase monogrammed with my father's initials. The handle was broken and a dog collar buckled through the two metal loops. Inside was a jumble of my first-grade printing exercises, whole pages filled with small and capital *E*'s, a white photo album with a yellow pressed bud rose in it, a list of classmates who might like me, a faded Band-Aid—colored hospital identification band from when my mother was in Saint Peter and Paul's for me, photos of me naked with a beach ball in little cardboard frames—I quickly flipped them shut, then I found a yellowed onionskin paper report on me.

Ann is an average child. Her teeth have white marks, possibly from a fever in infancy, making her inappropriate for close-up facial photography. Her hair and olive skin are rich and promising, and her long bones might bode well, but her expressions are sometimes blank and unpredictable. In play skits, with other children, she was sometimes shy and melancholy, looking off somewhere into the distance. Other times, she became aggressive and out of control.

The report was a tissue carbon, on letterhead stationery, green on yellowed white. Ann Hatfield August. Age 2½. The Glory Jones Agency on Park Avenue in Chicago. I held it in my hands and read it over and over again, as if there might be more about me. I didn't remember any of it. I didn't know I'd ever been in Chicago.

It was a watery day, windy, not raining yet but it would, and I was walking to Three Corners. I waited on the old cracked sidewalk, outside the wire fence of Saint John's School. Mary Griling was going to meet me at ten o'clock. I didn't know how she'd get out of her classroom, recess wasn't until 11:15. I guess she said she needed to go to the lavatory. Anyone would have believed Mary.

Chalky yellow light came from all the windows in the old red brick school. Dry leaves blew up against the fence by my feet. I felt in my pockets. Mary's passion this year was for marbles. The popular girls in her class were girls whose fathers worked in the ball bearing factory up the Fox River in Pulaco, girls who brought huge, shiny ball bearings to shoot with. They called them steelies. I had a steelie and a package of colored cat's-eyes.

I stood there and cars went by and then finally I saw her, com-

ing out in her indoor clothes, a jumper, a white blouse, knee
socks and clean, polished saddle shoes. Her collar was neat and
crisp, folded down like two envelopes. She had her badge pinned
to her jumper over her left breastbone; it was a silver metal
eagle on a white satin ribbon. Mary was awarded it in assembly for being the best female pupil in her class. She ironed
the satin ribbon at night and put the pin back, fresh, every
morning.

The sharp leaves touched our legs through our socks as they
blew against the fence while we talked. I gave her the marbles
and steelie and she put them in her pocket, keeping her hand
there, holding them. We scuffed our shoes on the pavement.

"I guess you better get back," I said.

"Yes."

"Remember those pictures I took a long time ago in our new
house?"

"Uh-huh."

"I'll get rid of them, burn them someplace."

"Okay."

"I'm sorry."

She shrugged. "I don't care."

"Just go ahead and find Benny if you want anything," I said.
"Don't be afraid of him."

"I won't. I like Benny."

I never said anything to the rest of them, to the boys. She stood
there and I put both hands on the shallow indentations of her
shoulders. We kissed softly, both of us, the way I'd seen my
cousin Hal kiss my mother once, looking at her mouth, so carefully, as if he were afraid he could miss.

"This way, we won't have the house, but we'll have a car to let
people know who we are a little," my mother was saying. She'd
managed to get the Lincoln Continental after all. "Maybe out
there where everyone's in apartments, it goes a little more by the
car. Because we won't have a house or anything, but maybe this
will help. They can see we came out of something."

When we slid into the new car, it smelled like lemon wax. The leather moved below us, soft and rich. We both wriggled, shrugging, to adjust ourselves. It felt like our bodies would make permanent impressions, the leather seemed that moist. My mother opened her purse and took out a bag with two long leather gloves in it. She held each of her hands up, taking a long time pulling them on.

Then it was an Indian summer day and everything was already done. We stood in front of our house on Carriage Court, alone, light, carrying nothing, already packed. Ted had left for the rink very early. The house was empty and clean, the windows washed. Everything inside had been accounted for. The grass was cut. There was a stake with an orange SKLAR REALTY—FOR SALE sign stuck in the front lawn.

"Comemeer," my mother said, "I want to show you something." We were standing on the front sidewalk, by the new car, which glistened in the sun. I didn't want anyone, any of the neighbors, to step out of their house and see us. Across the street, the garage door was rolled up and one of the boys stood over a work table. A radio came on. I just didn't want him to ask anything we would have to answer.

My mother lifted the lid off a garbage can and grabbed the back of my neck. Her other fist held a fan of pictures over the can like a hand of cards. She dunked my head gently.

"I was packing your closet and I found these."

In the pictures, Mary looked simple, very young. She was much older now. The boys looked frightened and excited, eyebrows pushed together, dark uneven lips. The boys seemed guilty, caught. My mother peered down, looking at me looking at them. Her voice was very gentle, as if she were afraid.

"Don't ever do that again, Honey. Seriously. It's against the law. Because they could really sue you and put you in jail if the parents ever found out."

The garbage cans were clean, hosed off, and ferns bright with new tight fronds curled against them.

"What for?"

"Just because." She shook her head. "They just could. Take my word for it. And believe me, they would. So don't ever do that again, Honey, because you could get in big, big trouble. Really."

She ripped the photographs into pieces. They'd yellowed, they looked old and simple. Mary, in them, was nothing, just so young.

"We'll forget about it," she said, quietly, letting them fall into the garbage can. Then, she bent down and retrieved the torn bits. "Actually, let's not leave them here. You never know who looks around. We'll throw them out somewhere else, on the road." She unclasped her purse and dropped the shiny scraps of paper inside.

Then we walked down to the car, stopping on the lawn. My mother frowned. "You know you were right when we moved in. It is an ugly house. It really isn't anything much. Just a little shoe box with no windows."

I turned around and looked. It didn't look to me like a shoe box anymore.

The leather smelled new and old at the same time as we sank down into the car's front seat. My mother seemed nervous, driving. She hadn't told the family about the Lincoln Continental and now they'd all see it. They'd have to. When we turned onto the gravel of Lime Kiln Road from the highway, the sky was blue, the clouds white and thin, the telephone poles pitch-black. High leaves on the trees glittered, sharp, dark green. The sky was a deeper blue than most pale summer skies and the wind moved like bright transparent banners around the branches. My grandmother's house looked trim and neat as we drove up the driveway, the dark front bushes shiny. Birds sat on the tin tops of the mink sheds on the lawn, the cornfield was yellow and dry. Behind the old barn that once housed the butter factory, the highway looked dull, pure gray. And when we drove up and parked, my grandmother and Carol came out of the house. They seemed drawn to the car. Carol and Jimmy each touched it, running their hands over the sides.

My grandmother didn't say anything. She smiled with her teeth together and she was squinting, the way she did in the sun.

"What's that, a Lincoln Continental?" Jimmy said to my mother.

"Mark III," my mother said.

She had packed neatly, and with an eye for color. Through the windows the inside looked spare and orderly. The trunk was full and the backseat had only our best suitcase, and on the tan leather, there was a printed red box and each of our summer sweaters. That was all we were taking with us to California for the whole rest of our lives.

Hal was gone already, at boot camp in Texas. The night before he'd left for the air force, I'd sat on his lap, pretending to shoot beebee guns in the air. I had looked outside over the dry lawns. All our lives we'd collected skeets from the fields. It was supposed to be good when you found a whole one.

Inside, the kitchen was buzzing with sun. It was after eleven in the morning. Jimmy Measey had already driven to breakfast at Bob's Big Boy on the highway, then to the water softener store and back again. Carol stood pouring coffee for everyone while my grandmother served squares of rhubarb pie, just made this morning, still warm. Jimmy sat on a high stool drumming his hands on the table.

That summer, because we were leaving, I'd stayed afternoons and watched, trying to learn how to bake. The crust must be made in the morning; the parts not set, but the flour, lard and water mixed on the kitchen table, rolled out thin on the cutting boards. Nothing was measured, nothing kept. My grandmother washed and picked over the fruit, chopped the rhubarb, peaches, tossed in handfuls of berries and beat up eggs and sugar and fresh nutmeg in a blue bowl. Maybe vanilla, if we remembered. We poured the liquid into pie crusts, lining the square tin pans, and it smelled as clean as milk. We dallied over the crusts, ruffling the edges with two wet fingers for a long time. When they were in the oven, there was a fine dust of white flour in the air. I'd watched and studied, taking notes.

"Would you like milk?" Carol set the glass down, hard, in front of me on the table. Then she walked to the counter and wiped her hands on her apron. She seemed to be trying not to get in anyone's way, she stood studying her knuckles.

Carol would have my grandmother to herself now. My mother eyed Carol suspiciously, a little bitter, as she slowly ate her square of rhubarb pie, examining each piece on her fork before she put it in her mouth, as if it were a complicated wonder.

And Carol looked at her sister, who still had her figure, a young face. (Why was it—she seemed to be puzzling—that Adele's face stayed clear long past the age when Carol's and all Carol's friends', women who used masks and facials and creams, accepted lines?) Who knew what Adele could get for herself, what we could do in California? We already had the new car and Carol must have wondered where we got the money for that. (Later, she would hear from the former owner, the dentist's wife, who belonged to clubs, about the matter of delinquent payments.)

But my mother's optimism must have seemed stamped on her clothes and even on mine, like labels. Carol glanced down shyly at herself, leaning against the counter, and she slouched, looking frumpier. She rubbed at her mouth with a napkin, as if she had eaten something sweet and oily and there were crumbs on her face that would stay no matter how hard and how many times she washed. Her thighs rubbed against each other as she walked and she seemed to wish we would leave. She moved as if she hardly ever thought about her body from the waist down. She paid no attention to her legs. Except when she saw my mother.

But it would only be a little while now. Carol closed her eyes and when she opened them she looked out the window. She could wait, she knew, she must have said it to herself without words, she was a waiter, she always had been, always would. The oblong silver water tank gleamed like the Goodyear blimp on the grass, in the untimely sun. Carol would have remembered Benny and me in our baby sunsuits climbing on the rough silver, scratching our chubby legs. It was all so new to us then. "It's funny what kids like," Carol said, "the most ordinary things, like water." Water tanks, things after a while my mother and I forgot and didn't even see anymore. Carol shook her head. It was too bad for Benny that I would be gone. All summer, Carol had found Graham crackers hidden in stacks in Benny's room, when she'd gone in to dust. She hadn't said anything. She'd left them.

Carol must have known she would always change the towels, screens in summer, storm windows in fall, the plain things, putting both hands on Benny's shoulders; only when she thought of that, she probably pictured his squirmy body below her fingers and a small boy escaping under the kitchen table. Now, to touch Benny's shoulders, Carol had to reach. And he would still grow more.

My grandmother wasn't young either, and when she was old and when she could no longer take care of herself, Carol would be right there, right next door, here. Carol would come every morning for coffee and ask her what she wanted to do that day, in the same careless, flat inflection our grandmother had used with her and she had used talking to her own children.

Carol would keep her mother clean, she would keep the sheets fresh and smelling of rainwater. Every day she'd come and push the windows open. She would take the time to wash the doilies on the windowsills underneath the African violets and iron them, just to put them back again where they'd been. Never in a million years would my mother do that. No matter what she said.

When the sky clouded and turned gunmetal gray with the blue, Carol would walk by herself over the back lawn in a hurry to the clothesline between the two pines. She would put the wooden pins in her pockets and her mouth and fill her arms with sheets.

These were chores my mother and I had done, had dreamed about doing always, but now we wouldn't anymore. We wanted other things.

When my grandmother was old, I would be away at college, my mother could be anywhere and Carol would be there, here, home. We already knew it that day. It worked out like numbers in arithmetic. Carol was already wide in the hips, she and my grandmother went to the same girl at the Harper Method Beauty Shop every Friday, a standing appointment, for the same all-around-the-head permanent curls. Carol's face had become rounder, with kindness, as she'd grown into middle age. Her voice had the bland, even quality of an unselfish nun. It was only around my mother she had an edge.

And my mother, tasting the coffee go bitter and dry in her mouth, having eaten her two pieces of pie, felt full and still sure there was not enough. She stared at the half pie left in the tin pan. Carol was always born first. Her mother already had a daughter when she was born.

It was almost noon and there was a breeze lifting the thin summer curtains off the sills. My mother set her cup in its saucer and it trembled, chiming a little as she looked around the kitchen. Simple views. A corner. The refrigerator. Broom closets, the clean white stove. The mangle. With her chin in her hands, she closed her eyes a second, perhaps believing that if Carol were not next door (the dark darker, the edges of her eyelids tight), her husband, the Arab, my father, gone nowhere, a new hard star in the night sky, it would have been only herself, she would be staying home with her mother. She would be the one. The night sky chipped with light would be bordered with windowsills like a framed doily.

Then she opened her eyes and all the silver in the kitchen—faucets, fixtures, the tin bread box, handles on the cupboards—was glistening with maintenance and care and it would someday be Carol's and if my mother wanted it more than everything, if she picked the first star in the sky every night of her life and wished, she still could not have it, ever.

The screen door slammed and it was Benny. He stamped in, heavy on the floor, hands at his sides, grinning. He wore glasses now, small glasses with thin gold rims. He was shy because he had a present. Just Benny in the room, standing, tall and awkward, breathing like a light lift of sawdust, seemed to let Carol's shoulders relax. He justified the position of the land.

I took my present from his hand. He hadn't wrapped it. He'd been over in the garage, working, he'd finished just this second. It was a metal box, tin, with a hinged lid. Inside was a cushion of blue satin. I kept staring into it, I didn't want to look anywhere else, it was perfect.

"It's for jewelry."

"He made that all by himself." Carol nodded.

Benny and I ran outside, to the lilacs and the pussywillows behind the garage. We were too old to play anymore. We just stood there, our bare arms long and weak, kicking dirt. Our parents were coming out now, down the porch to the car. We could hear the dog yapping at their heels.

"Oh, you shush now, you," my grandmother said to him. I imagined her bending down, patting his back. He had to be quiet. He would be here forever; in a minute, we would be gone.

They couldn't see where Benny and I were and they hadn't thought yet to call or look. We were behind the garage, in the bushes, left alone a secret there. There was wind that day that seemed to make you want to move; I thought after we drove away that Benny would start running. The sky was plain and clear, the air where we were was old. There was nothing in the birdbath. Everything was in its place just where it was.

Suddenly, we heard our mothers, each of them, calling our names.

"Ben-ny."

"Ann. Ann."

They were calling loud, as if we were farther away than we were. Their two voices echoed in the air off the trees. They must have been cupping their hands. We looked at each other, suddenly scared, and hard. We had a minute—they thought we had farther to come—before they would start looking for us.

Then it was black and Benny was hugging me and we were dizzy, turning, standing up. That was something about Benny, always. He could hug you so hard, hanging on as if he were dying, falling off the spinning planet, out of the earth's fall, and his fingernails bit into you and you were there, black, for a second.

We fell to the ground then and apart. We opened our eyes on the grass. I looked at him one second, then ran to my mother.

"Well, well, there you are." They were slow still, by the car, a family in a picture, in blue and white sailor suits, the dresses rustling in the breeze. Then I saw behind her glasses my grandmother was crying, the tears slow on her skin like drops of water on a peach. My bike was leaning against the garage, my bike that Benny was going to give the Grilings.

We stood by the car with the door open, the wind was there all around us, we heard a thin distant constant moving wind. My grandmother came in close. Everyone else was farther back, like croquet balls, anything colored and still, scattered on the grass.

There were three pairs of shoes, my grandmother's, my mother's and mine, all white. "Here," she said, and far above, she handed my mother a blue envelope. "It's nothing much, just go buy yourself one of those little portable televisions with it once you get there."

Her hand slapped against the skirt of her dress to call her dog away, away from the white wheels of our car, us, the open window, the gravel white and sparkling as we were driving away.

"Well, remember," she said, and then there was just the wind louder and the indifferent changing sky and Benny was running somewhere on the edge of the lawn and I saw nothing and we were gone.

LILLIAN

. . .

4

THE AGE OF THE YEAR

■ □ ■

My mother had seven sisters and they all lived near us in Malgoma. I can still remember them on my hands: Hattie, Clara, Ruth, Irene, Alma, Ellie and Jen. My mother was Ida, right in the middle. They were all married except Ruth, and Ruth lived at home with their father. So each one had her own house. Once a week I went to those houses because they'd decided I could make piecrusts. They used to say you were born with a feel for it, like with gardening, especially there near the water where the air changed so much day to day. Their mother was one such a one and Hattie, but Hattie had arthritis. I never used a recipe. I just mixed flour and water, sugar and lard, sometimes a speck of spice or nuts. It would take me all morning every Saturday, going from house to house. The aunt would generally sit with me, talking, and doing something else, sewing or sorting the wash. There was a lot more housework in those days. You had to do everything by hand.

I carried notes between the sisters. They sent everything back and forth—recipes, gossip, what the one was making for supper that night. And if someone spilled something that made a stain, she'd write a note and ask what would take it out. They were each different but they all got along. You don't see that so much anymore, close sisters. Alma was the pretty one. She wasn't the youngest, but she was a baby. She was always the father's favorite and the others knew it. They envied her, especially Ruth, who stayed there cooking his meals and cleaning up after him, but they never held a grudge. They were just the opposite. They fawned over her.

I remember the older ones brushing out and braiding her hair. She would just sit there and let them fuss. Alma loved to be touched. Sometimes, when I was there, she held out her arm and asked me would I tickle her. But she had her share of hard luck, too. She married a vaudeville piano player and he was gone a lot, always on tour. First he was in John Johnson's band, then it was Hans Hansen. And by the end, she lost all her hair, poor Alma. I used to visit him in the nursing home. Alma had passed away long ago. He still had his two pictures—one of her, with her long hair, and one of him with his band. They aren't allowed to have anything in there, so his doctor prescribed two shots of whiskey a day, that was Frank's best medicine. Even into his eighties Frank was still a handsome man. The ladies there liked him too and they tried to get him to play the piano. But he was a loner. He said, what do I want with those old biddies? And every time I visited, he'd tell me the same stories again and again. He'd fingered those two pictures so much, the edges were ruffled like fluted pies.

Each one of the sisters had a real different kitchen. It was like having eight houses, I knew my way around each one. I knew where to find the sifters, where they hid the cherry bounce. We had the smallest house. It was only my father and my mother, my brother Milton and me. My father was a welder and they worked long hours. And when he was home, he was a quiet man. My mother really ruled the roost. I don't think she was too proud of him, either. I think she wanted him to be something better. I know she would have liked to have more children. She played the piano, she embroidered such hairpin lace on the pillowcases and sheets, she made all her own doilies. I suppose she thought she would have made a good doctor's wife or banker's wife. But she only had us. So she paid a lot of attention to Milton, she spoiled him. He was her favorite and he was a pretty boy. It would just have to be a boy that got those curls. And such blond, blond hair. He had long eyelashes too. I didn't have hair like that, mine was straight as a board, until I learned how to braid it. Then it curls when you take it out. Now it's been braided for so many years it curls by itself. I wouldn't know how to make it straight again.

The place I grew up was fifty miles from here. Now it seems like the next town over, but then there were five or ten villages in between. None of them have names anymore. They were just carriage stops really, a hotel and a drugstore and a few houses. There was that huge fire in the canning factory, that closed down Pulaco and Suaminee. And the rest, the people just moved, I suppose. They had to leave to find work. A few farms are still standing, but most of those houses look empty.

We were a small family for that time—all those around us had more. And I always wished for a sister. Then, for a while, we had another girl in our house. I was down by the railroad tracks cutting pussywillows for a tablesetting, one night. It was in the fall, around five o'clock, just before supper. There was a girl and a cat behind her, walking on the coals. We were out there a little while and then a storm came real quick and it started pouring. I turned to go home, but when I looked back, the girl was still there, on the rails. I shouted, did she want to come with me to my house? She didn't look like she heard me, so I went down and took her wrist and then she understood. She followed me, both of us running. I held the pussywillows close to my side and she was carrying that cat up under her dress.

It took us awhile to decide she was dumb. She was filthy dirty, you could see when she was inside under the light, with coal on her arms and face. She had long black hair, all matted. It was thick hair, so when you looked down into it, under the lamp, there were all different colors, blues and greens. I remember that because we brought her into the bathroom and washed her in our big tub. Milton carried in the hot water from the stove and helped us hold her down. You wouldn't believe the ants that came out of that heavy hair, thick streams into the water.

"How old are you?" my mother shouted at her. "Do you hear me now, say if you understand." The girl just stared straight ahead. She looked pitiful and small in our big tub. We figured out that she couldn't talk. She looked to be about seven or eight, she was the same size as I was, and we had no idea where she came from. We thought someone may have just left her off, migrants, maybe, going south for the winter. She was pretty then, once we'd fixed her up. We'd washed her and combed her hair and put her in one of my dresses, like a doll. I'd tried to keep the cat out in the yard, with my boot, but she wanted him in, so he was drinking milk from a saucer, under the kitchen table.

The next day my mother and I went to the convent. We knew there was a nun who taught the deaf. They all went to school together in Malgoma, the deaf, the blind, I suppose they were lucky to go to school at all then. We waited at the door while the novice went to get Sister Mary Bead. We had a cherry kuchen with us; we never went anywhere without something baked. We told the Sister about the girl and she said she'd take her into her class and then we had to pick a name. My mother said Louise. That was what she had wanted to name me, but my father thought it sounded like an old woman. Too much like one of those sisters you already have, he'd told her. I wanted to call the girl Penny and they let me have my way. I suppose so she was more like a sister.

Sister Mary Bead used an old one-room school, with a stove in the corner and a dunce cap up on a bureau. I went to regular school with three rooms. Three rooms was big stuff in those days. Not everyone went to school then. Some of the farmers needed their kids to stay at home and help out. And if they lived too far in the country to walk, they stayed home, that's all there was to it. And in school, it was nice, the older ones helped the little ones. I always had my brother Milton in my class.

On the way home for noon lunch, Milton and I stopped to pick up Penny. Sometimes we stood in the doorway and watched. They went very very slowly. It wasn't noisy like our class. Sister Mary Bead held something up in her hand and the class—there were only four or five there—would try to say the word. Paper. Pencil. Ordinary things. They'd make funny, strange sounds trying to say it. I suppose it's different learning to say a word if you've never heard it.

Then one day in December, I went there by myself. It was a blizzard and my mother had kept Milton home. I walked, reciting

my poem to keep my feet from freezing. Did we learn the poems!
I must have known fifty. "The small rain down must rain." When
I stood at the door Sister Mary Bead was holding up an orange. It
was like a little globe in that classroom, against the blackboard
and her brown and white habit. Then there weren't oranges like
now in the supermarkets, so you can get them all year round.
They had to ship them in freight trains from California and Florida and they only came in around Christmas. And even then, they
were expensive. Milton and I each got one in our stocking and
that was it for the year. But oh, did they taste good. They were
darker, almost a red, and heavy with juice. They tasted sweeter
then. It was a special meal for us Christmas morning; when our
presents were open, there was still something left.

For a long time, Sister Mary Bead stood in front of a teacher's
desk, holding up the orange. Strange sounds came from her pupils, every time she said the word. Penny sat with her hands
clasped in front of her on the wooden desk. She was louder than
the others. I could understand what she said, more than I could
the rest, but maybe it was because I was used to her. Outside the
windows, snow was falling as if it were stitching such even seams
on the darkness and the wood stove whispered in the corner. They
spoke in unison and their voices wobbled, almost like singing. By
the end, the sound of the class seemed rounder, finished, like a
word. Then Sister Mary Bead took out a pearl-handled knife and
peeled the orange, holding it in one hand, between her thumb
and first finger. The skin came off in one curled ribbon. And they
passed it around among themselves, down the rows of desks, and
each one took only a section, so there was more than half left at
the end. Sister Mary Bead offered it to me. I took a section, too.

We all went to church on Sundays and there we had to be good,
because any one of the sisters could shush us or slap our hands,
it was like having eight mothers looking down on us from all over.
And they were each one tall. All we knew then was that Penny
didn't like church. She didn't want to go. At first my mother just
made her. But then, once the service was on and we were all
kneeling, singing the hymns, Penny scooted out. We couldn't get
up and chase her. After supper, that day, she came home again,

all dirty and full of burrs. The next Sunday, it was the same thing. She left when my mother walked up for communion. That day, when we went home, a blueberry pie was missing from the kitchen. I'd baked two pies that morning and left them to cool on the mangle.

Later on, we found cans and mason jars missing from the cellar. Ellie's husband, my uncle Shaw, worked for the Great Lakes Railroad Company and he got us dented cans for almost nothing. They couldn't sell them in the stores but what was inside was still good. And we did our own canning from the garden every fall. We didn't notice in the cellar for a long time, though, and Penny was probably going into it every Sunday. She stopped coming to church altogether and Sister Mary Bead told my mother just to leave her be.

Wherever Penny went, that black cat followed along. The cat slept under her desk at school and up on the foot of her bed. We named the cat Silk, but I don't remember anyone ever saying its name. Then one day that spring, the cat bit Penny on our porch. It bit her in two places, on the calf and just above the knee. She came in bleeding and crying, choking noises we'd never heard before. Right away, Milton said, Where is that cat? He understood the cat would run away. Well, the bites were nothing, they weren't deep. We washed and bandaged them and she was all right, they'd heal, but she was frantic all night over that black cat. When she was in the tub and we were cleaning her off, she tried to get up and go outside after it. She slipped away from us— she was so darn skinny and slippery then with soap—and my mother had to stand at the top of the stairs and yell for Milton to catch her. He got her, naked on the front lawn, and carried her upstairs kicking.

My mother sent me with a note to the doctor, this was before we had telephones. The doctor was just Ross Smittie, Clara's husband. I went in through the back door, the way I always came to their kitchen. Their kitchen was the biggest and they had a new pantry, all black and white tiles and cookie-cut woodwork. I told them what happened and right away he said he worried about rabies. He walked back over with me and looked at Penny's leg.

He said she'd have to have rabies shots, one each day for fourteen days, unless we found the cat.

I think maybe holding her naked and kicking like that had given Milton ideas. They were such opposites, the two of them; him so white and her dark. But every day, the minute school was out, he went running in the woods to look for that cat. See, if we had the cat, they could test him for rabies. But after three days were up, we hadn't found him and Penny had to start in with the shots. The doctor walked every day to our house. He stood by the window filling his syringe. Ugh, I hated to see that yellow liquid flowing from the little bottle. They were such long long needles. Penny would lie back on my bed while he kneaded her stomach and then pressed the needle in, her legs hanging down over the dust ruffle, still as if they were dead. All that time, she never once cried.

Wouldn't you know it, Milton found the cat two days after the shots were done. And that was when we found out everything. Penny wasn't alone, she had a father. He was living in the foundations of an old house out by the railroad depot. He had a tent strung over the top for a roof and down inside he got the furnace working. He cooked his meals right there. Milton said he found all our dented cans, empty, piled up neat in one corner. The man was apparently clean. But Milton hadn't said anything to him; he'd turned around and run home, without even taking the cat. He'd been scared to death, he said, he'd never seen anyone so ugly.

So a group of men went, my father, the doctor, three or four of the other sisters' husbands. They left that same night, with lanterns, the doctor carried Penny piggyback. It was summer already and warm late. My mother and Milton and I stayed out on the porch, shucking corncobs, waiting.

And when they came back, they had a story to tell. Penny's father could talk and hear. The men explained about having to test the cat, that there was a possibility it was rabid and the man was happy to give him up. The man had offered them coffee— coffee my father recognized as ours from the dented Holloway tin. He told them they were Oneidas from up near Locknominee.

Penny was half Indian, her mother was dead. Then he showed
them what he called his laboratory and in there he had needles
and alcohol, all such stuff, and books. Ross Smittie was amazed.
Penny's father had performed plastic surgery on himself, he'd remade his own face. His tribe of Oneidas had always thought he
was the ugliest man they ever saw. Even when he was a little boy,
they wouldn't look at him. He had lived with his wife, she was a
runaway from the orphanage in Traverse City, outside the tribe,
but in those same woods. Then when his wife and two Oneida
children died of polio, the Indians decided it was him. His own
people stoned him and chased him away. He took Penny and they
left—they got a ride on a cart with some gypsies up to Michigan,
they picked cherries with the migrants all summer and then they
rode the freight trains here. But what was really so hard to think
was that this man found a way to sneak into the public library at
night—see, he was afraid for people to see him—and read up all
about plastic surgery. He wanted to remake his face to be better.
He got a hold of needles and suture somehow and from studying
those books, he changed himself. I suppose he used mirrors to
see. He said it took months, most of the winter. He had to wait
for one part to heal before touching another. And he did it. Well,
you can imagine the ruckus—Ross Smittie wanted to call in re-
porters from the newspaper and write to other doctors from all up
and down the state to come and see. He said it was a miracle the
man hadn't killed himself, but there were no infections Ross
could find, only clear, healed scars.

Now that there was a big to-do, they moved to Clara's house,
Penny and her father and the cat. They had more room there and
it was nicer, I suppose. There was a write-up with a picture in the
newspaper and a couple other doctors came to see. But it all died
down, because the truth was, he still had such an ugly, ugly face.
It was scary, I could see how the people were scared.

In all the hoopla for him, nobody did anything with that cat.
Finally, my mother went over one day and got him. She had him
tested and there were no rabies. But at that time they had to kill
the animal to test him for rabies. They cut their heads off. I suppose they found the rabies somewhere in the brain. And we knew

just where they put the animals, too, in a big metal drum out in a field of the dump. We sat on the porch that day thinking of the drum, our cat inside limp like a rag.

It was summer and school was out and so I only saw Penny on Saturday mornings when I went over to Clara's to make crusts. Penny knew more words and now she could read lips. She put her hand right up against your mouth to feel while you were talking. Her fingers always had a taste, what was it, like apricots, I think. Well, Milton was prettinear all the time over there. He had a real crush. Clara teased about it, she said he chased Penny around in the backyard, pulled her skirt up to see her panties. They were just kids, eight or nine years old, but ooh, was my mother mad. That's the only time during all those years I saw her mad at him. She got mad at me plenty, I was clumsy and knocked things over and she didn't think I was quick as I should have been, but she always thought Milton was perfect. To her he was really something.

She gave him a spanking with a willow switch on the kitchen table with his pants pulled down. I watched and he cried, oh ye gods, he cried, you could hear him two yards down. Then after, while he was resting in his bedroom, sulking, she went right to work mixing the batter for his favorite cake. We could smell it coming up from the oven; I sat with Milton on his bed trying to make him laugh, pushing his kneecaps through the covers.

"Smell," I said and we both sniffed the air. "She's already trying to make up with you. She likes you better."

Well, that made him smile, it just came out like he'd been holding still purposely before.

"It's 'cause I'm a boy," he said. He was glad it was true, but I suppose he felt bad for me. He knew it wasn't fair.

"I know," I said. And there we both sat.

He got his cake but she told him that he was forbidden from playing with Penny ever again. He did it anyway, they snuck. My mother never caught them that I know of. I saw them once in Swill's barn. I followed him and lay on the ground, looking in one of those low windows. They were close enough so I could hear most everything they said. They were playing doctor.

She lay down on a bale of hay the way she used to on my four-poster bed. He pushed her blouse up and the band of her skirt down. He kneaded her stomach and I watched her muscles jump and sink under his hands.

"And all around the mulberry bush, the monkey chased the weasel. And all around the mulberry bush, pop goes the weasel."

At pop, he stuck a finger down in her belly. That's all they did, again and again. Lying on that prickly hay, I got bored, but I was afraid they'd hear me if I stood up. I wanted them to be done with it, so I could leave, but every time I looked in again, I got a feeling like goose bumps, I wished it was my stomach giving under his hands like dough and me submitting without ever once crying. But I'd been around all his life. Milton hardly ever noticed me.

Then that fall a circus came to town. We all went to see. They had a big green and white striped tent in a field. It was Indian summer and it was hot. I got sick from being in there, Lan-knows what all we ate, and my father took me outside the tent so I could throw up in the grass. I remember the stagehands standing smoking, the stars and their lit cigarettes and fireflies near the ground by the ropes.

When the circus left, Penny and her father went with them. The two brothers who ran the circus gave him a job. He had a side tent with a two-hundred-twenty-pound lady, and a banner that said MAN WHO RECONSTRUCTED HIS OWN FACE. Ross Smittie wrote the story that was going to be painted on a placard. They made a wooden cutout for his face.

The day they left town, Milton and I got up early. Milton shook me awake. There was still dew on the ground when we went out to the barn. Milton rode me on the handlebars of his bike. It was the only time I remember us sneaking together like that. In the barn, he'd found a litter of kittens. He had a cardboard box and we filled it with hay, then lifted the kittens in one by one. Their eyes were still just bulges grown over with fur. I had to hold the mewing box on my lap on the bumpy road home.

My mother didn't come, she didn't want anything to do with it, she and the sisters all thought circus people were dirty and they were

none too sorry to see them leave. But my father walked us to the
parade, one on either side. The elephant led, then the carts, then
the zebras my mother said were painted ponies. When we saw Penny
and her father on the back of a covered wagon, we waved and Milton
ran to catch up with them. He gave her the box of kittens and that
was the last time we ever saw them.

I've often wondered about that and whether that might be why
Milton turned out the way he did. I suppose he loved her like kids
do and then her going off all of a sudden, away into nothing, as if
she'd hardly ever been there. Sometimes people did that then, it was
harder to communicate; they'd just disappear and you'd never see
them again and it was like they were dead. Worse than dead. You
didn't even know a place where they were buried.

Something else happened to Milton that I didn't know at the time
and it might explain some, too. My mother told me fifty-odd years
later. I guess once, when Milton was a little boy, this was before
Penny, when he was real young, my mother was in the kitchen canning peaches. We had two peach trees in our backyard and they had
big good peaches. She used to put them up in mason jars and she
made jam. It must have been a Saturday morning because I was
somewhere else, baking. My dad would have been out at work. Our
kitchen was nice; it was a mint green with nice white counters. We
had a white mangle by the window, with a doily. My mother was
proud of her kitchen. It faced the backyard and it was sunny and it
was always spic and span, real clean. She polished so all the silver
on everything and the white of the sink and stove just shone.

Well, it was a summer day and she was canning and I suppose the
mason jars, some filled already, some waiting, were lined up on the
counters. The peaches boiled in a big white pot on the stove. I was
at an aunt's house, my father was at work and Milton sat on the
kitchen table, swinging his legs below him. He'd just gotten a splinter from lifting the crate he wasn't supposed to touch, the crate that
held the milk bottles on our porch. He'd wear just his knickers, no
socks, and his bare legs would dangle from the table. He liked to sit
like that. She took the splinter out with a needle and a knife. She
was good at it. She could get deep ones in one piece and it only hurt
for a second.

She told me she didn't know what happened but the weather changed outside. One minute it had been raining and then it was fair and drops lit up against the window. She had been looking there at a spiderweb outside shining with colors. Milton had his eyes squeezed shut. "Is it going to hurt?" he asked her. She laughed because it was all over. She showed him the sliver on her palm.

"Lil, I was so happy all of a sudden, I don't know what came over me." She said all at once she felt real happy alone by herself and with Milton. I guess she sat down on a chair and took him in her lap—and my mother wasn't that way. She told me, he hung on to the back of her neck and started kissing her and she was distracted, thinking of something else I suppose or nothing, not thinking, and she didn't know how much later, maybe a minute, she realized her eyes were closed and she had been kissing Milton like a man. Their mouths were open and he tasted like peaches, she said. She supposed they both did. He was sucking her chin like nursing again almost. She pulled him against her shoulder then and shuddered when she thought what she was doing. She said she found her hand just laid soft over his britches. It all seemed terrible, wrong, like an accident. Then she set him on the floor, stood herself back at the stove and slapped her hands together. She used to do that whenever she finished something, even when she got real old. It was a habit with her.

And nothing happened. The day went on, no one knew, I suppose she finished her canning. And later on, when she thought about it again, it didn't seem to matter so much. Milton had gone outside and played in the afternoon, it was just one minute in the kitchen, in with so many others. He was so young, too, she didn't suppose he'd remember anything. And at that age, they didn't know yet what you are and aren't supposed to do. After a while, she said, she didn't think about it anymore. She wasn't even sure it happened. Or maybe only a few seconds.

But when she finally told me, she said she sometimes wondered if it could be the reason why Milton went away. She didn't know, it wasn't much, she said she sometimes had a feeling. What did I think? Did I think it could have mattered, something less than a minute, so many years ago?

"Oh, no, shucks no, Milton is Milton," I told her. We sat in my kitchen then. "He always wanted to go away. He wanted to see the world and now I suppose he's seen it."

That seemed to make her feel better. She nodded. "Yes, I suppose he is seeing it."

We were drinking tea that day and we stopped talking. She was already old, in her eighties. But I still sometimes wonder whether that might have had something to do with it. Because Milton always loved his momma, he loved her but he had to get away.

There was a boy who came and helped my dad with the yard. That was Art. He lived on the other side of town, poorer than we were. He was a year older and that seemed like a lot to me then. One night, he baby-sat for us, it was in summer, and my aunt Ruth was having a garden party. My mother and father left, all dressed up, carrying a rhubarb pie I'd baked that morning, a deep dish, with a fancy lattice crust. Rhubarb grew in our ditches, all over. It was like a weed. Milton and I used to hide in it when we were real little, behind those huge leaves. It grew bigger than we were then. In summer, we ate it for a snack, just plain. We dipped the stalks in a bowl of sugar before each bite and the sugar would get real pink.

That night we had to be in our beds early, when it was still light out. I could hear water dripping down from the pump onto the cement in front of our house. Then Art walked into my room. I don't know why, maybe I went down first and asked for a glass of water, but he sat in my little rocker, with his bare feet on the curved runners. I'd never seen that before. All my boots were dainty, lined up pointed straight front in the closet. He told me a story. Oh, and I just loved it. I still remember how it went. He said an old hobo and some kids were playing down by the tracks and in one of those fields, they found a trunk. And the trunk had three compartments. They opened the first compartment and there was ice cream in it. And they all ate and ate the ice cream. And then the kids went home. And when they came back the next day they ate more ice cream—they figured out no matter how much they ate, there was still the same amount left. It was a

magic chest. Things didn't get used up. The ice cream knew how
to replenish itself.

Well, so then they opened the second compartment and it was
filled with all kinds of candy. And that was what we loved. The
kids ate and ate loads of candy and it was still full to the brim
when they went home. The next day they opened the third compartment and that was full of golden coins. They ran their hands
through the coins and laughed. They filled their pockets until they
bulged and they ran home to their families. The hobo waited until
the sun was down and came back to the chest with a sack. He
filled the sack with coins and ate candy and ice cream until he
couldn't eat any more and then he jumped on a train. He remembered the stop, he wrote the name of the station down on the
inside of his cuff, so he could always come back and get more.
He vowed to himself never to tell anyone about the magic trunk,
even if he fell in love and found a wife. But he died that very
same night. Thieves came into the car he was riding and killed
him for the money. They filled their own bags with the golden
coins and threw his body in the sack, by the side of the tracks.

The kids who had found the chest made a pact; they could each
use it, take as much as they wanted, but they could never tell
anyone about it, ever. And they kept their word and always went
back and took from it. Their families and friends wondered how
they got their treasures; in fact, the families worried. They each
had a secret idea: each one decided he would tell his own child
about the chest, so that after he died, his family wouldn't go without. When they were children and first found the chest, they were
two boys and a girl. And later, the men watched anxiously over
their wives, waiting for them to show, and the woman prayed and
prayed to have a child, but she couldn't have one. They each died
true to their word, childless. And there was a drought in the place
where they'd lived and the town got poorer and poorer, but no one
else knew about the magic chest and there it sat in the field, full
to the brim with ice cream and candy and golden coins.

Lan-knows where he got that story, I suppose someone told it
to him. I just loved to think about it, I pictured that chest out
there in the field, like my mother's big steamer trunk in the base-

ment, and it always made me happy. I suppose when you're a kid like that, just going to sleep at night, you think, even though you know better, Well, maybe you can find it. Art sat on my bed and wrote my name on my back with his fingers. L-I-L-L-I-A-N. He traced each letter big and I felt it through the cotton of my nightgown. His letters made big circles that put me to sleep.

I suppose that was when I first started to like him. It happened slow, he was always around, you didn't really notice it. I don't think he really thought anything of me then, I was just a little kid to him. Most of the older boys had a few younger ones to follow them around and help, if they were the least bit nice. That's the way we did it. I suppose he knew I had a crush, if he ever thought about it, but no one took those things for much. I saw him every day around our house and this wasn't for a month or two, this was years. And he saw me every which way—with leaves in my hair, all dirty, when we helped him rake and burn, dressed up nice for church, when I first learned to put on rouge. Heck, he still gave Milton and me our bath together, so he saw me that way too.

Milton and I both thought he was just the greatest thing we ever saw and we followed him around when he'd let us. They used to shoot rifle practice in a field back of Swill's barn. We weren't allowed when they had guns, but we'd listen from our porch at night and the next morning before breakfast, Milton and I would go and see if we could find skeets in the field. We found plenty of broken pieces, but we didn't want those, we needed whole ones, ones somebody had missed. When we found one, oh, then we thought we had a prize. We brought them home and gave them back to Art, the next time he came around. He never said anything about it, he just smiled and took it with him in his pocket. I suppose they just threw them in the air again the next time they shot, after all our hard looking.

I think the thing that finally made him look at me, like a girl not just some little kid, was a picture. There were traveling photographers in those days, just like musicians—the little towns couldn't support such stuff on their own. There wasn't the business. But once a year they'd come and line us all up outside of

school, the girls together. Cameras were huge then, big wooden
boxes, and they brought their own umbrellas and all. When I was
a senior, after the class picture, the photographer asked if he
could come to my house and take some more pictures of me alone.
Well, I had to ask my mother and then I went the next day and
said, Why sure.

When he came to our house, my mother had us all ready. I was
wearing a white lace dress, all pressed and starched and my boots
were polished so the buttons shined. She'd braided my hair and
pinned it and she'd dressed up Milton too. All the furniture in the
house had been oiled. She had flowers from the garden set out in
silver vases. My little dog, Blackie, had a big blue satin ribbon
around his neck. My mother asked the photographer if he didn't
want to take Milton in the picture, too, but he said no, and so it
was just me sitting on the piano bench, holding Blackie on my
lap. He came around the next day with the picture all mounted
on fancy black paper and he left it with us. It was nice of him.
My mother had already been figuring out how she could scrape
together the money from our food allowance, but he just gave it to
us and went on his way.

Then, after that, every time anyone walked into the house, they
had to see my picture. Why sure. I was big stuff then for a week
or two. And that's when they all got the idea that I was pretty. I
was just a little runt before, but now they all thought I was swell.
I could tell, because they treated me a little different. Even my
mother, she was careful. She looked at me more. It made her
think of me better. Everyone but Milton. It didn't make one bit of
difference to him, one way or the other. He didn't care what I
looked like.

But what I worried about was with Art. You know, at that age,
you don't think so much about your family. You think they'll always be around and you can forget about them for a while. Art
was the one I wanted to look at the picture. And he finally did.
All that summer, I palled around with Art and his crowd of older
kids. They were from big families most of them and they had to
work—they picked strawberries for Swill, the nurseries could
hire kids cheaper then than the migrants—and after their day,

we'd all do something. They'd be tired from kneeling under that
hot sun, so we'd just walk around town, maybe buy an ice cream
if we had a little money. Then ice cream was more of a treat, they
made it in molds, like cookies, so you'd get a new shape every
time. A clover or a heart or a flower. And each one would be a
different flavor.

And then on the weekends we had our real fun. We went swimming in the quarry or down by Baird's Creek. We'd each take a
sandwich and a towel and we'd wear our bathing suits under our
dresses and hike out there. We hung our dresses on the branches
alongside the creek. I loved to swim, that feeling of getting all
wet and drying off so quick in the sun, and then sliding in again.

We could have gone on like that forever. We didn't worry then,
like kids do now. Both my daughters worried so much about themselves. More than I ever did. And the granddaughter is the worst,
yes you are, it's the thighs one week, and of course the breasts
aren't big enough, next thing you know, it's the knees or the
ankles. Pretty soon it'll be the ear, you just wait.

We were too shy to think about our bodies. And we wore bathing suits that came almost to our knees, so you couldn't see much
anyway. I still have mine; it's a blue with white buttons, I don't
know why I keep all such stuff.

And in the country, there where we were, it was quiet. Quieter
than it is anywhere now. We didn't have the cars and the trucks
or the highways. Once in a very long while we'd hear a train go
by and you'd stop whatever you were doing and listen because it
was a change. It always seemed sort of sad, a train, but an every-
day sadness. To me it did. It made you think of the things you
didn't know. Most of all day it was silent, except what noise we
made ourselves, diving in the water, splashing. I remember lying
flat on a rock for hours under a tree that would sway, just the
littlest bit, in the breeze. We could have gone on like that for
years, and it was my fault that we didn't. That was my one big
mistake, but what did I know?

For my seventeenth birthday, I made a big cake and we had a
party. It was just girls, that was the way they did it, with ribbons
hanging from the ceiling, and all the aunts came. My mother's old

steamer trunk sat in the front parlor, repapered inside, and they each brought something for me to take along to college. I'd already gotten in for the next year, at the Catholic college in Marquette, it was all set I was going to go.

I suppose I was so puffed up from the party and everyone giving me something that I said yes when I really shouldn't have. When Art came that night and gave me his present—it was a black pin, I still have it—he asked would I go swimming with him the next day and I said yes.

And wouldn't you know, sure, that was when it happened. He was young, too, just eighteen, he didn't know any better. He'd never been alone with a girl before, except maybe his sisters. First we swam and then after, it was still morning, we were lying on that rock, under the tree. The way the branches moved, the air went on your skin like from a fan. All of a sudden he came and lay on top of me and I didn't know what was what. All the time I was growing up, I thought a soul lay in your chest, I even thought I knew what it looked like. It was a wide, horizontal triangle like a yoke, made out of white fog, like clouds are. I thought married people had babies by somehow pressing their chests together so their souls touched. That's how dumb I was. That was as much as I knew. I was pretty sure it had something to do with kissing, and so I was careful we didn't kiss. I hadn't really pictured more than that—but there it was, our chests felt real warm and pressed next to each other, so I could feel his sharp bones. It was uncomfortable, but not an altogether bad feeling either.

Then the other began. Neither of us said anything. I was afraid to move, I was ashamed of how much I didn't know. That's how dumb I was. And he was different, too, I was afraid of how his face looked, stern and sealed like a stranger's, like a profile of a man you see a distance away, working up on a power line.

He started rubbing me all over and I knew you weren't supposed to let them touch you. I didn't know exactly why and to tell you the truth, I didn't know how to stop it. Then he reached under my back and opened my swimsuit. Then all of a sudden, I was a little smarter, because I knew enough to know it shouldn't go much below the waist. At first it didn't. Then he reached down by my left leg and went up under the band around one thigh. It hurt, like something sharp, the edge of a thing. I kept hoping nothing more would happen. Then he pulled the suit down so above my waist was bare. Right away, I thought, all right, that's done now, just as long as he doesn't pull it down any further. I kept thinking like that, nervous, until it was all off. Then when he was right there, over me, I understood more. I cried a little, I suppose most people do, especially like me when they don't know what's coming and feel that first burning, oh it hurts, but then it went on and on and I closed my eyes and all I thought of was my mother.

I thought of her room. I could exactly picture the furniture. The high bed, square and neat, with the white chenille spread, the tassels just touching the floor, the mirror, the white bureau, the one fern and then the white curtains, blowing at her windows. I had gone into my mother's room alone in the afternoon. The white walls had a bluish color, like light around an egg. I thought of my mother with my father in that room and the white cotton nightie she wore to bed and how she must have wanted to touch her soul to his and I tried to feel that way and be that way with Art, my chest pressed right under his, collapsing, so we could both feel the warm.

And that's when I got pregnant with Carol, from that one time. We did have bad luck, that I'll say. I had wanted it, though, I was thinking of it. Wanting it made the pain seem important, for that one second the whole thing seemed holy, like a sacrifice. Maybe you get pregnant easier when you think like that.

My mother and father sure weren't happy. Oh, no. My mother had worked hard saving and fixing up my college trunk and she never liked Art so well anyway. She wanted Milton and I both to marry better families, families she knew. Cousins even.

I got married in a dark blue dress. My mother didn't come, but I went home after, alone, she wouldn't let him in the door again. She was just wearing a housedress. She was sweeping when I came in. I half kissed her, she moved her cheek away and for a long time I remembered her face inside the oval glass of the door. I felt my braid swish on my back as I walked down the path. She was watching me and I left that day. Art met me down the road. Art was scared too, but there we were married. We had no choice but to do it.

For him it was a kind of adventure. And he never did have to go to a war. He went and tried to enlist for the first one. They sent him back because he was too young. Then, by the second, he was too old already. I was born in May 1900, Art in 1899, so between us, one was always the age of the year. And he had an idea that we had more fun somehow because it was the beginning of a century. He told that to Adele once and oh, was she mad. We had the whole century in front of us. He always liked gadgets, balloons, fireworks, everything new. See, I didn't learn all his crazy ideas till then when I was stuck with him.

We moved sixty miles to Bay City and at first we lived on top of a store. It was all new people. I wrote to my mother and dad, one letter a week for more than a year before she would even answer me. I don't think she ever really forgave me. She had to some later, when she was sick and living with me. But she never liked Carol because of it. As if Carol could help what we did.

Then a year after we left, Milton ran away. That must have been hard on my mother. He went off to San Francisco to join the merchant marines. From what I heard after, we were the only ones in Malgoma who were the least bit surprised. And when I knew, it seemed right, it made sense. He had always wanted to get away. Even when he was a little, little boy and I had to watch him, he'd crawl off the blanket, under the fence, out of the yard, away from where he was supposed to stay.

Milton's birthday is September first, the same as our Adele's. And they are a lot alike, so I've often wondered if there isn't something to that. There's one such a one like Milton in every family. One who thinks he has to get away.

We lived above a little grocery store, which was a help to me with the baby. Art was gone all day and some at night, too, he was just starting up, trying to make a go of it, and he was still young enough to want some fun. So I took the baby downstairs and sat in the store with Mrs. Sheck. She knew babies, she had three schoolchildren of her own. She'd hold Carol, too, and we'd talk all day about babies, she'd show me one little product or another. We got through.

Art began as a photoengraver just when they were starting up the newspaper. He worked Sundays and all night sometimes to get it out when he was supposed to. I still have the first year of newspapers all bound up in such a book, this big. I should call the museum, see if they want the old thing. I just haven't wanted to lug it out to the dump.

Then, when we'd saved a little money, after the first few years, we bought the land for this house. We rode all over, looking at land. I picked out this spot for the oak tree. I liked that big tree in the front yard. The land was cheap then and this was nowhere. We were the first on Lime Kiln Road. Art bought past where the barn is now and all the way down to the tracks.

"That swamp?" I said. "What are you ever going to do with that swamp?"

I should have kept my big mouth shut, because now that land is worth a lot of money. It was outside of the city limits, part of a new little town, Ashland they were calling it then. Art was already thinking he wanted enough land so when Carol grew up she could build and live here, too. He was hoping if we built a nice house, others who wanted to live in the country and were just getting a start would move out. He thought we could all pitch in and help with the work, women and men. The newspaper gave him his ideas. He started town meetings and they drew up a plan for every house to have sewer and water and electricity.

Then he got into the mink and was that a lot of work. He built that barn in back prettinear by himself. And they were temperamental, those mink. If you didn't do every little thing just right, they could die and then you were out.

By that time, too, other people built on our road like Art wanted. Mack Griling moved in down where they are now and he built a house, and the Brozeks came across the road. They built a house and that little apartment above the garage, for her brother who was in the navy, for when he came home.

See, all the time Carol was growing up, we were so busy, thinking of other things, trying to make a go of it.

And we were still so young. Lot of other people our age didn't have children. I made friends with the other mothers, though, even if they were older. Amber Brozek across the street—she had Chummy—and I was even friends with Mack's first wife. Tinta was her name and ooh, was she a pack rat, every inch of that house was full of junk. And she painted paintings too yet, all of them landscapes from around here. So every little spot on the wall that wasn't full already, she covered with one of her paintings. Some were so small like a postcard. That end of the road was never any good. I was sorry they moved there, I still am. Ugh, I didn't like going with Carol into all that dust and dirt, you knew there were plenty of germs. I don't think Tinta ever cleaned. And when she opened a drawer once, I saw she had her clothes all rolled up in little balls. But, still, she was a neighbor too, and we didn't have very many. Amber and I went with our babies once a week or so for tea. We'd dress Carol and Chummy in their oldest clothes before we walked down and then, after, we'd let them play in the dirt. That's when they made their mud pies. They loved that, sure. And then we plunked them right down in the tub.

Art hired two men to help him out with the mink. Only one was married, the other still lived at home. Art palled around with them, after work too. They used to go to the Morley Meyerson Building, it's not there anymore, but it was one of the first old buildings, right along the river. They climbed up to the top, five stories, and they jumped off the roof into the Fox River. The Fox River was clear in those days, cold, but you could swim in it. The bay, too. People swam all over in summer. And they had the nice beaches. Now that's all gone because of those darn paper mills. But they give the people the jobs, that's the thing. I didn't like to hear it, Art taking risks like that, five stories, and me with a daughter barely walking at home, but I knew he had to get it out of his system somehow, being young. And so I didn't say anything. We wives didn't say too much. I suppose he had to have his fun, too. He worked very hard for his money. And we were lucky. Lots weren't as lucky as we were.

When my father died, we hired detectives to go find Milton. We had to hire detectives when Dad died and then again for my

mother. They found him in a one-room over a tavern in San Francisco. The detectives had a picture we gave them and they said
right away, coming off the ship, they knew it was Milton. He still
had those yellow curls. But I hardly recognized him anymore, he
changed so. He was a real solid man at the funeral, people looked
and wondered, is that Milton? He had to borrow one of Art's suits
and it hardly fit him. He wasn't thin anymore. But he did still
have those curls. If we hadn't found him and sent him money to
come home, he never would have known his father was dead. He
stayed for a while and worked on the mink farm, but that didn't
go. He didn't like that. I suppose he'd been around the world
prettinear by then, he'd seen all kinds of things. He was used to
more excitement. And he drank. As soon as he had a little money
saved up, he'd go blow it in the taverns. I remember once it was
Thanksgiving. He had gone the night before, from tavern to tavern
by taxi, and when we were just sitting down for Thanksgiving, he
staggered up the road. He was shaking when he came in and he
asked Carol to get him a glass full of whiskey. She was eight or
nine then and she did it. She got him a water glass full and he
just gulped it down. And the way he ate, he was a nervous person.
He ate real fast and greedy. He never used to be like that. I
suppose on the ship maybe they had to be. Then, after us, he
went home to Malgoma and lived with Granny for a while and that
was a disaster, too.

A year or so later, after he'd left again, he sent us a big coconut, with painting on it. That gave Art the idea for the Polynesian
bar in the basement, oh ye gods. Yes, we have Milton to thank for
that, the colored lights and all. The fish was our fault, that was
from Florida. I wanted to go to Florida, and he caught it there
and had it stuffed. And every once in a while, we got a postcard
from Milton. I stopped reading them because I found out things I
didn't necessarily want to know. He went on about the Silver Slipper, oh, he ranted, he must have been drunk when he wrote some
of those. I wouldn't be the least surprised.

Carol was eleven years old by the time we had Adele. Everything was different by then. Adele was born in 1929, she was a
child in the depression years, but she was too little to tell. By the

time she was old enough to know anything, we had some money
again. And she got plenty, much more than Carol.

Carol was like a little mother, such a help to me. Those years,
for a long time, we had hamburger every night and we did all
kinds of things with it, Hamburger Surprise, Hamburger Su-
preme, Hamburger Royale. We mixed in potatoes and ketchup,
different canned vegetables, anything to stretch out the meat. I
still have that metal box of recipes we used then, things we cut
from the paper.

Carol changed Adele and watched her, everything. Carol was
always serious. I thought because we had her so young, she
stayed afraid of things. I was afraid when I was pregnant with her.
That Tinta said her mother took up mail-order watercolor lessons
only once in her life, when she was pregnant with Tinta, and here
Tinta turned out to be a painter! And I suppose, too, when Carol
was little, she could tell how scared I felt. She always kept quiet,
that didn't worry me because I was like that, too, but really, I
think she had a hard time of it. She was always short and dark,
and then she would have Art's big nose. Neither you or Adele
have that nose but Carol sure enough got it.

And everything Carol didn't get, Adele did. When I think of it
it makes me mad. Because we were older then and then we really
wanted a child. We were the right age then for one. And we had
more money. Art never really took the time to spend with Carol
when she was little, he was building up the business and those
years we were so poor, scraping and saving, but later, when Adele
was born, he could like a baby, he'd come in and play with her,
oh, for hours. When she was still in diapers, he'd carry her out
to see the mink.

And of course Adele would just be pretty. She always had
blond, blond hair—she got that from my mother—and such perfect creamy skin. Just like Milton. She didn't get the freckles
until later. She's the only one of all of us who got my mother's long
legs. And dimples. And so you can imagine she had the clothes
and the kids over and the parties. Able Hansen had moved in by
then and they had kids she could play with. And Amber had Phil
and Lacey, where when Carol was growing up, there was only

Chummy, and Carol was always too shy to play much with a boy. Carol used to stay inside by me.

Adele, when she was old enough, trouped out there with the worst of them, a real tomboy. She was always a regular dickens, into everything, in the swamps, all full of coal from the tracks, whatever they could find to collect dirt and tear their clothes, they found. Of course, those years I had a wash machine already, in the basement, back of his Polynesian bar. When Carol was little she had to be careful to keep whatever she had nice, because if that went, there wasn't the money for new. Adele had a horse when she was thirteen, fourteen, that's what that shed in back was from. That's where Adele kept her horse. It wasn't fair and I know it. It just never was fair. Adele got more.

But even with that, there was always something not quite right with her. I remember there was something far back, I think even when she was a baby. She was never all there. She did odd things even when she was real, real little. I often feel bad that we spoiled her and I know we did spoil her, but I think there was something else the matter, always.

Of course with two daughters so far apart in age, you have to expect they'll be different. And we had some good times, too, the family. When we first got the car, we'd drive to Kewaunee and stop at the old dime store and buy the girls those little wax bottles with syrup in them. They made them to look like little Cokes. And we'd have picnics on the beach all day long. Once we sent the girls off to Mackinac Island. They took the train up to Michigan and then a ferry—it was a big trip for them. I remember them all dressed up with their lipstick on, going. I'm still glad we planned that, that was nice for them. There haven't been too too many times when they were close, as sisters.

Adele was alone then for a long time when Carol went into the army. She was my only one at home. Of course, when she was that age, out of high school, Adele went to college, the works. These days they go to graduate school and get so smart you can't even talk to them anymore. But when Carol finished with high school, we didn't have the money for college, so she had to stay home and work. I still feel bad about it. Because she would have

liked that, too, she would have gotten something out of it. I've
told her many times, I'd pay for her now to go, but she doesn't
want to be in with those young kids.

When the war came, she went into the Wacs and she was over-
seas, so I suppose she saw something there, too. I know there was
a fellow she liked over in France. Both of my daughters went in
for the foreigners. I suppose they wanted something a little different. I always wonder if it wasn't from Milton that they got the
idea.

Oh, it was a shock for me when I first found out Carol had
signed up. She was twenty-four, but I wasn't ready yet to lose a
daughter. I was home baking one day in the kitchen, I had a
sponge cake in the oven and I went out to get the mail. And there
was a summons for Carol. It was wartime already, but they didn't
enlist the women. She must have signed herself up and never said
a word. Well, there was no more deciding about it, like it or not.
It said she had to report, with her clothes, to boot camp in Cedar
Rapids, Iowa, December 18. Before Christmas. Carol worked
downtown then, at the Harper Method Beauty Shop, and I called
her on the telephone. And I said, "What in heavens did you do?"

But she just kept still. That's the thing with the quiet ones.
They can do it to you, too. Finally, she said she'd written away
because she wanted information.

And here she was stuck, before she knew it. And wouldn't it
just be Art's Elk night. He joined with a couple other fellows from
the mink. I called the Elk Lodge and they wouldn't tell me where
he was, only that the men had gone out to have fun. Oh, that
made me mad. Well, I had an idea. There was a house on Irwin
Street that was never any good. I'd heard the men out by the mink
cages talk and laugh about it and then they always hushed up
when I came near.

So I took the bus and then walked the eight or ten blocks towards the bay. That neighborhood has never been good and it still
isn't. That house is still there, it's a supper club now. Small's
Paradise. Then, it was for the men to go and see a show. They
had a stage in the living room. Lan-knows how much they paid to

get in and then I suppose they got stuck for drinks too. Well, I looked in at the window and I couldn't see anything. The grass came up to my knees, they must never have cut it, and I tore my stockings on a thistle. Then I just walked right in. I'm still sorry I did. That taught me a lesson. I'd never seen the things that I saw that night on the stage. There was a woman up there with a donkey. Yes, a donkey, and they were doing just what you'd think, the worst you could imagine. I wouldn't have thought it was possible. It made me sick just to see it. They did that here in Bay City. Carol's Jimmy says they still have stuff like that going on down in Mexico.

I saw Art's face for a moment before he saw me. He was leaning forward from a table with two other fellows, laughing.

Well, sure enough, Carol went into the army—there was nothing we could do—and I got myself used to the idea. Art and I never talked about it. I went on, same as usual, but after that I kept the whole business of the Wacs between Carol and me. We talked about it, we got her clothes and cosmetics and toiletries packed. It was the first time I had a project like that alone by myself—before we'd done everything together. And I didn't want him getting funny with me anymore either. Not after what I saw. Not if that's what he thought of me.

But then after a while you forget. Carol went away and we got letters home, from camp first and then from the base. Adele was getting to be a teenager, lovesick around the house. She went with her girlfriend to see *Gone With the Wind* and they were fits and sighs and giggles in every corner, after, all secrets.

Pretty soon we were back to the usual, but then sometimes at night in bed, he'd be breathing on top of me, I'd have my chin tucked over his shoulder, looking at the ceiling, the way we did, and I couldn't think of my mother anymore. Our room now looked just like hers, the same white everywhere. I'd think of the girl with the donkey, she had such dark legs, like an Indian almost or a gypsy, and she was wearing something like a red girdle. Her eyes the way she looked straight ahead without blinking, opened all the way open, I wondered if she could be blind.

□

I was glad enough never to have more children. Two was enough, and then the grandchildren. I suppose when you have daughters, you end up with the families. I think when you have boys, they go off and make a start by themselves, but your daughters always come back to you. They bring their children home.

Carol is like me. She went into the army, then pretty soon after the war, she came home and went back to work at the beauty shop. And we had some fun then too. We miniature golfed and we gave each other manicures. Then she met Jimmy at the country club and not too long after they were engaged. When they got married, we had the reception right here, we put tables out in the backyard. They built the house next door. Amber's Chummy did the same thing when he got married; he and June built on the lot next to the old Brozeks. So Chummy and Carol ended up both next door to their mothers. Carol always worked, she kept the books for Jimmy at the water softener store and she was a very good mother with her sons. The only thing I wonder is if she didn't make the same mistake I did, having them too far apart. But she and I get along. We still do.

Adele I will never understand. She was seventeen when Jimmy and Carol got married, old enough to be jealous.

But then Adele went away to college and did she have the clothes. And shoes and furs, you can't imagine. And they needed formals and she could never wear the same one twice. Oh, she got plenty, believe me. And even in college with all that she had—and she was in a sorority, she won some beauty prize, she was the lilac queen of this or that, she was on the dean's relief committee, her picture in the paper—all that wasn't enough for her. She got in with that Lolly, and sure enough they got themselves in trouble. Oh, it was a big scandal, I'm still ashamed. They went up and posed half-naked for a fellow who put out topless bathing suits. They wore them in pictures for a mail-order catalog. Someone Jimmy worked with saw it, Carol didn't even want to tell me. Now, why would she want to do a thing like that?

Then after college she wanted to stay and get her master's degree. She went out to California, the first time in 1954. I remember because that was the year Art got sick. He had cancer of the colon. I thought it was because he wouldn't take the time, when he was out with the mink, to come and go to the bathroom when he had to. He worked so hard, he would just wait and hold it. But now his brother and two sisters died of it too, so it must have been in the family. He was young to be so sick, only fifty-five.

We had to go to the Mayo Clinic and the doctors there did what they could. But they told us it wouldn't be long. They couldn't say just how much, but less than a year, they were almost sure of it. So right away, we called Adele—we had a hard time getting her, too—and we asked her to come home. And she wouldn't. I never understood why she didn't then—because she and Art were always close, he did loads for her. She was just like Milton. So far away and her own father dying. She kept postponing and postponing, she said she had a test, then her orals. I was scared she wouldn't make it before he died, and oh, he wanted to see his Del. And for months there at the end, he wasn't so good. But she did make it. That's one thing I have to say for Adele. She is lucky.

Then right after Art passed she wanted to marry this Hisham. I probably should have stood up to her more, but I didn't know either. I was just plain tired after a year of nursing him. And it's not easy to stand up to her. She gets mean when she doesn't have her way. I'll tell you, many times I've been afraid of her.

That last summer before Art died, Carol and I drove out by the bay and picked a stone. He had worked very hard all his life for his money and I wanted to get him a nice stone. I was glad that I could. So then after I spent lot of time planting flowers. I went out almost every day to water. And it is a nice stone. I always think that pink granite is the prettiest. It stays.

You want to know about your mother and I suppose that's natural, sure, a person wants to know about their family and you haven't had too too much of one. But I don't know what I can tell you. She's always been a mystery to me, too. I just don't know about her.

Well, after they were married, they moved around for a while, here in Bay City, always renting. They got a lot of Granny's nicest furniture and her good china dishes and I'd like to know what they did with it all, because Adele hasn't got any of it anymore. Then they were flying back and forth from his family in Egypt, too, I think for a while they thought they might live over there. But your mom couldn't take it. She couldn't eat the food. The food that was their equivalent to butter, she couldn't keep down.

I was there once too, oh, she wanted me to go and see his family. When I went on the tour with Em, I stopped on the way back from Austria. I'll tell you everything was so dirty, everywhere was dust and they just sat outside in their dirt. She said his parents were real wealthy like kings over there, but not that I could see. It was just so very very dirty.

Your mom got pregnant over there. I'll tell you, Ann, you're lucky to be healthy, because your mom was real sick when she came home. I didn't believe her when she told me she was seven months. She was down to nothing, eighty or ninety pounds. She said she couldn't eat the food over there, she couldn't keep it down. I suppose that's why you turned out small, because your dad was tall, six foot something. And then you were early, in an incubator. Your dad made it just a few weeks before you were born. I remember him down by the sidewalk and the little bit of lawn outside Saint Peter and Paul's. He was smoking a cigarette and looking up at the windows, I suppose trying to see in your ma's.

He was a funny one, the things he said. You couldn't always understand him. "So congratulations," I said to him. "How does it feel to be a father?"

And he was always shaking his head. "Beauty is a betrayal," he said. "It's always for itself, never for you." Now do you know what that meant? I didn't either. I still don't.

For a while when you were a baby, they lived in one of those little cottages by the bay. Well, I don't suppose you'd remember, you were real small yet then. You lived in that red cottage at the end. He taught classes over at Saint Norbert's College, but he couldn't make a go of that. He made a speech out there once and they all said it sounded just the slightest little bit on the communistic side and they didn't ask him back the next year. Then, he

was selling Volkswagens and pretty soon, Jimmy got him started
with the vacuum cleaners.

Once I went over to visit your mom in that cottage. It was during the day, and your dad wasn't there, he was out working, I
suppose. Well, here it was middle of winter and you were toddling
around in just a diaper. On that bare floor. With no socks or
shoes. And there was hardly any heat in those cabins, either.
Well, we went to the bureau and got a little jumpsuit to put on
you. But when we came to the feet, Adele told me she didn't have
any shoes for you. She told me, "Hisham says that babies don't
need shoes." Well, over there, the babies probably don't *get* any
shoes.

So I don't think you had the easiest time. But then I suppose it
didn't hurt you. I went out that day and bought you socks and
shoes, three or four pair. I thought that would last a little while.

Then it wasn't too long and you all moved in by me. I suppose
they couldn't keep up with the rent on that cabin. And the house
wasn't so empty anymore then, the way it was with Art gone. I
think it was better for you, too. We had Benny right next door, he
was just a year ahead, and even when you were both babies, you
always played together nice.

How old were you, three or four, when your dad left? He came
and went a couple of times—Adele gave him money to fly back
and forth from Egypt, they thought he could get money from his
parents, but I don't think that ever came to much. Then, the last
time, he charged up all those bills. That time he went to California. I guess he thought he could get famous there. He was a
handsome man. For a long time, I watched for his face on the
television. The bills started coming a couple weeks after he left.
Then we knew he wouldn't come back. Expensive luggage, tai-
lored suits, shirts, shoes, socks, hankies—I suppose everything
he thought he'd need for a big, fancy trip. He and Adele were
good for each other that way—they both liked to live high on the
hog.

Well, I just paid the bills, we didn't want the talk. We paid it
all, and it was steep, and then that was the end of it. And not too
long after, my own mother got sick, your granny. So I had to go

down to Malgoma and settle her things and move her up to my
house. Oh, was I mad. Before I got there, just the week before,
two such antiquers, young men, came and cleaned her out. She
gave them her best pieces for almost nothing. Between what
Adele got and sold Lan-knows where and those antiquers, there
was hardly anything left. But there were two things I wanted. The
piano was still there, that I used to practice on when I was a girl,
and it had such a nice round bench. I wanted that bench. And
above the piano hung one frame with eight oval holes cut out of
the paper and pictures of the eight sisters inside.

Well, my mother was a tough one, such a one. Two things I
wanted, neither worth much, and she wouldn't give them to me.
She made sure the piano and the piano bench and that picture
stayed with the house when she sold it. That was the way she
wanted it to be, and what she wanted she got. When she came to
live with me, she was the boss, even sick. You probably don't
remember her much because those years she stayed to herself.
She didn't like kids anymore. She just didn't have the patience. I
used to buy presents for Ben and you at Christmas and try and
say they were from her, but she shouted from the den, no, no,
they're not from her, she didn't buy you anything. And she
wouldn't come in and see the Christmas tree. She stayed alone in
her room. Do you remember we had goose for Christmas? Granny
always liked goose.

Then Carol's Hal got that horse. Oh ye gods. Hal always had a
scheme and it never went right, ever. He was sixteen years old
and we went to a church bazaar, here at Saint Phillip's. They were
auctioning off a pony. I remember I fought that day with your mom
because once we got there and each gave in what we brought,
your mother and that Lolly started giggling and giggling. Oh, they
thought something was so funny.

"Well, what are you laughing at," I said. "Why don't you let us
all in on the joke."

It turned out those two had baked a pie and when they were
done and it was in the oven, they figured out they'd forgot to put
in sugar. They each thought the other had put it in. But then when

they took it out of the oven, it looked just fine, and so they brought it and gave it in anyway.

I told them that wasn't at all nice and that just made them giggle some more. Ugh, when they got started, watch out. I was thinking, Well, what if a poor family bought that pie, one that really couldn't afford it, but just said, oh, the money goes to the church and it would be a nice dessert for Sunday supper. And then they got that sour thing. Well, I let them laugh and I went all over, to all the booths, and tried to buy that pie back. But I couldn't find it, no, somebody must have bought it already. I just hope to God it was a family that could afford to throw it out.

For years already, Hal had been collecting silver dollars. Whenever any of us got one in our change, we'd save it for Hal, for his collection. When they announced the winner of the big auction that day at the bazaar, they said Hal's name for the pony. Carol almost fainted. "What am I going to do with a horse?" she said. He'd spent all those silver dollars on that pony, seventy-three of them. He thought he'd take the neighborhood kids on rides for a nickel or a quarter and that way earn some money! He always had a scheme. I told him, if he'd just once hold on to his money.

It was a brown and white spotted pony, not trained or anything. Some farmer must have donated it. We called him Silver Dollar. Well, pretty soon, when it didn't all pan out the way he'd thought—there weren't many kids in the neighborhood and they didn't want to pay to ride that pony, it was slow, they could go quicker on a bike—Hal lost interest in it. We had to nag him even to feed it and brush its hair. It lived in that old shed where Adele's horse had been.

Wouldn't you just know, Granny was the one who took care of it. She got up at five every morning and hauled out that big pail of water and oats. She was the one who brushed that pony. Even after they took the leg off, she hobbled out there on crutches. She was a tough one, such a one.

I'm still sorry I let them take that leg, I think that's why she died. She just didn't want to live anymore when she couldn't move around. They said her heart was like a girl's, she could have lived lots longer. But she'd had the tumor in the leg. That they had to get rid of. Those last months were hard, with her in bed, I got up all hours of the night, changing the bedpan, she was so ashamed, she wouldn't let anyone but me in there. And then she was losing her hair, too. She was a proud, proud woman. It was hard for her.

She died on your seventh birthday, in the morning, before any of you were awake. I wasn't sorry. She'd lived a long, long life, she was ninety-one when she died and she didn't really want any more. I was up with her all night. We didn't talk much. We weren't ever close and she wasn't one to pretend. But I'd taken good care of her all that time and she knew it. She never had bedsores, she always had her things around her, I fixed her just what she wanted to eat. She had to admit I'd been good to her. And I was glad to have done it. Then when she died, at five thirteen in the morning, she looked happy, she got this big smile and her hands just opened at her sides. Carol was there then, too, she saw it. And then I knew, that was the end of something.

Adele and I talked and we decided to go ahead with your party. Why not, it didn't make any difference to you kids and she had everything already planned. She had a cake from the bakery in the icebox. And because Granny was so old, we weren't sad. She would be happier where she was.

So I sat on the phone to the funeral parlor and with the priest. And then again, too, we had detectives looking for Milton. They'd been looking this time for weeks already. And I saw outside the kitchen window, Hal taking you kids for rides on Silver Dollar. He went round and round the garage, so slow. I suppose your mom paid him something, that was probably the only time he made his money on that horse. Not long after Granny died, we had to give the horse away. Some people on a farm took him, where they had little kids. They came in a truck and got him.

You were wearing white that day. A white eyelet blouse and shorts and white anklets and white tennies. I remember from the picture: you had a big white bow in your hair. Your mom planned a nice party for you. Some of Chummy and June's came, Hansens, and that Stevie Felchner, whose parents rented the little orange cottage in back by the barn, and those Griling kids. You can see in the picture, after all these years, you can still see how the other little children look clean and had decent clothes and shoes and those Grilings didn't. There were the two girls your age, Theresa and Mary, and the one they didn't have too much longer, that retarded girl, Annette, who went away to school for them up in Okonowa. I remember they each brought you presents. Everyone's was nice, something the mothers bought and wrapped, except the Grilings'. They each brought something they'd just bought, in the bag from the store. I suppose the dad or whoever gave them their money, gave each one fifteen cents or a quarter and they each went in and picked out what she wanted. I don't remember what Theresa or Mary brought anymore, jacks or something, you know, a regular present. But this Netty brought you such a cellophane bag of chocolate candies. I suppose that's what she would have liked for herself. She couldn't play with toys much. But it was a warm day and they were all outside and I suppose she was carrying it around, holding it in her hands, and by the time you opened your presents, hers was all melted, just one gooey bag of chocolate and the kids laughed.

Your mom had all kinds of things planned: games, pin the tail on the donkey, she'd bought firecrackers that came out like red, white and blue parachutes you kids could chase across the yard. So while you were all busy with that, she came in and found me. She had a supper planned for the kids after, she'd ordered that cake from the bakery a week ahead. She had sparklers and those black firework snakes for you kids to light after you ate.

She came and told me about Netty's chocolates; we both felt so bad.

"Pyuk," she said, holding the bag up and dropping it, with a thud, in the wastebasket. "Mom, you don't think you could just whip up something chocolate for a cake, so we could take it out and say it was made from Netty's candies? You wouldn't have the time?"

"Why sure," I said, "but won't Annie expect the storebought? She knows you went to pick it up." The cake from the bakery was real fancy, I bet she paid quite a bit for it. She'd brought one of your crayon pictures of a swimming pool and they'd copied that, with the frosting.

She said she'd take you aside and explain. You always were good like that, she could talk to you and tell you the truth. She knew you wouldn't cry or fuss or throw a tantrum like a lot of children would. You were mature, more than Benny was. Carol couldn't talk to Benny like that. Your mom talked to you almost like a grown-up.

"We can have the other with Benny and Hal tomorrow," she said.

And I was glad to do it. When someone dies, it's like you've been hit hard in the stomach; you lose your breath for a moment and everything stops. Then when it all comes back, you have an empty house. I'd made the phone calls first thing in the morning. Now there was nothing left to do. The house seemed so big and quiet. And do you know what I did? I fetched that bag of chocolate from the wastebasket, it was sealed with such a cardboard strip on top, it was perfectly good, just melted, and I used that as the start of your cake. And believe me, I'm telling the truth, did that cake ever turn out good.

I took my time. I had all afternoon. I baked three layers and then while they were cooling on the mangle, I made a filling with nuts and a separate maple frosting. Your mom had the idea to put seven sparklers in like candles, and we lit them just before she carried it out.

We'd set up two card tables in the backyard, and your mom had covered them with paper tablecloths. Red, white and blue. Everything had to match. It was just dusk then and Carol and Hal were there too, and your mom and Lolly and we all sat down and had that cake on paper plates. Your birthday is in June and the mosquitoes mustn't have been too bad then yet, because we stayed out late and watched while you kids drew with your sparklers on the air. You and Benny played tick-tack-toe, but whichever one won, it always faded before you could draw the line through. Ben was teaching Netty to write her name. She wrote the same letters over and over. She had the letters right, but she was too slow. I went and made a pot of coffee to bring out and we ladies kept drinking the coffee and eating the cake. Then, one by one, at eight or nine o'clock, the mothers would step out on the porches and call their kids home, and family by family, they'd go. First Hansens, then Stevie Felchner, then finally June came over to get hers. Pretty soon all the mothers had called their kids in, except the Grilings, and they looked embarrassed because they had no mother. That little Mary got the older ones by the sleeves and they said they better go home, too, their father would be missing them. And by the time we folded the card tables up and went in, all that cake was done for.

I've thought about that many times. That was good of your mother to think of, on that day when she had so much to do. That Netty went away, I don't know, a year or two later. I remember when they came and took her in the car. I watched by the window. It was two women with short hair, they looked like church women, and just an ordinary car.

ANN

■ □ ■

■ □ ■ □ ■ □ ■ □ ■ □ ■ □ ■

5

SOUTH OF WILSHIRE
■　□　■

When we moved to California, we didn't know anybody. For the first three weeks, we stayed at the Bel Air Hotel, but that was too expensive, so we moved to another, smaller hotel on Lasky Drive. Lasky was one of the quiet, mildly commercial streets south of Wilshire Boulevard in Beverly Hills. It seemed to be a clean hotel, inhabited mostly by older single people who rented by the month. Our room in the Lasky House had a double bed with a faded, flowered bedspread, gray carpeting and old wooden venetian blinds.

We went to the same place for dinner every night, the Hamburger Hamlet in Westwood, and we tried to sit in the same booth. We ordered the same food every night, too. There was enough else new in our lives.

"Well, it *is* beautiful." My mother sighed as we drove away from the Lasky House and Beverly Hills and the car coasted down a hill on wide, bright Wilshire Boulevard into the sun. Tall, glorious apartment buildings stood on both sides of the street, their stripes of window catching light from the late, red, falling sun. We saw young boys in huge white leather tennis shoes on skateboards. Two rabbis walked on the sidewalk with a three-year-old girl in a pink dress. A couple in sweatsuits jogged.

We didn't know how they could do it; live, eat, look like that. For us, it seemed so hard.

My mother was going to be a special education teacher in the Los Angeles Public School District and her classes started a day before mine. We got up early when it was still dark. She took a long time dressing and left an hour to drive. As she went out to the elevator, she told me to stay inside our hotel room. I asked if I could just walk around the block.

"Honey, I've got a lot on my mind. Just do what I say this once."

So I made the bed and stayed in the room, watching TV, pretending I was an actress on each of the shows. I kept calling the desk to ask the time. I wanted to go out but I didn't. Here I was too scared to disobey.

And when my mother finally came back, something was wrong. She knocked things over, moving quickly. It seemed everything had changed. I didn't even know if we'd get dinner. She exhaled, snapped on the overhead light, kicked her shoes off and began undressing, hanging her good clothes neatly in the closet.

She looked at me for the first time that afternoon. "You won't believe what I've been through today, you just won't believe it," she said. Then she went back to undressing.

Except for the overhead light, it was dark in the room because the blinds were down. We never raised the blinds. We didn't want anyone on the street to be able to see us.

"I can't teach there, Honey. They sent me to Watts. That car going in the parking lot with barbed wire all around. They have electric fences. I'm telling you, Ann, we're lucky I'm alive."

Her voice sounded small. I'd never heard her so scared. It made me feel light in my stomach. I lifted up an edge of the blind. It was reddish outside, dark only in the centers of bushes.

"They have a big wire fence around the school, it's like a prison. They give you a card you put in to open the gate. And Annie, those kids were like this, taller than I am." She was standing in just her bra and underpants. She whispered, "And all black. I can't go back there, Ann."

"Don't other people go, too? I mean, what about the other teachers? It couldn't be that bad."

"With this car? Wait'll you see. They scratched it. Somebody scratched it with a piece of broken glass. He must have taken something and gone all the way down the side. One day there and the car's ruined. You'll see." She sat on the bed and turned off the overhead light, even though it was only five o'clock and reddish outside. We could still hear the day from the sidewalk below, other people's day.

"Won't they send you somewhere else, somewhere safer?"

"I doubt it. They're probably all booked. School's started. They've got their staffs lined up. See, that's how they get you. That's what this school system does. They get the poor person from out of town and stick them there in the ghetto, where no one else will go. And I suppose they can get away with it. People come all the way out here, and then what are they going to do? And if it's a man and he has a family to support? But I'm too old for that, Honey. I'm sorry, Honey, but that I just can't do for you."

I remembered how we were the day we found out. We whirled around in our stocking feet, our hands together in the middle, screaming "Weeeeeeeeee!" We'd been alone in the house on Carriage Court, skidding on the black and white checked kitchen floor, no one heard us. When we stopped, she had looked shy. "You don't know, Annie, but there aren't many women my age who have an MA," she'd said.

She probably remembered that too, and it made everything worse. We felt like dupes now, for having been proud. And she probably went back to thinking what she usually thought about herself, that she wasn't quite right in the world.

"We'll have to go home if I can't get another job. I can't work in that school, Honey. I'd get hurt. I wouldn't get out alive."

"Are you just not going to go tomorrow?" Tomorrow was my first day of school. I didn't even know if we were having dinner. I started to hang my clothes up, too, neat in the closet. I always get neat when I'm scared.

"I'm calling first thing in the morning, believe you me. We'll set the alarm. But the other teachers said, sure, they wanted to leave, too. Everyone wants to get out of there. I'll tell them I just can't teach there and see what they do. And otherwise, I guess I'll look for another job."

I didn't say anything for a while.

"I don't even know where to look here. I mean the LA School

System is it, they're all over. I don't know, but I need to make money. We have to live."

It was still only afternoon, but I pulled on the T-shirt I slept in and crawled under the covers. My mother sighed and sat down next to me. We had the one double bed and I always stayed on my side, near the edge. She shook my foot through the blanket.

"Come on. Get up, Honey. Let's go get a bite to eat."

I had to know. "Do we have enough money?" I asked. "If you're not going to have a job?"

"Well," my mother tried to laugh. "We have enough for one dinner, silly. Don't worry so much. Come on. It'll work out. I don't know how, but it will."

I felt something like a metal bar in my chest as I stood up, going from my heart to my neck.

But outside the Lasky House, there was a breeze. The air was bright and cool. I looked at the other people walking on the sidewalk. They seemed amazing to me. Then, I saw the scratch on our Lincoln. We both looked away from it.

"Should we try somewhere new, closer, or would you rather just go to the old place?"

"Hamburger Hamlet," I said.

We ordered sunflower sandwiches, the same thing we ate every night. They were cheese, tomato, and sprouts on wheat bread with little porcelain dishes of sunflower seeds on the side. They had always enchanted us. We knew from the menu that the mayonnaise was safflower. But tonight the sandwiches weren't wonderful. They were food. When we'd finished the sandwiches, we ate every sunflower seed from the small white porcelain bowls.

We drove past the long strips of park in Beverly Hills, lawns that separated the commercial district from the lush, residential streets above. Papery late summer poppies bloomed, red and tall, moving in the little breeze.

"One of these nights I'm going to come with a scissors when it's dark and cut a bunch of those." My mother laughed a little, mimicking the mischievous vigor she'd always had, effortlessly, in Bay City. It was a weak try. We were both far too afraid to do anything like that here. And if we did steal the flowers we would have no vase to put them in, nothing but the paper-wrapped water glass in our hotel bathroom.

The next day was my first day of school and I had to go anyway, even knowing we might not stay. My mother was driving to the Los Angeles School District office to try and talk to someone. We both wore our best clothes. My best dress from Wisconsin was navy blue wool, with a red belt, a little hot for this weather, but my mother said to wear it anyway. "They always remember what you wore your first day." While she dabbed makeup on in the bathroom, I pulled up my first pair of navy blue nylons. At home in Bay City, we girls all bought our own nylons at K-Mart down the new highway. We hid them in our school lockers, changing out of our knee socks from home every morning. When my mother finished her own hair, she braided mine and tied on a red ribbon.

"Are those kids going to *school* like that?" My mother peered over the steering wheel to get a better look. We were early, parked across the street. "They look like they're going to the beach."

They wore long, wide-bottom jeans, ragged at the ends from dragging on the ground, leather sandals and T-shirts. The girls' hair fell down over their faces onto their arms and backs, thinning to points at the ends like vines, as if it had never been trimmed.

"I have to change," I said. "I want to go back to the hotel."

My mother shook her head slowly. "We don't have time, Honey. I have to get going and, anyway, you'd be late. You don't want to be late your first day. And I wouldn't send you to school looking like that, I wouldn't."

"I'll walk back."

"There'll be the nicer kids and those girls will be wearing dresses. Believe me, Annie, I know. Go on, you look real cute. Really, or I wouldn't tell you."

I got out, carrying my clean new notebooks. It was nothing like schools in Wisconsin. It was old. The plain stucco walls were painted pink. All the roofs were red tile. There was a square steeple, as if it had once been a church.

Everything seemed strange: the small, old desks, the pale but bright blue walls. I thought it might always seem odd to me; I might leave before it ever grew normal. From where I sat in the class, I could see a palm tree, its huge leaves fluttering a little near the window.

Two girls in my class wore dresses, but I could already tell that they weren't the ones I wanted to know. I liked the thin girls with long panels of hair like curtains on both sides of their faces. They smiled and laughed, knowing things. But I wasn't even sure if I'd come back here tomorrow. I thought of my mother somewhere asking the LA School District for a different school. I imagined her in the district office like a court, pleading her case. She was asking for our two lives. The person who decided was a man. He sat and listened behind a large, wooden teacher's desk; he played with a pencil between two fingers. She was standing in high heels, pacing, occasionally running her hand through her hair, pushing it back. She moved precariously, in those heels. He deliberated, listening. The sleeves of his judge's robe dragged on the desk. She talked on and on, a whine in her voice. At moments, she broke into a cry, while he sat calmly looking down at his clean hands.

The teacher asked me a question and I said, I'm sorry, I lost my place.

She moved on, kindly, to the next person. Finally, the lunch bell rang. I followed behind the crowd down to the basement cafeteria, but I didn't have any money, so I walked around to some trees in front of a smaller playground, with low gym equipment for the little kids. The air was hazy, hot but not clear, and cars moved on Wilshire, a block away. I didn't know if I would ever like it here. It wasn't the way I'd imagined.

I stood there, looking at the empty painted playground toys. I was thinking of my mother, where she was. Two girls walked up in front of me. One was tall and messy, messy hair, knee socks too thin for her legs and a large mouth. The other was small. They were the two girls wearing dresses.

"You new?" the big one said.

"Yeah."

"Where do you live?"

I knew the right answer. But I didn't live on Roxbury or Camden or Camden or Rodeo, or on any of those streets with the pretty names. I didn't live anywhere.

"I don't know," I said. "I don't remember the name of the street."

The big girl bent over her open palm, concentrating. "Is it above or below Santa Monica?"

I shrugged. She used the lines on her palm as a map. "Say this is Wilshire, the next big street is Santa Monica and above that is Sunset. You don't know which one you're closer to?"

"I think Sunset, but I'm not sure."

The bigger girl looked down at the small one. "She probably lives near Sunset."

A bell rang then and we moved towards the door.

"What does your father do for a living?" the taller girl said, her hand on my arm.

Two answers came to me. "He's a doctor," I told them. The first thing I'd thought was, He's dead.

The teacher stood drawing a map with colored chalk on the board, her dress lifting to show her strong, tan legs as she reached, and outside, a buzz saw tore the air. I read the part in the book and I liked it. School was so easy. I had darker things; the judge's sentence on my mother and me, the word no. I would have given anything that day to be twelve and I was twelve.

The two girls in dresses turned up next to me in the hall, after the last bell rang. Now that I'd lied to them, they bugged me. I wished they'd go away.

"You know what you could do to be really pretty? I think you'd be really pretty except for your teeth are crooked. You should get them straightened." She looked at the smaller girl. "Don't you think she'd be pretty with even teeth?"

The smaller girl nodded avidly.

"You should go to an orthodontist and get braces."

In the surprise of sun, I was wondering where I could walk that wouldn't show I was going south of Wilshire. I'd never thought about my teeth before. I'd always thought my teeth were fine. I'd looked at my face hundreds of times in the mirror, looking at it different ways for when I would be on television. Always, the best angles were ones only I saw. When I was alone and no one else could see. Now I worried about my teeth. I made my mouth go narrower.

Then my mother's car pulled over by the curb and I was so glad to see it, I ran and got in and she started driving before she even said anything. It was something she'd picked up from the summer. She drove to relax now, just anywhere, just to drive. We rode through the quiet residential streets with big houses and green slatted tennis courts. We both liked to look at those houses. What my mother had thought before in Bay City was true; it helped to have a car we weren't ashamed of. There was so much else we had to hide.

"Well," she sighed. "It looks like we can stay. They gave me another school in West Covina. I went out there this afternoon and saw it already. It's in the Valley, it's a long drive every day, but it's a white school, middle-class, all houses. So, I guess we'll have to really start looking for an apartment."

"Isn't that good? Aren't you happy?"

"Well, I'm tired. It's an hour and twenty minutes there, and another hour and a half back. I've been driving all day. Let's go get an ice cream cone."

We parked in front of the Baskin-Robbins and my mother gave me five dollars to buy our cones. She would never go in herself. At night, she said she wasn't dressed well enough and she didn't want to run into anyone. As if we knew anyone to run into. But today she had on her best suit.

We tried to meet people. My mother asked about kids at school and about their parents, but nothing seemed to come of it. We called a family named the Flatows, who'd moved from Bay City a few years ago, when Mr. Flatow's company transferred him to Beverly Hills. In Bay City, their family owned an expensive children's clothing store. I remember shopping there with my mother when I was little. The saleslady would take out a drawer full of socks which were all your size and they would be folded up so they looked like colored eggs.

My mother and I sat in their apartment for an hour, having tea. They lived south of Wilshire, too. They had a daughter a year younger than me, but she left to go to a dog show a few minutes after we arrived. Her parents asked my mother about news in Bay City and my mother told them what she could, but they didn't seem to know the same people. They praised the Beverly Hills High School, where we kids would all eventually get to go, and encouraged us to drive by. "It's like a college campus," they said as we left. Nothing came out of that visit, either. We didn't see them again.

We met Julie Edison the way we'd met other real estate agents. My mother called and said we were looking for a house. Weekends, we toured Beverly Hills mansions for sale. We saw houses with five bathrooms and only one bedroom, houses with tiny kitchens and ballrooms, a house that had once belonged to William Holden. We saw where the Monkees lived for a while. We walked through houses with more than one real estate agent. That was when we were living at the Bel Air Hotel. When we moved to the Lasky House, all of them but Julie stopped calling. She kept showing us houses, and the places she took us to were smaller and smaller. Finally, she showed us a house we really liked.

It was a normal house, with two bedrooms, just above Santa Monica Boulevard on an old, unimposing street. None of the houses were big or fancy. This one was white brick with a red chimney and bushes out in front. It had two stories, a fireplace, a nice kitchen with windows looking over the backyard. We fell in love with the house.

We'd seen it twice already. It was the picture I held in my mind at night when I was trying to fall asleep. My mother told Julie what she'd told other real estate agents, other times: that we'd come ahead to start looking, but we were waiting for a husband to join us. After a while, my mother stopped returning Julie's phone messages. They came on little pink slips the man behind the reception desk handed us when we walked into the Lasky House. My mother stuffed them in her purse.

While we licked our ice cream cones at night, we drove by the house. Once, my mother parked in front. We just stared.

"It really is a beauty, isn't it? It's small, but elegant. It has charm, more charm than a lot of these that have been added on to and added on to so they end up one big hodgepodge. I'd do it all in white wicker and chintz. It's really the perfect little place for two girls. And in the winter, we could make fires in the fireplace. We could go to the woods and collect pinecones, remember how nice they burn?"

"But we can't afford it, can we?"

She sighed. "I don't see how. But who knows, we'll see."

"It's a hundred thousand dollars. How much is that you'd have to put down?"

"I don't know, twenty, thirty."

"And we don't have that much?" I had no idea how much money we had.

"Honey, we've got barely enough with what I'm making to pay the Lasky House and our food every night. Plus your school clothes and when we get an apartment, we'll have to give a deposit, plus, plus, plus. I can't do all this on my own."

"So it's out then. We can't afford it."

"I *told* you, we'll see. I just don't know right now. Who knows, Gramma might even give us something."

We parked on the street in front of Julie's condominium, a new high-rise building.

"Now, you know, this might be the last time we see her, once she finds out we don't want the house. She knows she won't get her commission then," my mother said.

We'd called home, collect, to my grandmother many times.

"I know, I don't care."

We sat in the car. It was October and a little cool in the evening. We had the heat on.

"Okay, as long as you know. So you won't be disappointed." My mother hadn't wanted to return Julie's messages. She thought the

best thing would be to drop it and just run into her again sometime, later, when we were all set. It was my idea to call.

We rode up the elevator in silence. When she opened the door,
Julie was standing, holding a phone to her ear. A thirty-foot extension cord dragged behind her. She ushered us in, smiling, all
the while saying, "Right, right," into the receiver. She was wearing a man's long-sleeved shirt rolled up to her elbows and purple
panties. Her fingernails looked newly polished. There were cotton
balls stuck between her toes.

We sat down primly, waiting for her to get off the phone. We
liked Julie.

"So, how are you," she said, as she hung up. "I've missed you,
I've been calling."

"Well, we've been busy, haven't we, Ann?" my mother said.
"And I have some unhappy news. My husband won't be coming.
We've decided to get a divorce."

Julie pounced on the couch beside us, her fingers spreading on
my mother's back.

"It looks like he won't be joining us. I've decided to leave and
so . . . we're on our own."

"Oh, no, I'm sorry."

"Well, I am too. I'm really sorry for her. And she's being a very
brave girl. But I think it'll be for the best. I've really known that
for a long time. And I just don't think I can live with him again.
I just can't."

"Jesus, let me make some coffee."

My mother said she'd decided to leave; she thought turning
down money was a claim in itself. I'm sure to Julie it made no
difference. Julie wasn't a snob. She was a practical person. If you
had the money, you bought a house. If you didn't, you rented.

"I can't do it, it's just not right," my mother yelled into the
kitchen.

"Maybe then it's not bad news," Julie called. "Maybe it's really
good news. Or it will be. If you'll be happier."

"I think we will, in a little bit, when we're settled. But unfortunately, I'm afraid it means we won't be able to swing the house.
On our own, we just won't be able to do it."

"There'll be other houses again when you can. That one was a particular steal, but if you can't, you can't."

"I'm just sorry for all your trouble."

"Oh, don't be sorry about me, that's my business." Julie squeezed my shoulder. "Ann, I've got a half gallon of Jamoca Almond Fudge in the freezer, why don't you dish it out for us." She yelled after me. "If there're no spoons in the drawer, they're in the dishwasher."

"Oh, none for me, please," my mother said, "I really shouldn't."

"You shouldn't. I shouldn't." Julie slapped a thigh. "Come on, Adele, you *should*."

"Well, a wee bit."

"So, you're going to need an apartment." From her pink lacquered file cabinet, Julie took out a map of Beverly Hills. She squeezed between us on the couch. We each ate our ice cream staring down at the map on the coffee table. We listened and memorized, alert, to all she could tell us.

"The bottom line is you want to keep her in Beverly Hills for the school district. But I think we can do even better than that. In high school—they're all together. But this year, for seventh grade, there's four elementary schools. And if you can get her in with a good group of kids, she can just keep on with them."

"RIGHT," my mother said, hitting the table. "It'll just carry over. That's why I wanted to get her in now, while she's still in the seventh."

Julie traced the map and its districts with her pink fingernail. The names enchanted us. Trusedale Estates and all the long, wide streets with palms down the center belonged to Hawthorne School. Cañon, Rodeo, North Elm Drive.

"I'd try to keep her in El Rodeo. Beverly Vista is mostly apartments. And see, Horace Mann's way over here. That gets into La Cienega."

My mother reached over and ruffled my hair. "We'll keep you in El Rodeo."

Julie snapped her fingers. "I have a friend who has a daughter

in seventh or eighth grade in El Rodeo and she's in with a real
chic crowd. She's the only one in her group who doesn't live in a
house. All the others live above Sunset. Should I call her and ask
if she has any advice?"

"Would you?" My mother dabbed the corner of her eye. My
mother loved being grateful. She crossed her fingers while Julie
dialed. I turned away.

"Okay. Good." Julie stood on one leg with the other foot crushing down a sofa cushion. "She should. Okay. One sec." She
looked at us. "She says she should work it in the conversation
that she's from Wisconsin. A lot of the new kids are just from
other schools in LA and that's a bore. But Wisconsin's different,
so see if she can mention that."

Excitement built on my mother's face. She loved social strategy, careful planning. It was one of her lifelong passions.

"Oh, Annie, I've got it," she said, hitting her hands together.

"What."

"You can say, how's this, she can say, Gee, in Wisconsin,
where I'm from, by now, by this time of year, I'd be wearing my
bunnyfur coat. It'd already be so cold." One of the great prides of
my mother's life will always be that when I was ten, I owned a
real rabbit coat. "Say, Every year I was wearing it by November.
Or even October. Say October."

"I'm not gonna say that."

"Why not? Or, let's see, you could say, Boy, is it ever warm
here. I wonder if it'll ever get cold enough to wear my bunnyfur
coat. In Wisconsin—"

Julie's hand slapped over the mouthpiece again. "And she
should be a little shy, aloof. Don't chase them. Let them come to
you."

"Yes. Let *them* come to you. Do you hear. Don't PUSH. Wait.
Just let them come to you in their own time. Because sometimes
you push."

"No I don't."

"Yes, you do. I've seen you."

That was a theme of my mother's. She thought I was too aggressive. She tried to teach me to be feminine. The art of waiting. I thought if she were a little more aggressive, we might know people and have a place to live.

"Why don't you worry about making friends yourself? I don't see why you're so worried about me."

"Where am I going to meet anybody? You're the one who can."

Julie found us a one-bedroom apartment on South Elm Drive, just inside the El Rodeo border. It had nice windows overlooking the street and gold shag carpeting throughout. We lived there with no furniture except a queen-sized Sealy Posturepedic mattress and box spring we'd ordered over the telephone.

My mother was obsessed with paint. The first few weeks, she found spots the painter had missed. She called the landlord, a large-breasted woman who lived north of Sunset and drove down to our building in a brown Mercedes once or twice a week. The landlord had also promised my mother white shutters for the windows. My mother became enraged each succeeding week they were late. She began to doubt that they would ever come. Every day, I arrived home from school before my mother. And when I saw the windows still bare, I got nervous, knowing my mother would yell for a while when she came in from work. She had long, angry telephone conversations with the landlord at night. Sometimes, the landlord put her husband on. I could hear the change in my mother's voice. She was softer with a man.

Finally, the shutters arrived. The landlord had promised white shutters and they were white, but a shade off from the color of the walls. My mother felt heartsick and furious. After two nights of phone calls with the landlord, the same painter came back to repaint.

"It's cheap. She got the cheapest bad paint and slapped it on. With all this cheap stuff around not right, I don't even want to be here. I JUST CAN'T LIVE LIKE THIS!" my mother screamed.

I stood there. I used to make myself peanut butter sandwiches on toasted English muffins and eat them standing up.

The second day the painter came back to match the shutters to the wall, I stayed home sick from school. I wanted to offer him something, but we didn't have the usual things, like coffee. All we had were sunflower seeds and peanut butter and English muffins.

Then the landlord walked in and I hid in the closet. The painter knew I was there, but she didn't.

"Just impossible," I heard her say.

"Oh, she's all right once you get to know her," the painter said. "I think she's really a good person underneath."

I didn't know if he was saying that because I could hear. He and my mother used to talk, though. She'd cry and tell him how frustrated she was, how hard everything was for us here, at the same time pointing to spots on the wall and saying, "Oh, oh, you missed" or "This little bit looks thinner, would you mind, just to even it? Thank you."

"Well, she may be wonderful as a person, but as a tenant, she's a nightmare."

When my mother came home, the landlord was in the front yard talking to the gardener. My mother bounded upstairs to see the painted shutters and then marched down again. "Well, the shutters are better, it's an improvement. But now what about the carpets? They were supposed to be cleaned two months ago. I don't even want to walk around without socks and shoes. They're filthy."

I watched from the window upstairs. The landlord dropped the green hose she'd been holding.

"I mean, Geraldine, I JUST CAN'T LIVE LIKE THIS!"

"Adele, it's been shampooed twice already and let me tell you something. You say you can't live like this, with the shutters a shade off color, and meanwhile you can live in an empty apartment with no furniture, with a daughter in school for three months."

"Well, the furniture's all picked out, it's just WAITING at Sloane's to be delivered. I just want everything RIGHT before it comes."

They talked a while longer in low voices and then the landlord slid into her brown Mercedes and drove way. But she'd gotten to my mother that time. At dinner, in our booth at Hamburger Hamlet, my mother seemed distracted. I tried to talk about different things. She had a piece of her hair between two of her fingers and she kept turning it, studying.

"Split ends," she said, in the middle of my sentence.

I stopped talking and she seemed to notice. She looked up at me. "You know, she's right, Ann, living all these months with no furniture and I'm worried about the carpets. She's right."

I loved her then. I was so glad, that seemed so normal and reasonable. I thought now we might start living the way other people did.

But the next thing that happened was my mother found another apartment. It was smaller, but cheaper and already furnished. "I mean, it's not great furniture, but it could be cute. I can see already. We could make it real cute with some felt draped and different things around," she told me.

So maybe that was it all along. Maybe we just couldn't afford our apartment.

"But she could sue us for the whole rest of the year," my mother said. She was scared about our lease. So we moved out late at night, carrying all our stuff in bags and suitcases to the car and driving to the new apartment in the dark. "I want us all out of here, before she knows." Even without furniture, it took hours before everything we had was moved. We left the bare, almost new mattress and box spring. The studio had only one room, with a small alcove to sleep in, and the alcove already had a bed in it.

When we finished moving, we didn't go to sleep. The new place was still too new and we didn't want to look around carefully, then. We drove out Sunset in the dark to see the beach. We parked on the Pacific Coast Highway, and sat in the car with the doors locked, looking at the waves. We did that whenever things got too bad. You couldn't see much, the ocean was just black, but you could hear the waves and sometimes we saw foam. We waited until it was light and the sand changed and then we drove back to town and had big breakfasts at Nibbler's. My mother called in sick to her school. We were both going to stay home and work on the new apartment.

Then, when it was nine o'clock, we drove right up to the landlord's house. We'd never been inside, but we knew where it was, we'd driven by. I pressed myself hard against my car seat. But then we were there parked in front and my mother was taking off her seat belt, saying, "Okay, here we are. Let's get it over with."

There was a long lawn in front of the house. The grass seemed wet from the night. It was a pinkish brick house with white statues by the drive. There was a fountain but it wasn't running yet. The whole house looked closed as if the people inside weren't up.

"Can I stay in the car?"

"Hon, I think it would be better if we both went. I really do." Her voice was kind. She was being nice. "Come on, Hon. Let's go."

We stood there on her porch, our car far away over the lawn, knocking on the brass knocker. We must have looked like refugees. We'd been wearing the same clothes all night to move, we hadn't slept. I could feel my hair matted in the back.

A maid answered and then we waited for a long time while she went to get the landlord.

Finally, the landlord walked to the door. We'd never seen her like this, she was barefoot, wearing only tennis shorts and a T-shirt. She was obviously surprised to see us, her eyebrows pressed down, but her voice stayed measured and pleasant.

"What can I do for you?"

My mother started shaking her head. "Geraldine, we have to talk. It just hasn't worked out for us, the apartment. The rug, the shutters, everything. And I think I have grounds to get out of the lease, given all that's been done and what was said would be done."

"You want to get out of your lease? Is that what you want?"

"Well, yes, I think given—"

"Fine. I'll be happy to let you out of it. No problem. I'll rip it up right here."

My mother and I looked at each other, following her into an office. The house seemed large, solidly furnished, quiet. It must have been wonderful to wake up in the morning and walk around heavy things like that.

The landlord scribbled on the lease and attached a note to the top, signing it and stapling the pages. "Fine, just let me know when you'll be out."

My mother laughed oddly. "Well, actually, we're already out."

The landlord looked at us fast and hard when she heard that, her head steady in one position, as if we really were crazy. "Okay," she said, slowly. "I'll write you a check for your deposit, then."

"Believe me, Geraldine, we left it clean as a whistle. You can ride right down and look."

Her dark head was already bent down, writing. "I believe you," she said and handed us the check.

The next place was worse. I never liked it. But we cleaned and then we got used to it. At least there was furniture. My mother had plans; she wanted to make new curtains and slipcover the vinyl couch, but for a while we didn't do anything.

We had a loud, cheap alarm clock that rattled on the floor when it rang. Every night, my mother sighed as she set it. She sat on her side of the bed, next to the telephone, naked except for a T-shirt, and handed the clock to me. We never had our work finished, so sleep always seemed a small surrender. Our work was as simple as my homework for school, the books piled up on the tiny, wobbly, dinette table and whatever my mother was supposed to do with the stack of manila files she carried in from the car every evening and then brought back the next morning. Our work was simple, but it hung over us so constantly that we lost track of what exactly it was we hadn't done. We always knew we were behind. So my mother set the alarm for five o'clock. We both felt so tired at night we could excuse ourselves, with the idea of the long empty hours that would hang in front of us when we got up.

I knew when my mother turned and sighed in the night, I had radar for her. I always moved before she inched anywhere near me. I slept with a closed fist full of blankets and sheets. Our life together made me selfish.

We kept the clock by my side of the bed and when it blared

out, rattling, in the morning, my mother would turn and say, "Five minutes. Five more minutes."

This happened six or seven times. Then at eight or eight thirty, she'd bolt up to a sitting position and say, "Oh my God," with a low hardness that made my heart stop.

"Hurry up," my mother yelled while I sat on the edge of the bed, pulling on my knee socks. She stood naked, across the room, pinning her hair up into a showercap. She paced. I just looked straight back at her, pulling my sock on slowly.

"Okay, fine, you can make fun, but I'm leaving without you if you're not ready."

I was ready twenty minutes before she was, the same as every morning. I sat on the edge of the bed with my schoolbooks ready on my knees.

"I'm going as fast as I can, Honey."

"I'm going to be late again."

"Well, so am I then, and believe me, my job is more important than the seventh grade."

When we stepped outside, it was already too bright and my mother's heels clicked on the raked cement going down to the garage. As she drove the Continental up, pumping gas with her shoe, it scraped the cement side of the ramp. The space we had to go through was almost exactly the same width as the car and so, every morning, it made an awful, shrieking noise.

"Damn," my mother said.

"Could you please shut up."

"Jeez. You think you've got something a little decent once that you've paid a lot for, and then, before you know, it's just another piece of junk, too."

I did feel bad about the car. I knew how she thought. We were one by one getting the things you needed for a life. We didn't expect to get ahead or get extra things, not since we'd moved. We just wanted what it seemed everybody else already had. But things didn't keep. We'd never have them all at once. It made me think of the junk in Griling's front yard, back on Lime Kiln Road. All those parts of things. I could understand it when my mother sighed. When she did that, some part of me opened and closed again.

I did weird things, too, by myself. At night, when we went to dinner, I said I had to go to the bathroom and walked upstairs to the wall of phones and phone books. The Hamburger Hamlet had thirteen different phone books for LA. I looked in two or three a night—that's as long as I thought I could be gone before my mother would miss me—for the first three letters of my father's name. I'd gone through every phone book and it was never there, but still, any time I was anywhere near a phone book, I had to check again, as if it could be. I was never surprised when I didn't find it. I didn't think about it too much. It was just something I did.

The last day of school before winter vacation, Daniel Swan started walking home with me. I guess like my mother said, it was easier for me to meet people. He was a guy in my class. He always kept a stash of square Kraft caramels in his jacket pocket, sometimes he'd give me one, sometimes not. I didn't want him to see where I lived, so every few blocks, I'd stop and say, This is out of your way.

He'd start ahead of me, digging his hands in his parka pockets. "I'll go a little bit farther."

Finally, we stood in front of my apartment building. "Okay, I'm going to go now." I put out my arm like to shake hands.

But he didn't leave. I didn't invite him in, even though I had my key in my hand, and he didn't ask. Our apartment was on the first floor, you could see our front window. But I didn't tell him which door was ours, or anything, and we just sat on the landing doing nothing. He gave me a caramel and started opening another for himself, the cellophane one small glitter in the dull late afternoon sun.

Then I heard the scrape that was my mother's car going down into the garage. It made an awful sound. I just sat there.

"Hi, you kids!" my mother shouted as she hurried up the ramp, pitched forward because of her high heels. She dabbed the edge of her eye with a sleeve. She was carrying a stack of files, as usual. It was December, but in Los Angeles, December can be like autumn. The air was dull and cool and smelled as if the earth were about to change.

"Hey, why don't you help me carry in groceries!"

We both ran down the concrete to the garage, glad to be told what to do. Then, I was grateful for the car. The leather smelled rich and good. I was glad my mother kept it clean.

My mom had gone shopping, so she could offer us things to drink. She'd been to the Linville Nutrition Center and bought pomegranate juice and carrot juice and celery juice and three kinds of kefir. Daniel seemed used to that kind of thing. When she asked him, he said he wanted peach kefir.

My mother brought out bags of cranberries and brand new needles and threads. She told us she'd seen gorgeous strings of cranberries on a Christmas tree in a store window, prettier than popcorn, and so she thought we should make some. They were opening lots already, all over Westwood, the trees bundled together and stacked against walls.

We sat on the floor and started stringing. It was hard. The needles seemed thin and flimsy against the berries. We pricked our fingers and broke the cranberries and after a half hour, we each had only a short little stringful to show for it.

"Well, we're going to have dinner at the Hamburger Hamlet, Daniel. You're welcome to join us, if you'd like. Or if you can, if your mom's not expecting you."

"But you mean, we're going to give up on the cranberries?"

"I think we should, don't you?"

Daniel stood and wiped his hands on his pants and followed my mother to the sleeping alcove where she pointed to the phone. In the little space between the bed and the wall, there wasn't room for two, so she moved out of the way for him.

"The Witch will still be working, but I'll call the rest of them. They'll be glad I'm not there. More food for them."

"Oh, Daniel." My mother laughed as if that were a joke.

In the living room with just me, she sighed and her shoulders dropped and she looked tired again.

We crowded in our regular booth at Hamburger Hamlet, all three of us.

"Hmmm. They've raised their prices, I see," Daniel said.

Neither of us ever would have said that. It seemed odd and happy for someone to talk about money.

My mother put her menu down and smiled. She was charmed. It was a relief to know other people thought about money, too. "You may have whatever you'd like, Daniel."

"Hmm, I always like their halibut, but it's gone up since the last time I was here."

"Oh, go ahead. Get it," my mother said.

On our week's vacation, my mother and I wandered into a store on Brighton Way and bought two suede jackets to give each other as presents. They were expensive, but they were on sale and my mother said they would be good forever and you need one or two smashing things.

So we had those and there weren't going to be any surprises. We'd received wrapped boxes of presents in the mail from home in the middle of December and we opened them as soon as they arrived.

We didn't know what to do with ourselves during vacation. We saw Julie once and we took an old woman from the Lasky House to the Hamburger Hamlet for dinner. Beverly Hills put up elaborate decorations on the streetlamps, but except for them you wouldn't have known it was Christmas. When we drove out of the commercial district, the long residential streets looked bright as always. The lawns were thick and tended, green, the palms tall and dry, and we heard the hollow thonks of volleys on hidden tennis courts.

My mother said we could get steaks for five dollars at the Charthouse, a new redwood restaurant on the water, so Christmas Eve we drove down to the beach. We argued, I thought the place would cost more. But by that time our car was looping on Sunset over Westwood. From the hills, the pink roofs of UCLA looked quaint.

But I was right. When we stood inside the Charthouse, waiting, my mother raised her eyebrows and said, "Let's go."

I wanted to stay. You could see the waves through a glass wall. It was warm and softly lit, the Beach Boys sang from the corners, a woman had already taken our names.

"I *told* you," I said.

We walked out on the gravel parking lot to our car. "Honey, they've gone up. You used to be able to get a steak here for five, six dollars," my mother said. "Well, anyway, it was a nice ride."

We drove back to the Hamburger Hamlet. Later that night, my mother rewrapped the presents we'd gotten from home in better paper, paper that all matched, and she wrapped our jackets and whatever empty boxes we could find around the house. "Just to make it a little Christmasy." She'd bought thick shiny dark green paper and red satin ribbons.

Then, at ten o'clock, my mother decided she didn't want to do any more decorating until the house was clean. "Let's just stay up and finish it. Then we can wake up in the morning and it'll be all done."

"Can't we do it in the morning? Why don't we just put the felt up and the cookies out and go to bed."

"Well, I don't care what you do but I'm staying up. I couldn't sleep with that kitchen floor the way it is."

"You've slept fine every other night."

"Honey, I'm not going to fight with you just because I want something a little nice once in my life, at Christmas. I'd like to wake up Christmas morning and have the place clean, okay?"

I didn't argue anymore. My mother started on the kitchen and put me in the bathroom. She told me to scrub every tile and then the insides of the tub and the toilet. I was down on my knees with a pail of water and ammonia and a plastic cylinder of Comet. I swiped pieces of dirt and strands of hair from the corners. I stopped for a second and looked down into the toilet water, blue from Comet. Then I went into the kitchen to get something to drink.

My mother knelt, fiercely scrubbing the floor.

"Don't tell me you think you're done already." Some hair fell out of the rubber band and a vein in her forehead was raised. She looked strained and awful, like a dog pulling against its leash.

"I just wanted to get something to drink."

"Oh, okay."

"You bet, okay," I said, carrying my glass back to the bathroom.

"Shhh, the whole building can hear you, these walls are like nothing."

"I don care," I shouted. And then I turned the shower on before she could say anything else.

The bathroom did look nice, the tiles glistened, clean, but there was something about our apartment that still didn't seem worth the work. It felt like a toy apartment, nothing was big enough, and whether it was a little cleaner or a little dirtier, it still wasn't right. That was the thing about working hard on it— while you looked close at one little thing, scrubbing, you forgot. Then when you finished and stepped back, it was always a disappointment you couldn't change more.

At two thirty we quit. We peeled our clothes off right onto the laundry pile. We still didn't have a hamper. It was another thing, like ice cube trays, that other people always had. The clothes smelled the way a refrigerator smells when you defrost it.

My mother sighed when she handed me the alarm. "I set it for six," she said, in the dark. "We'll feel better when it's clean."

We slept a groggy sleep until eleven. When we woke, the apartment was warm.

"Are you up?" my mother said. She sat, hugging her knees under the blanket. From where we were, we could see the opposite white wall, where the paint was cracking, and the bathroom door. "Well, Merry Christmas, Little One. Should we open our presents now or should we best leave them wrapped a while? They look so nice wrapped."

"We can leave them. We know what they are."

"You know, I know I said we'd go out to breakfast but we slept so late I'd almost rather just stay here and finish so it's done. Then

we can go to your friends' this afternoon." We had been invited to
one Christmas party by a friend of mine from school, who lived
near us in an apartment. Her mother and stepfather were giving
an open house. It was the only Christmas thing we were doing.

"I'm hungry."

"Have a little eggnog, Hon, and let's get started."

"What do we still have to do?"

"Not too much, really. We've got to vacuum, and especially the
closets, because they're full of dust. Then the windows and polish
the silver and that's it. Then just decorate." She shrugged. "I just
can't really relax until it's done."

For maybe the first time in my life, I went without being asked
to the closet and took out the vacuum cleaner. I began in the
bathroom, banging on walls.

My mother walked past, still wearing only her sweat shirt,
drinking from a carton of eggnog.

I pulled the plug on the vacuum cleaner.

"Could you PLEASE not drink from the carton. Could you just
pour it in a glass?"

"I can see you're in a pleasant mood for Christmas."

"There's germs."

"The other one's unopened. Drink from that."

I plugged in the cord again and pounded against the floor-
boards. A few minutes later, my mother tapped my shoulder. I
jumped. "Honey, we should really call home. Let's do that now."
She sat on the bed and crossed her legs. "You know, I don't know
why they can't call us. It's later there, you know."

I opened the new carton of eggnog, poured some into a glass. I
took the carton to the living room closet, where I kept my schoolbooks.

"So did you get the sweater?" my mother was saying, into the
phone.

"Let me talk," I said softly.

"You didn't! You've got to be kidding. Well, they sent it two
weeks ago! You *didn't* get a sweater? Are you sure? It was a, a
brown sweater. Are you sure, a brown sweater, with, let's see, a
shawl collar and yellow buttons! Oh, it was beautiful, Mom."

The way she was yelling, my grandmother must have been holding out the phone.

"It's not her fault," I said, but my mother didn't hear me. I was sitting on the floor, gulping. I didn't know if there really was a sweater. I'd never seen it or heard about it. She could have gone and done it without me. But then, why wouldn't it have gotten there? Other people's things always worked.

"It was from Saks. They said it would get there for sure. Oh, I'm sick, I'm absolutely sick. It was a beautiful sweater, gorgeous wool. Oh, and it had pockets. Well, you'll see. It should come any day now."

The sweater never arrived. Neither did Carol's nightgown or Jimmy's scarf or Benny's sweat shirt or Hal's blazer. And my mother did it again and again, every holiday. It got to be a joke with the rest of us, "Did you get the sweater?" And it got so my mother didn't trust the United States Postal Service. If you said you were going to send her a letter, she wanted you to insure it.

We went back to cleaning. Every few minutes, she would stop and shout. "She could do a lot more to help you, you know? You'd think she'd want to help, her own daughter. But no, not her."

By the time the apartment was ready, it was after three. I ran to the kitchen to throw away the dirty paper towels from the windows. The open house at my friend's was from one o'clock until six. We had to hurry.

Then my mother handed me the car keys to get the cedar boughs from the backseat.

"Can we do that later, we're going to miss the party."

"Honey, it's going to take three minutes. This is the very last part. Just let me feel like it's finished, so I can at least think we're going to come back to a clean house. Here. Go on, Ann."

I squeezed the keys in my hand so it hurt and ran outside. The street was deserted and the air was cool so my arms had goose bumps. It felt good. The light was soft and gray, as if it might rain. In another window in the building there was a huge fake tree with colored lights that blinked. An older woman lived there alone and she hardly ever came out.

Most of the cars were gone. I sat inside ours for a while, smelling the clean air from the cedar. I put my hands on the steering wheel. I wished I could drive. I knew how, but my mother would never let me. Benny drove lawn mowers and tractors, over the fields in summer.

I piled all the cedar branches in my arms. Needles fell on the car carpet, but my mother could worry about that later. I didn't care. I dumped the branches just inside the door in one heap.

My mother stood placing her gingerbread house on a polished silver platter. We'd draped a card table with green felt. Then she began sticking the cedar boughs around it for a wreath. She draped cedar boughs on the moldings a foot down from the ceiling, on the bathroom mirror, anywhere she thought they would stick. She was right, they did change the apartment. The air felt like the outside. It seemed the ceilings were higher. You could feel it in your lungs. It was clean.

Finally, she finished. The last cedar branch was placed. We both stood back to admire it.

"Well, there. Now we just have to vacuum up these needles and we're done."

I started stripping my clothes off. It was four o'clock, there wasn't even time to take a shower. I pulled on clean knee socks. "This is the one fun thing we can do for Christmas and it's going to be over in an hour and I'm not sitting here and vacuuming."

"Okay, don't. You don't have to. I'll do it." And she dragged the old Electrolux like a dog out from the closet. And then I knew that she'd never get ready. There wasn't time. Because after that was done and put away, she needed her hour-long regime for dressing.

I yelled so she could hear me over the vacuum cleaner. "I'm going. I'm writing the address down here, so you can come if you want."

"No, don't bother. I won't come. I wouldn't go in alone. I'd really rather just finish here. To tell the truth, Honey, that's what'll make me feel best. Just so I know it's done. But you go on and have a good time." She didn't seem mad.

I walked outside. The clouds were moving fast above me. I jammed my hands in my pockets. I walked down the sidewalk and everything looked closed. You couldn't see inside the apartments. I thought of the door opening, the noise and color when I first walked in. All of a sudden, I didn't want to go. I turned towards my friend's street though, anyway. I'd walk around the block and then see. I walked all the way to the high school. It stood there empty and cool like a castle over the tiered lawns. Two men ran back and forth playing tennis on the green courts. There was no one else around. I was wearing my best jeans, which I'd ironed for this, and high platform shoes and now I wished I had on my sneakers so I could walk over the lawns. For some reason I wanted to put my hand on the pale pink stucco of the school's walls, as if I could leave a handprint. But walking across the wet lawn would have ruined the suede of my Korkease. And I thought of things like that.

I turned towards home and walked slowly. There was no hurry anymore. The apartments looked like everyone had left for Christmas, as if only people who owned houses stayed. I didn't want to see anyone. I started to cry, the tears stinging my skin, for no reason. It was pretty outside and calm and I felt glad to be in new clothes.

When I walked back to our building, I didn't go inside. I sat by our door for a long time, staring at the street. I didn't think about anything, I just didn't want to go in yet.

Finally, the door opened and my mother shrieked. "Oh, Ann. You scared me. I was coming to look for you. How long have you been here?" She wore a coat, opening the door, nothing on her legs. Her hair was still pulled back in the pink rubber band. She was carrying keys.

"Come on, let's jump in the car and just get an ice cream cone."

"Now?"

"Mmhmm. I'm just in the mood."

We turned the heat on and I realized as my mother's coat fell open that she wasn't wearing anything. She was planning to have me run in and get her cone, as always. But the Baskin-Robbins was closed, a small crooked sign in the glass door.

"Damn. Damn, I really wanted one after all that work. We should've just spent the money and had our steaks. And I want an ice cream cone. Damn."

My mother bent over the steering wheel and she wouldn't stop crying. I kept looking out the car windows at the empty street. Then I'd shake her shoulder and say, "Mom, Mom?" but that only made her heave harder.

I took the keys out and walked around to her side of the car. I pushed her over to the passenger door and drove home, dizzy, wobbling some, down the deserted wide streets. My mother was quiet now, her eyes closed.

A long time ago, once, in the cab of Jimmy Measey's red truck, it was a bright afternoon and the fields were blue with snow. On the highway, Benny perched up on his father's lap driving. I remember his green and yellow striped shirt. There were times when we were happy. Then, turning onto our road, Jimmy said, "Ann's turn, Ann, do you know how to drive?"

I said yes, but I was terrified. I didn't know how. I didn't know where things were, anything. I knew we would all die, but then someone lifted me up on Jimmy's lap and I could see: the telephone lines for miles, patches of mud in the field, tall grass poking through, snow sparkling out the windshield all the way to the barn, I was so high up. I turned the wheel with Jimmy's hands outside my hands and felt the car move on the road, as if we were sliding. I could feel Jimmy's weight behind me, his hands hovering on either side. They let me steer, swiveling up the road, the great truck rocking with all of us in it, under the power of my hands.

In front of our apartment, a policeman stopped me. I looked up at him as he bent to our window. He was staring at my mother, crumpled against her door. He asked me where we lived. I pointed. He shook his head, Okay, and tapped my shoulder with a piece of paper rolled up. He let us go and drove away slowly, on the empty, holiday street.

I opened the door with my own key. We left the room dark,

except for the tree lights. I went over and took a Christmas cookie, tree-shaped, with red and green sprinkles on top and sat on the felt-covered sofa. My mother hung up her coat and got into bed. I sat there and ate my Christmas cookie, slowly, each bough of the Christmas tree first until it was just a blob. When I was done I looked down at my empty palm and licked off the crumbs.

"Was it over?" my mother said. She was propped up in bed, using both pillows.

"What?"

"Your party."

"I didn't go." I hated admitting that. Instantly, I wished I'd lied.

"I know just how you feel. I'm happiest right here in our own cute little place. Just relaxing. It *is* cute now." She yawned and stretched. She was still wearing her gray nighttime sweat shirt. All that Christmas Day, she never did get dressed.

6

LAS VEGAS, DISNEYLAND, EGYPT
■ □ ■

It felt like two hands of air opening inside my chest when my father lifted me on the bottoms of his feet. He lay on his back, his legs sticking up, supporting my belly, his hands holding my hands. I swam in air and light. Kaboosh was what we called that game, Kaboosh, Kaboosh. I didn't know whether it was a word in Arabic or something he made up.

I didn't know anything until he was gone. And then it was like any death: absolute and very slow. My father left while we were still sleeping. He drove away in our brown Valiant, without his vacuum cleaners or vacuum cleaner attachments. He took a new suitcase with new clothes.

The door would have been locked and the air outside must have felt cool. His footsteps would have broken the web of dew on the lawn. The six-fifty train went by every day, setting the bushes and trees trembling in the yard like teacups. Perhaps they surprised him and he looked back at the house, remembering each of our round faces. Rows of old mink sheds sagged in back of the clotheslines, with patched red tented roofs. There may have been sheets, white and fluid, on the line. Everything would have seemed pure and distinct in the waterless, early morning light. He must have rubbed his eyes and then left.

He had to turn at the end of our road, onto the highway, our white house in his rearview mirror shrinking to the size of the building on the back of a penny, then nothing, a spec of dust on the glass. The sound of our car, now his, mixed with the other traffic, which we always heard and would hear, even in sleep.

□

We woke up late and dizzy the next morning. The sun felt high and generous, soaking the white curtains and softening the corners of the room. Lilacs seemed to beat against the screens.

"Where did he go?" I asked my mother. We were tucking a corner of the white chenille bedspread into the dark wooden frame. Together we bunched the cloth down, her hands pressing over mine.

"He's gone," my mother said.

"For how long?"

"Oh, I don't know." A string of hummingbirds moved on the lilac bush outside, where someone had tied a red scarf. Flies in slow orbits hit against the screens. My mother started ironing. All her summer clothes that year were seersucker and cotton.

"He's gone to California to make us money," she said. "But he'll be coming back."

"When?"

For a moment, her mouth wavered and her face began to lift. Her hands stalled on the iron. She picked up a blouse, held it across her shoulders and then took it to the closet. There was a row of empty hangers. Her chin snapped back into a straight line and she began pushing the iron again, over the perforated pink and white fabric.

"I don't know," she said.

I sat on the floor, waiting. She ironed carefully, starting every blouse at the collar. When the last one was hung up and buttoned again, I asked her what we were going to do.

She didn't answer. She turned off the iron and looked out the window, her hand resting on the dresser. "What, Honey?" she asked a moment later.

"I said, what are we going to do today."

She yawned. "I don't know. I'm a little tired, how about you?" She reached out her hand and found mine. We stood there a moment and then she sat on the bed. "Come on up, let's just close our eyes a minute."

We lay there on our backs. It was where she'd slept with him.

□

Before we went to sleep, my mother hummed one of my father's tunes. My father wanted to be a songwriter. That was why he'd gone to California. People told him he was a handsome Arab. He thought he could make money in the movies. As far as I know, songwriting was the only one of his aspirations to remain constant for most of his twenties. Later on, he gave up on music, too.

After my father left, my mother and I slept in the same bed. My mother would slide under the sheet, in her slip that she slept in, and tuck her hands under my arms to get warm. That year, my mother went to bed with me after supper and when I crawled out in the morning, she was still asleep. My grandmother and I tiptoed around the house until noon, when she woke up, and then we were quiet again after four, when my mother took her naps.

The three of us drank large quantities of milk. Our milkman delivered two cold bottles every morning. African violets on the mantelpiece thrived, perhaps because my grandmother and I stopped several times a day to check the moisture of their soil with our fingers. The house seemed to stay effortlessly clean.

And while my mother rested, my grandmother and I stole out of the house on expeditions, to see the maple syrup tapped out of trees in fall, to feed ducks and geese cans of corn at the Wildlife Preservation Center in winter, to search in spring for trilliums and wild violets in the fields. Perhaps my grandmother and I could have lived like that forever, moving quietly, playing, she on top of the kitchen table with her cards, me underneath with my colors; but by summer, my mother regained her strength. We watched it happen. One day she stopped taking naps. The next week she didn't go to bed with me after supper. And by that time, she was already bored.

She enrolled the two of us in figure skating classes Saturday evenings. She bought us matching short dresses made of stretch fabric and skin-colored tights. The rink seemed silent, the only sound was a humming, like the inside of a refrigerator. The ice was divided into eight rectangular patches and my mother and I shared one.

We concentrated, our necks bent over like horses', as we followed the lines our blades made. My skates had double runners. Then, at eight o'clock, scratchy music started up on the PA system and we free-skated, wild around the rink.

"This is how you really lose the pounds," my mother called, slapping her thigh, "skating fast."

A man did a T-stop in front of her, shaving a comet of ice into the air. They skated off together, while I stood there, wiping the melting ice from my face. That was the first time we saw Ted.

When the music stopped, my mother pulled me over to the barrier, where we ran our skate tips into the soft wood.

"See, when you're older, you can bring a boy you're dating here to see you skate. He can watch you and think, hey, she's not just another pretty girl. She can really do something." She nodded up to the rows of empty seats. They were maroon velvet, with the plush worn down in the centers. My mother looked at me with a slanted gaze as if, through a crack, she could see what I'd become. I knew what I wanted to be: I wanted to be just like her.

But my mother felt restless, waiting. We drove slowly through the winding streets of the good neighborhoods by the river, her friend Lolly from college in the front seat. We ate soft ice cream cones which melted fast, the chocolate dripping down our shirts.

"Boy, wouldn't you love to live there?" my mother said, slamming on the brakes.

Behind a long dark lawn stood a house with white pillars. "But, go on, Lolly."

They spoke in low voices. "Who would have thought, here in Bay City? Would you, the next time, I mean, before the, shall-we-say, ring? You know what I mean?"

"I know what you mean. And I think I would," my mother said.

"And so do I know what you mean," I yelled from the backseat, although of course I didn't. I just felt left out and I wanted them to stop.

They sipped coffee outside on the back porch. I pretended to be taking apart a lady's slipper, studying it, setting the soft red pieces out on the boards between my legs, so they wouldn't think I was listening. They were talking about how many times a week Lolly should wash her hair and how many shampooings per wash.

My mother sighed and looked out over the fields. Serrated red and yellow leaves stuck in the grass, and all the corn was down.

"So have you heard anything from, a-hem, California?"

My mother didn't talk for a while. I didn't dare look at her. I moved the stem of the lady's slipper up and down on my palm. My father had been gone for two years.

"Ann, go inside and watch TV with Mom," she said finally. "Go sit and keep her company."

I dragged my slippers on the boards. They were quiet until I was gone. My mother had both hands around her coffee cup and she stared down into it, blowing. The living room was dim because all the curtains were closed. I sat on the floor next to my grandmother's legs.

I liked the smell of nylon stockings. They were everywhere in our house: hanging from the shower curtain rod, brushing my face in the bathroom, tucked in the top drawers of dressers next to silver cases of lipsticks, which, at that time, had their own rich waxy smell. The stockings smelled different with legs inside the nylon, they smelled like something burnt.

"Well, now, let's get up and do something," my grandmother said, at the commercial. "Not just S-I-T in front of the TV all day. Should we drive out to the cemetery and water? We can stop at the dairy on the way and you can get your chocolate milk."

"Okay, Gramma," I said.

While my grandmother backed the Oldsmobile out of the garage, I stood on the porch, listening to my mother and Lolly again.

"And so he said, he said to me, Well, come on, Adele, you've been married before. Let's try and see if we like it. Like it? I said, Like it? Well, what happens if I don't?"

My mother and Lolly bent over, hugging their knees, laughing. A hawk drifted in the sky.

"Why is that funny?" I said. "Will someone please tell me what's so funny about that?"

They looked at each other and laughed some more. I started walking to my grandmother's car, my hands trembling at my sides.

"It's something that's only funny for grown-ups," my mother called.

I slammed the door and then turned, smiled at my grandmother. The tin cans we used for watering at the cemetery rattled in the backseat. I was glad we were going because I didn't want my grandmother to stay inside all day and get pale and soft like an old person. She thought she was taking me for my benefit. Neither of us imagined that we were the one in any trouble.

Once, when he was still at home with us, my father tried to mow the lawn. In the morning, he left from the back door, with his black case of vacuum cleaners and vacuum cleaner attachments. My father was a salesman then. He loaded the trunk of the car, our Valiant, the color of root beer Popsicles.

The lawn mower was a piece of furniture, orange metal like a tractor. It was the kind you sat on and rode. Grass sprayed off in a fountain from one side.

My cousin Benny stood on the driveway, bare-legged, fidgeting by the lawn mower. Even as a child, he was always moving. When he had to wait for us, he'd go out in the backyard, with a stick as tall as he was, spinning, and you could run up to him and clap your hands and he wouldn't hear. He was blond as an unlit wick.

"You wanna ride?" Benny's sneaker stuck up against the orange metal, bracing to pull the cord. Jimmy Measey walked out of the garage carrying a tin can of oil. It was still on the ground, empty, after.

"Me?" My father's fingers opened on his chest, lightly. He'd been in Wisconsin five years. In Egypt, where he came from, they had no lawns.

Just then the metal of the screen door rang. My grandmother walked outside with a hoe and a white cotton glove. She wore men's clothes, overalls, plaid shirt, a different plaid scarf. Since her husband died, she'd begun to get up early and she had taken to wearing his clothes.

My father wavered. Jimmy Measey told me later he was trying to impress my grandmother.

"Sure," my father said. He looked down at Benny, touched the chalky yellow of his hair. My father was always sorry I wasn't blond. I looked like him, not my mother. "Would you like to ride along?"

"Can't. Only one person at a time."

"All right."

"Here's the gas, here's the brake," Jimmy Measey explained, swiveling the wheel.

Benny snapped the cord and my father shot off, his backbone a ruler, taking the ride hard. He went in one straight line. All of a sudden, the velvety grass turned bumpy. My father's hand waved, the arm flapping back behind him.

"Hey, get off, slam the brake!" Benny's yell scratched a sharp red line on the sky. I saw it years, a long time, after.

"Jump off," Jimmy Measey said, running after the lawn mower. "Jump."

No one understood what my father was yelling, and he went through the hedge, crashing corn stalks. Finally he fell off. Silky corn hair stuck on his collar when Jimmy Measey caught up to him, on the ground. The mower was still going, towards the barn. Benny chased it. My mother started out of the house then, her high heels catching in the grass.

"I don't know why you didn't just slug on the brake." Jimmy Measey demonstrated, crushing a corncob under his boot, even though my father was walking, towards the house and my mother. Jimmy Measey felt impatient to go, he was late. He liked to drive to Bob's Big Boy on the highway before work and order coffee and unbuttered toast. He liked to sit at the counter and hear the other voices, familiar and unfamiliar at the same time. He'd made a rule for himself, to be in the water softener store by ten. Jimmy Measey was a salesman, too. But he never left. He might have looked at cars on the highway overpass, wishing he were a stranger in one of the small windows, going west. But even in imagination, he always returned, back to Lime Kiln Road.

"What have they done to you?" my mother screamed, but my

father shrugged her off his elbow and walked ahead fast and alone.

Benny rode the mower in, his sneakers bouncing up off the sides. Benny loved machines.

Jimmy Measey's hands rocked my shoulders, tilting me back. "You miss your dad, don't you? You miss your daddy, I can feel that in you." We stood outside, by a fire, burning leaves. Jimmy Measey was behind me, I felt all his weight. Benny stood there too, impatient to move, his blue sneaker pawing the ground. Smoke poured into the sky.

My eyes closed, I was dizzy. When I opened them again, we were all still standing, watching the light black ghosts of leaves escape, up into the air. Across the road, a light came on in the kitchen. Old Mrs. Brozek set her table. From where we were, it all looked like wax. Jimmy Measey put his hands over my ears.

"See that hole?" He pointed my head. His fingers pressed into my temples, as if they were denting them. "That's where your dad went through the hedge."

It was an ordinary hole, just a lapse in the dark bushes.

"He's yelling away something in Egyptian, whatever they talk over there. You couldn't understand it. I tried to stop him."

I felt the fat jiggle on Jimmy Measey's belly, warm and deep.

"Practically needed a lasso. He went right through the hedge."

Our oak tree was over a hundred years old. We'd been raking for days. That year the leaves were the size of Benny's and my hands. We'd knelt on the ground, matching them. From the noise in the wind and the silvery outlines of branches swaying, there was something enormous above us. There were still about a million leaves.

We stood there watching leaves collapse and fizzle into light black ash. A rusty sunset streaked the sky for miles, making our houses look small.

"Whenever I look out my sliding glass doors and see that hole, I think of your dad," Jimmy said. "I wonder where he is now."

I'd been staring at the oak tree, the patches of the sky through the fists of dry, curled leaves. They rattled like brown paper bags being crumpled.

"Dad," Benny said, his sneaker rubbing the soft lawn. "When are we going to eat?"

All of a sudden, I thought of my mother and wondered where she was. I left them there and ran inside. My grandmother stood up to her elbows in flour. Flour seemed suspended all through the kitchen, mixing in the soft yellow air. I found my mother sitting on the bathroom rug in a shortie flannel nightgown, tweezing. She was holding a small round mirror up to her face.

"What is it, Honey," she said, studying her left eyebrow.

"Uncle Jimmy asked if I still missed my dad."

Now she was doing the lip. She pulled it down over her top teeth.

"Oh, Honey, you didn't even know your dad. You were too young to really know him. How could you miss him?" She sighed. "When people ask you that, you just say, No, not really, I'm very close to my mom. That's what you say."

"Okay," I said and still stood there.

"I'm the one who misses my dad," she said. "But you never had that real total love. Maybe you're lucky, you know, maybe it'll be better for you. You'll never know enough to miss it."

I walked into Jimmy Measey's house without knocking. I let the screen door slam. Jimmy Measey sat in the kitchen, holding a beer can beaded with water.

"Is Benny here?" I asked.

He lifted the can of beer and took a drink. Then he looked at me, grinning, and held up his hand. "I hit him," he said. "I smacked him a good one." For an instant, he seemed to be licking his lip. Then he swung his chair to face the wall. "He's in the bathroom," he said.

Benny stood on the plush-covered toilet seat examining his cheek in the mirror. There was a big red handprint on his nose and over the left side of his face. He carefully dabbed cold cream on the indentation. He looked solemn as if he were adjusting, as if it would never go away. His mother stood helplessly below, holding up the open jar of cream.

"Jimmy hit him," she said, shaking her head.

Benny turned around to look at me. "I was bad," he said.

I was afraid of Jimmy Measey, but sometimes he was different. He took Benny and me for a walk down to the railroad tracks and when Benny ran ahead and got a milkweed stem, saying "Lookit this, Dad," I wanted to remind Benny of the red handprint and, at the same time, I wished Jimmy was my father too.

Before we'd left the house, my grandmother tied a wool scarf on me, her knuckles hurting under my chin as she made the knot. Benny didn't have to wear a scarf because Jimmy Measey thought we didn't need them, but he let my grandmother put mine on me. I was the women's and Benny was his.

Near the ditch, Jimmy Measey took my hand. His hand felt dry and hard, like a foot. Down the tracks, two kids balanced on one rail, their arms out to the sides. We knew who they were; they were Grilings.

Jimmy Measey rummaged in his pants pocket and took out a dime and handed it to me. "Here." He looked down the tracks. I thought he wanted me to give it to Grilings, so I started running on the coals.

"Annie, no."

"I'll do it, Dad." Benny stooped and left the dime on the rail. The kids were still a long ways down the tracks in what was left of the sun.

We heard from my father in the middle of winter three years after he left. There was a long-distance phone call from Las Vegas and it was him.

"We're going to Disneyland!" my mother said, covering the mouthpiece with her hand. Into the phone, she said she'd take me out of school. We'd fly to Las Vegas and then the three of us would drive west to Disneyland. I didn't recognize the voice when my mother held out the phone. It sounded like someone I didn't know.

I held on to the edges of the kitchen table. I wanted to go to school the next day. I shrugged and wouldn't touch the phone.

"You'll know him when you see him," she said.

We waited three days for our summer linen dresses to be dry-cleaned. "It's going to be hot," my mother warned. "Scorching," she added, with a smile. It was snowing dry powder when we left; we saw only white outside the airplane window. Halfway there, we changed in the tiny bathroom, from our winter clothes to sleeveless dresses and patent leather thongs. My mother brushed blush on our pale winter shoulders. With her eye pencil, I drew freckles on my nose. It still felt cool in the plane, but my mother promised it would be hot on the ground.

It was. The air swirled with visible heat and dirt. A woman walked across the lobby with a scarf tied around her chest for a shirt.

My mother spotted my father in the crowd and, holding my hand, pulled me towards him. We pretended I recognized him, too. He looked like an ordinary man. He wore tight black slacks, a brown jacket and black leather slip-on shoes. His chin stuck out from his face, giving him an eager look.

He had our brown Valiant parked outside and my mother sat in the front seat. We passed motel swimming pools and the tinge of sky hung over the water like a line of dirt on the rim of a sleeve. My father parked in front of a low pink stucco apartment building. When we walked up, three men crowded on a porch, leaning against the iron banister.

"He told us you had long hair," one said.

"You look like your dad."

"A real brunette."

"She's prettier than her dad."

My father smiled and the gaps between his teeth made him look unintentionally sad, like a jack-o-lantern. He touched my hair, looking down at it, and I knew he was proud of me. I loved him blindly then, the feeling darkening over everything, but it passed.

"Don't you want to introduce your friends to me, too?" My mother pushed our suitcase onto the porch. She smiled the smile she practiced in front of the mirror, sucking her cheeks in to make her bones seem higher.

The men wore V-necked T-shirts and their skin was dark like my father's. The way they bent and leaned and shuffled while they stood made them seem dangerous, like teenagers. My father introduced each man and each man smiled. He said they were his roommates. Then he gave me a present: a package of six different colored cotton headbands. They made me think of Easter eggs. I held the package carefully and didn't tear the cellophane open.

My father worked as a waiter in a hotel restaurant. My mother and I went there for supper, our first night. We ate slowly, watching him balance plates on the inside of his arm. He sat down with us at the end of our meal, while my mother sipped her coffee. He crossed one leg over the other, smoking luxuriously, when my mother leaned closer and whispered in my ear.

"When are we going to Disneyland?" I said, saying what she said to say but somehow knowing it was wrong.

My father put out his cigarette and looked up at my mother. "You're late," he said. "It's Friday. You're four days late."

My mother pushed her hair back with her hand. "Well, we were busy. There were people we had to see. We canceled plenty as it was." My mother could hold her own. "So, when are we going?" she asked gamely.

"When you didn't come Monday, I lost the money I'd saved." He said this matter-of-factly, looking around the room.

"In four days, how?"

"On the tables."

My mother's voice gathered, "You, you can't do this to her."

Back at my father's apartment, they sent me outside to the porch. There was a book of matches on the ground and I lit them, one by one, scratching them against the concrete and then dropping them in the dirt when the flames came too close to my fingers. Finally it was quiet. My father opened the screen door and I went in.

They'd put sheets on the living room couch for me. They both undressed in my father's room. My mother looked over her shoulder, while she unzipped her shift. Then she came out to say good night. She looked down at me hard, as if she were trying to judge whether I was young enough to forget things I didn't understand. She sighed, finally deciding it wouldn't matter.

"Now, don't say anything to Gramma that I slept in his room. But there's nowhere else to go here." She rubbed my back absentmindedly for a second.

The next morning my father and I woke up early. We walked to the hotel coffee shop and sat on stools at the counter. I was afraid to ask for anything, so I said I wasn't hungry. My father ordered a soft-boiled egg for himself. We didn't talk. I watched his eyes catch on the uniformed waitress, the coffeepot tilting from her hand, a white purse on the other end of the counter. He seemed happy.

He whistled the refrain to his song, a song we all believed would be a hit. I sang along the words to myself. "Oh, Ringo Starr on top of my tree, Oh, Santa bring the Beatles to-oo me." Ringo was my mother's favorite Beatle. "He's so homely he's cute," she always said, clicking her fingers against her thighs when she and Lolly danced in the den.

The egg came in a white coffee cup. He chopped it with the edge of a spoon, asking if I'd ever tasted a four-minute egg. I ate a spoonful and I loved it. No other egg was ever that good. I told my father, hoping we could share it. But he slid the whole cup down, the spoon in it, without looking at me and signaled the waitress for another egg.

Walking back to the apartment, he kicked sand into the air. He turned to me suddenly, as if he'd just then thought of something.

"How do you like school?" he asked.

"Fine," I said. "I like it."

"That's good," he said. Our conversations were always like that, like lighting single matches.

I sat on a towel by the hotel pool while my parents tried to win back our money for Disneyland. When my mother rubbed lotion into my shoulders, she pointed to a woman sleeping on her back, with a washcloth covering her eyes. A child squatted next to her head, brushing the woman's hair with a toy brush. A boy, asleep next to them, had a white bar of soap hanging from a braided cord around his neck; his fingers moved over the soap, as if he were dreaming on it.

"Those kids are in the shows at night. Look at that," my mother said. "The kids make the money and the mother just lounges."

Later, when my parents went into the casino, the little girl pulled the woman's hair.

"Shhhh," the woman said. "And let him sleep. He was up late. Go in the water, Honey."

But the boy woke up and ran onto the diving board, the muscles in his stomach jiggling like a bowl of shaken water. The sound of his yell made the woman sit up and lift the washcloth off her face.

His feet flapped on the surface of the water, then he stopped and shook. His mother and sister and I all stared but he didn't seem to notice us. He seemed to be splashing with other, invisible bodies in the pool.

I watched the boy most of the afternoon, hoping he would look at me. He stood gurgling water, his head tilting up, soaping himself with bubbles from the bar around his neck. His mother would pull to a sitting position every once in a while, taking her sunglasses down from the top of her head, and smile, watching him, look nervously over to his sister; then, having counted each of her children, she would sigh, sinking back to her towel, opening a magazine over her face.

I waded in the shallow end. My mother said I could play with these children so I knew I could, but I didn't know how to start. It seemed too hard. I closed my eyes, tumbling through the water, and thought that when I went home I could write letters to them. Months later, back at my grandmother's house, times when I wasn't even thinking of my father, I felt like writing a letter to that boy. But I didn't even know his name.

"So we'll go to Disneyland next trip," my father said, walking me back from the pool. There were no lawns in front of the parked trailers, but the sand was raked and bordered with rows of rocks. My father's black slip-on shoes were scuffed. He was holding my hand but not looking at me.

"When?"

Suddenly, I wanted the name of a month, not to see Disneyland but to see him. Taking long steps, trying to match his pace, I wanted to say that I didn't care about Disneyland. I dared myself to talk after one more, two more, three more steps, all the way to the apartment. But I never said it. All I did was hold his hand tighter and tighter.

"I don't know," he said, letting my arm drop when we came to the porch.

On the plane home, I held the package of headbands in my lap, tracing each one through the cellophane. My mother turned and looked out the window.

"I work," she said finally, "and I pay for your school and your books and your skates and your lessons."

She picked up the package of headbands and then dropped it back on my lap. "A seventy-nine-cent package of headbands," she said.

I hid behind a tree, watching my grandmother walk down the driveway, the back corner of her scarf whipping in the wind. The red metal flag stood up on the mailbox. I watched her shuffle through the mail and shove it into her pocket. She didn't hold any of the letters in her hand or look at one for longer; that meant there was nothing unusual. Then I ran up to her.

I thought I still wanted to go to California, but later. My blood ticked from running, the damp air touched my temples, the wind was a battle in my sleeves. Twigs lifted off the ground as we headed towards the backyard, where the wash was still moving on the lines. I helped my grandmother gather the sheets, collecting clothespins in our mouths and pockets, to carry them in before the rain. The sheets that night felt stiff on our beds, smelling of soil and cold water. When it started to rain, we hauled out our buckets to collect in the yard, under the eaves troughs. My grandmother believed rainwater made our houseplants grow. At night, we listened to the sounds on the roof. It was a different life from my father's, from what we imagined was California. I didn't know whether I watched for the mail because I wanted a letter from my father, or because I was afraid and hoped he would stay away, so we could keep what we had.

At Bob's Big Boy, one day in the summer, my mother and I pressed together in the phone booth and emptied her purse out on the metal ledge. There were hundreds of scraps of paper, pencils, leaking pens, scuffed makeup tubes, brushes woven with a fabric of lint and hair, a bra, and finally, my mother's brown leather address book, with the pages falling out. We wanted to call my father in Las Vegas. It was already over a year since we'd flown there. The number was written, carefully, in brown ink.

My mother dialed, saying Hold your thumbs, here's hoping. She said a quick, mumbled Hail Mary, rounding off the four points of the cross to a touch on her forehead and three quick taps on her chest. I scraped all the coins from the bottom of her purse. When the operator came on to say how much the call cost, my mother lifted me up and I dropped in the money. We both waited, our mouths together by the receiver. A sleeping male voice answered.

"Yeah?"

My mother asked if my father was there.

"No," the man said. "Wrong number. Nobody here by that name."

"Well, do you know where he went? He used to live there, we saw him there."

"Not since I've been here."

"Would one of your roommates know?"

"I've been here the longest."

"Oh," my mother said. "All right."

We called information in Las Vegas then and gave my father's ame, but they had nothing listed.

□

Sunday was the day my mother took over the house. My grand-mother woke up early and drove to church. Everyone on our road went to church except us. In the morning, when our neighbors were driving into town, the women holding the clasps of their purses in their laps, Lolly drove on the same highway, in the other direction, with the car radio on, and a box of warm cinnamon rolls open on the passenger seat.

She went to Krim's, Bay City's best bakery, early, before the after-church crowd and bought twelve of the large soft rolls for just us. They were expensive and we loved the extravagance. By the time Lolly stamped to our back door, my mother was up and around the kitchen singing "I'm Gonna Wash That Man Right Out of My Hair" and the pitcher of dark, thick orange juice was slowly filling. It was my job to squeeze the oranges.

Lolly tore open a new carton of cream and walked out to the porch. "So did you try it?" she asked my mother.

With my grandmother gone, they didn't even send me inside when they talked. We ate slowly, on our second rolls each. My mother and Lolly sipped their coffee. They gave me a mugful just to warm my hands. I took small drinks and it tasted like dirt. I was trying to learn to like it.

"Why do you ask?" my mother said.

"I just thought, it seemed last night on the ice, there were some, shall-we-say, new jumps?"

"Well, yes. Mmhmm. I did try it."

"You did?"

I was bouncing my slipper on the edge of my foot, over the side of the porch, and it fell. The ground felt cold when I hopped down to get it.

"Where did you go?"

"Nowhere. Just here."

"In the bedroom, with the troops upstairs? You're kidding. With Mama in the house?"

"We watched Carson. Everyone was asleep."

"And?"

My mother sighed, blowing on her coffee and looking out over the yard. The grass seemed faded and the fall light was whiter than in summer. "It was fine. It'll be fine," she said. Sometimes my mother seemed older.

Lolly scanned her face as if there was something different she couldn't quite put her finger on. Finally, she looked at me as if I knew. My mother seemed slow and collected, it seemed she'd come to some resolution. When the train passed and her coffee cup chattered in its saucer, she looked down and smiled, as if the noise were music.

"So what about California?"

"I don't know," my mother said, looking straight at Lolly, holding her cup in the air, "but with a man like that, who can? Who does know?"

"You haven't heard anything?"

"Not a thing."

"And you don't think you will?"

"Oh, I think so. I'm sure of it, in fact. Someday, he'll have a record out or they'll cast him in a movie and he'll come into some money and, then, I'm sure he'll call us. But who knows when?"

"I know what you mean."

"And she's growing up. I can't just stay here forever." My mother nodded at me.

As soon as she said that, I wished I was younger. I fell out onto the grass and started doing cartwheels. My hair knocked against my cheeks. I walked on my hands.

"Did you see, Mom, did you see me?"

My mother and Lolly both sat with their coffee cups in their laps, not talking.

"Do it again, Honey," my mother said.

Skating the next time, I didn't get off the ice. When the music stopped, my mother and Lolly stepped delicately onto rubber mats at the exit, my mother taking a few last breaths, as if she were leaving precious air. The Zamboni, a machine that cleared the ice, already stood growling at the other end of the rink. I took one last run around the ice, skating as fast as I could, my arms flailing. The Zamboni followed close behind because the man who drove it believed I needed to be taught a lesson.

It was like being chased by an animal; I heard the thing behind me, I couldn't tell how near it was. I was ready for its paw on my back, to tip me over, any second. My mother stood at the exit yelling and I saw her but I couldn't hear. The Zamboni behind me, I raced, running on my tips, trying not to fall forward because if I did I'd be caught underneath the machinery. I raced for my life, believing I could die and that if I tripped and fell and the Zamboni ran me over, it would be fair, because I shouldn't have been on the ice.

Maybe I wanted to die. I ended up ramming against the barrier at the exit, falling hard into the wood.

And just then, my mother and Lolly looked at each other, turned and walked downstairs. They refused to acknowledge me; they wouldn't encourage such behavior. Besides, my mother felt embarrassed because of Ted. She wanted Ted to think she could make me mind.

I had some pride. Instead of running after them, I stood at the exit, kicking sheets of ice off my blades. Another mother, there to pick up her children, hugged me against her belly, a strong arm pulling me in. She whispered, "Tell me, does your ma hear anything from your daddy?"

"I don't know," I said.

"Awww," Mrs. Bayer whispered, rubbing down my hair.

For a moment, but only for a moment, I let my eyes close.

"You must miss your daddy," she said, her face dropping into a loose expression of pity.

I pulled away. "No."

Taking the skates off on the bench was pure joy. My work was done. My shoes seemed sizes too big for my feet and my ankles felt filled with air. Walking over the thick rubber mats, my body seemed to start at my shins. I was light. I'd done what I could do.

We heard from my father again two years after my mom married Ted. He called my grandmother first. He didn't know about Ted or the house on Carriage Court. He seemed to suppose we stayed

the same the years between his phone calls. He told my mother
he lived in Reno, with a new wife. So, apparently, he still hadn't
made it to California. He told my mother he wanted to take me to
Disneyland.

"Well, I don't know. Do you think we'll really get there this
time?" She snorted into the phone.

"Oh, no, you don't," my mother said then, after huffs and
pauses, impatient sighs. "Nothing doing. I'm not taking her out
of school to fly out there alone. Either I come too or she's not
going."

My father wanted to have just me. Finally, he agreed to send
the money for two tickets. Then, she covered the receiver with
her hand. "Ann, his new wife has an eleven-year-old granddaughter. She's never seen Disneyland and they thought they
might bring her along. Would you like that or would you rather it
be just us?" She whispered, "If you'd rather just us, then say so."

"I'd rather be just us," I said.

My mother took her hand off. "She feels she'd rather not have
another child there." I hated the way it sounded like that, loud. I
hopped around the kitchen in a circle and yelled, "I don't care. I
don't care who comes. Bring her."

"Don't worry, I'm sure he won't bring her," my mother said. We
stood in front of the open refrigerator, eating slices of cold châteaubriand. That way there were no dishes to wash. "What do you
think, a granddaughter your age. His wife must be as old as
Gramma."

"Why couldn't I go alone?"

"Honey, there's a lot of things you just don't know, okay? Believe me, I'm a lot older and I know this man."

She waited and I didn't say anything. I had the salt shaker. I
shook on salt.

"Ann, he could get you on a plane to Egypt in a couple hours
and who'd ever know? Yeah, you didn't think of that, did you?
And let me tell you, you wouldn't like it. They'd get you married
and pregnant in no time. Over there, they educate the boys, not

the girls. There's no such thing as a high school girl. Your dad was just darn lucky."

My mother and father wanted to take me out of school and fly to Disneyland right away, but Uta, the new wife, insisted we wait for Easter vacation. That gave my mother and me three weeks to shop. We bought new dresses and my first stockings and white gloves.

Then my mother read about something she wanted: a new Sony portable color television. A jewel. They were small; she showed me the picture she cut out of the magazine. She wanted a white one, she felt sure they came in white. The article said they wouldn't be available in the States for another year, but my mother thought they'd have them in California. "I'm sure of it," she said, "it's right across the water from Japan. I bet they'll be all over the stores."

My mother had stopped telling Ted about the things she wanted, because he tried to get them for her and he made mistakes. For Christmas, he'd bought her a console record player instead of a stereo with component parts. He surprised her with a dishwasher, just after she'd bought hand-painted plates. She shuddered talking about what he'd come up with if she told him about the Sony: a big, cabinet-sized Zenith or RCA.

She picked me up after school and we drove downtown to Shreve's. We browsed on the electronics floor, watching all the televisions. They had Sony black-and-whites but no colors. All the colors were huge things, whole varnished cabinets.

"Can I help you," a young woman said, her hands in the pockets of the brown store smock.

"Oh, no, thank you." My mother nudged me as we walked to the parking lot. "We'll have the first one in Bay City."

Ted walked us outside to the aluminum steps of the plane. It was a windy, wet afternoon. My mother hooked my hair behind my ears and then put her hand on her own head. She wanted to go inside the plane, so we wouldn't get mussed, but Ted just stood there and so we waited.

His smile seemed different to me that day, higher on the left side, bent, not like a zipper.

Our airport wasn't large. You could see runways going into the fields and around the perimeters; behind the blinking lights, trees started again, birches and pine. The inside terminal was small, too, with one coffee shop where high school girls worked as waitresses.

"Well, you have fun," Ted said. He laid one arm on my shoulder and his other hand reached under the back of my mother's hair.

She sighed. "Well, I don't know if it'll be fun, I doubt it, but necessary. And it'll be fun for her, you're right, for her it should be fun."

My father sat with his legs crossed, staring as if he wasn't seeing anything, in a plastic, molded airport chair. A woman stood behind him, with a hand on his shoulder. Her other hand was cocked over her eyebrows, as if she was looking for something far away. It seemed they'd been waiting a long time.

"John, is that them?" I heard her say. But John was not my father's name.

Then my mother waved, he stood up and we all met. The granddaughter stood there, too, a girl whose legs were so thin it looked as if something might be seriously wrong. She kept shaking my hand up and down.

The five of us were going to eat right away in a restaurant in Beverly Hills, Uta told us. She had already made the reservation. But first, my mother wanted to use the ladies' room. She asked me to come along.

"Don't feel bad about the granddaughter," she said, in front of the mirror. She brushed out our hair. "Because I'm sure *he* didn't want to bring her. *She* insisted. Did you see how *she's* the one with the money. *She* made the reservation. *She* had the camera around *her* neck. It's like she's the man and he's the woman. So don't feel bad."

They had a rented car and my father drove. He and Uta sat in the front seat. My mother had to climb in the back with the granddaughter and me. Her high heels made it hard to balance, getting in. She put her hands on her lap and smiled right away and you could tell she didn't like this.

"So, Hisham, do you still have the Valiant?"

He chuckled a little. "No, I had to get rid of that."

I thought of our Valiant in a Nevada dump somewhere. Benny was good with cars. Even though he was only eleven years old, he drove up and down Lime Kiln Road in his dad's truck. I'd been to the dump in Bay City where they put the old cars; Griling ran it, walking around with a stick. The machine dump covered two sides of a hill and a long valley. It wasn't just cars, there were old wash machines and refrigerators, their doors open, and warm from the sun. Cats lived on the empty wire shelves.

"I'm calling myself John now," my father said, glancing over at Uta. Uta nodded, looking down at her purse.

"John," my mother mulled. "How come?"

My father shrugged. "People recognize it. They know how to spell it." He laughed. "I'm applying to be a citizen."

Uta took a small white box from her purse and gave it to my father to give me; it was a gold bracelet, with one charm, a tree with turquoise leaves.

"Well, it's real, all right," my mother said, examining it later under the lamp. We stayed at the Disneyland Hotel, my mother and me in one room, them in another. She showed me the tiny stamp of 19K printed on the gold. "It must have been expensive. But it's gaudy, you know, she's got money, but no taste. That's one thing about us, Ann, we have taste. We can go anywhere and they'd think, Hey, what a great-looking mother and daughter. And that's class."

For years, I'd watched "The Wonderful World of Disney" on TV. Sometimes in bed, before I went to sleep, I imagined us—my father with more hair than he had now, my mother's swooped up on top of her head, held with a diamond pin, and me, blond like my mother and prettier than I am—in our old brown car, with rounded fenders, floating down a long canal. A fairy with a wand of flies' wings perched just at our backs, touching the tops of our heads. I'd feel her fingers on my spine and lean against her knee, but I wouldn't turn back to look at her, for fear she wouldn't be there. The brown car drifted slowly and trees above us bent down with the weight of their fruit. When we touched it, it was ours, the way, when you cup your hand outside the window of a moving car, you imagine something solid and then you feel it. We passed animals on the banks of the canal and at one turn, I saw an elephant carrying the Las Vegas circus children dressed in leopard skins and sequins. The lighted castle stood in the distance. The banks of the canal were a simple yellow, the trees green, the sky and water blue. Disneyland looked like the crayoned city I'd drawn on my grandmother's floor when I was a child and we floated in the Valiant, farther and farther in.

I'd wanted to see Disneyland for so long and now I was there. All day the five of us bought things. My father and my mother kept peering down into my face and saying, "Having fun?" I felt like they could see all the things I'd imagined to myself, the private things I'd pictured with my eyes closed, in the dark. I'd shrug and say, "Yeah," and look at the granddaughter. I turned out glad she was there. The two of us got to pick out the restaurants we wanted and what we wanted to order in each one. Nobody talked about money. Uta always paid.

They all kept looking at me and asking what I wanted to do next. I shrugged and said, "I don know." But that made them nervous. My father walked with his hands in his pockets, looking high up, towards the sky. Then he talked to my mother about cutting my hair.

"We've thought of it, but I think it's better long," she said.

He seemed to agree. "No, she'd have to be thinner if it were short."

"Sometimes, I think about bangs," my mother volunteered.

On Saturday, Uta rented a limousine to drive us to a famous restaurant. It was on top of a tall building so we could see lights of the whole city below us. One side was pure black and my father said that was the ocean.

My father spoke French to the waiter—I watched my mother and Uta look at him and sink back in their chairs. There were some things women couldn't do and those were the things my father was good at. My father ordered for all of us, something I'd never heard of, tournedos.

When Uta went to the ladies' room, my mother laughed, leaning over so her face came close to my father's in the reddish light. She picked up the candleholder in her hands and looked up at my father.

"John, I'm trying to see you as a John," she said.

He laughed, moving the salt shaker. The granddaughter looked at me. "When you go home, we can write letters to each other and be pen pals. Will you write to me?"

As I watched my mother laughing, I wasn't sure if it was a real laugh, from happiness, or if it was for our TV.

I was full before my tournedos came. But they were steak and delicious. I asked my father if I could wrap them in a napkin and take it back in a doggy bag. He stamped his cigarette out and looked at my mother, smiling. "No, Ann," he said. "Not here."

My mother joined in quickly, "Oh, no, Honey, not in a place like this."

"Is she yours?" a man asked.

My mother answered, "She sure is, she's my little one." We stood in a dark hallway. Uta was paying someone to find our coats.

"A very pretty child," the man said. He was short and bald, fat, in a dark suit.

"Yes, isn't she? And she's nice, too. She's a real nice girl, aren't you?" My mother stroked my hair.

"No," I said, looking down.

The fat man was not alone. He lifted a silver stole off a woman's shoulders and followed her into the restaurant. My mother bent down to me. "Do you know who that was? *That* was Robert Wise, the producer of *Sound of Music*. Did you see the way he looked at you? You're going to make it, kid. I can't believe it."

"How do you know it was him?"

"Believe me. I just know."

In the lobby, my father spoke to the headwaiter. He took a salt shaker from his left pocket and a matching pepper shaker from his right and gave them to me. "A little memento of tonight."

I said thank you and held them the way he held them, in my coat pockets, and looked up, overly grateful. My father always had nerve.

My mother just smiled grimly and thanked Uta and my father, as we crowded in the backseat of the limousine, my mother's heel catching on the carpet. We felt cowed by their money, both of us.

I worried about the New Sony. We were leaving tomorrow and we hadn't done anything. All day, I brought up the subject of televisions, but the only one who answered was the granddaughter, who told me that her favorite program was "Gilligan's Island" and that we could write to each other what our new favorite programs were in fall when the listings came out.

And it wasn't only my mother, it was me, too. When I slipped my hand in my father's, I wasn't sure why. It seemed easier to have another reason. Otherwise, we felt like fools.

My mother and father and I seemed more like a family that trip than we'd ever been and that was because of Uta, because she thought of things. She took pictures of me with my dad. My mother and father each went along with it, but they didn't seem to like her ideas. They did things because they had to.

It was Uta's idea that my father and I should meet before dinner the last night, so we'd have a chance to be alone. My mother shrugged as Uta suggested it, as if to say, what for, but she didn't have the nerve to do anything. In our room, before I was supposed to go down, she brushed my hair out across my back.

I was nervous. I wasn't used to being alone with my father. I didn't know what to say to him.

"I'll bet they've got one right here," my mother said. "In Disneyland." We both knew what she was talking about.

"I haven't seen any in the stores."

"I think I saw one," she said, winking. "A white one."

"Where?" I'd been looking all week. It was the only thing I'd known to do.

"In one of those little shops downstairs."

"Which one?"

"I'm not sure, exactly. But I saw it."

"What should I do?" I knew I had to learn everything.

My mother shrugged. It seemed easy for her. "Tell him you're saving for it. He'll probably just buy it for you. Suck in your cheeks," she said, brushing blush on my face. She was having fun.

I didn't want to leave the room. I wanted to close my eyes and keep feeling the spokes of the hairbrush on my back. My mother gave me a short push out the door. I tried to remember everything.

I saw my father's back first. He was standing by the candy counter in the hotel drugstore. Every time I saw him I went through a gradual series of adjustments, reconciling the picture I held in my imagination to his appearance, as I recognized him. He was almost bald now. He was heavier than he had once been. His chin still shot out, but it no longer made him look eager. He seemed mildly dissatisfied, bored. His lower lip seemed to hang a fraction too far out, it didn't match his upper lip. He was buying a roll of Life Savers, peeling the wrapping paper off one end. He peeled it in a string.

Then he saw me and smiled. "Would you like anything?" he asked, tilting his head to indicate the rows of candy on the counter.

I thought for one wild moment. I could abandon the plan and say yes. Yes I want a candy bar. Two candy bars. He'd buy me two of the best candy bars there and I could stand and eat them sloppily, all the while gazing up at him. If I smiled, he would smile. He would bend down and dab the chocolate from my mouth with a handkerchief moist with his own saliva.

But I knew I'd remember. And then I would hate my best memory because it would prove that my father could fake love or that love could end, or, worst of all, that love could exist weakly, without the power to dominate a life, his life. And I couldn't believe he'd write me letters, I just couldn't believe it. I thought of my grandmother, years and years, walking out to get the mail.

"No," I said, "I'm saving up my money."

"What?" My father smiled down. He was still unraveling the paper from his Life Savers. He hadn't heard me. I had another chance.

"I'm saving my money for a new Sony portable color television," I blurted.

He had been looking at me and he stopped. He didn't move but he lifted his eyes up to something over my shoulder. Then he glanced at his watch and scanned the drugstore.

"Oh," he said.

I think at that moment he relinquished me to my mother. He was humming "Raindrops Keep Falling on My Head"; he'd been humming all weekend—other people's songs.

On the way home, neither of us mentioned it.

"Look at the mountains," I said.

"Yeah, mmhmm." My mother wouldn't even move her head.

It's funny how we were. The bracelet my father and Uta gave me turned out to be worth money, more than what the televisions cost when they came out a year later. It would have taken a miracle to convince us.

When the plane landed, we didn't even call Ted. We took a taxi home, my mother clicking her nails against the window. When we were inside, she collapsed on the blue-green couch and looked around disapprovingly. Our suitcases lay scattered on the floor.

"You know what he told me when we left? He said after all he did you didn't even say thank you. He said he'd open doors and you'd just walk through, he'd offer to buy you candy and you just said no. Not even no thank you. Just no. I've taught you how to act and what do you do there? Nothing."

The days with my father flashed like cards. I hadn't said no-thank-you.

"And here you use big words all the time and complex sentences. You should hear yourself joking around with Ted. You didn't say ONE BIG WORD the whole time we were there. I couldn't even stand listening to you. Un-huh. Yeah-uh. I don know. You didn't say one smart thing in front of him. Let me tell you, Kid, you sounded dumb."

"My name is Ann," I said.

She turned over and sighed. It sounded like air coming out of a balloon. "Sure, Ann. Call yourself whatever you want, I don't care. Go out and play. Go out and play with your kids."

I opened the refrigerator door and looked. Ted had made a châteaubriand by himself and sliced it. He'd stacked the rectangles neatly on a plate. Behind me, my mother turned over and knocked the cushions onto the floor. Her shoes dropped, one at a time.

"And you didn't even smile. Here, you're sharp and funny. There you slumped and looked down. And you talk about getting on television. You really just looked like any other kid around here. Well, fine. It's a good thing we're back because I can see now that this is just where you belong. Here with all the mill workers' kids. Well, good."

I walked outside without a jacket, looking for one of my friends. On Carriage Court, kids didn't knock on each other's doors. We just went outside and waited. But no one was there. It was a gray, cold day and it looked like it might rain. I was walking when a mother, from down the street, honked. She rolled down her window and asked if I wanted a ride. I got in the station wagon though I didn't know where I was going. She didn't even ask me. She just dropped me off at the skating rink. By that time it had started raining. The guard nodded as I walked in and from the lobby I saw Ted on the ice. Just then, I realized it was a workday, a schoolday, Monday. That was why none of the kids came outside. Ted was giving a lesson, bending down and holding a woman's ankle, pointing her foot into a figure eight.

I walked to his office and took the key for the rental room, from under a certain bench. The rental room was small and covered with cubbyholes, with the sizes of skates painted in yellow. I took a pair of knicked, worn gray fives, with the brown rental stripe in back. When I'd skated, I had my own good skates. In these, the ankles were broken down.

I put them on and ran on points, wobbling because of the skates. Then I stepped onto the ice and skated; I crashed into Ted and held his sweater. He put a hand over my head and told the student something I didn't hear. When I pulled myself off, the student was gone. I opened my eyes and looked up at Ted; it was different than with my father. I couldn't bury my head in Ted's sweater and forget. Here, I knew exactly where I was. Ted was still Ted, standing in front of me. I didn't expect him to understand.

"You're back," he said. That was all. Ted would never know, unless I could find the words to explain myself, one by one. It seemed too hard.

I looked across the empty rink. The ice was gray blue, the hockey lines pale underneath like bruises. My father was gone for good and Ted was just Ted, another man in the world who had nothing to do with me.

"Would you like me to teach you to do loops?" he asked. His teeth were grinding, you could hear that, it was so quiet on the ice.

I couldn't say no because of the way he looked, standing there with his hands in his sweater pockets. He started skating in tight, precise loops. I hadn't figure skated for years and my ankles felt shaky. I was tired. I didn't have the concentration or drive I'd had before; then I'd been trying to improve. Now, the quick, beautiful loops seemed pointless in the empty arena. I glanced up at the stands around us. But Ted's hand was tight around mine and I began to follow his lines on the ice. I didn't know. I thought maybe I could learn.

Ted had an office, deep in the arena, underneath the rink, in a basement hall with no windows. When my mother and I had first met him, his office was like a home. He had an oak wardrobe with clothes, mostly sweaters, all warm things, and a stereo with his favorite records. In the years since he married my mother, those records ended up warped and misplaced, and the office wasn't neat and tended the way it had been. When we left and put the house up for sale, he began to spend all his time there again, sleeping on the cot against the far wall.

I guess that time in Disneyland was the last time I saw my father. I'm not sure. He didn't die or anything. For a long time, we thought we would see him. There wasn't a day. We just never heard from him again. I still wouldn't be surprised if he found us.

7

A SHOPPING CENTER
SOMEWHERE IN THE VALLEY

■ □ ■

We used to drive around at night, we didn't have anything else to do. We didn't like to be in our apartment. There weren't places we could sit and do things. If I read my homework on the bed, there wasn't anywhere for my mother to go. The sofa in the living room was old and uncomfortable. I didn't like both of us to be on the bed. So we drove around in the dark. We drove down Sunset and slowly through the quiet northern streets in Beverly Hills. Sometimes we parked and beamed the headlights over one lawn. Houses in Beverly Hills still amazed us.

After we sat for a while, peering out trying to see movement inside the frames of fuzzy, lighted windows far back on a lawn, my mother would sigh and turn on the ignition. "Someday," she'd say.

"Yeah. Right."

"I believe it. We'll have a house. And clothes. You'll have everything a teenage girl could want, Puss." She'd reach over and slap my thigh. I'd move closer to the door, stiffening. "I just have to meet the man and catch him. Should we stop and get an ice cream quick before bed, for a little energy? Maybe it'll even get us up and working. That little sugar in our blood."

One night, we drove to Will Wright's, because my mother was dressed up. It was our favorite ice cream place. You could sit down in it. It was overpriced and old-fashioned, the garden circled with Christmas tree lights all year long. We sat outside in

the courtyard at a small, wobbly table; I stuck a wad of gum under
the metal base to even it. The round pink top was marble and the
chair backs were lacy, heart-shaped wrought iron.

"You know, it's really something, when you think of it. Weather
like this in March." That was one of the public things my mother
said. When we were out, she only said things that could be overheard.

"Yeah, so."

She gave me a reproaching, corrective smile. "It's nice." She
forced a laugh. "In Wisconsin now, you'd be freezing cold. You'd
be in your bunnyfur coat."

Ice cream was my mother's favorite food, and in it she loved
contrasts. Icy vanilla with scalding hot, hot fudge. Will Wright's
served tiny sundaes: little silver dishes with a scoop of exquisite
ice cream, flecked with black shavings of vanilla bean. The scoop
was the size of a Ping-Pong ball. Two separate porcelain pitchers
came with it: one of whole almonds, the other of hot fudge, which
my mother spooned on, a bite at a time, to keep the maximum
hot-cold contrast.

A tall man swaggered over to our table and, yanking a chair
with him, turned it backwards and sat on it like a horse.

"Howdy, ladies," he said, extending his hand. "I was wondering if I could, uh, borrow a match."

"Honey, do you have a match?" If I had had a match, my
mother would have killed me.

"Honey, I asked you a question."

"You know I don't."

She smiled at the man. "I'm terribly sorry. I'm afraid neither of
us smoke." She rummaged in her handbag. "I sometimes carry
them, for candles, but I don't seem to have any just now."

The man stayed. He didn't ask other people around us for
matches and he didn't go back to his table in the corner.

"So, my name's Lonnie," he said. "Lonnie Tishman."

My mother stepped on my foot, hard, under the table.

"I'm Adele and this is my daughter, Ann."

"Your daughter? You two look just like sisters."

"Oh, no."

"You sure do. I said to my friend over there, I'll ask those two gals. They look like they'd be smokers."

"I'm twelve years old," I said. My mother kicked me, then pressed her shoe over my foot again, driving in the heel.

My mother and Lonnie Tishman were both moving. He stood up and turned his chair around and sat on it the regular way, then he crossed one leg over the other, like a woman's. He seemed rubbery, all joints. His top leg bounced off the other knee. His fingers drummed on the marble tabletop. My mother seemed to be in slow motion, her spoon abandoned on the saucer, her ice cream melting in a puddle, no hot-cold contrast anymore. She gradually realigned herself so everything, her legs, her shoulders, her hands, faced him.

I was the only one still. I'd learned when I was young to be very still and not move when I wanted something. I wanted Lonnie Tishman to leave. My knees pressed into each other. Later, I found tender bruises. But he stayed, breathing loudly. Lonnie was a mouth breather.

"So how are you gals tonight?"

"We're great, aren't we, Annie? We were just saying how we *love* this weather. We're new to LA and we really love it."

"Just got here? Where're you from?"

"We're out of Bay City, Wisconsin."

Lonnie slapped his top knee, setting both legs jiggling.

"Golly. Wisconsin."

My mother looked down at the table and lifted the tips of her fingers.

"So, what are you two gals doing out here?"

"Well, I teach. I'm a speech therapist in the LA Public School System." There was something tiny about her pride. It killed me, I loved her. "And she's an actress," she said.

I stared down at my ice cream as if eating required all my concentration. They both looked at me hard, as if they were tracing me, drawing outlines on the sky.

Lonnie whistled through his teeth. "She's an actress." His chin

fell down and the way his face turned, I could see, in his cheekbones, he was handsome.

"Mmhmm." It sounded like my mother could say more, but
wouldn't. It was her imitation of modesty. Of course, there was
nothing more to tell. I wasn't an actress. I only wanted to be.

"Whewee, a kid actress, huh? I knew a guy whose daughter
was on TV. Little blond kid with the braids down the back. What
was that show called. Her name's Linda, I think, or Lisa. Lisa
Tannenbaum."

"Do you know her, Honey?"

That was harsh, like a twig snapped at my face. There wasn't
any possible way I could have known Lisa Tannenbaum. "No," I
said.

"Where do you gals live?" Lonnie pushed his chin close to my
mother. He had short bristles on his face, which made me think
of an electric field, things crackling, lightning on dry ground. I
wished my mother would feel it, too, and pull away. It was something about men. When I was a child, I went to my cousin's
house. I locked myself in the bathroom and looked at things. It
was all different from ours. I felt something like electricity when
I put their towels to my face. I thought it came from men, the
smell of men. I imagined it had something to do with shaving.

"In Beverly Hills," my mother said quietly, dropping the
words.

"Well, hey, what do you say, why don't we get together sometime."

"Sure," my mother said.

"Why don't you give me your phone number and I'll call you
and we'll hook up?"

"We're 273-7672."

Lonnie took a pen from his shirt pocket and wrote our phone
number on his wrist. He stood up, shoved the chair in towards
the table, pulling the back to his leg. "Well, I'll be a-seeing ya,"
he said.

My mother put her hand over the bill. "Should we get going?"
I'd finished my ice cream; my mother no longer seemed interested

in hers. She quickly looked over her shoulder to see he was gone
and then bent towards me, her face greedy with excitement.

"You know who that was, don't you?" There was something
hard and individual about her face; her beauty was her beauty,
her luck was her luck.

"No." I ground a stone under my shoe.

"Didn't you hear him say his name? That was Tishman: Lonnie
Tishman. Haven't you seen those signs on Wilshire where they're
building? That's all Tishman. They're everything. All the high
rises. Those condominiums in Century City where we drove by,
don't you remember? I said the top ones would be gorgeous. Who
knows, I'll bet he'll give us one of them. He's all over. Believe
me. *Ev*-ery-where." There was something about the way she said
it. I can't explain.

I knew I was supposed to be glad and excited; if I were excited,
it would be like praise. She would shake her hair and bask. But
I didn't believe her. He didn't look rich. Something about the way
he rubbed his hands on his pants when he stood up.

"You know what this all means, don't you?"

"No."

My mother sighed, dragging her spoon in her coffee. "Boy, can
you be dumb sometimes."

I was quiet, knowing I could be. I looked up at the sky and
understood, without exactly thinking, that it was late on a school
night again, eleven or twelve o'clock, and that I hadn't done my
homework and I wouldn't do it. That tomorrow would be like other
days, the hall of my school with old wooden doors, closing and
closing, me coming up the stairs, alone and late. The sky was a
dark blue, through the branches of the trees. The stars seemed
very dim.

"You're going to make it, kiddo. Why do you think he came up
to us?" My mother's voice curved; it was like a hook. She was
scolding to get me back.

"He liked you, I suppose." I hated saying that. Her face lit up
from her eyes.

"You think so?"

"I don know."

"Did you really think he liked me? Tell me, Ann."

"I guess."

"Well, he's going to put you on television." My mother clapped.
From a lifetime of working with children, all my mother's emo-
tions expressed themselves in claps.

"He's not an agent." I said that, but I could feel the beginning
of something in her insistent, lilting voice. She worked with that
voice, as hard as if she were building something both of us could
see. Sometimes, I felt my mother climbing up a long, long series
of stairs, above what seemed true—my school, the hum of electric clocks behind closed wooden doors, my steps, late, the messy
locker, my books, heavy and unlooked at, and I followed her to
up to the clear air. At the top, there was a sky, but when she
pushed at it, it broke like so many sheets of colored tissue paper.
She began to climb to the other side. I stood still below, next to
her legs, but I could see air, feel the wind, from the other side.

"Oh, come on. Didn't you hear the way he said, he has a *friend*
whose daughter is on TV? What do you think that meant? He was
just testing you. That was his way of asking, do you really, really
want it? You know, a lot of kids *say* they want to be on television,
sure, but then when it comes right down to it, they don't have the
commitment. Not really. We're different. We really do have it.
This man's not the agent, but I'll bet his friend is, the one he was
sitting with. I'll bet *he's* the agent and this Tishman's the producer. We'll just have to wait and see, but he has our number. I'll
bet you land a TV show. And now it's all in the offing."

"When?"

I pulled closer to her and waited. She didn't have to build
anymore or fight: we were there. Now, she could be slow. I needed
every word. I moved close and watched her face, attentive, like a
person holding a bowl, trying to catch single drops of rain.

She tilted her head for a moment, thinking. Her cheekbones
seemed high, she looked thin, as if the bones in her face were
very frail. When I was little, I'd once held a velvet-lined box with
a glass cover, a perfect bird skeleton laid out inside. My grandmother had lifted the lid with her fingernail.

"I would say soon. Very soon."

It was all different now, where we were. I didn't snap or mope or sulk. I sat at the edge of my chair, leaning across the table to be near her. She was distracted, aloof—sure of me.

The night had the same blue perfect air as the inside of a bubble. I felt elated to touch the marble of the table under my hand. I slept that night easily, thoroughly pleased, the knowledge dissolving in me.

Lonnie Tishman called the next day. I answered the phone. I recognized his voice and for a moment I believed it was the call that would deliver me. A sound stage. Cameras. A voice would say, You have been chosen. You. But he just asked, "Your mom around?"

Then the usual came back. Brown doubts and suspicion. The wooden backs of doors.

"It's for you." I shoved the receiver away.

My mother, three feet to the left on the carpet, stood still in her tracks for a full minute. Then she walked the four steps to the night table, breathed in and picked up the phone. The mattress jiggled as she squirmed. She changed her legs, from the left to the right, on top. She laughed, but I could hear she was puzzled. She was trying, with her pauses and tones, to weld whatever he was saying into the shape of a normal date.

"Well, okay, I suppose. But actually, I don't cook very well." With one hand, she redistributed bobby pins in her hair. Her mouth was working. "Oh. Oh. Well, really, it's our kitchen. To tell the truth, I think I'd just as soon go out." This—a more aggressive statement than she liked to make to a man, especially at the beginning—was followed by an avalanche of helpless giggles. "Okay," she said, finally, bouncing her shoe off her toe. "We can do that."

She stood and clapped after she hung up the phone. "What do you know, Ann! We've got a date this Sunday night."

I stayed on the bed, doing nothing.

"Hey, Little Miss, you better paste a smile on that face, because this could just be your big break."

"Oh yeah. How's your date going to be my big break?"

She stuttered a second. Even speech therapists stutter. "He probably wants to check me out first and see if I'll really let you do all this. You know, a lot of mothers wouldn't cart their kids around to rehearsals and tryouts and to the studios. But I will. I really will. And that's probably what he wants to know."

We both got haircuts. My mother only let me get a trim, half an inch of split ends, so I was finished a long time before she was. I sat under the turned-off dryer and leafed through old movie magazines. I studied the dotted pictures of dark men. I thought it was possible I'd see a picture of my father.

"So this man wants to hide it," my mother said, to the woman teasing her hair. At the same time, she watched her curls fall around her face in the mirror. She tilted her head to the left. My mother held her face like a jewel, always moving a little to glance off another facet of light. "He doesn't want me to know."

"Could be," the hairdresser said. "There's supposed to be one Tishman brother left and they say he's a little nuts."

"This is the man. I know it."

By the time we left, it was raining outside. My mother took my magazine and tented it over her head as we ran to the car.

"These people play down their money. Because they want you to like them for *them.* Lots of people are probably after him for his money. Sure. And this is his way of testing us." She nodded, preoccupied, as she warmed up the car. "Mmhmm. See, at first, I was upset, because he didn't want to go out to eat, and then when I kind of suggested it, you know, he wanted this Love's Bar-b-que, a really cheap place. No atmosphere or anything. Here, I thought, well, with all his money, he can take me somewhere a little better. But I can see now that he wants to find out if we really like him for *him.*"

Again, the car screeched going down into the garage. "After all, we met him in the Beverly Hills Will Wright's. And anybody in there is somebody."

"What about us?" I said.

She shrugged. "You're right."

□

Sunday was the date. It was all we did. We woke up early, at six, when the alarm clock rang, for once. We cleaned, then shopped. We bought candy to put out in a bowl and things he could drink if he wanted to. In the afternoon, I sat on the bed, watching my mother dress. She'd already taken her bath. She moved around the small floor space in her bra and pantyhose, running from the closet back to the bathroom mirror.

I picked up a book to read, but every two minutes she interrupted, and I was glad to quit again. This was fun.

"Ann-honey, tell me something. Which way, up or down, what do you think? The hair, come on, concentrate a second. Down? Are you sure? Why?"

"Makes your neck look longer."

"It does, good. Are you sure?"

It occurred to me that my mother had never been alone. At home, she'd had Lolly, probably even before I was born. Lolly had always been there, bigger, quiet, sitting on the edge of some bed, watching my mother become shinier and shinier, enclosing more and more light in her body on a dull, late Saturday afternoon, getting ready to give herself, brilliant, to one man. For the first time ever, I felt sorry for Lolly. I remembered her scratchy plaid Bermuda shorts, her head bent, looking down at her big hands. At least I was younger. I could still be pretty myself someday.

I was asleep when they came home that night, but I heard the key work in the door and Lonnie's loud, raucous voice and her hushing him. And then I heard her giggles. That was the worst thing. I was awake then and I waited for it to stop. I wanted him to leave, so it would be quiet again. But he didn't. He never did. For the first time in that apartment, my mother didn't sleep with me in the bed. They opened the sofa; I heard the metal mattress frame scraping the floor.

"Shhh, you'll wake her."

"I forget you've got a child in here."

We'd never opened the sofa bed before. It must have been a

dusty mess. The dark green vinyl sofa was a problem. At Christmas, we'd tried to drape it with a bolt of green felt, but it had looked wrong and you couldn't sit on it. We'd finally settled for cleaning it and draping a red mohair afghan over the back.

My mother stood a foot away from me, lifting sheets out of the closet. I held absolutely still. As a child, I'd dreamed of burglars coming in at night from the train. In the dream, I'd have to be still. Later, the burglar lined us up in the cellar. He was stealing our television and my mother blamed it on me. The burglar pointed a rifle at us and Benny saved everything by putting his finger in the hole at the end of the gun.

They must have been making the bed. It sounded like they dropped twenty shoes and tripped over each other each time. It seemed it would never be quiet.

"Shhh," my mother said and then giggled.

"Hell, I thought you said she was asleep."

"Well, she is, but she's a light sleeper."

Another shoe dropped. For what seemed like hours, layers and layers of time, I thought I heard something; the sheets moving, the metal of the bed. The sound of his mouth-breathing changed the whole air. I didn't want to close my eyes.

But I must have finally fallen asleep in the morning, because I missed the alarm. I put my hand over the buzzing clock, to stop the noise, but I didn't reset it. My mother woke up on her own and came and sat next to me on the bed. She moved her hand on the blanket, over my back.

"Get up, Honey. It's time to get ready for school. Upseedaisey. Really, Honey. It's time now."

"Is he still here?"

"He's sleeping."

I pulled the covers and bedspread around me, and walked into the closet. I put my jeans and T-shirt on there. My mother stepped in and grabbed my arm. There wasn't room for two. Our closet was small and full, with clothes on hangers and linens on the shelves.

"Ann, I didn't sleep with him," she whispered. "I mean, I slept with him, but I didn't. He didn't touch me, we just slept. I swear to God, Ann, that's all we did." She lifted her palm up like a child, scout's honor.

"I don't care what you did." I walked around him to the bathroom. There was almost nowhere to walk. Opened up, the sofa bed took the whole room.

My mother followed me to the sink. "Well, I care. And I didn't."

We were alone in the apartment, making my bed. My mother shook a pillow down into the pillowcase. We'd driven to a laundromat in Pacific Palisades. Of course, there were closer laundromats, but my mother had found this one and it was clean and there was a health food snack bar next door. The main thing was my mother didn't want to be seen in a laundromat. In Pacific Palisades, it was okay. We didn't know anybody there. And now that I had friends at school, I felt the same way. I didn't want them to see me doing wash. When we finished my bed, my mother opened the sofa and put sheets on. I didn't help her with that and she didn't ask me.

"The tingling is over. What can I say? That real excitement, the fantasizing—I just don't feel it anymore. So, let's just hope some money comes in on one of his deals so we get a little something. And soon."

Lonnie slept here every night now. We no longer pretended Lonnie was an agent or a producer. Now, it was supposed to be enough that he might have money and give us some, to help us out. And it was enough. We adjusted.

"What about all these buildings that say TISHMAN on the scaffolding? I saw another one today on the way to school. On Roxbury."

She sighed. "Could you come and help me here a second? Just tuck the other side." The sofa bed felt flimsy, metal springs and a three-inch mattress. Sometimes in the night I heard a crash when the metal legs buckled and collapsed. "This man wants to make it on his own. He doesn't want to just be the son of someone who made it big. But I think if one of his deals comes through, if this shopping center makes it, *then* he'll go back to his family and say, See, this is what I could do, alone."

"Are you sure it's even the same family? There're a lot of Tishmans in the phone book."

"Honey, I'm sure."

"How do you know? Did he tell you?"

"Ann, I just know. Okay? You just have to learn that I know some things you don't. Okay? I'm a grown-up."

"At least he could pay rent."

"Honey, he does pay rent. He pays rent on his own apartment in Hollywood."

We'd seen his building. It was dark red brick, old, set far away from the street. Once, after dinner, my mother had stopped there, outside his building, so he could run in and get clean clothes. While we were waiting for him in the car she pressed the button that locked our doors.

"He's never in it."

"Well, let's just cross our fingers and hope it comes through soon, okay, Honey? Because I need it too. Believe me. Believe me, I'm getting tired."

I dropped it.

I developed sores on my head; small red bumps with scabs. My mother thought it was either lice or some weird disease. She decided I'd caught it from Lonnie. She called and made an appointment with a doctor in the Valley, an hour's drive away.

"You never know, people talk. Word gets around. Beverly Hills is really a very small community. And it's not the nicest thing to have, you know." My mother always worried that people would think we were unclean.

After school, we drove to the Valley. Sometimes, I really liked my mother. She drove easily, with one hand, as she pumped the gas with the toe of her high-heeled shoe. We looped on the freeway ramps smoothly. She talked to me and drove almost unconsciously on the six-lane highway with a freedom and confidence anyone at home in Bay City would have admired if they could have seen her. I remembered our first day in Los Angeles, how she'd clutched her whole body an inch away from the steering wheel. Her voice, when she told me to turn off the radio, fell stern and quiet. She'd been afraid for our lives. She'd driven on the right-hand side, almost on the gravel by the high aluminum fence. Her lips had moved and I thought she might have been praying. Now, she changed lanes and told me to look at the sun, just over a Coke sign on a dry hill. There were things to be proud of my mother for. I doubt she ever thought about it, how she'd learned to drive here.

She knew the Valley; she drove out to work every day. I didn't know much about her life without me. And my mother seemed shy and a little ashamed of what she did all day. Driving to the doctor, I asked her what she'd done at school. "Oh, nothing. You know. Just the usual," she said.

I imagined her in a room, plants on the windowsill, with tall boys and fat sloppy girls. With her they would all be timid. I imagined her standing close to them, holding their faces by the chin and looking in their eyes while she said the word. "Say thick. Th-th-th-thick." Their mouths wobbled crumbled sounds, trying to copy her lips.

We were speeding, my window cracked open, the sun a fuzzy line over the brown hills.

"There's my exit," she said, real joy in her voice, as if she were showing me the building where she worked.

The doctor didn't seem horrified by my head. My mother and I always felt calmed by doctors. They made us feel clean, like everyone else. He diagnosed the bumps as scabies, said I could have picked them up anywhere, probably in school, and matter-of-factly wrote out a prescription for Quell Lotion. He told us to wash my hair every day for eight days and put on the pink lotion afterwards. My mother nodded while he explained this, as if she were receiving critical and difficult instructions. That was all. He let us go. We bought the lotion downstairs in the pharmacy and then went for an early supper at the Van Nuys Hamburger Hamlet. We ordered big dinners and we each had dessert. It felt good to be alone, just the two of us.

We could have gone home after that and I could have washed my hair in our shower, but my mother panicked over anything having to do with uncleanliness, and when she panicked, spending money made her feel better, so she took me to her hairdresser. The hairdresser washed and blow-dried my hair so it looked thick and good, and then we had to ruin it, rubbing in the lotion, which made it greasy and rumpled.

"Ever hear from that Tishman fellow?" the hairdresser asked my mother.

"Mmmhmm, sometimes."

The next day she took me to a different beauty parlor.

After my last treatment, it was almost dark when we left the beauty shop. We drove to our apartment to pick up Lonnie, and then we drove farther out into the Valley than I'd ever been. We didn't have time for dinner because we were late. Lonnie had an appointment to meet someone for a business deal. He was supposed to be building a shopping center.

My mother drove and Lonnie sat in the front seat creating a chain reaction, hitting one hand on the other hand, which in turn hit his knee. My mother let him play the radio while she drove. I was sitting up against the back door with a book open, trying to do my homework. I was trying to improve my life, do what I was supposed to do. My efforts to make myself better never went anywhere. I didn't really believe they would.

The land changed outside our car windows. It was brown and flat, the hills seemed lower, and buildings were small and scarce. It reminded me of little towns in the desert when we drove into California. We stopped at a light and a man in a cowboy hat crossed the road. There were no sidewalks, just highway and gravel on the sides. There were more trucks than cars on the road with us. Gray-brown tumbleweed dotted the hills above the shopping center, where my mother finally slowed the car.

There was a McDonald's in the shopping mall and Lonnie told my mother and me we should wait for him there. When we all got out of the car, he walked in the other direction, towards a bar, where he was supposed to meet his partner. He walked away, rubbing his hands on the front of his pants. We stood on the blacktop and my mother seemed distracted until she said, "Wait here a second, stay right here," and ran up to Lonnie, her purse hitting the side of her thigh as she ran. They weren't far away. "She can wait in the car. She'll study. Are you sure I shouldn't come along?"

I stood still, growing cold up from my feet.

"Hey, hey, comemeer a second, Woman. Let me give you a kiss before I go."

They stood there in the middle of the parking lot like two movie stars, her hair falling over her back and her stockinged heels rising up out of her shoes.

I looked the other way, at the window of a closed knitting store. I felt like I was nothing and I never would be. Then my mother came running back. She slapped her thigh when she stopped. "Come on. Let's hurry it up."

We sat against the inside glass wall of the McDonald's. There was a field on the other side of the highway, except for one gas station, nothing. My mother sipped coffee from a coated paper cup. We thought if we were going to sit here, we'd better buy something and we didn't want to spoil our appetites. My mother pointed on the glass.

"See, over there. That's where they're going to put the shopping center."

"Why?"

"What do you mean, why? So we can make some money, that's why. And buy a house, maybe. So I don't have to run myself ragged—"

"I mean, why there?"

"Oh, I don't know. They know where the best places are. This man is *the* expert on shopping centers. He's already made millions."

The sides of the highway were marked with glowing red circles on three-foot wooden stakes. It was just brown field on the other side, nothing, land that could have been anywhere. I didn't believe it. I couldn't believe Lonnie being in a bar down the mall with some guy would make a shopping center grow there.

I thought of something I hadn't remembered for a long time: the city I'd drawn under my grandmother's kitchen table with crayons. I'd planned houses and swimming pools, buses. I could

easily draw for hours, working on one thing for my city. Now I
looked outside and imagined the colored structures I'd drawn,
huge and built, on the field across the street.

"But there's one already, across the highway. This one."

She sighed, tired and preoccupied. "I don't know, Honey. I'm
not the expert. They are."

"What kind of people have business meetings at night, in the
middle of nowhere, anyway?"

She didn't get mad. "Shhh, Honey. Just be quiet a minute. I've
been working all day and I'm tired." She put her purse up on the
plastic tabletop and unclasped it. "Here," she said, handing me
a dollar. "Go get us french fries. But just a small because we
don't want to spoil our appetites. If this meeting goes well, he'll
take us out somewhere nice. We'll get you a good steak. Really,
Honey."

We were still eating the french fries, not talking, when Lonnie
came in, rubbing his palms on the front of his pants.

"Hiya," he said to my mother. He did that a lot, acted as if he
was with just one person instead of two. He was wearing the same
thing he wore every day. A velour pullover and a blue zip-up vinyl
jacket.

I looked out the window at the dull field across the highway.
Businessmen didn't look like this. Neither did millionaires.

Lonnie was nuzzling his flecked chin against my mother's neck.
She hummed "mmmmm" with a noise that sounded vaguely electric.

"So, how's about a little supper?" he said.

"Okay. What do you feel like? Should we stay somewhere
around here or head back towards home?" Then, she winked at
me from over his shoulder.

"How's about here? I'd take a Big Mac and fries, how 'bout it.
How 'bout it, Ann? Hamburger?"

"All right," my mother said, sliding back down onto the plastic
chair.

There was an apology in her eyes as she turned and held her
face in both hands, but she never would have said anything in
front of Lonnie.

"Let's get it to go," Lonnie said, fidgeting at the counter.

My mother's car had changed. She never would have let me bring McDonald's into the cream-colored leather interior. But she let Lonnie. We ate on the way home, my mother asking me to hold her milkshake for her on the freeway.

"So what was the gist?" she was saying in the front seat. I had the ashtray in the back lifted and I was trying to read my homework by that little light.

"That's one proud man, I'll tell you," Lonnie said. He lowered his window so a whistle of air came in and he rested his elbow on the glass.

"So, do you think it'll go or not so much?"

"Hey," Lonnie said, beating his hand on his chest so the windbreaker made a rattling noise. My mother was driving, I held her milkshake, Lonnie's hands were free. "What kind of guy do you think I am, anyway? 'Course it'll go."

"Ann, you can hand me my malt now. Thank you."

I had my book propped as close to the ashtray as it would go. It stayed steady there as long as the car went straight on the freeway. I didn't look up until the book fell.

"This isn't our exit, Mom." We were past Beverly Hills. The streets where we were driving looked dark and unfamiliar.

"We're going to stop at Lonnie's apartment for a second."

Yellow lights shone from his building. My mother and I stayed in the car while he ran out to get a change of clothes. His apartment building looked very old. We had buildings like that in Wisconsin, the orphanage and paper mills along the river. Dark brick buildings, small windows, built in the last century.

"So what happened to our nice dinner?"

She turned the heat on. The doors were locked and the motor was still running. "Honey, I'm trying to get rid of him, too. Don't you think I'm scared? But let me do it slowly. I know how to manage this man."

Someone walked by on the sidewalk, a kid. My mother stiffened, clutching the wheel, watching him all the way away in the rearview mirror.

"I don't even like him anymore, believe me," she whispered. "I think he's on drugs. But he could hurt us, Ann. He's in with people who could really hurt us. Do you know what the Mafia is?"

"Some kind of straw?"

"No, no, that's raffia. Like we had at your birthday party the year with the piñata. That was fun, wasn't it?"

"I don know what it is then." The trees here scared me. Otherwise I would have lied. I didn't like admitting things I didn't know.

"Well, it's gangsters. Awful, awful people. Criminals, but whole gangs together. All over the country. They kill, they cheat, anything. And I think he's part of that. I'm worried for my life. And your life. This other man he met tonight could kill me."

Lonnie started across the lawn, holding his bag in front of him with both arms.

"What about the police?"

"The police can't stop them. Nothing can. So just let me take care of it, okay?"

I didn't say anything, I was too scared. When he came back into the car, with a wash of cold air and the sinister click of the locks after him, it was almost a relief. He was just Lonnie. He'd brought his clothes in a brown paper shopping bag, a white shirt on the top.

In bed that night, trying to sleep, I couldn't get warm. I thought of the shapes of my crayoned drawings, built, on a field of dull grass. I was scared to be in the same room with Lonnie.

We'd driven by Century City on the way home; a few floors stayed lit in the tall buildings. I thought that in offices there, in rooms with typewriters and metal desks, shopping centers were being planned. I believed and I didn't believe my mother. I was beginning to distrust her promises but I still believed her threats. I believed Lonnie was a criminal.

I barely slept that night. And in the morning, I got up when the alarm rang. Light was coming in through our faded Christmas green felt curtains, making delicate lacy patterns over the apartment. My mother and Lonnie were asleep in the middle of the room. Nothing looked so dangerous anymore. I bent down and shook my mother. For once, I wanted us all to be up on time.

"Why don't you get up already so we can eat some breakfast for a change."

"Shhh. He's sleeping. Five more minutes. Please, Hon."

"Fine, I don't care what you do." She turned over and pulled the blanket to her eye.

I took a shower and dressed. Then my mother got up. She stood by the bed, wearing nothing but Lonnie's T-shirt.

"You know, you're not the only person in the world," she said.

"So." I was buckling my shoes. I picked up my books. "I'm leaving."

"Just hold your horses. You have time. I'll be ready in a second. Sit down."

Lonnie was awake now, too. He looked tiny in his white jockey shorts, the leg holes stretched and bagging. He held his slacks out delicately as if he might trip stepping into them. His hair was a mess.

"I'm leaving," I said again.

"Just wait." My mother was yelling. "You'd think SHE's the only person in the world."

"I don't always have to wait for you just because you don't want to get up on time and eat breakfast and live like a normal person. I'm always waiting for you." I guess I was screaming, then.

"Oh, you, you—" My mother came at me, tripping over the huge sofa bed between us. She tripped and hit her knee, which made her madder. "I work, I slave, I run myself ragged, so SHE can live in Beverly Hills, so SHE can be a movie star, and what do I get? What do I get for thanks? A whole lot of guff from a stinky mouth."

"Who's a movie star," Lonnie said, one leg in his pants, one not.

"Thanks a lot."

"Hey." Lonnie lifted his hand in a grand gesture intended to silence us both. He looked at me, his face slack. "Your mother is a lovely woman," he said, his chin weaving slowly left and right, "you ought to treat her with respect."

My mother was still wearing nothing but the T-shirt, standing with her hands on her hips.

"I'm leaving."

Lonnie staggered up onto the bed, so he stood there, with his pants unzipped. "Hey," he said, loudly, raising his hand again. "Everyone quiet."

He didn't have a chance. Neither of us paid any attention.

"Oh, ohh, you lit-t—"

I was almost to the door when Lonnie jumped down and caught my arm, hard, twisting the skin. "Hey. Listen. I don't want to see you upset your mother like this." He looked back at her, she sat on the bed, crying now.

I twisted away. "Get your hands off me. Don't touch me. I'm leaving and I'm not coming back."

"You go ahead, you should. Go on and get lost. You don't deserve your mother. She's a lovely woman and you're nothing."

"Fuck you!"

My mother followed me to the door but I was already outside, down the sidewalk. She stepped for a moment onto the landing, wearing just the T-shirt, the toes of one foot on the other, shyly, shouting my name.

I kept walking. I heard the door slam and then I heard her shrill voice and Lonnie's low bellow. But they diminished as I walked, replaced by the small sounds of birds, slow tires, the first hammers on a construction site a few blocks away. The air felt kind, mild, windy as it touched my skin. I checked each of my pockets. I had everything I needed for a day. My hair was clean, just now beginning to lift a little as it dried, I had my books, money in my pocket. For once I had left early for school. The clean fronts of apartment houses, cars on the streets, the fountain at the corner of Wilshire and Little Santa Monica, all seemed indifferent and kind.

I'd been taught all my life or I knew somehow, I wasn't sure which, that you couldn't trust the kind faces of things, that the world was painted and behind the thin bright surface was darkness and the only place I was safe was home with my mother. But it seemed safer outside now, safer with indifference than care.

I decided I could go to Nibbler's. I had money, I had time. I could eat breakfast and then go to school. But my mother and the apartment had something on their side, a card to play against the bright, moving air: night. I had nowhere to go.

I kept walking. The air was cool on my skin, a leaf dropped on me—it tingled, the serrated sharpness of its edge like a scratch, then softness, a belly. I turned around. I kept expecting someone to stop me. But no one did and so I kept walking, now afraid to look back at the apartment.

Then I came to the street Nibbler's was on; it seemed large, a decision. I turned. Now if my mother or Lonnie left the apartment, I would be out of sight, gone. I was halfway there when I heard a car behind me that sounded like my mother's. I didn't have the nerve to turn around, because it seemed like something I'd made up, but I bit my lip and stood still. The tires sounded like ours. Then a Mustang pulled in front of me, forest green. My heart fell several inches lower.

I started walking again. I could hardly believe this was me. The noise of Wilshire Boulevard came closer. The day seemed to start in many places, like gears catching and moving, a huge machine. Beverly Hills was a city all of a sudden and I had six dollars and some change. I walked past the glass reflecting door of Nibbler's and stopped at Wilshire Boulevard in front of a purse shop. Then, somewhere behind me a car skidded and I heard heels and my mother was there, grabbing my arm, her fingernails biting my skin.

"Annie, Honey." She hugged me, her rib cage heaving, I felt her breasts move through her blouse. I just stood there and didn't say anything and then it was back to normal. "Let's go and park the car right and we'll have some breakfast at Nibbler's. He's gone, Honey. He's all packed. I told him he had to get out and he's gone. So it's just us again, thank God. I told him when he yelled at you like that, that was the end. No one, not anyone, can get between us." My mother's face seemed shallow and concave, like the inside of a pan.

"I'm hungry," I said. I started walking fast. Now I was thinking of time again, of not being late for school.

"Well, okay, wait a minute." She grabbed my arm. "We have to go a little slower. It's these damn heels." She lifted one foot and pushed something with her hand.

I felt the money in my pockets, the soft paper of the dollars. The buildings were just buildings again, what they seemed, familiar. The city looked beautiful and strong now, bright and silver, like a perfect train, drizzling light off its wheels as it moved. We could hear the fountain splashing behind our backs.

Lonnie was gone and we ate a big breakfast and I still had my money.

She paid.

8

A DOCTOR'S APARTMENT

■ □ ■

The cake was my idea. Daniel Swan and I were both bad students, underachievers, according to our mothers. Neither of us did any homework. We were weeks late handing in our maps of Johnny Tremain's Boston. We made the cake with mixes, cut it in the shape of Boston and drew in the streets with a fluted frosting tin. For the first time I could remember, I got an A on something. The class laughed and the teacher left the room and came back with a serrated knife and brown paper towels from the bathroom. She cut the cake in little squares and gave them to the first person in each row to pass back.

They were good. Sweet and airy. That's the thing about mixes; they are good the first day. After that they get hard.

From then on, Daniel Swan and I baked cakes for all our high school projects. We stopped using mixes. We tried out different recipes and our cakes improved. I kept a notebook and wrote to my grandmother to ask why things turned out the way they did, to learn about icing.

There was an annual high school bake sale and everyone was supposed to bring something. So I was at Daniel's house, high in Benedict Canyon, making the Milky Way galaxy, all the planets and planet rings and moons in round cake tins. It was a big project. We mixed a different kind of batter for each planet and they'd all have to be frosted. My mother had bought us the ingredients. She'd taken us to the store the night before. Daniel had raised his eyebrows when the checker totaled the bill.

"That's pretty high. You shouldn't have to do all that, Mrs. August. I can ask the Witch."

"Oh, no, don't be silly, it's your kitchen."

My mother was serious about the cake. Except for the one old woman at the Lasky House and Julie, the real estate agent, my mother didn't have any friends. It seemed easier for me to meet people. I had school. She was hoping for a divorced father. Or a widower, better still. Maybe one where the wife ran away. For good, of course. She didn't know, but she'd already planned what she was wearing. She had a new dress, yellow, with her ivory jewelry and black pumps. She was counting on the auction. And she felt glad I was up at the Swans' baking cakes. "See and this way, we'll at least know the Swans," she'd said.

"I know other people, too."

"Well, I hope," she'd laughed. "And I hope they have fathers. Single."

We slid three round cakes in the oven. I mixed batter for a yellow cake while Daniel melted unsweetened chocolate. There were two ovens, one regular and one microwave, built in. Whatever seemed new and expensive and could be built in, the San Ysidro house had. When I looked at the long row of ingredients, the colored boxes and bags and jars, I felt bad my mother had spent so much money.

"So maybe we can all go together, your family and my family."

"You want to go with the twins and Rod, you go ahead. They're terrible. They're uncivilized."

"And your mom and dad."

"They won't go. Maybe the Witch, but she's probably got something for work. And the Failure'll be in Mexico."

"When's he coming home?"

"Depends on the deal. But probably the end of the month. No. Definitely the end of the month. Because to come home sooner than the end of the month, something would have to go right. And that's impossible."

I sifted. It felt quiet in the house, we were almost alone. The twins were at Scouts and Rod was visiting his best friend, Harold.

But from the room off the kitchen, a wedge of bluish light came from the TV and we heard the steam of Darcy's ironing. Riley sat at the low kitchen table, the children's table, doing his homework. His glasses dropped to the bottom of his nose and he sometimes looked at me from over them. At the same time his shoulders shrank down and he sank in the chair under the table, his black high tops sticking out the other side.

"Riley." Darcy pulled him up by the collar. "Get to work now." Riley was Darcy's son and she was harder on him than she was on the Swans. "You children makin another cake?"

It was hard not to smile at Riley. There was something about his face. When you looked at him, you felt like you knew what he was feeling. He was already rich from commercials; the Witch's advertising agency had started him when he was three years old and now he got parts on his own. But Darcy cared about school, too, even though he didn't. We all understood why. He'd have plenty of money. Darcy drove all the Swans and Riley to El Rodeo and the high school in the station wagon every morning.

The house seemed empty while we worked, but it was a house that always felt empty. Dull white ceramic candlesticks with hinged doves stood on the windowsills. Frank Swan was a land developer in Mexico. He took trips down there two months of the year, but nothing had come of them yet, nothing worked. "He doesn't make any money," Daniel simply said. "The Witch makes all the money and the way they spend it, even that's not enough." He called his mother the Witch to her face, but he never would have called his father the Failure.

We both looked around the house while we mixed, grateful and helpless. "It's nice that your kitchen is so good," I said.

"We may as well use it while we have it."

Daniel said the Swans might lease the San Ysidro house and move to another, rented, place, if the Failure's deal didn't come through. They'd lived in a lot of houses before, all rented. This one they had built. I never could talk about our money problems, even though I worried all the time. But Daniel had seen our apartment. It seemed different for us. It was obvious. You could see what we didn't have.

"Here," he said, sweeping the walnuts into a blender. And we watched the dust coming up, whirling against the glass.

When we set the last cakes in the oven, Daniel asked Darcy to watch them for us and we climbed the back steps to Daniel's room. The children's hallway was narrow, littered with socks and T-shirts and baseball cards. Another stairway led to the parents' room. They never came to this part of the house. Paper blinds moved a little from the open window. Outside stood a pool house that was supposed to be for the kids, but so far, it had only one big bean bag chair. Nothing in the San Ysidro house was done yet.

"Last year, somebody paid two hundred dollars for a stupid model of the school. And they didn't even frost the roof, they used licorice."

"Not that we'd get to keep the money."

"No way."

A radio snapped on outside to "Jeremiah was a bullfrog." Home again, the twins splashed in the water. I never got to listen to rock stations and we didn't have a stereo, so I tried to remember what I could. I admired people who knew about songs. It was like dancing, one of those things like being rich or smart in school or good-looking. I always tried to remember and write the names down when I got home. I kept secret notebooks, neat charts, Group, Song, Album, Refrain. I studied these like I never studied school. It seemed people were born with it, you got it like long legs or an older brother.

"Why, what would you buy? More shoes?" Daniel reached over and touched the platform of my Korkease.

I looked down at my feet. I was wearing good socks and shoes, they looked normal, nothing to be ashamed of. I wasn't the least bit insecure about those shoes because they weren't mine. I'd stolen them a week ago from a girl's open locker. I figured I could get away with it because every girl at school wore these same shoes. I had another pair, older and beaten up, with platforms not as high. The shoes cost sixty dollars.

My mother noticed when I had new things but she never asked

about them. "They give you that height you need in the thigh," she'd said.

I wore them every day. They seemed like mine now.

"You mean, if they gave us two hundred dollars? I don't know. I guess I'd give it to my mother."

I reached down on the floor and picked up a card of Uranus. Daniel had cards of the planets and constellations. He went with other guys to Mount Pinos every weekend. One of the fathers drove. There was a telescope at the top. I thought skies weren't much to look at, in Los Angeles. I would have liked to see stars.

Then Daniel stretched a rubber band between his hands and stared at it. He sat next to me on the bed. "So when are we going to?"

I knew what he meant. His mouth went a certain way.

"What?" I was a girl.

"You don't know?" He looked at me skeptically, but I wasn't scared. I said what I was supposed to say and anyway, sometimes being caught lying isn't as bad as being caught with the truth. "I can't believe you. You're so naive. Don't you know where babies come from?" Daniel made fake kissing noises.

"Kissing, you mean." I looked down at my feet. My feet looked irreproachable. Packaged. "I think we're too young. I'm not going to do it until college."

"What about more than kissing? When are you going to do that?"

"When I'm thirty."

Daniel snapped the rubber band across the room. "You're hopeless." He picked up his jacket from the floor and took out one Kraft caramel.

"Can I have one?"

He raised his eyebrows. "Ask nicely."

"Can I *please* have one."

He tossed it to me.

We heard Darcy downstairs, opening the oven door and shutting it again. A breeze came from Daniel's window and lifted a paper airplane from his desk to the carpet. There was a sugary smell of caramel on both our breaths.

Daniel stuck out his arm in front of me. "Here, rub my arm."

We scratched the hard tops of each other's arms, from our elbows down to our hands. Another person's fingers feel different
on your arm. There seemed to be sparks, tracing down my skin
and lasting about as long as something you write with a sparkler
holds in the sky. Then Daniel took my leg and pushed my sock
down to my ankle, my shoe in his lap. They were precise fine
sensations.

When Darcy called us, we jumped and ran. She and Riley were
standing in front of the microwave and we stood, too, looking in
the glass window watching the pale belly of our cake rise.

The Witch bounded in, calling, "I'm ho-ome," carrying two grocery bags like any mother. Darcy hurried over to help. "Oh, thank
you, Darcy, I'm so tired. Hello, Ann, how are you? I bought
dates."

The twins ran in from outside and fought for their mother's
arms.

"Let's go." I liked the noise and disorganization of a family, but
Daniel wanted to be alone. I followed him to the living room. The
living room seemed to be why they'd built the San Ysidro house.
The kids' bedrooms were tiny like closets, Darcy and Riley's room
was normal, even the upstairs master bedroom was just nice. The
living room looked like a ballroom; two stories high, and banked
on both sides with tall windows. A fireplace grew out of the
stucco. The floor was red clay, Mexican tiles.

There was absolutely no furniture unless you call a grand piano
furniture. There were niches on the side walls to sit in, but the
cushions were put away in a closet.

It was a house for crowds. The Witch and Frank had given a
party that winter, a benefit for musicians who'd written a musical
called *Year of the Mushroom*. The living room had been lit with
candles, torches lined the drive and everyone sat on the smooth
floor, listening to the kids in tie-dyed clothes pound the grand
piano and shake their heads and sing.

"It's going to be the next *Hair*," my mother whispered.

They planned to perform around the country in mushroom-shaped tents, with seating for five hundred. My mother wrote out a check. I tried to stop her but she was excited. It scared me a little, her attraction to them. She wouldn't have wanted me to be like that.

Daniel and I sat together on the piano bench. Daniel had studied piano for eight years and then quit. The whole reason the Witch liked me was that I somehow got Daniel to practice. The living room was cold. I'd never taken piano or any instrument in my life and my fingers didn't know where to go. Daniel was trying to teach me. He'd played three or four pieces through, after sorting out the dusty stack of music under the piano bench, slapping the books against his thigh.

Then he played this piece. I made him stop. I loved the melody. It made me think of something in nature. This was the piece I wanted to learn.

Daniel wanted to teach me so we could play it together. But it was really hard. We hadn't gotten three bars down yet. My fingers seemed to have no memory. We went over and over the same nine notes, going as far as we could until I made a mistake, but I never got tired of it, because I loved hearing the melody, even a piece of it, every time. I liked to think I was learning how to do something, improving myself. Then I saw my mother's white car pull up outside the front window. She got out, pushed her hair back with both hands and ran to the door. We slipped off the bench and walked to the kitchen, passing Riley. Then we heard the sound of a rough scale. Riley was beginning to take lessons. He wanted to start a rock band when he was eighteen.

In the kitchen, our mothers each had their hands in a plastic bag of dates. "Mmmm," my mother was saying.

"Adele, I have to take you down there. They're so cheap. Don't you think they'd make a nice present, in some kind of basket?"

"With a bow. Absolutely."

"I have so many clients. And they all have to be Christmased." My mother touched my hair and kissed me. "Hi, Darling."

"You're lucky she lets you kiss. I wouldn't dare touch Daniel, would I?"

Daniel shrieked and ran around the counter. "Ouch! Stay away from me, Witch!"

"So, Adele, Ann tells us you ski."

"Well, mmhmm, we really haven't here. To tell the truth, I'm a little scared of skiing on this western snow. They say it's different."

The Witch pulled up another plastic bag of dates for my mother to sample. Daniel and I snuck out. They'd talk awhile. We still had time. "To tell the truth," my mother was saying again, as we skidded through the dining room on just our socks.

But she didn't tell the truth. To my mother, Cassie Swan wasn't the Witch, she was a woman who lived north of Sunset on San Ysidro Drive and so my mother was all dull formality. My mother wasn't scared of western snow. It was money. It was always money.

Daniel said, Move over, and Riley looked at us, over his horn-rimmed glasses that were too big for his face, and kept on with his scales. "Come on," Daniel said. Then finally, he shoved Riley off onto the floor, clearing the piano bench for me. I saw Riley's face for a moment when he fell, he looked up at me, it was awful, something I never forgot. Then, a minute later, on the floor, he did a back somersault, and landed, smiling goofy again, all charm.

Both mothers walked in to watch. They each slid one foot out of one high heel.

"Isn't that great?" my mother said.

"Daniel could be so good if he'd only practice. If he'd only once stick to something."

"Oh, he should, he's obviously talented. Obviously."

"I wish he'd listen to you."

Under the piano, Riley bent over, pounding away at the tiles like a keyboard, with his genius for mimicry.

At the cake sale my mother fell in love.

"Did you see when we walked down the hall and he walked down the hall?" I was carrying the square marble cake we'd bought and my mother kept elbowing me in the ribs.

"I looked and I saw this HANDsome man, I mean, boy, is HE good-looking, I mean REALLY, and I thought, Hey, he's not with another woman, he's here alone. He must be divorced or even a widower. I'll bet a widower, the way he walked with his head down. And every few minutes I'd be walking along and he'd sort of look at me, like, Hey, who's she? And I'd sort of look at him and he'd look at me and sort of smile, you know. So then, we were both in front of your cake—say, wasn't that something, a hundred dollars. You should be proud. You and Daniel should both be proud—"

My mother unlocked my door. "Oh, Honey, do we really want to put that gooey thing in our nice car? Let's not, Ann. Really. Why don't you run over and throw it in the trash. There's a can. Nobody's going to know and I can just see if I have to brake, it'll be all over the leather. And that'll never come out."

"I'll hold it on my lap."

"Honey, just throw it out. We can go get ice cream cones if you're hungry for a little something sweet, but I don't want that messy thing in my car. I'm sorry, Ann, but I just can't. I'm not. I have to keep this car nice."

I crossed the street and dumped the cake in a garbage can. It was a good cake, it smelled like mint. A girl named Isabel had made it and her cakes had a reputation for being messy, but good. She used liqueurs in her batter.

"We paid seven dollars for that," I said, when I sat down in the car.

"Oh, Honey, the money's for the school really, not for the cake. Ooops." She braked as a man holding a child's hand walked in front of the car. She was always a distracted driver. "Tell you what. Let's go get ice cream cones. That's better for us anyway."

"I don't want ice cream."

"Well, I think I could go for one. Anyway. Where was I? Oh, in front of your big galaxy. I was standing and he was standing, but not saying anything. And that's when you came up with your friend, and she said, 'Oh, Ann, this is my father, Dr. Spritzer'— that's interesting, isn't it, that she said Dr. Spritzer, not just my dad, she must be real proud of him, obviously. You know, Hon, you should really introduce me as Dr. Adele August in situations like that."

"You're not a doctor."

"I am. I have honorary PhDs from a couple of places."

"Where? I've never seen them."

She sighed, steering with two fingers. "I don't know, packed somewhere. Maybe at Gramma's. I really have to get all my things organized. But anyway, it doesn't matter, because you were real cute the way you said it anyway, real nonchalant, just, 'This is my mom.' Really, you did it just right."

"I'm relieved."

"And boy, did HE look then. 'Oh, what kind of doctor are you?' I said, but just real casual."

I'd heard all this—I'd been standing right there, but you couldn't stop her once she'd started. I looked at houses out my window as we drove.

"And when he said, 'Orthodontist,' I said, 'Really. That's funny, because I've been looking for an orthodontist to see if Ann's going to need braces.' Remember, Hon, how you came home your first day and said the girls told you you needed braces? It's a good thing they did. Lucky."

Right there, in front of our cake, Dr. Spritzer had leaned over, taken my head in his hands and opened my mouth. He had doctor's hands. While he held my head, I felt like sleeping.

"Yup, I'm afraid she will," he had said. "She's got some pretty big toofers in that little mouth."

I thought he and my mother should get along. They both used the same dopey slang.

"So, did you hear when he said, 'Bring her in anytime and we'll see what we can do'? And then he sort of winked at me. Real subtle. Sort of half a wink. I suppose he didn't want you kids to see. So. We'll just have to wait. But I think in a week or two I'll call his office and see about braces for my little Bear Cub."

She reached over and patted my knee and I stiffened. She parked in front of Baskin-Robbins.

"You really don't want one? Just a single dip."

"No."

She held out money to me. "Well, I'd like a double, the top
scoop chocolate almond, the bottom, pistachio. On a sugar cone."

I just sat there.

"Come on, Honey. Just run in and do this one thing for me.
After all I do for you. Go on." She pressed the money into my
hand.

In the two weeks before the appointment, we dieted. We ate sal-
ads at Hamburger Hamlet for dinner and my mother gave up ice
cream altogether. The Saturday before the appointment, we went
shopping on Rodeo Drive. In one of the dressing rooms, a room
that was so big and pretty we could have lived in it, my mother
sat down on the love seat and cried, quietly, so the salesgirls
hovering in the hallway wouldn't hear. She lifted the beige ticket
from the sleeve of a suit she was trying on. It cost seventeen
hundred dollars.

"Well, so why don't we go somewhere else?"

"There is nowhere else." She shook her head, unzipped the
skirt and began to step out of it. She looked ruefully around the
room, glancing at herself from different angles in the mirrors,
flexing and arching her foot. She looked over her shoulder at the
backs of her thighs. Then she sucked in her cheeks.

"I'm pretty, but that's not enough. Nobody wants a woman my
age who doesn't dress."

"I thought he liked you. You said he winked."

"Well, he saw me in the yellow. He only saw me in my best
thing."

"Oh, come on."

"Don't kid yourself, he's no different from the rest. He can have
anyone he wants, let me tell you. They want rich women. Not a
schoolteacher with a child to support."

I started putting the clothes back on their hangers. The skirt
kept falling off.

"Just leave it," my mother said. "They'll do it. It's their job."

□

"I'm just going to cancel," my mother said. "Oooh." She swerved, just missing a garbage can. "I don't have anything decent to wear. He's not going to want me in these old fuddy-duddy clothes."

"Why don't you wear the blue?"

"That's out of date. The collar's no good."

"Well, should I come home or not?" The appointment was for two o'clock, I'd have to miss an afternoon of school.

"Just come home and we'll see. I'm not making any promises. We'll just see."

When I walked in, at noon, my mother's six best dresses were lying out on the sofa. She stood in her lace underwear with her hair in rollers.

"Tell me, Honey, what would the other kids' mothers wear, do you think?" She stood soaping her face with pink organic geranium soap. "What do you want me to wear?" I sat on the arm of the vinyl couch and she sat next to me, still soaping. "I even thought of calling Cassie Swan and asking her. Should we go, Honey, or not? Or should we just cancel?"

She felt frightened of people here. I'd gone to school and made some friends. But she still didn't know anybody. The women we met all seemed to have about twenty times more money than we did. She tried, but it wasn't like with Lolly. My mother thought they would be judging her, picking her over for faults. We'd come all the way here and now she was scared. And she'd had so much courage in Wisconsin.

"Wear the blue, it's pretty," I said. But I wasn't sure either.

"You think? Even with that collar?" My mother looked up at me as if I could save her life.

"I think it's pretty. He won't be looking at your collar."

She went back to the sink to rinse. Then she started on her eyes. Suddenly, she banged her hand down on the counter. "I've got it. I'll wear the Gucci scarf. That'll cover the neckline and then it'll be smashing." She started crying again. "Oh, that's it, Ann, we're going to make it here after all. I know it. I really do."

We stood in the elevator. "Look once, Honey. Do I have any on my teeth?" We'd arrived forty-five minutes early to Dr. Spritzer's building and so we'd eaten hot fudge sundaes in the drugstore downstairs.

"Open a little wider, Honey," Dr. Spritzer said. He looked even better than he had at the cake sale. His good face seemed to pop out of the tight-necked green smock.

"So how did you survive your cake?" he asked my mother over my head.

"Ours was very tasty, actually."

"Let's see here." He moved something suspiciously like a pliers in my mouth. "Well, it looks like she's going to need some braces for da teef, I'm afraid."

"She is." My mother patted my shoulder. "Well, Honey, it won't be too bad. I guess you're just going to have to have them." She tried to look concerned and suck in her cheeks at the same time. "How long will she have to wear them, do you think?"

"We'll just have to see how fast her teeth respond." He shook my jaw. My mother didn't say anything about the price and Dr. Spritzer called a girl named Pam to come over and make a plaster mold of my mouth.

"Hi," my mother whispered. I was asleep, then I opened my eyes and made out the shape of her back. "Are you up? Unzip me, would you? I'm stuck."

She wriggled closer to me on the bed. My fingers felt heavy with sleep and they wouldn't move. Finally, the zipper sprang free in my hands. I opened it down to her underpants. My mother stood and hung up her dress in the closet.

"It feels so good to be out of that. But it was absolutely the right thing, the dress. It was perfect. Couldn't have been better."

It was coming to me: we'd gone to Rodeo Drive and she'd bought a dress for her date with Dr. Spritzer, and now she was home late, and happy.

"How was it?"

She pulled on a T-shirt, then sat down. "Well, you won't be- lieve it, Ann. It was marvelous. Just marvelous. We met for drinks. Here at the Left Bank, we sat at the bar, and he was sort of smiling, you know, and I smiled, and then he said, Hey do you feel like a couple of lobsters? I said sure, why not, and he took me to this place. Ann, we've got to go there sometime, you'd love it, you would ADORE it, but it's expensive. It was RIGHT on the beach. And we got in and everybody knows him there. They all say, 'Oh, hello, Dr. Spritzer, Hi Josh.' And he's short. I didn't realize it before, but he's this little itty-bitty man. It's a good thing I wasn't wearing higher heels. Boy, is that ever lucky, when I think about it. I almost wore the black. Even in these, I came right up to here on him.

"So we talked and talked and we just agreed about everything. I don't know how, I don't know why, but we really clicked, you know? Sometimes that just happens, you just CLICK with someone. And here we were eating these lobsters and you know how they're messy and the butter was dripping down my face, oh, God, I thought, here he's going to remember me with a shiny, buttery chin."

"What time is it?"

My mother went to the front window and pulled the felt curtain and let it close again. There was a damp spot where she'd been sitting on the blanket, darker than the rest of the wool. I rolled over and picked up her underpants from the floor. They were wet. I dropped them back, I didn't want her to see.

"It's pretty late. Almost time to get up. Should we jump in the car and ride down to the beach for a little? The sun will be just coming up. And I bet Alice's would have a good breakfast."

My legs still felt weightless and empty inside.

"I'll just throw on some clothes and we'll go." My mother walked into the bathroom and the toilet seat clicked against the wall. "Should we do that, Honey?" She always left the bathroom door open; she liked to keep talking. The toilet paper roll creaked. "We can get some strong coffee. Come on, get up. We'll have fun. Come on, Ann."

She clapped her hands while I put on jeans and a loose, old sweater, warm clothes I'd feel ugly in at school, when it was light. But now I needed comfort and these clothes made me feel regular.

It was still dark when we drove up, out of the garage. We could just see the shapes of the trees and buildings in the weak street light. My mother turned on the heat. Bundled in soft clothes with my sneakers up on the dashboard, I was glad to be driving. I didn't care how far we went.

My mother crossed Wilshire Boulevard, onto Arden Drive. She slowed and then stopped in front of a house. "This is where his kids live. And the ex-wife, Elaine." The street was dark and empty. We could sit there and stare all we wanted. Beverly Hills seemed as small and innocent as Bay City, as anywhere.

"We should always get up early," I said.

"He put a lot of work into that house. A lot of work and a lot of money. He did that whole hedge, he told me. He says he still goes over to do the gardening."

"You don't think he'll ever want to go back?"

"Oh, no. I'm sure of it. He loves his kids, though. He'll always see his kids, I'm sure. Apparently, he worries about Amy. About her weight. Apparently, she's very insecure."

My mother started the car again and we drove south. Even Wilshire Boulevard was empty.

"I'm going to drive you past his apartment for a second. It's gorgeous inside, absolutely gorgeous. See, he had the big house with the garage and the pool and the yard and all, and he said to me, now, for the first time really ever, he's living alone. So he wanted something small and neat, without a lot of stuff around."

She parked across the street from one of the new Century City high rises and rolled her window down.

"He's up there on the fourteenth floor. See his window?" She craned her neck and bent out.

"No."

"It's dark now," she said, sighing. "He turned his lights off. He's probably gone to bed. Sweet." She smiled to herself.

The car rumbled softly and in the field next to us, already staked for development, light was beginning to come up from the ground. Down Wilshire, in the distance, the Veterans' building gleamed like a knife. We turned up to Sunset and drove on the wide, clean, loopy road for a long time. There's a place where Sunset meets Pacific Coast Highway. You turn at a stoplight and then you're there at the beach. We parked the car alongside the road and got out, to walk. The sand was still more gray than yellow. You couldn't see a sun yet. But it was lighter than it was dark. The water looked choppy. There were whitecaps. It was cold, we kept our hands in our pockets.

Close to the shore, the water seemed clear. The boom of waves crashing and the plate of green water, washing up on the sand, seemed to wipe out what we said and start the world over, new and clean, every minute.

Farther out black figures of surfers moved, appearing from where we were like letters of the alphabet.

"Look at how early they come out. That's great. Can you believe we really live here now?" Our hair blew in front of our mouths. "I'd love a house on the beach someday, Josh says that's what he wants, too. He's had the house in Beverly Hills with the kids, he's done that. Now he'd like something else."

"What about my school?" Beverly Hills kept a strict district. That was why we had to live where we lived.

"There must be a school out here somewhere."

"Do you think he'll want to get married again?"

"I don't know, Ann. We'll have to wait and see. We'll just have to see. He's already paying alimony and child support, you know. And those two will have to go to college, too, still. So I don't know. It was just a first date. Let's hope."

We walked north, against the wind. Sand blew up on my jeans, making a ripping noise.

"He did say, though, at the end, he walked to his balcony and he leaned back and said, Adele, I have never had a first date like this in my life. This was more dynamic and more, close, you know, than any first date in my whole life.

"And I said, I was thinking just the same thing. And it's true. Really, Ann. I never, never really feel anything on a first date. I told him, it usually takes me a long time to get to know someone. But this man really, really cares about me."

"Did he say he loved you?"

"Oh, no, Honey, he couldn't. Adults who've been married before just don't say that to each other right away. That takes a long time."

"A month?"

"Even longer. A year, maybe. That's almost like an engagement, saying that at our age. You might not even say it until you just went, Say, here, I bought a ring."

That made me remember Lolly and her shall-we-say-ring. My mother never got a ring from Ted. They'd decided to put the money towards the house on Carriage Court.

"But he did something. He did something last night that grownups do sometimes that shows you really, really care about someone."

"What?"

"Oh, Honey, it's something adults do in bed. But not many people ever do it. It means you really, really like the woman. You'll know when you're older. It just means they're really, really serious about you. They wouldn't do it with just any woman."

"How will I know if you don't tell me!"

"Well, I hope you're not planning to go to bed with anyone for a long, long time, Little Miss. Because, let me tell you, it wouldn't be a good idea with boys your age. The men really still want you to be innocent if they're going to marry you. They may say they don't, but they really do. It's different with me, Honey, because I've already been married."

"So when I'm married, how will I know?"

My mother laughed. "You'll just know. No one ever told me. The way you know never changes. It'll just happen. And you can tell. You really can." She sighed. "Boy, can you."

Farther up, a line of surfers in black wet suits walked towards the shore. In the shallow waves, they rode one hand on the boards, which bobbed ahead like dogs on leashes.

"So whatever this special thing is that Dr. Spritzer did, my dad didn't do that?"

"Oh, Ann, your father. Honey, your father loved me and he

loved you, too, but he's an irresponsible man. It wasn't just us. He left his jobs, everything. He's a selfish, selfish man."

The waves broke huge, about ten feet and rounded like perfect glass.

"But, don't worry, because there'll be other men in our lives. I'll catch another father for you, you just wait. Who knows, maybe it'll be Josh Spritzer. Wouldn't that be fun to have a doctor and a doctor like him, who looks like that? Everybody likes him, Ann."

"Even if you marry him, he won't be my father, though."

"I don't know. I think he would. I'll tell you, a father is some-one who DOES for you and GIVES to you. Not just take, take, take. I mean, what makes your dad your father? Just a little sperm. And genes. What did he ever do for you?"

I shrugged and pulled my collar up. She was right. I couldn't say anything to that.

"And I'll tell you, if we play it smart with Josh Spritzer, he may end up being THE adoring dad. Just watch. He told me last night that his kids give him OODLES of trouble. You can't even imag-ine, Ann. These kids really have problems. After dinner, we were having coffee and we talked and talked and talked about how worried he is with Andy. He doesn't even know if Andy can get into college, with his grades, Ann. Can you imagine, with a school like Beverly High and money? You'd think he'd have everything going for him. And he can't even get the grades. Not even for UCLA. But don't say anything to any of your kids. Even to Amy. They're trying to keep it quiet. I really shouldn't be tell-ing you any of this, because he hasn't even told Amy. But he thinks Andy may be on drugs.

"Then, at the end, we were just going to leave, he looked at me and smiled—he's got this huge, bright smile—and he said, 'I've been talking and talking about my kids, and you haven't said a word about yours. You must have problems with Ann, too.'

"And I said, 'Well, no, as a matter of fact, I don't.' He said, 'You don't?' And he looked at me, like this, you know, and said, 'You don't worry about drugs or her getting in with the wrong group of kids or anything?' And I said, 'Well, actually, we have pretty good communication. When she has a problem, she tells me and we work it out together.'

"And let me tell you, he was impressed, Ann. He was thinking to himself, Why aren't my kids more like her? You can bet."

We kept walking. She had no idea. I didn't tell her my problems. But I just jammed my hands farther down in my pockets. I wasn't going to fight now. I liked Dr. Spritzer.

She yawned. "I'm getting hungry. Should we trek up and see if Alice's is open?"

The pier seemed a long way off, but we could see the restaurant, with its shingled turret, from where we were. We started diagonally up the sand.

"Wouldn't you love a dog on the beach? Maybe we should get a dog!" My mother's voice boomed loud. The ocean always made her optimistic.

The sand became darker and dirty, when we got up near the restaurant. We stood and looked until we found our car, more than a mile down, by the side of the road.

My mother slapped her thigh. "Well, we can eat whatever we want and the walk back will work it off. We need that little exercise."

She grabbed my hand, right as I turned from the water, to follow the pebbled path to the door. "You know, we made the right choice, coming here. It was hard at first, but look at us now. Look at you. You're getting braces. With your teeth straight, your face will be just perfect and you're in Beverly Hills High with the richest and the smartest kids in the world. Really, Ann. The very top, top kids in this world. We never could have had any of this in Wisconsin."

She stood looking down at my face, waiting for something.

"I'm hungry," I said.

"You're really going to be somebody some day. These kids you meet now will be your connections, your milieu, for the rest of your life. I only wish I'd had the chances you'll have."

Where we walked in there were overturned chairs stacked on tables. A broom was pitched against the wall. At the front, farther down on the pier, a waitress walked between tables with a coffee-pot. Her thongs flapped loudly on the floor.

We took a table next to the window. There was one surfer, far away. "He shouldn't be out there all alone," my mother said. "Do you see another one? They're always supposed to have a buddy."

The waitress came to give us coffee. She didn't ask, she just slapped two mugs down and filled them. The skin on her face seemed tight and her toes looked old with wrinkles. But her hair was bleached white and her legs and arms were downy. She probably wasn't much older than I was. Her name, on a plastic pin, was Dawn.

"Isn't this great being up early? It's just seven now. We're not usually even up yet. Look at that. Did you see that wave? Absolutely amazing."

We ordered huge, sloppy omelettes that came with herbed potatoes and raisin wheat bread.

"We'll get a good breakfast and start the day with protein," my mother said. After one date, we already felt richer.

"So, when are you going to see him again?"

"Next Saturday night. He's going to take me to the opera." My mother sighed. "I'm going to need clothes for all this." She started biting her hand. She did that when she was nervous. It made her look terrible.

We felt rich for about as long as it took us to eat our food. Then the dread came back. All we'd have to do. Our plates lay almost empty; only crusts and the rind of a pineapple slice. It would be light in Dr. Spritzer's apartment now. He would be up, moving around. Loose.

"I'm going to have to have clothes and get my nails done. Let me tell you, Ann, there are plenty of women who'd give an arm and a leg to go out with this man. And they can spend all day in the beauty parlor with the manicures and the hairdressers and the leg waxes. And I just can't."

"But he liked you."

"I know. But let's face it. He saw me in my best thing. The green. And that's really all I have that's new."

"I need clothes, too."

"Oh, no, Honey. You really don't. You're just a child. Remember, I'm the one who has to catch us a man."

"I'm almost fifteen."

"I know you are, but believe me, I'm the one who has to find you a father—you really don't need clothes now. When you really need them is in college. You're not going to marry any of these boys you know now. They don't really get serious about you until college. And don't worry, because by then, you'll have the clothes and a great big house to bring your kids home to. I think we will by then, Ann. I really do."

She stared down at her plate and dutifully ate her crusts.

I looked around the restaurant. Then I saw three girls from my school, their black flippers on the floor next to their feet, their hair wet and combed. I panicked. It felt like my mother at Baskin-Robbins. I didn't want them to see me. They sat across from each other, talking and sipping coffee. I wanted to leave.

"There's some kids from school behind you. But please don't look now," I whispered. Now I hated the clothes I had on.

My mother immediately turned. "Where?"

"Over there, but would you please—"

"Well go say hi to them. Go on, I'll pay the check and you go over and say hi. Go on. You look real cute."

"I don't want them to see me."

"Don't be silly. Go on. You know what it is, it's your insecurity. And you shouldn't be insecure. You look darling. Really."

For a second, my eyes lifted, and at that moment, one of them saw me.

"Hi," she mouthed. "Come on over."

"They see me," I said in a low voice.

"Well, I'll pay the bill, you go on."

While my mother walked to the cash register, I skipped up the two steps to where they were. They pulled over a chair for me. One of them got up and took a cup from the waitress's station and poured me coffee. They moved quickly and easily, rearranging themselves and changing like the waves outside.

Huge breakfasts lay in front of them on the table. They each had omelettes with potatoes. There was a bowl of fruit and yogurt and a large plate of thick french toast with powdered sugar in the middle. They had a side order of ham. I felt hungry again. They must have seen me looking.

"Surfing makes you eat a lot," Leslie said. "We've been here since five."

"They got me out that early."

"Feels good when you're in though."

Windows surrounded the table and the light played now from here, now from over there. They were girls I knew from school, smart girls, who sat near the front of the class and asked questions.

"I better go, I think my mom's ready to leave." She stood by the cash register holding her closed purse in front of her. When I looked at her, she smiled.

"That's your mom? She's a fox."

"You guys surf?"

"Leslie surfs. We swim. It just feels good to be out in the morning. What are you doing here? Having breakfast with your mom? You do that a lot?"

"No, she had a big date last night, her first big date in California. So she woke me up and we came here so she could tell me about it."

Their chins sank on their hands. Their mouths fell loose. They leaned forward on the table.

"She *tells* you?"

I nodded. "We're pretty close."

"Did it go all right?" Leslie whispered. "The date?"

"So far. But you never know. They're so innocent." I turned and looked at my mother. "You could break her heart with a blow dryer—you guys don't want this food?"

"You hungry? Here. We'll order more. Isabelle's got her dad's credit card."

"Do you think she slept with him?"

I nodded. "She did."

Susan gasped, then caught herself. "Today's assembly, you know. We don't have to be there for first section. Until ten. We could give you a ride if you want."

"Yeah. Stay with us."

They picked at their food carelessly.

I walked down to my mother. She smiled at me. For once, it was me who touched her arm.

"See, that wasn't so bad, was it? You looked like you were all having fun up there. I was just watching you. Real cute girls. We'll do something with them once maybe. I'll take you kids out to dinner or a movie."

My mother was walking to the door, as if we were leaving. I followed a little back, trying to slow her. Finally, we were there at the door. She opened it.

"Come on, Pooh."

I shrugged. "There's an assembly today, we can come late, so I'll stay here with them and they'll give me a ride."

My mother's mouth twitched, then remade itself, but differently. "How can those kids drive? They're only fourteen."

"Susan's a junior. She has her license. She got a car for her birthday."

My mother ran her espadrille on the sand. She was outside already.

"I don't know if I want you going back in that car with them. We don't know how she drives, anything. You could be dead." She shook her head. "I'll worry all day. Why don't I just drive you and we'll take them out some other time. I could even bring the bunch of you here to the beach. Some Saturday or Sunday. You kids can lie in the sun. I'll bring a book and go sit by myself a little so you kids can talk alone."

"If you drop me off now, I won't have anything to do until ten."

"You could study in the library. Get ahead with your work."

"I want to stay," I said.

"Oh, okay," she said. "Well, have a good time." She looked enviously back at the restaurant. "I have to get going or I'll be late. You make sure she drives carefully. Okay, promise me that."

"I will."

She walked a few steps then turned back. "Wear your seat belt."

I'd never worn a seat belt in my life. My mother and I never used them. "Okay," I said.

I stood at the door watching her. When I turned back towards the table, I couldn't help thinking of how she was walking alone, all that way back to where our car was.

CAROL

■ □ ■

■　□　■　□　■　□　■　□　■　□　■　□　■

9

HAPPINESS AND ACCIDENTS

■ □ ■

When I look at those old pictures I hauled out for you, I see things I didn't see at the time. Mostly Hal, I guess. How unhappy he was. He's always got some goofy expression, holding his fingers up, rabbit ears over your head or making a face. Never anything just sincere or natural. Never a smile. I suppose Hal had it hard. Jimmy traveled three, four days a week those years, when Hal was growing up. He went on the road selling water softeners. Jimmy was Northeastern Regional #1 for Aqua-Max. And even just Brown County is a lot of little towns. I knew his route by heart in those days and I used to keep a little patch from the Wisconsin map torn off and taped up by the telephone. I put pins in it, so Hal would always know where his father was.

Benny was just happier, you can see it, in all the pictures, he's got that grin. That just looks like Benny to me. There he is in his costume by the boat. He was ring bearer for Brozek's wedding. You know, we did a lot, we really did things, when the boys were young. We had the boat and the snowmobile, and then for a long time we went up to the trailer.

We went to Disneyland, the four of us, we drove out in the mobile home. That was the first trailer and it wasn't a big one, but we had fun in it. It had bunk beds where they each slept and a kitchenette. We saw a lot that way, driving. Didn't you go to Disneyland too once with your mom and dad? I thought you and your mom flew out there. She was like that, whatever we did, you had to do, but better. So, if we drove the trailer out, you flew. But it was the same Disneyland we saw once we got there.

We traveled a lot then because Jimmy won trips as bonuses. And did he ever sell the water softeners! That was a good time for us and we liked the water softener people. They had fun. When you went somewhere, like a convention with them, they partied. We'd go out. These people with the Rug Doctor are all Jehovah's Witnesses. And they really sort of stick together. They come with their families, they bring the kids along to everything. And they don't drink or dance, so there's not much you can really do with them. They're nice and all during the lectures and the meetings, but then, after, in the evenings, they don't really socialize with you if you're not one of them.

And you, too, look at you. You're real happy in those old pictures. You can tell you and Benny are friends, even though you're not looking at each other—you're each holding up your toys, he's got his roller skate hanging down and his drum, you've got your deer. And all those packages behind you. Your mom always went overboard at Christmas. I think we still have that dollhouse somewhere in the basement. But look at your eyes and mouth. You look so grateful, like you're almost going to cry. I remember how you were. You and Benny had a good period when you were little, lot of people don't even have that.

I think you did change after your dad left, you and your mom both. Or who knows, maybe it was just getting older and going to school. You seemed quieter. I think you always studied a lot. But you didn't have that smile with the open eyes that you had when you were real small. When you were small, you always looked so grateful, nothing like your mom. I think Benny always kept that, but then Benny had it easier.

I worried about you. We felt bad for you with your mother. We thought you'd be the one to have it hard.

I remember once you wanted to go to school with Benny. He was in kindergarten then, not even real school, and I wrote a note and so you went. And Ann, you loved it, you just always liked school. You wanted to go again, and you went once or twice more. Then they were having a field trip. They were going to go on a bus to see Hansen's Dairy. The teacher sent a note home, the parents had to sign permission, a few days before. Oh crumps, all those years of notes and permission forms, every time you're absent, you have to have an excuse when you're sick to get out of gym. They really are hard on kids. Harder than needs be.

Well, I wrote your name in, too, and signed it, but when you came off the school bus that day, you and Benny both had notes pinned to your sleeves from the teacher. You weren't a five-year-old, she said, you weren't in the class, no, you couldn't come, you'd have to wait until next year. Now that seems mean, doesn't it? I don't know, maybe she had enough in her class already. But you wouldn't think one more would be any trouble. They had those ropes with the loops on them and you kids would each put your hands in one loop and go like that, roped together, when they took you across the street. It looked pretty in spring, when all the girls wore their nice summer dresses. I suppose they took those ropes along on field trips. So they never had to worry about losing you.

I remember telling you that, that you couldn't go to the dairy. You had to stay home. You were just mortified. I said it real fast, I didn't think it would be such a big deal, I was probably doing something else, unloading groceries, who knows what anymore. Well, your chin puckered up and wobbled, I could see you just trying your hardest not to cry and you didn't, not that I saw. You walked out of the screen door, with your hands real stiff by your sides and your head high. Your mother probably taught you that.

But with all your mother's messes, you turned out okay. Our kids were the ones who had the trouble. I will say this, your mom was right about one thing: education.

We didn't put as much stress on school. Hal had good marks all through grade school and the highest in his class on the Iowa Basics. I always thought that was why Adele liked him; she figured they were two of a kind, both smart in this family of averages. Benny always came home with Cs. I tried to help Ben with his schoolwork, but Jimmy didn't care too much. After work, he'd take Ben outside and toss a football until it was time for supper. He thought they should learn more outdoor things. Sports. I suppose that's normal with boys.

□

I sometimes wish I had a daughter. I would have liked that, I think. You know, going shopping and just talking, the things you do with a girl. You were a little like a daughter when you lived here.

I remember once you had a part in the school play. You were going to be Mary. I guess it must have been the Christmas pageant. I don't know anymore, but it was something they had in the auditorium and they invited all the parents and the grandmas. The mothers were supposed to make the costumes. So your mom was going to send you in your summer sandals and this long muslin robe, just a beige thing, like a bedspread or a curtain really, that your dad left in a closet. It was from where he came from. She didn't make a veil or anything. That was going to be it.

"For Mary?" I said to your mom. "For a boy, maybe, one of the shepherds, but not for Mary."

She always had an answer for you. "Well," she said, "that's what they wear over there, in Jerusalem. That's where it happened, you know."

You couldn't say a thing to that, because she'd been there and I hadn't. That much at least was true. But this was Saint Phillip's in Bay City, Wisconsin, and I *had* been here plenty. I don't care what they wear over there in Egypt, I knew they didn't wear that *here* when they were Mary in the Christmas play. So I bought some nice thick velvet, a remnant, it was a beautiful color with your hair, a deep, rich blue, and I sewed you a gown. She didn't mind, she just shrugged and let me do it. And we made you a white veil and a thing around your neck out of a starched sheet. You looked real nice. Your mom went and clapped and all, but here you were Mary and she seemed distracted. After, she came up and pulled on your collar. "You look like a little pilgrim," she said.

But she was funny because the next year you were an angel and she made a tremendous costume for that. I remember because she did it in Gram's garage and she got that gold glittery paint all over everything. On the lawn mower and the wheelbarrows. Gram said she never had been able to get it off the floor. The cement is still gold under the car.

"And how many people get to drive in on a yellow brick road,"

your mom used to say. She got it from that Lolly. I didn't think it
was so funny. I saw Gram's point.

One of those Griling girls was an angel with you, and your mom
made a costume for her, too. Your mom took sheets and old white
gloves and your tennies. Each of you had to give a pair of your
old tennies. Then she bought big pieces of tagboard and she cut
out wings. She untwisted coat hangers and made you each haloes
that stuck way up over your heads.

She laid it all out on the garage floor once when Gram was at
church and she spray-painted it all with gold. You can still see
the angel shape from the cement that's not gold on the floor.

Well, it did look good, just great. You two were the best angels
Saint Phillip's had ever seen. I think they even gave you some
extra lines to say—I suppose they couldn't have such well-
dressed angels just stand there doing nothing. You read real well,
nice and clear, even then in the second or third grade.

And after the pageant, the Griling girl came running up to us,
crying. I think it was Theresa. They'd gotten Bub Griling to come,
the older sister brought him, she was the only one that had any
sway, they said she looked like the mother.

Theresa was so proud, here she was in a play and with a nice
costume like that and he came, drunk. He went up to the stage
practically in the middle of the whole thing and shouted, "Now
what did you do to your shoes?"

They had to lead him out, the sisters. I remember the oldest,
the pretty one, with that wavy blond hair, she was wearing red
shoes. He was yelling, oh you can imagine how Theresa felt on
her big day, her family all leaving by the side door because her
sisters had to take her father home. And I'll tell you, Ann, he
stank.

So Theresa stood by us afterwards, when all the kids went with
their own families. And she was heaving and crying because he'd
said she'd have to go barefoot the next summer because he wasn't
going to buy new ones just because she'd gone and ruined her
shoes. Or she could wear them gold, he'd said. He was drunk.

So she tugged at your mom, asking, Will it come out? Could
she get it off somehow? Oh, those kids were pushy, but I guess

they had to be. He never took care of them and their noses were always running, they looked dirty. You know, you tried to be nice to them, but you finally think, Gee, he doesn't do a thing for them and they're his kids, heck, why should I?

Well, it was the last day of your school before vacation and the assembly was over early and they just let you go. So your mom and I took you and Theresa and Ben down to Shaefer's and bought you all new sneakers for the spring. We told Mr. Shaefer to give them to you each big so your feet could grow a little. It was snowing outside downtown and they put the streetlamps on early, it was a dark, wet day, and we were the only ones in the store. You three walked around the carpet in your new, white tennis shoes. You'd think it was the most exciting thing you'd ever had. You walked so delicately, as if you were stepping on the moon. That was what was nice about little kids. It didn't take much to please you then. Keds sneakers and oh, then you were all set.

You wanted to wear them outside, but we didn't let you—they would have been ruined in that slush. Mr. Shaefer wrapped them up nice, you each got your own shoe box to carry. Your mom insisted she pay for all the tennies and she stood up at the counter, giving him her check.

Theresa wanted to keep her gold shoes. I don't know what she ever did with them, threw them out probably, when she got home. They shed those gold sparkles all over wherever you stepped.

Later on, Mr. Shaefer called, her check bounced and I had to pay it. I never told Jimmy, he would have been mad. He called there at Mom's house first and it was just lucky no one was home and then he called me. So I drove down and gave him the cash that same afternoon. He was real nice about it, quiet. He gave me back the check and I folded it in my purse. I never did tell Adele. I talked to Mr. Shaefer a little while by the counter. He had people in the store that day, trying shoes on their kids. It was right after Christmas, I remember.

I only had a few times I was close with Adele, the way you and Benny were fifteen years. Once, really, that I remember, and that was when we were already grown. I sure remember fighting with her. That's most of what comes to mind.

But once my parents sent us both off to Mackinac Island for a holiday, just the two of us, alone. I think Milton wired the money and said to buy something for the girls. He always thought of us like that, as real little girls, even when we were grown. And we had just a wonderful time there. Your mom was already in college, she was going back for her sophomore year and I already had Hal. We took him with us, in a stroller. And he was good. He was an easy baby. Benny always tried to climb out of things, he hardly ever slept. But you could take Hal anywhere. So I never really felt hampered.

We went up on a Friday and you go from the train to a ferry and then over there on the island they don't have any cars. Just horses and buggies. Apparently, the people did own cars, it wasn't that backwards, they just figured out it was a better tourist spot with the buggies. So they passed a town ordinance banning the cars. Can you imagine! What they won't do to make the money. I think maybe they could have cars in the winter, when the tourists went home, but in summer, when we were there, you didn't see a one.

All the roads were that nice old-fashioned brick. We stayed in the Grand Hotel—there was the one big hotel in the center of everything, with pillars and long white steps going up to it. Oh, Ann, I think they were marble. And the horses and buggies would line up in front. It was real swishy. We came on a Friday night and we got all dressed up in our room, and I mean dressed up, we wore long white gloves that buttoned and gowns when we walked down those stairs. Oh, such stuff we had. Those gloves are probably still in the basement, but where would you ever wear gloves?

We did all kinds of things that week. We walked around, we shopped. Lake Michigan was too cold to swim already, it was Labor Day, the end of the season, just before the summer stuff really closed up. But we'd go and walk along the beach.

I remember one morning I woke up real early. It was the Wednesday, I think, we were taking the ferry home the next evening. Well, Adele always slept in, you didn't want to talk to her until noon, but I was used to getting up early from having a baby. They don't let you sleep. So I dressed real quiet and I dressed him and we took a walk. I left a note for Adele at the desk, to meet me for lunch. There was sort of a special bakery we liked and this was going to be their last day open. Most of the summer people had already left.

It must have been eight or nine in the morning. I pushed Hal in the stroller and we came to this painter by the side of the road, painting the woods. I recognized her because she worked at night in the lobby of the Grand Hotel, drawing portraits in oil pastels. I knew because Adele had had herself drawn in her long gown and gloves. Hal and I had been standing, waiting for her. I'd shookled him, rocking, saying, "See, oh, look, see she's drawing a picture of your Auntie Adele."

The artist was dressed differently now, she just had on pants and a shirt, and a cap, I suppose for the sun. I recognized her but I wouldn't have said anything because I didn't want to be a bother, but she said hello and put down her brush. She had her whole easel and palette set up there. It was really something to see, the spot she was looking at and then the way she'd painted it with her colors. Those silvery birches. It was really something. She had a thermos of coffee and we passed the metal cup between us. I rocked the stroller a little with my foot, to keep Hal quiet.

She said this was what she considered her real work, this outside-painting. She painted the water on the beach, too. I thought that would be hard, don't you think? Because it's always moving. It never keeps still. And she said yes, it was hard, she said she had to look a long time at it. She did the drawings in the hotel to make her living. She wasn't married or anything and she lived here on the island all year long. She said she painted outside every day she could, when the weather was nice, the summer and fall. Then in winter, she stayed in a garage and made bigger pictures from the ones she'd done all summer. She said every year she felt so glad when it was spring. In summer, sometimes after her work in the hotel, she painted at night, too, by the moonlight. She said she took the ferry over to Traverse City and painted tents at the county fair.

"Tents are so beautiful," she said. I never forgot that. Because they are pretty, but it's just not something you'd think of.

She was short, but you could see she wasn't real young. She must have been about my age and she had a real soft way about her. I remember thinking that she might never marry. And here I was with my baby, you know, and I thought, What a wonderful life. She seemed so independent.

She asked if I'd like her to keep Hal there awhile so I could walk around by myself or take her bike and ride a little. And I said, Okay, sure, why not. I had another sip of her coffee. We finished off the cup and I went and rode on her old black bike. Now when I think of it, that was selfish of me, using up her free time and taking her bike and her coffee, but then with a baby I felt so glad when somebody offered a favor. And I expected other people to ask me things, too. That's the way it was with young mothers.

And it was so nice riding. I was the only one on that road, a nice, wide, blacktopped road with a bright yellow line like chalk down the center, and sumac on both sides. I had on a short-sleeved white blouse and a skirt I'd ironed with a little travel iron that morning in the hotel and I felt the air rush up under my arms, so I must have been going pretty fast. I just pedaled, it felt so good, I don't know how long it had been since I'd ridden a bike. Then pretty soon I came to a big lawn for a school—a new, one-story building with all the windows on the same level. I stopped at the curb to tie my shoe. I was the only one anywhere around. It was a still, bright day. And across the street the sumac and the aspen trees and pines looked to me just like they did in her painting.

Then I stared down at my shoe, on the curb. Where the cement ended, there was ordinary dirt. A fringe of such tough grass started an inch or two in. I rubbed that dirt with my foot. And it was all dotted with such scraps, rubbish. Little bits of paper. Just junk. I don't know what it came from, wrappers, beer tops, junk

like you saw everywhere. It made me feel awful, like there was
no place special, there would always be this dirt. And what I'd
seen before, the pretty thin trees and like in her painting, that
seemed a small part where all over there was loads and loads of
this dumb dirt. Isn't that for the birds, thinking like that on a
holiday? I had to make myself lift my eyes up to those trees again.

That afternoon we met Adele at the bakery we liked and we stayed
a long time after lunch. It was their last day. Kids came over from
the mainland to work the summer and they were all going home,
back to school, I suppose, their regular lives.

Adele had made up a little paper chart and we were figuring
out her schedule of courses. She switched back and forth every
which way and we went over and over it. It seemed like a game
to me. Economics on Wednesday mornings, English from four to
six. And people would walk by and look at Hal and I'd take him
up out of the stroller. It was the end of the summer and we had
suntans. Adele and I were both young.

We sat there for so long we got hungry again. It was outside, in
a little area closed off with a wrought-iron railing. We sipped ice
water with flowers frozen in the cubes. Those glasses, I don't
know what it was, they were thick maybe, they just felt good in
your hand. We ordered coffee and blueberry tarts.

The coffee tasted strong and they brought real cream. And
those blueberry tarts were delicious. I remember taking mine out
of the little wax paper ruffle and slipping it on the plate. They
printed the wax paper with gold and they made the tarts with
mounds of blueberries under a currant glaze and custard—then
a thick layer of chocolate just above the crust. I wish I had the
recipe for those. Adele could probably tell you, just from tasting,
what was in it, what spices. But she would never remember anymore.

The paper doilies from under the pastry blew onto the brick
patio in a little breeze, they were white with gold fluting. They
had gray marble tabletops, with dark green iron chairs.

Hal stood up in his stroller blowing soap bubbles. These were
really the last few summer days. At the curb under a tent of green

leaves, I watched an old man put his hand under his wife's elbow and ask if she wanted an ice cream. They crossed the street in a diagonal, slow, to the cart on the other side. Michigan chills early. They get the Canadian winds.

That chocolate in the blueberry tarts was such a surprise. Oh, they were good. I've meant to try and make them like that a hundred times, but it would be a lot of work. I even bought those little tart pans, I have them here somewhere. I think they put in something special, nuts, I'm sure, and maybe a little lemon in that crust.

People walked past us and some at other tables stood up and left. We just stayed. Behind Adele, a girl who worked there sat with her legs crossed. Their uniforms were red and white, like candy stripers'. She had her hair pulled back off her face in a plain rubber band and she took a long time smoking a cigarette.

Adele would every once in a while bend down and try and teach Hal something. She'd wave her fingers in front of his face to make his eyes move and say This Little Piggy on his toes.

"He's very bright, Carol," she said. "He'll be a bright, bright boy. You'll see. I'll bet he's reading at two or three."

That meant a lot to me from her, but I tried not to show it. Even being sisters, we were shy sometimes.

"So, you think he'll be all right?" I laughed a little. "Smart like you?"

"Smarter." She sighed. "The boys always are. The lucky dogs."

"So you don't think I did too much the wrong thing marrying Jimmy and staying home."

She nodded her head real slowly. Hal stood up in his buggy. We'd bought him that bottle of soap bubbles with the wand. I held his hands, trying to get him to sit down.

"No, I don't think you did the wrong thing, Carol. I think you'll have a good, happy life."

I never forgot that. My chin swelled, I could feel the blood coming there and my lip was doing something funny—I'd had no idea before I cared so much what she thought. I glanced over to see if she was noticing, but she looked away. I suppose she was worried about herself.

"And I think you will, Adele. You've done so much already, at your young age. You'll get your degree, maybe even go to graduate school. I think you're going to have an exciting, exciting life. You'll go places. I know you will."

She smiled at me, but one of her distant smiles. I suppose she thought there was a lot I didn't know. And there was. Plenty I couldn't understand. She hasn't had the easiest time. I suppose even then she must have worried. You could see. A girl that pretty and nervous, beautiful, really, looking all over, scattered, putting on lipstick there at the table.

"Should we go?" she said.

"No, let's stay." For once I acted like the leader. You'd think I always would have been, but even eleven years older, I never was with her. The waiter strolled by and all of a sudden I felt in a festive mood.

"We'd each like another tart," I said. "Two more. And two more cups of your good coffee." That brought us both back to normal. We laughed and laughed. Adele lowered her voice the way she does when she's joking around, trying to be stern, saying, "Carol, you really shouldn't have," but we both wanted more. She slapped her behind. "Why not?" It was our last day of vacation. We were going home tomorrow and then Adele would leave for college. We had plenty of money, extra. We felt like rich girls. And we didn't worry about weight or health or any of that yet either. We were young. And we were both pretty enough the way we were, we knew that. I was married already. That was the least of our worries.

He brought the coffee first in nice china, with pink morning glories painted on the cups. We poured the cream in, it was that old-fashioned heavy cream, almost brownish, and it just swirled and swirled. We watched it a long time, longer than ever needs be. But then we had the time.

For a while everything seemed to be going good with us. Hal really did seem okay, except in school. We had the trailer at Pine Mountain and we went up every weekend skiing. For once, Hal and Jimmy agreed on a sport and Hal could do it. Ted and your mom drove up, too, and stayed in the lodge, we'd always end up there together. You got to be a good little skier, you had your white bunnyfur jacket, remember your mom bought you that? She took a lot of flack for it, believe me. Gram, everybody, thought she would spoil you.

She and Ted and Jimmy and I were all drinking in the lodge bar the night when we found out Hal broke his arm. Your mom and Ted tried to keep apart a little and have their own social group, but they really couldn't. It was small enough so everybody knew everybody. We each sort of liked someone else. I sat on Paul Shea's lap in that cocktail lounge. Jimmy flirted too, with Barbie Shea. That's really as close as we ever got to anything risqué. But we were all there together, so nothing too much could ever happen.

And one of those nights in the bar, they came and told us Hal broke his arm. Safety patrol was up bandaging him on the slope and they'd have to take him to the hospital for a cast. It was that night skiing—I never liked it. It wasn't safe.

So Hal couldn't ski that whole winter he had the cast. We still drove up every weekend, we had a whole social life there by then, and Hal moped around in the trailer. You were a little wizard. You were a real good skier, jumping down those moguls. Well, Ted was good, and he'd taught you. Benny really couldn't keep up and he was always naturally so good at any sport. But I remember him maneuvering his snowplow. You used to dare him onto the tough slopes with you.

One night we were in the lounge and you came in to find your mother because you'd hurt your nose. You kids had been playing on those metal bars for the lines in front of the lift pass windows. You used to twirl on them like monkey bars and I guess you were turning and you just smacked your nose, hard. You had your hand over your face when you ran in.

Of course, your mom got hysterical. "Oh, no, what did you do to yourself? You've ruined your nose."

She held your face to the side and cried, it was ridiculous, we hadn't been near so upset with Hal's broken arm. She was sure your nose was broken and your whole life was down the drain because now you wouldn't grow up to be pretty and no one would want to marry you.

"I TOLD you not to play on those bars," she kept saying.

"You did not." By that time she had you crying, too, she'd convinced you that you'd ruined your chances for a decent life.

Ted and Paul Shea inspected you. They thought it wasn't broken. Ted ordered your mom another drink. She wanted to call an ambulance and take you twenty miles to a hospital. Paul said they didn't do anything for broken noses, anyway, they just had to heal. It's a good thing Ted was there or God knows what she would have done. I told her, too, it probably wasn't anything but a bump, but she didn't listen to me. With your mom, you really had to be a man for her to listen.

She still thinks you broke your nose that night and that's why she wants to get you a nose job. She blames us for not letting her call the ambulance. She begged me, Carol, tell her, tell her *you* did it and tell her how crooked her nose is. She doesn't believe me. Well, it doesn't seem crooked to me. I told her that and she just sighed, ogh, you know, like everyone's against her.

We skied three winters and the year Hal broke his arm was the last time. That March, towards the end of the snow, when we thought there'd be one or, at the most, two more weekends, Hal skied. He knew he wasn't supposed to. The doctor had told him time and time again. He still had the half cast and a sling on that arm. But he had to ski, he had to show he could do it with one arm.

We all saw him at about the same time. Your mom and I were in a chair lift together going down. We went on the high slope where I was scared to ski, but there was a lodge at the top and I'd wanted to go and have hot chocolate. So your mom had talked the lift man into letting us take it up and back again. We were the only ones on the whole lift going down, all the rest were empty chairs. That's one thing your mom is great at, if you ever want to do something that's not allowed, she can talk the person into it. She gets a kick out of it. Behind us, going up, Jimmy sat in another chair with Barbie Shea. Ted was giving a lesson at the top of the mountain, demonstrating the pole. He punched both poles hard into the snow. Across from him a row of skiers copied. First we saw you and Benny, standing where the moguls were way too high for you. They were just a little smaller than you were.

"Oh, my God, look where they are, Carol," your mother said, grabbing my arm. She leaned so far over the chair tilted and swung and we practically fell out.

You seemed to know you were over your heads. You both moved real slow, snowplowing around the moguls, leaning in so your skis were almost horizontal. You looked like you were afraid to look down. You were going first and Benny followed behind you.

"Now, don't yell. Or they'll get scared and then something *will* happen."

"They should take their skis off and walk down. I'm going to tell them to do it. Ann," she shouted. "Ann. Benny."

The chair lift moved pretty quick though. You looked like you heard us but didn't see where we were. All of a sudden, you were staring somewhere else and then we stared too.

There was Hal on an orange stretcher, with his cast on his chest and the other arm out in the snow. Three Red Cross Safety Patrol boys knelt bandaging his leg. We had to keep riding down the chair lift, we couldn't get out. Ted was skiing down to him, neat smooth slalom jumps. He'd left his class, with their poles stuck in the snow, at the top of the mountain. You and Benny looked down and tried to steer towards him, but you could barely move as it was. Then I looked over my shoulder and I saw Jimmy. He was the only one who didn't know. I saw his hat and the back of his head. He was getting ready to jump off the chair lift.

So then Hal had a broken arm and a broken leg and we didn't ski anymore. He really had a hard time of it. That leg was in a cast eight months. He stayed out of school all that spring and I stayed home from the store, too. He mostly read and I'd watch television in the breezeway, but we would eat together. I liked having him home again. Sometimes Gram would walk over and have a cup of coffee with us. She'd bake a cinnamon ring or a blueberry buckle and carry it over warm, covered with a dish towel.

Then when Hal went back to high school, they took his

crutches away and kicked him down, those big boys. They could really be mean. And I don't think he ever caught up after the time he missed for the leg. Then when he finally had the cast taken off, he got in with a bad crowd.

When Hal was a freshman he stopped writing his name. At first it just seemed like some stunt a teenager would pull—but he kept to it so darn long. Then pretty soon he didn't write at all—even those tests with the little blue circles you fill in with a pencil, he turned them all back empty.

So they called us, they said specifically that both parents were supposed to come, so Jimmy and I went, one morning, and talked to the principal. They said Hal should see a psychiatrist and they wanted us to both go, too, the psychiatrist wanted the whole family. Now you read about that a lot, but I'd never heard of it then. Well, that was just too much for Jimmy. He banged his fist on the table and said, "No son of mine is going to any psychiatrist. There's nothing the matter with him. The only thing wrong with him is he's stubborn. And he's lazy." Jimmy took the truck and drove back to the water softener store. I apologized for him, but it didn't really do any good. I walked down those halls and the sound of my heels echoed so. But Jimmy's mind was made up. And when he gets like that, it's no use trying to talk to him. What I remember now about that day are those stone hallways and that I was wearing a hat with a feather on it.

He started up with that Merry. We weren't happy, no family would have been, really, I don't think, if it was their son. It wasn't just that she was poor, that wasn't it. But she was dirty. That was really the thing. When Ben went out with Susie, it was a completely different story. We wouldn't have said a thing if he'd decided to marry her. We would have been glad. And her parents weren't rich either. They both worked. But they were nice people. Clean.

But with Merry's family, it really wasn't so good. You know, you hear things. Her mother was gone somewhere, I don't know where, but she wasn't dead. She lived somewhere up north, Escanaba maybe, working as a waitress. And the father drank. I drove by the house once or twice on the way to the cemetery. They lived on Spring Street and their house was one of the worst. It was an old, gray house and all the basement windows were cracked. We heard that Merry had a sister who was sixteen or seventeen that the father had kicked out. She was living on her own, in an apartment above a store, and still going to the high school. Some at church said she was pregnant. So it wasn't all the nicest.

We probably shouldn't have said a thing. Adele used to call us and yell, DON'T tell him not to go out with her, that'll just make him REBEL. Say, Hey, she's a great girl. Have fun!

And then when he graduated, we thought at least he'd go to college and meet other people. You were still here, when Hal finished high school. We were all at the graduation in the gym, when he was number 563 in his class. Merry wasn't going to college. She was going to stay at home and work in a shop. I think she ended up at McDonald's. Whitewater wasn't much of a school, but we thought he could at least get on his feet there. If he applied himself for a year he could transfer to the University of Wisconsin. But he drove back home almost every weekend and partied with the kids from high school. And that was all during Vietnam. So lots of them were signing up. Their parents couldn't pay for college, so they went in and then when they came back, they had the GI Bill. Griling's boy and all those Brozeks went into the service right after high school. Most all the kids around here signed up—the kids you and Benny played with, too. But see by then there wasn't a war.

Well, in April or May, Hal came home and said he wanted to drop out. After Gram's already paid for the whole semester. We tried to talk him out of it, we all did, Adele came over and talked to him for hours about college education, college education.

"So where did a college education get you?" he said. "It got you married to a college professor who left you with a kid to raise by yourself."

Now God forbid if I said that, but when he did, she laughed.

We found out then, too, that he was flunking—Adele got that out of him, he didn't say that to us, so that pretty much had to be the end of it. So we thought, he could come home and work for a

year or two and when he'd grown up a little he'd miss the fun of
school and then he could go again and maybe apply himself more.

Then he let out the real bombshell. He wanted to get married
to Merry. They were in a hurry. Well, that was almost worse than
dropping out. That was permanent. Oh, did we fight. We did
everything we could to talk them out of it. And for once we all
agreed—your mom and I and Jimmy all thought it would be just
dumb for him to marry her so young.

Gram didn't like her either, but she wouldn't say anything. She
said he was hearing enough bad from all of us, she could just
keep her mouth shut. But she hoped too that we could talk him
out of it. "At least wait," she used to say when I'd complain to
her. I went over lots during that time and had coffee with her in
the middle of the day. Hal was at the store, helping Jimmy. Jimmy
thought if he wasn't going to be in school and if he wanted to get
married too yet, he'd better learn to earn his keep. And I think
Jimmy worked him hard. Every morning, they were yelling and
fighting before they even left the house. Oh, it wasn't nice. It was
really awful. Benny got real quiet. I suppose he didn't know what
to do, he liked his brother and he liked his dad, so he'd get up
real early and I'd fix him breakfast before they were dressed. He
sort of snuck around, he was afraid to get caught in someone's
way.

So I tried to be extra nice to Ben. I'd be up early, anyway. I
really couldn't sleep, so I'd get myself up and make a cup of
coffee and pretty soon Benny'd come down to the kitchen, all
dressed with his books ready. I'd fix him cinnamon toast or an egg
and he'd eat it real fast and gulp his milk and then he walked
over to Gram's. And Gram would feed him a second breakfast.
He had such an appetite and he always stayed thin. It would just
be a boy to have those long legs.

We all went over there to her house when it got rough. I'd go in
the middle of the morning to have some peace. Jimmy and Hal
called me to complain about the other one during the day. Jimmy
called from his office and Hal called from a pay phone, but if I
didn't answer, they hung up. They wouldn't call me at Gram's.
And Gram would fix a pot of coffee and we'd eat a little some-

thing. She had her house so nice, she had the two bird feeders hanging, one outside each of the kitchen windows. And every once in a while when we were talking a bird would come. We'd stop and watch.

I told her about how dirty Merry was. You'd think if you were going to meet the parents of the boy you wanted to marry, you'd at least wash your hands, wouldn't you? Even if she wasn't going to take a bath. Her fingernails were so dirty, I can't tell you. There was a black line under each one. And I told Gram that the once I'd gone over to her house with Hal, there were dishes in the sink, and in the drawers, when she went to get a sweater, I saw everything mixed up, scrambled like in a washing machine.

Gram's teeth rubbed together the way they did when she was nervous. She told me old Tinta Griling, Bub's mother, was like that. She kept her clothes in the drawers rolled up in little balls.

Well, your mom drove over with Ted and talked to Hal. That didn't work. Finally, we had everybody together. We had the priest from Saint Phillip's, your mother, you and Benny were back playing in Benny's room.

Jimmy and I had practically given up. We'd tried everything. They were lots calmer than we were. She sat there on the couch with her short, funny hair and her dirty nails and just acted polite. Can you imagine sitting in your fiancé's house with the parents and everyone telling you they think you're too young? But she wasn't the least bit affected. No, they both said the same thing, they were in love and they wanted to get married.

"So how do you think you're gonna make a living?" Jimmy must have yelled that ten, fifteen times.

And Hal just said he was ready to work, he'd go out and find a job. Merry had been working now a year already. We could see the priest gradually coming around to their side. And we couldn't really stop them. They were both of age. They didn't need our permission.

But Adele wasn't going to let it drop. She always thought Hal was like her and she wanted him to go to college and really make something of his life. I suppose we'd already given up on some of that. I couldn't picture him going back to school, really. He hadn't been paying attention most of high school. He'd have so much to catch up. And then we didn't go to college either.

Jimmy and I sat with the priest in the kitchen, I fixed coffee, Jimmy stood looking out the glass doors to the backyard. He was on his second vodka gimlet. We were exhausted. Adele was talking to them in the breezeway. We could hear her, her voice was still energetic after all this time. She seemed so young to me, always.

"So, tell me why, really, you have to get married. Why can't you just keep dating? What's really the big deal?"

"Say we want to go to bed together."

I put my hand over my mouth. That was our Hal. I'm sure the priest heard, but he didn't move, he stared down at his coffee mug. It was still empty. Right away, I poured. Then, for sure he heard the next thing my sister said. When she gets excited, her voice is like a bell.

"So why don't you just go to bed together? Let's face it. It's 1968 and people go to bed together before they're married. Plenty of people. You know that. So why the charade? Go on and go to bed together. Take a roll in the hay."

My sister. With a priest in the house. I said, "Oh, crumps, you never know with her." I thought I had to say something. Jimmy turned from the window, slow and grinning, looking at the priest. I think we were both waiting to see if the priest would say anything.

"Leave it to Adele. She's not shy." Jimmy's grin got bigger. "I say she's right, let 'em go ahead. I wouldn't say the same if it was my daughter. But she's not my daughter."

"Oh, sure, and just wait then till she gets pregnant. That'd be real nice, sure."

The priest looked up at the wall telephone. "Let's hear what they say."

"It's a sin," Merry said.

"We want to be okay in the church." That was our Hal.

"Oh, come on, the church looks the other way. Don't you think plenty of people at Saint Phillip's are going to bed together? Why, sure they are. You should hear the half of it. And the church'll change its mind. A few years ago we couldn't eat meat on Friday, now we go to McDonald's. That's no reason to get married."

She went on and on, long after we stopped. She wanted to write Hal recommendations to the University of Wisconsin, Madison, where he hadn't a chance of getting in. She ran all around town, she lined up an appointment for him to go to a psychiatrist. I don't remember anymore what all she did. She did try to help him. But he wasn't going to listen to anyone. We all said we wouldn't go to the wedding if they had one and so they took the bus up to Escanaba one weekend and got married there.

Jimmy went around saying they were living in sin because they weren't married in the state of Wisconsin, but six months or so later, it wasn't long, when she was pregnant, they had another wedding in the backyard and Gram baked a cake and we all went. So that was the end of it. Hal was working at Fort Adams paper mill then, she was still at McDonald's and they had a trailer over by the airport in that lot the Indians own. Those Indians want to put up a hotel there now. Yah! That's their land, they say. Can you imagine?

And then Hal had to go into the service. It was really one thing after the other. He never had any luck. He ended up enlisting because his lottery number was fifty or sixty something—high up. It was 1969 and he knew five or six boys who'd been killed already. He thought in the air force he had a better chance of staying here and fixing engines or something. Jet mechanic. I don't know, maybe he thought being married would help. It didn't, I don't think. He thought he'd like the air force better than the army or the marines. A lot of his friends from high school were already in. Lot of Bay City boys fought in Vietnam.

Hal had to go to boot camp with Merry still pregnant and that seemed real sad. We thought he wouldn't even see the baby or only once or twice, before he left. Adele had a fit again, oh ye gods, she was on the phone with us every day with a scheme. First she wanted to get some kind of student deferment, then she heard somewhere that you could get out of it if you had them put braces on your teeth, she thought of everything.

But we didn't know if it would even be such a bad thing for him

to be in the service. Jimmy thought it might make him grow up. I
didn't really know, one way or the other, but he was out of the
house and I thought it wasn't our business anymore, so I didn't
interfere. But this time Hal went along with Adele. He wanted to
get out too. They tried the whiplash and the flat feet and the
allergies, and whatever else they could say, but it didn't work. He
had to go in.

And after all that fuss, he was only gone nine weeks. He went
to the Lackland Air Force Base in Texas at the beginning of the
summer. And I guess the boots there didn't fit him quite right.
Hal was always flat-footed. I've read now that that could have
been helped some if we'd gotten a certain kind of shoe with metal
arches when he was little, but we didn't know about that then.
Your mom read up on such stuff. So you and Benny had good
shoes, Stride Rites, all the most expensive. But then Shaefer said
your arches got ruined anyway with some red pumps, real fash-
ionable, that your mother bought you in Milwaukee. So, she might
as well have let you wear shoes from K-Mart. The ones from Milwaukee were just as bad.

I guess in Texas they were all marching along in some field.
He was overweight then. And they shaved his long hair off right
away and put him in something called Motivation. They made
them march and march. He lost fifty pounds in that nine weeks.
Hal with his flat feet in boots that didn't fit him right and pretty
soon he tripped over a pothole and I think he even bumped his
head with the rifle. So he wasn't there a week even, and we got a
telegram that he was in the hospital, he'd torn a ligament in his
leg. And then I guess they let him out and made him march again
too soon, before he was really better, and so the leg got worse and
he fell again, from walking on that bad leg, and that time he
slipped a disk, too. And so there he was in the hospital again. He
was in for a week or two and then they had him out marching.
Every time the leg got worse. They were doing something wrong
or maybe just making him march too soon before it was healed,
but he said at night his leg would swell up over the knee, as big
as a basketball. Finally, the doctors said they wanted to operate
on the leg—that was the same leg he'd broken skiing—and he

said no, he wasn't going to let them. Well, we wouldn't give permission either, not with what happened to Granny, so he stayed in the hospital there and then they finally let him out. He got honorable discharge, medical deferment. They decided he was costing them too much money.

I often wondered if Hal didn't feel bad about being home. I'll tell you, I was glad, and Gram, too. Jimmy was a little ashamed, he didn't say it, but I knew. I hope to God Hal couldn't tell anything. But with Jimmy it was that he'd been in the war and that he'd always tried to get Hal going with a sport all his life, and it just never took. Hal probably should have been the bookworm type, but he got off on the wrong track with that, too. We didn't talk about it once he was home, but I know there were people who probably teased him, because all around here I could tell from the way they asked that they didn't respect us for it. We told them it was honorable discharge, but they still thought less of us. Chummy had two over there, one in the army, one in the marines. And Bub and Chummy had high school boys planning to sign up right away when they graduated.

You and your mom were gone before our real trouble started. We were worried about you still, thinking you'd be all alone with her in California.

I thought maybe that was where Hal got started with the drugs, down in Texas. You read so much now about the soldiers getting hooked on dope. Lot of them got killed because they were over there high on drugs. The Vietnamese wasn't high, so he shot our boys first. Sure. And now all those little Vietnamese we were fighting against are here in Bay City getting money from the government.

But Hal says they were already in the drugs before he left. We didn't see, we just heard about it later. That's the worst part of being a parent. All the dangerous, important things happen to your children without you. You hear about them later, too late. Apparently, he and Merry were in it together. No, it wasn't just the marijuana. We didn't know anything about it. He had his hair long and wore those dirty jeans, but then they all looked like that. And we didn't go visit the trailer. For one thing, she never invited us, for dinner or a housewarming or anything, so we saw them when Gram had something doing and we all went over there. On Christmas and Easter, we did something. Either at our house or we'd take everybody out. After you and your mom left, there wasn't much of a family.

I'd seen the trailer once or twice. I always told Merry I'd baby-sit for Tina when she was busy and a few times she called and said could I come pick her up. Merry had a job at the canning factory then and that is hard work. They all say it. Hal was on at the paper mill. I think she had a shift so she was working most evenings, too. I was glad to take Tina. I was glad to get her out of there. The trailer was truly filthy. I don't think she ever cleaned. There were candles burnt halfway down on the table and they'd just let the wax go right into the wood. And anywhere you'd step there were clothes all over the floor. I bet they just picked their clothes up off the floor in the morning and put them on.

Now Hal says all that time they were in the drugs, so that explains a lot of it. Things got real bad. Hal said sometimes they'd each go out to bars separately, he and Merry, and leave Tina next door with the neighbor. Oh, that still makes me mad. We would have gladly taken her. We would have loved to and I hate to think who those neighbors were, I saw them once, they were no better than Hal and Merry. The husband had such long wavy hair and those tiny little glasses they used to wear on the bottom of his nose. It still makes me mad to think of it.

But he said they'd each find somebody else at one of those bars and bring them home to the trailer. He said whichever got there first, that one got the bed. And the other couple had the couch. So it wasn't good. And who knows when they remembered to go next door and get Tina—then, in the middle of the night, or in the morning with four people milling around that little trailer. He says when she was still in diapers, just learning to talk, Tina knew the word peyote. I guess they had to tell her when they took her over here or to Gram's just what she could and couldn't say. I asked him lot of times if he gave her anything to take and he says no, but I wouldn't be surprised. Or if Merry did during the day to keep her quiet, while she was tired, from the night shift. They say Bub Griling's mother used to give Bub whiskey when he was a baby to make him sleep. But Tina's all right, she's a smart girl and a good girl, so I guess that's the main thing, whatever happened.

We didn't find out until everyone did. You were lucky you weren't here then. It was all over. Election year and the drugs had been coming in and the kids with the long hair, the hippies, and people got fed up. People had had enough and they wanted to crack down. And wouldn't you know, Hal was the one who got caught.

He says now he was set up and I believe him. But he admits that he was breaking the law. He was taking the drugs and he was selling them. He says they were in it for the money. He thought he could make money fast. And sure, look what happened. But he always had to have a scheme to get rich quick. He couldn't just wait and save like everybody else.

We saw it on TV at the store. It was the whole front page of the *Press Gazette* that night and the big story on the local news. FOUR BAY CITY BOYS ARRESTED IN DRUG TRAFFIC. Hal says one of the people who gave the drugs to him was caught for something else, assault with a deadly weapon, and so they really had him, and he was the one who told.

Gram was down in her kitchen, playing solitaire, and she heard it on the radio and she had the stroke. That was her first stroke. We found her right away because Jimmy drove over from the store to tell her, we were scared she'd see it on the television. Really, that was one of the worst things of my life, seeing Hal on the television. Jimmy said he thought the same thing. We recognized him and we heard it and we just couldn't fit it all together. We were really in a daze then.

Jimmy found Gram leaning over unconscious against the counter with the radio still on. I guess she stood up and went closer to the radio, probably thinking the same thing, Could this really be our Hal? But they gave the address and all. Hal Measey of Oneida Parkway, son of James and Carol Measey, Rural Route #1, Lime Kiln Road.

So we had my mom in the hospital, we didn't know if she was

going to make it, we had Hal in jail with a twenty-thousand-dollar bail. And we had to get a lawyer. Well, we mortgaged the house. We did it that same day. Jimmy and I went home, it was three o'clock, we'd left Gram in the hospital, we'd locked the shop, and Jimmy called Shea on the phone. When he got off he looked at me and said, "Carol, we're going to have to mortgage the house. That's the only way we can get that kind of money." I said, "Okay, Jimmy," and we drove downtown to the bank and did it.

By the next day, everyone knew. The women neighbors came over to say they were sorry about Gram and could they help. They didn't say a word about Hal. I'll tell you, they were real funny. And when I think now how long we'd lived there—here we'd been twenty-one years already; they'd known Hal all his life, the way I'd known their kids. It wasn't nice, Ann, it really wasn't nice. They thought we were foolish to put up the house and to this day I think it's the best thing we ever did. That's what turned Hal around, that his father would do that for him.

Later, Hal found out Chummy across the street had called in to the police and said there was something going on over here and so they already had a record of complaints against him. That was when Jimmy and I went away for vacation, from the water softener bonuses. Hal and Merry and Ben would throw a party. Well, I suppose they were a little wild. I never knew because they always had it cleaned up nice by the time I got home. But Hal said he used to see Chummy standing over there at the window, watching, holding his curtain back with one hand. And can you imagine calling in to the police without ever once saying a word to Jimmy when we came home? And I'll tell you, I remember when Chummy was in high school, he was one of those with the hot rods and the fast cars. He was a greaser. You wouldn't know it now, but he went through a period when we were young.

And they all thought we were just crazy to mortgage the house. They said if he skipped town then there we'd be and we wouldn't even have our house. But we didn't think twice, we did it and Hal listened to the lawyer. It was someone who worked with Shea. The other boy in with Hal had the trial and he went to prison. He was in the penitentiary for five years. Hal pleaded guilty—the lawyer said with that judge and a jury and here in Bay City, it just wasn't going to go—but he didn't tell on anybody else. He said he just wouldn't do that because that was the thing that made him get caught. They sentenced him to two years in jail, nights and weekends. He had to check in by seven o'clock and they let him out the next morning to go to work.

And that's when he and Jimmy started to get closer again, because of course, Fort Adams fired Hal when it all came out, and in order to make it so he could leave and work during the day, Jimmy said he'd give him a job at the store. That was around when we were getting out of the water softeners and getting into the pressure cleaners. So Jimmy gave Hal all the soaps. He sold the soaps. And it was a step up for him, I think. He was off the drugs and he had a job again. Merry used to bring Tina in at lunch and they'd sit in the back there and eat. I have to say, she was good. A lot of women would have just let him be, but I suppose she was in on the drugs, too. At least she knew about it. I told them a couple times, I'd give them money so they could go across the street and eat lunch at the Big Boy—he worked so hard all day, he really did—but they didn't want to. They just stayed in that little back room. I suppose they were so down in the dumps they didn't want to see anybody. She'd either pack a lunch or stop at McDonald's and bring them all burgers. So at least he saw Tina every day.

I wasn't at the store too much then because I was taking care of Gram. She came home from the hospital and she wasn't so good. She didn't lose anything, she remembered and she was just like herself, but she shook. She cried more. But that first one wasn't too bad.

And you know, even then, she was just so pretty. You weren't born yet when my dad was alive, but then she was really something. How can I describe her? I don't know, except to tell you that we all knew. It was like a fact of the world and it made a difference. When she came into a room or stepped out onto the porch, you felt special, like something was going on there. And I'll tell you, Ann, I don't know what it is, but we're getting smaller. Granny was a big tall woman with enormous breasts and hips. Her bust was a size D. And Mom was tall too, thin but tall. She was the same size as Dad. That's why, when he died, she could just wear his clothes. You know, around the

house. And I'll tell you, even in his old overalls that he used to wear
out to the mink, she'd be on her knees in the garden, wearing those
and an old old shirt and her hair braided and pinned up in the
back—and even like that she was beautiful. She was weeding like
that once, after the stroke, and the meter reader asked her out on a
date. Well, Adele and I were each pretty, I think, but we weren't
either of us what you'd really call beautiful. And we are both smaller.
I'm five foot four, she's only an inch or so taller. And even before the
mastectomy, I had no bust, really. And you, you're the shortest yet,
smaller than both your parents. And a figure almost like a boy.
Maybe that's because your mom didn't have enough to eat when she
was carrying you. I remember they had you in an incubator. But still
your Granny was so tall.

We really weren't friendly with them across the street for a long
time. And then later, we found out when Dicky and Ralph came
back from the service—Jay didn't go to Vietnam, the war was
over by then, he was too young—they brought back dope and they
got Chummy to try it once when they were all up north camping.
I thought that was something, too. But I suppose that was the
difference those five years made. And who knows what we would
have thought if it had been one of their boys, or one of Griling's,
instead of ours, who was in the trouble?
    Now Hal says he's glad he didn't go to Vietnam. It's the boys
who went who are sorry. He still knows quite a few of them, Brozeks, too, they're pals now, and he and Merry both knew one who
died. And they all say that none of the ones who went came back
the way they were before.

We got through. Even that first stroke of Gram's, it sort of all
happened and we got over it. It wasn't so bad after the shock. We
still had plenty of good times after that. That's when my mom and
I got close. That's when I really got to know her and like her as a
friend. We used to take a day and drive up to Door County and
go in all those little stores. Jimmy doesn't really like to do that.
Most men don't. And then we talked more like sisters. The age
difference wasn't so much anymore.

And Hal changed. He really did. He grew up. He's real thin now, he runs. I tell him he looks better than he did ten years ago. I was sorry after all they'd been through together that he and Merry couldn't make a go of it. And of course, you're always sorry for Tina's sake. But a lot of other kids are in the same boat, even at Saint Phillip's, and some a lot worse off than she is. She has two parents who really love her and she knows it. And they still get along. Merry's real cute now. She works in town at Echeverry's. She's got her hair real short. And the way Hal looks at her, I think he still likes her. But she's got someone else. She remarried. And when that Bob, he's the new one, was out of work, Hal gave him cleaning jobs out of the store; he did that until he found something permanent. I see Merry a couple times a year. She comes when we have a party or to pick Tina up. And I like her now.

All those things changed and I was sorry at the time, but I changed too, and it worked out better than I thought. I had a lot of nice times with my mother after her first stroke, we still had lot of laughs. Hal used to say we were terrible parents, oh he said awful mean mean things when we fought, but he's taken that back. I think he's a real good person now. I'm glad to have him around here. I guess you can forgive just about anything, if you're still nearby, you know.

But with Benny it is just the opposite. It never changed or went away. It's like a stone. It's been years now and it's still there. Now, it's almost like it always was. Some things you never do get over.

ANN

■ □ ■

10

HOME

■ □ ■

Once, a long time ago, we had a home, too. It was a plain white house in the country, with a long driveway, dark hedges rising on either side of it. Years before, my thin grandfather, who wore glasses, a white shirt and suspenders in each of his photographs, had built the wooden house for his family. In the photographs, his mouth is delicate and nervous, framed by deep lines, like his wife's. In summer, they put up green and white striped awnings on all the windows. I can imagine him standing on a clean ladder, my grandmother below in a blue dress, holding the two legs firm, while his white shirt billowed and filled with wind.

My mother and I lived in the house on Lime Kiln Road until I was nine, when she married Ted, the ice skating pro. The years I grew up there, I spent time outside, hidden, where no one could see me, trying to talk to the trees. It seemed then that the land around our house was more than owned, it was the particular place we were meant to be. Sometimes I thought we would stay there forever, that all the sounds of the yard would teach us about the world. But the trees never answered.

My mother had been born there, on an old kitchen table, but she saw it as an ordinary house on a dusty dead-end road off the highway, with a tavern on one side and the Land Bank on the other. It was out of the way, surrounded by unused land. She thought it was chance, bad luck that brought us here. She always meant to move.

□

For a while though, we rested. We lived with my grandmother.

One afternoon, like so many others, my mother and I lay together on our backs. The room was warm and swimming with
light. I propped myself up on an elbow, watching her because I
wasn't tired. It took willpower for me to keep still. A smile formed
slowly on her face until she was asleep and it seemed as unconscious and without meaning as a dolphin's smile. I knew I
shouldn't wake her so I just waited, watching for her to blink her
eyes open and remember me again.

Asleep on the white chenille bedspread, her hair fanned out
over the pillow, my mother was almost beautiful, prettier than she
was the seven or eight times a day she looked in the bathroom
mirror. She thought her nose was too long and she wasn't happy
with her hair. But asleep, her features settled into a calm order.
She had pale skin with freckles on her face and hands and arms
and knees. Some of the freckles were much darker than the others, so it seemed you could see through her skin to deeper and
deeper layers.

I crept off the bed and tiptoed to my mother's makeup bag on
the dresser and stole a brown sharpened pencil to draw freckles
on my own arm. It took a long time to make them look real. I
wanted to connect the dots on my mother's knee, making pictures,
the constellations of the stars, but I was afraid the pressure of the
pencil would wake her up.

I was used to waiting. Our life in that house, where the furniture seemed to pin the floors to the ground and dense shafts of
sunlight came alive with particles of dust, despite my grandmother's conscientious cleaning, seemed to be a temporary ar-
rangement, like an unscheduled delay in a remote train station,
best slept through. My father had never wanted to be there. My
mother didn't want to stay either. They thought of it as a place to
spend time we would forget about as soon as we left, as if it had
never happened. I was the only one who liked it.

And I knew about losing time. Drawing freckles on my arm, I
watched the clock on the dresser while my mother slept. I knew
if she didn't get up soon, there wouldn't be time to go out and do

anything. Then, as my mother's breath stretched and seemed to enter a freer, wider plain of sleep, my grandmother knocked on the door.

"Come now, if you're up. You can come in the kitchen and draw."

I tiptoed out, glancing back at my mother, my head heavy and dizzy from lying down. While my grandmother played solitaire on the kitchen table, I sat on the floor in a rectangle of sun, drawing with my set of sixty-four crayons.

The house stayed quiet except for the hum of the wall clock and the slap and shuffle of my grandmother's cards. I took all my crayons out of the box in direct disobedience of my mother's instructions, to take out one at a time and then put it back. I had a plan for a city, and half of it was already made. I lifted my construction paper from the cupboard. My city had a population of sixty-four and it was somewhere in California. Every family had its own house and yard and every crayon drew its own room. Some of the crayons fell in love. The darkest red was the father of his family, the palest, his youngest child. The Lemon Yellow drew a school bus and was the bus driver every morning. On the side, he grew lemons. Sky Blue painted the sky and filled swimming pools in backyards. Greens worked as landscapers and park builders. They sodded everyone's lawn and planted rows of palm trees on the streets. Shades of gray paved the highways and Yellow Orange painted the divider. Reds made chimneys and grew rose gardens.

I shaved bits from each crayon onto a sheet of wax paper. Today, my city needed a church. The grays made a stone building and I sharpened each crayon to contribute shavings for the windows. The crayons were getting haircuts.

When I had a colored honeycomb of shreds, I folded the wax paper and took it into the other room. I plugged in the iron. My mother's breathing made a high uneven hum. That first year after my father left, she was always resting. Now that I was doing something, I didn't want to wake her. I lay the iron on the wax paper and counted to one hundred. The sheet of paper felt warm and stiff when I lifted the iron. The colors had blurred and become transparent. I carried the paper back to the kitchen floor.

My grandmother looked down at me over her bifocals. "What all have you got there?"

I showed her roads, the school, the parks and the houses. "These are the stained glass windows for my church." I traced the empty arched holes in the building.

Then, when I finished explaining, I stared down at the flecks of color in the linoleum floor. I was embarrassed. I knew I shouldn't have told anyone. This wasn't the way you were supposed to play with crayons.

My grandmother pushed her glasses on closer and looked down at my papers. They were just papers now and a mess of crayons. I scooped up the crayons from their seats on the school bus and started shoving them back in the box.

I turned and asked, "Do you think I'm dumb?"

My grandmother shook her head. "It's good. It shows you have good imagination. I guess you'll turn out smart like your mom and dad."

That moment, relief spread from my chest like a pill finally dissolving. My back was warm. I just sat in the square of sun. I didn't feel like drawing anymore, but I didn't want to move. This was happiness, the warm sun on my bare legs. This was happiness. My grandmother went back to her cards, sweeping them together and shuffling the deck.

"Well, they all came out so it's going to be a good day," she said.

My mother slept. I didn't want her to get up anymore. She could sleep until my father came back and kissed her eyes awake. I didn't draw because I was afraid I would spoil it. I held up my windows to the real window; the sun came through, casting reflections on the white refrigerator door, the light sparking souls in all the colors.

The first real city I ever saw was Milwaukee. My mother and Lolly drove there to go shopping and they took me along. In a huge department store, my mother found a pair of red children's shoes, flat with pointed toes, Capezios just like her own. I wanted everything of mine to be like hers. The three of us stood staring down at the shoes for a long time, but my mother wouldn't buy them.

When we got home, I threw a tantrum. I felt nothing would be right again until I had those shoes. It was as if I'd lost something, although I'd never seen them before. I'd never imagined there were tall, peaked buildings, a place like Milwaukee. The next day I still felt agitated. I got up early from a bad night of sleep and dressed myself, tied my sneakers and said I was running away to Milwaukee to get my shoes.

"And how are you going to buy them when you get there? You've got no money," my grandmother said. She stood in the kitchen ironing. The ironing board came down from the wall and blocked the doorway. I had to crawl under, brushing her nyloned legs, to get through. The stockings she wore were thicker and orange, you couldn't see her skin.

"I'll get some," I said.

"Well, who do you think is going to give it to you? Sit down, why don't you, and I'll fix you an egg. And let me button your blouse on right."

But nothing my grandmother said was consoling. My grandmother wouldn't understand about fancy shoes. This was between my mother and me. I walked out the screen door and let it slam. A few minutes later, my mother stood on the porch. "Come back here! You get back here this instant!"

I marched over the lawn to the road. I was four years old, I don't know where she thought I could have gone. Everyone on Lime Kiln Road knew me. But she came running across the yard, her bathrobe flapping open, and her fingernails bit into my arm.

"Come on, get back in there." When she pushed me through the kitchen door, a box with the new shoes lay open on the table, the brown paper wrapping ripped apart.

"Are you happy now?"

I just looked at the shoes, the shoes I was going to walk to Milwaukee for. There they were, mine. I was relieved and then they were just shoes again.

"Aren't you going to say thank you, now that you got what you wanted?" My grandmother shook her head, ironing harder.

"You just can't surprise her with anything, Mom, she just won't wait."

I began to know I'd done something wrong. I didn't even want the shoes anymore.

"Well, you've got to teach her. You can't give her every little thing she wants. Let her try and walk to Milwaukee once."

"But then she cries."

"Well let her cry."

That day my mother drove past the dry cleaner's to the edge of town by the river and stopped the car on the side of the road.

"We're at the orphanage," she said. It was a dark brick building with tiny windows at the top of a hill. My mother reached over and opened my door. There was a ditch full of waxy, perfect buttercups.

"I brought you here because I'm telling you, Honey, you can't act the way you've been doing. I'm warning you. This is where you'll end up if I can't make you mind."

I sat as long as I could, looking straight in front of me out the windshield, maybe a moment longer, and then my chin wobbled and I started to cry. My head was wet and in my sweatered arms. My mother reached over and tried to hug me in her lap, even though I was too big and she hurt my back against the steering wheel. She started to cry, too, and she kissed me. "Don't worry, my Little Bit, I'll never give you up. Don't you ever worry." Then it seemed as if all she'd ever wanted was to make me cry.

She reached over and closed my door again. The buttercups blurred together now in one smear of color and we could hear crickets starting. Lights came on in the orphanage's small windows. Her face was over me. She looked down at me hard, as if she were looking at her own reflection in water. One of her tears dropped into my eye.

For the millionth time, when we were children, Benny started running through a field, shouting ah-a-ah-a-ah-a-ah-a-ah-a, with his arms out to the sides, until I couldn't hear him anymore. My cousin Benny was always running, he ran anywhere, just to run. Later on, he rode snowmobiles, plows, dirt bikes, motorboats, and cars. I didn't like him running away like that, but I didn't want to scuff behind, looking down at the ground, so I ran too, as if I'd felt like running all along. But Benny could run forever and I got tired. I stopped in my grandmother's yard and lay down to listen to the leaves.

Sometimes I thought I could hear the earth spin and I dug my hands into the ground and held on. The sound of the leaves there went on forever, but you had to run and then stop to hear it. The earth was like a shell you put your ear to. Then I turned over and looked straight up to the ceiling of leaves, big as hands, and the spots of blue sky between them. I even put my tongue out to taste the ground; it tasted like rusty metal. But that was as far as it went.

I always wanted more. I ended up running to Benny's house to see if he was home yet. If he wasn't there, I would have gone to look for my mother. The wind was always the same. It was like loving someone who didn't know my name.

Aunt Carol said, yes, Benny was in his room, she would go get him. She opened the sliding glass door, asking would I like to come into the breezeway, but I said no, and leaned against the back of the house. The sky was enormous with pink and gold-veined clouds. It was almost suppertime. With Benny on his way to see me, walking through his house, I felt I didn't need anyone, anymore. I didn't mind being alone. I could look at other things. I suppose it would have been that way with my father, if he was there. I looked and as far as I could see, the sky was all there was. I imagined a whole continent of men, stopping and leaning on implements, looking up.

We went to school far away, in town. Benny was a year older, so he went first. A school bus came in the morning, and picked him up at the end of Lime Kiln Road.

On Benny's sixth birthday, Carol wrote a note so I could go to school with him and safety-pinned it to my sleeve. That day the class made hats. I loved it. I glued a lace veil and plastic lilies of the valley to a blue construction paper oval. The boys made black top hats. We posed in the afternoon outside the school in our hats. In the photograph, we look old, like tiny country men and women.

Benny and I lay next to each other on our mats during rest period and when we woke up, the teacher brought out a cake in the shape of a lamb, with flaky coconut frosting. My grandmother had baked it that morning and driven it to the school in a box. The teacher passed around napkins with two tiny squares of cake on each one.

The first bite tasted better than anything, it was so sweet and soft. Then I remembered my mother and felt bad, so I wrapped my second piece carefully in the napkin and slipped it into my jacket pocket to take home to her. That day I didn't mind parting with Benny at the edge of our lawns. I had gone somewhere too.

"Well, sit down and tell me what all you did." My grandmother's back was to me as she poured a glass of milk.

"We made hats."

I was feeling the napkin in my pocket, trying to assure myself that the cake was still there. I'd held the piece inside my pocket all the way home on the school bus. I'd held it tight. I was worried now; the napkin was still there, but it seemed empty, the cake must have somehow slipped out. My fingers dug into the pocket, touching every part of the lining. It seemed amazing, impossible. It never occurred to me that I might have crumbled it, holding too hard. Finally, while my grandmother dealt cards for double solitaire, I took the napkin out under the table and spread it open on my thighs. There was nothing but a pile of crumbs.

While my grandmother shuffled, I got up and threw the napkin away. I had nothing to give my mother now, and I wasn't even going to mention it. Without the cake, she wouldn't understand.

The next year, when I started school, a hygienist came to my class and passed out new boxed toothbrushes.

"How many of you have your own toothbrush already?" she asked.

Most of us raised our hands. The few who didn't kept their hands folded on their desk tops and looked down. But Theresa Griling was bold in her dumbness. She got into trouble because you couldn't humiliate her. When people didn't like her, she dared them.

"I got one that's my brother's, too. It used to be my papa's," she said.

The hygienist sucked in her breath and looked at Theresa Griling as if she'd said something so wrong that the best thing to do was to keep very, very quiet. She walked to Theresa Griling's desk and stacked two more boxes of toothbrushes.

"Kin I have a red and a green instead of two greens?"

The hygienist silently made the exchange. "How many people are there in your family?" she said, then.

"Five, six counting my papa."

"Four, five, six. There. You can give them each a present."

"But my papa don't use one no more."

"*Any*more," the nun said gently, from the back of the room, her beads clicking softly in her hands.

The hygienist smiled enormously at Theresa. "Well, perhaps you can persuade him with your good example how important brushing is. He could lose his teeth prematurely."

"He already did. That's why he don't brush."

We laughed out loud and the hygienist looked around herself, touching her skirt, as if there were invisible flies. Theresa won that time; we could see it. The hygienist lost control. She walked to the front of the room and looked at Theresa with pure hate. The hygienist had huge, square teeth. She pointed to the blackboard where she'd drawn a picture of a cavity. Her face was perfectly colored with makeup. "I'll get you in the end," her large smile seemed to say. She was wearing a neat belted navy blue dress with matching navy blue shoes. Theresa's blouse was yellowed and her gray anklets sank down below the heels of her shoes. I was thinking of Theresa at home, where we lived, the flat fields and long rails.

I told my mother about the hygienist that night. We were driving around by the river and her friend Lolly was in the car with us. "You watch out for those Griling kids, because they are filthy, let me tell you," my mother said. "He is, Bub is. When their mother died and he just let them run around like they do, the city

came out and took them away. They put them in the orphanage."
She was talking to Lolly now, in the front seat. "And the nuns
gave them baths and combed their hair; they said their hair was
all matted and one of them had burrs in her skin. And they
cleaned them all up and gave them new clothes and fixed their
hair nice, you know how the nuns are, but the kids ran away and
went home again. And when the social workers came to the
house, the kids said they'd rather stay with their dad. No matter
how terrible, kids just always want their parents."

"Isn't that funny," Lolly said.

When we came home from Las Vegas, the winter I was seven, my
mother seemed to lose interest in me. She spent more time with
Lolly. I went outside after school, and stayed sometimes into the
dark. I ran and played with the kids on Lime Kiln Road because
of Benny. Benny was my cousin and that gave me something.

After school, I skidded into the kitchen, my grandmother
flipped up the hood of my sweat shirt and then I ran through the
yard to the fields. I met Benny and the other kids from our road
down by the tracks where the rails were empty and dull silver
as far as we could see. We got down on our heels and hit rocks
on the rails while we thought about what we would do. We only
played made-up games. We didn't use anything bought. Around
us, the country seemed so big. Later, when I moved to Carriage
Court, the kids played sports on the street with names: Capture
the Flag, Red Rover, Kick the Can.

Finally, we started running. At the top of a hill, Benny turned
and fell and rolled with his arms spread open. I lay down and let
go after him, my arms crossed tight over my chest like a prayer
and we turned, rolling, trusting it all, trusting the swatches of sky
to come back, the sweetness of grass in our mouths, the bumps,
rocks hitting off our heads, our feet coming unfurled and, finally,
Benny and I were tangled together in the soft muddy ditch at the
end.

We woke up in each other's arms. We'd played all our lives,
but we were conscious now when we unfitted ourselves. We were
older. I spit out the grass and my spit was mixed with green. We

ran to the top again and this time we skidded, our arms out, our chests falling in front of us, to gravity. We tripped over roots and rocks, the steepness pushing our speed, like a hand on the smalls of our backs. The breath cleaned out of our lungs, we fell, rolling onto our backs, looking up at the sky. We lay in the ditch, holding on, as if our own arms braced the land and air in the hurling speed of the planet's fall. We dug our hands into the soft grass until our nails were crammed with dirt.

Benny crawled over to where I was and sat with his knees on my knees. He held my wrists down and wrestled with me and we turned and fought and as we moved, the ground felt hard under us, like another body.

Then from far away the train whistle started and we all ran back to the tracks. We laid pop bottle tops and nickels in rows and we knelt there with both hands lightly on the rails. There was a humming. The metal was warm, holding in the last sun and giving it back slowly; we lay our cheeks down so whole halves of our faces vibrated with the coming of the train. From our ears to under our chins, it felt like a helmet of air. Benny said we should all close our eyes.

I didn't close mine. I knelt there, the field of vibration growing a thicker layer under my cheek, and watched Benny's face, his eyes shut smooth, his mouth moving as he breathed. It was best to be the last to leave but I wasn't that brave. I went back when Theresa Griling yelled; we were the first to go running up the hill, pulling our hair, screaming, so glad to be free, and scared, shouting the names of the boys still there, and we could see the train then, the big front light like an eye. The boys peeled off one by one, rolling down by the ditch and tripping up again, running.

The train came, a moment of pure vision. You couldn't think, you couldn't move, you couldn't see. That moment of suspense; noise of the highway, shudder of the train before we knew—yes, every day we were forgotten again. The wind pushed up and there was a whirl of steel and colors, the last sun drizzling the rails, and we hung on to the weeds by the road with our fists and the rest of us let go. Your face moved without you, your voice just went as if someone was pulling it out in one string, your body shook and you were left in a heap on the dusty road when the train was half a mile up in front of you, a train again, something you could wholly see, something your eye could end.

We gathered the flattened pop tops in our pockets as if they were money.

My mother and I made up a secret. It started one evening, a usual evening in our house, when my grandmother and I sat watching "Family Affair" on television. A branch beat against the wall. I walked to the window and saw the same blue light cast from front windows over the yards on our road. In every house the TV was on. There was comfort in that.

My mother stayed in the bathroom, wearing only a slip, practicing with makeup. She stood for minutes, fully absorbed, looking at her face in the mirror as she pushed up the cartilage on the tip of her nose. In the kitchen, she had Kris Miss Facial Herbs boiling in a pot. She steamed her pores open and then ran to the bathroom, where she had her mirror. During one of her migrations, she stopped in the living room and stood for a few moments watching TV with us.

"Ann, come here. I want to talk to you for a second.

"You know, you're cuter than Buffy," she whispered, looking down hard, as if she were appraising me. She took my face by the chin and turned it. I stood very still, my arms straight at my sides. She clicked her tongue. "You know, I've been thinking. We ought to get you on TV."

That moment something started.

"Come here." She began to brush makeup on my face, holding my chin with two tight fingers. "Like this." She puckered her lips. "Close. Now open." I felt her warm breath on my eyelids. "Let's see." She stood up to look from different angles. "You're going to make it, kid, I'm telling you, you are going to make it." Then she peered into the mirror and sighed. "And I'm not so bad myself, for a mother."

"You're beautiful," I said, meaning it.

"Do you really think so?" Her face was poised, waiting.

I nodded my head hard, up and down.

"Close your eyes," my mother said, smearing shadow on me with her fingers, so I saw colored lights inside.

We decided we would go to California, but it was our secret. I knew I'd have to be different from other children. I'd have to be better than the other kids to be picked and make all that money. My mother started to read to me from magazines at night. We knew all about the children on television. We knew how much money they made, we knew about the Jackie Coogan law, we knew that the camera adds ten pounds.

"Maybe your dad can even help," she whispered.

The next year at school, Theresa Griling walked behind me in the lunch line and every day she stepped on my heel, crushing my saddle shoe down. We ate at two long tables, watched by a novice who stood at the door.

My mother fixed me lunches that were always too big. I got a sandwich so thick the pieces fell apart when I tried to eat it, two eggs that weren't hard-boiled enough, bakery cookies, a bag of sliced carrots, celery and radishes, a banana, an apple and an orange. On both sides of me at the table, girls had standard lunches: a thin sandwich which pressed down even thinner while they ate, and a Hostess Twinkie. Theresa Griling had just one thing every day: a battered apple or a candy bar, sometimes a chicken leg or one slice of bologna. I longed for the other lunches. I was full after half my sandwich. Even my bag sitting open in front of me was bigger than the other bags. It looked sloppy and wrinkled, like an old elephant's thick leg. I threw most of my lunch out, tossing the whole bag into the garbage bin we passed on our way to the playground. It didn't look like the other lunches and some girls stared at me.

One recess, an older girl tapped my arm while I turned a jump rope. She said the Mother Superior would like to see me in her office. I glanced up from the playground; the sky was bordered and fenced with power lines, planted with three-story buildings and the steeple. The girl led me up two flights of stairs and opened a wooden door.

The Mother Superior stood by a window of honeycomb glass. I

knew I was probably in trouble, but I thought it was possible I'd
be told I'd done something good enough to change my life. Only,
I couldn't think of anything I'd done yet. Maybe a Hollywood
agent had come to our lunchroom and seen me eat with good table
manners. Then I noticed something familiar on the edge of the
Mother Superior's desk: a large, brown, wilted lunch bag, like my
own.

The Mother Superior nodded, letting her eyes close. The older
girl began, pulling back three fingers.

"First thing. Do you like apples?"

"Yes," I said, not knowing what this meant.

"Do you like . . . oranges?"

"Yes."

Then the bell rang. The older girl held on to her index finger,
waiting until the noise stopped. All through the building there
was an echo of steps, my classmates marching single file down
halls, upstairs and into classrooms.

"Last thing," the girl said. "Do you like bananas?"

Bananas. Bananas. I thought hard, deliberating. The room was
still. I was sure the question meant something else and that the
answer would determine the rest of my life. If I would be a child
star or just me. The older girl and I were breathing together, our
ribs moving out in unison, like fish hanging in an aquarium.

"Yes," I said.

The older girl picked up the wrinkled brown bag. "Then, how
come, in your lunch today, did you throw out a banana and an
apple and an orange?"

The Mother Superior's hands, folded on the desk top, looked
smooth as those of a statue. I understood now; I'd been caught. I
pictured the garbage bin and all the lunch bags. They must have
fished out mine.

The older girl led me down the stairs, past closed classroom
doors, to the lunch table. A novice stood there, waiting. They set
my bag at the place I ate my lunch every day. I started peeling
the orange. I took out all the little packets in my lunch and set
them up, like a village.

□

"Everyone else gets a sandwich and a Twinkie. And that's all. Nobody else gets a fruit."

"Honey, other mothers don't put in the time I do. That's why. I can see now you don't appreciate it. You'd rather have a piece of cheap lunch meat slapped between packaged bread. I stay up late, after working all day, and how many mothers do you think work?"

"Hush now. I'll fix her lunch," my grandmother said. "You two just go to bed."

"Mom, why should you have to, just because she—"

"Let Gramma. I want Gramma to make my lunch."

"Okay, fine. Go ahead. I can see no one needs me around here."

We looked at the door my mother slammed. My grandmother pulled out the cutting board and began to make me a sandwich. My mother was banging drawers shut in the bedroom.

It is always the people like my mother, who start the noise and bang things, who make you feel the worst; they are the ones who get your love. When I opened the door, the lights were off and my mother was already under the covers. I climbed up and crawled over her and as I moved, I hit her knee. It made a creaking sound, like wood.

"Watch it, why don't you?"

I slid under the covers, facing the wall. "I'm sorry, Mom."

She didn't say anything. It was as bad as I'd thought. When it seemed she was asleep for sure, I turned around, put my hands on her shoulders and curled against her spine, but she shuddered, shrugging me off. I couldn't get comfortable. My eyes hurt behind my eyes. My arms didn't seem joined to my shoulders right. I turned and turned. I couldn't seem to do anything to get warm.

Finally, I crept to the bottom of the bed, slipped down and walked out of the room. With each creak of the steps as I climbed, I felt safer and more sleepy. The upstairs was like another house. The air seemed colder and clean. While I was pulling the heavy quilts back to crawl into the small bed, my grandmother's sheets rustled.

"Sleep tight," she said, but maybe I only imagined it.

My mother added coffeecake squares to my lunches, squares she bought specially from Krim's, as if all she remembered about our fight was that my lunches should be better, which to her meant bigger. One morning that fall, on the school bus, Theresa Griling sat next to me and pressed up close against my ribs. "I heard you got in trouble with the Mother Superior." She shifted in the seat, moving her legs. "I got a bag, you can give me half and I'll trade you for my apple." She held a small, very creased paper bag in her lap. Out of her pocket, she pulled a bruised crab apple, from one of the trees in old Brozek's yard. I had my enormous lunch propped up on my schoolbooks. It stood as high as my head. Then as if she'd been holding out, she produced a Milky Way, the brown wrapper twisted, making white lines, and set it on the bag next to the apple.

"You want my stuff?" I said.

"Sure." She studied the ribbed rubber floor of the bus, she waited after she said it. It was the first time I'd ever seen her like that. She used to stare at me behind my bag on the bus in the morning. There were others who'd looked at me in the lunchroom at school. I'd always thought they were making fun, because my lunch was different and silly. Now I saw: they were hungry.

I nudged Theresa's side and we dug our arms in the bag. From that day on we had a deal.

In the spring, a boy from on television was coming to town for a cerebral palsy benefit. After the rains, posters of his face peeled off telephone poles, next to larger posters of Leonard Nimoy. My mother drove the twenty miles to the telethon through a storm. Inside the Civic Auditorium, on a stage, tables of women answered ringing telephones, taking pledges. The boy from on television walked with the cerebral palsy children, who looked complicated and stiff and fragile, as if you wouldn't know where to touch them.

Leonard Nimoy, in Spock ears, sat in the orchestra pit, next to a huge bin. People lined up around the auditorium to shake his hand and throw in their coins and dollars. My mother nudged me into line. "See that little girl? You're cuter than her. Sit on his lap like that and just ask him how he got into show business. Say you were wondering because you'd like to act, too."

"I don know."

"Go on. You have to get discovered somewhere. Who knows? Maybe it'll be here."

Onstage, the boy from on television stood at the microphone singing. He belted out "Every Little Boy Can Be President," opening his arms toward the cerebral palsy children, who were lined up behind him in a row of plastic chairs. On television, he played Buffy's brother. His real name was Timmy Kennedy.

My mother stuck a dollar into my hand. In front of me two boys in matching shirts pushed each other's chests, fighting for the first place in line. I stood straight, thinking about looking right and talking right. When it was my turn I walked up, but I was afraid to sit on Leonard Nimoy's lap. I stood close enough to smell the foreign, chemical smell of his shaved cheek, a man's smell, like the electricity around Jimmy Measey's towel, and I whispered into his ear. "How did you get started as an actor?"

He turned and looked at me, puzzled. "Just a minute." A child handed him her autograph book and he signed, with big loopy letters, smiling. The line moved forward but I stayed.

"Because I'd like to get into show business, too," I said.

He looked at me a little regretfully. "Oh, Honey, it's a long story. Too long for now." He gave me a sideways hug and then turned back to the line. "Bless you, thank you," he was saying, as I walked out towards my mother. I was ashamed. Leonard Nimoy hadn't taken an interest in me. I wondered if he would have if I'd sat on his lap.

Onstage, the celebrities led the CP children around in a circle. The boy from on television walked bending over, to reach the

arms of a much smaller girl. The children sang, in partial, shrill
voices, looking at their braced feet as they marched.

> LOOK AT US, WE'RE WALKING
> LOOK AT US, WE'RE TALKING
> WE WHO'VE NEVER WALKED OR TALKED BEFORE
> BUT THE FIGHT HAS JUST BEGUN
> GET BEHIND US EVERYONE
> YOUR DOLLARS MAKE OUR DREAMS COME TRUE
> THANKS TO YOU, THANKS TO YOU
>
> LOOK AT US, WE'RE WALKING
> LOOK AT US, WE'RE TALKING
> IMAGINE WALKING TO THE CANDY STORE . . .

My mother found out what flight the celebrities were taking back
to California and we drove to the airport that night. We discovered
the celebrities sitting quietly in an upstairs waiting room like
other people. Leonard Nimoy had taken his Spock ears off, he
was reading a magazine. The boy from on television sat playing
checkers. He was wearing a velour shirt with a zipper, just like
any other kid. But I knew he wasn't. I'd seen him on television.

His father told my mother that he was a gym teacher and that
his family was Mormon.

"Mother used to do all her own canning and of course that's
had to stop. One or the other of us travels with him. He has eight
brothers and sisters, and they've had to make sacrifices for him
to be on the show. So with part of his money, we've taken out
insurance policies for each of them."

The father asked the boy to say hello to me. He looked up
politely from his checker game and smiled. He seemed anxious
to turn back to the magnetic checkers. No matter what my mother
said, I wasn't pretty enough.

The boy's father told us that Buffy snubbed Timmy on the set.
In real life, she was years older, almost in junior high.

"You wouldn't happen to know a songwriter out there," my
mother asked. She said my father's name.

"I can't say that I do." He shrugged.

We watched the airplane wheels start spinning as it ran down the runway. "They must be tired," my mother sighed. When we couldn't see the lights anymore, we walked out to the parking lot. I huddled against the outside of my door. We both felt solemn for a moment, watching the plane in the sky. We both wished we were on it, in one of those small yellow windows.

My mother clapped. "Well, should we go get some sundaes to celebrate?" She unlocked our doors and rubbed her hands together.

"Celebrate what?"

"Well, I think I should give his agent a call, don't you?"

"What?"

"Didn't you hear me asking him who their agent was? She's apparently *the* agent to go to. All the child stars have her. Her name is Ellen Arcade and she's in Riverside. So I think she's the one we should get for you." My mother bent down closer to the heat vent. "A high school gym teacher," she mused. "What do you know."

Benny could be impatient, but sometimes in summer you saw him taking a long time reading to one of the neighbor kids, a story from her cardboard children's book. He helped littler kids with their math problems, pondering the elaborate boxes of numbers on their papers for hours. He tried to teach everything he didn't understand. If you asked him how he made a stone skip seven times on the surface of a pond, or where he found the birds' nests he carried home, perfectly whole, in two hands while running, how he balanced on water skis, he would shrug and grin, I dunno. He couldn't teach you because he had no idea how he did these things. I once asked him to show me how to dance. We put Hal's 45s on the console in their living room. *Would you like some of my tangerine?* Ben moved and shuffled. "How do you do that?" I looked at myself in Carol's huge, gilt-edged mirror. I was all wrong.

"You're fine, Ann," he said. "Forget it."

□

Once, at night that summer, Benny rode me on his handlebars,
down by the tracks. We let the bike fall on the ground and we
walked to the creek. Then Benny ran back to his bike and took
off.

He threw me his flashlight so it landed in the field.

I screamed no, but he rode away anyway, the light on the front
of his bike farther and farther away like a match going out.

I was afraid of the dark. Benny knew. A dog barked in the far
distance. Then the country seemed immense, as if there were
only small houses far apart and small clearings around them, not
networks of electricity, of sound. It felt like a randomly settled
wilderness, where you could disappear and no one would know.
Then, I picked up the cold flashlight from the ground by my feet,
touched the metal, fumbled it on and the night changed. Benny
was right. It wasn't him. The world softened instantly in light. For
the first time I could imagine angels, the halo looked so real. I
walked slowly and the sounds receded to crickets and a hum of
far-off power lines. With the flashlight, you could see one thing
at a time, the fitted seeds of one weed, a rough milkpod stem.

When I came to our road, I could see the shades of gray with
just my eyes. I turned the flashlight off. The fields went on to the
bare plain barn, a pure black. The land seemed different at night,
another place, belonging to anyone who saw it. The light changed
everything, made it look still and permanent, meant, like a city.

At the edge of our lawn, I stood on the worn spots by the mailbox. My thin grandfather and my grandmother, my own mother
and Carol had walked exactly here, secrets in their hearts, opening the mailbox door, and now it meant nothing, the dirt had no
memory, they were separate days, different years, all our thoughts
were gone, lost on air. My grandfather had taken long walks at
night. He had walked over his lawn, touching the tops of weeds.
In blizzards, he had liked to strap on snowshoes, walk out and
listen to the quiet under one of his trees. People we wouldn't
recognize, strangers, would touch the land after us, pack down
the same earth, without ever knowing how beautiful we found it,
how troubling.

Sometimes I thought it was Benny who gave me everything. When I ran into the yellow-lit kitchen, he sat eating an orange. He shrugged.

Every fall, when we went back to school in town, they lined us all up by the nurse's room to test for ringworm. You went in one at a time, to a closet, where two hygienists shone a black light on you. If they found ringworm, they would shave your hair off right there and they'd give you a cap to wear when you walked out into the hall again. You knew the kids at school who had the ring-worm, they wore stocking caps until their hair grew back. Some-times, during a wet recess, you would see a gleam of white skull on the playground, when kids ganged up and pulled a cap off. You'd see the kid snatch it back right away, picking it out of the slush and putting it back on.

In line, in front of the nurse's office, I thought I could feel something on my head. Theresa Griling, behind me, stepped down on the heel of my saddle shoe and I had to bite my lip not to cry. I loved my hair. It was my most prized possession. My mother told me that hardly any other kids in America had hair like mine. It was going to help me get on television. "It's the best hair to have," my mother had whispered. "Your black. The very best."

Walking back, I touched my hair lightly. It had been over in a minute, the black light, the hygienist asking my middle name to fill out her form. In the classroom we were supposed to wait in our seats for all the pupils to return. Sitting there, doing nothing, I thought a terrible thought; my mother herself had blond hair. I looked at the other girls around me, the redheads, the blondes. Maybe they could be beautiful too. The Hollywood agent might not pick me.

Theresa Griling walked into the classroom then, not crying, wearing a stocking cap. She just sat down at her desk.

A nun called the girls from the bottom of a wide scrubbed stair-case, the steps soft and nicked and scarred. We were picking up orphans from the orphanage for Christmas. We got two girls every holiday, never the same two, and despite my persistent request for boys. A scraggly, flocked wreath hung at the top of the staircase, over a window.

"Probably donated," my mother whispered, seeing me look at it.

Every holiday, the girls bounded down, slumped over, shy and eager in fancy dresses too light for the season and short socks that they were too old for. They usually had sturdy, women's legs. Their hair was pulled tightly off their foreheads, so their white faces seemed startled, like naked bodies. They looked clean. The nuns didn't care about pretty, but they wanted you to know their girls were clean. The year before, we got Mary and Theresa Griling. Bub had taken off somewhere, to Florida, and they had been in the orphanage again.

This year, their names were Dorie and Diane. My mother, who usually slowed the car to an almost halt in front of every expensive store, made only one stop; we all got out to see the Christmas windows at Shreve's. The orphans stood with their hands in their jacket pockets, their legs turning dull red between their dresses and their socks.

"Isn't *he* lovely?" my mother said. "Aw, look at that little wolf. Wouldn't you just like to bring him home?"

The orphans frowned between their eyebrows. They must have been cold. We stood in front of each mechanical scene too long, like people in a museum who look at each painting for an equal length of time, people not intimate enough to laugh and sigh in relief when they can leave.

My grandmother was rolling out dough on the table when we came in the back door. Carol stood rubbing her hands together, meaning to help. "Well, how do you do, I'm Carol. I'm the mother."

My mother snorted in the corner. She sat there, dialing Lolly on the phone.

"Yes, Adele too, sure. I'm the boys' mother. Now, we haven't had you two before, have we?"

"*No*, Carol," my mother said; then she started whispering into the mouthpiece.

"Oh, no, you're right. Now I see. But this one looks a little, you look a little like one we had last Easter and was she ever a pretty girl. What was her name now? I just can't think of it. Was she a Linda? Well, what is your name?" Carol extended a wet, doughy hand.

"This is Dorie and this is Diane," I said.

"Oh, no, it wasn't a Dorie. I'm sure I would've remembered a Dorie."

My mother snorted again into the phone. She was talking to Lolly about why it had been a good idea not to invite Ted for Christmas. Ted didn't have any family in Wisconsin, and he would be eating at a restaurant. "There's no reason he has to see it all, before," she said. "And he'll get a good prime rib, rare the way he likes it." Lolly seemed to agree.

I took Dorie and Diane upstairs to their bedroom. They had their nightgowns and toothbrushes along in one brown paper bag. Dorie hit the window with the back of her hand.

"You got a lot of room," she said.

Dorie's fingernails looked scrubbed clean, transparent. I'd seen where they lived, the huge rooms with rows of bunk beds in the orphanage. The cement floor in their bathroom sloped down to a metal drain. There were ten sinks, all on one wall. She smelled like dust or the air in a closet. Like something clean but old.

In the living room, Jimmy Measey yelled at Carol for stepping in front of the TV. She was standing next to the window, trapped, bunching the curtain in her hand.

"Well, Jimmy, I just wanted to look a second and see if they had their Christmas tree lights on." She let the curtain go and started to walk back towards the kitchen.

"Wait till the commercial, Carol. You can just stand there and wait," Jimmy said. "Don't you dare move while we've got the ball." Looking straight at the screen, he asked the orphans questions.

"What grade have they got you in over there?

"Do you like it with those nuns?"

They answered quietly, in unison, staring down at the rug.

"Fifth and sixth.

"Yes."

"Are there boys in there with you, too?"

"Yes, but more girls."

"More girls, huh."

"The boys run away."

"How long you been in there?"

Jimmy's eyes followed the game, the slow motion accidents and gentle falls, black and white on the television. While the girls talked, answering his questions, our team intercepted and he began yelling, thumping his knees, as Dorie said she'd been in the orphanage since she was eight years old. When the replay was over, Jimmy turned back. "Oh, 'scuse me. I had to see that. But go on."

"What happened to your parents?" I said.

They looked at each other and shrugged. "Mine are dead. They had a car accident when I was just a little baby," Diane said.

"What about yours?" I asked Dorie.

"I never saw my dad. But my mom's dead. Got to be, I used to get cards from her but not anymore for a long time."

"You remember your mother, you're lucky," Diane said.

"Yeah, me and my mom, we used to get up every morning, go buy the newspaper and a box of Milk Duds. We'd share them. She always had Black Jack gum in her purse."

"What happened to her?"

"Ann, shut your mouth. They'll tell you what they want to tell you," Jimmy said.

Benny walked in, carrying a bowl of potato chips. "Annie loves orphans because when she was little she thought she was one," he said. "She used to go around telling everybody she was adopted because her mother's got blond hair. She used to paint fake freckles on herself so she'd look more like her mom."

A commercial flickered onto the television, a waxed floor, and a woman on her knees. Then a vacuum cleaner, and the woman stood up. Jimmy said, "Okay, Carol, now you can go."

□

We set a plate of broken cookies out on our shoveled porch. "Oh, Honey, Santa doesn't mind, he likes the pieces," my mother said. "He likes to know we're only *hu*-man."

The new snow blew on the ice under the porch light like tiny balls of styrofoam. I opened a box of C & H sugar cubes from Hawaii for the reindeer. Then we put on our coats and hats and trekked over to Carol and Jimmy's house. Hal led the way, stamping a single channel of footprints in the snow. Benny and I were still light enough to walk on the high crusted banks with our arms out to the sides for balance. It was like walking on water, we stepped softly, feeling the peaks of the ridged banks. We stood as tall as our parents.

Snow lit the dark. It covered the fields as far as we could see. Small, sharp stars seemed embedded deep in the sky and the noise of the highway was muffled and far away. There were only a few headlights, they must have been trucks, long-distance interstates, carrying perishables, winter fruit.

Ahead of me, Carol slammed the screen door and began to pull off her boots. She walked through the house in her nylons, turning on lights. Carol and Jimmy owned one of the first artificial Christmas trees in the state of Wisconsin. It was expensive and innovative when they bought it, and each year they added new lights. This year, families of colors blinked at different times. Carol passed out Tom and Jerrys, and Jimmy told her to sit down. Then she brought in my grandmother's cookies on a plate the shape of a Christmas tree. She'd made the plate in a ceramics class and Jimmy had installed tiny electric lights around its rim. She set it on a low table near an outlet.

"Now, sit down," Jimmy said.

But she walked on her knees to the tree and selected packages for each of the orphans. The rest of our presents had name tags. She gave Dorie a pink plastic cotton-ball dispenser, a coin purse and a scarf. Diane opened a toy gumball machine and a set of lipsticks made to look like peppermint candy. Lippersticks, they were called.

Carol went shopping for the orphans every year at end-of-the-summer dollar sales. She also kept a cardboard box full of wrapped general presents in the closet, which would do for any occasion. Diane and Dorie sat quietly on the carpet, holding their gifts in their laps.

Hal opened the first large box; it held a snorkel and flippers, a new installment in the series of sports equipment Jimmy bought for his oldest son. Jimmy thought sports would make Hal normal; he immediately ordered Hal to try the flippers on. Carol stood to throw away the tissue paper. "Sit down, Carol," Jimmy said.

My mother gave me a blue velvet skating suit. I ran my finger over one of the embroidered flowers.

"Did you make it?" Dorie said. She was sitting at my mother's knees and staring up at her. My mother liked attention, she liked to be watched.

"Oh, no, Honey, it's much nicer than I could do. It's made in Switzerland," she said. "But don't touch. The velvet's very delicate. Real fine."

My other present was a chemistry set. It looked too hard for me. It said on the box ages eleven through fourteen, and I was only eight.

"What's that you got?" Jimmy took the box from me and studied the drawing inside the lid. It said you were supposed to prick your finger and look at the blood through the microscope. Jimmy rummaged in the box. He lifted a needle, about two inches long, in a sealed clear plastic packet. "Here, give me your finger."

I sat on my hands and shook my head.

He stood up. "You shouldn't even have a chemistry set if you're going to be a baby. If you can't prick your finger, you're not old enough."

"She can grow into it," my mother said.

"You spoil her, Adele. It'll hurt her a second and then it's over."

"Not on Christmas, Jimmy."

He looked at the orphans. "You two, hold out your hands. Come on."

They each opened one hand, slowly, palms up, uncurling close to their bodies.

"See, they're old enough. It'll do her good to see that."

Neither of them cried when he pricked their fingers. He didn't set up the microscope. He couldn't find the glass plates in the box. "Well, it's good for her to see," he said. He left the two drops of dark blood glistening on their fingertips.

Carol lifted up a black lacy slip from a rectangular box.

"Oh, Jimmy, now when am I ever going to wear such a thing. I don't think it'll even fit me."

Jimmy fumed. "If you don't want it, Carol, take it back. The receipt's in the box. Don't tell me about it, just take it back."

"Well, Jimmy, I only meant, I think it's too small. Are you trying to tell me something? Maybe I should go back on that grapefruit diet." She laughed an old woman's laugh. Carol's jokes were like the nuns', there was no mischief in them.

"Look at how nicely it's made," my mother said, fingering a seam. "That's all hand-sewn. It'll be smashing on you, Carol."

"Ogh," Carol said, "I don't know."

My mother shook her head. "She never appreciates anything. And he has nice taste, you know?"

Hal came back, in the flippers, stepping carefully between boxes and wrapping paper. Benny looked up at him; he was sitting in a big chair with his legs dangling down, quiet because he hadn't been given anything yet. Benny would get the flippers, though, he got all Hal's equipment, a few months later, when Hal never used it.

Carol passed Jimmy a small red box and he pulled the ribbon off slowly and let it flutter to the floor. His lips closed as tight as a berry and his cheeks puffed out. What Jimmy wanted and believed he deserved couldn't fit into this box.

Jimmy was our big spender. The Measer, he called himself at Christmas. Every year he waited until the day of Christmas Eve and then he went out and used cash. That year, he'd gone to Shopko and the downtown Shreve's. He'd bought a dishwasher for Carol. It had come in a truck early that afternoon. Jimmy had made it perfectly clear that what he wanted for himself was a new black Easy-boy chair with a lever to adjust the seat back's angle. But he'd snooped around the house and he hadn't found it anywhere.

His cheek trembled when he lifted the white cardboard lid and saw the watch. The watch looked expensive enough to mean that it, and not the chair, was his big present for the year.

"Carol, I already have a watch. You know that, Carol."

"Jimmy, I know you have a watch but I thought . . . here, let me show you, this has an alarm on it. Where are the instructions? He told me at the store how to do it, but—"

"I don't need an alarm on my wristwatch."

My grandmother shook her head and opened her own purse. She passed out sealed envelopes with ironed five-dollar bills to Dorie and Diane. She called Benny and me to come sit next to her and our heads pressed together in the small circle of light. Under the lamp, her unpolished fingernails looked yellowish like pearls. She showed us the new green entries stamped in our savings books. She had an account at the bank for each of us. "See the interest," she pointed, her fingernail tapping the paper. "You're each collecting interest."

Carol was whimpering now, wiping tears with the cuff of her sleeve. "Take those fins off and help me, Hal. Jimmy, I just thought you'd like another watch. At the water softener store, and all over, they said this was the newest thing. And you know you always like the newest thing." She leaned over, scattering the crumpled wrapping paper on the floor, still looking for the instructions to set the alarm.

My mother pressed tiny bottles of perfume into the orphans' hands. "It's what I wear, smell." She pushed her wrist up near their faces and they both bent down, sniffing her arm like puppies nursing.

I went over and stood by Benny. He swung his legs below the chair. His parents were fighting and they hadn't noticed him. Then, Jimmy saw.

"What's the matter, Benny, you didn't get anything from Santa Claus? Look, Ann's comforting him because Benny hasn't got any presents."

Carol stood in the doorway, shaking her head while she zipped up her jacket.

"No," Benny said. He looked down, afraid of his father. I could tell from the way his cheeks went, he was about to cry.

"You just weren't good enough, that's the trouble, Ben. I don't know any other reason that Santa'd forget you. Lookit, Annie's got presents and these two, Diane and I'm sorry, what's your name? They both got presents. What happened to you?"

"Dorie," Dorie said quietly.

Jimmy's voice grew. "You must've been bad."

Then, Carol and Hal struggled in, carrying the enormous Easy-boy chair. It had been in my grandmother's garage, next to the old lawn mower.

"Oh, Carol," Jimmy sighed. His relief seemed great enough to almost equal happiness. They lifted the chair in place and Jimmy sank into it, working the lever, cranking himself up and down.

Now, Carol took out her handkerchief and blew her nose. "Oh, Jimmy, I'm so glad you like *some*thing I got you this Christmas." Carol always carried ironed handkerchiefs and she had unfolded a white one, embroidered with green and red holly.

Jimmy leaned down and picked up the wristwatch. "You'll have to show me how to use this alarm." He buckled it onto his arm.

My grandmother stood up stamping her feet. "It's getting to be time for B-E-D."

Benny was still sitting, clutching the arms of his chair. Jimmy maneuvered the Easy-boy to an upright position. "Oh, listen, Ben, would you do me one favor?" He tossed Benny a set of keys. "Would you go and look in the garage for me? I think I left something there. By mistake."

Benny's face flew into an anxious happiness and he ran out through the breezeway. Then he came back, letting the garage door slam and lunging into Jimmy's arms. I hated to see them like that, pasted to each other, as if you couldn't pull Benny off if you tried.

"Here, you sit down a minute, Carol," Jimmy said, giving her his chair. He followed Benny. The two of them ran into the garage and we heard the motor putting. When the rest of us left, to walk back over to our house, Benny was still in the garage, riding around in circles on his dirt bike. And when we came to our porch, the broken cookies and the box of C & H sugar cubes, which had been under the light, were gone.

□

I stood at the window and watched Benny's garage, the chalky yellow light seeping out of the seams. I wanted it to be dark again. I heard my grandmother walking through our house, turning off lights. My mother came into our room, slipping her hand underneath my pajama top, and telling me it was time to go to sleep. She led me away from the window and pulled down the shade. I lay banked and quiet on the bed, only breathing, not moving otherwise, trying to feel nothing but her fingernails on my back. The sensations were black, delicious the way a cut can be.

It seemed it would have been easy to die like that, doing nothing, feeling nothing but pleasure, like underwater sounds or lights inside the dark bowls of closed eyes.

But I knew that it would always end and I would need it again and wanting it so made me smaller. After she left, going into her closet and pulling on the light or down to the kitchen to call Lolly, I couldn't summon and recall the pleasure I'd just felt. I couldn't remember pleasure and that was why I needed it so often and succumbed, again and again.

Because it was not easy anymore. The night my mother pushed my pajama top down off my shoulders and felt the soft hairs under my arms, I became less than a baby, a blob, a primitive living thing she could do anything to as long as she fed me with tickles. She liked to pull off the sheet, push down my pajama pants and pat my buttocks, they clenched at her touch. She wanted to look at me and blow air on my tummy with the full pride of possession. She kissed me on the lips and I shirked. When her hand reached down to the elastic of my pajama pants, I stiffened and bucked away from her. "Don't."

"I don't know why not," she said. "Why won't you let me look, you've got such a cute, twussy little patutie. Can't I be proud of your little body that I made?" When she stared at me like that, it seemed she could take something, just by looking.

"Could you talk like an adult, please."

She sighed. I was already beginning to accept the back rubs I needed, with one eye open, guarding myself from my mother taking too much.

I thought of the orphans in the upstairs attic room. They didn't belong to anyone. The nuns had clean dry hands, light on the tops of our heads. I knew nuns.

"Well, good night then," my mother said.

A swallow of cold air came in when she opened the door and left. I thought of the orphanage, worn sheets, the one rough blanket, how in winter they may crawl into a bunk together, both girls thin and dry, one of them might wet the bed.

The next day, at noon, the orphans were served enormous portions, as if they had been underfed all year and this was our one chance to make up for it. During a lull in the conversation, my mother suggested that our family sell the land behind my grandmother's house. That started an argument—my mother against everyone else.

It was an old fight. My mother suggested we put the barn on the market and everyone else started screaming. We kids all were sent to the downstairs bedroom, where we balanced our plates on our knees and tried to cut without tipping them. Dorie and Diane sat with their shoulders touching, making quiet references to the nuns, and to some other girl at the orphanage, as if to remind themselves they had a life.

Before, I'd thought Dorie might have scrubbed her fingernails clean in the cement-floored bathroom to impress us, with her manners, her pleasantness, with how little trouble she would be. She might have lulled herself to sleep thinking of flaky yellow light in a kitchen. But it seemed she was just now understanding that her private wish would not be realized, not only because we would not keep her, but because we were not a family she would want. They both seemed tired, anxious to leave.

In the kitchen, my mother was shouting. "I don't want to be stuck here all my life! I CAN'T LIVE LIKE THIS!"

"Adele, it doesn't have sewer and water. What do you think we could get for it now?"

Dorie spilled a cranberry on the white chenille bedspread. She looked up at us with terror, holding the berry between two fingers.

"Don't worry, we won't tell," I said. Benny reached down carefully to get his milk from the floor. We didn't look at each other. None of us said anything. We just waited, eating as if eating was our duty.

Then Benny mumbled something.

"What?" I said. We were all jumpy.

"Salty. This turkey's salty."

Dorie and Diane walked upstairs to get their brown bag of clothes. Their beds were neatly made. It was as if they'd never been here. Their presents lay on top of the dresser, with the wrapping paper folded underneath.

"Can we leave these here?" Dorie said. "If you could keep them for us, because if we bring them back to Saint Luke's, they'll just get stolen."

"Yeah, someone'll take them for sure," Diane said. "They take everything."

"Took a necklace watch I had from my mother."

"Okay," I said, and then we waited in the backseat of our car. When my mother finally came, she was sniffling and she didn't say a word to us. She slammed the door shut and started driving. I pressed my cheek against the window, knowing as sure as I knew anything that these two girls would never come back to our house to get their presents. My aunt Carol would probably keep them and rewrap them for next year's orphans. They would wait in her closet of all-purpose gifts.

I looked over at Dorie and Diane. I wondered if they knew the minute they stepped out of our house that they would never come back, if they'd already forgotten their presents on the upstairs dresser, or if they kept complicated accounts, cataloging their possessions, remembering the names of the streets they would return to when they left the orphanage, to collect the things that would help them in their new lives.

Their faces told me nothing. They were closed and solemn as if they were counting to themselves.

One night, the last summer we lived on Lime Kiln Road, Hal and his friend Dave drove Benny and me out to Bay Beach. It was a night when the air was moist, almost beginning to rain. I felt a mouth of wet like a kiss on my arm and then nothing as we walked through the crowds looking up at the lighted rides, and I waited, expecting it again.

Hal had money to buy tickets for Benny and me. They came ten for a dollar in a long green paper string. Benny and I wanted the Ferris wheel, we always wanted the Ferris wheel, and while the man strapped us in, with the old soft wooden bar, Hal and Dave stood at the fence.

We went slowly at first, our hands light on the bar, as the car tilted back and forth gently. Other people were still getting in, their bars snapped shut, it wasn't really going yet. Then it started, lifting up from under in one cool swoop of wind and we were swinging at the top, stretching, the tilt knocking air out of us. On the way down, falling softly, all the lighted small houses came closer and more real and then the next time up was faster and faster until it was like breathing, our air sucked in and out, our eyes opening and closing, the blur of landscape and lights and dark trees, and our nails biting into the soft gray wood until, finally, our car coasted down. The man swung open the bar and we walked out, dizzy and light, down the runway, where Hal and Dave stood ready to take our hands and lead us through the dark paths. We were happy to follow then, everything was shaken out of us.

We walked to the pavilion, a damp dim building where we weren't allowed, but Hal knew the way we were, half asleep and happy, we would never tell. There was a big barn door at one end that exhaled a breath of water. The bay started right there, down old wooden steps, cold and deep and dirty in one smell.

Girls and sailors moved on the dance floor, the boys in full white uniform, with hats. More sailors leaned on the refreshment bar that sold hot dogs and Nehi Orange. There was something about those girls. It was their dark lips, the glitter on their ears; their hair was not like our hair, it was thick and it swept up, and their legs looked tiny in their shoes. Dave took me on his back and Hal had Benny's hand as we went through the crowd. We could have been lost but we trusted them.

We walked past the games lined with sailors, where there were machine guns, colored ducks, everything with bolted rifles, and went to watch the bumper cars. We stood there listening to the hard thwacks of cars until the showers of sparks slowed above and the power began to drain. I closed my eyes and opened them again to look up at the sparks on the netted ceiling. The blue and white fire seemed magic, like sparklers, and it held a few minutes after in your eyes.

They took us farther into the woods. It was dark but there were noises all around us. Hal seemed to follow the invisible sounds to a place.

Then we were standing in a clearing on pine needles. I could feel the damp tall trees above us. The stars hung tiny in the sky. There were other people on the ground, five feet away, but we didn't know them. A girl was lying on an old army blanket, her knee out facing me like a face. A guy leaned on top of her. There was a flashlight on the edge of the blanket and the beam hit the marbled orange/yellow bottoms of her feet, hooked over the boy's white back. He fell, grunting, as he drove her into the ground. It happened again and again. That went on for a while and then he screamed, high like a girl, and he was still for a second, his neck lifted, thick and dead, but his right eyelid and right foot were flinching.

He rose to his knees and she still clung onto him. She lifted a few feet off the ground, her butt spread into separate muscles, her legs around him, hanging on. One by one, he took her hands off his shoulders and let her slide back to the blanket. She sat there picking at the wool. She bent down and I saw her face for a moment. She looked like Rosie Griling. I thought I recognized her; at the same time, I thought it couldn't be. Her lip was bleeding, she was pretty. A strand of her hair fell over her mouth.

Then another boy stepped out of his pants and lowered onto her, like someone starting pushups. He was still wearing his socks and T-shirt. She rearranged herself under him. I didn't like watching. It felt funny being a girl.

A flowered dress bunched up under her armpits. Her underwear lay twisted, a few feet away on the dirt. I looked back at Benny like I wanted to go home and he put his hands, lightly, on my shoulders. It felt safe and good to be in layers of old clothes, the same clothes as the boys wore. I was thinking they would never do this to me, I was family. The girl looked all yellow and white and the boy kept pushing her down. Another boy tore open a package of wieners. They got on their knees by the blanket. The one who was on top of her moved. They passed the package of wieners between them, someone threw down the cellophane wrapping. It glittered in the flashlight light. They stuck the wieners in her, first one, then another. She shuddered, then started to sit up, her hands coming to her face.

I turned around and said I wanted to go home.

Nobody had been talking and those boys heard me. They stood and wiped their hands on their pants. Those boys weren't old. They looked like regular boys, except we didn't know them. They were dressed in good warm clothes and they started circling around, their bike wheels wobbling in the dirt.

Hal lifted me on his shoulders. "We'll go now."

She was still sitting on the blanket, her stomach wet and shiny. She sat there with her legs sprawled out, patting her belly like a baby, as if someone would have to come and dress her. Her hair fell and covered half her face.

"Come *ON*, if you want a ride," one of the boys yelled to her.

She hung her head farther down.

"Where's my lipstick?" she said. She looked up at them and then around. It seemed the first time she saw the trees.

"We're getting out of here, now," one of them said.

"You guys want her?" He was talking to Hal and Dave, who were still standing with us on their shoulders. "Go ahead. You can have her. She likes it." The boy looked back at the girl. "Maybe they'll buy you your lipstick."

They rode away, handling their bikes roughly, standing up and pulling. I watched the lights on their handlebars draw jagged paths through the dark and then I closed my eyes against Hal's back.

The last night of summer, Benny and I slept outside. Benny stood there, scuffing his sneakers on our porch, at midnight, when he was supposed to. We took a blanket and a box of Graham crackers and walked across the yard to the hickory tree. Benny had climbed out his bedroom window and left it open. It was easy for me to get away. During that summer, Ted often stayed late, watching television with my mother in the living room. I crawled out of the downstairs bed, when I couldn't sleep, and woke up in the tight, cold twin bed across from my grandmother in the attic. Anyway, my mother wouldn't miss me. She was a heavy, greedy sleeper and nothing woke her.

We settled the blanket on the tall, uncut grass and opened the box of Graham crackers, passing it back and forth. We felt hickory roots under us. There were so many noises; some were insects, some were the highway, and some we didn't know. It seemed busy outside, like daytime, except for the dark.

It wasn't cold. The alfalfa field had been plowed and the corn was all picked, but there was a rich smell, like hay, that seemed to come from the ground. Even though school was starting, the air still smelled like summer. And the sky that night washed low and near us. There were white traces, as if the stars had moved and left trails of themselves, chalk dust on the black.

I chewed the end of a weed. I wasn't tired.

"You shouldn't care, you like school. You're good in school," Benny said.

"I don like it."

"Yeah, you do."

"You have a lot of friends," I said.

Since Theresa and I made friends, other girls didn't talk to me at school. When they invited me to their birthday parties, they didn't invite Theresa. And I was afraid of boys. An older boy had come up to me on the playground and teased me, and I'd hit him so hard his lip bled. He'd told and I'd been in trouble with the Mother Superior again.

"I'm afraid of them at school."

"You have some friends."

"Theresa."

"You get nervous," he said.

"Yeah, I get nervous." I felt relieved and happy, having said that. It seemed unimportant now that I'd ever been nervous and I couldn't imagine feeling afraid again.

"S'cause of your mother."

"What?" I'd never thought of that and it seemed awful, all of a sudden, for us to talk about her that way. And it was such a night, I didn't want anything wrong.

"Your family's different."

"No," I said. "She's fine. It's just me."

"Shhhh." He put his hand on the inside of my wrist, where the pulse is, and he went to sleep like that, his fingers on my arm. Everything outside seemed wonderful to me, and falling asleep took a long time. I kept sliding down in the dark and then my eyes opened again. I don't know what was more amazing: that our land was so changed and beautiful at night, or that it was familiar. It was our old barn, standing crookedly, casting a pure black shadow, and they were our houses in the distance with their porch lights on, but the sky was shining as I'd never seen it and each stalk of long grass seemed to hold an identical stem of moonlight on its side.

I woke up first and watched the daylight come into the sky. I propped up on an elbow. I heard the six-fifty train. I had never seen a sunrise and I've never forgotten that one. I must have moved, because Benny woke up, cranky because he felt cold and sore from sleeping on the ground. He ran home, dragging the blanket behind him. But I was happy. I felt incredibly light, walking over the field. I ate the last Graham crackers from the box. I felt I'd discovered something new that would change me and that my old problems, being nervous and afraid, were gone; already they seemed strange and silly to me.

The fall before we moved to Carriage Court, I wanted to go trick-or-treating with Benny, but my mother said no. She offered to take me in the car; she and Lolly would wait by the curb while I ran with my bag to the doors. But I cried and so she finally let me go.

Theresa Griling came, too, she was the only other girl. Their father had driven back from Florida and they were home again. None of us ever talked about when he was gone. That was when they took Netty away, at the end of the summer when he came home. At the railroad tracks, we all started running across the plowed frozen fields in one line. I could feel the hard ridges through the rubber soles of my tennies. After a while I didn't know where we were. The band of my mask hurt my chin and I had to hold up a bunch of sheet with one hand so I didn't trip.

Then there were dim streets where we didn't know anybody and the boys pressed up to the screen doors first. They were down to the next houses before Theresa and I got our bags open. But the heavy drop of candy in the paper bag was a pleasure, it seemed we were making progress. When we ran, the hard candy knocked on the sides of the bags and the bags banged against our thighs.

Later, we lost the boys and sat on a curb where we couldn't even find a street sign. I don't know how long we stayed there. But finally, the boys came back out of the fields. New guys were with them, riding wobbly circles on bikes. Some of them were smoking.

"Where's Benny?"

"I dunno," someone said. "Went somewhere with David."

"He's supposed to stay with us."

"Who says?"

"My mom."

"Her mom says." The smokers giggled, cigarettes dropping in the dark.

We started running again, Theresa and me in front this time and the guys on bikes bouncing over the fields. Then they came right up next to us, almost hitting us with their wheels.

"Watch out." I didn't know yet what they were doing, I didn't know I couldn't say no, that they didn't care. "That's my foot."

They pushed us down in the dirt and we both screamed. One pulled up my sheet and grinned at me. He had a crew cut and pimples and dirty hair on his upper lip. There was nothing in him that I recognized.

The other guy was pressing down Theresa's shoulders. He leaned over and kissed her, making fake smooching sounds like farts.

"Stop it," I screamed, kicking, before he did anything. My ears were cold and humming. I had a headache like one jagged line. He bent down and clamped his hands over my wrists and he was sitting on my legs. But when I looked up, I thanked God, because there was a circle of boys and I saw Benny.

"Benny. Make him stop."

I was so relieved to see Benny I closed my eyes, but then when I opened them again, he was talking to the guy next to him as if he hadn't seen me.

"Benny!"

But he didn't look down at me. He wouldn't. Then, all of a sudden, I felt it. A cold blade against my cheek, under my hair, on my neck. It was a scissors. The guy was cutting my hair. I heard the scissors clicking, the short, snuffling noises the hair made when it came off. Benny knew about my hair, he knew I'd been growing it all my life. It was unusual. Everyone said that about my hair. It was pure black. It was going to be one of the things that would help me get on television. My grandmother said it was so dark you could see other colors in it. I started to cry, but quiet. I didn't even care about Benny helping me anymore. It was too late. My hair was half gone. I just wanted it to be a dream, but I knew it was true. I just wanted my hair back, that was all I wanted and all I could imagine ever wanting.

The two older guys got on their bikes and rode away. That was the way they were, older kids, worse than lawless. They could just come out, get you alone and hurt you and then ride away. The rest of the guys, our guys, the guys we knew, started running across the uneven field. Theresa staggered up, she was crying, too, but she started following after them.

"Stevie," she was yelling and running, "Stev-vie, you're gonna be in troub-bel, I'm telling Da-ad," but she was falling forward, tripping and then getting up again, heaving harder, and I doubt her brother even heard her, she was so far behind.

I just stayed on the ground till they were far away. There was noise from trucks on the highway somewhere, but I couldn't see it. Then somebody was running back towards me. It was Benny, but I didn't want Benny then. He stood ten feet in front of me and screamed:

"Come on. Get up. You want to stay here all night, that's your business, but I'm supposed to bring you home."

I'm not going to say anything, I was thinking, I knew I didn't have to. There was nothing anyone could do to me now because I didn't care.

"Please, will you please come on. Just this once." Benny knelt down in front of me, moving his hands, wanting me to look at him.

I was trying to collect all my hair from the ground. The pieces felt light and soft and it was hard to see them in the dark. Mostly, I was doing it by touch. Benny scratched under his sock, but I didn't care what he did. He took off running then, yelling so the rest of those guys didn't go without him. I let him. Let them all go. I was wadding the hair in my hand and then dropping the balls in the bag with my candy. At least they didn't take my candy. The hair wadded up in balls, it was neat, it just made these puffs with air inside. When I reached, my knee touched the scissors. They were still there, little rounded elementary school scissors, the same kind I had at home. They lay open, a thin blue metal. I wasn't going to touch them.

"Come on, you coming or not, last chance!" I thought I heard Benny but I wasn't sure anymore. I was lowering my head to the ground, it was almost there, then there. My head felt intricate like an ant farm. I thought I could hear blood moving in tunnels.

But in a while my joints got wrong. My arms felt twisted in the shoulder sockets. I knew I'd better get up. It had been a long time, the trucks were still running somewhere and there was nobody else around, there hadn't been anybody for hours maybe. I'd have to do something myself. So I started walking with my bag towards the lights, the nearest lights, which were far away.

Ringing the doorbell, I almost fell asleep and a man came and let me in to use the phone. The kitchen gleamed bright and I didn't even have to think about the number. It was there, the first thing I knew. My mother answered and when she heard it was me, she started screaming. I couldn't listen to it and the phone dropped down so it was just hanging, knocking against the wall.

The man who lived there picked it up. I sat in a kitchen chair.

When he put the receiver back on the wall, he told me she was on her way.

"She's got the address and all. It won't be long for you now. You're pretty far from home, you have to be careful on Halloween, you know, the things you read."

A chair skidded back on the linoleum and he was across from me at the table, wearing black plastic glasses, with corn-colored hair. My eyes slumped to sleep. I didn't want to bother with anything, talking, nothing. It seemed she would be there as soon as I opened my eyes.

"Would you like an apple?" Something in his voice made me lift my head and see his hand lingering on one of the apples in a bowl between us. They were red, streaked with beads of other colors, beautiful all of a sudden. I wanted one but I was afraid. I couldn't decide what to do and then lights washed in the front window and I recognized the sound of my grandmother's brakes, like a voice. I thanked God it was my grandmother's car. I ran out with my bag in my arms and got into the backseat. Then we were all inside, my grandmother driving, my mother in the front bending over and looking at me.

"Oh God. Oh, my God, give me strength." She was kneeling on her seat then and pulling the short hair out from my face.

"What have they DONE to you? Who did that, tell me right now, who did that to you. Gram, would you look at her? They've ruined her hair, they've just ruined her. I can't believe it. How could you let them do this to you?

"You were the one, you had to go out. You were so smart, you thought you could keep up with the big kids, well, look at you now, just look at you. Sure, now you cry. Well, you'll have to live with it. It's your head, not mine. How could you let them DO that to you? Couldn't you run and call home? Couldn't you call me? Tell me, Honey, what happened?"

I was lying with my face pressed into the crease of the seat, eating my own breath back like another person's. I could taste the vinyl. I knew my mother would go on and on. She'd just keep yelling and yelling and pretty soon all we'd hear was her voice going up and down like a siren.

It was all noise. She was mad, she hated my weakness and wanted to beat it out of me and then she'd knock her hands against her own chest, killing the air there, too. I felt dry. I was a piece of wood. My grandmother just drove. We did things while my mother felt. We were still. Furniture. She took up the room in the car, sucked all the color out of us, eating the quiet for herself and all we heard was her collection, and we hated it. We could have punctured the air with our hate, it was that sharp, it had been turning for so long.

In the house, my mother marched right to the bathroom and called me. "Ann, come in here a second."

My grandmother grabbed my arm before I went. "Listen here, you, don't you worry. Tomorrow, I'll take you to the Harper Method and she'll give you a good cut. It's good to get rid of that heavy hair, anyway. It'll look real nice short." We stood in front of the bathroom. I gave my grandmother my bag of candy before I went in.

In front of the mirror, my mother combed my hair. She closed the door and locked it.

"I mean, it's what MADE you special. It was your crowning glory. You talk about going to California and auditions for television, well, let me tell you, other kids are cuter. Your hair was what you had going for you. Without it, I just don't think you'll stand out."

She shook her head, pulling a strand of my hair up and letting it fall back on my face, but even then, she couldn't resist looking at herself in the mirror and sucking in her own cheeks.

"People say my eyes are nice." I looked up at my mother.

"Who?"

"Lolly said and the ice skating pro said so too."

"Oh, Honey, they were just saying that. Ted said that, really, because he likes me. Your eyes are green, but some kids have a deeper, richer green. Your green is kind of ordinary."

My mother herself had blue eyes.

The next morning, my grandmother was waiting at the kitchen table. She had braided the hair she found in the brown bag of candy and sewn the two thick braids into the back of a yellow straw hat. "With the hat on, they'll all think you still have your long hair," she said.

I hadn't seen my mother yet.

That afternoon, my mother leaned against our white Volkswagen, her voice high above, far, her eyes on the telephone wires. "I think I may just go away somewhere, California maybe, maybe just away. You don't need me here."

I pulled her blouse, hard, trying to tug her down. Her face tilted up to the sky. "I do, Mom," I said. Her blouse that day was pink gingham, her initials embroidered over the pocket in white, fancy letters. The sky was pale blue, with a few clouds, the telephone poles, brown and scarred. She looked down at me, took off the straw hat and tossed it on the grass. She ruffled my hair. "You do, huh? Well, okay."

It only took the smallest thing. No one else in the world, nothing mattered.

11

LIME KILN ROAD

■ □ ■

There's a place in Beverly Hills where my mother and I lived for a little more than a year. From the outside the building looks like sandstone. The concrete seems gold, instead of gray, the slight difference in color of sand, when the sun comes out. On either side of the entrance, a molded lion's head holds a brass ring in its mouth.

At night, small lamps hidden in ferns lit the lions' heads. My mother and I always thought the building looked very elegant. For one thing, it was a move up for us, from our furnished studio. The apartments were like ski condominiums—there were six units, two floors each, on either side of a courtyard—and they seemed to be newly built. We felt proud to move in. My mother hired Daniel Swan's twin sisters to help us pack and clean. We threw out our unattractive odds and ends and we lined the new kitchen drawers with checkered paper. We had high hopes. We wanted to live like other people.

The apartment retained a just-built feeling, even after we moved in. Maybe it was because we had no furniture. The long, newly painted white walls of the downstairs and the beige carpet throughout, its nap still even to one side, stayed bare. But it was more. The insides of closets smelled like fresh-cut wood. We moved a bed into each of the bedrooms. My mother's room had built-in dressers; I just stacked my clothes in the closet. Ted's huge radio sat alone on the living room floor downstairs.

We often leaned on the carpeted steps in the middle of the apartment and looked at the light coming in through the porch's glass doors, hitting our living room walls in spikes and patterns, sometimes splintering into colors. We both felt pleased with the apartment, with the fact that there was an upstairs and a downstairs. We kept the bare place very clean. We ate most of our meals out and when we stayed home, we balanced plates on our knees, sitting on the carpeted stairs. I did homework on my bed.

My room had a cubbyhole, where I stored things. A door opened out of the wall, and inside, there was a plywood shelf. Every night, I put my schoolbooks there. Slanted two-by-fours sloped from the ceiling down into the foundations of the house. The boards were rough and unsanded, light wood. Perhaps they kept the closets smelling new. Between beams was nothing. You could put your hand through. I tried to be careful when I laid things on the shelf, so they wouldn't fall.

I don't know why the space was left there. Probably it should have been tamped with insulation or more wood. Perhaps the chute was a carpenter's mistake, someone else's careless harm. I've thought about that odd construction many times because one day that winter, after months and a habit of nervous care, I knocked my elbow on a corner and my jewelry box fell down.

"Why on earth did you put it there? I told you to watch that edge, for God's sakes. You knew it could go right through."

But that came afterwards. First I was just stunned. I didn't know why. I thought, Why would I leave something precious in the only unsafe place in the apartment? Perhaps there was a simple reason: it was a shelf. I had no dresser or desk for small things. But I could have put it on the floor.

It was the thing Benny gave me before I left, a tin box, with a hinged lid. Inside, I'd nested a ring, a handkerchief, a rolled-up list of my friends' names. That chute led to nowhere, there was no basement in that apartment. Things that fell down the chute were irretrievable. I imagined the tin box lying on its hinges like an opened clam, still, on the dirt floor among bare foundation beams.

Several times I went to ask the manager. After we moved out, I walked by the building. I've written letters to the investment company that owns it. I don't know what it would mean to me now, the box and its contents recovered. Ben has been dead for years, the box was a collection of childhood things. Still, it must be there at the bottom of that building like the real ticking heart of a huge machine. You remember the places you've lost to.

The night Ben died, we still lived in the small furnished studio where my mother and I slept in the same bed. She shook me awake, her hands rough and gentle at the same time. She squatted near the floor, rocking on her heels, the phone to her ear. It was still night and she was screaming.

She told me he'd been in a car. Jay Brozek had been driving. Jay had been speeding and he ran into a tree. Jay was fine, just a scratch on his cheek.

A smile grew on my face, I didn't have the strength to stop it. I felt the muscles rippling in my cheeks. Her face went crooked with pity. "Awww," she kept saying, "awww, poor Annie, poor poor Carol." When we hugged, we both squatted on the floor. I tasted her hair, a burnt taste, and her breasts moved against mine through our T-shirts.

We dressed and waited at the Western Union office with our suitcase. Carol wired us money for tickets. It was still dark out, when we drove to the airport. We didn't tell anyone where we were going; my mother phoned in to both our schools and said we were sick. It was a Monday morning. We left our car in the airport parking lot. This was our first trip home since we moved.

In Chicago, we changed to a small, older plane with scratchy, red plaid upholstery on the seats. The stewardesses seemed different, too. I recognized their voices. For the first time I heard that we had accents where we'd come from. It was in the way they said their o's. The stewardesses all wore the same maroon nail polish, matching their uniform belts. Their faces were not as delicate or chiseled as their counterparts' on the coastal flight. Maybe airlines chose stewardesses for features and the larger, less balanced profiles were left here, caught in the narrow local triangle above the ground where they grew up. Those voices, their ready nasal friendliness, sounded homely. And then I thought of how we spoke, my mother and me. I didn't think we talked that way anymore. From then on, I started being careful of my o's.

My mother turned in her seat. "Sounds familiar, doesn't it? Sort of a dumb accent, when you listen. Uneducated," she whispered. She bent over me and peered out the window. "But look at all those little farms. It really is pretty land."

The plane shuddered into its descent. Over the microphone, a stewardess asked us to buckle our seat belts.

Her voice hummed with pride and capability. Theresa Griling had wanted to be a stewardess, either that or a hairdresser someplace where rich people lived, Beverly Hills or Florida. When she'd talked like that, it had sounded brave and dangerous, something I'd never do. But, now these stewardesses seemed perfectly safe. Even in the air, even if they slept with a married pilot when the plane was grounded in Chicago for a snowstorm, even their adventures would be innocent. They would probably end up married and living somewhere within a couple hundred miles of the place they were born. They'd grow firm, righteous, the way good mothers become, their young optimism satisfied and thickened. Even those who'd chosen flight and travel, lightness, the air— you knew, listening to them, they'd never get too far away. Gravity sunk in the bottom of their voices, like the thumping of feet on the ground. Their flights would keep a tight perimeter between Chicago, the Twin Cities and Green Bay. We seemed different, already. I didn't know what would happen to us.

The runways of the Bay City Airport were just clearings in the low woods, rimmed with aspen and pine. When the plane shuddered and rumbled and bumped, we closed our eyes, clinging. When I opened my hand, a few moments later, my mother's nails had bitten in so hard there was blood. We both felt terrified of landing.

We walked into the airport slowly, dragging our one heavy suitcase. We saw Betty Dorris, the fat woman, still standing behind the ticket counter, wearing a blouse with a white ruffled collar. She had written my father's plane ticket when he'd first flown away. Betty Dorris had always liked my mother's men. The last year we'd lived in Bay City, she had invited Ted over to dinner. Now, she wouldn't look at us.

"God," my mother said.

Years ago, in December, my mother and I drove to her house and bought Christmas tree ornaments, styrofoam balls she had covered with velvet and lace. We bought them out of pity and then gave them away.

"I think it's rude that she doesn't say anything. She sees us," I said.

"Oh, of course she does. But you know, it's her way of snubbing me. I suppose she figures Bay City's hers now that I'm gone. Well, she can have it."

We braced ourselves, waiting for someone to find us and take us to a car. We didn't know who it would be. It was a relief not to see them yet. I knew the minute one of them looked at me, it would all begin.

My mother slipped the bag off her shoulder and set it on the floor.

"God, doesn't it all look small?" She looked around and then back at me. "I mean, the airport, everything, just seems TINY."

It's funny how close you get, closer than in life, except for the seconds you touched, and then you were both moving, not seeing, exactly. Looking down at Benny, I thought there was something wrong with the way his nostrils joined his lip. They looked strange and fishlike, inaccurate. I leaned over to kiss him and tasted powder on my mouth and felt the hardness just underneath, like metal.

It was a brass-banded cedar box, lined in pleated pale blue satin. A piece of lace I recognized from my grandmother's house lay under his head. It had always been draped over the davenport.

Carol stood on the carpet in her nylons, her high heels next to her feet, facing forward.

"They used to water the greens," Jimmy was saying. "See, then they let them golf free. So he was there with Susie and a whole group of them. And Jay Brozek was there too, he had his own car. So Ben got in the one car with Susie and all the rest."

"He was *in* the car?"

"He was *in* the other car and then Jay called him and said, Hey, Ben, come on over and ride with me, I'm all alone. So he did."

My mother crossed her arms over her chest and then she wiped her glasses on her silk scarf. She was wearing a black pantsuit, belted. "In the millions," she said, frowning. Pews lined the center of the room, so people gathered at the edges, where floral arrangements stood on the carpet. Smaller bouquets were set on draped tables. "Absolutely, they'll be rich from this."

"He can sue for companionship, for loss of income." Hal bent back his fingers, counting. "He'll be able to retire."

Carol moved from her shoes, which were still planted on the carpet, facing the coffin. "I wanted you to see." She pushed the back of my neck, dunking me over a bouquet of long-stemmed dark roses. They looked tinged, almost black. "From that little Susie." My aunt looked at me. "See, I always said, if Ben grew up and wanted to marry that Susie, we would have been glad, Ann. And they're not rich either, the parents both work. But it's a clean nice family."

The couple who owned Krim's bakery tapped Carol's shoulder. Grilings shuffled behind them.

"When you were little, you always thought you were adopted," Theresa told me, "because your mother had blond hair and you had dark." She reached out to touch my hair, the way she always had, as if black hair were amazing.

I asked Theresa and Mary how they liked the academy. "Fine," they each said quickly. "Good." They had known Benny, too, more than I did the past few years.

They told me Rosie had gotten married and moved to Milwaukee and Stevie had gone into the navy. He was on an aircraft carrier going around the world. Theresa said she planned to enlist in the air force when she graduated. On her coat, she was wearing small tin silver wings, from American Airlines. I recognized them, they had been mine. A stewardess gave them to me once when my mother and I flew home from Las Vegas.

"You're going to join the army and leave Mary all alone?"

"There's my dad," Mary said quickly.

"Air force," Theresa corrected.

Then Jay walked in the back door, flanked on either side by Chummy Brozek and his second wife, Darla, who was so fat she had to make her own clothes. She wore a huge brown smock with regular terry-cloth house slippers.

"She probably can't get shoes that wide," my mother whispered. "Look at that. Each foot is like a little dog."

Jay hovered taller than his father, but his neck wilted, he looked bad in a suit. His dark hair seemed wet and there were cracks and scabs on his lips. You could see the tremble. I stared at the scratch on his cheek. The three of them moved together, sideways, into a pew.

"I know it," Carol said, somewhere behind me.

All our lives, Brozeks had lived on Lime Kiln Road, Chummy delivered Morning Glory milk.

"Older," Jimmy said. "They've got two in the marines, one in the air force. The air force one is stationed somewhere in Germany, the other two are over in Vietnam. But they're all alive."

"He's going to be a pallbearer, Jay is," Hal said.

"No," my mother hissed. She shoved her fist in her mouth.

"That's what we said too, but Benny would have wanted it this way."

I'd never seen her before, but I recognized her from the school photograph my grandmother had sent, with *Benny's girlfriend Susie* written on the white border. They'd met working on a float. They'd stuffed thousands of square toilet paper tissues into chicken wire to make the top of a covered wagon.

"But the phone rang in the trailer and Carol got it. And they told us he'd been in an accident. They had him in the hospital at Bailey's Harbor. We had to decide right then if we wanted to fly him down to a big hospital or let the doctor work on him there. Hell, we didn't know. He was unconscious when we got there. And this dumb doctor is fussing, working on the leg, pinning the leg, and here he's concentrating all his energy on the leg and the heart stops."

"But—" I couldn't finish. I couldn't imagine Benny without a leg.

"I don't think he was too much on the ball. You figure, a country doctor up there."

"A GP probably," my mother murmured.

Carol, still without her shoes, clasped a hand on Jimmy's arm. "Look, both of the parents came and brought that Susie. They work, so they must have both taken off."

"See, if that was you, I would have had you on the next plane to Chicago to *the* best doctor," my mother whispered as Carol and Jimmy walked away. "A specialist. Some dumb country doctor sitting the night shift. No wonder, you know."

"Then he could have died on the plane," I said.

My mother pushed her face next to mine. "That's why we moved. So we could be there, *living* with the very best. Of everything. You should be grateful once in a while, you know? For all I've done for you. You don't see now, but you will someday."

Susie inched into the pew behind Jay, and laid a hand on his shoulder. They were friends, there was a whole system of love and danger nobody who wasn't young would see. I was thinking of Benny speeding in the dark, swimming at night with his friends, holding their cigarettes up over the water. All I'd missed the three years since we'd moved. Undressing Susie, screwing her on the dirty sand. Things I didn't really know, drinking, drugs. I looked at Hal. There was definitely something. All of a sudden, I felt so jealous: Benny had known everything first. Then, as soon as the return of a breath, I hoped he'd done it all, the things my mother most feared, the worst.

Susie wore suede fringed moccasins, tied around her ankles, under her dress. She had thick ankles and the moccasins made them look thicker, but she didn't seem to know. Benny wouldn't have ever noticed either and that made me think that life here was simpler than ours in California. We felt acutely aware of everything wrong with us. I'd been studying with a guy named Peter from my school, and his maid brought us a tray of cookies. "They're good, you should have some," he'd said, "or on second thought, maybe you shouldn't." The next time I'd stood up and crossed the room to sharpen a pencil, he cupped his hand on my thigh. "That's where you put it on," he'd said. My mother and I weren't the hits we'd hoped to be.

At the back of the room, Hal's wife, Merry, handed Tina over to Hal's arms. Merry and Tina lived in a trailer now, twenty miles up out of town.

"They were nice together, that Susie and Ben. They were good kids." Carol sighed.

"Better than Hal is," Jimmy said.

Behind us, two women were talking about Darla Brozek's cooking, how for a long time, she'd had to cook for twelve every night, five of them big boys. One woman started on Darla's recipe for chicken: you bone and skin two big chickens and lay the meat out in such a glass baking dish. You pour over two cans of soup, cream of mushroom, cream of celery, one of the creams. And then on top of that, she spread out those Pillsbury frozen biscuits and baked at 350 for an hour and oh, was it good.

"The Tet Offensive," Chummy Brozek said. "Yes, a medal. No, Hal never went. He was here the whole time."

I walked over to where Hal was standing, against an accordion wall.

"Where's the gramma?" someone asked.

"They've got her sedated, she's in the hospital." The time she'd seen Hal on television was the first stroke. Since then, she'd had two. The first time, Carol called us and said we didn't have to come home. She was already in the hospital recovering from the second stroke when they'd had to tell her about Benny.

That afternoon, when my mother and I had gone to visit, she seemed indifferent. I sat in the corner of the hospital room, watching as she tossed in her bed, my mother hovering over, saying, "Mom, you look great, how do you feel?" her voice loud and bright, as if my grandmother were deaf.

"Leave me be," she'd said.

Carol stepped back up into her high heels. People were beginning to leave and she had to stand next to Jimmy and shake their hands. She told Jay where the pallbearers would meet and he looked desperately grateful. He kept repeating, "outside back door, eight o'clock in the morning" as if the words were his duty for the rest of his life.

While Jay walked Darla to the car in the parking lot, Chummy lingered inside. "Go ahead and sue me," he said to Jimmy. "We've paid our premiums all our lives for something like this, first Junie and I paid and now Darla and I do. Go ahead and sue me."

"He'll have to live with this, Jay will," Hal said. "Just like I do."

"What he did is worse," I said. "You didn't kill anybody."

"Didn't get a chance."

He meant the war. Whenever Hal brought up Vietnam, the rest of us didn't say anything.

For a long time we all stood there at the door. We watched people we knew go down the dim hallway into the brightness. It was after Labor Day, but hot outside. We were the last ones there; Carol walked around picking dry flowers from the bouquets. She stepped out of her shoes again. "Do you think we should turn off the lights?"

"They do that," my mother said. "Leave it."

Carol rubbed the arch of her foot. "Do you want me to give you my keys?" she said. "You can drive to Dean's and pick up hamburgers for all of us." She was the only one who could dare talk about food.

I turned so our knees touched through our nylons. "I don't have a license."

"Oh, no, sure, I guess you wouldn't. You're a year younger, always."

We sat near the door a little longer. They gave my mother Jimmy's keys, but we were all of us shy to go out into that brightness.

Carol shook her head. "You know, I just can't help it. He was the one drinking. And now he'll get married and go to college and do all the things." No one answered. "Thank God, we gave Ben the skis last Christmas. At least he got some fun out of that."

My mother shoved her knuckles in her mouth. She wiped an eye with one end of her scarf.

"Oh, Adele, don't, you'll ruin it. Silk stains and that's such a very pretty scarf."

We drove fast, the two of us, windows down, my arm out damming the air, along Bay Highway, past factories and then the fields, in no hurry to get home. I fumbled with the radio knobs. It was September, an Indian summer day, and the fields smelled rich like corn.

We passed Bay Beach and the rides were still going. My mother skidded to a stop and we sat there, parked on the gravel, watching the slow-moving machines.

"Should we just go once?" she said.

Our seat bobbed and then we were high, at the top of the Ferris wheel, suspended while the boy below hurried children down the runway and fastened them in. You could see all the land, in clear geometry, the baby pool set like a gem in cement. The amusement park rides looked quaint and small, painted colors faded and old-fashioned. We were still at the top rocking, tilting. It wasn't falling that scared me, but the slow band of time as you're beginning to go, when you can still see the world in clear patterns, the web of lawns, and your fingernails cut into the soft nicked wood and everything in your body screams Stop. But you're moving.

The car tilted down and I was screaming, probably a long time before I heard it.

When we took her out of the car in the back parking lot of the hospital, the pavement sparkled and she planted her feet far apart, her ankles stiff as if she were on ice. In her room, she felt glad to get out of her clothes. She asked us to close the blinds, the bars of light on the blanket hurt her.

"Don't you want to talk a little before you go to sleep, Mom?" my mother whispered through the metal poles of the bed. "We haven't seen you for so long."

"No," she said. "Let me be."

□

After the funeral, my mother drove downtown to get her divorce. She took a long time dressing for it. Her lawyer told her there would be problems in the way of bills from Ted's credit card. Ted had ended up paying for our Lincoln. My mother skipped the cemetery. The rest of us went and then followed in a slow caravan back to Lime Kiln Road. Women put on aprons in the kitchen and stood cutting cakes on Carol's counters. Jimmy stayed outside, tending the barbecue pit. Hal lugged things—silver kegs of beer, trays of chicken for the grill. There was one round table under an umbrella where the priest sat with his feet up. He wore white athletic socks under his sandals.

There was a small stand of pines between my grandmother's house and Carol's, in the common backyard. I walked over and stood there, my heels puncturing the dry brown leaves and pine needles. My grandmother once told me that during storms her husband had fastened on snowshoes and trekked out to stand in this grove of trees, watching the snow come down. Protected by the high branches, he stood and watched. She said he loved the silence. The pine smelled sharp and good. This was the place Benny and I buried our pets; a bird with a broken wing we'd fed from an eyedropper, a lame squirrel. We'd sat in here for hours. We'd felt invisible then, inside a dome of different air. Now it was a few scraggly pines. We'd marked the graves with crosses made from clean licked Popsicle sticks and now they weren't there anymore.

I picked up a handful of dirt and let it fall down off my fingers. Things didn't stay and for no good reason. My father's hole in the hedge was a shabby lapse now, almost grown over, as if the bushes were slightly diseased. I thought about our crosses; wood wouldn't dissolve into the ground, not in five or ten years. No one would take them, but they were gone. Things just disappeared and we weren't even surprised. We didn't expect them to last.

When I walked back to the patio, someone was passing around a large gray rock. "It's a rock from Pikes Peak," Hal said. It was labeled in my grandmother's even penmanship, *Rock From Pikes*

Peak. "I took a trip to Colorado and Ben said he wanted a rock from Pikes Peak."

"Oh," the women said, in low voices, as if they were holding a dangerous and beautiful secret.

The rock passed from hand to hand on the back patio, the story repeated in different voices. "He said he wanted a rock from Pikes Peak," Jimmy said.

Right then, I wanted it to take home with me to keep. I wanted it a lot and I couldn't think of anything else for a while.

The women stood in the kitchen again, rinsing the dishes and stacking them. Everything outside seemed very clear, the dark green hedge, the corn, the red barn and the highway overpass. The sky was a tender blue with slow pink clouds. Ordinary objects looked precious and defined the way they do sometimes in cold air. It was still early in the afternoon and it seemed as if nothing would change, as if the fields and light had settled into a permanent weather.

The screen banged and my mother tripped, her heel catching in the netted doormat. She let the air out of her cheeks slowly. She stood on one shoe, the other stockinged foot at her knee, her arms crossed over her chest. I was sitting on the warm white stones of the barbecue pit. I waited for her to find me.

Then she saw me and shrugged. "Well, we're free," she said. "We didn't get much, but it's over. We're single."

The trouble with serenity is that it can turn. The trees seem to lose their souls and look again like painted scenery. You hug your knees and kiss them as if chilled. You pinch yourself. Then you turn to other people, talk, you trust only human beings again, as if nature has abandoned you. Christianity must have been born in twilight.

Only the family and Lolly and the priest still sat outside, on the back patio, when the air began to lose its light. The priest lit a cigarette.

I was thinking of Ben again, I imagined him drinking margaritas, banana daiquiris, the way he danced, stamping his feet, spinning, lightly touching Susie's breasts by the side of the house, driving, speeding in the night. "You can smoke?" I said to the priest.

"Sure."

"He's a super-duper-modern priest," Carol said. "They give guitar masses now. Oh, it's all changed since you left. They go to Michigan on retreats. I've seen this one in blue jeans."

The priest laughed, his soft voice dissolving quickly in the air.

"Can you drink?"

He nodded.

"So can you screw now, too?"

"Ann," my mother said. She and Lolly warmed their hands over the barbecue pit. "I don't know where she learns that language. Two days here. She doesn't talk like that in Beverly Hills."

"Some things haven't changed," the priest said.

Jimmy leaned over the table. "Annie here asked you, Father, because she was interested."

"Oh, Jimmy," Carol said.

It was too early for crickets, but it seemed we could hear the night coming slowly, before the light dimmed, a shifting of the earth. The trees moved as if they were pulling into themselves.

"Oh, and he's a good preacher, too, Ann. You should hear him. They come all the way over from the West Side."

"We go at night now," Jimmy said. "Guitar mass."

"You didn't know your aunt and uncle were such swingers."

"Me, I don't go to church," Hal said. "I pray by myself. God knows what I'm saying. I just ask him straight. None of this bullshit."

Nobody paid any attention to Hal, but that was normal. We were all used to ignoring him.

"Different for you," Hal said, pointing to his daughter, Tina. "You have to pray out loud. And you know why? Because I said so."

"I do," she said.

The five o'clock train came, a long faltering wail in the distance.

□

"Are you too cold?" Jimmy asked me.

"No, it's okay."

"'Cause I can go get you a sweater. You'd fit in one of his." It broke my heart, Jimmy like that, kind.

"So do you like California?" the priest asked my mother. His forehead had no lines, he seemed so innocent, local.

She shrugged. "Well, yes and no. I do and I don't." Her arms spread out, glamorous, over the pit. "I mean, I work nine hours a day and drive two more and just so we can live in one room where she goes to a decent school. So there's no time, really, or money, for me to have any fun. But, yes, I'm glad to be doing it. I'm glad to be giving her this opportunity."

No one said anything. The ice cubes knocked together in Jimmy's glass. Even Lolly seemed embarrassed, looking down. Our leg waxes, the days of facials, hours in tight pink masks, then the steam room at Elizabeth Arden's. I got to go, too, Saturdays and her date days with Josh Spritzer. The opera dress with windows of sheer fabric, revealing printed scenes of other cloth. Palm Springs, the ocean, the desert. We had fun. But I didn't say anything, either.

Jimmy stood up, he was always the worst with my mother. Carol seemed to have a genetic patience for her.

"Let me tell you something, Adele. We all work too, we—"

"Jimmy, don't," Carol said.

"I'm going to go get another drink." He went in through the sliding glass doors he'd built himself, years ago, when Benny and I were pests, underfoot.

My mother appeared injured. "Well, sure you work, too, but you have the house, you have the trailer—" My mother moved her face, looking around at it all.

I stared at her. "You wouldn't want it," I said.

Lolly reached out and touched my mother's arm.

"Just today, let's not have any fighting once," Carol said.

My mother and Lolly started whispering between themselves. "Well she . . ." my mother was saying, as I moved away.

□

The night before, we slept in my grandmother's house. We needed to be alone. We'd snooped around, opened drawers just to see the things once again where they'd always been, picked at food in the refrigerator. My mother sat on the kitchen floor with her legs spread out, searching the bottom cupboards for hidden cookies.

"They're in here somewhere." She'd been happy. I could have let her look, but she had this grin that bothered me.

I told her. "She stopped making them years ago."

"No," she said. "Those round flat butter cookies. She hides them in here somewhere."

"With the ground hickory nuts and powder sugar on top." I shook my head. "It hurt her eyes too much to pick the nuts."

"Oh."

An hour later, my mother came and touched my shoulder and said, "How did you know she stopped making those?"

I shrugged. "I just knew."

"Oh. I didn't know that," she said.

Then she called Josh Spritzer. The way she talked there was no possible way he could imagine our kitchen. She sat in the corner, her bare feet up on the vinyl chair. The electric clock above the stove buzzed, the cuckoo thugged, the refrigerator churned and the fluorescent curved tube of lights over the table hummed. The inside of houses in the country were like that then. Because of the silence, like a long throat, outside.

I could tell from the way her voice rose in waves of enthusiasm—too much music, nerve and light—that Josh Spritzer didn't want to be listening. Her breath gathered as she began each sentence. "And my sister, on the day of the funeral, was counting the flower arrangements." She laughed, trying to make it light.

After, she went humming through the house, filing her nails. But the phone call hadn't gone well; when she hung up, she'd stayed where she was and stared ahead at the wall for a full minute.

"Maybe we should go back early, huh?" She stopped in the living room doorway and looked around. "Our life isn't here anymore, you know? It's there."

□

Tina was fidgeting and when Hal yelled at her, she started to cry. He picked her up, then, and spanked her and her yelps escalated to screaming. Our heads bent down over the table.

"Hal, just leave her be once." That was Carol. "Ogh, Hal, she's overtired."

He pointed, with the hand not holding Tina, to his chest. "She's *my* kid, mine. She's not yours. I'll do what I want with her." Tina stopped crying. She hung still now, limp off his shoulder.

Jimmy was standing at the sliding glass doors. He let them pass.

"I mean, if I'd had half the help *she* did from my father." My mother had been talking to Lolly but her voice rose loud in the pause. "The house and every year a new car."

Jimmy just stood with his drink, inside the open glass doors. "Adele, come here a second."

She looked up. She was sitting on the edge of the stone barbecue pit, a leg swinging over the side. "What for?"

"I want to show you something."

"Show me what?"

"I want to show you the deed and the mortgage for this house I've been paying on for twenty-one years and that I'm still paying."

My mother shook her head. For a moment, I blushed. I thought she was ashamed. But she looked up again. No one could beat my mother. "You know who helped me when I got married? Nobody."

"Come in here."

My mother started crying. "I'm not going in there with you, Jimmy. You'll hurt me. I know that's what you want."

The priest sat chewing on the end of a weed and the evening train went by, a low crooked moan from the tracks. The young priest looked wistful then, as if he wished he were going somewhere.

Carol stood and held her elbows in her hands. Her mouth opened, but she must have thought better of it. She just shook her head.

"You've got your chance to see. Either look at it or shut up from now on."

My mother lifted her head. "I won't be talked to like that, Jimmy, by you or by anyone. I'm going home to Mom's now, because really, I'm very, very tired."

She started walking. Lolly stayed a moment longer, staring down at the fire. Then, reluctantly, it seemed, she stood and followed my mother over the lawn. A little smoke rose from the pit, and I watched the light from the priest's cigarette.

My mother was almost to my grandmother's porch. Then she turned and called me. She slapped her thigh the way people do calling their dogs in from outside. Lolly stood halfway across the dusky lawn and then she turned and walked to her car. It was almost dark. I stayed in my chair. In back of my grandmother's house the fields spread still and empty. A dirt road ran to the barn, then the highway, above the little houses with yellow lights on for suppertime, where a wagon and a wheelbarrow lay tipped. There wasn't much.

The land—it was the same, only small, the trees seemed lower, the houses simple compared to those we'd seen. Still, I understood things here. I knew how to be comfortable. We weren't doing so well in California.

My mother stood across the yard, her elbows pointing out, hands on her waist, like a harsh letter of some other alphabet. She was waiting for me. And I wouldn't move.

"You can stay here," Carol said, "I'll put sheets on his bed for you." Jimmy nodded and closed the glass doors. They hadn't even been in Benny's room yet. Years later, when I came back on a Greyhound bus, it was exactly the same, his size 14 boy's sweaters folded in the drawers, his model cars on shelves, airplanes hanging on strings from the ceiling.

My mother called me again. Everyone waited. Cars on the highway moved slowly, nothing else changed. The barn looked old, unused for years. My grandmother had seemed tiny in the hospital. I looked down at my legs, in dark pantyhose, good high-heeled shoes. The names and prices of these seemed like secrets

I would be embarrassed to tell. I couldn't stay here. There was nothing. I'd be like my mother, always wanting to go away.

I looked up. The priest was still chewing a weed. Carol bit her cuticle, her hand close to her mouth, Hal poked the coals of the fire. I did what they all knew I'd do. I followed my mother.

She yelled over the sound of pipes in the bathroom. "You know, I never realized how backwards they still are. They've got the faucet for hot and the faucet for cold and you can't really ever get it right."

I opened a drawer underneath the telephone on the kitchen counter. The half-sized pencils my grandmother used had ridged tips from the way she sharpened them, with a knife. I'd seen her many times, her broad back hunched in concentration over the wastebasket. Deep in the drawer, I found a folded communion veil, a box of oil pastels, a deck of cards with a scene of Canadian wilderness on their browned backs. There were other things: a tiny Bible with four-leaf clovers pressed inside, so their outlines stained the pages; numerous finished tick-tack-toe games; address labels; glue; a cookie cutter in the shape of a hammer. I flipped through one of the small notebooks. It was mostly grocery lists in faded pencil. *A stick of butter, chicken pie, bread, a vegetable.* Then I came across a list of the names of my grandmother's friends. Mabel, Jen, Ellie, April, Sarah, Jude. The women, now in their seventies, she called the girls. She'd sat down once with this little spiral-topped notebook and one of her soft-leaded, knife-sharpened pencils and made a list of her friends. It was something I'd done in Beverly Hills, where I didn't have many, where we weren't as impressive as we'd hoped. I couldn't stand to think my grandmother ever felt the way I did. From the drawer, I stole an old implement, something I didn't recognize that said Callodean's Tin in wood-burned letters on its side. It was just some old tool that fit the hand but had no use. I wanted it. I slipped it in my pocket.

My mother hollered from the tub. "And who do you think'd take care of you here? Your grandmother's in the hospital, she'll probably die, Carol and Jimmy are being nice, sure, but they'll get over it with their money and you just watch now that they'll have something, they're not going to give it to us. You'd think they'd help me after I've been alone all these years, but will they? No."

"You're selfish." I said it quietly, in the kitchen, but she heard me.

"Oh, I can see, it's you too now. All my life, all I've ever done is give to you and do for you and now you go against me with them, too. Well, I can see from now on, I'm going to give to ME."

I was tired. "I'm not going against you, so let's just be quiet."

"I'm not going to be quiet," she yelled. A second later, she stood dripping in front of me, her face crumpled. "You know I've given you everything I could," she said. She was looking at me, pitiful, I can't describe it.

"I know," I said. It was true.

We left the next morning, days earlier than our tickets said. We all seemed subdued when Carol drove past the Oneida land to the airport. I kept thinking that they'd paid for our plane; we were leaving so soon, they might feel like they paid for a convenient divorce. But then again, Carol seemed tired. She probably wanted to be by herself. She was getting like my grandmother. When something was wrong, they wanted to be closed up in their houses, alone.

Carol drove very carefully and slow. Her lips wove, she kept licking them, and her mouth constantly rearranged itself as if any position felt uncomfortable. We wanted her to just drop us off, so she could drive right home, but she wouldn't, she parked and waited until we boarded the plane.

Once we were in the air, we felt giddy. We both loved airplanes; they were like doctors; they made us feel rich and clean. We were dressed in our best clothes and new stockings charged at Shreve's. No one seeing us would know anything true.

In Chicago, we bought magazines. We drank Kahlua and creams. We felt like busy celebrities rushing home to our lives. And that's the way Carol must have seen us, too, as she lugged our big suitcase up the ramp, while we held our short dresses down, walking onto the plane. But when we landed at LAX, no one was waiting for us and we had to find our own car parked in the ridiculously complicated system of lots and after we got home, scraping the car so it shrieked against the concrete embankment of our driveway, my mother said she didn't want to call Josh Spritzer, that she'd wait for him to call her. And the phone didn't ring at all that night or the next night either.

Once that fall, my mother drove with the Witch to Palm Springs. They came back with bad sunburns and three hundred dollars' worth of dates. Dates and figs and other dried fruits. Daniel Swan and I sat on the porch steps of the San Ysidro house, watching them haul the bags in.

"Come on, kids, give us a hand," my mother called.

"We're absolutely broke." I turned to Daniel, my cheek on my knee.

He laughed. "We can beat you there. We're in debt."

Halfway between home and Palm Springs, a place called Hadley's sold discounted desert dates (and figs and other dried fruits). My mother decided they were a savings. She and the Witch said they'd freeze them all, then fix them in cellophane and fancy baskets at Christmas and give them as presents to the people they worked with.

"Listen, that's part of your job," my mother said, later, as we unpacked the plastic bags into our freezer. "And you don't know how much things cost around Christmas." The new apartment had a clean, large refrigerator. We'd moved not long after we came back from Wisconsin.

My mother got home late that winter, sometimes at nine or ten on school nights. We never had much food in the house, so we went out to dinner. Sometimes, when we felt too tired or broke, we'd skip supper and just go to bed.

I started breaking into the stash of frozen dates. I tore open the plastic bags and stood by the freezer when I was hungry, eating handfuls of them, frozen. My mother began to do it, too. We'd stand in our clean, empty kitchen, the freezer open, chewing hard. It was just something we did in that apartment. Every household has its habits. The dates were good but tough. We worried about chipping our teeth.

By November, all the bags were torn open. Sometimes my mother would shake her head. "A hundred ninety dollars on *snacks*," she'd say and sigh.

But we kept doing it anyway. She did it too. We were hungry a lot of the time.

Even though we both liked that apartment, everything went wrong in it. I invited three girls from school over for dinner and when I put the chicken in the oven, we discovered the gas was turned off. My mother had to go knocking at neighbors' doors until she found one who'd let us cook my chicken. She had to do it, I was too embarrassed.

And around Christmas, the day I had my first real date, my mother called, falling apart, somewhere on the highway.

My date was with an older guy named Ronnie. Daniel Swan and I—kids our age—couldn't drive yet. This guy had a blue Porsche and he skied, he had that white-eyed, raccoon tan. He'd run for school president and I'd worked on his campaign. His mother's greatest ambition was for all her sons to be admitted to Stanford. She'd hired a rock band to play at his campaign parties and she liked me because I'd drawn his campaign poster, a huge oil pastel on butcher paper. Probably as compensation, he'd asked me out.

It was a dark day, cool, even for winter. I rode my bike home right after school and washed my hair, taking an hour to blow-dry, curling it under. Then my mother called.

"It's me, your mother," she said.

"Where are you?"

"I'm on the highway, can't you hear the cars?"

I touched a wall. "Where are you calling from?"

"Boy, are you dumb sometimes. I just told you. I'm at a filling station out in the middle of nowhere. Listen to me. I'm not coming home." Her voice was odd and flat. I tasted metal in my mouth.

While we were quiet then, it came over the phone—the roar of trucks and cars.

"Now, listen. When they call you, I want you to say you don't know anything. And I'm going to tell you now about the insurance policy. The papers are wrapped in tinfoil at the bottom of the freezer. Underneath the dates. You'll get twenty-five thousand dollars for me. So take care of yourself, sweetie. You're going to have to from now on. 'Cause I won't be around. But I know you. You'll manage fine."

I couldn't talk at first. My lip was flickering.

"I'm going to have an accident." Her voice sounded make-believe and serious at the same time.

"Why, Mom?" That was all I could choke out. I looked around the room, the empty walls, the dark windows.

"You don't love me and so I—"

I whimpered. "Mo-om, I do, I love you."

"No, you really don't, Ann. I know. And I've tried, believe me, I've tried. I've done all I can do. And I can't help you anymore. You'll be better off without me. You're strong, you're stronger than you think. I know you. I tried to get us a Christmas tree, I got this huge, big beautiful tree. It was expensive, but I thought, Well, this once we'll really have something nice. At least I can do that for her. Don't you think I've felt bad that I couldn't have furniture for you and give you clothes and money like other parents give their kids? But I couldn't, Annie. I was all alone. I didn't have any man to help me. And I said to them at the lot, I said, Tie it on tight, because I've got a long way to drive. And they said, Yeah, yeah, sure they would. Sure. Well, they didn't. Here I'm driving on the freeway and it falls off. This big beautiful tree bounces on the road and it splintered into a million pieces. And that's where it is, all over the highway. A million smither-eens. I paid my last money for it. That tree was forty dollars. I couldn't even do that for you. I couldn't even get you a Christmas. I'm giving up. I'm driving up the coast and off the cliffs at Big Sur. It's supposed to be pretty there. Remember I always wanted to see them? I'm just going to have an accident."

"Mom, please, don't. Please come home. I need you." My voice wasn't the same either. I'd never heard it before. I sounded like her.

"You're just scared," she said. "You don't know what you'll do without me. That's why you think you love me now, but you really don't, you're just scared to be alone."

That stopped me for a second. It seemed true. Then I lost some grip and it started again. I sounded like a baby. "Mom, please, no, no, come home, I'll be good, whatever you want, just please—"

She hung up.

I opened the freezer and grabbed dates from the bags, the biggest, most expensive kind, medjools.

I paced the apartment, eating, watching the phone. I expected her to call again. Ticks of the minute hand followed me, pinpricks on my back. Then I sat on the floor and dialed the highway patrol. I waited a long time for them to answer. A man told me he couldn't say anything for twenty-four hours. "You call the hospitals, they'll tell you the same thing," he said. "But if she ends up there, in Emergency, they generally call you."

"I haven't heard anything."

"No, huh?"

"But she should be home by now. Usually." I obeyed what she said. I didn't tell him she'd called.

"Yes." He cleared his throat. "'Course a lot of them they can't identify right away. You say a white Continental? What does the driver look like?"

"Oh, well, she has . . ." My voice went dry. It was very hard, all of a sudden, for me to talk. "Blond hair. Freckles. Blue eyes. She's, I don't know, small. And pretty. She's real pretty." I felt like I was giving him what he needed to take her away from me.

There was an awful pause. "I heard about a Continental and something like that on 1 tonight, but I think it was a redhead. You're just going to have to sit tight and wait. Don't worry, if something's wrong, they'll call you."

I climbed upstairs and took off my new pantsuit. I pulled on a nightgown and crawled into bed, but I couldn't get warm. The alarm clock sat on the floor next to me. It was almost seven and

Ronnie was coming to pick me up for the movie at seven. I just waited in bed. I didn't know what would happen.

At seven, I went to the window in my mother's room and looked out over the front door. All the lights were off. I was wearing my nightgown and knee socks and my running shoes. I knelt by the window, listening for the Lincoln. Then I heard a door slam and I knew it was Ronnie's. I would have recognized the sound of ours.

I watched him walk up to the door. He was wearing boots that seemed to bind his legs and turn his feet out. He stood there on our doormat, and with both his hands, he rubbed down his hair; for a moment I felt elated; he liked me. But then the bell echoed through the wall and I ducked down under the window ledge. I didn't move, as if I could be caught.

There was a long silence, but I didn't hear footsteps. It was excruciating. He still stood there at the door. I thought in a panic if the door was locked; it was, I'd checked. He would just stand there and then he would leave. He would have to leave.

I felt like we were breathing together, on opposite sides of the wall. He didn't move, I didn't move. I didn't dare peek out anymore. The doorbell rang again, a long ring, making me shudder.

Then something horrible happened. I heard my mother's car screeching to a halt on the street. I knew it was ours. Suddenly, I felt absolutely furious at the way she drove; she never could learn to use a brake. She'd careen along, looking at everything but the road, and then, a second before a collision, she'd say, "Whoops," and smash on the brakes.

I heard the quick nervous clatter of her heels on the pavement and I crawled fast, galloping on the carpet, to my room to put my clothes back on. My hair was a mess, there wouldn't be time for makeup. I flipped the light on and opened my algebra book. I was zipping up my jeans when I heard the key turning in the door downstairs.

"Uh, Ann. Ann? Where are you, Honey?"

"I'm up here, Mom." I tried to make my voice sound cheerful. I brushed my hair furiously. Then I bent down to buckle my shoe. I went downstairs holding my open book in one hand, I must have looked about as casual as Hamlet. Then I stopped, halfway down, and said, "Oh, um hi, Ronnie."

He jammed his hands in his parka pockets and smiled up at me. He really is cute, I was thinking to myself, and just then I remembered that the entire apartment was empty. I'd thought of that before, this morning, which seemed like years ago now. I'd planned to meet him at the door, dressed and ready, smiling, sailing out with one line, like "We just moved in and our furniture's not delivered yet. Such a pain." But here we were, looking down at the expanse of beige carpet. No furniture, with the exception of Ted's big radio. And that was a danger, too. I could sense my mother veering towards it. I thought I'd die if she turned it on to her easy-listening station, I'd truly die. "Smoke Gets in Your Eyes" with orchestration, or "The Impossible Dream." This night was already way too weird for Ronnie. And his parents owned a rock 'n' roll record company.

He was looking around at the bare walls. "Did you hear me, Ann? I rang the doorbell."

"No," I said. "Just now?"

"Yeah. I rang it twice."

"I don't know, I was studying."

My mother smiled, radiant. "You must have just nodded off for a second. Well." She clapped her hands together. From a life of working with children, my mother believed in applause. "You kids won't believe the tree I've got." She winked at me. "It's more gorgeous than the first one even. But I think I'm going to need some help getting her in."

It felt good to be told what to do. We followed her outside. It was cold, a clear black night, with a few rare stars. I stood on one side of the car and Ronnie leaned on the other. We started untying the ropes. I was just following along. The air seemed tender. I felt so, I don't know, grateful. Like Ronnie and I were still just kids.

"Isn't she a beaut?" my mother said, and looked at me, smiling.

I shrugged and looked down. "It's tied to the fender, too."

My mother sighed. "Gee, I wish I had something in the house. Some hot chocolate or cider." She clapped again. "Say. We could all go out and get a little something. I'll take you kids out for some dessert."

"We're going to a movie, Mom."

"Oh, all right." She rubbed her hands together. "I just thought it would be a nice night for a little something hot. Brrr."

"Actually, I think we missed the movie," Ronnie said, lifting his sweater and looking at a watch. "It's starting now."

The three of us lifted the tree onto our shoulders. We stood it up next to the glass doors. The branches trembled and then fell into place. It was a huge, beautiful tree.

"So, what do you say? Should we go out and grab a bite to eat? I could go for a little something. It's up to you kids. Whatever you want."

Ronnie and I looked at each other.

"Okay with me," Ronnie said, his hands jammed in his pockets again.

I said, "Sure."

"Let me just change my clothes and we'll go." My mother ran up the stairs, clapping.

We both leaned against the car door, shuffling our feet on the curb. Ronnie's Porsche was down the block. It gleamed under the streetlamp.

"I'm sorry about tonight," I said.

His lip lifted in one place, as if pulled by a string. It was a kind look. "Is something the matter?"

"My dog died," I said. I didn't have one. "His name was Danny. He got run over."

"You should have told me," Ronnie said.

I bit my lip and my cheeks started shaking. I felt it starting. He stepped closer and rubbed my hair behind my ears.

Then my mother called. "I'm com-ing."

We climbed into our car, the three of us in the front seat.

"Should we have a little music?" my mother said, her hand on the knob.

"No!" I shouted, much too loud. I tried to laugh. "I mean, not now."

Ronnie looked out the window. His face seemed chiseled, set. I knew I'd blown it for being his girl friend. This whole night was too weird. It would be even worse, when he was home, away from us.

But right then, driving, the dark glass on three sides of us, I leaned my head back on the leather seat, it was one of those times I felt like driving all night. A clear sky, stars, the three of us could drive to Michigan or Canada maybe. Somewhere it would be cold.

12

A BACKHOUSE ON NORTH PALM DRIVE

■ □ ■

Not too long after Christmas, we ran out of money and moved. My mother quit her job during the fall teachers' strike and took work as a maid for an entertainment lawyer. We moved on a week Josh Spritzer was away, skiing in Colorado with his children, and we managed to keep the same phone number, so for a while Josh didn't know. We would be working for the Keller family, who lived on North Palm Drive, and we moved into their backhouse, behind the tennis courts.

My mother knew the Kellers because of me. Peter was a boy in my high school, a year younger, who asked me over a lot. Sometimes, his mother offered my mother mineral water when she picked me up, and that gave my mother a chance to talk about Josh. In a way, Nan Keller had been in on my mother's romance with Josh Spritzer from the beginning. The first time she dropped me off at Peter Keller's, we were all standing in the hallway and my mother had said, "Do you think I should have braces put on her? What do you think, Nan, aesthetically. You're the artist." I'd stood there like a horse while the two women pulled at my jaw and examined my teeth and gums. Nan Keller had decided we definitely should.

During the teachers' strike, I told Peter my mother was worried about her job, and that if she was laid off we'd have to move back to Wisconsin. In school the next day he said I could eat dinner at their house whenever I wanted. As if that would help our finances.

I suppose along the same idea, Peter called me up and invited me to his house for Thanksgiving. I said I didn't know, I'd have to ask my mother. When I walked into her bathroom, she was sitting on the rug, polishing her toenails, a magazine propped open against the tub. She clapped her hands when I told her. "He did? Great! Definitely we'll go. What do you mean, say no? We haven't got anything else to do." Josh Spritzer planned to take his children skiing, that time in Canada, Lake Louise.

"I don't know. He didn't mention you." That was hard to say.

But my mother didn't seem to mind. "Oh, well, she must expect me, too. She knows we wouldn't separate on a holiday."

I called back and asked Peter if he meant my mom, too. He said he didn't think so. I yelled upstairs. Now she was running water for a bath.

"Well, tell Peter you'd like to, very much, say, but that you don't think you can because you wouldn't want to be without your mom on Thanksgiving. So you'll have to go with her somewhere else she was invited. Say that."

"Did you hear?" I said.

Peter ran to ask. "Okay," he said, when he came back, breathless. "It's okay. Your mother can come, too."

It was always like that with the Kellers.

The afternoon of Thanksgiving, my mother and I arrived and stood in front of the huge door, checking each other over before we dropped the knocker. "You look really great," she mouthed to me. We both pulled up our pantyhose, still standing there on the porch, hoping none of the other guests would come and see us. Then my mother took a deep breath and knocked.

A maid in a short black dress led us to the drink room, a room entirely paneled in salmon suede. About a dozen people stood eating scampi out of little white ramikins. Only Peter walked over to us. He offered to take my coat.

"Should I give Peter your coat, Mom?" I whispered.

She pulled it over her shoulders. "No, Honey, I think I'll keep it."

Peter's grandmother lounged in the corner, talking about grilles on Rolls-Royces between the years of 1957 and 1970. She had a habit of marrying millionaires, who then died. She'd lost the last one recently, so she was wearing red. Peter told me she always wore red when she was in mourning. She wore black when she planned to leave a man. She believed Rolls-Royces hadn't been the same since 1970. She had three of them, each belonging to a dead husband. She herself drove a Bentley Silvercloud.

Peter also told me that she disapproved of Mr. Keller for being a lawyer, and for being a Russian instead of a Viennese Jew. Not that she herself admitted to being any kind of Jew. Whenever the Kellers fought, Peter's grandmother offered her daughter immediate and lavish refuge in her house, three blocks away on Elevado.

A famous movie star leaned on the salmon-colored wall as Nan Keller talked to him about mineral water.

Mrs. Keller had once been a painter. She sometimes spoke, romantically, of San Francisco, and the Art Students' League. It seemed she remembered painting on the sidewalks near Ghirardelli Square. But her mother, not Bert Keller, had come to fetch her home. Through the suede drink room's archway, we could see several of her recent paintings, standing in the living room. She painted with acrylics on clear huge stretched pieces of lucite, so the paintings served as room dividers as well. They seemed mostly abstract. She favored colors in the family of red. What was recognizable tended to be bloody.

"We bottle our own from a little island we found off of Panama," she was saying to the movie star. "Tell me what you think, Tony. It's not too bubbly. We like it clear." Tony Camden was the movie star's name.

"I'm in speech pathology," I heard my mother say next to me at the table. I noticed she was staring at the movie star, four people removed on the other side. Before I could stop her, she leaned forward, almost knocking over Mrs. Keller's centerpiece, made of bones, goat skulls, orchids and tall, burning beeswax candles.

"May I ask you a question?" she said to the movie star. "Your skin is so wonderful. Is there anything you do for it?"

But the movie star seemed pleased. He looked down at his young wife and she smiled back, lifting a piece of her hair behind an ear. "We have a little secret in our house," he said. "Every morning, Jan squeezes our own fresh orange juice. And we drink it with a tablespoon of cod liver oil and a tablespoon of wheat germ oil."

"Really," my mother marveled. She fumbled in her beaded purse, an heirloom. Then she had a piece of paper.

Mrs. Keller engaged the movie star's young wife in a discussion of tennis, how no one could ever be good unless they'd learned their form when they were seven years old and that's why she told Peter, every day, he should be out there with the machine, hitting balls, he'd be sorry later, he'd grow out of those political tracts he stayed inside reading and then he'd wish he'd learned tennis.

"Excuse me, would you mind saying that again," my mother asked. "I'd like to write it down. Now, it was *one* tablespoon of wheat germ oil, *one* of cod liver oil and that's *in* the orange juice? I see, mixed in the orange juice."

"As Winston Churchill said, anyone who isn't a Democrat before thirty hasn't got a heart. And anyone who's a Democrat after thirty doesn't have a brain."

Mr. Keller, a dark, lean man with a prominent Adam's apple, was roaming around his living room. He had a hard time sitting still at meals, so he tended to roam, with his pipe, through the house. Odd lamps pointed out at weird angles in the living room, highlighting some object or another as if it were a sort of store window.

"Oh, Isabelle," the movie star's young wife said. "She's not sure if she's a girl or not."

Mrs. Keller shrugged. "I don't know why, she looks great as a girl." Mrs. Keller kept a crystal bell next to her water glass, which she rang to call the maid. "Do you like pumpkin pie?" she asked, suddenly, after the maid had been told to bring out dessert and to corral Mr. Keller back to the table. It was the first question she'd asked my mother all evening.

"Oh, yes, I love it!" my mother cried, believing, as she had all her life, that in situations of some awkwardness, it was best to be enthusiastic.

"Do you," Mrs. Keller said, as the maid wheeled the dessert cart beside her. "Thank you, Marie. Because we honestly don't. All three of us just hate it. And we don't like mince either. Can't stand it. So, I found this recipe for a Portuguese ginger pudding that we serve with a hard sauce. Please tell Marie how much sauce you'd like." She turned up to the maid and spoke to her in Spanish.

My mother waited to start eating her pudding, watching her hostess's spoon, the way she'd been taught when she was a girl. Unfortunately, Mrs. Keller was fussing with the coffee service on the second dessert cart. My mother looked to her right and her left, where people sat eating, and she smiled with anticipation, fanning her dessert napkin out over her thighs and folding her own hands politely on her lap.

Outside, in the open air, walking down the street to our car, my mother grabbed my arm. "Did you *see* Tony Camden, how he kept looking at me? I'd turn the other way and then I'd peek back and he'd look again. This dress was really great. You know, it was expensive when I bought it, but boy, every time I get looks."

"Mom, he's married."

I kicked a wheel of our car, hands in my pockets, stamping. We were shouting because my mother walked eight feet away on a driveway so she wouldn't wet her heels on the grass.

"Boy, he sure is and did you catch how much younger? But I'll tell you, he was attracted to me, Ann. And does HE look great for his age. I'm going tomorrow and get us some wheat germ oil and cod liver oil and we're going to start. Now, what did he say, a tablespoon of wheat germ and a teaspoon of, or no, was it the other way around? Anyway, I have it written down."

She opened her side of the car. We both stood there a second. "Honey, look at the stars. It's a real clear desert night. Dry. Feel that air."

"Mom, open my door. Let me in."

"You're really not romantic, are you?" she said, looking at me, perplexed.

"Just cold."

She shuddered loudly, sliding in the car and turning on the heat. "Brrr. Me, too.

"I'll tell you, Honey, that Peter is in love. The way he looks at you."

"Do we have to drive by Josh Spritzer's tonight? You know he's gone," I said.

"Oh, let's. I feel like a little ride, actually."

The next time I saw Peter Keller in school, he told me, "They all liked you. They didn't like your mother, they thought she was strange, but Tony Camden said you were cute." Peter looked at me with a tilted face, as if he were offering something. I felt like pushing him so he fell hard on the concrete floor of the hallway.

But I didn't. I was scared of them, too. I smiled back and made polite conversation.

I probably picked the wrong time to ask. It was a weeknight and my mother seemed tired. We licked our ice cream cones, driving past Josh Spritzer's apartment. He'd been home from Canada four days and she still hadn't seen him.

"When are we going to call that boy's agent?" I was trying to sound casual. I remembered the boy's name perfectly well. Timmy Kennedy.

"Well, Honey, to tell you the truth, you've got to take off about ten pounds." She slapped her thigh. "Right here. I've been kind of waiting to see when you would, but you just gobble down the milkshakes." That night we'd eaten dinner at the Old World, which claimed to make milkshakes with entirely natural ingredients.

"You're the one who drags us out to get ice cream cones every night."

"Well, one little dip isn't going to hurt."

□

My mother drove to the Linville Nutrition Center, a wholesale
health food store decorated in old-fashioned pink. She bought an
electric juicer and huge bottles of cod liver oil and wheat germ
oil. The grocery bags said KEEP IN THE PINK.

"So, I just don't know about this man," my mother said, her legs
crossed, leaning out of her chair towards Mrs. Keller. They sat on
the terrace overlooking the yard. I'd been on the courts with Peter,
trying to learn to hit the ball. Now Peter rallied with his teacher,
starting his daily lesson. Mrs. Keller offered me a glass of lemonade from a cart as I sat down, eyeing the court while she
poured.

"Hi, Honey," my mother said to me. "He's just not stable, Nan.
You know, one minute he says one thing, the next minute, it's
something else. I can't plan. Sometimes, I even think of just calling up his psychiatrist and saying, 'Hey, what's going on with this
man?'" My mother laughed, an asking laugh.

Mrs. Keller responded with a smile that was less a show of
support than an act of charity.

Encouraged, my mother went on. "I'd like to tell his psychiatrist a thing or two."

My back stiffened and I pulled my knees up to my chest. I
knew my mother shouldn't have been telling Mrs. Keller those
things. Mrs. Keller stirred her drink and put the swizzle stick
down on a napkin.

"You know, Adele, he does have a reputation as something of a
ladies' man. I'd be careful of him." Her gaze drifted back to the
tennis court. "Good shot, Peter," she said softly.

My mother took Mrs. Keller's remark as an invitation for further disclosure. She thought about Josh Spritzer so often she
needed to talk. The less she saw him, the more she craved talking. Just saying his name seemed to calm her.

"Well, I heard that too, before I started going out with him.
But he wants to change, he told me that at the very beginning. I
have to say this for Josh Spritzer, that he WAS honest, he told me
he had a fear of commitment. So I suppose, for a while it was fine.

But now, I think he's getting scared. He got himself in deeper than he planned."

"Hmm," Mrs. Keller said. "Well, are you seeing anyone else?"

My mother fell back in her chair, her hands loose on the armrests. She could have talked for ten straight hours about Josh Spritzer, speculating, analyzing the intricacies of his character and planning strategy. She would have loved to.

I wondered if she ever thought of Lolly and our old porch, looking over the fields, with the constant running sound of the highway. Maybe that was the real happiness in her life, sitting with a friend, easily plotting, yearning, planning out romances—more than the romances themselves. My mother's two passions were for difficult men and expensive clothing, neither obtained by the usual methods, but with a combination of luck, intuition and calculated risk. She could also talk for hours about how she acquired an Alan Austin green leather coat from a cleaner's in Covina for almost nothing, how an old woman gave her a Chanel suit, twenty years ago.

"Oh, sure," she said, recovering. "A few. There are a few other people." She didn't feel quite happy with that, though. She wanted to turn the conversation back to Josh. She wanted to turn every conversation back to Josh. "But you know, Nan," she whispered, leaning forward, "I really don't care for any of them."

"Well, you never know what'll happen," Mrs. Keller replied. With that, she stood up, carrying her drink, and walked over to the terrace ledge. "Look at those lime trees. We pay a three-quarters-time gardener and I don't know what he does all day. Plants weeds. The help situation is impossible. And when you think, really, of what they get. The pay's not bad and our backhouse is quite a nice place to live, when you consider what's on the market."

"Oh, it's fabulous!" my mother burst out.

We all stood, looking over the yard, Peter and his tennis teacher swinging languorously, the still pool behind them under the trees. No one said anything for a while.

"Well, I suppose we should skedaddle, Ann." My mother slapped her hand lightly on her side.

She left it so Mrs. Keller could insist we both stay for dinner, but Mrs. Keller didn't. She just turned around, mildly smiling. "Good-bye."

When we got desperate for money, my mother decided I was thin enough to see Timmy Kennedy's agent. "Who knows, maybe you'll land a series and then we can buy some decent furniture. Who knows?"

I wore tight ironed jeans and a pale green midriff shirt that left two inches of my belly bare. My hair hadn't been cut for a long time, and the ends of it curled under, so it touched my back on the bare spot. It felt creepy, like fingers there.

We started early because we didn't know exactly how long it would take to get there. Ellen Arcade's office was in Riverside. All the way, my mother just drove and we didn't say anything. I hadn't eaten much since my mother made the appointment. And for the past week, I'd sat out in the sun every afternoon, my towel on the overgrown grass of Roxbury Park.

We stopped at two gas stations in Riverside to get directions. And when we parked on the lot in front of the building, we were still a half hour early. It was a huge gray complex and around it were wasted fields and overpasses. I scooched up on the seat to look into the car mirror. All during the ride, I'd kept my eyes closed and my face aimed at the front windshield so my cheeks would get some color. We both sat in the car awhile, back against our seats. We didn't want to walk in too early.

My mother put some makeup on me. She brushed mascara on my lashes, patted on blush. It was a relief to close my eyes and give my face to her. Then I marked on freckles over my nose, with a sharpened eyeliner pencil. With the car door half open, my mother unzipped her pants and tucked in her blouse again. I bent over from the waist and underbrushed my hair, the way girls in my class were doing it that year.

The agent's office was on the third floor and her waiting room was tiny and full. Black and white glossies of children, signed in loopy, slanted penmanships, crowded the walls. Most of the girls' names ended in *i*'s and several were dotted with hearts. Some of the photographed faces smiled, some pouted, a few even cried. In one, a starburst glittered inside a tear. Around us, children squirmed in their chairs. A Mexican baby screamed in his grandfather's arms. One woman, the obvious mother of four blond, freckled children, patiently knitted.

The receptionist gave my mother a clipboard with a form questionnaire. We filled out my name, age, height and weight. I lied about my weight. My mother said I was a year younger than I was. They also wanted to know what languages I spoke, my grades in school and my measurements. When we turned the form back, we were called in, and the others waited, as if they were used to waiting. Ellen Arcade, a woman in her fifties with blond hair, sat behind a large desk in the inner office, stamping a cigarette out in a glass ashtray. She read over my questionnaire on the clipboard, smiling and nodding along. My mother slid me a complicitous look.

"So, how do you like Beverly High?"

"I like it," I said.

"Well, everything here looks good." She shoved the clipboard in a drawer. "Would you read something for me, Ann?"

After, the agent leaned back in her chair. My mother pressed forward, cheeks lifted, listening.

"She'll need pictures," the agent said. My mother nodded, staring at her. While we sat there, Ellen Arcade called a photographer and made an appointment for me. That seemed lucky, because it cost money. If we'd had to do it ourselves, we wouldn't have. My mother would have changed her mind. With arrangements set, Ellen Arcade looked ready for us to leave. Her arm listed towards us, but my mother wanted to talk. She gripped her chair.

"We're out of Bay City, Wisconsin, and once there was a telethon there and that's where we met Timmy Kennedy. Bay City actually has the biggest CP telethon in the country . . ."

"Isn't that something," the agent said. "He was quite a kid, Timmy."

"Is he still acting?" my mother asked.

"No, he's on the football team at Santa Monica High. Had enough of it." She lit another cigarette, then stood up and held each of our hands in a firm, quick yank. I wanted to say, Wait, does this mean you're taking me?

But all she said was, "We'll be in touch."

We did have the pictures done, and Ellen Arcade selected two for portfolio blowups, which I got to sign. Then nothing happened and the photographer charged my mother a hundred dollars. Which contributed to our financial ruin.

The backhouse was next to the pool behind the tennis courts. It had two big rooms and, up three steps, tiny bedrooms off a hallway and a bathroom with a portable shower. It had been built, originally, to be Nan Keller's studio. But since she rented a loft in Venice, they had made the studio into a game room. A felt-covered pool table stood prominently when you walked in and there was a working pinball machine in the corner. They left what furniture there was for us: Nan's old drafting table, the chairs and a couch. There was no kitchen, but there was a bar with an elaborate soda fountain. We had a half-size refrigerator and we always meant to buy a hot plate.

We moved on a week Josh Spritzer was skiing, so we had only the Swans to help us. At first my mother and I cleaned the big house together. We spent long afternoons fighting upstairs over who got to vacuum and who got to dust. Both of us felt embarrassed and we tried to understand each other's weak points. I never wanted Peter Keller to see me. So my mother did his room and bathroom while he was in school. Then, after a few weeks, I stopped helping. I left it for my mother to do during the day. I went to high school and tried to forget about it.

My mother didn't last long as a maid. It turned out she didn't know how to iron. She spent an hour doing each of Mr. Keller's shirts. He wore two a day, all in shades of white and the palest blue.

"How do you iron your clothes? You must stay up all night," Mrs. Keller asked.

"Well, actually, since we moved and I was working, I dry-clean," my mother said.

Another time, Mrs. Keller found my mother standing in her dressing room, with no possible purpose, her arms crossed over her chest, surveying the rows of dresses and shoes.

"What are you doing here?" Mrs. Keller asked.

"I just made the bed," my mother said. And she had done that—beautifully, with a corner folded down and a water glass of hydrangeas on the end table. The trouble was my mother and Mrs. Keller liked to do the same things, the little touches, graceful additions. Mrs. Keller needed someone good with a mop. It's amazing we lasted as long as we did. Finally, Mrs. Keller found my mother crying in the kitchen with the cook, both of them on their knees looking for the piece of my mother's fingernail that had broken off.

"If I bring it in, he can fix it, he has a sheer, sheer fabric he glues it on with."

The two-hundred-and-fifty-pound cook crawled on the floor, searching, her arm around my mother, to comfort. The roast sat bloody in the sink, uncooked, and the next day Mr. Keller walked over the tennis court to the backhouse and spoke to my mother about the possibilities.

My mother broke down and cried and talked about her master's degree, moving her ring around the finger with the now-patched nail. They discussed other possibilities for speech therapists: private practice, convalescent hospitals. They decided we could stay in the backhouse, but that my mother would get a job and we would pay rent.

For three weeks she worked as a hostess in the downtown split-level Hamburger Hamlet, wearing long skirts and walking through every night in a terror, afraid that someone who knew Josh Spritzer would come in. Finally, Mr. Keller arranged for an interview at the convalescent hospital where each of Peter's step-grandfathers had lived, briefly, before he died. My mother got the job.

□

I found a job, too, as a wrapper in a clothing store. I went in every day after school and all day weekends. During the holiday rush, my mother asked the manager and they hired her on, too, for Saturdays. We measured our Saturdays, not from our salaries, but from what we took. The way we did it was easy. I would wrap huge packages and send them down with another customer's bags to the pick-up ramp. My mother would write up a receipt for one small thing. We picked the packages up downstairs when we punched out. It didn't feel like stealing, exactly. We owned clothes now, thousands of dollars' worth. Clothes seemed easy, not a big deal. Once I opened a drawer and found a little cellophane bag of rings, untagged. I took the whole bag. None of it seemed dangerous really, it was just a small thrill, something that made you suck in your breath a moment so your rib bones rose. And when we drove home as it was turning dark and the streetlights flickered on, you could touch the clothes on the car seat next to you and feel like you'd gotten something out of the day, something you could use later.

But even though we both had jobs, we were never good with money. The first time we couldn't pay the rent, my mother called Mr. Keller on the telephone and cried and sent me up to the front house carrying mixed flowers and a check they couldn't cash until two weeks from Wednesday. Mr. Keller was a kind man. He looked at me, put his hand on my arm, his Adam's apple bobbing up over his collar, and said, "Okay, Ann, tell your mother thanks. And don't you worry, huh?"

As I turned to go, Mrs. Keller called, "Bert, ask Ann if she's had anything to eat."

I was standing at the back door of the kitchen, the door that led to the fenced tennis court, which separated the big house from ours. A cake, with a third cut out, showing its layers, was standing on a cake plate. The smell of roast beef lingered on its tin foil, left, wrinkled on the counter.

I hadn't had anything to eat yet. My mother was so upset about the rent, we hadn't gone to get dinner, but I just said, "No thanks, I'm not hungry."

Not that I was any saint. I scuffed my feet along the tennis court and when I walked in, I plopped down onto the sofa, my hand on my belly.

"What did he say?" my mother asked.

"I'm starving," I said. "My tummy hurts."

"Ann, just tell me what Mr. Keller said. Then we'll get something to eat."

"He said okay."

My mother began to beat her chest with an open hand, like a pigeon preparing to take off. "Oh, thank God. Thank you, God," she said, her head tilted up to the low ceiling.

I groaned. It made me sick when she got grateful. Everybody else had a place to live and you didn't see them thanking God for it.

"Okay, okay. Let's go. You're just not sentimental, are you? Well, I am. I'm thankful when people are nice like that. Get your jacket."

We had the half-sized refrigerator but we never kept much food in it. Every night we went out for dinner.

"Brrr, come on, hop in," my mother said. We parked our car in the alley, behind the backhouse. She stood staring up at the sky. I walked around to my door with my fists jammed in my parka pockets. My mother kept quiet because she was making her wish. Forty-four years old and every night of her life she made a wish on a star.

"It's clear tonight, Ann, look at those constellations." My mother clapped her hands. "It's going to be a great day tomorrow."

A Great Big Beautiful Tomorrow. Many of my mother's enthusiasms could be traced. We turned up the heat full blast in the car and I looked out the window, dreaming to myself. I was always dreaming to myself in those days. I wanted so many things. We drove, slowing the car in front of Josh Spritzer's old house in Beverly Hills and then, not finding his Thunderbird in the driveway, my mother headed towards his apartment in Century City.

"What are you thinking, Bear Cub?"

"Nothing."

"Come on, you can tell me."

"Nothing," I said.

"You know, you could say something once in a while, have a conversation."

It was hard to find restaurants that time of night. Usually, we didn't have cash and not too many places took checks. But we'd go into one of those restaurants with the little metal "No checks, please" plaques over the cash register and sit down and eat a whole meal. At the Old World on Sunset, there was a bulletin board in the back of the restaurant, with all the bounced checks pinned up on it. Two of ours were there. You passed it on the way to the bathroom. When my friends from school wanted to eat at the Old World, I didn't have the nerve to say no, but I sat scared, extremely conscious, the minutes any of them left the table to go to the bathroom.

When the bill came, at the end of a meal, my mother would start writing a check. The waitress would usually look flustered and say, "Oh, but we don't take checks."

"You don't! Why not?"

"We just don't. Restaurant policy. There's a sign there, right where you come in."

"Well, this check is good, I can assure you."

"I'll have to ask the manager."

"Please do get the manager."

My mother would fold her arms and smile at me over the table. I'd shove my chair back and put on my jacket. "I'm going outside."

"Okay, Hon," she'd say. "I'll just be a minute."

Then I'd wait for her, leaning against our car. I let her do it alone.

We didn't say anything about it, but we knew we had to avoid the places we'd ever bounced a check. My mother had two dollars in change and she just shrugged.

"Let's go and see if that little French place is open." There was a place on Pico we liked, a small restaurant, that served food like

my grandmother's; sweetbreads and pork roasts. "You get your
little soup and your salad and a little dessert. I could just go for
that tonight," my mother said. But the windows looked dark when
we passed. She sighed. "Should we drive over and get ice
cream?"

Some nights we skipped dinner and just ate sundaes. We were
usually on diets, so it seemed all right. My mother parked under
the trees in front of Baskin-Robbins and felt around the bottom of
her purse for stray dollars.

"Here, you run in," she said, pressing three damp dollars into
my hand. She would wait in the car with the motor running. I
knew which flavors she wanted and extra nuts and whipped
cream.

Tonight, though, I minded. "You go in and get them. Why
should I always go in?"

"I can't, Ann." There was real panic in her voice. "Someone
could see me like this." She was wearing a terry-cloth jogging suit
and tennis shoes. Her hair was pulled up in a ponytail.

"Someone could see *me*." I had on sweat pants and a T-shirt
and sneakers. My hair was wet because I washed it every night.

"At your age it doesn't matter," she said. "Anyway, you look
cute. At my age, they expect a woman to dress up a little. Remember, I'm the one who has to catch a father for you."

"I already have a father."

"Yeah, well, where is he?"

She had me there. "Hell if I know."

"Come on, Ann. Please. Just this once. Run in and get it
quick."

"No."

We sat there under the trees. "Please, Honey."

I shook my head. My mother started the car with a jolt and we
drove home. For a while, she didn't speak to me, but when I came
down to the living room later, for a glass of water, she was standing by the open refrigerator, eating crackers and sardines, wearing the sweat shirt she slept in.

"Want some sardines?"

I shook my head and went back to my room.

"Ann, come and try some. Come on a second. It's good."

I heard her lift out the milk carton and drink from it. I hated it when she drank from the carton. I couldn't stand the idea of her saliva in my milk.

"I don't want any," I yelled. "And I'm trying to sleep."

"Okay," she called back. The crackers made crunching noises. "But it's very good. Very, very good."

I was hungry. My stomach seemed to acquire consciousness. It wanted things. Steaks with melted butter. Fresh rhubarb pie. Being hungry made me cold and slightly dizzy. I remember that feeling of going to bed hungry and waking up light as if it happened more often than it really did. Most of the nights we didn't eat, we could have. We were on diets. We were always on diets and neither of us ever got skinny. But years later, it's hunger we remember.

That night I woke up to find my mother sitting next to me on my bed, looking down at my face. "I was just thinking to myself how lucky I am to have a daughter like you."

None of the rooms in the backhouse had locks. After she left, I got up and shoved my dresser against the door.

My mother's room was right next to mine and the construction of the backhouse seemed flimsy. Even with the door shut, I could still hear her breathe on the other side of the wall. I imagined her curled up, pushing into the plaster, trying to make a cave and bore through.

She knocked on the wall. "Good night, Sweetie."

I slept on the outermost edge of my bed.

Josh Spritzer seemed to be dropping my mother. Her dates with him were down to once every other week. Even now that she had better clothes. And he seemed to be taking more out-of-town vacations.

"I think I *will* call his psychiatrist," my mother said one morning, while I ironed my jeans before school.

There was another man who asked her out. His name was Jack Irwin and his head was flat and bald as a nickel. He lived with his mother, who was almost a hundred and who had lost control.

When we went to visit in their apartment once, she wobbled in her chair, her face jiggled, her eyes loose, wandering, her hands opening and closing, roaming the air for substance, finding nothing, and, at the end, her mouth opened to about the size of a penny and she left it there and said, "Eh," not like a question but like a word.

My mother had met Jack Irwin in the convalescent home. His mother had broken a hip. Since those days in Palm Manor, Jack Irwin talked about Solvang all the time. "Lovely little village. Rollicking, rolling green hills. And the Swedes. Everything maintained by the Swedes." Apparently, he'd been there with his mother in 1961.

"He wants to take me there," my mother said, one night. She'd come home from a date with him and she sat on her bed, curling off her pantyhose. "For a weekend. I can't even kiss him. Could you come here a second, Ann, and undo my bra?"

"I'm in bed."

Then there was the slam of a drawer. "'Course I suppose he could do a lot for us, with all his money." She sighed and I could hear her sit down again on the mattress. "He always asks about you, Ann, he thinks it's great you're doing so well in your school. He wants to talk to you about your college."

I heard her settle into bed. "Well, at least it was a good dinner," she said through the wall. "And he'll take us out to breakfast on Sunday."

The weekend they went to Solvang, my mother seemed very grown up. She snapped the buckles of her suitcase shut when she heard his car in the alley. She seemed older. She wore a suit, with her hair pinned up neatly in a bun.

"Here," she said, pressing a twenty-dollar bill in my hand and closing my fingers around it. "That's for food. Call Leslie and go out." When she opened the sliding glass door and Jack was there, we both felt disappointed. He stood, hands at his sides, wearing a plaid jacket and a white turtleneck sweater. Every time, we couldn't imagine beforehand how ugly he really was.

"All set," he said, clicking his heels together.

"I'll try to get you a present," she whispered. When she hugged me good-bye, for some reason I didn't know, I started crying. I wetted my mother's collar.

"Sshhh," she said, kissing me next to the eye. "I'll be back on Sunday."

They both looked slow and proper getting into the car. He lifted the trunk and put in the suitcase and opened her door first. She sat in the passenger seat and folded her hands. I threw myself on the couch and pulled up the mohair blanket. And it was me who usually never cried.

The next morning, Saturday, Peter Keller called me on the telephone from the front house. "I want to kiss your lips," he said.

Peter Keller was a year younger and we rode to school in the same carpool. He wasn't the kissing type.

"What for?"

"I don't know."

"Well, not if you can't think of a better reason than that," I said and hung up.

An hour later, he called back.

"I thought of another reason. I'm wild about your warm lips and I want to squeeze you tight." I heard pages moving, but it didn't sound like a joke.

"Yeah?" I was eating a carton of ice cream from the freezer. My mother had stocked up before she left.

"I want to part your lips with my tongue."

"Yeah?" I dragged the phone to the couch and lay down. "And then what?"

"Can I come over now?"

"Sure," I said. I didn't even think of changing my T-shirt, which was spattered with chocolate ice cream. When I came home from school every day, I took my good jeans off and hung them up in the closet. Peter was one of the kids I played with in my old clothes. If another friend of mine called on the telephone, I'd get rid of him fast. I didn't feel bad about it. He was a grade lower.

When he came to our sliding glass doors, he looked the same as always, his hair capping his face. But he squinted and his hands were opening and closing at his sides.

"So?" I said.

"Maybe we should go out some night?"

"Go out some night? What about what you were saying on the phone? Where did you learn that?"

"From a book," he admitted.

"No," I said. "We're not going to go out some night. Come in. Lie down over there and undress."

I hadn't planned anything, I was making it up as I went along. I felt taller and powerful, like a teacher, reaching up to the top of a clean blackboard.

"All right," he said. He untied a sneaker and held it in his hand. "Don't you want to talk first? It's not even dark out," he said, looking at the doors.

I shook my head. It was a spring day. The wind moved in the tops of the palm trees outside. No one was around. Peter undressed, holding his shirt and pants balled up in his hands, as if he were afraid I was going to take them. His arms hung pitifully at his sides.

"Aren't you going to take yours off, too?"

His underwear looked white and new as a child's. One of the things that amazed us when we'd cleaned the big house was the Kellers' surplus. They all kept drawers of new underwear, some in the packages, unopened. In the bathroom closets, there were rows of soaps and shampoo, more than one of everything.

"You first," I said.

He sat down on the old blue and red striped couch and pulled off his underwear. Guys are so shy, I was thinking.

"Okay," he said, looking up at me. He took in a breath and held it. He seemed scared, as if I would hurt him. He was very thin and almost hairless. He seemed frightened, like a woman.

I kicked my tennis shoes off with my heels.

"Lie down," I said.

I sat next to him on the couch. "Okay, you can kiss me, but

not my face." He fumbled, trying to take my shirt off, so I stood up and pulled it over my head. I unzipped my jeans and dropped them on the floor. Then I sat on top of him.

He closed his eyes but I didn't. I looked around, out the sliding glass doors, while the veins in his neck rose up like a map. The pinball machine sparkled, metal and glass.

"Have you ever done this before?" he asked.

I hadn't. I hadn't even thought of it. Not even with Daniel Swan, whom I loved. We tickled the backs of each other's arms and I thought of wearing a soft white sweater and Daniel kissing me once on each eye. But I wasn't going to tell Peter Keller.

With Peter, it was different. Touching him was like touching myself. I never thought about him. It was broad daylight.

He sat up, facing me, and took my hand. He looked at me as if this were something big in both of our lives. "Lie back down," I said, pushing his shoulders. It was amazing the way he sunk back. You don't think you can do that to another person.

The air didn't move. I made a ring of my first finger and thumb and took him in my hand. It felt soft, the softest skin I ever touched. I watched. His hands fluttered by his sides. In the slits of his eyes, all I could see was white. He had no anger in him.

I don't know how I knew what to do but I did.

I put him inside me. His eyebrows pushed together as if he was working hard. A sound escaped from him. His face looked pure as something new. I felt it, he felt it. Then he started to move, lifting his hands to my waist.

"Lie still," I said. "I'll do it." Peter's dog rattled the metal garbage cans against the wall outside. I looked down; my own leg, the way it tilted, seemed different, separate from my body.

So this is what it is, I thought, not much. I pulled up to my knees for a second. There was a spit of blood on my leg. At the sight of it, I stopped.

"What's wrong?" Peter asked. "Did it hurt?" His fingers fluttered near my face.

"No," I said, crushing his ten fingers in my two hands and starting again. "No."

His face seemed limp on his neck. It would be so easy to kill another person, I was thinking. You'd just reach down. People just walk up and give themselves away to you.

All of a sudden I started moving and I was going faster and faster and I closed my eyes and then, I wasn't doing it anymore, he was holding my waist and I was afraid, so I tried to be still. I hung on to his shoulders like the edge of something and clung to one word, trying to keep it, quiet. Then, just as sudden, it was still again. And slow. I opened my eyes. My feet flickered the way fishtails sometimes beat a few last moments after they're dead. It was like falling. My arches and my knees ached and I felt light and tired, but I didn't want Peter to know anything.

Then I got up and ran outside to the pool. "Hey," he yelled and started to laugh. "Hey." And then he was next to me in the pool, his arms around me underwater.

"I love you, Ann," he said.

He looked at me, waiting. Flat brown leaves floated on the surface of the pool, beginning to disintegrate. The water below felt thick and filmy. I lifted an arm up to the air and it was shiny, as if in a sheer rubber glove.

"I'm taking a shower," I said. All of a sudden, I climbed out and ran into the backhouse. I latched the flimsy lock on the sliding glass doors. A minute later, when he knocked, I wouldn't answer. I thought of him watching me as I ran, naked, my breasts and thighs jiggling, him seeing that and it making him smile.

But he was naked, too. He must have run through his own yard and somehow snuck back into the big house.

My mother came home that same night. A door slammed, she ran in and flipped the light on in my room. She unlatched her suitcase and started unpacking right there, on my floor.

"I just couldn't do it." She stared at her open suitcase, shaking her head. "I couldn't touch him. I let him kiss me and he swished his tongue around in my mouth and I just couldn't. I practically gagged." She walked to my bed and looked down at me. "I'm sorry, Honey. Even for you, I couldn't do it. We slept in the same bed last night and he'd reach over and touch my side and I'd just cringe. I can't stand that man."

She walked to the bathroom and brushed her teeth. Then, she lifted a purple sundress from her suitcase with two fingers. "Well, here. I brought you a present. I went through a lot to get you this so you better like it. Here. Try it on."

I was thinking of the weak, pale folds of skin, like rippled batter, under Jack Irwin's belly. I thought of his mouth, rolling *r*'s against her ear.

"I don't like it," I said. "I don't want it." I really didn't. It had a low back and frills. I looked at the dress and hated it.

My mother examined the hem herself. After all she'd said, she seemed surprised and hurt that I didn't like the dress. "I picked it out. I think it's adorable. Try it on. You'll see how cute it hangs."

I grabbed it and went in the bathroom to change. When I came out, she touched my bare back, inside the long U of the dress.

"Oh, it's adorable. Go look at yourself. It couldn't be cuter, Honey." She sighed. "Well, at least we've got that. And it is cute, Ann, it really is."

My mother seemed to relax then, as if the dress had been worth it, after all.

That night I couldn't fall asleep again. I got up, it must have been two or three in the morning, took the dress from my closet, balled it in my hands and crammed it down the garbage can in our back alley. It was scary and peaceful out there, dark, with a low wind, moving the palms, making them spill small hard dates on the pavement. The next morning I felt settled and pleased when I heard the clatter of garbage trucks in my sleep. But it was Sunday. The only sounds I could have heard were church bells.

I'd invited Leslie over because I thought my mother would still be gone. Finally she left to drive to the convalescent home. Leslie had never seen our house. She came to the front; I sat, waiting on the curb, and led her through the gate, past the courts, to the backhouse. I'd thought all morning of how I could make it seem the big house was ours.

I did that whenever people dropped me off. They just dropped me outside the big house and I dallied by the fountain and then walked around the block. Mrs. Keller asked that I not use the front gate. We were supposed to walk in from the alley.

Inside the backhouse, I'd shut all the doors, so you could only see the big room. We sat on the old red and blue striped couch, sipping Cokes. I looked at the white closed doors. It seemed to me there could have been long hallways, terraces, dens and bedrooms following off behind them in every direction. I hoped that was what Leslie imagined.

She stared at the pinball machine. "Does it work?" she said. I nodded.

"Is it just you and your mom, here?"

"I have two brothers," I said. I gestured with my arm up at the closed doors, indicating their rooms, their wings. "But they're at camp." It was April, but I didn't remember that until later.

"Oh," Leslie said.

We played pinball three or four times. I was anxious for Leslie to go, because I hadn't told her my mother had come home. I didn't know how to explain it, and I was afraid she'd walk in and open the doors. Especially now that I'd said that about brothers. Finally, Leslie said, "Since your mom's not home, you want to eat dinner at my house tonight?"

I shrugged. "Sure." I liked Leslie's house. It was pink brick with ivy. Any time of the day, when you walked in, there was a hum of quiet activity somewhere behind doors. Once in the afternoon, while she was changing to tennis clothes, I'd stood and stared at the dining room table, the six chairs.

They were brown wooden chairs. There was something permanent, meant, about their placement, the way the trees had seemed to me, back home. Every day, these chairs waited, absorbing light all afternoon, while in the kitchen, soft clicks and knocks of bowls and the whirring of beaters progressed, the evening meal in preparation. I stared at the back of one chair. It seemed the security of a whole childhood. It stayed there, all day, the wood worn and glossed like a held chestnut.

When Leslie had come down, swinging her racket in the still air, I'd been startled. "I like your chairs," I said.

She shrugged. "These?" She squinted, as if looking at her dining room table and chairs for the first time. A bowl of peaches sat in the center of the table. "You always love everything so much," she said.

That afternoon, I didn't leave my mother a note or anything. We ran up the alley and through the back gate to Leslie's house, over her lawn, into the kitchen door, where she shouted, "Rosario, I'm ho-ome and Ann is staying for dinner."

Later, I remembered: we'd walked around our pool to the alley gate. Leslie had seen our house from the outside, she must have known how small it was.

It got worse with Peter and me. We did it all the time, always sneaking off. I got meaner and meaner. He did everything I told him. Sometimes he just rubbed me. I would turn over on my stomach and he'd rub my legs.

My mother and I were invited to more dinner parties at the Kellers' and for Easter and Christmas and Thanksgiving. My mother started calling Mr. Keller Bert. After that, she always left the rent check on their hall table by the first of every month.

In the big kitchen, afternoons with Peter, I felt free to eat. I ate and ate and ate. Everything I wanted.

And Peter got money from his father to take me to restaurants. Peter's father liked me, Nan Keller didn't. But we rode in taxis to expensive restaurants where I could order anything I wanted. I picked the most expensive thing and two desserts. Peter didn't like desserts, so it looked as if we were each having one. I ate the cake in front of me first and then we switched plates. I worried more about what the waiter would see than what Peter would think of me.

After I was laid off from my wrapping job, I got Peter to buy me clothes. He had a charge account at the store where everyone from our high school bought their jeans. At first, he seemed reluctant. But I showed him the slip. "It just says the price. It doesn't say boys' or girls'. It doesn't even give the size."

We went in every few weeks. I wore a larger and larger size. At the cash register once, Peter patted the swell at the top of my thigh. "We should start playing tennis," he said. I felt furious. He'd touched me like I was something he owned.

"You sound like your mother," I said.

That day as we were leaving the store carrying bags of clothes, we passed a girl from our school named May. She was tall and thin, with long blond hair, wearing a pale blue shirt with clouds on it, and matching blue jeans. Seeing her, I felt a wave of humiliation. I was embarrassed to look the way I looked.

I turned to Peter, urgent. "Let's go to the Konditorei for tea." Tea at the Konditorei meant a silver tray of intricate tidy pastries. Mint green cakes, strawberry kiwi tarts inlaid like mosaic floors. It was four in the afternoon.

"Are you sure you want to?"

"Yeah, why?"

He was watching May's hair sway as she walked up the sidewalk. He looked back down at me. "That's okay. I like you the way you are. I like your ass," he said.

That year, Peter's parents sent him back east to a prep school, with strict instructions for the tennis coach. His mother wanted to get him away from me. But when he came home for vacations, we'd start again. Any time of the day in the small maid's room off the big kitchen, the ironing board in the corner, a faded flowered bedspread that held dust which rose like chalk in the sun.

I was less and less nice. I gritted my teeth. I thought of him as anyone, any boy. But the colder I was, he didn't seem to notice. Holding my waist, when he looked up at me from the bottom of the bed, his eyes half closed in devotion.

During the time he was away at school, I started to have normal dates. Leslie and I traded clothes, I had more than she did, from my job at the store. Some nights, Daniel Swan called me late from the phone in his room and we talked and didn't hang up. We put the receivers by our pillows and fell asleep, to the other's breathing. My mother came to my room in the middle of the night and put the earpiece back in its cradle. She thought it was adorable, but she didn't want to tie up our line all night.

All the while, I had tried to diet. But it wasn't until Peter went away to Exeter that I finally lost the weight. And then it came off effortlessly.

It was a June day, the summer I was leaving. I was lying on my back on the single bed in the maid's room with the window cranked open, so we heard the distant slow thonk-pong of tennis balls as my mother took her lesson, and the occasional rousing bark of Groucho, Peter's dog. My mother took her lessons in the middle of the day, when no one else wanted to use the courts. This doesn't count, I was promising, no one will ever know, I won't tell anyone. I was leaving for college. The east. Rain and yellow slickers in cafeterias. Books. Clean things. I won't ever tell anyone, I was thinking, I'll make him swear not to tell, it'll be as if it never happened, this is only sort-of happening . . .

"Ouch," I said, jerking away.

"What's wrong?"

"Your fingernail, it hurt."

Peter stood up and unlocked the door. He walked into the maid's bathroom. I heard the soft clicking sound of him clipping his nails. When he came back I was standing up and dressed, shorts and a T-shirt over my swim suit.

"I don't want to do that anymore," I said.

"Okay." He sat down on the bed, where we were, spread out his hand on my impression.

"Ever." I walked into the bathroom and closed the door. I felt like I'd lost the day already, though it was still early, just noon. I washed my face and ran the maid's plastic brush through my hair. There was a window over the sink and I looked outside. My mother lunged for the ball, all in whites, all heart. Everything else seemed still, hazy in the heat. The clippings from Peter's fingernails were floating in the toilet bowl. I didn't flush them. I left.

13

A DOCTOR'S OFFICE

■ □ ■

"I have to learn this stuff, Mom. Kids at school have stereos, they know the names of all these songs. It comes up."

"Okay, okay, but not loud." She sighed and turned the car radio back on. That was one thing about my mother. She could understand your wanting to fit in. "I can't bear those drummers," she said.

Josh Spritzer still seemed to be dropping us. Her last date with him was almost three weeks ago, on a Wednesday. But we kept driving by his house every night, before we went to Baskin-Robbins. First, we drove past the high-rise apartment. My mother couldn't look for his white T-Bird there because he kept it in an underground garage. You needed a special card to get in, and Josh had never given her one. She had to park on the street. So we craned our necks, counting floors by their balconies in order to find his windows. If my mother saw a light, she sank back in the car seat and exhaled, comfortable at least for an hour.

But now, the windows of Josh Spritzer's apartment looked dark and she leaned over the steering wheel biting her fingernails. I felt furious, all of a sudden, that he didn't have a lamp with an automatic timer.

My mother turned the car around in the middle of the wide Century City boulevard and headed towards the house where Josh's ex-wife and children lived. She snapped the radio off. She drove at sixty miles an hour through the residential streets of Beverly Hills to find the soothing sight of his car in front of his children's house.

"But Mom, even if he is seeing his kids, he's still not seeing you."

"Shhh, be quiet." We raced down Little Santa Monica. My mother knew herself. All she needed tonight was to forget those dark windows—to relax, enjoy her ice cream cone, sleep.

It seemed strange that my mother didn't feel jealous of Josh's ex-wife, Elaine. When Josh visited, he often sat for hours in the living room of the Arden Street house, having a drink with Elaine. We sometimes saw them as we drove by at night, two silhouettes at a low table.

But my mother had very specific fears. As it turned out, she did not consider Elaine Spritzer pretty. Elaine was short, only a little over five feet, with muscular arms and legs. My mother described her hair as frizzy.

The fact that Josh had apparently once found Elaine attractive enough to marry seemed to escape my mother's attention. And I sure wasn't going to remind her. We each held our breath as we went over the bump in Arden Street that would give us a clear view of Elaine Spritzer's driveway. And tonight we were lucky. The T-bird was there.

My mother parked our car in front of Baskin-Robbins and fumbled in her purse for dollars. That night I didn't fight. We felt relieved, it was late, we were both tired.

Nan Keller knocked on our glass doors. She seemed bored now that Peter had gone away to school. And the backhouse we lived in had been built to be her painting studio. Now, she rented a huge loft in a renovated Venice hotel on Market Street, but she seemed to harbor affection for our place. Every time she came inside she looked around at the low ceilings and close walls and smiled as if they reminded her of things.

"I brought you some sketches," she said. "I was just drawing. I thought you might want to take a look."

My mother made a face, scanning the backhouse. The place looked a mess, but we had to let her in. She was our landlord.

They laid the sketches out on the pool table.

"Can I get you anything?" my mother asked, veering towards the half-size refrigerator. "We don't have much, but I can make some lemonade, or I have carrot juice."

Nan Keller waved her off. "We had a dinner at Ma Maison and I'm absolutely stuffed."

"Oh, they're Ann." My mother stopped, seeing the pictures.

"They're *almost* Ann," Mrs. Keller said. "I was sketching other noses, just to see what could happen with a surgeon. I think this one would be fabulous. Turn to the side, Ann." Mrs. Keller pointed, her cool fingernails touching my face. "A little off, here and here. Just straight. I think it would be smashing. See, she's got a little bump from somewhere."

"Her father," my mother mumbled. My mother's hands dug in her pockets and she stared up and down from the sketches to me. She started nodding. "I think you're right, Nan. Just a little and she'd really be something." Her eyes opened wider in awe of my potential.

"It's not inexpensive, but now's the time to do it, the kids all get them in high school, over the summer or even in fall, it's no big deal. You see them at Beverly with bandages, the boys and the girls, no one minds, it's like braces, it's almost a stigma *not* to have them. And then when they go to college, nobody ever knows. And when the braces come off she'll be all set."

"Who would you take her to, Nan?" My mother became studious. It was easy to imagine her in college, with the tortoiseshell glasses, long since replaced with constantly lost contact lenses, her pencil neatly scribbling, following the teacher's instructions. My father had been my mother's professor.

"I don't know, there's a Doctor Brey on Roxbury. He's popular, he did Lexie's daughter, but I think he does all the same nose. It's a nice nose, but it's becoming a cliché, you know?"

"Oh, we don't want that." My mother acted so humble with these people.

My mother and Nan Keller continued to talk about plastic surgeons, those who did one tract nose and those who thought they were artists and wouldn't listen to what you wanted. One took nitrate photographs of his noses before and after and had bequeathed them to the Los Angeles County Museum of Art, where his wife served on the board of directors, active in volunteer fund raising. Another looked like Ernest Hemingway; recently divorced, he lived in Malibu.

I excused myself. "HE sounds good to me," my mother was saying.

Later, when I came down for a Coke from the half-size refrigerator, Nan Keller was still there, sitting on the old red and blue striped couch. On the floor in front of them stood the bottle of Courvoisier we'd moved to all the places we'd lived in California and never opened, my mother not being a drinker. We had the one suitcase we'd taken in our trunk when we left Wisconsin. It was printed with my father's initials, and missing a handle. We'd kept it together with a belt around it and a dog collar clipped to the handle loops. In it, we'd carried a jumble: our precious things and our old ice skates, and this bottle of Courvoisier. We'd taken it all the way from Wisconsin and then from apartment to apartment and now Nan Keller sat drinking it.

"Well, it's only a rumor, but apparently, he's been seen with her by a few people at Hillcrest."

"Damn. That man," my mother said.

"Who are you talking about?"

"This isn't for you, Ann, go to sleep," my mother said, tapping her nail against a front tooth.

I could have killed Nan Keller.

My mother shook me awake the next morning. "Come on, we're cleaning up a little." She squatted down in front of a cupboard, taking out pans and setting them on the floor. The house looked more of a mess than last night. She was wearing her gray sweat shirt and her hair strained up in a ponytail. A sponge rested where she'd started to wash the cupboard. Our suitcase of old photographs, mementoes, my skates from when I was five, lay on the sofa, unzipped. Whenever my mother was upset, she took things apart and unpacked.

She didn't look at me. Her arms rummaged in the cupboard.

"Take that garbage out this minute," she said.

Four bags sagged against the doors. I carried two. I could hear her starting to bump things and yell as I opened the gate to the alley. "A damn thing around here. I work and work and slave . . . who does she think she . . ."

I lifted the other two bags, slower this time. Birds made small noises in the trees. A white truck whooshed on the clean empty road a block away, at the end of our alley. I leaned against the wall, in back of the house. I didn't have anything with me.

"Made of money, it's a thousand for her teeth, now two thousand for her nose and meanwhile, I have nothing, NOTHING!"

I slipped back in and snuck to my closet and took all the money I had, shoving bills in my pocket. It felt good, the slightly oily paper. I crushed it in my fist.

She ran to my room and stood, veering at the door.

"Why don't you go find your father, you treat me like filth after all I've done. I'll tell you why, because you're scared. You'd rather stay and sap me. Sure, your dumb mother will always drudge for you. For your bikinis that you HAD to have and never wore after I bought them for you, and your pictures when you thought you were going to be a movie star. Yeah, uh-huh. Well, you've got another thing coming, kid, because you don't respect me. You don't love me after all I do for you, how hard I work."

She was waiting and I just stood there for a long curved minute, one rotation.

"Oooh, you—" Then she was coming and I backed into the closet, my arms in front of my face. I knew what I had to do to stop her. Talk. But I held still, I wasn't going to move. I was a piece of wood. My body turned empty, porous, that was what got her.

Something hovered on the ceiling, a scrap of cloth, I saw everything below, slowly, indifferent, like the blades of a fan, moving at a constant speed. I didn't want anything. Except to be away, east, somewhere cool. It seemed clear and true. I didn't love her.

She hit me once, bad, my cheek vibrating like hard metal, and I was falling against the closet wall, the brass hook knocked my head and I was thinking, this is it, it's sharp like a deep cut, one red scratch in the sky: she could hurt me so bad we would never forget.

And then it turned adult and clean. This person coming at you, lunging, her mouth opening and closing, teeth an ecstasy, and all of a sudden, you know and then, whack, on your forehead and she's moving and the picture you saw breaks like crystal.

She hates you. She hates you more than anything she is and she's tied until she kills you, it's that deep in her. She will stay. And you know you have to get up. You want to close your eyes and be dizzy, let this blur dark, tasting the blood in your mouth like a steak, and let her come back to you and touch you softly, lead you to your bed, tuck you in, care for you.

Now, still in the closet, but a million miles away (a hawk flying over a blank western sky), you start sobbing. You hear yourself as if it's someone sitting in a chair across the room.

I stood up and shuffled past her to the door. She pressed right behind me, breathing.

"It's me or nothing, kid," she is saying, her voice laughing and crying. She looks at me, slack, her face sags with an intimate apology.

I slide the door shut and I am outside. We look at each other, stunned, for a moment through the glass. Stunned that I would choose nothing.

I slumped in the alley, next to clean garbage cans, mad at myself because I was so weak. My ears were ringing and they seemed to ring through all the other days. Everything looked sharp, the willow branches over the alley fence so brittle they could cut the sky.

"Come on, get in," my mother said. She slid over and opened my door. She moved quickly now, dressed and businesslike. She sat in the driver's seat, the passenger door hung open. Then she got out and stood with her hands on her hips. "They turned off the phone and we have to go down there. So if you want the phone to work, when your kids call, then you better get in."

We sat in silence while she drove. She waited in the car and I went in with our papers, the bills rumpled from being in my mother's purse. She counted out the cash she gave me to the dollar, and then she asked me for change. But she was right. I would have stolen from her.

I just went to the people at the desks and gave them everything. I didn't say a word. My mother would have made excuses, told them our tragic life story, tried to make them like her. But they already knew us, that's why she stayed in the car. I went in every month. They just did it for me, right away, without questions.

When I slid back in, my mother was sitting sideways on the edge of her seat, looking at her profile in the rearview mirror. She pushed the tip of her nose up with a finger.

"I need a little, too. Just a touch off the tip. Nobody'd even know." She sighed. "Maybe we'll both go in."

My mother finally did call Josh Spritzer's psychiatrist and he refused to see her. She succeeded, however, with Josh's son's psychiatrist. She drove to see him at his office, three afternoons a week, each time dressed as if for a date. After a while, Josh Spritzer stopped calling altogether, but my mother nonetheless remained cheerful. She seemed to be home a lot more.

She spent time on our half-size refrigerator. She polished the glass and the plastic and the chrome and she bought expensive jars of things which she lined up, according to size. Vinegar with herbs floating upside down, mustards, chutney, maple syrup. She pared and peeled carrots, celery, jicoma and green beans for a platter on the second shelf. The parsley was arranged in its own ceramic pitcher. An elaborate fruit bowl, the apples polished and decorated with sprigs of mint, daisies poking out between the oranges, held the prime spot on the top shelf. I caught her rubbing brown eggs on her sweat shirt. And above the glistening eggs, she rested a small Steiff toy chicken.

I took an apple one day after school and lay on the couch, eating. I was happy. I liked having all that food.

Just then I heard my mother's car outside in the alley. "Honey," she called. "Come help me, would you?"

The backhouse yard was small enough so we could hear each other from anywhere. In the alley, she bent unloading dark green shopping bags. They were light. I took them all in one hand. Then she stood at her dresser, smiling, concentrating on a small, flat box. She untied the green satin ribbon. She opened the box and held it out to show me. It was a man's tie, deep red, with tiny blue dots.

I shrugged. "What's this?"

She kept grinning. It was the middle of the afternoon. She must have been out shopping all day.

"Isn't it pretty?" She stared down at the folded tie in the palm of her hand. "It's silk."

"Who's it for?"

She sucked in her breath and pulled her chin up. "It's a present, Ann."

So that was how it was going to be. I went to my room and closed the door. A few minutes later, she called me again.

She stood in front of the open refrigerator. "Honey, when you take an apple, take it from down here." She pointed to the produce drawer, crammed full of bagged apples and oranges. "I don't mind you eating, but I arrange the basket so it looks pretty."

I didn't say anything and she kept on.

"Do you understand? Because I'd like to keep it nice. It took me three hours the other day to get this refrigerator decent."

"So you're not working anymore."

"I'm working."

"When?"

She smiled. She wasn't going to tell me. I turned to go back to my bedroom. I kept wanting to hit that smile.

"Don't you worry about that," she yelled. "That's my worry. And believe me, everything's fine. Everything's finally going to be just fine." She started humming to herself and I heard glass clinking, jars being moved inside the refrigerator.

Jack Irwin still called. He took us out to dinner in formal, expensive restaurants I'd never heard of and which didn't seem to require reservations. These restaurants had in common white tablecloths and an extraordinary number of small courses. Everyone in those restaurants seemed old, old waiters in black cotton suits and women in long dresses that showed whole U-shaped sections of their paper-thin, crinkly backs.

Would the young lady like whipped cream on her gâteau, the ancient waiter would ask.

"Yeah, tons," I'd say, loudly. But no one looked at me.

"Yes, thank you," Jack would tell him, "the young lady would like a bit of cream."

The backhouse seemed more tended every day. Like before, when I came home from school, it was usually empty. My mother would rush in an hour or so later, perfectly dressed, with a new haircut or a new blouse or a new color on her nails or a mysterious package which I assumed was another present.

She seemed happier than I'd seen her for a long time, but distracted.

My mother couldn't keep her secret for long. "It's going to be wonderful," she said. She sank down against her car seat after she told me, her chocolate almond cone almost touching her chin. "You're finally going to have everything. We'll have a big house and you'll have all the clothes you want." She said that she and her psychiatrist, a Dr. Leonard Hawthorne, had fallen in love. Apparently, they were going to get married.

Her eyes half closed and she licked the cone neatly, around in a circle.

"And I'll get a car?" I said.

"And you'll get your car," she said.

I still hadn't seen Dr. Hawthorne. He didn't call or come to the backhouse. From what I could tell, the only times they met were their afternoon sessions. But that seemed to be enough for her. She remained happy in a talkative way. She'd be dusting the inside of a cupboard, she'd look up and say, "Aren't we lucky, Annie-honey? Aren't you glad something nice happened to your mother after she's worked so hard all these years?"

Every night, she sat at the dining room table—which was Nan Keller's old drafting board covered with a new white cloth—and wrote letters. She used red stationery, red envelopes and a quill pen, which she dipped in white ink. She wore a new, floor-length, peach-colored silk robe with cuffs that folded back and a long, round collar.

When she completed a letter to Dr. Hawthorne, she sealed it with beeswax. She'd bought a stamp that said "Joie d'Adele."

For my birthday, I wanted a car. Every kid in LA who didn't have one wanted a car.

My mother kept smiling weirdly and humming before the day. "Don't worry," she said, in a singsong lilt.

The morning of my birthday, she gave me keys. Her face seemed radiant, spilling. "Yes," she nodded, "it is," and watched me fly into happiness.

A few minutes later, after hugs and giggles, I asked where the car was.

"I wanted to get it today for you, but they couldn't have it till next week. But don't worry, Puss, it's on its way."

"What color?"

She hesitated. "White," she said, then nodding too much. "Mmhmm, it's a white one."

A Tuesday night, she took off her peach-colored robe and dressed again. I thought she wanted an ice cream cone and I got dressed right away, too. I thought she might be coming around to her old habits. I actually missed driving by Josh Spritzer's houses.

But when we slid into the car, she seemed distracted. She didn't talk to me or tell me where we were going. It was eleven o'clock and we drove all the way out to Santa Monica. She parked the car across the road from a high-rise apartment building. Outside, the beach palms moved in the wind.

My mother turned to me quickly, for the first time since we'd left the backhouse.

"Do you have a dollar?"

I felt in my pocket, but I already knew what was there. "I have one dollar, but it's my last money."

"Give it to me."

I kept my hand clutched around the soft paper in my pocket. I sweated and the dollar felt damp. "I need it for school tomorrow."

I knew all the arguments: worked all these years, slaved, she supported, etc. But she didn't even start. She just stuck out her hand. "Come on. Give it to me."

She ran to the building across the street in her high heels. I saw her with a man just behind the glass door. Later, she told me she needed my dollar to tip the doorman. Dr. Leonard Hawthorne lived in the penthouse and she wanted her letter delivered by hand.

She looked relieved and looser when she sank back in the car, her hair messy and glamorous from the wind. She rolled down her window. "Oh, smell that air, would you?" She took a deep breath and for a moment, she seemed like herself again. "Should we run and get an ice cream cone? Oh, we don't have any money, do we? Drat. I could really go for a chocolate almond. Do you think they'd take a check? Why not? Huh? They know us. We've been going for years."

Leslie and I walked, as we did every day during morning recess, down the open plaza of the fourth floor New Building, to buy sweet rolls and coffee in the cafeteria. We'd learned to like coffee. We practiced, drinking it with two packets of powdered cream and four Sweet'n Lows. Every day, we found it delicious again.

During class, I'd rifled through all my pockets and purse, but I had no money. I'd used all my change the week before. I would have to lie.

The sweet rolls smelled warmer and darker that day, they'd just been taken out of the oven, the white sugar frosting melted so they stuck together when the ladies behind the counter lifted them with spatulas from huge tin pans.

"I don't think I'll have one today," I said.

Leslie took two, the heavy rolls flopping on the flimsy paper plates. "Come on, you can't let me get fat alone."

I looked down. This was hard but necessary. We stood in the line to pay. Leslie was pouring our coffee. "No, I don't want anything."

Leslie opened her leather wallet and took out a five-dollar bill. She paid for both of us. "I'm forcing you," she said.

We walked back over the fourth floor terrace slowly, careful not to spill, talking quietly, under the eaves where pigeons nested. I kept looking over at her. Sometimes, like at the Pacific Gas and Electric Company, people seemed so kind. Then I thought the world would be easy. But thinking that confused me about my mother.

"Oh, my mom's getting married," I said. A splash of coffee spilled on my suede shoe.

I lied to people on buses. Dumb lies, only things that didn't matter. I told a man I came from a family of seven children, my father worked in a bakery. The man nodded, not the least bit surprised.

My mother took me along on one of her sprees. We got up early and looked at linen suits on sale. She found one that was rust-colored and I found a blue.

"Aren't these too much?" I said, rubbing the cardboard ticket.

"They'll always be good. They're a classic cut. Really classic."

My mother stood in a pool of light from the high arched windows of the store. The brick floors and vaulted ceiling made us feel peaceful. But she hadn't worked in months. The drawer with our bills wouldn't open, it was packed so full.

"Do we have the money?" I whispered.

"Mmhmm," she said. "I think so. For something of this quality, at this buy, yes."

And I let her walk to the antique bar used as a desk and write a check, for mine, too. On the way out we found purple hats, hundred-dollar purple hats.

"Absolutely adorable," my mother said, flipping one on me.

We bought those, too.

I thought, with all the money we owed, a couple hundred dollars wouldn't make a difference. If I tried to be careful, my mother would just spend it anyway, so I'd collect things now while I could. As if you could stock up on purple hats.

□

When my mother was upset, she turned graceless. She bumped into corners, her elbows jabbed walls. She hurt herself.

"Damn," I heard her say. It frightened me how much she could pack into that small word.

All her knocks and wandering would end up in my room, but there was nothing I could do except wait. There were no locks on any of our doors. Finally, she came. She wasn't wearing anything but a dirty gray sweat shirt. She squatted on my carpet, bare-legged, rocking.

"I don't know, I just don't know. SHE'S the one who had to come to California, SHE was going to be a movie star, and I work and work and slave and it's high time I get something for ME once instead of you, you, you and more you. And you don't even like me. I can see the way you look at me."

She covered her hand with her sleeve before she hit me.

I used everything, hitting hard, loose, not seeing what I was doing. And in a few minutes she fell off the side of my bed. I was getting stronger than she was.

She stood up and walked to my door. She crossed her arms and spit, her saliva arching over the carpet, falling a foot short of the sheet.

My mother didn't forgive me right away. When I came home from school, she was standing in front of the full-length mirror on her closet door, wearing an unfinished wedding dress. A seamstress knelt pinning the hem. I recognized the ivory beaded satin. It was one of our things from Wisconsin. She'd bought it, years ago, in Egypt.

"What are you doing?" I said.

She wouldn't look away from the mirror. "We're busy now, Ann." I just stood there, watching. The woman crawled around my mother's feet, taking pins out of her mouth and sliding them into the thick fabric. My mother kept changing the position of her mouth and watching the effect in the mirror.

"Look what she did to me." She rolled back her left sleeve. Her arms stretched long and thin, light brown. My mother bruised easily. "Look at those marks. She's like a little animal."

I sat in the alley. A few gates down, three boys pedaled out on bikes, with baseball bats and mitts in their baskets. They still had high light voices and I watched them ride off, pedaling standing, beautiful boys with careless voices.

An hour later, at dusk, my mother marched out and asked me if I wanted to put on a sweater, so we could go have dinner. She didn't seem at all surprised to find me slumped in the alley. I sat there a lot of times now. The dressmaker had gone and my mother looked tired. I pulled on an old sweater and she didn't complain. We both just settled in the car.

"Well, so, what are you thinking?" she said at the restaurant. She propped her face on her fists, tried to smile.

"Nothing."

"Nothing at all?"

I shrugged.

She reached over, put her hand on my forehead. "You're a little warm."

"I'm fine."

"You're just tired." She sighed. "Well, it won't be long now. Pretty, pretty soon, I think, things will be changing for the better. The much better."

"Do you still think you're going to marry Dr. Hawthorne?"

"Mmhmm," she said, reveling in the adjustment of her smile, all the while studying her nails. "No, I really don't think, Honey. I know."

I crossed my arms on the table. "So if you're going to marry him, why doesn't he ever call? You never go out on dates."

"Honey, you don't understand." She leaned closer. "It's all part of the therapy. Remember the first time when I was upset? Well, he was bringing me through my father and all that pain. I've suffered a lot, Ann, you really don't know. And then the next time it was your father and that was a hard one, boy, I can tell you. Then I had to go through Ted Diamond. But I'm through it all now. It's over. And he's stopped seeing me, as a patient. It's like he's saying, Hey, you're done. You're finished. Now we can go ahead and just date."

"So when do you think you'll get married?"

"I'd say, oh, about a month. Maybe three weeks, but probably a month."

"When will he start calling and coming over and stuff?"

"Any day now, Honey. Certainly by the weekend."

But he didn't call by the weekend. And the next day, my mother's red envelope, addressed with white ink, came back in our pile of mail on the washing machine top, *Return to Sender* scrawled on it with an ordinary ball-point.

"Give me that," my mother said.

I followed her to her bedroom and watched her slip it in a drawer. I saw a flash of red. "If he's going to marry you, why did he send your letter back?"

My mother gave me a patient look. She opened the drawer and took the letter out again. There were dozens of red envelopes in there.

"Look-it, Honey. This is addressed to *Doctor* Leonard Hawthorne. See." She ran her fingers over the indentations his ball-point pen had made. "See, he doesn't want me to write to the doctor. The *doctor* doesn't want to see me anymore. He wants to know me as Len Hawthorne the man, not the doctor. And believe you me, so do I!"

That night, my mother wrote a long letter to Len Hawthorne, The Man. She addressed it to his home in Santa Monica and used twice as many stamps as necessary.

"This is Adele August. I'd like to—okay, okay. But please. It's an emergency." She sat in her bedroom with the door closed, but I could hear through the wall. That was the day when the envelope addressed to Len Hawthorne, The Man, came back in our mail.

Since she'd stopped going to her job, my mother slept in. She almost never woke up before I left for school. Mornings, I stood at the half-size refrigerator, looking at all the food. My mother

kept it perfectly clean and well stocked now, as if she feared a
surprise inspection. I used to stand in the quiet, light backhouse
with the refrigerator door open. I stared at the fruit. I almost
didn't want to touch it. I wanted it to stay the way it was, cold and
hard, the apples beaded with strings of faceted colors.

Then one morning, my mother was moving behind the soda fountain in her peach-colored robe when I woke up. She made us
bananas on cereal. She smiled at me weakly while I ate. "Is that
good, Honey?"

"Yeah." When I finished, I brought the bowl to the sink and
washed it. We didn't have dish towels, so I dried it with a paper
napkin. Then I went to get my books.

"Oh, Ann," my mother called. "Could you please stay home
for a while this morning. I'll write you a note. There's something
I need you to do."

"I should go to school, Mom." I wanted to go.

"Honey. This is important. I need you to call somewhere."

"Can't I do it now?"

"Honey, it doesn't open until nine."

I sat back down. I thought of missing Nutrition. It wasn't even
eight yet.

"You'll be glad you waited. This is for your good, too."

At exactly nine, I said, "Okay, let's do it now."

"Well, just give them a second. I said they *open* at nine. Let
them put their things down and get a cup of coffee."

If I rode my bike to school, I'd be there for Nutrition. I said,
"I have to go."

"Okay, okay, let me find the number." She was stalling. She
knew it by heart. She dialed and handed me the receiver.

"Now, say you need to talk to Doctor Hawthorne. Say your
name is Amy Spritzer. Go ahead."

I didn't want to do it, but she was looking at me. A woman
said, Good morning, and I said, Hello, this is Amy Spritzer,
Could I please speak to Dr. Hawthorne? Just a moment, please,
she said. It was working.

"What should I say to him?"

My mother's eyebrows lifted. "Is he coming?"

I handed the receiver over. "Hell-ow," she said, in a high, soft voice. "Ye-es."

I went to her purse and took out two dollars, and held them up for her to see. She shoved me away with her hand. It wasn't going well.

"I just felt, really, once more . . . Well, I feel I have some things I'd like to talk to you about. With you. . . . Oh, all right. I know."

She hung up the phone and looked straight at me. "See, he just got in. This wasn't the right time. We should've waited an hour. Damn." She bit her cuticle.

"Mom, if he's going to marry you, why won't he talk to you? People who marry you talk to you."

"You don't understand," she said. "You don't know anything."

I walked outside to where I left my bike. My mother followed me. She stood across the pool, holding her robe closed over her chest.

"You better hope it's true," she said, in a warning voice. "You better hope Leonard Hawthorne loves me, because if he doesn't, believe me, there's nothing for us. Nothing, do you hear, nothing!"

She walked towards me on the cement, and I took off on my bike. I stood up, pedaling, giddy. She couldn't seem to realize, it didn't matter what I thought.

My mother said she was going into the hospital for an operation. Something in her voice made it sound like a lie. I tried to hold my own, I didn't believe her.

There was something about the way she said things, about the way she was vague—it made her always seem wrong. You couldn't be sure. It was hard to tell what my mother did and didn't know. She didn't use facts. But then, things that had seemed to be her whimsy, in the past, back in Wisconsin, things I'd laughed at with the rest of our family, turned out to be true here. Like the way my mother had wanted to get Hal excused from Vietnam by putting braces on his teeth. People had laughed and laughed. But

that's what Leslie's brother Dean had done and now he was at
Stanford.

"What kind of operation?" I said.

She acted like she didn't want to tell me. Then she lowered her
voice to a whisper. "Cancer," she said, as if it were a secret.

"Where?"

She slapped a hand on her left breast. "But never mind, never
mind."

She did go into the hospital. She stayed overnight. Jack Irwin
drove and I rode along in his car to pick her up. She was wearing
her peach-colored robe with a white blanket on her lap when a
nurse wheeled her out into the parking lot. I climbed over to the
backseat. She acted extremely kind to Jack. And for years that
was all I heard about her cancer.

I called Dr. Hawthorne from a pay phone at school and gave the
receptionist my real name. He came on the line the same way he
did when I'd said I was Amy.

"Yes, Ann, what can I do for you?"

A lot. Too much. That was the problem.

"My mother thinks you're going to get married and I wanted to
know if that was true." My voice sounded small, peculiar.

"I could see you at three o'clock. Can you come in then?"

I said I could and I didn't go back to class when the bell rang.
I walked around the back of the typing building, where smokers
ditched and leaned against the wall. I didn't have a watch. Every
few minutes I got up and looked at the clock over the track.

Dr. Hawthorne's office was on the ninth floor of a Century City
high rise. I leafed through a newsmagazine in his waiting room.
It felt really odd to think how many times my mother had been
here. I could imagine her, distracted, twisting and biting a piece
of her hair.

Dr. Hawthorne wasn't handsome. He was very thin, he wore
glasses, and his mouth seemed to hold a permanent expression of
distaste.

I sat down in a large, padded chair and looked around. I

waited. I'd already asked him on the phone if he was going to marry my mother. I was waiting for his answer.

But he didn't say anything. "You have a couch and everything," I said finally. I tried to sound normal and kidlike.

He acknowledged my comment with a smile that was more like a wince and then he was silent again. He looked at his hands intently.

"So are you going to marry my mother?"

He shook his head and something collapsed in me, a faint rumble, the beginning of a very long sound. I hadn't known how much I'd believed my mother until just then. Everything was going to be different.

"She sees what she wants to see," Dr. Hawthorne said. He held his hands tentatively, forming a basket of air. "My interest in her has always been strictly professional. I've told her that many times."

My mother hadn't worked for months, those bills jamming the drawer.

"I've done everything I can. I've stopped therapy. I refuse her phone calls. I am denying any pleas for contact. I feel that's the best thing."

I just looked at him.

"In fact," he said, staring at his fingertips, lifting them slightly back, "I haven't received payment for the last five months of treatment."

"I'm sorry," I said. Somehow, that seemed the worst thing yet.

"It would be best for your mother to see another therapist."

"Isn't there anything you can do?" My throat swelled up on the inside, it was hard to talk.

"I feel this is the best thing. The only thing."

"What should I do?" I tried to keep my chin in, tight, to lock my jaws.

"Do you have any contact with your father?"

I was surprised that after all those sessions with my mom, he didn't know. I shook my head.

"No contact?"

I shook it again.

"Well, that makes it harder." He looked at me, squinting.
"How old are you?"

"Seventeen."

I found myself concentrating, as he did, on his wrists. His cuffs
seemed amazingly white. "Try not to depend on your mother very
much. She's not responsible enough to take care of herself, not to
mention another person."

My chin wove.

"What are your plans after high school?" he asked finally. I
suppose I should have stood up to leave.

"Oh, I don't know. College. Back east maybe." The way I was
going now, skipping school, forget it. My grades weren't great. I'd
be in more trouble.

"That's shooting pretty high. Well, good for you."

I held on to the arms of my chair. I didn't go. "I don't know
what to do." That came out like a yelp. "I mean, I lie sometimes,
too. I lie to people I'll never see again, and my friends, they don't
really know me."

He looked at his watch, on a thick gold band, loose on his
delicate wrist. He seemed to be thinking I was her daughter after
all. I was screwed up, too.

"We'll have to stop here." He cleared his throat. "I'm not going
to charge you for this session."

I still didn't move. I took off one shoe and pulled down my
knee sock and dug into my pockets, collecting all the money. I
didn't trust anywhere in the backhouse anymore, so I carried my
money around with me.

"Will she kill herself?"

He shook a little, wincing, I guess that I surprised him. He
frowned. "I don't think so. Your mother hasn't shown signs of a
suicide."

"Oh." I looked at him, grateful for that. "Could you see her
one more time and tell her you're not going to marry her? Just
once."

I sat there with all the crinkled money from my pockets and
straightened the bills on my thigh. I offered to pay for one more
time. I guess that got to him. He shook his head again and said

he wouldn't take the money. He said the appointment my mother used to have was already filled but when there was a cancellation, he'd have his receptionist call.

I didn't go home. On the high school track field, kids from the four classes competed against each other in sack races and egg relays, an athletic carnival. I found Leslie on the top bleacher, drinking coffee with our sixty-two-year-old French teacher, Madame Camille. Outside the announcer's booth, there was a five-foot stack of white pie boxes, from the House of Pies.

My mother had been so enchanted when we'd first moved to Beverly Hills and driven around at night. In Bay City, every block or two had a tavern, an old house with a sign outside. "Here, you don't see the taverns, they all go out for dessert," she'd said. We had marveled at the House of Pies, Lady Kelly's, all the ice cream stores. My mother felt she was finally in her element.

Exhilarated, sick of being goody-goods, Leslie, Madame Camille and I stole a pie and sat on the bleacher sideways, eating it with our fingers, half watching the colors move on the field below.

Later, an announcement blared over the loudspeaker.

"The junior class is disqualified because several members of that class—you know who you are—stole one of the prizes. It's too bad that just a few people ruined the whole class's fun."

We stood up, stunned. Madame Camille walked precariously on the bleacher in her high heels. "I will buy another pie," she said, lifting her white patent leather purse over her head and moving as fast as she could to the control booth. "I will pay."

I didn't tell my mother I'd seen Dr. Hawthorne. We went out to dinner that night, the same as always, and after, we drove to Baskin-Robbins. Now, the furtive run inside with the five-dollar bill moist in my hand and back to the car parked in the dark, under the trees, carrying the two cones like torches and eating them in the front seat with the heat turned on, listening to my mother sigh and talk about what we'd have in the pretty-soon future, acquired a settled sadness. Those trees dropping blossoms on the car top and my mother not taking them for real because she was waiting, waiting to be married and to see them as a wife, a doctor's wife. I knew that I would leave her here, still waiting.

When we called home to ask for money, my mother always had me talk first. My grandmother asked me questions about school. Then, I had to stay near the phone, so close we touched, while my mother begged. My grandmother would ask if we really needed it and I would have to say yes. We'd already gone through the green book of my grandmother's account for me.

Ellen Arcade finally called us. She screamed into the phone. "You didn't *tell* me you knew Cassie Swan, we were talking the other day, and your name came up for this commercial, but we have something even better, there's a series and with the influx of the Iranians, oh, you know, Adele, you read the papers, *any*-way, Ann is just perfect, with her coloring. I want her to read next Wednesday . . ."

My mother held out the phone and we both listened. I scribbled notes of the time and place. It was an address in Westwood on the seventeenth floor. An audition. My mother and I wheeled around the room, falling down dizzy, when we hung up the phone, and I stopped eating for the next five days.

The morning of the audition the phone rang while I stood in the shower. I hadn't washed my hair for five days. I'd noticed if I let it get totally horrible first, it looked better after I washed it. My mother was talking; I thought I must have heard wrong. "Two o'clock, okay, let me ask you one more thing," she said. "Not one question? Oh, okay."

I bent over, shaking my hair dry upside down to make it straight. My mother knocked on the door. "Hurry up in there. I need a shower, too."

An hour later, she was dressed. "I'm sorry, Ann, but my work is just more important than your audition. We have to live and you don't even know if you'd get the part. It's your first one, you probably wouldn't. Let's face it, you don't really look Iranian." She stood by the door, her purse over her shoulder.

"You said you'd take me." My face fell loose. "You haven't worked for months."

"Well, Honey, I'm sorry, but something today came up and I just have to go."

"You're not going to take me?"

"Try and call and ask them if they'll schedule it an hour later, and I'll come pick you up if I can when I'm done. But I've got to run. I'm sorry, but I've got to do what's best." Her polished purse, her heels, the patent leather gleamed as she tripped to the car. I heard the gate slamming. I ran outside undressed, banged on the car windows. She opened her door. "See if you can change the time."

"I can't," I screamed.

She shrugged, looked in the car mirror, frowning, then smiling again, arranging her face. Then I guessed. "You're not going to work, you're going to go see Leonard Hawthorne, who doesn't even want to marry you or anything; that's where you're going! It's not to work for money. You promised!"

She shrugged again and started rolling up the window. "I'm not going to talk to you while you're like this," she said and drove away, out of our alley.

Peter Keller was in Massachusetts. I called Daniel Swan, but only Darcy and the twins were home, she didn't know where Daniel was. I even called Leslie, but her mom said she was out taking her tennis lesson and I wouldn't have ever said anything like this was important enough for her to hurry and call me back, I never would have done that. When you called Leslie's family, they answered in another zone and you had to kind of respect their slow time. Then it was a half hour to three o'clock and I stuffed my dress and makeup and hair things and all the money I had in bags and ran down to the corner, stopping every few feet in the alley to bend over and underbrush my hair, and when I came to Elevado, I hitched and a milk truck picked me up. This was 1975 and there weren't milk trucks any place in the country anymore, except Beverly Hills had these stores called Jurgensons and for

about three times the price of anywhere else, they delivered your
food in these white, old-fashioned trucks.

The guy drove me to Wilshire, two blocks from the place, and
I took my Korkease off and ran. Then, just before I went up in
the building, I was sitting on the curb, buckling my shoes, and I
saw this orange, flowered baseball cap with a big bill in the window of a jeans store, on a ladder actually, and I liked it and on a
whim, I just went in and bought it for six dollars. It was something
I would have never done if my mother had brought me, I would
have been checking my makeup in the car, all perfect, and this
seemed like something just personally me, and I slammed it on
my head and went up the elevator.

I thought once I got there, I could check in with a secretary or
casting girl or I didn't know what and then I thought I'd find a
ladies' room and go and wash up and change and put on my
makeup and everything. But when I walked in, it was this ordinary, glass-doored, impressive-looking office, with a big desk,
and a big, manicured blond secretary, and when I said who I was,
she said my name into an intercom and in like a second, they
showed me into this enormous room with windows and striped
thin blinds and a view of the whole world and two men were sitting
in chairs, leaning back with shirts and ties, saying my name.

They motioned me over to an empty part of the room and I stood
there with all my bags just on the carpet and they were laughing,
one of them smoked, he leaned down to light his cigarette again,
and said, "So, okay, what have you got in there, in all those bags."

And I don't know what happened, I went dark. Pigeon-toed and
knock-kneed, I bent down and started pulling things out of my
bags. "A dress, a ladies' room, please. Just because I want to
clean up a little doesn't mean I don't, I have Dignity. Yes Dignity,
with a capital D. I may not have money, but class." I was tripping,
leg over leg, and it went on a long time, I put on makeup without
a hand mirror, I changed without a bathroom, pulling my dress
over my head, I faked those air machines that blow your hands
dry. "There," I said, landing on the floor, my stuff a strewn pile,
my makeup smeared, hair two panels in front of my face. "Don't

you feel better clean? Yes, I do, much, much, better. You can seat us now, please."

I'd mimicked people all my life, but that was the first time I'd done her. I looked up again. My legs felt like Gumby. The men had been quiet, both of them, and now they were laughing. One clapped. I had screamed. I thought they must have felt terribly sorry for me. But I was a little elated, too. I knew there was a chance I'd done something good, good enough to change my life. "Okay," the one with the cigarette said, taking out a gold case, lighting another. "Do they teach you to read, too, over at Beverly Hills High?" The whole time there, I forgot I was wearing that orange hat.

When I came out of the building I spent the whole three dollars I had left on a hot fudge sundae at the Westwood Will Wright's, and I ate it in about a minute, standing at the takeout counter. I was so hungry all of a sudden. Then I went to go home. Nobody picked me up on Wilshire, this time, when I hitched. I stood at the corner of Westwood Boulevard, in front of two huge office buildings at a bus stop, still carrying my bags. About fifty people in gray business suits milled, waiting for the bus. I went up to each one, I swear, each one, I said, "Excuse me, I live in Beverly Hills, I go to the high school; I lost my wallet and I don't have any money. Could I possibly borrow forty cents for the bus and if you give me your address I'll send it back to you?" I got two nods, fast, flickering, almost like sleights of hand. Other people just looked away, into the hills you couldn't see for the smog, as if they didn't hear me. I ended up walking home. I got there at eight o'clock and stood looking in the refrigerator. It was empty. My mother must have thrown out all the food.

After a while, I knocked, lightly, at her door. "Mom, are we going to get some supper?"

"Leave me be, Ann. Just go away." Her voice was flat and totally different. I scuffed up to the Kellers' and went in the back and the cook fixed me a ham sandwich.

□

What I was afraid of never happened. My mother just talked about
Dr. Hawthorne less and less. In the evenings, she still wore her
peach-colored robe, but she tended to lie on the couch flipping
through magazines. I didn't find any more red envelopes in our
mail. I'd been walking around waiting for the day she'd fall apart.
But she didn't. She hadn't with Josh Spritzer, either.

One afternoon, late, she rushed in dressed up, her white lab
coat over a pantsuit.

"Well, I'm back at Palm Manor and guess what? They gave me
a party, they were so glad to get me back. They said no one else
they'd had in either convalescent home was good with the people
the way I was."

A tear formed on the corner of one eye.

"Control yourself, Mom." I could be such a pill.

She dabbed her eye with a sleeve. "Well, I suppose I understand these old people. A lot of them are out here from the midwest or somewhere else, you know, and here they are in a home.
All alone."

"I'm glad you're working again," I said. I was so cold. I walked
away to my room. She should just work and make money to pay
for my school and clothes and for college. For me to go away. I
didn't want to hear about it, about her trying, how she felt. She
should just do it and make it look easy.

"'Course I suppose they've got it pretty good there. There's a
lot worse, I'll tell you," she said, mostly to herself.

The gas and electricity was cut off again and I stayed home from
school to pay the bill. We both did it rotely, something we were
used to. Now, the people in Pacific Gas and Electric knew my
name.

"I'll catch a father for you yet, Ann, you just wait." My mother
patted my knee. We sat parked in front of Baskin-Robbins and
she sighed.

"Not for me, anymore. You should look for a husband for you.

But I don't need a father anymore." We both knew I would go away in one year.

My mother sat up straighter. "Well, sure you do. For when you're in college, you can have parties and bring your kids home. And just to have a man you can look up to a little and talk."

"Even if you marry someone, he won't be my father. I had a father."

"Yeah, well where is he."

I shrugged. "Anyone else'll just be your husband. I won't really know him that well."

"Just wait and see. You plan too much. You're thinking and analyzing, you've got to learn to just be. And besides, you might like to have a man to look up to, to ask for advice once in a while."

A piece of my mother's hair hung near her ice cream cone. I reached over and hooked it behind her ear.

"I have you."

"Yes, but you need a man, too. You'll see." She started the engine of the car. "Who knows, maybe you'll be better off not growing up with a man all the time. Because with my father, you always compare and nobody else ever has that real closeness you did with him. Maybe you're better off never knowing it. I think so. I think everything's just going to go right in your life."

We got the call, union scale, sixteen weeks shooting the first season. The part was Marie Iroquois on "Sante Fe." They'd changed me to an Indian.

We had habits, but we never admitted them. We ate out every night, but every night, it was as if my mother felt freshly surprised that driving in the car and finding a restaurant was, at ten o'clock, our only alternative. We never bought food for the half-size refrigerator anymore. All we had in the house was carrot juice and wheat germ oil.

It was stubbornness. My mother didn't want this to be our life. She'd do it a day at a time, she'd put up with it, but she wasn't going to *plan* for it. We didn't pay bills, we didn't buy groceries, we bounced checks. Accepting our duties might have meant we were stuck forever. We made it so we couldn't keep going the way we were; something had to happen. But the thing was, it never did.

My mother had to pick me up from work now, in Studio City. She came late a lot of times. I'd hang around with this boy, Clark, a guy from the Valley.

It wasn't anything like I'd thought it would be, television. I just had to stand around and say lines, once in a while I got to say one word more than another word to make people laugh, but it didn't really matter what I did. It was work, like my sophomore part-time job in the PE office. Mostly they wanted pictures of black hair. Before, I'd imagined the movies were the center of the world, and people loved you, people like my father came up and saw you and told you you were beautiful. But this was like nothing. The places we shot were in the Valley, just gray lots and studios, trailer dressing rooms. We stood around waiting most of the time. Nobody thought we were anywhere. Even people like Clark, who wanted to be actors, and who walked funny, he sort of bounced to make himself seem taller, they all just wanted to get somewhere else.

But other people, outside television, treated you different. Teenaged girls on Beverly Drive giggled behind, turned shy if I stopped, and looked up at me.

I was still going to leave her. I'd go to college, a clean, safe, normal escape. I'd have the money. Before, she used to tell me I had a trust fund. I asked her about it a lot. The first time, when I was fourteen or something, it was, "Don't worry, I arranged this with your father's family when you were a baby. There was money set aside for your college then, from Egypt."

"Like the whole country of Egypt is just going to send me money."

"Don't worry, I've worked it out. On your seventeenth birthday, it'll come."

The second time, it was, "Well, I'm worried, I haven't heard anything from the Egyptians and I'm very worried." I asked about papers, documents, even names. She had nothing. The next time I asked was the June before Marie Iroquois. We sat in the car, licking ice cream cones. She put her fingers to her throat. "My jewels are your trust, Ann, so just be quiet." Once the checks started from "Santa Fe" I never mentioned it again.

The point of the fight was always, "I don't know why you can't go to UCLA like all these kids I see, they're getting good educations, they're studying to be nurses and lawyers and female doctors. I see them in the convalescent homes."

I had no answer so I didn't give one. And the fights always passed.

I got into a better school than I deserved, with my lousy grades. But even colleges thought you were different if they saw you on TV.

We both knew I would go. We joked about it.

"You know after we've worked so hard all these years, you could really just stay a while and help out a little, so we could get ahead once, you know, after I've worked nights and at Hamburger Hamlet and as a maid, and everything, you know? It wouldn't kill you."

I knew.

Something I found when I was packing to go away: a newspaper clipping, in a shoe box where I kept things, from the *Beverly Hills Courier*, March 2, 1972.

13-YEAR-OLD SEEKS HOME. NEAT, WELL-BEHAVED OKAY STUDENT. B + PRETTY (DARK HAIR, THIN). DOES NOT SMOKE AND HAS NO INTEREST IN EXPERIMENTING WITH DRUGS. PLANNING TO GO TO COLLEGE. I WOULD HELP AROUND THE HOUSE. MAY BE THE DAUGHTER YOU'VE ALWAYS WANTED. NO TROUBLE. PO BOX 254.

I remembered I wouldn't let the guy who took my money for the ad open the envelope until I left. He was cute, red-headed, he looked like a college kid and he flirted with me, but

after he read my ad, which must have been as soon as I walked
out of the office, I didn't want to see him again.

I never went and checked my post office box for replies.

Another time, I rummaged through the jumbled suitcase from
home. It was a little library of me. First-grade report cards, average, average, average, one above-average—in penmanship—a
list of friends to work on stuck in a book (some who already liked
me, some who might), a large photo album with one entry, pressed
yellow roses and a faded orange clear hospital identification
band. Wisps of hair curled in envelopes. Baby teeth in eyedropper bottles. Beach ball photographs.

I remembered it only dimly, the place on the highway, Kelly's,
a small brick store with a house in back. Mostly, they developed
film, you parked your car on the gravel and went in to pick up
your packet of snapshots. It was a dim rainy day when we went,
a carpeted room in back. The man looked young and dull. My
mother was the brightest thing there, full of light and authority. I
wore an orange raincoat with pink dots over my tiny swimsuit and
thongs. I remember them posing me with the beach ball, remember lying on the carpet, arching up, for them to slide the swimsuit
off. I don't know, I must have been six or seven. I hated the way
my hair looks in the pictures, up in a bun, and my forced big
smile, the way my leg tilts, posing. It's funny for me to think of
us in that little dim place by the highway, taking nude pictures of
a seven-year-old with a colored beach ball. At one point, my
mother took a powder puff out from her purse and powdered me.

She still has that little orange and pink raincoat. She keeps it
in dry-cleaning cellophane at one end of her closet.

Leslie and I shopped together for college. Used clothing stores on
La Cienega for broken-in Levi's, we tried on hundreds from the
wooden apple barrels, chose the ones that fit and then tore the
knees. We bought tiny used T-shirts with numbers on them which
we wore so tight they bound our chests and a strip of skin escaped
uncovered above our belts. Her parents kept asking me over to

dinner, but her family got on my nerves. It was the same every night. Her father, her mother, her little brother, where they sat, the bowls of food moving around the table like a clock.

They all kept quiet, only Leslie complained. "So why *don't* we do these things, why *don't* we boycott grapes?"

But Leslie's parents never yelled. They remained soft-spoken always. "You have to choose your causes," Leslie's mother murmured, "we can't do everything for everyone. Or we'd be boycotting the whole store. We'd have nothing to eat. Your father and I have chosen the Jews. When you go away to college, you'll find the one or two things that mean the most to you."

Leslie rolled her eyes at me. Later, in her room, she shook her head, "I'm counting the days. Sometimes I think all my mother cares about is getting her nails done and her legs waxed. She's like a mannikin in a store window." That's what I thought of Leslie's mother too, I would have agreed if I didn't know that kids really love their parents.

When we walked downstairs later, a huge fight started between Leslie and her father over Häagen-Dazs. Häagen-Dazs ice cream was just new in the stores. Leslie's parents said they wouldn't spend two dollars on a pint of ice cream, no matter what. Leslie screamed, Dana's father bought it for his kids.

I just wanted to go home. My mom and I sometimes bought two pints and each ate one, right from the carton, with a spoon.

One day I brought the rent check up to the big house. I went through the kitchen and while I stood talking with the cook, Mr. Keller walked in. I realized I'd never seen him in the kitchen. He looked slight there, out of place among the huge stainless steel sinks and counters.

"May I have a word with you, Ann?"

We walked through the living room to the back terrace. We stood looking over the lawn and the tennis court. His face twisted. "Do you have all the money you need, for college?" he said.

I shook my head, yes.

"If you need anything," he said.

I looked back towards the empty house. "Where's Mrs. Keller?" I asked.

"In San Francisco for the day."

Daniel Swan wasn't going anywhere. The San Ysidro house stayed the same: the Failure's deal still hadn't come through in Mexico, the Witch still whipped around the corners like a wind, late and busy. The only one making money was Riley, who had already started a rock band. The summer before we'd been in a commercial together. The Swans weren't moving, but they didn't have the money to send Daniel away to college. He was going to stay at UCLA. He didn't seem to mind. We sat on the steps in back of the house, our heads on our knees, staring at the plain dry canyons. "My grandfather's jewelry business, he sells diamonds, I might do that and make a ton of money. Or I could work in a bank like my cousin. I might do that or developing. I'd like to buy my own boat, then you don't have to worry about anything, a sixty-foot yacht and you could live on it and go around the world."

"What about astronomy? I thought you were going to major in astronomy."

"I'll do that too. I could go to school at night, if I make all that money I won't need a degree, I'd just want the classes, I don't know, I might do anything."

Before I left for college, it seemed my mother was working all the time. One night we parked in front of a house on an empty wide street north of Sunset. The palm trees seemed to whisper over the lawn. "Too bad Idie's dead," my mother said as we made our way up the driveway. A Mrs. Dover invited us into the kitchen. We followed her as she slip-slopped through the cluttered house. "The shanty Irish," my mother mouthed.

I sat next to my mother at the kitchen counter, listening while Mrs. Dover made tea and talked about Melly's heart. Melly's heart this, Melly's heart that. Mrs. Dover moved slowly, like a fat person. Mrs. Dover said she could cook only some things now and not others, now they could walk but never too fast, they took rides but not far and all because of Melly's heart. We listened nicely, my mother smiling as if she understood the moment before Mrs. Dover said it.

"It's all the same heart," Mrs. Dover whispered over the kitchen counter, as if she was afraid of being overheard. "Idie was a year younger when she, you know. He's sixty-five now."

"But you forget, Trish, that he's in good shape." My mother's voice scolded with conviction. I didn't know whether she was telling the truth or not. "Idie was fat, Trish. And she didn't exercise. And do you know what she ate?"

"So you think he'll hang on a while?" Mrs. Dover laughed a short laugh.

"She ate doughnuts. Jelly doughnuts. That's all she'd eat. The dietitian forbade the aides to give them to her but she wouldn't touch anything else. Sure. Jelly doughnuts with powder sugar on top."

"I didn't know that."

"Well, of course. He'll live another ten years, Trish. At least. *At least.* Now, you're the one who needs more exercise. You know, when Melly's seventy-five, he's going to be in good shape and he's going to want a wife in good shape, too."

"You think so?" Mrs. Dover looked up at my mother.

My mother and I ran down the gravel driveway to the car, giggling. She drove fast through the residential streets to the store windows on the way to Baskin-Robbins. "Boy, would you look at that suede suit. Isn't *that* elegant. That's what I need, a few good suits that'll take me anywhere."

"I'm sure it's incredibly expensive." Clothes had been so easy when we worked in a store, like a game, getting more and more, making outfits. Now, they seemed hard and important again.

"Yes, but it's quality. That's what I've always done. I've always bought the best, good fabrics and with a good cut that's really well made. And then it lasts forever."

"Fine if you can afford it in the first place." I worried about my mother managing her money, after I was gone.

She sighed. "You can't even let me have a little fun, imagining, can you?"

□

As if it were something unconnected to my leaving, incidental, my mother would mention her plans to kill herself.

"I might just drive over . . ."

"You'll get the insurance."

"You'll be *fine*."

"I want you to invest that, it'll be a lot of money."

"You're a survivor."

I did not believe her and I did. I knew my leaving would make a difference, could make a difference.

Anyway I left.

The Saturday after my last shoot for "Sante Fe," I made an appointment to get my hair cut. I told my mother in the morning.

"What are you going to have, a trim?"

"More like a cut."

"Oh, Honey, no. Don't, Ann. You'd be crazy to get more than a little trim. Why do think you got Marie Iroquois, that's what's cute about you, Honey. And don't think that doesn't matter at college, too, believe me. Really, it's the truth, Ann."

"I'm just telling you. For your *information*. I'm not asking for advice. I'm just saying, I'll be gone between eleven and noon. You better find something to do with yourself, that's all."

What she found to do with herself was drive to the beauty shop, sit and read magazines in the front, by the window. I'd never had my hair cut since those boys chopped it off on Halloween when I was eight. Just trims. I'd always had long hair. It had seemed important.

I watched the woman and her scissors in the mirror, the little wet pieces falling everywhere. A circle of hair stuck around my shoulders on the cotton smock and a wider circle fell on the floor. The little pieces felt sharp, they itched my neck.

My mother ran up. "What are you doing? She only wanted a little bit. Oh, Honey, look. You just wanted a trim."

They each stood over me, one of them holding scissors.

"That's not what I said."

"You sure did, that's what you told me at home this morning.

You said just a little. She's got six inches off already, it's going to look awful. What are you letting her do to you?"

"Please sit down, Mom." I looked at my hands lying there, on the beauty shop smock. They could have been anyone's hands.

My mother turned to the woman cutting my hair. The woman, pivoting on one foot, leaning close, cut in quick, decisive clips. "Why don't you at least undercut it, so it turns *under*, not up? That's just going to flip up when it dries. It's going to be awful."

"I am undercutting it," the woman said.

"Jeez, Honey, I could have taken you to the man who does me in Glendale. You should see the beautiful cuts. The girls your age come out with this full, long, bouncy hair. And it just curls. He cuts it so it goes under." She picked up a panel of my wet hair and dropped it back onto the cotton smock. "She's thinning it," she said. "You're thinning it."

"I am not thinning it," the woman said.

"May I ask you where you learned to cut hair?"

"Mom."

"I'm just asking her a question. She can tell me."

"I studied in New York and in London."

I smiled for pretentious Westwood, where PhDs worked at the post office and my hairdresser studied in London.

"Where in New York?"

"I studied with Christiane at Michel Heron and with André."

"Oh. I haven't heard of them," my mother said. "Oh, stop, please. You're not going to take any more off, are you?"

"I'm going to shape it, so from the bangs down to the shoulder, it's one line." The woman gestured with her comb. "Okay?"

"Oh, God. I don't know why you do this to me. Well, fine, it's your life. But you just have to rebel, don't you? You have to make yourself ugly. Don't you see, Honey, you're cutting off your nose to spite your face."

"My hair. I'm cutting my hair."

"Are you jealous of me? Is that it? Because, Honey, you shouldn't be. I'm your mother. I can help you. If you'd only let me. You should see the cute cuts they're giving."

She walked out of the border of the mirror. Then she came

back. "I can't stand it. I can't sit here and watch her doing that to you."

"You're not sitting," I said.

The woman kept turning on one foot and snipping. The hair was now an inch above my shoulders. I turned and saw my mother in the front of the store. She sat back down in her chair and opened a magazine.

Next to me, a man blow-dried a young girl's hair, pulling the brush tightly away from her face. The two hairdressers smiled. "Is she always this way?" The woman looked at me in the mirror.

"Just about my hair. She always wanted me to have long hair."

The woman turned her blow-dryer on. In a minute, my hair began to look beautiful, a neat thick clean line next to my chin.

My mother appeared in the mirror again, holding her magazine in one dropped hand, moving around the chair, circling me. I wouldn't look at her. She stared at my face in the mirror.

"You'll just let anyone be your mother, won't you? You let anyone but me."

I never did hear from my father. I used to think, he might see me on TV and write me or call me or something, but nothing ever happened. I don't know, maybe he tried or maybe he didn't have a TV or whatever. I suppose it could have been anything.

I left lightly. Everything my mother wanted, I gave her. She kept all my baby things, my first teeth in bottles, my skates from when I was five years old. There was a work shirt she liked, I gave it to her. She pointed to things and I left them in the backhouse. Anything to get away. And when she took me to the airport, she walked me to where I got on the jet, she walked to where they wouldn't let her come any farther without a ticket and when she kissed me, she looked at me, so I pulled out these new jeans I bought, they were Jag, and Jag was just a new name then, they were like my favorite thing, and she knew it and I gave them to her.

"You may not see me again," she said, real softly, because

other people were passing, busy, with little suitcases, and I guess they could hear.

I stuffed the jeans in her hands and she looked at me, eyes all grateful, huge like a pet's. But that night, when I called her from Providence, she answered the phone on the first ring, jangled, and said, Well, the pants didn't fit her, I'd obviously bought them for me not for her and I didn't understand the meaning of a present, I'd never learn how to give.

That night she talked about the insurance policy again, the cliffs of Big Sur. I called her back and she didn't answer and then I called her and couldn't find her for three days until I reached the Kellers, who told me she was out practicing on the tennis courts.

For years, I didn't go home.

CAROL

■ □ ■

■ □ ■ □ ■ □ ■ □ ■ □ ■ □ ■

14

THE STONE AND THE HEART

■ □ ■

It was like a stone, something in me. The way a hook needles a
fish, it hurt when I tried to move away from it. And then it
turned and I was worse. Love sunk like that in me once. Like a
hook so I couldn't think of anyone else.

It was a long long time, too long. And I was alone, dwelling. I
passed Benny's room every day, we kept the door shut and I was
the only one who went in. I said I had to clean and I did clean
every day, wiping dust with a soaked rag before it ever had a
chance to settle. I oiled that old wood dresser, wiped the windowsill. We'd built the house ourselves when we were married,
so it showed just how many years had gone, that wood. And then
I polished each one of his things. He had that fish hanging on the
wall that he caught in Florida, they each had their rifles mounted
over his bed, and then there were all his models. He spent hours
putting those together when he was little. He had such patience.
I started with the hotrods and I dusted them with a real soft piece
of chamois and then I stood up on a footstool to do the planes.
(He had planes and you had stars. He gave them to you—you put
them up yourselves on your ceiling, those glow-in-the-dark stars.
I remember because your ma was mad. She wanted me to pay to
repaint. But then, later, Gram and I stood in your room once—
after you'd gone and moved away—and we figured out those were
real constellations. We found Big Bear and the Little Dipper,
Pleiades. You must have stood by the window and copied it all
down.)

I used to take his shirts and socks out of the drawers and wash them in a special laundry. Then I put them all back where they were. I remembered exactly which T-shirt was on top that first day when I came in, and how each went underneath. It took four hours to clean the whole room and I always felt sorry to leave. I used to pick up that rock from Pikes Peak and just stand in the middle of the room and hold it. Those windows are small, I don't know why, that's the way they were doing them that year we built the house I suppose, so somewhere on the floor, there'd be one small square of light. I slipped off my shoes and stood on the light in my nylons and held that rock and looked down at it. It was an ordinary big rock, gray and dusty. It could have been from anywhere. But it was labeled *Rock From Pike's Peak* and Benny had held it, like I was doing. I don't know what I thought I'd get from that stone, holding it like that, in the sun. I looked and looked at it and saw the same thing: the dirt color, gray, the plainness. But I felt like something would come into me through my hands. I understood then the way I don't anymore about religion. It is a matter of concentration, a promise never to let anything else come between. I had that kind of bond, then.

I don't mean going to church and giving charity, none of that, that we still do. I mean the religion that is a private thing, trying to clean yourself out, so you're an empty house, a dustless vessel.

I've lost that. That I don't have anymore.

I spent half my day in that room for a year, the first year. Nobody bothered me much about it. Jimmy kept following his own map. We didn't have too much to do with each other. We'd always had the twin beds that made up together to be a queen. That year, I didn't even bother pushing them to the center in the morning. I started sleeping facing the wall. I liked that sour cold air in the crack. That's how I was then. It tasted to me like hosts on my tongue, dust dissolving.

Then once I was in Ben's room, cleaning, and Mary Griling was riding outside on the lawn mower. Jimmy hired her to help around the yard and I don't know why, with the noise and all, but I dropped the rock I was holding in my hand and it fell and shattered on the floor.

After that, I didn't go into the room. We could keep things the way they were more by not looking than by care. I shut the door then and nobody ever went in. I drove in the car and got a rock from the quarry and taped the label on and put it back. I never once touched it again.

Time hadn't stopped, I just had. The next year, eleven months, Jimmy went in the hospital for the heart. He was one of the first in Wisconsin to have the open heart surgery. I don't remember anymore if I was scared. I still lived in another world; the darkness. I didn't mind the waiting at all and in the hospital, that's most of what it was. I didn't mind anything as long as they left me alone. I'd settle in my chair and sink down and then I'd be off. It was as if I had work to do and when they left me alone I could take it out and begin unraveling and get started on what needed to be finished.

I thought about the leg. I worked that night over so much in my mind and every time it hurt. I was like a person with a loose tooth, running his tongue over the sore place again and again, activating the pain. If it was still there, I wanted to touch it.

We were in the trailer, Jimmy and I, the night they called. We were already asleep. The phone there was on a wall in the dinette. We both got up when it rang, we must have known, it was so late at night and we sat across from each other at that little dinette table.

Jimmy talked in the phone but he held it away, so I heard everything they were saying. Right then we had to choose. We could fly him down to Milwaukee to a big city hospital or keep him where he was, in this little Emergency Room. And we couldn't ask anybody, we didn't have time. I was wearing rollers, I touched them to make sure and then I remember staring at Jimmy's hand and my hand on the dinette table. Both our hands looked familiar and old, like gloves, something you'd wear every day that would take on a shape.

Well, neither of us knew.

And I was surprised, because for all Jimmy's wanting to be the man, he looked at me and asked me what to do. Real even. And I knew he'd listen.

"I don't know, Jimmy," I said. I looked and just begged for him to choose. We saw into each other's eyes and they went back and back and back and neither of us knew. He waited. And so I said, "Maybe we'd best keep him here."

He told the man on the phone and in no time, the next thing I knew, we were in the car, on the highway, driving. I don't know how we ever got our clothes on. Times like that, there are miracles you hardly notice.

I remember riding that night. It was eighteen miles to the hospital and Jimmy drove fast. We were the only car on the road. We didn't say anything to each other, but we had the windows open and I could smell. That was the only time in my life, there in the car, when I really felt the word married. We were married. Other times words like that meant other people.

Outside, earth rushing in, and the wetness of pine. Jimmy turned the radio on to country music, a woman singing, "I Fall to Pieces"; her voice whining like the whine of green air just out the windows, clinging. "Always," she sang. And I felt almost happy.

I'd been to the Emergency Room in Bay City so many times with Benny. He'd had to have stitches, he'd had sprains and once the cast. When he was real small, he'd tried to jump off the garage roof. He wanted to fly like Peter Pan. He had you up there too, but we didn't know. I'd found him, curled and bloody, and raced him off to the hospital in the car.

You had been afraid to jump. You kept so quiet up there that even after we came home in the station wagon, nobody knew to get you down. I fixed cinnamon toast and Benny was watching cartoons in the breezeway, and it was Benny who remembered you all of a sudden.

No one else ever died. Granny didn't. It was the same leg, the left, and they took it off just above the knee. Mom thought a long time whether it was the right thing, but there was a tumor, they had to get it out. They operated in winter. And I remember the shock in spring, when I first saw her walking out with the crutches. She wore big high rubber boots on the one leg and a jacket. But she wasn't wearing any stockings and you could see where the leg ended against the fabric of her skirt. The skirt was blue, a real girlish print, and the leg was white and wrinkled and old. It came to a point and a knot, they tied her skin at the end like a sausage. She went outside every day to feed that pony. But Mom said later what broke her spirit were those crutches. She couldn't ever get used to walking that way. She was ninety-one years old. And once she couldn't be outside, running everything, bossing the world, then she didn't want to live anymore.

With Hal in the army, that was the left leg too. He said those army doctors thought he was crazy, that second time he came out of the hospital. They made him march and at night, when they couldn't see, his knee swelled up to the size of a basketball, and it hurt him. But then, when he went to the infirmary in the morning, it fell down again. They made him march. Finally, he said if they'd give him a camera he'd take a picture. And then those doctors wanted to operate and he said no. Who knows what they would have done, those army doctors. And once he came home, it healed by itself. It still hurts him, when it rains I notice a limp.

Jimmy got to be the strong one, after he'd had the operation. When he came home from the hospital, we both worked together and that's when we really got started in the health. That's how I learned the vitamins, he had to take so many pills every day. I made an effort to do the right things. I took them, too, we changed our whole way of eating. I did everything the way we were supposed to, fruits and vegetables and fibers. I threw out the frying pan. And Jimmy really was good. They told him to lose thirty pounds and he lost it. They told him one drink a day, that's it. And that was it. He had to walk five miles and he did, all the way past the tracks on the new road over on Brozek's land, where they put the developments. He got to know some of the people in duplexes on those spoon-shaped drives. They'd wave at him when they went out to water their lawns. He bought the walking machine and he walks in the laundry room when it's too cold outside. He built muscle, he kept telling me he was in better shape than he had been for years. And I think that gave him a new lease. I think that was the turning around for him.

People told me, after the operation, a heart gets scars and creases, wrinkles, lines like a hand.

He took an interest in new things. He read up on solar. He dreamed the idea for a swimming pool. He'd walk in his aerobics clothes past Brozek's land and come home wanting to sue.

"Not yet," I told him. "Nothing doing."

I was still in the dark, with a long way to walk before the end. I'd be doing the dishes, my ring on the sill, looking out the window to the backyard and I'd try to imagine how Ben would have walked on the grass, without the leg. Sometimes I'd see him walking on water, crooked over the wavy green. Then I'd have to rub my eyes. I couldn't imagine him with crutches, even limping, I couldn't imagine Ben slow. He always loved speed, for the feel of it. When he was real little, he used to haul a stick in the backyard and spin, he'd go so fast, he wouldn't hear you if you called. He got like that sometimes when he ran. And then later, the machines. The minibike, dirt bike, tractors, lawn mowers, snowmobiles. And then the car. I think, truthfully, Benny sped, too, on those empty peninsula highways late at night, sure. It wouldn't have had to be Jay. It could have been Benny alone. He loved anything that went fast. Nobody could keep up with him.

I thought and I thought and I didn't get anywhere. I felt a place in me where it hurt every time I touched, the stone. It was the darkness I swallowed.

I told myself: he could have died those minutes on the helicopter in the air, between the peninsula and Milwaukee. But the way it was was the only way it was: while that old doctor fooled, fussing with the leg, pinning it, the heart stopped.

You were the one who let Gram see him. When a person thinks the same thoughts again and again, they each take on a shape and a color, almost a taste in your mouth. And my thinking, Well, at least Gramma saw him, was clear relief, like green-white air, antiseptic as an after-dinner mint from a nice restaurant, that cleans out all your head. It let me go on to other things.

That day in the hospital was a court of law. Gram was already in for a stroke and then we'd had to tell her about Benny. And even under the drugs, she was fighting us. She wanted to go and see her Ben.

Her arms pushed up, beating out of the blankets, and Adele was standing on one side, keeping her down. When I watched that I remembered years ago, opening the bathroom door and you were standing in the big clawfoot tub. It was the same thing—you were hitting, fighting to come out, and your mother stood pushing you down.

In the hospital, Gram was yelling. "You let me alone. Get away you." But from the drugs, her voice sounded different, real small and far away. "Get," she said, as if she were spitting out the pit of something.

"Mom, you've got to stay here," Adele said.

"I want to see him once more and I'm going to," Gram was saying, but she really wasn't all right. She bit her own lip so hard it bled. I was on the other side of the barred bed from Adele. I saw that bright blood trickling down her chin and I wiped it off with the hem of my dress.

I think maybe what really hurt Adele was Gram didn't seem the least bit interested to see the two of you. It had been years already since you'd been gone. That, I'm sure of it, was the drugs. She could only think of one thing at a time and that was, going to see him.

You sat away from us all, in a chair in the corner. Your mom stood on the one side of the bed with a young doctor in those mint green clothes they wear. He kept fingering his stethoscope.

I had the priest over by me. He was fingering his beads. But neither of them said anything, they let us fight over her.

I wanted Gram to go. It was selfish, because I didn't really know how sick she was either, but I wanted her to go, no matter what. I wanted Adele out of there, back in California. This was our life here. She'd left it.

"She's got to stay, Carol. She could have a stroke and DIE," Adele said. Right there, over Gramma.

Gramma started crying, fingering her sheet. "I am *not* going to die," she said.

Adele turned to the doctor. It was like an instinct in her, turning to men more than women, looking up, and to MDs more than ordinary men.

The doctor dropped his hands from the stethoscope. He seemed reluctant to say. "We can give her another sedative, but it is a risk."

"Do you really want to go, Mom?" I said. Here I was leaning over and shouting loud as if she were a child. Her hearing was just fine. "You know, if you aren't so good, you don't have to go. Benny would understand."

"OF COURSE he would," Adele interrupted, yelling. "In fact, he'd RATHER. He'd rather you not go."

"I want to go and I'm going," she said. She sat up on the bed. "I told you. I want to see him."

I looked at my priest. He bent his head down so I could see the freckles on his balding head. He prayed.

"Carol, I just don't think she should go. It's not going to help Benny anymore and it could, you know—"

I just didn't know. "I don't know," I said. "I just don't know."

Your mother turned all of a sudden and looked at you. "What do you think, Ann?"

We all looked at you then, in the corner. You were wearing scuffed-up cowboy boots, like they wore around here, and your legs crossed. That was the first time I'd noticed you'd grown up. Your legs were long and you moved your arms like someone definite.

"Let her go," you said. You recrossed your legs, put the other one on top. Your boot was worn down in the heel. "She should go."

"You really think so, Annie?" your mom asked.

And you nodded.

So she had a sedative and we held her, me on one side, Adele on the other. Just that walk from the station wagon to the back door of Umberhum's, it seemed like a long ways. I parked as close as I could to the door. The sun was so bright she couldn't look. We walked real careful but her face was confused, as if she thought her ankles were going in different directions, out of control.

I'd driven by Umberhum's Funeral Parlor a million times, but that day I felt like I owned it. Adele and I almost carried Gram in, she was so light, like nothing on our elbows, as if we were fooling, playing the Emperor's New Clothes, and everyone stepped back, hushing, for no one who was there.

Then her weight seemed to fall back into her in a heap from the sky when she knelt on the pew by the coffin. For the first time she seemed to me an old woman, the way she settled on that pew. She reached over and touched Benny's hand. I was thinking how weak and helpless she looked, that we still had to get her up and back, and maybe Adele was right and this was a mistake. I couldn't tell from her face if she knew anything that was going on. She stayed a long time before we realized she'd fallen asleep.

But it wasn't a mistake. She didn't die, either.

I didn't like anything, anymore, for a long time and that's why I had to go away. I saw the bad in everyone around me. As soon as she was well, my mother bored me. Her life seemed like a windup toy. She traced the same steps, through the same little rooms, bedroom, kitchen, bathroom, every day. She ate her meal off the same dish and then she washed it. And that's all she talked about, what food she put on that same plate in that same kitchen and how much she paid for it.

Hal was worse. Merry left, Tina was gone, they lived in a truck up out of town by the bay, with Merry's new boyfriend. And Hal had a girl, that Patty, who I'd always liked, but he treated her like dirt, like nothing. I saw him hit her, plenty, he used to hold her jaw and slap her. And she didn't even fight back. She just stood there and her bangs shook.

There was nothing I did. I went into the store one day to balance the books. I had a cup of coffee from the Big Boy, I was just going to concentrate down in the darkness and do the numbers of the books. I wasn't going to pay any attention.

Then Hal walked in. "How's Patty?" I said, trying to be nice.

He shrugged. "I only like her because she goes down on me."

I shut the drawer in my desk that was open and got my keys out of my purse. I went out to the car and drove home. For a long time, the books didn't get done.

Adele always called, always asking for money. Once she said she had cancer. She sent Gram a Polaroid of herself opened up, in operation on the surgery table. I'm not sure why, but I knew right away she was lying. That made me so mad, she gets you down. It was the first thing Jimmy and I did together for a long time. We needed to find out for sure. She'd told us the hospital she'd been in and from them we found the doctor. He confirmed it to us: there was no cancer. My sister was a fine, healthy woman. Her operation had been purely cosmetic. He turned out to be a plastic surgeon. Apparently, sometime in college, your mother had silicone implants. One had shrunk and now she was having her breasts evened out.

Well, we told Gram and, that once, Adele didn't get her money.

See, it was around that time I found the stone in me, that hardness I'd swallowed. I felt it, a cold dark, it pressed back against my fingertips. I didn't tell anyone, I hoarded, kept it to myself. It stayed under my left breast, always. The hook was there. As soon as I found it, it stopped hurting. I touched it many times, to test. I couldn't sit still, I always wanted to be alone. I excused myself four, five times in an hour to go to the ladies' room to touch it. I went into a trance like that, I didn't think. Touching the stone in me.

I went away to their retreats. In the woods in Michigan, Minnesota, I even drove up to Ontario. Never once to a doctor. For a long time it was my secret. I read the Bible. I memorized: *the fear of God is clean, enduring forever.*

We are strangers before thee.

I came to know my own wickedness, how I hoarded. Around campfires in pine woods, clearings like our own in the Vale of Valhalla, painted rocks in a circle, I knit and felt alone. The others, nuns and churchwomen, fell in together and did good. They darned the priests' socks. They made potato salad, they gossiped and laughed, washing pots and pans. I wouldn't join. I prayed. I pleaded for cleansing, there in the north. I wanted the cold to come and burn the dust, everything impure out of me. A crystal agate, something forced by fire. I touched the stone while I prayed, the stone I wanted to save. It was the deepest part of me. My fire. My good.

But the others complained. Priests took my hands and asked me to forget. One of them read my palms; the right hand and the left, what you are and what you were born to be. *There is a time to mourn and a time to forget.* I yanked back. Father James sat me down and gave me suggestions, how to make my way with the other women, as if I were an unpopular girl.

That was when I finally went back home. The women stood in front of a silver trailer, opening bottles of relish and ketchup for a barbecue. All of a sudden, they looked mismatched and shabby to me, the nuns in their hiking clothes. Socks under sandals, the red acne scars on their skin, they were women who had never been pretty, women who would never have sons.

I didn't want to scrub with them on the ground, in a campsite. I'd wanted silence and cold, I'd wanted to climb. Gossip, cooking—those nuns played bridge on picnic tables—all that I could have with my own.

I drove home. And when I got there, I knew I'd given in. I was tired, I unloaded all my gear and dumped it in the basement. I made a call for an appointment with the doctor.

And what did I see that first day back from Canada, when I opened the newspaper, but a picture of Ben's little Susie engaged to marry to Jay Brozek. All five of those Brozek boys came back from Vietnam. No one else ever died. The Brozek girls were pretty, three or four of them went to college, all on scholarship. Sheila got married and now she lives across the street. Every year, Christmas Eve, they sent their youngest with a basket of cookies to Gram. Phil and Jimmy talked when they met on the yard, Phil told Jimmy to sue. It got me down.

I cut out the picture and put it under glass on the desk top where I paid my bills. I went into the bath and soaked for a long

time. I looked at my breast, felt for the stone. I seemed so different now that I was back and given up, I almost thought it wouldn't
hurt, I wouldn't find it. But there it was, rubbery, mobile, the
same as when I'd first touched it and I knew then that it was
something bad they would take away from me. I'd have to go in
the hospital for them to cut it out.

I don't know what I thought, that that Susie wouldn't ever get
married. She was only sixteen when it happened. She had to go
on and have a life, too. I kept looking at that picture every month
when I paid my bills, it's still there, under the glass. And now,
you know, it doesn't bother me. Because around the eyes and the
mouth, Jay turned out to look like Benny. She must have seen
that, too.

I was glad about you but you weren't here. The season you were
on TV, we bought a machine to tape your show. During the daytime, I'd put you on and just look at you. I thought of you every
once in a while and thought that you'd turned out to be a nice
girl. I was glad to have you for a niece. But I never wrote. I could
have, I had time. I could have at least sent a card. I should have,
I was still too much by myself, I wasn't near as good as I should
have been.

You came the one Christmas from college on the Greyhound
bus, you saw Hal and Jimmy fight. Gram didn't feel too well, she
wouldn't have even stayed up if you hadn't been here, but Hal
came late and then he played rough with Tina. Poor Jimmy said,
maybe next year we could all get to Florida and Adele could come
and meet us there.

And Hal said by next year, he'd be a millionaire and he'd have
a helicopter. He said maybe he'd visit us for a day in Florida and
then go to Haiti.

That Patty put up with all of it, his drinking, everything, and
all the while, she worked too. She typed for a pediatrician. Now,
she won't even speak to him, he says, she won't say hello when
they run into each other in the mall.

That night, your mom called and I think she felt bad because you were here and she was alone then out in California. Well, she started in on Gram. Did you get the sweater, Did you get this, Did you get that. Oh, we were so used to it by then, it didn't get us down anymore. Gram and I just said no, no, not yet, real quietly, but we blamed it on the Christmas mail, said we were sure it would come tomorrow or the day after. And that seemed to calm her down.

She wanted to talk to Hal and I shouldn't have let her, he'd already been so rude to the rest of us, he was drunk. Well, he got on the phone and all of a sudden, he was yelling, I couldn't hardly even listen, he could be so mean. "You're a liar," he shouted. "You didn't send anything and you know it. That's bullshit. And every year since you've been out there you call and say the same damn thing and you know damn well you didn't do it! I don't care if you don't send anything, just don't give me this bullshit."

Jimmy finally tore the phone away from him. Then I guess you went and talked to her on the extension in the bedroom.

Hal and Patty left that night not so long after, Hal still drunk. He'd been drinking since I don't know when, he'd had a beer in his hand steady since he walked in our door.

And we wanted to keep Tina with us, put her to bed in Ben's room. I said I'd take her home in the morning.

But Hal said no, she was his and she was going with him. He grabbed her like he did by the hair so she was almost crying.

I took that Patty aside and asked her if she couldn't just drive or talk him into staying over and she said, no, she felt the same way, but she didn't dare fight. That really got him started, she said, the best thing she could do was go along with it.

Jimmy couldn't take it anymore, he went into the bedroom and said good night. That was it for him. And you and Gram and I stood like a little chorus huddled together in our boots there under the porch light. Patty sat on the passenger side, her face all flat and sour, and Hal took a long time unlocking his door. He drove a Ford pickup then. I bent down to Tina and said, "Where do you want to sleep tonight? Do you want to drive with your dad like this or should we fix you a nice bed and I can take you over to your dad's house in the morning?"

She wouldn't look at me. She squirmed, from one leg to the other.

"I don't know," she said.

All of a sudden, she went to the bathroom then, standing up, I guess she was scared. She couldn't hold it and Hal glared at me saying, "See, now look what you did. Trying to take my kid away from me."

She looked at the little puddle in the snow by her foot and then she started to cry, late, the way kids do sometimes. "I want to go with my dad," she said. And he hoisted her in and we stood and listened to the motor gunning and then watched the headlights make dizzy paths down the road, much too fast. All night, I jerked at noises, waiting for the phone. But nothing happened. They didn't die. Nobody else ever died.

Do you eat carrots? The doctor told me young girls who have cancer in their families should eat a carrot every day. There's something in it that prevents, the same thing that makes the carrot orange. I eat a carrot every day now and it hasn't come back yet. I go in for X-rays every six months and so far nothing has shown. He says I'm like a normal person again now. But they took so much out because I didn't go in right away. If you ever feel anything, you go right in because they say they can do it now and still save the breast. I wear a falsie and then in Florida, I have a bathing suit with it built right in. But it's in our family, both; the stones and the heart.

Hal went through a lot before he straightened out. For a long time, even when he was young, he always had to have a scheme. He tried to sell things around here to the neighborhood kids, he tried to get them to buy his creepy crawlers, he wanted them to pay to ride that horse. Well, in town, maybe so, but no kids out here were going to pay to get up on a pony.

Then, after Benny, he started taking his vacations out in Colorado. He likes it there. He's always said he might like to move someday. I hope he does, I hope he makes it. Well, he was in at the beginning of Breckenridge, before you heard about it as a place. Then the names you heard all the time were Aspen and Vail, Sugarloaf. Well, he put lots of money in, all his savings, and he borrowed from Gram and from us too, for this development. And it really seemed it ought to go. He went in with five or six others. It was a good idea, but somehow, when it all came through, it turned out the others owned the land and Hal owned the snowplows. And the snowplows broke down and that cost money to repair and pretty soon they rusted. In a couple years, he ended up paying someone else to take them off his hands.

He was behind from that for a long time. But he kept working at the store, ten, twelve hours a day until he got ahead a little. The next thing was those houses. He bought two little houses and he was going to renovate and fix them up and sell for a profit. And he worked on those too, Patty helped, he had Tina over there after school painting. But they were right by the railroad tracks, so nobody wanted to buy. He took a loss on those too.

He started the Chinese restaurant and the Frozen Yogurt and then one time he tried to get the Wisconsin franchise for some new Sony gadget. None of it panned out. He just doesn't have the knack for making money.

It's a good thing Jimmy got him started in the Rug Doctor, so at least he's got that and the pressure cleaners. His plans all came to nothing. He still talked, for years he was going to be a millionaire. Nothing he did ever worked.

Jimmy and I were back to normal, then, we had things in common. The health. We both take the Herbalife vitamins in the morning and we eat our cereal with wheat germ and brewers' yeast. You came quite a few times on your vacations, Gram was always glad about that. Each time, you went home with junk from the basement, nothing valuable, our old coats and Villager sweaters. You like that old stuff, I don't know what you do with all that junk. I kept hoping my old coat would turn up on TV. The once you wore those crazy earrings.

I remember, I overheard Jimmy talking to you in the breezeway. I was coming up from the basement with a load of wash. "She doesn't want to," he said. "Not once since Ben."

I stood still there on those steps. I didn't want to hear more.

"Maybe," you said and I could almost see you shrugging.

The next day, we put you on the Amtrak train, Gram and I. You had a duffel bag and a huge sack of peaches from the yard. That was the time, you told us, you fell in love, you wrote that you stayed up all night with him, eating peaches and watching the stars in the observation car.

Well, I didn't have hair then. I was still wearing the wig. All my burns from the trailer fire healed but I still didn't have my hair back. Such a thin down grew all over my head. I've seen it on some women with cancer.

That night, I stayed up late, Jimmy was out, it was his Elks night, they played poker. He kept up a social life, more than I did. When he came home, I heard him on his side of the room, undressing, hanging his clothes.

"Jimmy, are you hungry?" I whispered.

"You up, Carol?"

He switched the light. I was wearing an old nightie and I still had my wig on. "Let's have some ice cream," I said.

In the kitchen, I spooned out from the carton. He opened the sliding glass doors, never mind the bugs, the air smelled sweet, alfalfa and the hay. It smelled like a million dollars.

"Should we go outside and eat it?"

I took the blanket from the davenport in the breezeway and we spread it on the grass in the backyard. I dug out some Hershey's chocolate syrup back in the pantry from before we started the health. It was a loud summer night. The crickets were loud, the stars were near. Everything was dark around us. Next door, Gram had been asleep for hours, Griling's was dark, too. Bub had been gone quite awhile already then.

All of a sudden we were living on a road with mostly old people. We finished our bowls of ice cream and then Jimmy said, "Want some more?" He went in and brought out the whole carton and we ate from that with our spoons. Then that was done for, too.

I shivered a little and Jimmy rubbed his hands on my arms to warm me. All of a sudden, I felt shabby. It was an old flannel gown and I didn't ever bother with the falsie at night.

We lay down there on the grass and we started to sleep. I didn't know if he'd even want to touch me like that, the way I was. It wasn't like when we were young. But then it started. He put his hands under the nightie and rubbed my legs. He pulled the whole thing over my head. The wig caught on the collar and came off.

"Oh, Jimmy," I said.

"Shhh. Nobody's up."

I felt like our voices were drowned out by crickets. I remembered, I didn't want to kiss. I tucked my chin over his shoulder, I felt our legs moving on each other, crossing, and recrossing, the wetness of the grass.

We did everything but kiss. That seemed silly to us, maybe, kid stuff. When we woke up, it was still the middle of the night and the ground had grown cold beneath us. My shoulder was wrong. Jimmy said his hip hurt. So we lugged everything in and went to bed. We didn't find the wig, but we didn't look hard, I said, just leave it, we'd get it in the morning.

And we went in Ben's room and both slept in his little bed. We seemed smaller that night. In the morning, the whole room turned shades of gray, us too, our arms, our legs. I woke up and went to get breakfast ready, I left Ben's door open, Jimmy was still asleep, and then when I was standing in my robe by the counter mixing a blender drink, I remembered my head. I looked out the glass doors to the backyard and it seemed fresh and strong, the way the fields and grass here get in July. July is really our nicest, and it all looked the same, as if we'd never been there. Then I thought I saw a dark impression in the middle of the lawn. The grass was pretty tall, so it was darker there, crushed down. But I didn't see my wig and I wasn't going to go outside and look for it in daylight.

That morning, Jimmy talked to me, reminding. We paid for Adele's divorce, we were still at the store, trying to make a go of it, get out of the hole. He wanted to retire and build. A swimming pool, a Jacuzzi, the solar, a house in Florida. He wanted to give the Rug Doctor to Hal, for Tina's college education.

I felt something dissolving in me. Jimmy turned, made me look around. "We could have a nice life yet, Carol. We don't have much time left."

I said okay. We sued.

There where we'd slept, that's where Jimmy put in the swimming pool.

I come about once a week and water the flowers. I pray. I talk to him. I talk to Benny all the time. Oh, I don't know, I say, "I suppose you're real disappointed in me, in what I've been doing. You must not be too proud of your mother."

Jimmy wants ashes, he wants to be cremated into that dust. He says I should scatter him in the backyard. He never stops at the cemetery, even when he's driving past. But he doesn't really think Ben is here. I do, see.

Gram had seven strokes in all. After the first one, she snapped back in twenty-four hours. With each one it took a little longer. And she'd lost some by the last. "Ben, aren't you dead yet," she'd say to me, when she thought I was Benny. "Ben, I thought you died, Ben."

That last time, your mom called, she talked to all the doctors in the hospital and she had her doctors in Los Angeles give them orders. Gram had things in her hair, test things, wires she really never should have had to have. And all those years, Adele never visited, never once sent a card. But that was your mom. She yelled at me, ooh, in the hospital, it wasn't nice. But you know, we get along now.

They had to move Gram near the end. That night I stayed up and talked to her. They say the hearing is one of the last things to go. I don't know anymore what I said. That last night, I was holding her hand, she didn't seem happy, her mouth looked bitter and she kept calling Adele, Adele. She cried that name all night before she went.

She had a restless time. She'd turn around and toss and switch back and forth. She couldn't get comfortable. I was there when Granny, your great-grandmother, passed away and she got this

big, beautiful smile on her face. And I was waiting for something
like that to come to Gram. But it never did. I asked the doctor, I
asked, why couldn't that have happened to her, Granny was really
sort of a mean woman, and my mother was so good, and the doctor
said, Everyone does it in a different way. Every one is different.

Benny and my mother and my father all share the one granite
stone.

Somebody else finally died.

ANN

■ □ ■

■ □ ■ □ ■ □ ■ □ ■ □ ■ □ ■

15

A NEW CAR

■ □ ■

Christmases I did nothing. Holidays in repertory houses, huge silver and black, beautiful LA romances on the screen, sipping expensive coffee. I was in love, but I wouldn't go to his house, either. By that time families bugged me. Other people's as much as my own. We'd make out, touching each other's clothes; the same jeans, flannels, soft, worn-in things. We loved the movies; they were black and white, beautiful—everything we needed. We sat in the dark, audiences raucous from displacement, all of us away from home, gay men, foreign students, Jews, laughing wildly at *Sullivan's Travels*, *The Navigator*, or *Seven Chances*, gasping through *Hiroshima Mon Amour*.

No matter what, I wouldn't go to LA.

"Some people remember birthdays," my mother said and hung up the phone.

Finally, my mother and I rented a car in northern California, a compromise. She said she'd always wanted to see the wine country. We sat in the car, my mother straight in her seat, staring at her hands, looking deserving. I told her Leslie lived in Berkeley and I'd call her, she could come with us or not, whatever my mother wanted.

"I thought you said it would be just us."

"That's fine."

"I'd rather be just us," she said.

It was spring. We hadn't seen each other for five years. It was interesting just to look at her.

All day, my mother talked about retirement. "I know just what I want," she said. "I'll do it all in French country. I'll have a brick wall in the kitchen. Just real homey." In a restaurant, she tilted her head. "What's this? Is this Bach? I love Bach. Do you know Des Pres, Honey? Well, I mean, he's dead, but there's this record. I learn these things from Daniel Swan, he's a double major in music at UCLA. You wouldn't believe all the things I'm learning." She nodded in time. "This *is* Bach."

She snuck little pieces of bread into her mouth. "I've already started to get things. For the house," she whispered. "See that blackboard up there? I bought two old school blackboards like that. Even nicer. They're in the Swans' basement. And the pine chests I told you about are for the house, too. They'll eventually go in a bedroom. I have another armoire in Nan's garage. See, and then what I'll do is I'll have a big open kitchen and when you bring your kids home, a boyfriend or someone special, or no, just your kids, you always have nice friends, like Leslie and all of them, I'll have the menu written down on the blackboard so when you come down in the morning it'll all be written out."

"Where are you looking for this house?"

Her cheeks lifted. She folded her arms on the table. "I want somewhere where I can see the mountains and the ocean. The whole wide scope of things. It doesn't have to be a big place, I just want a little house, something simple."

"'Cause aren't houses in LA like a fortune now? I mean, hundreds of thousands of dollars?"

"You wouldn't believe it. Remember that little house I wanted to buy from Julie Edison? Eight hundred thousand dollars, they're asking now. Remember how I used to drive by? I could shoot myself now. I knew that area was going to be big, I knew it, if I'd have only trusted my instincts—"

"But we never had the money."

She seemed clear that day, her face intelligent and thin. Her arms refolded, rueful. "No, you're right. We never had the money.

But I do now. And I'm saving. So just wait. Someday your mom'll have a real great place for you to bring your friends home to. By the time you're in graduate school. That's when you really need it anyway. That's when the kids in your generation really start to get engaged. I hear it all the time on 'LA Good-Morning.' They're waiting even up until the thirties. Like my dentist."

"I don't know if I'm going to graduate school. Anyway, I'm living with this guy."

"This Henry." She shrugged. "I wish you'd waited. Pretty soon I'll have something you could really show someone."

"Well, I mean, I don't know if it's going to work out."

"But all the others there in Providence must see you're living with someone, all the real choice boys."

"Nobody really knows."

"Sure they do, don't kid yourself. And they don't respect you for it either, Ann, no matter what they say. A boy doesn't respect you when you give him that for nothing. I just remember when I came home from college, what did I have for a boy to see? Lime Kiln Road. And Grilings."

The waiter came, we ordered dessert.

"Well, I don't know, I'm not tied to LA, either. And I'm getting sick of all the driving. Maybe I'll just end up near you, I've heard Cape Cod and what is it, something Vineyard, is supposed to be gorgeous, they say they're the prettiest beaches in the world. I mean, if you really like it there, if you want to stay."

"I don't know what I'm doing. I'll probably just work for a while, travel around. I might waitress at some truckstop."

"With your advantages." She laughed. "I can't really see you at a truckstop."

"It could happen."

"Well, don't you dare. You know I worked in a cheese factory all through college. It wasn't so much fun. Speaking of truck-stops, I got a letter from Lolly." She unfolded a sheet of peach-colored paper from her purse. After all these years and no trips home, Lolly still wrote to my mother. And I knew for an almost fact, my mother never sent letters. After years of saying her mail

was lost, my mother wouldn't trust the U.S. Postal Service. She
believed mailboxes in LA were obsolete, that no one picked up
from them anymore. She said she opened one and saw cobwebs.
If she absolutely had to send something, she'd drive to the post
office and pay nine dollars for overnight express. Paying made my
mother trust things more.

I'd heard my grandmother complain. "I never get a card, nothing. Even when she calls and I send money, I never even get a
card to say thanks." It wasn't exactly laziness. It wasn't that she'd
forgotten them. I'd seen my mother trying to write something
down. She would sit at the table with a card or a piece of fancy
colored paper and she'd write and cross out and finally give up.
She had it in her mind that she would get married and be rich
and then she could make up for all she didn't send by wiring a
plane ticket out for her mother to visit and taking her to see everything and buying presents. That's just the way my mother was.

She smoothed out the soft paper of the Bay City *Press Gazette*
clipping; a photograph of Lolly hitting the one-million-dollar
mark, lifting her left arm up to a chart. Lolly sold real estate now,
she'd gone to school and gotten her license the year we left. "Let
me tell you, in Bay City, that must not have been easy. That's a
lot of little houses to add up to a million." My mother scanned the
letter. "And she's still having this passionate, that's what she calls
it, affair with the ex-priest. She lost her virginity at forty-five, can
you imagine that?" My mother wrinkled her nose.

"Do you think she'll ever get married?"

"No, I don't think so. I doubt it. But who knows? She does
have boyfriends."

"It sounds like they're mostly ordained."

My mother laughed. "You *are* funny, besides being factual."

"Maybe if we'd stayed in Bay City, you could afford a house
there."

"Oh, sure, I could buy a house there now, a great house. But
I'd never go back. It's really nothing, you know, no culture. Nothing." My mother took a pill bottle out of her purse and broke off a
piece of seaweed for each of us. "At my age, believe me, I need
all the E I can get."

□

As we left the restaurant, my mother noticed a weathervane on the wall, an antique deer, she wanted. I told her it looked like a decoration, but she went back in and found the owner. He accepted her check. We carried the deer to the car. "He'll fit in a linen closet," she said. "For the time being."

My mother had gone to an accountant and now she carried a black checkbook the size of a three-ring binder.

We skidded in front of a church. My mother was driving.

"Since when do you believe in God," I said.

She told me she wanted to light a candle for my grandmother. "I go to church every Sunday now. The pink Catholic in Beverly Hills. On Little Santa Monica." This Sonoma church stood empty, plain, with simple pews and a pine altar. But all the candles were either lit or burnt down to the bottom of their glass canisters.

"I'll blow one out and you can light it again."

She shook her head no. "We'll just say a prayer." Then she dragged out her long black checkbook again. "Turn around, would you?" She wrote a check on my back and folded it up, stuffing it through the coin slot.

I didn't have to ask the question.

"Sure, it's charity. It's a deduction, I deduct all these things now. And they'll take my check. Gladly."

She slipped her arm through mine. "You'll never guess who I saw at church last month. Tony Camden," she whispered. "I walked in and I saw this very good-looking head. But I only saw the back. You know. He was in front of me. But I thought to myself, Adele, that's one *very* good-looking back of the head. So I sort of elbowed, genuflecting, you know, I think I was a little late, and I knelt down next to him, and I look and who is it but Tony Camden. He was kneeling holding the pleats of his pants. And I thought, Boy, would I like to know him."

"Mom, he's married."

"Is he still? I'm not sure, I didn't see her. Anyway, so I sort of smiled you know and then it was time to sit up and he sort of looked at me and he smiled and I'd smile again and then when

we walked out at the end, it was this huge beautiful day, real
clear, you could see the mountains just like that, and we're standing on the steps and he looked at me and said, Bye-bye, and I
looked at him and said, Bye-bye. So I'll tell you, I'm not missing
one Sunday."

Inside a dim, windowless room, on a cement floor, we undressed.
A woman with feather earrings handed us rough, chlorine-
smelling towels, her heavy hair brushing our arms. We'd stopped
at the sign that said "Dr. Hickdimon's Mud Baths." My mother
knotted a towel above her breasts, making an easy shift. My
mother's brilliance is in a lot of things you notice if you're around
a person all the time, but which don't count for much in the world.
While we talked, her hands moved through her hair, taking bobby
pins from the edge of her mouth, arranging a perfect bun.

"This will be just what we need," she said.

The woman led us to a room with two long bathtubs standing in
the middle of the floor. Mud filled them to their thick curled brims
and spilled over onto the elaborate claw feet. This wasn't ordinary
mud. It seemed blacker, and twigs and roots showed. It bubbled.
A wooden plank floated on the surface of each tub.

It took a long time to lower us in. My mother went first. She sat
on the plank, her belly falling into a small sag. It was a shock, to
see her naked. She seemed both thinner and looser and I noticed
on one of her teeth there was a black hairline like a crack in
porcelain.

"Eeeeeee," she said, sliding into the mud. Sweat glistened on
her forehead like a cobweb.

Her eyes closed. "That feel good?" the woman asked.

"Mmmhmm," my mother murmured.

Then it was my turn. The woman kneeled on the floor and
pushed the plank so my legs went down like a seesaw. She covered the rest of me slowly, with handfuls of warm mud. You didn't
sink. The mud was too heavy. I could have lifted an arm or a leg
but it would have been hard. Underneath you felt a thick cushion,
we floated like the wood planks. Over me, the mud was about the
same weight a person is, sleeping on top of you.

"We've really come a long way, you know, Ann, when you think about it?" My mother turned, her chin bobbing on the surface, her neck smeared with the mud. Then her eyes shut and she smiled.

I thought of what my mother once said about her dying. She didn't want to be buried with the rest of our family in the cemetery above Prebble Park. She wanted to be mounted in a glass case, like a diorama at the Bay City Museum, only it would be in her grandchildren's house. They would change her clothes and accessories according to the season.

I was with my mother the day she'd thought of wanting a scarecrow. We rode and rode past farms until she found the one she liked. It stood alone, set back in a cropped corn field. We couldn't see it without squinting. The wind still lived in the scarecrow's sleeves. The barn and farmhouse were miles away, tiny in the distance.

She bought the scarecrow from a farmer. He accepted her yellow check. The scarecrow's clothes were faded and patched, the thinnest cotton. "He's really a work of art, you should see in back, the way his overalls have been mended. It's like an old quilt. He's all hand done."

The scarecrow had made my mother think of having herself mounted. It had been a joke in Wisconsin, when she'd been full of mischief, when we drove to the cemetery where our family plots were already owned. Now she'd never go back. She'd probably want to be cremated, scattered on California land, somewhere you could see the ocean and the mountains. She hardly ever made fun of things anymore.

I pushed my hand up to the lip of the tub to find her hand, but I could barely feel through the wet mud. Her hand was like something solid your fingertips hit when you're digging.

I'd been back to Wisconsin a million times, on slow Greyhound buses during college, where there was always one very young woman in back, her hair in a bandanna, hitting her kid, saying "Shit-up," softly before each smack, her voice pure as resignation, the kid wailing, arching higher every time, screaming, all the way to Bay City, where I skipped down, light, onto the snow-dusted pavement in back of Dean's ice cream parlor.

I remember the winter town, my grandmother asleep in the country at nine o'clock. Taking the Oldsmobile and driving by the Fox River; the old, old buildings of the men's Y, buying chili and pie at the lighted diner. I sat on a stool smoking, looking out the window. And liking it so: the yellow streetlamps, coal and sulfur piles, smokestacks by the river. A girl going home to a mill town, the familiarity and the strangeness.

I drove to bars at night. Pool tables. Boys sheepish in army coats, home whole from Vietnam. Some. Bashful with me because they knew I went away. I'd gone to college.

To one I said, "I look much better at home." It felt easy here in the old bars, stained walls, the thick inside air. I knew these boys.

"Jeez, you must look great there because you sure look pretty now."

I almost got arrested for stealing a hot fudge pitcher at Dean's. A manager from somewhere else made me take it out of my purse, hurt my arm when I twisted away. Then I had to walk out of the store, in the aisle between warm glass cases, where the intricate-colored German cookies worth a million dollars blinked.

I always drove the Oldsmobile. My mother had never let me touch our Lincoln, even when I was learning. She felt terrified I would ruin it and then she couldn't get to work. I learned on Daniel Swan's ancient Triumph and on Peter Keller's Mercedes. But my grandmother walked with me to the garage, wearing her plastic rainboots, a clear scarf covering her head, and patiently got in at the passenger side and folded her hands in her lap. The Oldsmobile smelled like my grandmother. The tin cans with their coffee labels worn off that we used for watering at the cemetery rattled in the backseat.

It was a smooth, easy car, heavy on roads.

□

The last time I went, Carol picked me up at the airport, thin in a lemon-colored pantsuit, taking me to a new American car, a convertible.

"He builds now," she said as we pulled into their gravel driveway. When I stepped out, with my suitcase, Jimmy stood in work boots, on top of the roof, holding huge coils of something silver.

He'd retired from the Rug Doctor and now he built in their wide backyard.

It was nothing like it had been. There was a laned Olympic swimming pool, a garden, blond rocks planted among petunias, an elevated redwood deck, with a redwood ladder to the hot tub. It looked like pictures of California.

"That's the solar," Carol said. Jimmy stood installing the silver coils to heat the pool year round. He climbed down and shook my hand. His voice seemed breathless all the time now. He'd built everything himself, slowly.

Carol still kept the books for the store and now she also sold the Herbalife, a menu of vitamins she and Jimmy ate every morning at the white dinette table, looking out at the new backyard.

Hal was changed entirely. He was thinner and he'd moved back home, into the tiny bedroom he and Ben had shared when they were growing up. He slept in his own small bed. When I stayed there, I slept in that room too. Every day, Hal woke up and dressed while I was asleep. I heard him moving around; he seemed exceptionally neat now, spare of movement. He worked at Three Corners, managing the pressure-cleaning machines, renting out the Rug Doctor. He drove to work before seven in the morning. On the bedside table rested a large, hardback book with a pink padded cover like a Valentine's candy box. *Our Daily Helper*, read the title, and the pink satin ribbon was always placed in that day's prayer.

I told Carol my mother still had both breasts, the last time I'd seen her.

"I thought so," she said. "You know the funny thing is we get along now, your mom and I."

For some reason that made me sad.

Mostly, my aunt drove me around places. Museums, antique shops, flea markets, the huge untouched Goodwill and Salvation Army stores by the river. I liked to find old things.

Friday night, we went out for fish fry. The restaurants flew in the fish, frozen, from Canada because the Fox River and the bay were polluted by the paper mills. Carol said the Wildlife Preservation Center had cameras out from the local news; the ducks' beaks twisted, they were born mutated, from eating the polluted fish. "And you should smell the East River, does it stink," she said. "They say it'll take ten years to clean it up."

My grandmother's house, in the yard next door, had been rented.

"A young couple where they both work," Carol said. "He's a floor manager at the Shopko."

I looked at it every day I was there, a dark house with low windows above the ground. The grass had grown tall against the siding. Carol said they hired Mary Griling to mow both lawns.

It made me think of once when I sent my grandmother a blank notebook covered in fabric for a diary. When I helped Carol clean out the house, the dresser drawers, I'd found the book wrapped in wax paper, the pages thick and perfectly white.

I couldn't stand the food, after a day or two it drove me crazy. Not one thing was fresh. The lettuce, the iceberg lettuce, seemed old. Jimmy took us all for dinner at the new Holiday Inn. It was a buffet; sweet wine, too much food, races for the shrimp, everything else overcooked. I hated it and hated myself hating it.

I told Lolly, when she showed me her office. She worked for Dan Sklar now, we walked through his Japanese rock garden, our heels sinking in the moss. I told her how I couldn't stand the Holiday Inn buffet.

"On the west side, oh, you didn't like that? Oh no, hmm, well,

that's really my favorite place, they have a new chef over there."
She laughed her old sly laugh. "Oh, well, if you didn't like that,
you really have outgrown Bay City. Because that's really about the
best restaurant there is, here."

Lolly had some kind of diabetic anemia and she had to eat
protein every few hours. In the office, she took out a small package of tinfoil from her purse and unwrapped it. It was a cold sliced
turkey heart.

Once, from Providence, I'd called information and found Ted Diamond's number. He still had a listing in Bay City. It turned out he
was married, with five sons. His wife sounded nice on the phone.
When she put him on, he said he was okay, tired. "Your mother,"
he said with a bad laugh.

Carol told me after they'd put in the pool they ran into Ted and
the new wife somewhere. A week or two later, it was in summer,
the new wife called and asked if she might bring the little boys
over to go swimming. They didn't know each other, just that Ted
had been married to my mother once. Carol said no she had
bridge club and couldn't let them come when she wasn't there
because of insurance. The wife had called four or five times
again.

Once I found a Christmas card in the mail, one of those pictures,
with Ted and the wife and the five little boys dressed in identical
red blazers with gold buttons, in front of a big fireplace with five
red stockings. The wife had written on the bottom, "Ted sends his
love and he'll write you a letter after the new year."

The thing with Ted is I always know where to find him. And,
like with most people that way, since I could call him and talk to
him any time, I never feel like it.

They all got a kick out of what I wore, their old sweaters, earrings
from the thirties and forties. They thought it was hilariously
funny.

□

"I don't bullshit them," Hal said. "Whatever they want to know, I tell it to them straight. I tell them what that life did to me."

Hal lectured at Catholic schools in Bay City, about his troubles with drugs and alcohol. He told seventh and eighth graders how he lived with Merry in their silver trailer on the Oneida lot by the airport and what had happened to him.

I asked if it was still the same in school with drugs, wasn't it different then, with Vietnam, the times.

Hal said no, he knew from Tina there was still temptation.

"Tina, come out here and tell your cousin about the marijuana in school." He looked up at the small, added-on breezeway bathroom, one of Jimmy's projects years ago.

"Can I wait just a minute, Dad, I'm doing my makeup."

"She knows everything," he said. "She knows everything I did and she forgives me."

Hal told me he didn't write the lectures. He improvised. He said before he spoke to a class he needed quiet, he needed to be alone in a room. He said he stood in those coat closets, the white tangled safety patrol belts in a cardboard box on the floor, stacked cases of pencils, the gleaming pale green arm of the paper cutter, waiting to see what would come to his mind, some bit of conversation left from his marriage, some morning, drug-laden, in the dirty trailer.

Then Tina came bounding down the three stairs, the wings of her hair swooping out, her chin tilted up, offering us her face.

Carol followed behind. "Look at her, thirteen years old and a half hour in the bathroom already. When she first told me she wore makeup, I said, not around me you're not, but then I saw what little she did and it does look nice. Isn't it something, but you know, even at her age, I can tell the difference, she really does look better with that little color around the eyes. Even at that young age."

Tina flopped down on the couch and operated the TV by remote control.

"So this year, I'm going all over Ohio, Illinois, Michigan, Min-

nesota and Nebraska," Hal said. "And they're going to have me
do a record."

Jimmy and Carol showed me the blueprint of their home, in Hanger's Cove, Florida. They had a brochure with a model of the
houses in four color photos. But their house, though model B,
was not really like the picture. Jimmy had built onto it, he'd
added a patio and a second breezeway.

"We had to go to court and fight," Carol told me, passing Griling's
house. "They wanted to put in a junkyard here on Lime Kiln
Road, across from Guns. The city tried."
     Bub Griling was dead now, his dump overfilled, rotting, a haz-
ard.

Carol mentioned Indians and the Vietnamese. Part of the old
water softener store on Three Corners stood empty. The paint shop
that had been there closed. Evenings, Carol and I drove over in
the car, to show the storefront to prospective leasers who answered the ad in the *Press Gazette*.
     It was a shabby empty space, with concrete floors and low ceil-
ings, not carpeted like the Rug Doctor office next door. Carol and
I paced, waiting for a woman who wanted to turn it into a dance
studio. The rent was sixty-five dollars a month. "One of these
little Vietnamese wanted to rent it. Yah! He wanted to put a fruit
market in here and he wanted to write on the window, in *Vietnamese*. Yah! Can you believe that?"
     The week I stayed, I couldn't convince Carol and Jimmy that
the Vietnamese in Bay City were not the same Vietnamese we'd
fought.
     She stood, shaking her head, looking at her feet on the floor.
"We lose so many boys over there and then they come here and
get money from the government. Yah. All those little people.
There's lot of them, here, we have the H'mong.
     "And the Indians, now they want to put up a hotel, across the
highway from the airport. They gave them all that land, to the

Oneidas, they said that was their land. Yah! And now they want
to put a hotel up. They've got bingo games there every Saturday
night already."

Driving through the dark city, I saw apartments; old buildings,
pretty like New England, turn-of-the-century stone by the river
with glass windows and that yellow light. I'd think of coming here
and renting an apartment and living. It seemed amazing, how
cheap it was. I could easily afford a pretty place, little rooms off
a hallway, an old white stove in the kitchen, crannies, closets,
maybe a clawfoot tub. But I couldn't live there, I knew it. The
feeling always passed.

Every day, Jimmy got up at eight o'clock the way he had when he
drove to the store on Three Corners, ate breakfast and began work
at nine. He still took an hour lunch break, the only difference
was that now he hiked five miles, doctor's orders. He had a machine to walk on in the laundry room for days when it was too cold
outside. In the same room, Carol kept a machine which suspended her in the air, hanging her upside down on a series of
metal tubes and bars. She said it helped with her back.

I sat in the breezeway talking to Mary Griling, who'd grown up to
be six feet tall. She told me what had happened to everyone on
our road.
    Of the Grilings, Mary ended up being the one who stayed at
home. She took care of her father until he died. Now she lived in
the house with her brother and oldest sister, she worked in a
computer shop in town.
    She said she might go to Florida. "My dad's dead, there's noth-
ing for me here."
    "But you're close to your family. To Rosie."
    "I am, then I'm not," she said. "I am and I'm not. Not like it
was with my dad."
    After we'd left, she'd had polio. She limped a little and her
smile twisted up to the left. She was still very neat, careful. Theresa was the one who'd gone away.

"Coming tonight, Mare?" Jimmy walked through the breezeway, lifting a tray of chickens for the barbecue. Hal was giving a
party.

"Working. But Terry'll come. She'll come with the baby."

"Yah, Theresa's home," Carol said. "She was stationed in Japan and she met a fellow over there who can speak and understand Russian. Oh, and a real handsome boy. So he flies one of
those planes out of Japan and listens to what they say over there."

Carol stood on the porch hollering. "Handy! Handy!" She waited,
fists on her hips, until the dog came running through the back
field. She bent to pat him.

"You know Ralph Brozek, Jay's brother? Yeah, he was staying at
my place, freakin' out right and left, one flashback after another.
He couldn't get out of my bathtub once, he thought he was in a
ship on fire, that's where all the other guys with him died. I say,
'Hey, my brother's dead, too. They're in the same place.' But I
don't know one single person who came back from Vietnam the
way they started.

"My mom and pop think I got out because of the leg. But that's
not how it happened. Air force was messing with my head. They
decided they wanted to operate. I said no, you're not going to
operate. This went on, I don't know, six or eight weeks. Then I
was lying, they didn't know what I was talking about. I was seeing
the shrinkologist. I told them a little fairy tale. Asshole doctors.
I told them, I'm going to kill myself. You're going to find me
hanging from the rafters. I sat down. I couldn't control my emo-
tions. They sent me home."

We sat on the edge of the patio.

"So what made you religious?" I said.

"I needed more than just what was in this world."

Theresa and I stood breast deep in the hot tub, leaning against
the underwater benches with our hands. Theresa was tall now, a
woman, no signs of what she had been. She'd left the baby at
home with her brother's wife, she grabbed my arm and said we

had to talk. We sat for a long time in the hot water, steam rising around us, the party continuing, further on the patio near the pool, a stereo blaring in the solar house.

"I miss the trees," she said. She was holding her elbows and shaking her head. I recognized the expression. "I miss the open space."

She lived outside Kyoto and sometimes her husband was gone, flying, for two or three weeks. She took care of the baby herself. She lived on a base, though she was no longer in the army.

"Just a wife," she said. She told me the Japanese were very good with children, that they revered infants. She said she was studying Ikebana.

I looked at her and understood the crooked smile, the rue. We both sat staring into the dark yards, the old barn a pure black, vacant fields.

"They told me they rented out your gramma's house," she said. "That doesn't seem right." I shook my head. "They're putting my dad's house up for sale, too, and that doesn't seem right either."

The pool gleamed turquoise from underwater lights, tropical plants hung in the bathhouse. "It's so different."

"I guess when you go away, you want it to be the same, but when you stay you want it to change."

In the kitchen, before she walked home, Theresa wrote down her address on a square paint-color sample of Jimmy's. Theresa Lambert, FPO Seattle, 98767, Japan.

"You won't believe it. I bought a re-yall Seth Thomas grandfather clock, *signed*. Do you know how rare they are now? They're in museums, you just can't find them anymore. It's here already, in the closet for now, I don't want anybody to see it and get ideas, these doors are like nothing, but won't that be something when I have my little house? Someday. You won't believe, Honey, how beautiful it is."

She called me a lot, whenever she wanted to talk.

Someone from "Santa Fe" had sued, and they paid us all back royalties.

It was easy, sending the check, signing it over—then it was gone and I was only as poor as anyone else in Providence.

I remembered something I'd forgotten for a long time, the job I'd had in a department store wrapping packages. It was like a TV game show, a bonanza, where all around were prizes. My mother had come in on Saturdays as extra help. In three weeks, we ripped them off blind. We stole slacks, dresses, everything.

I still wear some of those shirts. That's one thing about stealing, you wear something long enough and it seems as though it was always yours. It's the same as if you bought it. Those years, I never felt scared. Now I think it's crazy, the risks we took. We could have been in the backseat of a squad car, booked on felonies, both caught. We did a lot for money, things meant so much to us. And it seemed hard for my mother. Since I've been gone, money has come to me. People have given me things. I always feel a little bad at how hard my mother tries.

The thing I keep thinking, when I remember my mother, is how young she was.

One day I read it in the newspaper, Buffy died. The girl who was an actress that everyone wanted to be when I was nine. She'd been nine too. She looked younger, she played a twin on "Family Affair" with two high blond pigtails. Mattel put out a Buffy doll and they also made one of Mrs. Beasley, Buffy's doll on television. Buffy was famous. When I lived in Bay City, I read everything there was about Buffy. I found an interview with her in *TV Guide*. I remember it said she lived in Pacific Palisades. She talked about working, she said once when she came home her brother had eaten all the strawberries. I knew she had a mother and no father, like me. I thought of her now, enormous, full grown, but with the pale thin legs and white anklets, a nineteen-year-old girl in blond pigtails. I kept thinking of paper around her, the long woman's legs, eerie where they met the white anklets, in a shoe box. She died of a drug overdose in an apartment on the Palisades. I guess she'd never gone too far away.

□

A while later, my mother talked about a house, how I had to come
home and see it.

Finally, I went to LA.

"I have everything," my mother says, hugging me. "There's all
different kinds of cheese and a salami in the refrigerator. And
fruit. I've got peaches and plums and watermelon and strawberries . . ."

She's still listing fruit as I set down my suitcase and walk over
the carpet to the sliding glass doors. We're on the ocean, in Malibu. Waves unroll below us on the sand, muscular and glassy.

"Kiwi and kiwi and kiwi . . ." My mother sticks on kiwi when
she runs out of fruits. "Oh, and I have white wine and red wine
and Kahlua, I remember you like Kahlua, and gin and tonic. And
oh, I have limes."

She is standing behind me, her fingers light on my back. Together, we watch the water. That's one thing about my mother, her
capacity for awe.

"Isn't it nice?" she whispers.

All her things are here, the things I've heard about for years, the
grandfather clock backed into a corner, hidden by ferns and a
Kensia palm.

"I don't want anybody to see it and get ideas," she says.

The pine bench, stripped blond and waxed, stands in front of
a couch, antique armoires are set with green Limoges plates, tiny
antlers, dried roses and orange peel. She shows me each thing.
The Tiffany lamp, its one original petal-glass shade, the other
replicated by a glass blower she met in Santa Barbara, every
piece collected slowly. I walk around the rooms and touch.

"It's worth three times what I paid," she whispers, her eyebrows lifting.

Sometimes when you walk in a house that has been newly, thoroughly cleaned, you feel light. You're eating, you're lounging on
a couch, spreading open the pages of a magazine, but you are a

small thing, in the rooms. You're living the way people live inside movies.

The carpet is new and even, the glass perfect. I'm surprised. I guess I'm even impressed.

This is what is in the bathroom: Porthault scallop-edged towels, organic geranium soap, aloe vera shampoo, fennel toothpaste on the spotless counter and a huge shell filled with natural sponges.

I sit on my mother's bed and let her show me things. The Tiffany lamp, half Tiffany, half Santa Barbara, sheds soft colored light on the wall. My mother's closet could be a museum. Each article is tended. The floors shine with oil, her shoes hang in felt bags, tucked in French cloth shoe-panels. Her dresses fall perfectly and sweaters, from Chanel to Lacoste, are stacked according to color, each in its own clear plastic zipper bag. She seems to own nothing old. Most of my mother's clothes are white.

She sits on her bed, next to the lamp, with her glasses on, mending a torn piece of lace on the hem of my skirt. It caught in my heel; the way I live, I would have left it to rip. I idly pull out one of my mother's drawers. There are rows of unopened Dior stockings, textured, not, sheer to opaque, in all colors, her silk and lace panties and bras. An antique coin silver evening purse, wrapped in a white felt bag, and a sachet, rose petals and orange peel.

"I make those myself," she says.

I'm thinking, my mother has changed. When I lived with her, she was more like me. She could walk out of the house looking perfect, nails buffed and polished, hands soft, everything on her bright, pressed, falling in gentle ruffles and folds, the patent leather purse dark and shining like a mirror, but she left a million little odds and ends behind. Old things, gray stained sweat shirts in the closet, clothes she kept for wearing when she was just with me. She didn't seem to own those anymore. She must have thrown them all out, everything stained. She used to have old purses, each one containing scraps of things, change, matted brushes, pictures, junk. They seem gone now, too.

She must have always wanted to live like this; from one perfect outfit to the next, nothing in between, every day crisp new clothes, nothing to be ashamed of, ever, anywhere. She always loved new things. Someone could always be watching.

The ocean feels so close and loud, I don't want to sleep. We drink Kahlua in tall glasses of milk and my mother tells me secrets about her clothes.

The next morning, the living room is a cage of sun. My mother stands by the oven, wearing white, poking at bagels with a fork.

"I have lox and cod and smoked salmon, and onion, tomato and cream cheese and, let's see . . ."

"You bought this house?" In the daylight, it seems too good. If my mother bought a house with the check I sent her, I imagined it small, a bungalow in the Valley, or towards Riverside, Pasadena. There are a million little LA towns. Tarzana, maybe. But not here.

Her back turns, there is a flinch of movement in her shoulder, under the loose white shirt. She stiffens and pauses a second.

"Mmhmm," she says.

Late afternoon, my mother sews over the hem of my skirt, all around, not just where it tore, to strengthen it. She is humble before the ancient delicate fabric, the new, Japanese style. A servant to a beautiful dress. It feels quiet in the house. Dim light. She is bent over, feet clumped pigeon-toed on the floor, knees pressed together, biting a thread. I drop down and do pushups. She is all deft concentration. The skills she's had forever. She studies careful invisible stitches in the weak light. She puts her glasses on.

"Adele, you have enough food for forty," Daniel Swan says, closing the refrigerator door.

"Here's the pasta and here's lemons," my mother calls.

Daniel unrolls white butcher paper with pink, round pieces of veal on it. There must be thirty medallions.

"That's okay, whatever we don't use, we'll keep." My mother sighs and lightly claps. "So."

I cut a lime for my gin and tonic. We've been drinking for hours. My mother washes vegetables, individually, in the sink, drying each mushroom with a paper towel. She stops, looks at us and smiles. "If I ever have a man around again, he's going to have to cook. You bet."

She moves past us to the table, her caftan brushing the floor. The centerpiece is a three-foot basket of fruit. Apples and oranges, cherries, strawberries, grapes and kiwi spill over the top.

I marvel at the kitchen. Tiny brushes stand next to organic soap, under a framed poster of "All rising to a great place is by a winding stair," Francis Bacon rendered orange and blue by Sister Corita. Herbs in a hanging wire basket, shells. "Blue! Blue! The butterfly counts not months but moments, and has time enough."

Foucon. A holy water ox. Orchids in ferns. An old lamp from Wisconsin. A bowl of lemons.

"Oh, come here, you two. Look." My mother stands on the balcony, letting her wine glass dangle off the rail like a huge jewel.

We watch the waves open, white and then transparent over the sand.

"And look at him, can you see that little porpoise? He's been visiting me all week. He looks just like a rock, but that's him."

My mother's hands move delicately under running water; she's a hardworking cook. But she has no sense of timing. The veal burns, curling up at the edges, smelling like milk. She scrapes the pan and sighs, taking the white butcher paper back out of the refrigerator, for more.

I stir the noodles. My mother put in too many and not enough water. I know her logic; it is a beautiful, if small, copper saucepan. But the noodles seem to be dissolving.

"Yuk," Daniel says, lifting the spoon. He rummages through

the cupboards for a colander. I notice him pausing, on his knees. He holds up a white grocery receipt over a foot and a half long.

I shrug and sponge a line of ants from the counter.

The food arranged on platters at the table, I go to look for my mother. I find her in the bathroom, slowly unpinning electric rollers in front of the mirror. Now she puts on her beads. She wears three strands. She lifts each one and lays it on her chest, then rummages under her hair until she finds the clasp. She doesn't fasten it in front and then tow it around, the way I do, living alone. We stand there like that a long time, watching her hands worry under her hair.

"Ann, make a list for me of what books I should read. Listening to you kids talk is great but I realize I've fallen behind. I just don't have the vocabularies you kids have. I used to. But I spend so much time reading in my field and writing those damn reports. I want to catch up again and really follow what's what in the literature and artistic field."

She looks at me from the other end of the table. "She's really beautiful, isn't she," she says.

"No," I say.

"That's what's so nice about her is she doesn't know. I'm so happy when you're here."

A silence falls like the silence after someone has said they love you. She waits.

The food is terrible, the veal, though perfect looking, is tough, the noodles are the texture of oatmeal. We eat slowly.

My mother stands and claps. "Well, what about dessert? Daniel, what would you like? We have carrot cake and I have everything for hot fudge sundaes, I have vanilla and coffee ice cream, and hot fudge and nuts, I have cream, let me think if I have anything to whip it with."

Now, the scraps of food seem solid on the dark plates. The candlelight makes it all look old.

"We'll do it, Mom. What would you like?"

"I think I'll have carrot cake," she says.

Daniel switches on the overhead kitchen light and my mother turns her chair towards the window.

I stack our dishes in the sink.

"Daniel, we wanted cake," I say.

He's balancing three bowls of ice cream on his arm, and nudging past me to the table. "We're having hot fudge sundaes," he says. I flick the light off again and my mother doesn't say a word about the ice cream, only "Mmmmmm," when she lifts the spoon to her mouth.

"Comemeer," Daniel says. My mother zigzagged, tired and glowing, to her bed. She doesn't usually drink, she never used to. Daniel and I clean the kitchen, the pots and pans, the plates. I start wrapping all the food in sight with Saran.

Daniel opens the garage door and squats on the cement. The carrot cake rests on the floor, untouched, perfect.

"Look." Daniel points.

Then I see it, my eyes adjust to the dimness. Ribbon-thick bands of ants surround the base, tunneling into its sides. The frosting is dotted with dead ones.

The next day, my mother shows me her new car. It is a white Mercedes station wagon, with silver everywhere, tan leather interior, a dashboard more computerized and beautiful than any stereo. She blushes. We are standing outside on the dirt Colony Road, overgrown with weeds. She backs the car, infinitely slowly, from the garage. Two tan, very blond children wearing shorts and bandannas chase a dog, also wearing a bandanna. Everything is bright. By the driveway leans one spent rosebush. I hear a motor churning, somebody's pool.

"When did you?"

She shrugs. "I realized, it was the only car I really liked. I looked at Toyotas and Jeeps, I almost bought a Jeep wagon with the wood sides, you know, but it ended up being more expensive than this was. So . . . I just picked it up last week."

"Why do you want a station wagon?"

She inhales, shuddering. "We-ell, I'd like to drive my grand-children around someday."

On the long streets of our old neighborhoods in Beverly Hills, new octagonal signs stand on all the lawns. WESTEC SECURITY: ARMED PATROL, they read. ARMED RESPONSE.

"Oh, come on, after all they've done for us. Besides, Peter wants to see you, poor Petey, he's been calling every day. He still likes you."

"The Kellers haven't done anything for me."

"Well, they have for me."

Almost a year ago, Nan Keller died in an accident. At Aspen, she was run over by a snowplow. She paused at the bottom of the mountain, between runs. The machine stood idle on top of a pile of plowed snow. Kids had been playing in it and they left the brake open. The plow rolled down the hill, over Nan.

Now, Mr. Keller was suing the ski lodge and arranging a retro-spective of her paintings. "I went out with him once," my mother says, "but I just couldn't do it. Ugh. I couldn't kiss him."

When Peter Keller calls, I won't talk. Every time my mother lies, says I'm in the bathroom, in the shower, taking a long bath, steaming. He must think I've become extremely clean.

Daniel pulls the strap of my suit down, then we are kissing.

"I didn't think this would ever happen," he says.

I duck underwater and pull off his suit; it tangles on his feet, but I get it somehow and loop it around my wrist like an enormous bracelet. We kiss hard, imprecisely. We bob. He lifts the elastic away from my leg and he feels enormous, and good, oh so good, inside me. I keep rising to the surface, he pushes my shoulders down.

Then, he yanks out of me, bites the package open, pulls the rubber on underwater. He'd been swimming with it in his hand. Now it starts again, random, hard, real inside me.

"Hi, you two!" My mother stands in yellow slacks and sun-glasses on the deck.

"Can she see us?"

"No, we're underwater."

But I can see our legs and stomachs, green but distinct, like hands in clear gloves.

I swim away and Daniel yells, hey, grabbing my ankle. A wave comes up over our shoulders, we're caught in it, tumbling, gasping, clawing the sand bottom, finally bobbing up again, ten feet apart, our hair bunched in our mouths. We can't find Daniel's bathing suit. I hold up my arms so he sees and we both start diving for it, looking.

I stand for a second on the ridged sand, closer in than Daniel. My mother bends over, watering geraniums with a hose on her balcony. "She looks so good in her house."

"The Kellers' house," Daniel says.

I start swimming in, hard, breathing underwater, to get Daniel another suit.

"The thing I like about swimming in the ocean is that you can pee whenever you want," he says.

I guess I should have known. She bought the car instead of a house. She's borrowing the house, maybe renting, whatever.

In the dark, my mother shakes me. "Hurry up, you're really lucky. The grunion are running. I have a schedule."

I pull on jeans and a sweat shirt from the chair. In high school, we went on grunion runs, late night rides to the beach in tiny cars, girls sitting on the boys' laps, our hoop earrings catching in our long hair. But we never saw any grunion. We'd walk on the beach with flashlights a few minutes, then pair off to make out in the sand. I'd always thought the fish were an excuse.

But my mother has a little pamphlet from the Coast Guard. " 'The female comes in on one wave and she twirls herself into the sand, so she's upright, half buried and half out. And there she lays her eggs,' " my mother reads. " 'Then, the male swims in. He circles around her and deposits his sperm.' If they're lucky, they swim off together on the next wave. But sometimes the female gets stuck in the sand and if she doesn't catch the next wave, she dies, poor thing. She can't breathe, I suppose. Aw."

"Why do people catch them?"

"They're good to eat, I think. I suppose you fry them."

We stand on the balcony and don't see anything. The sand looks the way it always looks, shiny and smooth, dark. My mother bends down to roll up her pants. "Come on," she says.

A few minutes later, she runs back up the redwood stairs, two at a time. "It's thick with them. They're all over. You just can't see them from here." She takes pails from the garage, stepping over the carrot cake, and we fill them with water from the hose. The buckets feel heavy and the slap of water on my leg is cold as we lug them down to the beach.

It takes my eyes a few seconds to adjust. But then, I see them everywhere, wriggling like corkscrews in the sand, silver on one side. The shore comes alive with them.

"You catch them with your hands," my mother yells, running, her arms low to the ground.

Holding a grunion is like holding a muscular beam of moonlight. It's that fast. They try to squirm up out of your fist. Some flop down, slithering back into the dark shellac of water. The ones we catch clap against the sides of our pails.

There are hundreds of them. When you put your foot down in a cluster of grunion, they spread away from you in starlike migration.

I look up at the bowl of the sky, alive with stars and stars. They seem to be wriggling, too, burning holes in the dark. My mother knocks the pail over, giving a slush of fish back to the water. We turn it right and start again. It seems we can go on all night. My hands grow quicker and bold.

Our buckets thump like hearts and we keep running. It seems they will come all night, the wet fish we can touch.

"So you didn't buy a house."

She sighs. "I really want a house in just the RIGHT spot, where I can see the mountains and the ocean, and where there's a little artists' colony and I can take a ceramics class and make stained-glass windows, all these various things. I'm just going to wait until I can afford a real choice place. The house can be little, cute, but small."

"You bought the car, though."

"Yes," she says, cautiously, not sure what she's admitting.

We leave the beating pails on our balcony and take our clothes off there, letting them fall in soft piles. I don't know what time it is. The sand still glitters with grunion. Now I see them everywhere. We run the cold hose water over our bodies, before we go inside.

In the morning, we take showers, still smelling of seaweed. I pack. We step over the carrot cake and the murky buckets of dead black fish in the garage, into the white car in the sun. I bring my suitcase with me. I'm leaving my mother to deal with the stink and dead things when I am gone.

"Today is Sunday. It is the third of March, 1979." There is a sign on the fourth floor of my mother's convalescent home in Santa Monica. The bright crayoned letters continue, "The weather today is mild and sunny. 'Nice.'" I follow my mother through the nursing station where she flips through charts, marking files. She moves with competence, the flaps of her lab coat brisk behind her. Everyone knows her here.

"I told you about Miss Eldridge," she says. "She's the one who had beautiful, beautiful things. This may be hard for you, but it's good, I think. You should see what happens."

My mother told me about Miss Eldridge; she came to Los Angeles from Medford, Oregon, during the First World War and lived with her fiancé, who was in the service. She waited for him and he was killed in the war. Then, she worked all her life as a legal secretary, never married.

The curtain is drawn, separating Miss Eldridge from someone else in the room. What I am not prepared for is her beauty. She sits up on the bed, perfectly clear, her hands the conscious hands of anyone.

"Claire, I told you I'd bring my daughter to come meet you and I brought her. Here she is, here's my Ann."

Miss Eldridge looks at my mother and then at me, and shakes my hand. Miss Eldridge is crying without any noise, and my mother begins to cry too. I go over to a bulletin board and study the pins. There are three postcards. I remember now that Miss Eldridge has no children. "I'll change it again this month," my mother says.

"Thank you for bringing her to see me."

"I told you I would. And I did. I brought her. And now she's off again."

Miss Eldridge nods.

We sit in the car.

"She'll never leave there," my mother says, "it's really sad, because she's mentally as clear as you or me."

My mother's open eyes are as motionless and blue as a fish's. "But they don't have it that bad, you know?" She looks down. "I feel like you're always leaving."

"I always come back," I say.

"But not for long."

I shrug. "That's what kids do, they leave."

I only left home once and that was years ago.

My mother drives a freeway to the Valley. She turns onto an exit I don't recognize and slows at a gas station. Across the street is a school, fenced with high aluminum.

She pulls up around the back and then I see it: our own Lincoln, up on cinderblocks.

"Do you want it, Ann? I've had them keep it for you. He says it'll only cost two hundred to spiff it up and it might still run a long time. I've got the keys for you."

She took them out of the glove compartment, but I say no.

"Are you sure? It's a good car still. You just may need it."

But we drive to the airport, leaving it.

In front of the terminal, I gather my suitcase. My mother doesn't want to park in the lot. "Somebody could really bump it, you know? Sit a second, we'll just talk, we'll wait here," my mother says. "You have time."

My flight is not for an hour. We sit, not moving, in the new car.

Against the window, she looks perfect. Her scarf falls and ripples at her collarbone, her hair curls under. For a second, I feel like she is leaving, not me. Then I glance down at her hands.

"My hands are my worst feature," she says. "These age marks. But they're getting better. I put E on them."

We turn and see each other.

She says, "Life is just too little, isn't it?"

"Mom." I kiss her, then I run out of the car.

CAROL

■ □ ■

16

A LOT OF PEOPLE'S SECRET

■ □ ■

Nobody knows it to this day, but my husband almost killed Hitler. That was the most exciting time of my life, those three years I was in the service. Before and after, I've been pretty much in the ordinary. I've stayed here close to home. My sister has had the excitement; she's been all over, she went to college, did everything. But my big time was during the War.

Before that I was real shy, not like Adele. My mother said even when I was just born, I was always a quiet baby. Apparently, I slept all the time. I didn't wake them at night, nothing. I was real easy. Well, I can attest that Adele was never that way.

I was eleven years old when they had Adele and I didn't even know my mother was pregnant. I was so dumb, naive. Just all of a sudden, I had a little sister. I didn't like it much, either. No. I had to baby-sit. I was the one who got up in the middle of the night to change her. And she cried plenty. There was always such an age difference, too. We were never really friends.

My parents didn't tell me anything. I remember when I first started menstruating, I didn't know what it was. I was in church and here I was bleeding. And when I came home I was still bleeding. Well, I was so upset, I didn't know what to think. I told my mother and she said to me, "Didn't anyone ever tell you about that?"

And I thought later, many times, Well, gee, who was ever going to tell me, if my own mother didn't?

When Adele was that age, she had plenty of friends to teach her the ins and outs. She always had a crowd. But I was too shy.

I never even had a date or anything and this was in high school. I was so shy that if I walked down a street and a fellow was coming towards me, I'd go all the way around the block to avoid him. Isn't that terrible? I think it is.

After high school, I wanted to go in training to be a nurse. But my mother didn't like the idea of nursing, I don't know why, she just didn't see me as a nurse. I still think I would have liked it.

But she knew someone who did beauty and that woman, a Mrs. Beamer, convinced my mother that beauty was really the thing. So I went to beauty school here downtown and then I worked at the Harper Method Beauty Shop. It was okay, it wasn't too bad, I didn't mind the work one way or the other and I got in with a nice group of girls.

It did help me with my own hair. Now I can go with once a week in the beauty shop and in between, I keep it up myself. I don't give myself permanents or tint my own hair, but everything else, I do. And when I lost my hair in that trailer fire, I knew how to style the wig.

And I learned a lot there, from the other girls. Upstairs from the beauty shop was a doctor my father knew. The doctor's brother was a veterinarian and my father had him out once or twice a year to look at the mink. Well, this particular doctor treated all the girls who lived at the Silver Slipper. That was a tavern at the end of our road. I'd meet them on the stairs as they went up to see Dr. Shea and we nodded. I'd say hello, they'd say hello to me. We'd seen each other on Lime Kiln Road. Well, eighteen years old and until the girls at the beauty shop told me, I didn't know what they were. My mother never said a word. She told me to stay away from there and I knew my dad was real mad when they opened the Silver Slipper Tavern and put the beer sign up, but I thought he was mad about the drinking.

I don't know why I was like that, so backward. Maybe because of my father. Because of what happened to them, having to get married, he was too protective. And I think they made me scared. Because I remember once, I was in fifth or sixth grade, we were living in the house on Lime Kiln Road and some boys came once and knocked on the door. They were just boys from my class. And my father answered and yelled to my mother. "They're after Carol, keep her upstairs," he said. "They're here after Carol."

Well. I suppose they just wanted to get my homework or for me to come outside and play. Oh, when I even think about it, they're after Carol. So he was a part of it, I'm sure.

Then, around that time, after high school, I first started going out a little. I was nineteen or twenty and I used to go with the girls I met working. We went out to Bay Beach. Then, Bay Beach was still real nice. That green and white pavilion was just new and all painted—it was a Public Works Project, for years the men were there building and then they painted those murals for the ballroom. Franklin Roosevelt came to Bay City when it opened. Now they just have those darn pinball machines and computer games. It's all games where it used to be a dance floor. And I remember, they were just putting in the bumper cars. They already had that little train that went along the beach. We saw beautiful sunsets over the Fox River with the silhouettes of the smoke stacks. Those piles of coal and sulfur would take on colors. The bus went right along the river, north to the bay. You went with the girls on a Friday or Saturday night and the fellows came separately. Our crowd from the beauty shop rode on the bus. There were no dates or anything. You'd just dance. And they got the good bands to come here to Bay City then. Tommy Hill and Sammy Kaye. I remember, Swing and Sway with Sammy Kaye. You'd stand by the sides with your girl friends and the fellows would come and ask you to dance and you'd think, Ooogh, he asked me, so excited. There was no go off in the car and do things, like now. It was a whole different way of life. Not everything sex, sex, sex. And then you went home on the bus again. If you did go out after, you'd go to Dean's and have a sundae with the girls. The boys went somewhere else.

The women from the Silver Slipper were actually older than they'd looked from a distance. They dressed young. I'd thought they were all in their twenties, a little older than I was. Now, up close when they went to the doctor, I could see. They were tired women, coming to middle age. They must have been in their late

thirties, one or two were past forty. They had such lined faces. A
few looked like Indians and I think those few were the only ones
who didn't dye their hair. When they climbed upstairs coming to
Dr. Shea's, you could see their dark roots. And they must have
done it themselves because no one had ever seen them in Harper
Method or Billings', that was the other beauty shop in town then.
You could see their veins through their nylon stockings. They
always walked looking down, with their hands in their jacket
pockets. As if they were ashamed, you know.

The girls at Harper Method told me Dr. Shea gave them birth
control. He deloused and defleaed them and gave them special
shampoo and soap for scabies.

When a woman was sick, Dr. Shea drove out to the Silver Slipper and made a house call. People said when one died, they buried her right there out in back of the tavern, in Guns Field. They
didn't even own that land. The girls whispered to me what the
rumor was: that he gave those women abortions. Of course that
was illegal then. No one seemed to have heard any more details,
though, and I know for a fact that there was at least one child
there at the time, a boy. He ended up at the orphanage.

Jimmy knew that boy later, one summer they worked together
on a farm. He said that boy and some of the others used to do
things with the sheep. Isn't that terrible? He said they put the
ewe's hind legs in the front of their boots, so she was stuck. They
wore such high boots then, up to the knees. And the sheep would
sort of buck to get away. Ogh. Jimmy never did that, but I suppose
the farm boys used to talk about it, I don't know. See, that's what
we thought about sex then: it was either real, real bad and a
secret, shameful, or there was none and that was all right. I don't
think my mother and father ever really did much of anything. No.

Then, the war broke out when I was twenty-three. It was around
Thanksgiving, I remember, I read something about the Wacs and
Waves. Become a Wac, you know, they were recruiting. And I
filled out an application and sent away to get their booklet. I
didn't tell anyone, I just did it. And then one day this letter comes
and says that I'm to be in Cedar Rapids, Iowa, on December 18,
no ifs, ands or buts. Then I had to go, I couldn't just change my

mind anymore. Well, my mother got that letter and she was furious. She called me at the Harper Method—something she never
did, my mother had such respect for any work or school, you
know, whatever we were supposed to be doing. Because she never
worked herself. She said to me on the phone, "Now *what* did you
do?"

But the service was a very good thing for me. It was the first
time I really had fun. That's when I finally got to know boys. At
boot camp, you had one locker—one locker—and in there you
had to keep all your clothes, your two uniforms, your cosmetics,
your hairbrush, everything. That was it. And there was one big
bathroom with a long mirror—so in the morning we'd all be in
there lined up, putting on our cosmetics and fixing our hair. You
learned some tricks that way, from the other girls.

The girls came from all over and most of them were nice. I
stayed six weeks in boot camp in Cedar Rapids, and then we went
to Evanston, Illinois. And there, it was a regular base. There
were men everywhere, all around us. There were two of us for
every ten of them, so we had a ball. And there in Chicago, we got
passes to go to plays and movies and musicals, whatever was
going on, you know. So even though I didn't go to college, I still
did get to see something. It wasn't as if I stayed home in Bay City
and just deteriorated.

I was in communications. We operated teletypes; we all knew
Morse code. I can still do my name on the clicker. The boys there
in Evanston were in training to be pilots. They had these little
yellow planes and the ensigns had to fly them to Jacksonville,
Mississippi, and then back up to the carrier in Lake Michigan.
There were a lot of deaths in those little yellow planes. And then
we had to send the telegrams to the parents. And that was the
hardest, I think, for the family, you know. If you lost a boy over-
seas, that was hard. But to lose him when he was still here in
training, before he got a chance to fight, well, then, you couldn't
even think he died for something. But when they made it, and
most of them did, then they'd come back with their wings and
their white uniforms all bright and nice.

I had some of the more interesting work there was for women

in the army. But communications was actually my second choice. My first choice was to be up in a watchtower, you did the radar for the planes. And I think that would have been interesting, too. But they were all filled up for that. And there was lots of work that wasn't so good. Some of the girls had to fix engines and that was dirty work. After that you could never get your hands really clean again. That grease stained the cuticle, around the nail. Like the people who work out at the armory say, they can never get that smell off their skin.

By then I wasn't so shy anymore. Then I was dating plenty. There was one warrant officer I dated, he was an Italian and he came from Chicago. Then he was stationed in the South Pacific. He wrote me to wait until he was finished and came home, but then already I was dating someone else. Quite a few of them proposed. I could have gotten married several times. I don't remember anymore why I didn't. I guess it just didn't appeal to me.

They sent our unit over to France. Some went to Hawaii, lots went to the west coast, San Diego, San Francisco, Monterey, and we got to go to Europe. First we went to England, then through the Channel and we ended up stationed in Normandy. Well, over there I met a fellow I did like.

And nobody knows it, but I got married over there. It was a real marriage, in the Catholic Church. He wasn't a Catholic, but he converted for me. He took his first communion the morning we were married. I never did tell Jimmy. He wouldn't like it if he knew. But I'll tell you something—he wasn't even the first. There were two in Illinois before him; an ensign and the warrant officer.

Before I went into the Wacs, I had to have a medical examination. I just went upstairs from the Harper Method to Dr. Shea. And he examined me and he said, "My God, you're still a virgin."

I said, "Well, crumps, what else would I be? What did you think I was?" So even then, it couldn't have been so unusual. But it was a big risk you took every time, because they didn't have birth control pills or anything. I never got pregnant, I guess I was lucky. I've often wondered what would have happened if I'd been pregnant when I came home from Europe. Then I would have had

to tell everyone I was married. I don't know, who knows what's for
the best.

He was a French Jew, he was born in Paris. But he spoke beautiful, beautiful English. Morgenstern was his name. His father
had been one of the moviemakers over there, but when I met him,
he didn't know anymore where his mother and father were. He
was living with a family who had a farm there in Normandy. They
sheltered him. You could tell he shouldn't have been on a farm.
He had such slender, slender hands. He was real delicate, you
know. But he'd learned to milk goats and make cheese. He joked
about it. He'd been there already a year and a half.

After we were married, we went to Paris. I had my discharge
and we were both going to go to America. The Americans had
France then and we were supposed to take a boat that went to
Texas. We had our tickets and all.

There in Paris, he left me in a candy store. I suppose he
thought that's where a young wife would like to go. He was going
to meet a contact from the Resistance. The man was to give him
a handgun. He would go over into Germany and attend a parade
from a street corner, where he could almost touch the Führer and
then he was supposed to shoot him and run.

He was there that day at the parade, with the gun in his pocket.
He told me later, there was a blond girl standing in front of him,
with hair that had tints of green underneath the yellow. He didn't
know her, but for some reason, he lifted his hand and touched the
little girl's hair. Hitler rode by on the car four feet in front of him.
He could have reached and kicked the metal of the fender. But
instead, he stroked the hair of an unknown child, touching the
gun in his pocket.

Hitler rode away, the parade went by, and before he came to
fetch me, he slid the gun down the dirty toilet of a public rest
room. That afternoon, we left for America, Texas.

All the boat ride, he was sick. Did I say before how weak he
was? He wasn't in good health for a long time then already. He
couldn't sleep at night and I stayed up with him. He had his coat
and my coat and still he couldn't get warm. Later on, he com-

plained about the boat ride. One day, he climbed down to the storeroom. He took me to see: there were rats in the barrels of oatmeal. After that, I never once made my children eat things they didn't want to eat. I had fights galore with Jimmy over that, but for once I stuck to my point.

We landed in Texas in the morning and there was this huge, huge horizon. I had never seen it like that before either. Black men moved with ropes there working the docks; that was something he hadn't seen. And a few minutes later, I was opening my purse for American money to buy chewing gum, my husband's first discovery in the New World.

We took a train from Texas that went all the way up to Wisconsin. Oh, was that something. It was all army. People standing up, women with little children and babies, trying to feed them and change their diapers. And my husband was still real sick. I had to ask people to give up their seat for him. And they did. Quite a few offered. Well, he died right there on that train. Yes, he died. It was the scariest thing that had ever happened to me in my life.

Later, the army did an autopsy and said it was a heart attack, but at that time I didn't know what to think. Here I had this young husband, he was twenty-seven then. He just passed out in his seat. It was mostly all women on that train and they all helped. I just cried and cried. I didn't know what to do. I was twenty-six years old and here I was just married and my husband was unconscious on the train. I couldn't think. All I could imagine was if he would only just wake up. I was so unrealistic. And then the terrible thing was nobody could do anything until the train's next stop. I still don't know how long that was because the woman in the chair next to him got up and gave me her seat and would you believe, at a time like that, I fell asleep? Yes, I did. I slept.

The next stop was some little place in Oklahoma called Gant. Three of the women, one with children, woke me up and led me out. They kept patting my hand and telling me it would be all right. "Poor dear," I heard them whispering. They got me into a hotel and I didn't even see him. They'd carried him out first and somebody had taken him to the army coroner's office.

They had him cremated. They thought that was the best thing.

I've thought many times since, I wish I'd had the presence of mind to see that he was buried. Then there would be some place where I could know he was.

It was nice of those women, they stayed overnight two days with me in that hotel. The morning we left, we took his ashes, they came in such a box like this, and we threw them out in the fields by the tracks. They kept asking me if there was anywhere special I wanted them and I said, no, no, I didn't care and I really didn't. I just wanted to get it over with and get back on the train. You see, I didn't connect them with him. The place in Oklahoma, the box, it was all funny. I felt like I was just going along with it. I knew those stones weren't really him.

Then it was a long ride north on the train and I had a lot of time to think. And I thought and I thought, should I tell my mother and dad that I'd been married. I didn't see what would be the good in it. I'd planned to just bring him home and introduce him, this is my husband. We're married. I knew they wouldn't be so happy about it, but I thought they would like him when they got used to him. Now, there wouldn't be any point.

And I thought I might forget about him faster if I didn't tell anybody. That's what they said in those days. When a girl was jilted, the mother would say, now, stop talking about him and pretty soon, you'll stop thinking about him too. Now I don't think that's true. I don't think that's true at all. But then I did. I remember straightening my hat and gathering all my things neat together when the train pulled into the South Bay Station. I'd be going home alone, there were people for me, family. I thought the army was another world I'd been in—and in this one it wouldn't be so hard not to mention it. Not just him, the whole war. I didn't really feel like talking about any of it.

Now I wish I'd talked about it then when I could, then right away, when it was natural. So many years later, if you don't forget, if you haven't forgotten like I haven't, you're too ashamed to bring it up. And then it's always your secret. I imagine the war is a lot of people's secret; you know, what happened to them then.

Paul was his name and he was a beautiful boy. He looked real, real young, much younger than I did. It's so long ago now; nobody

could be as good as I remember Paul. And you know, it's not a
good thing to have a secret like that. Something you care about
so much. A person you idealize who's dead. Because it takes away
from your regular life. You compare and it doesn't do you any
good, because no matter what you want or think, he's dead. You're
better off forgetting him and trying to be happy with what you've
got.

And here I think of him the way he looked then; well, if he still
looked like that, who knows, the way I am now, he wouldn't even
want me. But I kept thinking of Paul for such a long time, then I
couldn't even stop it when I wanted. Every time I'd have a minute
alone, my mind would sort of drift and I would picture things with
him. I always imagined that it had been a mistake, that it wasn't
his bones and ashes we threw away at Gant and that he stayed in
a little hospital there—a small stone building run by nuns. I had
the whole thing in my head, oh I was so silly, his room with the
plain walls, a cot with a navy blue blanket, just a simple wooden
cross above the bed. There were dandelions growing in the grass
outside his room. That's what he saw when he looked out the
window during that long time he was getting well. And every day,
the nurses brought him food and stood there while he ate it. They
didn't talk much. They folded their hands on the front of their
habits and they looked out the window, too. Sometimes, in that
field, there were cows.

Then, I always imagined, he found me. He wrote me a long
letter or he called me on the telephone and I had to get rid of my
life and of Jimmy. That was never too hard. In my daydream, that
part never took too long. Sometimes I confessed and told everyone. And then the priest had to come and tell my parents and
Jimmy that since my first husband turned out to be still alive,
Jimmy and I weren't really married. On other days, I didn't tell a
thing to anyone. I just got in my car before supper and drove
away. What I spent the most time sitting and dreaming about was
when we'd meet together again. He had thick lips and the top one
sort of pulled up over his teeth. If I knew how to be a sculptor, I
could still make his face. He had a smooth forehead, no lines,
high cheekbones like a woman's, and that straight, plain, even

nose. It was with him I understood that just the plain, the regular, was beautiful. It didn't have to be something special. It was just the ordinary, not having anything wrong. I suppose he had what people might call a weak chin. His face came to a point and the chin was small and hard, like the tip of an eggshell.

Oh, I'd close my eyes and think of us pressing together, kissing against the wall in a room. I always pictured behind us, one single bed, made up, the cover smooth. I tried to imagine the first instant, that urgency, and then after that—that ohgh—I couldn't do it anymore, I couldn't picture. I'd have to open my eyes and be wherever I really was. In the house or the yard, Mom's house or the water softener store. And then the air and the light in the room where I was seemed thicker and staler than before. I remembered each time then he was dead. That went on for a long time, for years. It didn't really stop until Benny was born. And then, I don't know why, it went away. I guess it was hard to want to imagine giving up my babies. And they were Jimmy's after all. And by then, too, it was just such a long, long time.

I don't want to make it all sound bad. I had good times when I came home, too. After V-J Day, the young people flooded back to Bay City. There were lots of parties that winter, lot of dances. It was a happy time. Overall, I think the war was a good thing for a lot of people's social lives. Of course, there were some wounded, but you didn't see them much. And then there were those like Phil Brozek, who went over to Bikini Island. When he came back, he picked up his milk route again that he'd had before the war. The swelling in his legs, the cancer, all that from the radiation, that didn't show until much later.

I met Jimmy on the golf course. He had been in the service, too, in New Guinea and then in Australia. He jokes that he should have met me before the war, when I was still a virgin. He knows that much, that it happened with both of us in the war. He grew up in Bay City, too, and we graduated high school the same year, but I never met him. He went to Central High and I went to Catholic, the Academy. We only met the boys from Premontre. He says he wants to go back to Australia sometime and see how many kids look like him; he says there weren't any women in New

Guinea, just those natives, but there in Australia, apparently, they had their fun.

I don't know, do you think I should have married him? I don't know either, I often wonder. Then, at the time, I suppose I thought, why not. I needed something new. Here I was back living at home again, sharing a room with my little sister. And she got into everything—oh, God, was she a snoop. She'd open your mail, go through your drawers, anything. One day she told me she stopped reading my diary because it was too boring to keep her interest up. Oh, she could be a little brat.

And my mother wasn't the same with me, either. I never told her I was married, but she knew something was different, she could tell. That last year, I didn't write as much. At the beginning, I'd sent presents from everywhere, but towards the end, I just wasn't thinking about home anymore. I remember on the train, I was an hour away, and I realized I was coming home with no presents for anybody. I got out at one town, I had only a few minutes, and I bought the first thing I saw that would do—a box of cookie cutters. They were nice cookie cutters, all unusual shapes and good stainless steel, but she must have seen that they were just from around here. But at least I had something to give them when I came off at the station.

I remember that night, the lanterns lit, it all looked real pretty and the town had changed so. I felt happy and sleepy all of a sudden. They took me out to Dean's for a sundae and they had the hot fudge, like it always was, in the little silver pitcher. The sky outside over the river turned violet, the lanterns and the piles of sulfur were that real pretty yellow. And you know, I was almost relieved to be alone. I was so tired I felt like a girl again.

But that didn't last. Pretty soon I couldn't stand it anymore. After all the excitement of the war, the travel, the uniforms—you know, sometimes it was like one long parade, you were always sort of tired and excited and you were usually around so many people—Bay City just didn't seem like much anymore. That first night when I was exhausted, it felt perfect, just the way you'd want a town to be. But then when I got some sleep it seemed too small. And here I was plunked back in the same house on the

same road. I was shampooing and styling again at the Harper
Method Beauty Shop.

And one thing I can say for Jimmy, he knew how to take a girl
out on a date. He always took me to a nice supper and then after
we'd do something; we'd go to a club and hear music or we'd go
dancing. And every couple of dates I'd get a corsage. I have them
all here, pressed in the dictionary. And he always had a big crowd
of friends and they gave parties. Twenty, thirty people over for fish
fry or chicken bouya. And my parents never did that. We didn't
have as many friends.

So we went ahead and got married. We had the service at Saint
Phillip's. Jimmy was a Catholic, too, so that was never a problem.
I think my mother and dad liked Jimmy, if they didn't, they never
said anything. And I was already twenty-eight. Maybe they
thought I wouldn't get any better.

And wouldn't you know my little sister managed to ruin my
wedding. She was a bridesmaid, with two others, my two best girl
friends from the Harper Method. I wore Granny's wedding dress.
See, my mother never had one. It was a beautiful dress, that old-
fashioned pearl-white satin with a long train. Adele walked behind me holding it up. I remember she had a white dress, too. I'd
wanted the bridesmaids in pink or mint green, but no, Adele said
it was either black or white. And so the others had to be white,
too, they all had to match. She herself got married in a suit, I
remember.

It was a small wedding, a hundred, hundred fifty people. We
had the reception at my parents' house, in the backyard. We had
tables spread out with white tablecloths and white and green balloons tied up in the oak tree. My dad's men from the mink had
rented tuxedos and they stood behind the tables pouring champagne. There was champagne everywhere and trays of food. My
mother had been baking for days.

She'd made the cake herself. It was a lemon cake inside, real
moist and tart, with a beautiful, fluffy white frosting. Adele had
decorated it that morning—and I have to hand it to her, it was
beautiful, she covered the whole thing with sugared flowers, real
flowers, violets and pansies from the yard, and with cookies in

shapes from those cookie cutters I brought home. She was always good at such stuff. But then, she didn't want us to cut it. She made them take about a hundred pictures, before she'd let us touch it. We have more pictures of that cake than of the rest of the wedding put together.

I do have a picture of the women, when I threw the bouquet. I still had my big nose in the pictures, so we don't put them out anywhere in the house, but we still take the book down and look at them once in a while. Jimmy says he liked my nose big, he says he didn't mind it.

All Granny's sisters were there from Malgoma and Granny, and all the neighbor women. My mother was wearing a peach-colored dress with a corsage. My dad had bought us each special corsages, he had them in the refrigerator when we woke up that morning.

Well, we didn't have a balcony or anything, so I threw the bouquet from the porch. It was just those couple of steps. In the picture, the ladies are all standing on the grass in a line; the married women closest to me, with their hands at their sides, they're not trying to catch it. My mother is the most beautiful one in the picture and you can barely see her, she's standing behind two of the aunts. She really had a perfect profile, like that on a coin, so even, and her hair grew thick and nice. Even then when it was turning gray, it turned that beautiful silver white. And I think she was happy for me. All that day, I'd looked at her from somewhere, when I was going down the aisle at church, later, on the lawn during the party, and her face was so nice, she was glad for me. She'd worked so hard on all the food and the house. And her cake turned out so good.

In the picture, she's got her hands behind her back and this big gorgeous smile. You hardly ever saw her smiling big like that. She was shy. She wasn't a smiler. You know, of my mother and my sister and me, I was the only one with a regular wedding and it made her happy, I suppose. In the picture, the bouquet is blurred in the air. It looks like I'm throwing it to my mother.

Two of my bridesmaids are in the front, crouched and ready like football players. Their knees bent, their arms out, their eyes are on the bouquet. They were both single girls and my age, they were ready, I suppose. Would you believe I don't know who they are anymore? My two bridesmaids, and I can't remember their names. And Adele is standing there, coy, her hands intertwined together. She is looking down at her shoe in the grass.

And she was the one who caught the bouquet. Seventeen years old and she caught the bouquet, sure enough, and without hardly trying. My dad was mad, he thought she was too young to even be in the line for it and he wanted me to throw it again. But she said, nothing doing. She wouldn't give it back.

Then she pulled her real stunt: she locked herself in the bathroom and took a shower! Well, all those people drinking all afternoon and only the one bathroom in the house. Pretty soon they were lined up into the kitchen. Adele was in there humming in the shower. Oh, ye gods. She washed her hair and set it, and so she was in there a long time, hour, hour and a half maybe. And was I mad.

Some of the men walked up the dirt road and went in the field by the barn. But a lot of people just drove home. The party started breaking up. The neighbors ran down the road to their own bathrooms. My father stamped in and rattled on the doorknob—we were afraid he'd break the door down. That was their worst fight I ever saw. When he couldn't get the door open, he went around to the other side of the house and yelled at her through the window. The next day, we went out and my mother showed me: he trampled her whole bed of lilies of the valley.

Well, it was a hot day and I suppose Adele thought she wanted to cool off. Can you imagine, a hundred fifty people, all drinking, and one bathroom, locking yourself in for over an hour? By the time she came out, most of the people were gone. Pretty much just Jimmy's family and our relatives from Malgoma were still there. And the bridesmaids. My sister always did manage to get herself right in the middle of everything. Jimmy still blames her for ruining our wedding. We were planning to party all night! My dad had set up a record player downstairs, in the basement, and his Polynesian room was all set for dancing. But everyone had gone home already! My mother cooked for the relatives and Jimmy and I went out with the bridesmaids and the ushers to a supper club, Jantzen's. I remember we drank lime bitters.

Really, outside of the war, my life has been pretty much in the ordinary and I suppose that's been okay with me. I don't think I would have liked moving around and always having to look right and talk right, like your mother does. But you know, I wish I had gone to college. I listen to Adele and to you talk and you just say things so very well. You know how to speak nice, you do.

We went to Niagara Falls for our honeymoon, just the typical thing, but we had fun. I remember the first night, I suppose from the excitement of the wedding and the party and then traveling, my period came on. It wasn't due then, it was over a week early. I told Jimmy and he said, okay, and said I should just put my hair up and do whatever I needed to do to get ready before bed. See, he knew, he had sisters. And we each got into our single bed and said good night. Every night then, when we came into the hotel room, he'd look at me and I'd say no, not yet. Then our last night before we had to go home, I winked and said, "Tonight."

I don't remember ever deciding to build right next door to my mom and dad, somehow we just knew that's what we were going to do. The land was there already, so at least we had that. My dad helped a little with the foundation, but mostly Jimmy built this house by himself with one other fellow he hired. He was already in the water softeners then. Sullivan Water Softeners. All those years, it was us against Kinsley. That was the other brand. I remember once after we were in the house, I looked out the window while I was doing the dishes and there were all these silver water softeners, shining like torpedoes, leaning against the back of the house. Well, of course, we put in a water softener and Jimmy gave one to Mom and Dad one Christmas. Adele would have gotten one too, but she was never settled down long enough anywhere.

I suppose if I could do it again, I'd build farther away from my parents. It really was just too close. But then, who knows, if I did it again, if I would even marry Jimmy.

And it was a help to me those first years with Hal, to have my mother right next door. And then when Dad was sick. Your mother was out in California at that time, doing something or other in school. We called and called and she wouldn't come home. She was lucky; she barely made it.

When she finally did come, your dad was up here all the time with her. I liked Hisham, he was a nice fellow. Not responsible, well, you know that, but nice. And oh, he was a very handsome man. Tall and dark, with big, big white teeth. I remember him at Dad's funeral. He didn't like the open coffin. He thought that was such a barbaric thing. In fact, if I'm not mistaken, he fainted. He was with Adele and she bent down to kiss the cheek and I'm pretty sure he fainted. He was just appalled. The Muslims didn't do that, see. Over there, they cremate them. I suppose maybe they don't have the room to bury.

We did something around here that my dad had started and all the neighbors took it up, too. When a baby was born, you planted some kind of bush. If it was a boy, you planted a bush that would have berries, if it was a girl, a bush that flowered. With Hal, we planted raspberries, with Benny, currants. Those raspberry bushes are still here, they've spread. The idea was for the kids to be independent. When they were children they could go outside and eat the berries and pick the flowers. My father always thought of things with big ideas; he thought if worst came to worst someone could live on nuts and berries. And then when someone died, we planted a tree. I don't know why a tree. For my father, my mother wanted two; a hickory and a birch.

When my father died, he left money in his will for me to get my nose fixed. He wrote a letter with it that said he had had a big nose all his life and he'd never done anything about it, but that he'd been the one to give it to me and he wanted me to be able to get mine fixed.

And I did. Here I was already married and with a five-year-old son and I went on the train to Chicago alone to have the surgery. There wasn't anyone who did it in Bay City. It was sort of a scary thing. I thought I'd better have a picture to give the doctor an idea of what I'd like; at the Harper Method we'd always told people to look through the magazines so they could show us what they had in mind. So I had my photograph folded up in my purse. It was a picture of Katharine Hepburn. I thought if I was going to get a new nose, I may as well go for something really good, huh? Why not.

Well, I went and it was really awful. Chicago seemed very different from what I remembered of it during wartime, and I was just alone and out of uniform. I couldn't just go anywhere like I did then. And I suppose, I was older.

I remember the night before, I ate dinner in my hotel room because I had no idea where else to go. Then, I still didn't know what to do, I had the whole night ahead of me, so what did I do, I sat down and wrote a letter to my mother. Oh, I was such a goody-good. I really was. I was really too good.

Then the next morning I woke up and I was so scared. All of a sudden, I liked my nose, and I thought, what if I end up with something worse? But I had the appointment already, the doctor was all lined up and I didn't know if I'd even have to pay him anyway, if I didn't come. So I left the hotel and on the way to the hospital, I walked by such an arcade. They had one of those booths where you put in a quarter and it takes your picture four times and they come out in a strip like an up-and-down cartoon. I took my picture. I decided I wanted four pictures of my nose. I still have them. It really wasn't too great a nose.

The funny thing about the operation was that the doctor put me under, but I could still hear him working—I wasn't completely asleep. I heard crunching noises, like the way my dad ate chicken, he cracked the bones with his teeth and sucked the marrow. Then I heard a clipping, like with a shears.

I'd given him the picture beforehand and he said he'd do his best. He told me he had to work with what was there. And I think he did a good job. I've always been glad I did it.

Still, I'll never be pretty like your mother. She has those long legs from Granny. And one thing I have to say for her, she always did keep up her figure and dress herself nice. She has a knack for that, anything with colors. She has that and my mother and Granny had it, too, but I never did. I've never been good that way. I never could just put things together the way they do. I've always had to buy the whole outfit.

And Adele always did the exciting things, too. She's been all over, she mixes with the real rich people. She's never been happy with just the ordinary. I don't think she ever really liked Bay City.

She called once when she was in California and said she was going to a party where she was going to meet George Cukor and Katharine Hepburn. Jimmy talked to her, he answered the phone. We didn't know who George Cukor was until she told us, but we knew Katharine Hepburn.

"Katharine Hepburn, Katharine Hepburn!" Jimmy was yelling. I think he'd already had his gimlet. "You know your sister has her nose!" Adele remembered the story, too. And she called the next day and said, yes, she had met Katharine Hepburn and that she was a very icy person, real aloof, and all night she'd sort of stood apart, but then Adele had gone up and said, Excuse me, Miss Hepburn, but I wanted to tell you that my sister has your nose. Adele told the whole story, about me working at the Harper Method Beauty Shop and taking in a picture and all and she said, for the first time that night, Katharine Hepburn smiled. So thanks to my sister, somewhere out there Katharine Hepburn knows that a Carol Measey in Wisconsin has her nose.

ADELE

■ □ ■

■ □ ■ □ ■ □ ■ □ ■ □ ■ □ ■

17

THE COURSE OF MIRACLES

■ □ ■

I don't plan anymore. I used to. I used to try to control. Now I just sort of let things go with the flow. I live in The Now. And I find, everything just comes the way it's supposed to.

I've learned To Give Is to Receive. And when I can, when my billings are up, I look around for things for her. Even when I shouldn't, I do. I saw an adorable Calvin Klein black and white evening dress at Robinson's. It isn't cheap, but it is ADORABLE, it would be just smashing on her, and she needs to have one or two good things. It's fine to be the intellectual, but once in a while, you should dress up a little, too.

I even thought of it for me, I drove out at noon and tried it on, but my arms are just too old for it, you need a young arms and back. So I put it on layaway for her, she may as well wear it now when she's young. When you've still got the good arms. And those little white outfits I sent her like mine, they're two twenty-five, two fifty, actually, no, they're two seventy-five.

It's the most important, beautiful, fulfilling thing I've ever done in my life, being a mother. And I look at her and think, Hey, I didn't do such a bad job. But she holds in her fear and her anger, she hasn't learned to let go yet of her fear and just love, the way I do. I have no guilt. Not anymore. I'm living in The Now. I've found a real inner peace and nothing can really disturb it. She hasn't learned to forgive yet. But, you know, I look at her and think, If I was such an awful mother, the way she paints me out to be with her friends, she LOVES to play the poor child, the martyr, POOR, POOR Ann, then she wouldn't be so great, what she is.

I see the kids right here in Beverly Hills where the mothers were too busy with their manicures and their thises and their thats, they never took the time to give the real total love, the emotional closeness I did. I see it, I see it all the time in the convalescent homes. I have two girls, one is nineteen, the other's twenty-six, and neither will ever walk again, from the drugs.

And I started from scratch, from nothing, she saw the house and the dead-end road I grew up on. I was on my own, raising her, when I was her age, who does she think helped me? When I think of what I grew up around, the old mink sheds, a dead-end road—nothing, and I look at what she's had. Beverly Hills High School, college. And the lessons. And the clothes.

I think to myself, How did I get out of there. Other people just stay in the same rut all their lives. It must be something in the genes, our genes, that pushes us ahead. My sister is the totally opposite of me. And yet, it's the gene characteristic that's so incredibly, magnificently universal. That makes me believe there has to be a master plan, a universal power. Something in the genes way back, whether it's centuries ago—and here we are that we, a few of us, all these chromosomes meet and become something. We're all only electromagnetic particles. And so is a rock, a fish, a bird, a butterfly. And that's how you know. That's how I know, that I'm more than just this lifetime.

I'm part of all that went before and all that went after me. These are my beliefs. They're very strong and very deep. I was always different. From the kids I grew up with. I was the same and yet I was different. But then everyone feels that.

Everything was meant to be and if she has to rebel to find her own independent self, then I can let her. And I know what I've done, I know it in my heart, in myself, I know she'll thank me someday.

She could have been a poor nothing girl in a factory town in the midwest. And here she's in with a great crowd, going to the best schools, she can go anywhere, mix with anyone. Absolutely anyone. She's really a member of the intelligentsia, the real cream, the upper crust. And she's there because I got her in when she was young enough to learn. I was already thirty-nine when we moved here. I was young and good-looking. Sure, she's smart and she's pretty and talented—the works, she's got it all, the best of everything, I tell her—but I'll tell you, there are plenty of them there in the midwest who are the same and you'll never see them, because they'll never get out and rise up. Like Lolly. They just sink.

They tried—to make me and more than that, my child, into their mold. I had to let myself and my daughter go free. And mold in another way. I didn't see the joys and the happinesses I felt life offered. If only to look at a sunset or to look at an owl on a fence or to see the glories of Yosemite. I think the real ordinary is just to be simple with yourself. But they weren't simple. They were highly complicated people. They lived by the negatives, rather than love and joy.

My mother could have come out once and visited me. Never once did they think that I could need. That has hurt me. But I also know it was Carol's doing. How selfish people can be! To think they don't have to do anything.

It's very hard to change social classes after a certain age. I have friends, the Swans are lovely really, and Bert Keller, they're very good to me, having me up for parties and dinners and screenings, brunches, whenever I want, really, but I'll never be in the way that she can. You really need the man and the house. And you don't just find a man at my age. They're all looking for a woman who has money. And like Nan Keller used to say, if you don't learn your tennis before a certain age, before you're twenty, you'll never get your form just right. But I'm practicing, with tennis I don't agree, I am learning.

She'll have the big house someday and the husband and the beautiful yard, all of it. And, I'm hoping, grandchildren. I'm ready to be a grandmother. I think it'll be one of the most satisfying emotionally, I mean, beautiful things. I don't worry about getting old. You're as old as you feel and I feel young. I'm ready for grandchildren right now.

I'm happy here in my little place, I've fixed it up cute. Some-

day, I'd like to buy, I'd like to have a little house where I can see
the ocean and the mountains, real choice. But it has to be the
right spot. I'm looking. I'm looking all the time. I'm going to move
pretty soon. I'm saving. LA has gotten too big and too busy. I'm
sick of all this driving.

And her going to Wisconsin, her doubts, all this playing up
how she was poor, working class—I tell her, Honey, you were
NEVER working class, your mother always had an MA, that's not
working class—at the time, it hurt me, it really just hurt me right
here in the heart, when she wouldn't dress up, even once, she
wouldn't put on the clothes I sent her FOR ONE DAY, just to
please me, but now I understand that was all just rebellion. And
I've learned to be patient, not to try and change people. And when
you do that, they come around by themselves, quicker than if you
try to influence. And she'll never go back to Wisconsin. Never in
a million years. She couldn't go back, after Brown. I couldn't
either, now. I really couldn't. There's nothing for us there anymore.

I remember all those stinky mink sheds—I used to go there
after school and talk with my dad. We'd stand and stick our arms
in, real quiet and still, that was how you got the mink to know
you. I'm the one who had my childhood there. And I wouldn't go
back if you paid me. I'd like to know where my furs are now,
though, and my dresses. There's one suit with a green velvet collar and the pinched waist, it's exactly just what they're wearing
again now, I'd give anything to know where that is now. But Carol
probably threw it out or kept it for herself. That's what happens
when you leave.

But it's worth it. You have to just say, you lose a lot of things
that should be yours, but it's worth it. They're the ones who are
stuck there.

A man? I'd like to meet someone real, real special someday, a
man I could really share with, but right now, I'm concentrating on
my work. I've got the convalescent homes, my patient load is up
again, thank God, and I've got a few other little things, I'm de-
signing a line of clothes for the bedridden, I have a partner and
we've hired a designer, this young Japanese boy who's going out

with Betsy Swan, and I'm writing a book. I don't go to a lot of
parties, I live a very quiet life. I'm actually a very shy person.
And before I really want to look for a man, I'm just going to get
ME organized first, type up those damn reports, it's the end of the
month again.

And I read before bed every night. I've gotten very involved in
the spirit, in giving and really feeling a oneness with the world. I
read this Course of Miracles and I hope and pray, she'll read
them. I sent them all to her for Christmas, with a few other things
of course, clothes and a little jewelry. She laughs. They may not
be Pulitzer Prize–winners but they show you the fullness and the
openness of life. They teach you to give. And let's see, what else?
I'm reading Zen, all these various philosophies.

Sure, she's going to rebel.

What I try to tell her is you can be BOTH—you can have the
high IQ and the real intellect, you can be the Female Doctor AND
you can dress up a little and act a little feminine.

I've done it all these years without a man. Not many women
have been father and mother both. And I've been through lots she
doesn't even know. There are many things she doesn't know, the
things I didn't tell her, just so she wouldn't worry, just so she
could be a child. I was in jail once for those damn parking tickets,
never again will I let them pile up, but for a while there, I was
back in school, getting my new California certification and I just
put them in the glove compartment when I got them. Well, it
happened twice and the first time, Frank Swan drove right down
and paid my bail. But the second time I was there till four in the
morning, the Swans were in Mexico, they couldn't reach the Kellers, the Kellers were at a party, four o'clock was when they came
home. Well, I was raped by a woman in there. Yes, so there's a
lot she doesn't know. I haven't had it easy either.

But I've learned to be at one with the world and to forgive. And
since I've let go of my fear, lots of good things have just flowed
into my life—all this furniture, the Tiffany, the Seth Thomas—
it's all just meant to be.

And I even see her coming around. She visited and I got a
place at the beach last year, for all her kids, so they could party.

And I watched her with them. I just had to say to myself, leave her be, even with the hair and the bitten nails and all, and the underarms and the legs, ugh, that I really can't go for. But those boys all looked at her, so I guess that's just how they wear it now. I don't think you have to, I think the really great girls now still have the long, thick hair and they wear a little mod jewelry or mod dress, not the punk hair that's going to be out of style in six months, but I just shut my mouth and smiled. And I hoped and prayed that like I did years ago, she'd find her own grace, with her eyes closed. And I think maybe she is. They all danced out on the sand, with their music, and can she ever dance! Well, I suppose with the ballet and the thises and the thats, the cotillions, all I gave her as a child. But I didn't recognize her at first, I looked down from the balcony and thought, who's that? And then I couldn't believe that it was me, I made that beautiful girl.

But she thinks too much, she's so nervous, she has that anxiety, she's got to learn to just BE. And for so long all I heard was bitch bitch, whine whine, that now sometimes, no always. Always her happiness surprises me.

I wish I could have brought her here when she was even younger, so she wouldn't have all these various feelings and yearnings for the midwest and her middle-class roots, but that was her father, not me. I never wanted to stay there. But he left. And now I've got my station wagon ready for my grandchildren. They'll be all this—all Beverly Hills. They'll be born into it—thanks to me.

When I was pregnant with her, we lived in Egypt. I didn't know anything, I was so young. But her father wanted to have a baby and so I thought, okay, maybe that would help him, settle him down. His family was there. They thought it would be wonderful. He had backing. Of course, later he changed his mind about that, too. But I'm over him now too finally. I think I could meet him again now and it wouldn't mean anything to me.

I lost so much weight, I was down to eighty-six pounds at seven months and I flew back. I wanted to be home with my mother. And so I could have her here in America with the very best equipment and hospitals in the world.

You carry a baby in the womb for nine months and then, when they're grown up, they call you collect, when they remember. She has her own life. And that's okay. I've learned to be patient. "Teach only love for that is what you are." The ups and down; I live with it. And I've got a lot ahead of me and a lot to be proud of. I know: she is the reason I was born.

ABOUT THE AUTHOR

Mona Simpson received a BA from the University of California, Berkeley, and an MFA from Columbia University. Her short fiction has appeared in *The Paris Review, Ploughshares, The Iowa Review, The North American Review,* and other periodicals. Her stories have been selected for inclusion in *Best American Short Stories* of 1986, *The Pushcart Prize XI: Best of the Small Presses,* and *20 Under 30*. She is the recipient of a number of awards, including a National Endowment of the Arts Fellowship, a Kellogg National Fellowship, and a Whiting Writers' Award. *Anywhere But Here* is her first book.

VINTAGE
CONTEMPORARIES

"Today's novels for the readers of today." — VANITY FAIR

"Real literature—originals and important reprints—in attractive, inexpensive paperbacks."—THE LOS ANGELES TIMES

"Prestigious."—THE CHICAGO TRIBUNE

"A very fine collection."—THE CHRISTIAN SCIENCE MONITOR

"Adventurous and worthy." — SATURDAY REVIEW

"If you want to know what's on the cutting edge of American fiction, then these are the books you should be reading."
                    —UNITED PRESS INTERNATIONAL

On sale at bookstores everywhere, but if otherwise unavailable, may be ordered from us. You can use this coupon, or phone (800) 638-6460.

Please send me the Vintage Contemporaries books I have checked on the reverse. I am enclosing $ _____ (add $1.00 per copy to cover postage and handling). Send check or money order—no cash or CODs, please. Prices are subject to change without notice.

NAME _____

ADDRESS _____

CITY _____ STATE _____ ZIP _____

Send coupons to:
RANDOM HOUSE, INC., 400 Hahn Road, Westminster, MD 21157
ATTN: ORDER ENTRY DEPARTMENT
Allow at least 4 weeks for delivery.

VINTAGE
CONTEMPORARIES